The Portable
FAULKNER

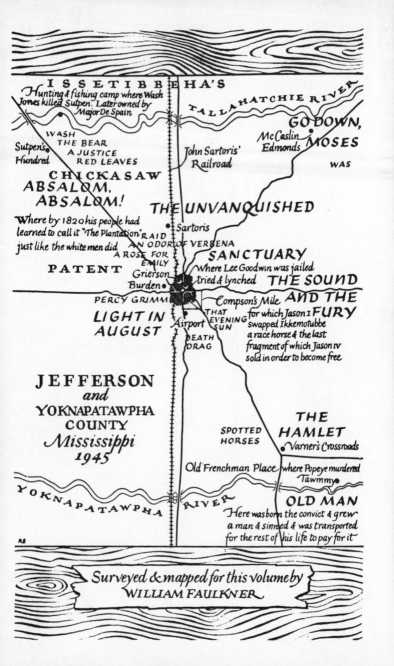

CONTENTS

INTRODUCTION

I wrote this introduction in the autumn of 1945, at a time when Faulkner's books were little read and often disparaged. He had a few enthusiastic defenders, but no one, so it seemed to me then, had more than distantly suggested the scope and force and interdependence of his work as a whole. I was writing to overcome a general misconception, and that explains why, at various points, my emphasis was different from what it would be today. Yet I find it difficult to change what I said, except in the comparatively simple matter of bringing facts up to date. The original text was written with a good deal of advice from Faulkner himself. It has some historical value, and I prefer to reprint it with a very few revisions, while saving my comments for the end.

I

When the war was over—the other war—William Faulkner went back to Oxford, Mississippi. He had served in the Royal Air Force in 1918. Now he was home again and not at home, or at least not able to accept the post-war world. He was writing poems, most of them worthless, and dozens of immature but violent and effective stories, while at the same time he was brooding over his own situation and the decline of the South. Slowly the brood-

ing thoughts arranged themselves into the whole interconnected pattern that would form the substance of his
novels.

The pattern was based on what he saw in Oxford or
remembered from his childhood; on scraps of family
tradition (the Falkners, as they spelled the name, had
played their part in the history of the state); on kitchen
dialogues between the black cook and her amiable husband; on Saturday-afternoon gossip in Courthouse Square;
on stories told by men in overalls squatting on their heels
while they passed around a fruit jar full of white corn
liquor; on all the sources familiar to a small-town
Mississippi boy—but the whole of it was elaborated,
transformed, given convulsive life by his emotions; until
by simple intensity of feeling the figures in it became a
little more than human, became heroic or diabolical, became symbols of the old South, of war and reconstruction, of commerce and machinery destroying the standards of the past. There in Oxford, Faulkner performed a
labor of imagination that has not been equaled in our
time, and a double labor: first, to invent a Mississippi
county that was like a mythical kingdom, but was complete and living in all its details; second, to make his story
of Yoknapatawpha County stand as a parable or legend
of all the Deep South.

For this double task, Faulkner was better equipped
by talent and background than he was by schooling. He
was born in New Albany, Mississippi, on September 25,
1897; he was the oldest of four brothers. The family
soon moved to Oxford, where he attended the public
school, but without being graduated from high school.
For a year or two after the war, he was a student at the
University of Mississippi, where veterans could then ma-
triculate without a high-school diploma, but he neglected
his classroom work and left early in the second year. He
had less of a formal education than any other good writer
of his time, except Hart Crane—less even than Heming-

way, who never went to college, but who learned to speak several languages and studied writing in Paris from the best masters. Faulkner taught himself, largely, as he says, by "undirected and uncorrelated reading."

Among the authors either mentioned or echoed in his early stories and poems are Keats, Balzac, Flaubert, Swinburne, Verlaine, Mallarmé, Wilde, Housman, Joyce, Eliot, Sherwood Anderson, and E. E. Cummings, with fainter suggestions of Hemingway (looking at trout in a river), Dos Passos (in the spelling of compound words), and Scott Fitzgerald. The poems he wrote in those days were wholly derivative, but his prose from the beginning was a form of poetry, and in spite of the echoes it was always his own. He traveled less than any of his writing contemporaries. There was a lonely year spent in New York as salesclerk in a bookstore; there were six months in New Orleans, where he lived near Sherwood Anderson and met the literary crowd—he even satirized them in a bad early novel, *Mosquitoes*—and then six months in Italy and Paris, where he did not make friends on the Left Bank. Except for writing assignments in Hollywood, the rest of his life has been spent in the town where he grew up, less than forty miles from his birthplace.

Although Oxford, Mississippi, is the seat of a university, it is even less of a literary center than was Salem, Massachusetts, during Hawthorne's early years as a writer; and Faulkner himself has shown an even greater dislike than Hawthorne for literary society. His novels are the books of a man who broods about literature, but doesn't often discuss it with his friends; there is no ease about them, no feeling that they come from a background of taste refined by argument and of opinions held in common. They make me think of a passage from Henry James's little book on Hawthorne:

The best things come, as a general thing, from the talents that are members of a group; every man works better when he has companions working in the same line, and yielding to the stimulus of suggestion, comparison, emulation. Great things of course have been done by solitary workers; but they have usually been done with double the pains they would have cost if they had been produced in more genial circumstances. The solitary worker loses the profit of example and discussion; he is apt to make awkward experiments; he is in the nature of the case more or less of an empiric. The empiric may, as I say, be treated by the world as an expert; but the drawbacks and discomforts of empiricism remain to him, and are in fact increased by the suspicion that is mingled with his gratitude, of a want in the public taste of a sense of the proportion of things.

Like Hawthorne, Faulkner is a solitary worker by choice, and he has done great things not only with double the pains to himself that they might have cost if produced in more genial circumstances, but sometimes also with double the pains to the reader. Two or three of his books as a whole and many of them in part are awkward experiments. All of them are full of overblown words like "imponderable," "immortal," "immutable," and "immemorial" that he would have used with more discretion, or not at all, if he had followed Hemingway's example and served an apprenticeship to an older writer. He is a most uncertain judge of his own work, and he has no reason to believe that the world's judgment of it is any more to be trusted; indeed, there is no American author who would be justified in feeling more suspicion of "a want in the public taste of a sense of the proportion of things." His early novels, when not condemned, were overpraised for the wrong reasons; his later and in many ways better novels have been ridiculed or simply neglected; and in 1945 all his seventeen books were effectively out of print, with some of them unobtainable in the secondhand bookshops.[1]

---

[1] I have let this paragraph stand, with the one that follows, as an accurate picture of Faulkner's reputation in 1945.

The Portable
FAULKNER

Revised and Expanded Edition

Edited by Malcolm Cowley

THE VIKING PRESS
NEW YORK

Originally published in 1946.

Revised edition first published in 1967 by The Viking Press
40 West 23rd Street, New York, N.Y. 10010

Portable is a registered Trademark of Viking Penguin, Inc.

Printed and Bound in the United States of America

Permission to reproduce the William Faulkner writings in this
volume must be obtained from Random House, Inc.,
201 East 50th Street, New York, N.Y. 10022.

An earlier version of Part III of the Introduction appeared in the
Sewanee Review as part of an essay entitled "William Faulkner's
Legend of the South."

Library of Congress Cataloging in Publication Data
Faulkner, William, 1897–1962.
The portable Faulkner. Edited by Malcolm Cowley. Rev. and
expanded ed.   New York, Viking Press [1968, c1967]
I. Cowley, Malcolm, 1898–   ed.   II. Title.
PS3511.A86A6   1968   813'.5'2   68-5863
ISBN: 0-517-478609

h g f e d c b a

Even his warm admirers, of whom there are many—no author has a higher standing among his fellow novelists— have shown a rather vague idea of what he is trying to do; and Faulkner himself has never explained. He holds a curious attitude toward the public that appears to be lofty indifference (as in the one preface he wrote, for the Modern Library edition of *Sanctuary*), but really comes closer to being a mixture of skittery distrust and pure unconsciousness that the public exists. He doesn't furnish information or correct misstatements about himself (most of the biographical sketches that deal with him are full of preposterous errors). He doesn't care which way his name is spelled in the records, with or without the "u"—"Either way suits me," he says. Once he has finished a book, he is apparently not concerned with the question of how it will be presented, to what sort of audience, and sometimes he doesn't bother to keep a private copy of it. He said in a letter, "I think I have written a lot and sent it off to print before I actually realized strangers might read it." Others might say that Faulkner, at least in those early days, was not so much composing stories for the public as telling them to himself—like a lonely child in his imaginary world, but also like a writer of genius.

II

Faulkner's mythical kingdom is a county in northern Mississippi, on the border between the sand hills covered with scrubby pine and the black earth of the river bottoms. Except for the storekeepers, mechanics, and professional men who live in Jefferson, the county seat, all the inhabitants are farmers or woodsmen. Except for a little lumber, their only commercial product is baled cotton for the Memphis market. A few of them live in big plantation houses, the relics of another age, and more of them in substantial wooden farmhouses; but still more of them are tenants, no better housed than slaves on good plantations before the Civil War. Yoknapatawpha County —"William Faulkner, sole owner and proprietor," as he inscribed on one of the maps he drew—has a population of 15,611 persons scattered over 2400 square miles. It sometimes seems to me that every house or hovel has been described in one of Faulkner's novels, and that all the people of the imaginary county, black and white, townsmen, farmers, and housewives, have played their parts in one connected story.

He has so far [1945] written nine books wholly concerned with Yoknapatawpha County and its people, who also appear in parts of three others and in thirty or more uncollected stories. *Sartoris* was the first of the books to be published, in the spring of 1929; it is a romantic and partly unconvincing novel, but with many fine scenes in it, such as the hero's visit to a family of independent pine-hill farmers; and it states most of the themes that the author would later develop at length. *The Sound and the Fury*, published six months later, recounts the going-to-pieces of the Compson family, and it was the first of Faulkner's novels to be widely discussed. The books that followed, in the Yoknapatawpha series, are *As I Lay Dying* (1930), about the death and burial of Addie Bundren; *Sanctuary* (1931), for a long time the most popular of his novels; *Light in August* (1932), in some ways the best; *Absalom, Absalom!* (1936), about Colonel Sutpen and his ambition to found a family; *The Unvanquished* (1938), a cycle of stories about the Sartoris dynasty; *The Wild Palms* (1939), half of which deals with a convict from back in the pine hills; *The Hamlet* (1940), a first novel about the Snopes clan, with others to follow; and *Go Down, Moses* (1942), in which Faulkner's principal theme is the relation between whites and Negroes. There are also many Yoknapatawpha stories in *These 13* (1931) and *Doctor Martino* (1934), besides other stories privately printed (like *Miss Zilphia Gant*, 1932) or published in magazines and still to be collected or used as episodes in novels.[2]

Just as Balzac, who may have inspired the series, divided his *Comédie Humaine* into "Scenes of Parisian Life," "Scenes of Provincial Life," "Scenes of Private Life," so Faulkner might divide his work into a number of cycles: one about the planters and their descendants, one about the townspeople of Jefferson, one about the poor whites, one about the Indians, and one about the Negroes. Or again, if he adopted a division by families, there would be the Compson-Sartoris saga, the continuing Snopes saga, the McCaslin saga, dealing with the white and black descendants of Carothers McCaslin, and the Ratliff-Bundren saga, devoted to the backwoods farmers of Frenchman's Bend. All the cycles or sagas are closely interconnected; it is as if each new book was a chord or segment of a total situation always existing in the author's mind. Sometimes a short story is the sequel to an earlier novel. For example, we read in *Sartoris* that Byron Snopes stole a packet of letters from Narcissa Benbow; and in "There Was a Queen," a story published five years later, we learn how Narcissa got the letters back again. Sometimes, on the other hand, a novel contains the sequel to a

---

[2] That was the tally in 1945. With one exception, all the books that Faulkner published after that year are concerned with Yoknapatawpha County. The exception is *A Fable* (1954), about a reincarnated Christ in the First World War. The Yoknapatawpha books, eight in number, are *Intruder in the Dust* (1948), about a lynching that is averted by a seventy-year-old spinster and a pair of boys; *Knight's Gambit* (1949), recounting the adventures in detection of Gavin Stevens; *Collected Stories of William Faulkner* (1950), containing all the stories in *These 13* and *Doctor Martino* as well as several not previously collected; *Requiem for a Nun* (1951), a three-act drama, with narrative prologues to each act, about the later life of Temple Drake; *Big Woods* (1955), a cycle of hunting stories, some of them revised from chapters of *Go Down, Moses*; *The Town* (1957), second volume in the Snopes trilogy; *The Mansion* (1959), concluding the trilogy; and *The Reivers*, published a month before Faulkner's death on July 6, 1962. In all, sixteen of his books belong to the Yoknapatawpha cycle, as well as half of another book (*The Wild Palms*) and it is hard to count how many stories.

story; and we discover from an incidental reference in *The Sound and the Fury* that the Negro woman whose terror of death was portrayed in "That Evening Sun" had indeed been murdered and her body left in a ditch for the vultures. Sometimes an episode has a more complicated history. Thus, in the first chapter of *Sanctuary*, we hear about the Old Frenchman place, a ruined mansion near which the people of the neighborhood had been "digging with secret and sporadic optimism for gold which the builder was reputed to have buried somewhere about the place when Grant came through the country on his Vicksburg campaign." Later this digging for gold served as the subject of a story published in the *Saturday Evening Post*: "Lizards in Jamshyd's Courtyard." Still later the story was completely rewritten and became the last chapter of *The Hamlet*.[3]

As one book leads into another, the author sometimes falls into inconsistencies of detail. There is a sewing-machine agent named V. K. Suratt who appears in *Sartoris* and some of the stories written at about the same time. When we reach *The Hamlet*, his name has changed to Ratliff, although his character remains the same (and his age, too, for all the twenty years that separate the backgrounds of the two novels). Henry Armstid is a likable figure in *As I Lay Dying* and *Light in August*; in *The Hamlet* he is mean and half-demented. His wife, whose character remains consistent, is called Lula in one book and Martha in another; in the third she is nameless. There is an Indian chief named Doom who appears in several stories; he starts as the father of Issetibeha (in "Red Leaves") and ends as his nephew (in "A Justice"). The mansion called Sutpen's Hundred was built of brick at the beginning of *Absalom, Absalom!* but at the end of the novel it is all wood and inflammable except for the chim-

---

[3] The Old Frenchman place was built in the 1830s by Louis Grenier, as Faulkner tells us in the prologue to the first act of *Requiem for a Nun* (1951).

neys. But these errors are inconsequential, considering the
scope of Faulkner's series; and I should judge that most
of them are afterthoughts rather than oversights.

All his books in the Yoknapatawpha cycle are part of
the same living pattern. It is this pattern, and not the
printed volumes in which part of it is recorded, that is
Faulkner's real achievement. Its existence helps to explain one feature of his work: that each novel, each long
or short story, seems to reveal more than it states explic-
itly and to have a subject bigger than itself. All the separate works are like blocks of marble from the same quarry:
they show the veins and faults of the mother rock. Or else
—to use a rather strained figure—they are like wooden
planks that were cut, not from a log, but from a still living
tree. The planks are planed and chiseled into their final
shapes, but the tree itself heals over the wound and continues to grow. Faulkner is incapable of telling the same
story twice without adding new details. In the present
volume I wanted to use part of *The Sound and the Fury*,
the novel that deals with the fall of the Compson family.
I thought that the last part of the book would be most
effective as a separate episode, but still it depended too
much on what had gone before. Faulkner offered to write
a very brief introduction that would explain the relations
of the characters. What he finally sent me is the much
longer passage printed at the end of the volume: a genealogy of the Compsons from their first arrival in America.
Whereas the novel is confined (except for memories) to a
period of eighteen years ending on Easter Sunday, 1928,
the genealogy goes back to the battle of Culloden in 1745,
and forward to the year 1943, when Jason, last of the
Compson males, has sold the family mansion, and Sister
Caddy has last been heard of as the mistress of a German
general. The novel that Faulkner wrote about the Compsons had long ago been given what seemed its final shape,
but the pattern or body of legend behind the novel—
and behind his other books—was still developing.

Although the pattern is presented in terms of a single Mississippi county, it can be extended to the Deep South as a whole; and Faulkner always seems conscious of its wider application. He might have been thinking of his own novels when he described the ledgers in the commissary of the McCaslin plantation, in *Go Down, Moses.* They recorded, he says, "that slow trickle of molasses and meal and meat, of shoes and straw hats and overalls, of plowlines and collars and heelbolts and clevises, which returned each fall as cotton"—in a sense they were local and limited; but they were also "the continuation of that record which two hundred years had not been enough to complete and another hundred would not be enough to discharge; that chronicle which was a whole land in miniature, which multiplied and compounded was the entire South."

III

"Tell about the South," says Quentin Compson's roommate at Harvard, a Canadian named Shreve McCannon who is curious about the unknown region beyond the Ohio. "What's it like there?" he asks. "What do they do there? Why do they live there? Why do they live at all?" And Quentin, whose background is a little like that of Faulkner himself and who sometimes seems to speak for him—Quentin answers, "You can't understand it. You would have to be born there." Nevertheless, he tells a long and violent story that reveals something essential in the history of the Deep South, which is not so much a region as it is, in Quentin's mind, an incomplete and frustrated nation trying to relive its legendary past.

The story he tells—I am trying to summarize the plot of *Absalom, Absalom!*—is that of a mountain boy named Thomas Sutpen whose family drifted into the Virginia lowlands, where his father found odd jobs on a plantation. One day the father sent him with a message to the big house, but he was turned away at the door by a black man in livery. Puzzled and humiliated, the mountain boy was seized upon by the lifelong ambition to which he would afterward refer as "the design." He too would own a plantation with slaves and a liveried butler; he would build a mansion as big as any of those in the Tidewater; and he would have a son to inherit his wealth.

A dozen years later Sutpen appeared in the frontier town of Jefferson, where he managed to obtain a hundred square miles of land from the Chickasaws. With the help of twenty wild Negroes from the jungle and a French architect, he set about building the largest house in northern Mississippi, using timbers from the forest and bricks that his Negroes molded and baked on the spot; it was as if the mansion, Sutpen's Hundred, had been literally torn from the soil. Only one man in Jefferson—he was Quentin's grandfather, General Compson—ever learned how and where Sutpen had acquired his slaves. He had shipped to Haiti from Virginia, worked as an overseer on a sugar plantation, and married the rich planter's daughter, who had borne him a son. Then, finding that his wife had Negro blood, he had simply put her away, with her child and her fortune, while keeping the twenty slaves as a sort of indemnity. He explained to General Compson, in the stilted speech he had taught himself as appropriate to his new role of Southern gentleman, that she could not be "adjunctive to the forwarding of the design."

"Jesus, the South is fine, isn't it," Shreve McCannon says. "It's better than the theatre, isn't it. It's better than Ben Hur, isn't it. No wonder you have to come away now and then, isn't it."

In Jefferson he married again, Quentin continues. This time Sutpen's wife belonged to a pious family of the neighborhood and she bore him two children, Henry and Judith. He became the biggest cotton planter in Yoknapatawpha County, and it seemed that his "design" had already been fulfilled. At this moment, however, Henry came home from the University of Mississippi with an older and worldlier new friend, Charles Bon, who was in reality Sutpen's son by his first marriage. Charles became engaged to Judith. Sutpen learned his identity and, without making a sign of recognition, ordered him from the house. Henry, who refused to believe that Charles was his half-brother, renounced his birthright and followed him to New Orleans. In 1861 all the male Sutpens went off to war, and all survived four years of fighting. Then, in the spring of 1865, Charles suddenly decided to marry Judith, even though he was certain by now that she was his half-sister. Henry rode beside him all the way back to Sutpen's Hundred, but tried to stop him at the gate, killed him when he insisted on going ahead with his plan, told Judith what he had done, and disappeared.

"The South," Shreve McCannon says as he listens to the story. "The South. Jesus. No wonder you folks all outlive yourselves by years and years." And Quentin says, remembering his own sister with whom (or with a false notion of whom) he was in love—just as Charles Bon, and Henry too, were in love with Judith—"I am older at twenty than a lot of people who have died."

But Quentin's story of the Deep South does not end with the war. Colonel Sutpen came home, he says, to find his wife dead, his son a fugitive, his slaves dispersed (they had run away before they were freed by the Union army), and most of his land about to be seized for debt. Still determined to carry out "the design," he did not pause for breath before undertaking to restore his house and plantation as nearly as possible to what they had been. The effort failed; Sutpen lost most of his land and was reduced to keeping a crossroads store. Now in his sixties, he tried again to beget a son; but his wife's younger sister, Miss Rosa Coldfield, was outraged by his proposal ("Let's try it," he seems to have said, though his words are not directly repeated—"and if it's a boy we'll get married"); and later poor Milly Jones, whom he se-duced, gave birth to a girl. At that Sutpen abandoned hope and provoked Milly's grandfather into killing him. Judith survived her father for a time, as did the half-caste son of Charles Bon by a New Orleans octoroon. After the death of these two by yellow fever, the great house was haunted rather than inhabited by an ancient mulatto woman, Sutpen's daughter by one of his slaves. The fugitive Henry Sutpen came home to die; the townspeople heard of his illness and sent an ambulance after him; but old Clytie thought they were arresting him for murder and set fire to Sutpen's Hundred. The only survivor of the conflagration was Jim Bond, a half-witted, saddle-colored creature who was Charles Bon's grandson.

"Now I want you to tell me just one thing more," Shreve McCannon says after hearing the story. "Why do you hate the South?"—"I dont hate it," Quentin says quickly, at once. "I dont hate it," he repeats, apparently speaking for the author as well as himself. *I dont hate it,* he thinks, panting in the cold air, the iron New England dark; *I dont. I dont hate it! I dont hate it!*

The reader cannot help wondering why this somber and, at moments, plainly incredible story had so seized upon Quentin's mind that he trembled with excitement when telling it, and why Shreve McCannon felt that it revealed the essence of the Deep South. It seems to belong in the realm of Gothic romance, with Sutpen's Hundred taking the place of a haunted castle on the Rhine, with Colonel Sutpen as Faust and Charles Bon as Manfred. Then slowly it dawns on you that most of the characters and incidents have a double meaning; that besides their place in the story they also serve as symbols or metaphors with a general application. Sutpen's great design, the land he stole from the Indians, the French architect who built his mansion with the help of wild Negroes from the jungle, the woman of mixed blood whom he married and disowned, the unacknowledged son who ruined him, the poor white whom he wronged and who killed him in anger, and the final destruction of the mansion like the downfall of a social order: all these might belong to a tragic fable of Southern history. With a little cleverness, the whole novel might be explained as a connected and logical allegory, but this, I think, would be going far beyond the author's intention. First of all he was writing a story, and one that affected him deeply, but he was also brooding over a social situation. More or less unconsciously, the incidents in the story came to represent the forces and elements in the social situation, since the mind naturally works in terms of symbols and parallels. In Faulkner's case, this form of parallelism is not confined to *Absalom, Absalom!* It can be found in the whole fictional framework that he has been elaborating in novel after novel, until his work has become a myth or legend of the South.

I call it a legend because it is obviously no more intended as a historical account of the country south of the Ohio than *The Scarlet Letter* was intended as a history of Massachusetts or *Paradise Lost* as a factual account of the Fall. Briefly stated, the legend might run something like this: The Deep South was ruled by planters some of whom were aristocrats like the Sartoris clan, while others were new men like Colonel Sutpen. Both types were determined to establish a lasting social order on the land they had seized from the Indians (that is, to leave sons behind them). They had the virtue of living single-mindedly by a fixed code; but there was also an inherent guilt in their "design," their way of life; it was slavery that put a curse on the land and brought about the Civil War. [I must add one remark in deference to an argument of Cleanth Brooks', in his very useful work *William Faulkner: The Yoknapatawpha Country* (1963). Although Sutpen had more than his share of the guilt, he never pretended to follow the code of conduct that in some measure atoned for it. Temperamentally he was less of a Southerner than a Northern robber baron out of his time and place; or he might even stand for the blindly ambitious man of all ages. To the other planters, he was always an alien. Quentin Compson, their descendant, regarded him as "trash, origninless"—so Faulkner told me in a letter— but Quentin also grieved the fact that a man like Sutpen "could not only have dreamed so high but have had the force and strength to have failed so grandly." Thus, it was not at all in his character, but rather in his fate, that Sutpen became emblematic of the South.]

After the War was lost, partly as a result of the South-erners' mad heroism (for who else but men as brave as Jackson and Stuart could have frightened the Yankees into standing together and fighting back?) the planters tried to restore their "design" by other methods. But they no longer had the strength to achieve more than a partial success, even after they had freed their land from the carpetbaggers who followed the Northern armies. As time passed, moreover, the men of the old order found that they had Southern enemies too; they had to fight against a new exploiting class descended from the landless whites of slavery days. In this struggle between the clan of Sar-toris and the unscrupulous tribe of Snopes, the Sartorises were defeated in advance by a traditional code that kept them from using the weapons of the enemy. As a price of victory, however, the Snopeses had to serve the mecha-nized civilization of the North, which was morally impo-tent in itself, but which, with the aid of its Southern re-tainers, ended by corrupting the Southern nation.

Faulkner's novels of contemporary Southern life—espe-cially those written before 1945—continue the legend into a period that he regards as one of moral confusion and social decay. He is continually seeking in them for violent images to convey his sense of outrage. *Sanctuary* is the most violent of all his novels; it has been the most popular and is by no means the least important (in spite of Faulk-ner's comment that it was "a cheap idea . . . deliberately conceived to make money"). The story of Popeye and

Temple Drake has more meaning than appears on a first hasty reading—the only reading that early critics were willing to grant it. Popeye himself is one of several characters in Faulkner's novels who represent the mechanical civilization that has invaded and conquered the South. He is always described in mechanical terms: his eyes "looked like rubber knobs"; his face "just went awry, like the face of a wax doll set too near a hot fire and forgotten"; his tight suit and stiff hat were "all angles, like a modernistic lampshade"; and in general he had "that vicious depthless quality of stamped tin." Popeye was the son of a professional strikebreaker, from whom he had inherited syphilis; he was the grandson of a pyromaniac, and he had spent most of his childhood in an institution. He was the man "who made money and had nothing he could do with it, spend it for, since he knew that alcohol would kill him like poison, who had no friends and had never known a woman"—in other words, he was a compendium of all the hateful qualities that Faulkner assigns to finance capitalism. *Sanctuary* is not a connected allegory, as George Marion O'Donnell condemned it for being[4]—he was the first critic to approach it seriously—but neither is it a mere accumulation of pointless horrors. It is an example of the Freudian method turned backward, being full of sexual nightmares that are in reality social symbols. It is somehow connected in the author's mind with what he regards as the rape and corruption of the South.

In his novels dealing with the present—I am speaking of those written before 1945—Faulkner makes it clear that the descendants of the old ruling caste have the wish but not the courage or the strength to prevent this new disaster. They are defeated by Popeye (like Horace Benbow), or they run away from him (like Gowan Stevens,

---

[4] The essay by O'Donnell, "Faulkner's Mythology," appeared in the *Kenyon Review* (I, Summer 1939). It is reprinted in Hoffman and Vickery, *William Faulkner: Three Decades of Criticism* (Michigan State University Press, 1960).

who had been to college at Virginia and learned how to
drink like a gentleman, but not to fight for his principles),
or they are robbed and replaced in their positions of influence by the Snopeses (like old Bayard Sartoris, the
president of the bank), or they drug themselves with elo-
quence and alcohol (like Quentin Compson's father), or
they retire into the illusion of being inviolable Southern
ladies (like Mrs. Compson, who says, "It can't be simply
to flout and hurt me. Whoever God is, He would not permit that. I'm a lady."), or they dwell so much on the past
that they are incapable of facing the present (like Rev-
erend Hightower of *Light in August*), or they run from
danger to danger (like young Bayard Sartoris) frantically
seeking their own destruction. Faulkner's novels are full of
well-meaning and even admirable persons, not only the
grandsons of the cotton aristocracy, but also pine-hill
farmers and storekeepers and sewing-machine agents and
Negro cooks and sharecroppers; but they are almost all of
them defeated by circumstances and they carry with them
a sense of their own doom.

They also carry, whether heroes or villains, a curious
sense of submission to their fate. "There is not one of
Faulkner's characters," says André Gide in his dialogue on
"The New American Novelists," "who properly speaking
has a soul"; and I think he means that not one of them, in
the early novels, exercises the faculty of conscious choice
between good and evil. They are haunted, obsessed,
driven forward by some inner necessity. Like Miss Rosa
Coldfield in *Absalom, Absalom!* they exist in "that dream
state in which you run without moving from a terror in
which you cannot believe, toward a safety in which you
have no faith." Or, like the slaves freed by General Sherman's army, in *The Unvanquished*, they blindly follow
the road toward any river, believing that it will be their
Jordan:

They were singing, walking along the road singing, not
even looking to either side. The dust didn't even settle for

two days, because all that night they still passed; we sat up
listening to them and the next morning every few yards
along the road would be the old ones who couldn't keep
up any more, sitting or lying down and even crawling
along, calling to the others to help them; and the others—
the young ones—not stopping, not even looking at them.
"Going to Jordan," they told me. "Going to cross Jordan."

Most of Faulkner's characters, black and white, are a
little like that. They dig for gold frenziedly after they
have lost their hope of finding it (like Henry Armstid in
The Hamlet and Lucas Beauchamp in *Go Down, Moses*);
or they battle against and survive a Mississippi flood for
the one privilege of returning to the state prison farm
(like the tall convict in "Old Man"); or, a whole family
together, they carry a body through flood and fire and
corruption to bury it in the cemetery at Jefferson (like the
Bundrens in *As I Lay Dying*); or they tramp the roads
week after week in search of men who had promised but
never intended to marry them (like Lena Grove, the
pregnant woman of *Light in August*); or, pursued by a
mob, they turn at the end to meet and accept death (like
Joe Christmas in the same novel). Even when they seem
to be guided by a conscious purpose, like Colonel Sutpen,
it is not something they have chosen by an act of will, but
something that has taken possession of them: Sutpen's
great design was "not what he wanted to do but what he
just had to do, had to do it whether he wanted to or not,
because if he did not do it he knew that he could never
live with himself for the rest of his life." In the same way,
Faulkner himself writes, not what he wants to, but what
he just has to write whether he wants to or not.

I V

It had better be admitted that almost all his novels have
some obvious weakness in structure. Some of them com-
bine two or more themes having little relation to each

other, as *Light in August* does, while others, like *The Hamlet*, tend to resolve themselves into a series of episodes resembling beads on a string. In *The Sound and the Fury*, which is superb as a whole, we can't be sure that the four sections of the novel are presented in the most effective order; at any rate, we can't fully understand the first section until we have read the three that follow. *Absalom, Absalom!* though at first it strikes us as being pitched in too high a key, is structurally the soundest of all the novels in the Yoknapatawpha series—and it gains power in retrospect; but even here the author's attention seems to shift from the principal theme of Colonel Sutpen's design to the secondary theme of incest and miscegenation.

Faulkner seems best to me, and most nearly himself, either in long stories like "The Bear," in *Go Down, Moses*, and "Old Man," which was published as half of *The Wild Palms*, and "Spotted Horses," which was first printed separately, then greatly expanded and fitted into the loose framework of *The Hamlet*—all three stories are included in this volume; or else in the Yoknapatawpha saga as a whole. That is, he has been most effective in dealing with the total situation always present in his mind as a pattern of the South, or else in shorter units which, though often subject to inspired revision, have still been shaped by a single conception. It is by his best that we should judge him, as every other author; and Faulkner at his best—even sometimes at his worst—has a power, a richness of life, an intensity to be found in no other American writer of our time. He has—once again I am quoting from Henry James's essay on Hawthorne—"the element of simple genius, the quality of imagination."

Moreover, he has a brooding love for the land where he was born and reared and where, unlike other writers of his generation, he has chosen to spend his life. It is ". . . this land, this South, for which God has done so much, with woods for game and streams for fish and deep

rich soil for seed and lush springs to sprout it and long
summers to mature it and serene falls to harvest it and
short mild winters for men and animals." So far as Faulkner's country includes the Delta, it is also (in the words of
old Ike McCaslin)

. . . this land which man has deswamped and denuded
and derivered in two generations so that white men can
own plantations and commute every night to Memphis and
black men own plantations and ride in jimcrow cars to
Chicago and live in millionaires' mansions on Lake Shore
Drive, where white men rent farms and live like niggers
and niggers crop on shares and live like animals, where
cotton is planted and grows man-tall in the very cracks of
the sidewalks, and usury and mortgage and bankruptcy
and measureless wealth, Chinese and African and Aryan
and Jew, all breed and spawn together.

Here are the two sides of Faulkner's feeling for the South:
on the one side, an admiring and possessive love; on the
other, a compulsive fear lest what he loves should be destroyed by the ignorance of its native serfs and the greed
of traders and absentee landlords.

No other American writer takes such delight in the
weather. He speaks in various novels of "the hot still pine-
winey silence of the August afternoon"; of "the moonless
September dust, the trees along the road not rising soaring
as trees should but squatting like huge fowl"; of "the tranquil sunset of October mazy with windless wood-smoke";
of the "slow drizzle of November rain just above the ice
point"; of "those windless Mississippi December days
which are a sort of Indian summer's Indian summer"; of
January and February when there is "no movement anywhere save the low constant smoke . . . and no sound
save the chopping of axes and the lonely whistle of the
daily trains." Spring in Faulkner's country is a hurried season, "all coming at once, pell mell and disordered, fruit
and bloom and leaf, pied meadow and blossoming wood
and the long fields shearing dark out of winter's slumber,

to the shearing plow." Summer is dust-choked and blazing, and it lasts far into what should be autumn. "That's
the one trouble with this country," he says in *As I Lay
Dying*. "Everything, weather, all, hangs on too long. Like
our rivers, our land: opaque, slow, violent; shaping and
creating the life of man in its implacable and brooding
image."

And Faulkner loves these people created in the image
of the land. After a second reading of his novels, you continue to be impressed by his villains, Popeye and Jason
and Flem Snopes; but this time you find more space in
your memory for other figures standing a little in the background yet presented by the author with quiet affectio..:
old ladies like Miss Jenny Du Pre, with their sharp-
tongued benevolence; shrewd but affable traders like
Ratliff, the sewing-machine agent, and Will Varner, with
his cotton gin and general store; long-suffering farm wives
like Mrs. Henry Armstid (whether her name is Lula or
Martha); and backwoods patriarchs like Pappy Mac-
Cullum, with his six middle-aged but unmarried sons
named after the generals of Lee's army. You remember
the big plantation houses that collapse in flames as if a
whole civilization were dying, but you also remember
men in patched and faded but quite clean overalls sitting
on the gallery—here in the North we should call it the
porch—of a crossroads store that is covered with posters
advertising soft drinks and patent medicines; and you remember the stories they tell while chewing tobacco until
the suption is out of it (everything in their world is reduced to anecdote, and every anecdote is based on character). You remember Quentin Compson not in his despairing moments, but riding with his father behind the
dogs as they quarter a sedge-grown hillside after quail;
and not listening to his father's story, but still knowing
every word of it because, as he thought to himself, "You
had learned, absorbed it already without the medium of
speech somehow from having been born and living

beside it, with it, as children will and do; so that what your father was saying did not tell you anything so much as it struck, word by word, the resonant strings of remembering."

Faulkner's novels have the quality of being lived, absorbed, remembered rather than merely observed. And they have what is rare in the novels of our time, a warmth of family affection, brother for brother and sister, the father for his children—a love so warm and proud that it tries to shut out the rest of the world. Compared with that affection, married love is presented as something calculating, and illicit love as a consuming fire. And because the blood relationship is central in his novels, Faulkner finds it hard to create sympathetic characters between the ages of twenty and forty. He is better with children, Negro and white, and incomparably good with older people who preserve the standards that have come down to them "out of the old time, the old days."

In the group of novels beginning with *The Wild Palms* (1939), which attracted so little attention at the time of publication that they seemed to go unread, there is a quality not exactly new to Faulkner—it had appeared already in passages of *Sartoris* and *Sanctuary*—but now much stronger and no longer overshadowed by violence and horror. It is a sort of homely and sober-sided frontier humor that is seldom achieved in contemporary writing (except sometimes by Erskine Caldwell, also a Southerner). The horse-trading episodes in *The Hamlet*, and especially the long story of the spotted ponies from Texas, might have been inspired by the Davy Crockett almanacs. "Old Man," the story of the convict who surmounted the greatest of the Mississippi floods, might almost be a continuation of *Huckleberry Finn*. It is as if some older friend of Huck's had taken the raft and drifted on from Aunt Sally Phelps's farm into wilder adventures, described in a wilder style, among Chinese and Cajuns and bayous crawling with alligators. In a curious way, Faulkner combines two of the principal traditions in American letters: the tradition of psychological horror, often close to symbolism, that begins with Charles Brockden Brown, our first professional novelist, and extends through Poe, Melville, Henry James (in his later stories), Stephen Crane, and Hemingway; and the other tradition of frontier humor and realism, beginning with Augustus Longstreet's *Georgia Scenes* and having Mark Twain as its best example.

But the American author he most resembles is Hawthorne, for all their polar differences. They stand to each other as July to December, as heat to cold, as swamp to mountain, as the luxuriant to the meager but perfect, as planter to Puritan; and yet Hawthorne had much the same attitude toward New England that Faulkner has to the South, together with a strong sense of regional particularity. The Civil War made Hawthorne feel that "the North and the South were two distinct nations in opinions and habits, and had better not try to live under the same institutions." In the spring of 1861 he wrote to his Bowdoin classmate Horatio Bridge, "We were never one people and never really had a country." "New England," he said a little later, "is quite as large a lump of earth as my heart can really take in." But it was more than a lump of earth for him; it was a lump of history and a permanent state of consciousness. Like Faulkner in the South, he applied himself to creating its moral fables and elaborating its legends, which existed, as it were, in his solitary heart. Pacing the hillside behind his house in Concord, he listened for a voice; one might say that he lay in wait for it, passively but expectantly, like a hunter behind a rock; then, when it had spoken, he transcribed its words—more cautiously than Faulkner, it is true; with more form and less fire, but with the same essential fidelity. "I have an instinct that I had better keep quiet," he said in a letter to his publisher. "Perhaps I shall have a new spirit of vigor if I wait quietly for it; perhaps not." Faulkner is another author who has to wait for the spirit and the voice. He is not so much a novelist, in the usual sense of being a writer who sets out to observe actions and characters, then fits them into the framework of a story, as he is an epic or bardic poet in prose, a creator of myths that he weaves together into a legend of the South.

AFTERWORD

Except for the minor revisions I couldn't help making, that is what I wrote about Faulkner in the autumn of 1945, on the basis of the seventeen books he had published. There would be nine additional books in the subsequent years, and eight of them would belong to the Yoknapatawpha cycle. In the same years there would be a Mississippi flood of critical studies dealing with various aspects of Faulkner's novels (most often with their symbolic elements). The question is how this introduction might change in emphasis if I were writing it today, in the light of his critical reputation and on the basis of his life's work.

A few of the statements I made in 1945, or quoted with approval from others, would have to be revised on the ground that they do not apply to the later novels. I note, for example, André Gide's comment on Faulkner, "There is not one of his characters who, properly speaking, has a soul"—to which my echo was, "I think he means that not one of them exercises the faculty of conscious choice between good and evil." Though broadly true in 1945, the statement would eventually be riddled with exceptions. Temple Drake, to mention only one of these, had been a morally supine creature from the beginning to the end of *Sanctuary*. Twenty years later, when she reappears in *Requiem for a Nun* (1951), she drives herself into making an agonized confession, and she makes it "to save my soul," which she has discovered for the first time.

Another statement contradicted by Faulkner's later career is that he "finds it hard to create sympathetic characters between the ages of twenty and forty." Again that is true of the early novels, but the later ones contain many characters between those ages who are meant to elicit not only sympathy but admiration. Nancy Mannigoe, for example—"a nigger dopefiend whore," as Temple calls her—is also presented as a martyred saint. The villains forgo a little of their villainy, and one of them, Mink Snopes, becomes the real hero of *The Mansion* (1959). There are even happy endings of the conventional type. Lucas Beauchamp is saved from being lynched (*Intruder in the Dust*, 1948). Temple Drake, having found a soul, goes back to her husband and her surviving child. Gavin Stevens (in *Knight's Gambit*, 1949) stops talking long enough to marry a woman to whom he had first proposed when she was a girl of sixteen.

In Faulkner's later novels, the Yoknapatawpha story is traced backward to the founding and naming of Jefferson, as well as being carried forward almost to the present day. They might be regarded as sequels to the earlier books, yet they almost seem to be written by a different novelist. The sense of doom and outrage that brooded over the early ones has been replaced by pity for human beings, even the worst of them ("The poor sons of bitches," Gavin Stevens says, "they do the best they can") and by the obstinate faith expressed in the Nobel Prize address "that man will not only endure: he will prevail"—all this combined with more than a touch of old-fashioned sentiment. I respect the later Faulkner, with most of his demons exorcised, but the younger possessed and unregenerate author is the one whose works amaze us, as they never ceased to puzzle and amaze himself.

Even in an introduction confined to those earlier works, I should, if I were writing it today, adopt a somewhat different emphasis. In 1945 I was arguing against the scandalous neglect of his novels. Not only were they little read at the time but it seemed to me, as I kept saying, that hardly any critic had looked for a general design in which one novel was linked to another. So it was the design that I chiefly emphasized: the imaginative effort to understand the present in terms of the past that led Faulkner to elaborate a legend of Southern history. In so doing I shifted my attention from book to book without pausing long enough on any one of them, even *The Sound and the Fury* or *Absalom, Absalom!* and without examining each of them as a separate achievement. Fortunately that emphasis has been corrected and overcorrected by a host of later critics.

Perhaps I dwelt too much on what is in the foreground, that is, on the story of a single county in northern Mississippi presented as, in Faulkner's words, "that chronicle which was a whole land in miniature, which multiplied and compounded was the entire South." Faulkner in his early novels is indubitably a Southern nationalist and an heir of the Confederacy—for all his sense of guilt about the Negroes—but he is something else besides, a fact that I failed to make sufficiently clear. What he regarded as his ultimate subject is not the South or its destiny, however much they occupied his mind, but rather the human situation as revealed in Southern terms—to quote from one of his letters,[5] "the same frantic steeplechase toward nothing everywhere." He approached that steeplechase in terms of Southern material because, as he also said, "I just happen to know it, and dont have time in one life to learn another one and write at the same time." There was of course another reason, for it was the South that aroused his apprehensions, that deeply engaged his loyalties (*"I dont. I dont hate it"*), and that set his imagination to work. He always dreamed, however, that his fables might stand for a universally human drama.

So I would have different points to emphasize if I were writing the introduction today. I would be able to use the cartographical studies of other critics instead of groping

---

[5] The one dated "Oxford. Saturday." (Early November, 1944.) See *The Faulkner-Cowley File*, pp. 14–17.

my way without maps—except those supplied by Faulkner himself—and stumbling more than once. It seems to me, however, that my introduction, combined with the selections in the present volume, continues to mark out the straightest path into Faulkner's imaginary kingdom, and the surest path for those who might otherwise get lost in the swampy places. Yoknapatawpha County is a region where every landmark has a story of its own, and every story goes back to earlier times. Accordingly the selections were planned to give a general panorama of life in the county decade by decade, from the days when the first settlers came riding westward from Carolina on the Wilderness Trail or northward on the Natchez Trace. So as not to distort the sequence, I included no complete novels, but there are three stories almost of novel length: "The Bear," "Spotted Horses," and "Old Man."

For this new edition I have not found it necessary to make many changes in the text. Faulkner's later books round out the Yoknapatawpha story, but without transforming it into something else. The principal borrowings I have made from them are two of the prologues that appear in the printed version of *Requiem for a Nun*. One of these, "The Courthouse," contains his most detailed account of the early settlers (and enabled me to omit a chapter from *Absalom, Absalom!* dealing with the same material). The other is "The Jail," which is Faulkner's most effective statement of how the past lives in the present: "It's not even past." Here as elsewhere I tried to make selections which are really (and not merely in the phrase from book jackets) "complete in themselves." "Thus," as I said in 1945, "the book can be dipped into as if it were a Faulkner anthology; but I also hope that some readers will go through it from beginning to end, following the characters and the sequence of events as if they were reading one continued story; and I hope they will find that it retains something of the organic unity of Faulkner's legend."

MALCOLM COWLEY

BOOKS BY WILLIAM FAULKNER

*The books are novels unless otherwise identified. If they
deal wholly or in part with Yohnapatawpha County, the
title is preceded by an asterisk.*

1924. *The Marble Faun.* Boston, The Four Seas Company.
A cycle of nineteen poems.

1926. *Soldier's Pay.* New York, Boni and Liveright.

1927. *Mosquitoes.* New York, Boni and Liveright.

1929. *Sartoris. New York, Harcourt, Brace and Company.
First of the Yoknapatawpha novels.

1929. *The Sound and the Fury. New York, Jonathan
Cape and Harrison Smith.

1930. *As I Lay Dying. New York, Jonathan Cape and
Harrison Smith.

1931. *Sanctuary. New York, Jonathan Cape and Harrison
Smith.

1931. *These 13. New York, Jonathan Cape and Harrison
Smith. Six of these stories deal with Yoknapatawpha County.

1931. *Idyll in the Desert.* New York, Random House. A
short story published in a limited edition.

1932. *Miss Zilphia Gant. Dallas, The Book Club of
Texas. Another short story published in a limited
edition and, like *Idyll in the Desert,* never re-
issued.

1932. *Light in August.* New York, Harrison Smith and
      Robert Haas (a successor firm to Cape & Smith).

1933. *A Green Bough.* New York, Harrison Smith and
      Robert Haas. Faulkner's second and last book of
      poems.

1934. *Doctor Martino and Other Stories.* New York, Har-
      rison Smith and Robert Haas. Fourteen stories.

1935. *Pylon.* New York, Harrison Smith and Robert Haas.

1936. *Absalom, Absalom!* New York, Random House
      (which would publish Faulkner's subsequent
      books and in time reissue most of the early ones).

1938. *The Unvanquished.* New York, Random House.
      Seven long stories that together form a novel.

1939. *The Wild Palms.* New York, Random House. A
      novel composed of two long stories told in alter-
      nate chapters.

1940. *The Hamlet.* New York, Random House. First
      volume in the Snopes trilogy.

1942. *Go Down, Moses.* New York, Random House. First
      published as *Go Down, Moses and Other Stories,*
      but Faulkner intended the book as a novel.

1948. *Intruder in the Dust.* New York, Random House.

1949. *Knight's Gambit.* New York, Random House. A
      cycle of five short stories and one novella, all
      dealing with the adventures in detection of Gavin
      Stevens.

1950. *Collected Stories of William Faulkner.* New York,
      Random House. Contains forty-two stories, all
      that Faulkner then planned to preserve, except
      for those fitted into more integrated volumes like
      The Unvanquished, Go Down, Moses, and
      Knight's Gambit.

1951. *Requiem for a Nun.* New York, Random House. A
      three-act play with a narrative prologue to each
      act.

1954. *A Fable.* New York, Random House.

1955. *Big Woods*. New York, Random House. Four hunting stories (two of them revised from chapters of *Go Down, Moses*), with interchapters to set the mood.

1957. *The Town*. New York, Random House. Second volume in the Snopes trilogy.

1959. *The Mansion*. New York, Random House. Concluding the Snopes trilogy.

1962. *The Reivers*. New York, Random House. Faulkner's last novel, published a few months before his death on July 6, 1962.

1965. *Essays, Speeches and Public Letters*. Edited by James B. Meriwether. New York, Random House.

1966. *The Faulkner-Cowley File*. By Malcolm Cowley. New York, The Viking Press. Contains twenty-six of Faulkner's letters.

The Portable
FAULKNER

THE OLD PEOPLE

Editor's Note

Here are four of Faulkner's stories dealing with early days in Yoknapatawpha County: with the Indians, the first white settlers, and the McCaslin plantation in the time of Uncle Buck and Uncle Buddy.

The Indians in Faulkner's country were Chickasaws. He paints them as being slow, brooding, cruel, serene, like the land itself, to which they belonged as much as did the wild creatures they hunted. The settlers disturbed this natural relationship. They found it easy to buy the Chickasaws' land—even to cheat them out of a hundred square miles in one transaction, as did Thomas Sutpen—because the Indians were psychologically unable to place a cash value on it. Then, having driven the natives westward and having peopled the land with slaves—to grow more cotton to buy more Negroes to grow more cotton—the planters set about creating their own aristocratic order.

Faulkner keeps looking back nostalgically to the old order, but he presents its virtues as being moral rather than material. There is no baronial pomp in his novels; no profusion of silk and silver, mahogany and moonlight and champagne. All the planters lived comfortably, with plenty of servants, but Faulkner never lets us forget that they were living on what had recently been the frontier. What he admires about them is not their wealth or hospitality or florid manners, but rather their unquestioning acceptance of a moral code that taught them "courage and honor and pride, and pity and love of justice and of liberty." The code was the secret lost by their heirs and successors.

"A Justice" is a story of the old days as told to Quentin Compson, who will reappear with Caddy and Jason in *The Sound and the Fury* and who will be the narrator of *Absalom, Absalom!* Besides presenting the Compson children, the story also introduces Sam Fathers, the Chickasaw hunter who lived among the Negroes. He too will reappear in later stories, but with other dates assigned to his birth and death; that is one of the inconsistencies mentioned in the Introduction. "The Courthouse" is from the printed version of Faulkner's play, *Requiem for a Nun* (1951), where it serves as a prologue to the first act. It introduces all the founders of Jefferson, including Thomas Sutpen (of *Absalom, Absalom!*), his French architect, and his wild Negroes from the jungle. "Red Leaves" is the most powerful of Faulkner's four stories that deal with the Chickasaws (the others are "Lo!" and "A Courtship"). With "A Justice" it was included in *These 13*, his first collection of stories, published in 1931. "Was" is the opening chapter of *Go Down, Moses* (1942). It introduces Uncle Buck and Uncle Buddy McCaslin, the two poker-playing bachelors who lived in a cabin built with their own hands, because —although they had inherited a big plantation—they refused to profit from the fruits of slavery.

1820

A Justice

I

Until Grandfather Compson died, we would go out to the farm every Saturday afternoon. We would leave home right after dinner in the surrey, I in front with Roskus, and Grandfather and Candace (Caddy, we called her) and Jason in the back. Grandfather and Roskus would talk, with the horses going fast, because it was the best team in the county. They would carry the surrey fast along the levels and up some of the hills even. But this was in north Mississippi, and on some of the hills Roskus and I could smell Grandfather's cigar.

The farm was four miles away. There was a long, low house in the grove, not painted but kept whole and sound by a clever carpenter from the quarters named Sam Fathers, and behind it the barns and smokehouses, and further still, the quarters themselves, also kept whole and sound by Sam Fathers. He did nothing else, and they said he was almost a hundred years old. He lived with the Negroes and they—the white people; the Negroes called him a blue-gum—called him a Negro. But he wasn't a Negro. That's what I'm going to tell about.

When we got there, Mr. Stokes, the manager, would send a Negro boy with Caddy and Jason to the creek to fish, because Caddy was a girl and Jason was too little, but I wouldn't go with them. I would go to Sam Fathers' shop, where he would be making breast-yokes or wagon

3

wheels, and I would always bring him some tobacco. Then he would stop working and he would fill his pipe—he made them himself, out of creek clay with a reed stem—and he would tell me about the old days. He talked like a nigger—that is, he said his words like niggers do, but he didn't say the same words—and his hair was nigger hair. But his skin wasn't quite the color of a light nigger and his nose and his mouth and chin were not nigger nose and mouth and chin. And his shape was not like the shape of a nigger when he gets old. He was straight in the back, not tall, a little broad, and his face was still all the time, like he might be somewhere else all the while he was working or when people, even white people, talked to him, or while he talked to me. It was just the same all the time, like he might be away up on a roof by himself, driving nails. Sometimes he would quit work with something half-finished on the bench, and sit down and smoke. And he wouldn't jump up and go back to work when Mr. Stokes or even Grandfather came along.

So I would give him the tobacco and he would stop work and sit down and fill his pipe and talk to me.

"These niggers," he said. "They call me Uncle Blue-Gum. And the white folks, they call me Sam Fathers."

"Isn't that your name?" I said.

"No. Not in the old days. I remember. I remember how I never saw but one white man until I was a boy big as you are; a whiskey trader that came every summer to the Plantation. It was the Man himself that named me. He didn't name me Sam Fathers, though."

"The Man?" I said.

"He owned the Plantation, the Negroes, my mammy too. He owned all the land that I knew of until I was grown. He was a Chickasaw chief. He sold my mammy to your greatgrandpappy. He said I didn't have to go unless I wanted to, because I was a warrior too then. He was the one who named me Had-Two-Fathers."

"Had-Two-Fathers?" I said. "That's not a name. That's not anything."

"It was my name once. Listen."

II

This is how Herman Basket told it when I was big enough to hear talk. He said that when Doom came back from New Orleans, he brought this woman with him. He brought six black people, though Herman Basket said they already had more black people in the Plantation than they could find use for. Sometimes they would run the black men with dogs, like you would a fox or a cat or a coon. And then Doom brought six more when he came home from New Orleans. He said he won them on the steamboat, and so he had to take them. He got off the steamboat with the six black people, Herman Basket said, and a big box in which something was alive, and the gold box of New Orleans salt about the size of a gold watch. And Herman Basket told how Doom took a puppy out of the box in which something was alive, and how he made a bullet of bread and a pinch of the salt in the gold box, and put the bullet into the puppy and the puppy died.

That was the kind of a man that Doom was, Herman Basket said. He told how, when Doom got off the steamboat that night, he wore a coat with gold all over it, and he had three gold watches, but Herman Basket said that even after seven years, Doom's eyes had not changed. He said that Doom's eyes were just the same as before he went away, before his name was Doom, and he and Herman Basket and my pappy were sleeping on the same pallet and talking at night, as boys will.

Doom's name was Ikkemotubbe then, and he was not born to be the Man, because Doom's mother's brother was the Man, and the Man had a son of his own, as well as a brother. But even then, and Doom no bigger than you are, Herman Basket said that sometimes the Man would look at Doom and he would say: "O Sister's Son, your eye is a bad eye, like the eye of a bad horse."

So the Man was not sorry when Doom got to be a young man and said that he would go to New Orleans, Herman Basket said. The Man was getting old then. He used to like to play mumble-peg and to pitch horseshoes both, but now he just liked mumble-peg. So he was not sorry when Doom went away, though he didn't forget about Doom. Herman Basket said that each summer when the whiskey trader came, the Man would ask him about Doom. "He calls himself David Callicoat now," the Man would say. "But his name is Ikkemotubbe. You haven't heard maybe of a David Callicoat getting drowned in the Big River, or killed in the white man's fight at New Orleans?"

But Herman Basket said they didn't hear from Doom at all until he had been gone seven years. Then one day Herman Basket and my pappy got a written stick from Doom to meet him at the Big River. Because the steamboat didn't come up our river any more then. The steamboat was still in our river, but it didn't go anywhere any more. Herman Basket told how one day during the high water, about three years after Doom went away, the steamboat came and crawled up on a sand-bar and died.

That was how Doom got his second name, the one before Doom. Herman Basket told how four times a year the steamboat would come up our river, and how the People would go to the river and camp and wait to see the steamboat pass, and he said that the white man who told the steamboat where to swim was named David Callicoat. So when Doom told Herman Basket and pappy that he was going to New Orleans, he said, "And I'll tell you something else. From now on, my name is not Ikkemotubbe. It's David Callicoat. And some day I'm going to own a steamboat, too." That was the kind of man that Doom was, Herman Basket said.

So after seven years he sent them the written stick and Herman Basket and pappy took the wagon and went to meet Doom at the Big River, and Doom got off the steamboat with the six black people. "I won them on the steamboat," Doom said. "You and Craw-ford (my pappy's name was Crawfish-ford, but usually it was Craw-ford) can divide them."

"I don't want them," Herman Basket said that pappy said.

"Then Herman can have them all," Doom said.

"I don't want them either," Herman Basket said.

"All right," Doom said. Then Herman Basket said he asked Doom if his name was still David Callicoat, but instead of answering, Doom told one of the black people something in the white man's talk, and the black man lit a pine knot. Then Herman Basket said they were watching Doom take the puppy from the box and make the bullet of bread and the New Orleans salt which Doom had in the little gold box, when he said that pappy said:

"I believe you said that Herman and I were to divide these black people."

Then Herman Basket said he saw that one of the black people was a woman.

"You and Herman don't want them," Doom said.

"I wasn't thinking when I said that," pappy said. "I will take the lot with the woman in it. Herman can have the other three."

"I don't want them," Herman Basket said.

"You can have four, then," pappy said. "I will take the woman and one other."

"I don't want them," Herman Basket said.

"I will take only the woman," pappy said. "You can have the other five."

"I don't want them," Herman Basket said.

"You don't want them, either," Doom said to pappy. "You said so yourself."

Then Herman Basket said that the puppy was dead. "You didn't tell us your new name," he said to Doom.

"My name is Doom now," Doom said. "It was given me by a French chief in New Orleans. In French talking, Doo-um; in our talking, Doom."

"What does it mean?" Herman Basket said.

He said how Doom looked at him for a while. "It means, the Man," Doom said.

Herman Basket told how they thought about that. He said they stood there in the dark, with the other puppies in the box, the ones that Doom hadn't used, whimpering and scuffing, and the light of the pine knot shining on the eyeballs of the black people and on Doom's gold coat and on the puppy that had died.

"You cannot be the Man," Herman Basket said. "You are only on the sister's side. And the Man has a brother and a son."

"That's right," Doom said. "But if I were the Man, I would give Craw-ford those black people. I would give Herman something, too. For every black man I gave Craw-ford, I would give Herman a horse, if I were Man."

"Craw-ford only wants this woman," Herman Basket said.

"I would give Herman six horses, anyway," Doom said. "But maybe the Man has already given Herman a horse."

"No," Herman Basket said. "My ghost is still walking."

It took them three days to reach the Plantation. They camped on the road at night. Herman Basket said that they did not talk.

They reached the Plantation on the third day. He said that the Man was not very glad to see Doom, even though Doom brought a present of candy for the Man's son. Doom had something for all his kinsfolk, even for the Man's brother. The Man's brother lived by himself in a cabin by the creek. His name was Sometimes-Wakeup. Sometimes the People took him food. The rest of the time they didn't see him. Herman Basket told how he and pappy went with Doom to visit Sometimes-Wakeup in his cabin. It was at night, and Doom told Herman Basket to close the door. Then Doom took the puppy from pappy and set it on the floor and made a bullet of bread and the New Orleans salt for Sometimes-Wakeup to see how it worked. When they left, Herman Basket said how Sometimes-Wakeup burned a stick and covered his head with the blanket.

That was the first night that Doom was at home. On the next day Herman Basket told how the Man began to act strange at his food, and died before the doctor could get there and burn sticks. When the Willow-Bearer went to fetch the Man's son and tell him that he was to be the Man, they found that he had acted strange and then died too.

"Now Sometimes-Wakeup will have to be the Man," pappy said.

So the Willow-Bearer went to fetch Sometimes-Wakeup to come and be the Man. The Willow-Bearer came back soon. "Sometimes-Wakeup does not want to be the Man," the Willow-Bearer said. "He is sitting in his cabin with his head in his blanket."

"Then Ikkemotubbe will have to be the Man," pappy said.

So Doom was the Man. But Herman Basket said that pappy's ghost would not be easy. Herman Basket said he told pappy to give Doom a little time. "I am still walking," Herman Basket said.

"But this is a serious matter with me," pappy said.

He said that at last pappy went to Doom, before the Man and his son had entered the earth, before the eating and the horse-racing were over. "What woman?" Doom said.

"You said that when you were the Man," pappy said. Herman Basket said that Doom looked at pappy but that pappy was not looking at Doom.

"I think you don't trust me," Doom said. Herman Basket said how pappy did not look at Doom. "I think you still believe that that puppy was sick," Doom said. "Think about it."

Herman Basket said that pappy thought.

"What do you think now?" Doom said.

But Herman Basket said that pappy still did not look at Doom. "I think it was a well dog," pappy said.

III

At last the eating and the horse-racing were over and the Man and his son had entered the earth. Then Doom said, "Tomorrow we will go and fetch the steamboat." Herman Basket told how Doom had been talking about the steamboat ever since he became Man, and about how the House was not big enough. So that evening Doom said, "Tomorrow we will go and fetch the steamboat that died in the river."

Herman Basket said how the steamboat was twelve miles away, and that it could not even swim in the water. So the next morning there was no one in the Plantation except Doom and the black people. He told how it took Doom all that day to find the People. Doom used the dogs, and he found some of the People in hollow logs in the creek bottom. That night he made all the men sleep in the House. He kept the dogs in the House, too.

Herman Basket told how he heard Doom and pappy talking in the dark. "I don't think you trust me," Doom said.

"I trust you," pappy said.

"That is what I would advise," Doom said.

"I wish you could advise that to my ghost," pappy said. The next morning they went to the steamboat. The women and the black people walked. The men rode in the wagons, with Doom following behind with the dogs.

The steamboat was lying on its side on the sand-bar. When they came to it, there were three white men on it. "Now we can go back home," pappy said.

But Doom talked to the white men. "Does this steamboat belong to you?" Doom said.

"It does not belong to you," the white men said. And though they had guns, Herman Basket said they did not look like men who would own a boat.

"Shall we kill them?" he said to Doom. But he said that Doom was still talking to the men on the steamboat.

"What will you take for it?" Doom said.

"What will you give for it?" the white men said.

"It is dead," Doom said. "It's not worth much."

"Will you give ten black people?" the white men said.

"All right," Doom said. "Let the black people who came with me from the Big River come forward." They came forward, the five men and the woman. "Let four more black people come forward." Four more came forward. "You are now to eat of the corn of those white men yonder," Doom said. "May it nourish you." The white men went away, the ten black people following them. "Now," Doom said, "let us make the steamboat get up and walk."

Herman Basket said that he and pappy did not go into the river with the others, because pappy said to go aside and talk. They went aside. Pappy talked, but Herman Basket said that he said he did not think it was right to kill white men, but pappy said how they could fill the white men with rocks and sink them in the river and nobody would find them. So Herman Basket said they overtook the three white men and the ten black people, then they turned back toward the boat. Just before they came to the steamboat, pappy said to the black men: "Go on to the Man. Go and help make the steamboat get up and walk. I will take this woman on home."

"This woman is my wife," one of the black men said. "I want her to stay with me."

"Do you want to be arranged in the river with rocks in your inside too?" pappy said to the black man.

"Do you want to be arranged in the river yourself?" the black man said to pappy. "There are two of you, and nine of us."

Herman Basket said that pappy thought. Then pappy said, "Let us go to the steamboat and help the Man."

They went to the steamboat. But Herman Basket said that Doom did not notice the ten black people until it was time to return to the Plantation. Herman Basket told how Doom looked at the black people, then looked at pappy. "It seems that the white men did not want these black people," Doom said.

"So it seems," pappy said.

"The white men went away, did they?" Doom said.

"So it seems," pappy said.

Herman Basket told how every night Doom would make all the men sleep in the House, with the dogs in the House too, and how each morning they would return to the steamboat in the wagons. The wagons would not hold everybody, so after the second day the women stayed at home. But it was three days before Doom noticed that pappy was staying at home too. Herman Basket said that the woman's husband may have told Doom. "Craw-ford hurt his back lifting the steamboat," Herman Basket said he told Doom. "He said he would stay at the Plantation and sit with his feet in the Hot Spring so that the sickness in his back could return to the earth."

"That is a good idea," Doom said. "He has been doing this for three days, has he? Then the sickness should be down in his legs by now."

When they returned to the Plantation that night, Doom sent for pappy. He asked pappy if the sickness had moved. Pappy said how the sickness moved very slow. "You must sit in the Spring more," Doom said.

"That is what I think," pappy said.

"Suppose you sit in the Spring at night too," Doom said.

"The night air will make it worse," pappy said.

"Not with a fire there," Doom said. "I will send one of the black people with you to keep the fire burning."

"Which one of the black people?" pappy said.

"The husband of the woman which I won on the steamboat," Doom said.

"I think my back is better," pappy said.

"Let us try it," Doom said.

"I know my back is better," pappy said.

"Let us try it, anyway," Doom said. Just before dark Doom sent four of the People to fix pappy and the black man at the Spring. Herman Basket said the People returned quickly. He said that as they entered the House, pappy entered also.

"The sickness began to move suddenly," pappy said. "It has reached my feet since noon today."

"Do you think it will be gone by morning?" Doom said.

"I think so," pappy said.

"Perhaps you had better sit in the Spring tonight and make sure," Doom said.

"I know it will be gone by morning," pappy said.

IV

When it got to be summer, Herman Basket said that the steamboat was out of the river bottom. It had taken them five months to get it out of the bottom, because they had to cut down the trees to make a path for it. But now he said the steamboat could walk faster on the logs. He told how pappy helped. Pappy had a certain place on one of the ropes near the steamboat that nobody was allowed to take, Herman Basket said. It was just under the front porch of the steamboat where Doom sat in his chair, with a boy with a branch to shade him and another boy with a branch to drive away the flying beasts. The dogs rode on the boat too.

In the summer, while the steamboat was still walking, Herman Basket told how the husband of the woman came to Doom again. "I have done what I could for you," Doom said. "Why don't you go to Craw-ford and adjust this matter yourself?"

The black man said that he had done that. He said that pappy said to adjust it by a cock-fight, pappy's cock against the black man's, the winner to have the woman, the one who refused to fight to lose by default. The black man said he told pappy he did not have a cock, and that pappy said that in that case the black man lost by default and that the woman belonged to pappy. "And what am I to do?" the black man said.

Doom thought. Then Herman Basket said that Doom called to him and asked him which was pappy's best cock and Herman Basket told Doom that pappy had only one. "That black one?" Doom said. Herman Basket said he told Doom that was the one. "Ah," Doom said. Herman Basket told how Doom sat in his chair on the porch of the steamboat while it walked, looking down at the People and the black men pulling the ropes, making the steamboat walk. "Go and tell Craw-ford you have a cock," Doom said to the black man. "Just tell him you will have a cock in the pit. Let it be tomorrow morning. We will let the steamboat sit down and rest." The black man went away. Then Herman Basket said that Doom was looking at him, and that he did not look at Doom. Because he said there was but one better cock in the Plantation than pappy's, and that one belonged to Doom. "I think that that puppy was not sick," Doom said. "What do you think?"

Herman Basket said that he did not look at Doom. "That is what I think," he said.

"That is what I would advise," Doom said.

Herman Basket told how the next day the steamboat

sat and rested. The pit was in the stable. The People and the black people were there. Pappy had his cock in the pit. Then the black man put his cock into the pit. Herman Basket said that pappy looked at the black man's cock.

"This cock belongs to Ikkemotubbe," pappy said.

"It is his," the People told pappy. "Ikkemotubbe gave it to him with all to witness."

Herman Basket said that pappy had already picked up his cock. "This is not right," pappy said. "We ought not to let him risk his wife on a cock-fight."

"Then you withdraw?" the black man said.

"Let me think," pappy said. He thought. The People watched. The black man reminded pappy of what he had said about defaulting. Pappy said he did not mean to say that and that he withdrew it. The People told him that he could only withdraw by forfeiting the match. Herman Basket said that pappy thought again. The People watched. "All right," pappy said. "But I am being taken advantage of."

The cocks fought. Pappy's cock fell. Pappy took it up quickly. Herman Basket said it was like pappy had been waiting for his cock to fall so he could pick it quickly up. "Wait," he said. He looked at the People. "Now they have fought. Isn't that true?" The People said that it was true. "So that settles what I said about forfeiting."

Herman Basket said that pappy began to get out of the pit.

"Aren't you going to fight?" the black man said.

"I don't think this will settle anything," pappy said. "Do you?"

Herman Basket told how the black man looked at pappy. Then he quit looking at pappy. He was squatting. Herman Basket said the People looked at the black man looking at the earth between his feet. They watched him take up a clod of dirt, and then they watched the dust come out between the black man's fingers. "Do you think that this will settle anything?" pappy said.

"No," the black man said. Herman Basket said that the People could not hear him very good. But he said that pappy could hear him.

"Neither do I," pappy said. "It would not be right to risk your wife on a cock-fight."

Herman Basket told how the black man looked up, with the dry dust about the fingers of his hand. He said the black man's eyes looked red in the dark pit, like the eyes of a fox. "Will you let the cocks fight again?" the black man said.

"Do you agree that it doesn't settle anything?" pappy said.

"Yes," the black man said.

Pappy put his cock back into the ring. Herman Basket said that pappy's cock was dead before it had time to act strange, even. The black man's cock stood upon it and started to crow, but the black man struck the live cock away and he jumped up and down on the dead cock until it did not look like a cock at all, Herman Basket said.

Then it was fall, and Herman Basket told how the steamboat came to the Plantation and stopped beside the House and died again. He said that for two months they had been in sight of the Plantation, making the steamboat walk on the logs, but now the steamboat was beside the House and the House was big enough to please Doom. He gave an eating. It lasted a week. When it was over, Herman Basket told how the black man came to Doom a third time. Herman Basket said that the black man's eyes were red again, like those of a fox, and that they could hear his breathing in the room. "Come to my cabin," he said to Doom. "I have something to show you."

"I thought it was about that time," Doom said. He looked about the room, but Herman Basket told Doom that pappy had just stepped out. "Tell him to come also," Doom said. When they came to the black man's cabin, Doom sent two of the People to fetch pappy. Then they entered the cabin. What the black man wanted to show Doom was a new man.

"Look," the black man said. "You are the Man. You are to see justice done."

"What is wrong with this man?" Doom said.

"Look at the color of him," the black man said. He began to look around the cabin. Herman Basket said that his eyes went red and then brown and then red, like those of a fox. He said they could hear the black man's breathing. "Do I get justice?" the black man said. "You are the Man."

"You should be proud of a fine yellow man like this," Doom said. He looked at the new man. "I don't see that justice can darken him any," Doom said. He looked about the cabin also. "Come forward, Craw-ford," he said "This is a man, not a copper snake; he will not harm you." But Herman Basket said that pappy would not come forward. He said the black man's eyes went red and then brown and then red when he breathed. "Yao," Doom said, "this is not right. Any man is entitled to have his melon patch protected from these wild bucks of the woods. But first let us name this man." Doom thought. Herman Basket said the black man's eyes went quieter now, and his breath went quieter too. "We will call him Had-Two-Fathers," Doom said.

v

Sam Fathers lit his pipe again. He did it deliberately, rising and lifting between thumb and forefinger from his forge a coal of fire. Then he came back and sat down. It was getting late. Caddy and Jason had come back from the creek, and I could see Grandfather and Mr. Stokes talking beside the carriage, and at that moment, as though he had felt my gaze, Grandfather turned and called my name.

"What did your pappy do then?" I said.

"He and Herman Basket built the fence," Sam Fathers said. "Herman Basket told how Doom made them set two posts into the ground, with a sapling across the top of them. The nigger and pappy were there. Doom had not told them about the fence then. Herman Basket said it was just like when he and pappy and Doom were boys, sleeping on the same pallet, and Doom would wake them at night and make them get up and go hunting with him, or when he would make them stand up with him and fight with their fists, just for fun, until Herman Basket and pappy would hide from Doom.

"They fixed the sapling across the two posts and Doom said to the nigger: 'This is a fence. Can you climb it?'

"Herman Basket said the nigger put his hand on the sapling and sailed over it like a bird.

"Then Doom said to pappy: 'Climb this fence.'

" 'This fence is too high to climb,' pappy said.

" 'Climb this fence, and I will give you the woman,' Doom said.

"Herman Basket said pappy looked at the fence a while. 'Let me go under this fence,' he said.

" 'No,' Doom said.

"Herman Basket told me how pappy began to sit down on the ground. 'It's not that I don't trust you,' pappy said.

" 'We will build the fence this high,' Doom said.

" 'What fence?' Herman Basket said.

" 'The fence around the cabin of this black man,' Doom said.

" 'I can't build a fence I couldn't climb,' pappy said.

" 'Herman will help you,' Doom said.

"Herman Basket said it was just like when Doom used to wake them and make them go hunting. He said the dogs found him and pappy about noon the next day, and that they began the fence that afternoon. He told me how they had to cut the saplings in the creek bottom and drag them in by hand, because Doom would not let them use the wagon. So sometimes one post would take them three or four days. 'Never mind,' Doom said. "You have plenty of time. And the exercise will make Craw-ford sleep at night.'

"He told me how they worked on the fence all that winter and all the next summer, until after the whiskey trader had come and gone. Then it was finished. He said that on the day they set the last post, the nigger came out of the cabin and put his hand on the top of a post (it was a palisade fence, the posts set upright in the ground) and flew out like a bird. 'This is a good fence,' the nigger said. 'Wait,' he said. 'I have something to show you.' Herman Basket said he flew back over the fence again and went into the cabin and came back. Herman Basket said that he was carrying a new man and that he held the new man up so they could see it above the fence. 'What do you think about this for color?' he said."

Grandfather called me again. This time I got up. The sun was already down beyond the peach orchard. I was just twelve then, and to me the story did not seem to have got anywhere, to have had point or end. Yet I obeyed Grandfather's voice, not that I was tired of Sam Fathers' talking, but with that immediacy of children with which they flee temporarily something which they do not quite understand; that, and the instinctive promptness with which we all obeyed Grandfather, not from concern of impatience or reprimand, but because we all believed that he did fine things, that his waking life passed from one fine (if faintly grandiose) picture to another.

They were in the surrey, waiting for me. I got in; the horses moved at once, impatient too for the stable. Caddy had one fish, about the size of a chip, and she was wet to the waist. We drove on, the team already trotting. When we passed Mr. Stokes' kitchen we could smell ham cooking. The smell followed us on to the gate. When we turned onto the road home it was almost sundown. Then we couldn't smell the cooking ham any more. "What were you and Sam talking about?" Grandfather said.

We went on, in that strange, faintly sinister suspension of twilight in which I believed that I could still see Sam Fathers back there, sitting on his wooden block, definite, immobile, and complete, like something looked upon after a long time in a preservative bath in a museum. That was it. I was just twelve then, and I would have to wait until I had passed on and through and beyond the suspension of twilight. Then I knew that I would know. But then Sam Fathers would be dead.

"Nothing, sir," I said. "We were just talking."

1833

The Courthouse (A Name for the City)

The courthouse is less old than the town, which began somewhere under the turn of the century as a Chickasaw Agency trading-post and so continued for almost thirty years before it discovered, not that it lacked a depository for its records and certainly not that it needed one, but that only by creating or anyway decreeing one, could it cope with a situation which otherwise was going to cost somebody money;

The settlement had the records; even the simple dispossession of Indians begot in time a minuscule of archive, let alone the normal litter of man's ramshackle confederation against environment—that time and that wilderness—in this case, a meagre, fading, dogeared, uncorrelated, at times illiterate sheaf of land grants and patents and transfers and deeds, and tax- and militia-rolls, and bills of sale for slaves, and counting-house lists of spurious currency and exchange rates, and liens and mortgages, and listed rewards for escaped or stolen Negroes and other livestock, and diary-like annotations of births and marriages and deaths and public hangings and land-auctions, accumulating slowly for those three decades in a sort of iron pirate's chest in the back room of the postoffice-tradingpost-store, until that day thirty years later when, because of a jailbreak compounded by an ancient monster iron padlock transported a thousand miles by horse-

back from Carolina, the box was removed to a small new
leanto room like a wood- or tool-shed built two days ago
against one outside wall of the morticed-log mud-chinked
shake-down jail; and thus was born the Yoknapatawpha
County courthouse: by simple fortuity, not only less old
than even the jail, but come into existence at all by
chance and accident: the box containing the documents
not moved from any place, but simply to one; removed
from the trading-post back room not for any reason inherent in either the back room or the box, but on the contrary: which—the box—was not only in nobody's way in
the back room, it was even missed when gone since it had
served as another seat or stool among the powder- and
whisky-kegs and firkins of salt and lard about the stove on
winter nights; and was moved at all for the simple reason
that suddenly the settlement (overnight it would become a town without having been a village; one day in
about a hundred years it would wake frantically from
its communal slumber into a rash of Rotary and Lion Clubs
and Chambers of Commerce and City Beautifuls: a furious
beating of hollow drums toward nowhere, but merely to
sound louder than the next little human clotting to its
north or south or east or west, dubbing itself city as
Napoleon dubbed himself emperor and defending the
expedient by padding its census rolls—a fever, a delirium
in which it would confound forever seething with motion and motion with progress. But that was a hundred
years away yet; now it was frontier, the men and
women pioneers, tough, simple, and durable, seeking
money or adventure or freedom or simple escape, and
not too particular how they did it.) discovered itself
faced not so much with a problem which had to be solved,
as a Damocles sword of dilemma from which it had to
save itself;

Even the jailbreak was fortuity: a gang—three or four
—of Natchez Trace bandits (twenty-five years later

legend would begin to affirm, and a hundred years later
would still be at it, that two of the bandits were the
Harpes themselves, Big Harpe anyway, since the circumstances, the method of the breakout left behind like a
smell, an odor, a kind of gargantuan and bizarre play-
fulness at once humorous and terrifying, as if the settlement had fallen, blundered, into the notice or range of
an idle and whimsical giant. Which—that they were the
Harpes—was impossible, since the Harpes and even the
last of Mason's ruffians were dead or scattered by this time,
and the robbers would have had to belong to John Mur-
rel's organization—if they needed to belong to any at
all other than the simple fraternity of rapine.) captured
by chance by an incidental band of civilian more-or-less
militia and brought in to the Jefferson jail because it was
the nearest one, the militia band being part of a general
muster at Jefferson two days before for a Fourth-of-
July barbecue, which by the second day had been refined by hardy elimination into one drunken brawling
which rendered even the hardiest survivors vulnerable
enough to be ejected from the settlement by the civilian
residents, the band which was to make the capture having
been carried, still comatose, in one of the evicting wagons
to a swamp four miles from Jefferson known as Hurricane
Bottoms, where they made camp to regain their strength
or at least their legs, and where that night the four—or
three—bandits, on the way across country to their hideout
from their last exploit on the Trace, stumbled onto
the campfire. And here report divided; some said that the
sergeant in command of the militia recognised one of the
bandits as a deserter from his corps, others said that one
of the bandits recognised in the sergeant a former follower
of his, the bandit's, trade. Anyway, on the fourth morning
all of them, captors and prisoners, returned to Jefferson in
a group, some said in confederation now seeking more
drink, others said that the captors brought their prizes
back to the settlement in revenge for having been evicted

from it. Because these were frontier, pioneer times, when personal liberty and freedom were almost a physical condition like fire or flood, and no community was going to interfere with anyone's morals as long as the amoralist practised somewhere else, and so Jefferson, being neither on the Trace nor the River but lying about midway between, naturally wanted no part of the underworld of either;

But they had some of it now, taken as it were by surprise, unawares, without warning to prepare and fend off. They put the bandits into the log-and-mudchinking jail, which until now had had no lock at all since its clients so far had been amateurs—local brawlers and drunkards and runaway slaves—for whom a single heavy wooden beam in slots across the outside of the door like on a corncrib, had sufficed. But they had now what might be four —three—Dillingers or Jesse Jameses of the time, with rewards on their heads. So they locked the jail; they bored an auger hole through the door and another through the jamb and passed a length of heavy chain through the holes and sent a messenger on the run across to the postoffice-store to fetch the ancient Carolina lock from the last Nashville mail-pouch—the iron monster weighing almost fifteen pounds, with a key almost as long as a bayonet, not just the only lock in that part of the country, but the oldest lock in that cranny of the United States, brought there by one of the three men who were what was to be Yoknapatawpha County's coeval pioneers and settlers, leaving in it the three oldest names—Alexander Holston, who came as half groom and half bodyguard to Doctor Samuel Habersham, and half nurse and half tutor to the doctor's eight-year-old motherless son, the three of them riding horseback across Tennessee from the Cumberland Gap along with Louis Grenier, the Huguenot younger son who brought the first slaves into the country and was granted the first big land patent and so became the first cotton

planter; while Doctor Habersham, with his worn black bag
of pills and knives and his brawny taciturn bodyguard
and his half orphan child, became the settlement itself
(for a time, before it was named, the settlement was
known as Doctor Habersham's, then Habersham's, then
simply Habersham; a hundred years later, during a schism
between two ladies' clubs over the naming of the streets
in order to get free mail delivery, a movement was started,
first, to change the name back to Habersham; then, failing that, to divide the town in two and call one half of it
Habersham after the old pioneer doctor and founder)—
friend of old Issetibbeha, the Chickasaw chief (the motherless Habersham boy, now a man of twenty-five, married
one of Issetibbeha's grand-daughters and in the thirties
emigrated to Oklahoma with his wife's dispossessed people), first unofficial, then official Chickasaw agent until
he resigned in a letter of furious denunciation addressed
to the President of the United States himself; and—his
charge and pupil a man now—Alexander Holston became the settlement's first publican, establishing the tavern still known as the Holston House, the original log
walls and puncheon floors and hand-morticed joints of
which are still buried somewhere beneath the modern
pressed glass and brick veneer and neon tubes. The lock
was his;

Fifteen pounds of useless iron lugged a thousand miles
through a desert of precipice and swamp, of flood and
drouth and wild beasts and wild Indians and wilder white
men, displacing that fifteen pounds better given to food
or seed to plant food or even powder to defend with, to
become a fixture, a kind of landmark, in the bar of a wilderness ordinary, locking and securing nothing, because
there was nothing behind the heavy bars and shutters
needing further locking and securing; not even a paper
weight because the only papers in the Holston House
were the twisted spills in an old powder horn above the

mantel for lighting tobacco; always a little in the way, since it had constantly to be moved: from bar to shelf to mantel then back to bar again until they finally thought about putting it on the bi-monthly mail-pouch; familiar, known, presently the oldest unchanged thing in the settlement, older than the people since Issetibbeha and Doctor Habersham were dead, and Alexander Holston was an old man crippled with arthritis, and Louis Grenier had a settlement of his own on his vast plantation, half of which was not even in Yoknapatawpha County, and the settlement rarely saw him; older than the town, since there were new names in it now even when the old blood ran in them—Sartoris and Stevens, Compson and McCaslin and Sutpen and Coldfield—and you no longer shot a bear or deer or wild turkey simply by standing for a while in your kitchen door, not to mention the pouch of mail—letters and even newspapers —which came from Nashville every two weeks by a special rider who did nothing else and was paid a salary for it by the Federal Government; and that was the second phase of the monster Carolina lock's transubstantiation into the Yoknapatawpha County courthouse;

The pouch didn't always reach the settlement every two weeks, not even always every month. But sooner or later it did, and everybody knew it would, because it— the cowhide saddlebag not even large enough to hold a full change of clothing, containing three or four letters and half that many badly-printed one- and two-sheet newspapers already three or four months out of date and usually half and sometimes wholly misinformed or incorrect to begin with—was the United States, the power and the will to liberty, owning liegence to no man, bringing even into that still almost pathless wilderness the thin peremptory voice of the nation which had wrenched its freedom from one of the most powerful peoples on earth and then again within the same lifespan successfully defended

it; so peremptory and audible that the man who carried
the pouch on the galloping horse didn't even carry any
arms except a tin horn, traversing month after month,
blatantly, flagrantly, almost contemptuously, a region
where for no more than the boots on his feet, men would
murder a traveller and gut him like a bear or deer or fish
and fill the cavity with rocks and sink the evidence in the
nearest water; not even deigning to pass quietly where
other men, even though armed and in parties, tried to
move secretly or at least without uproar, but instead an-
nouncing his solitary advent as far ahead of himself as the
ring of the horn would carry. So it was not long before
Alexander Holston's lock had moved to the mail-pouch.
Not that the pouch needed one, having come already the
three hundred miles from Nashville without a lock. (It
had been projected at first that the lock remain on the
pouch constantly. That is, not just while the pouch was in
the settlement, but while it was on the horse between
Nashville and the settlement too. The rider refused, suc-
cinctly, in three words, one of which was printable. His
reason was the lock's weight. They pointed out to him
that this would not hold water, since not only—the rider
was a frail irascible little man weighing less than a hundred pounds—would the fifteen pounds of lock even then
fail to bring his weight up to that of a normal adult male,
the added weight of the lock would merely match that of
the pistols which his employer, the United States Government, believed he carried and even paid him for having
done so, the rider's reply to this being succinct too though
not so glib: that the lock weighed fifteen pounds either
at the back door of the store in the settlement, or at that
of the postoffice in Nashville. But since Nashville and the
settlement were three hundred miles apart, by the time
the horse had carried it from one to the other, the lock
weighed fifteen pounds to the mile times three hundred
miles, or forty-five hundred pounds. Which was manifest nonsense, a physical impossibility either in lock or

horse. Yet indubitablv fifteen pounds times three hundred miles was forty-five hundred something, either
pounds or miles—especially as while they were still trying to unravel it, the rider repeated his first three succinct—two unprintable—words.) So less than ever would
the pouch need a lock in the back room of the trading-
post, surrounded and enclosed once more by civilization,
where its very intactness, its presence to receive a lock,
proved its lack of that need during the three hundred
miles of rapine-haunted Trace; needing a lock as little as
it was equipped to receive one, since it had been necessary to slit the leather with a knife just under each jaw of
the opening and insert the lock's iron mandible through
the two slits and clash it home, so that any other hand
with a similar knife could have cut the whole lock from
the pouch as easily as it had been clasped onto it. So
the old lock was not even a symbol of security: it was a
gesture of salutation, of free men to free men, of civilization to civilization across not just the three hundred miles
of wilderness to Nashville, but the fifteen hundred to
Washington: of respect without servility, allegiance without abasement to the government which they had helped
to found and had accepted with pride but still as free men,
still free to withdraw from it at any moment when the two
of them found themselves no longer compatible, the old
lock meeting the pouch each time on its arrival, to clasp
it in iron and inviolable symbolism, while old Alec Holston, childless bachelor, grew a little older and grayer,
a little more arthritic in flesh and temper too, a little
stiffer and more rigid in bone and pride too, since the lock
was still his, he had merely lent it, and so in a sense he
was the grandfather in the settlement of the inviolability
not just of government mail, but of a free government of
free men too, so long as the government remembered
to let men live free, not under it but beside it;

That was the lock; they put it on the jail. They did it

quickly, not even waiting until a messenger could have got back from the Holston House with old Alec's permission to remove it from the mail-pouch or use it for the new purpose. Not that he would have objected on principle nor refused his permission except by simple instinct; that is, he would probably have been the first to suggest the lock if he had known in time or thought of it first, but he would have refused at once if he thought the thing was contemplated without consulting him. Which everybody in the settlement knew, though this was not at all why they didn't wait for the messenger. In fact, no messenger had ever been sent to old Alec; they didn't have time to send one, let alone wait until he got back; they didn't want the lock to keep the bandits in, since (as was later proved) the old lock would have been no more obstacle for the bandits to pass than the customary wooden bar; they didn't need the lock to protect the settlement from the bandits, but to protect the bandits from the settlement. Because the prisoners had barely reached the settlement when it developed that there was a faction bent on lynching them at once, out of hand, without preliminary—a small but determined gang which tried to wrest the prisoners from their captors while the militia was still trying to find someone to surrender them to, and would have succeeded except for a man named Compson, who had come to the settlement a few years ago with a race-horse, which he swapped to Ikkemotubbe, Issetibbeha's successor in the chiefship, for a square mile of what was to be the most valuable land in the future town of Jefferson, who, legend said, drew a pistol and held the ravishers at bay until the bandits could be got into the jail and the auger holes bored and someone sent to fetch old Alec Holston's lock. Because there were indeed new names and faces too in the settlement now— faces so new as to have (to the older residents) no discernible antecedents other than mammalinity, nor past other than the simple years which had scored them; and names so new as to have no discernible (nor discoverable either) antecedents or past at all, as though they had been invented yesterday, report dividing again: to the effect that there were more people in the settlement that day than the militia sergeant whom one or all of the bandits might recognise;

So Compson locked the jail, and a courier with the two best horses in the settlement—one to ride and one to lead —cut through the woods to the Trace to ride the hundred-odd miles to Natchez with news of the capture and authority to dicker for the reward; and that evening in the Holston House kitchen was held the settlement's first municipal meeting, prototype not only of the town council after the settlement would be a town, but of the Chamber of Commerce when it would begin to proclaim itself a city, with Compson presiding, not old Alec, who was quite old now, grim, taciturn, sitting even on a hot July night before a smoldering log in his vast chimney, his back even turned to the table (he was not interested in the deliberation; the prisoners were his already since his lock held them; whatever the conference decided would have to be submitted to him for ratification anyway before anyone could touch his lock to open it) around which the progenitors of the Jefferson city fathers sat in what was almost a council of war, not only discussing the collecting of the reward, but the keeping and defending it. Because there were two factions of opposition now: not only the lynching party, but the militia band too, who now claimed that as prizes the prisoners still belonged to their original captors; that they—the militia—had merely surrendered the prisoners' custody but had relinquished nothing of any reward: on the prospect of which, the militia band had got more whiskey from the trading-post store and had built a tremendous bonfire in front of the jail, around which they and the lynching party had

now confederated in a wassail or conference of their own.
Or so they thought. Because the truth was that Compson,
in the name of a crisis in the public peace and welfare,
had made a formal demand on the professional bag of
Doctor Peabody, old Doctor Habersham's successor, and
the three of them—Compson, Peabody, and the post
trader (his name was Ratcliffe; a hundred years later it
would still exist in the county, but by that time it had
passed through two inheritors who had dispensed with
the eye in the transmission of words, using only the ear,
so that by the time the fourth one had been compelled
by simple necessity to learn to write it again, it had lost
the "c" and the final "fe" too) added the laudanum to the
keg of whiskey and sent it as a gift from the settlement to
the astonished militia sergeant, and returned to the Holston House kitchen to wait until the last of the uproar
died; then the law-and-order party made a rapid sortie
and gathered up all the comatose opposition, lynchers
and captors too, and dumped them all into the jail with
the prisoners and locked the door again and went home to
bed—until the next morning, when the first arrivals were
met by a scene resembling an outdoor stage setting:
which was how the legend of the mad Harpes started:
a thing not just fantastical but incomprehensible, not just
whimsical but a little terrifying (though at least it was
bloodless, which would have contented neither Harpe):
not just the lock gone from the door nor even just the
door gone from the jail, but the entire wall gone, the mud-
chinked axe-morticed logs unjointed neatly and quietly
in the darkness and stacked as neatly to one side, leaving the jail open to the world like a stage on which the
late insurgents still lay sprawled and various in deathlike
slumber, the whole settlement gathered now to watch
Compson trying to kick at least one of them awake, until
one of the Holston slaves—the cook's husband, the
waiter-groom-hostler—ran into the crowd shouting,
"Whar de lock, whar de lock, ole Boss say whar de lock."

It was gone (as were three horses belonging to three
of the lynching faction). They couldn't even find the
heavy door and the chain, and at first they were almost
betrayed into believing that the bandits had had to take
the door in order to steal the chain and lock, catching
themselves back from the very brink of this wanton ac-
cusation of rationality. But the lock was gone; nor did it
take the settlement long to realise that it was not the escaped bandits and the aborted reward, but the lock, and
not a simple situation which faced them, but a problem
which threatened, the slave departing back to the Holston House at a dead run and then reappearing at the
dead run almost before the door, the walls, had had time
to hide him, engulf and then eject him again, darting
through the crowd and up to Compson himself now, saying, "Ole Boss say fetch de lock"—not send the lock, but
bring the lock. So Compson and his lieutenants (and this
was where the mail rider began to appear, or rather, to
emerge—the fragile wisp of a man ageless, hairless and
toothless, who looked too frail even to approach a horse,
let alone ride one six hundred miles every two weeks, yet
who did so, and not only that but had wind enough left
not only to announce and precede but even follow his
passing with the jeering musical triumph of the horn:—
a contempt for possible—probable—despoilers matched
only by that for the official dross of which he might be
despoiled, and which agreed to remain in civilised bounds
only so long as the despoilers had the taste to refrain)—
repaired to the kitchen where old Alec still sat before his
smoldering log, his back still to the room, and still not turning it this time either. And that was all. He ordered the
immediate return of his lock. It was not even an ultimatum, it was a simple instruction, a decree, impersonal, the
mail rider now well into the fringe of the group, saying
nothing and missing nothing, like a weightless desiccated
or fossil bird, not a vulture of course nor even quite a

hawk, but say a pterodactyl chick arrested just out of the egg ten glaciers ago and so old in simple infancy as to be the worn and weary ancestor of all subsequent life. They pointed out to old Alec that the only reason the lock could be missing was that the bandits had not had time or been able to cut it out of the door, and that even three fleeing madmen on stolen horses would not carry a six-foot oak door very far, and that a party of Ikkemotubbe's young men were even now trailing the horses westward toward the River and that without doubt the lock would be found at any moment, probably under the first bush at the edge of the settlement: knowing better, knowing that there was no limit to the fantastic and the terrifying and the bizarre, of which the men were capable who already, just to escape from a log jail, had quietly removed one entire wall and stacked it in neat piecemeal at the roadside, and that they nor old Alec neither would ever see his lock again;

Nor did they; the rest of that afternoon and all the next day too, while old Alec still smoked his pipe in front of his smoldering log, the settlement's sheepish and raging elders hunted for it, with (by now: the next afternoon) Ikkemotubbe's Chickasaws helping too, or anyway present, watching: the wild men, the wilderness's tameless evictant children looking only the more wild and homeless for the white man's denim and butternut and felt and straw which they wore, standing or squatting or following, grave, attentive and interested, while the white men sweated and cursed among the bordering thickets of their punily-clawed foothold; and always the rider, Pettigrew, ubiquitous, everywhere, not helping search himself and never in anyone's way, but always present, inscrutable, saturnine, missing nothing: until at last toward sundown Compson crashed savagely out of the last bramble-brake and flung the sweat from his face with a full-armed sweep sufficient to repudiate a throne, and said,

"All right, god damn it, we'll pay him for it." Because they had already considered that last gambit; they had already realised its seriousness from the very fact that Peabody had tried to make a joke about it which everyone knew that even Peabody did not think humorous:

"Yes—and quick too, before he has time to advise with Pettigrew and price it by the pound."

"By the pound?" Compson said.

"Pettigrew just weighed it by the three hundred miles from Nashville. Old Alec might start from Carolina. That's fifteen thousand pounds."

"Oh," Compson said. So he blew in his men by means of a foxhorn which one of the Indians wore on a thong around his neck, though even then they paused for one last quick conference; again it was Peabody who stopped them.

"Who'll pay for it?" he said. "It would be just like him to want a dollar a pound for it, even if by Pettigrew's scale he had found it in the ashes of his fireplace." They —Compson anyway—had probably already thought of that; that, as much as Pettigrew's presence, was probably why he was trying to rush them into old Alec's presence with the offer so quickly that none would have the face to renege on a pro-rata share. But Peabody had torn it now. Compson looked about at them, sweating, grimly enraged.

"That means Peabody will probably pay one dollar," he said. "Who pays the other fourteen? Me?" Then Ratcliffe, the trader, the store's proprietor, solved it—a solution so simple, so limitless in retroact, that they didn't even wonder why nobody had thought of it before; which not only solved the problem but abolished it; and not just that one, but all problems, from now on into perpetuity, opening to their vision like the rending of a veil, like a glorious prophecy, the vast splendid limitless panorama of America: that land of boundless oppportunity, that bourne, created not by nor of the people, but for the peo-

ple, as was the heavenly manna of old, with no return demand on man save the chewing and swallowing since out
of its own matchless Allgood it would create produce
train support and perpetuate a race of laborers dedicated
to the single purpose of picking the manna up and putting it into his lax hand or even between his jaws—illimitable, vast, without beginning or end, not even a
trade or a craft but a beneficence as are sunlight and rain
and air, inalienable and immutable.

"Put it on the Book," Ratcliffe said—the Book: not a
ledger, but *the* ledger, since it was probably the
only thing of its kind between Nashville and Natchez, unless there might happen to be a similar one a few miles
south at the first Choctaw agency at Yalo Busha—a ruled,
paper-backed copybook such as might have come out of
a schoolroom, in which accrued, with the United States
as debtor, in Mohataha's name (the Chickasaw matriarch,
Ikkemotubbe's mother and old Issetibbeha's sister, who
—she could write her name, or anyway make something
with a pen or pencil which was agreed to be, or at least
accepted to be, a valid signature—signed all the convey-
ances as her son's kingdom passed to the white people,
regularising it in law anyway) the crawling tedious list of
calico and gunpowder, whiskey and salt and snuff and
denim pants and osseous candy drawn from Ratcliffe's
shelves by her descendants and subjects and Negro slaves.
That was all the settlement had to do: add the lock to the
list, the account. It wouldn't even matter at what price
they entered it. They could have priced it on Pettigrew's scale of fifteen pounds times the distance not just
to Carolina but to Washington itself, and nobody would
ever notice it probably; they could have charged the
United States with seventeen thousand five hundred dollars' worth of the fossilised and indestructible candy, and
none would ever read the entry. So it was solved, done,
finished, ended. They didn't even have to discuss it. They
didn't even think about it any more, unless perhaps here

and there to marvel (a little speculatively probably) at their own moderation, since they wanted nothing—least of all, to escape any just blame—but a fair and decent adjustment of the lock. They went back to where old Alec still sat with his pipe in front of his dim hearth. Only they had overestimated him; he didn't want any money at all, he wanted his lock. Whereupon what little remained of Compson's patience went too.

"Your lock's gone," he told old Alec harshly. "You'll take fifteen dollars for it," he said, his voice already fading, because even that rage could recognise impasse when it saw it. Nevertheless, the rage, the impotence, the sweating, the *too much*—whatever it was—forced the voice on for one word more: "Or—" before it stopped for good and allowed Peabody to fill the gap:

"Or else?" Peabody said, and not to old Alec, but to Compson. "Or else what?" Then Ratcliffe saved that too.

"Wait," he said. "Uncle Alec's going to take fifty dollars for his lock. A guarantee of fifty dollars. He'll give us the name of the blacksmith back in Cal'lina that made it for him, and we'll send back there and have a new one made. Going and coming and all'll cost about fifty dollars. We'll give Uncle Alec the fifty dollars to hold as a guarantee. Then when the new lock comes, he'll give us back the money. All right, Uncle Alec?" And that could have been all of it. It probably would have been, except for Pettigrew. It was not that they had forgotten him, nor even assimilated him. They had simply sealed—healed him off (so they thought)—him into their civic crisis as the desperate and defenseless oyster immobilises its atom of inevictable grit. Nobody had seen him move yet he now stood in the center of them where Compson and Ratcliffe and Peabody faced old Alec in the chair. You might have said that he had oozed there, except for that adamantine quality which might (in emergency) become invisible but never insubstantial and never in this world fluid; he spoke in a voice bland, reasonable and impersonal, then stood there being looked at, frail and child-sized, impermeable as diamond and manifest with portent, bringing into that backwoods room a thousand miles deep in pathless wilderness, the whole vast incalculable weight of federality, not just representing the government nor even himself just the government; for that moment at least, he was the United ˜tates.

"Uncle Alec hasn't lost any lock," he said. "That was Uncle Sam."

After a moment someone said, "What?"

"That's right," Pettigrew said. "Whoever put that lock of Holston's on that mail bag either made a voluntary gift to the United States, and the same law covers the United States Government that covers minor children: you can give something to them, but you can't take it back, or he or they done something else."

They looked at him. Again after a while somebody said something; it was Ratcliffe. "What else?" Ratcliffe said. Pettigrew answered, still bland, impersonal, heatless and glib: "Committed a violation of act of Congress as especially made and provided for the defacement of government property, penalty of five thousand dollars or not less than one year in a Federal jail or both. For whoever cut them two slits in the bag to put the lock in, act of Congress as especially made and provided for the injury or destruction of government property, penalty of ten thousand dollars or not less than five years in a Federal jail or both." He did not move even yet; he simply spoke directly to old Alec: "I reckon you're going to have supper here same as usual sooner or later or more or less."

"Wait," Ratcliffe said. He turned to Compson. "Is that true?"

"What the hell difference does it make whether it's true or not?" Compson said. "What do you think he's going to do as soon as he gets to Nashville?" He said violently to Pettigrew: "You were supposed to leave for Nashville yesterday. What were you hanging around here for?"

"Nothing to go to Nashville for," Pettigrew said. "You dont want any mail. You aint got anything to lock it up with."

"So we aint," Ratcliffe said. "So we'll let the United States find the United States' lock." This time Pettigrew looked at no one. He wasn't even speaking to anyone, any more than old Alec had been when he decreed the return of his lock:

"Act of Congress as made and provided for the unauthorised removal and or use or willful or felonious use or misuse or loss of government property, penalty the value of the article plus five hundred to ten thousand dollars or thirty days to twenty years in a Federal jail or both. They may even make a new one when they read where you have charged a postoffice department lock to the Bureau of Indian Affairs." He moved; now he was speaking to old Alec again: "I'm going out to my horse. When this meeting is over and you get back to cooking, you can send your nigger for me."

Then he was gone. After a while Ratcliffe said, "What do you reckon he aims to get out of this? A reward?" But that was wrong; they all knew better than that.

"He's already getting what he wants," Compson said, and cursed again. "Confusion. Just damned confusion." But that was wrong too; they all knew that too, though it was Peabody who said it:

"No. Not confusion. A man who will ride six hundred miles through this country every two weeks, with nothing for protection but a foxhorn, aint really interested in confusion any more than he is in money." So they didn't know yet what was in Pettigrew's mind. But they knew what he would do. That is, they knew that they did not know at all, either what he would do, or how, or when, and that there was nothing whatever that they could do about it until they discovered why. And they saw now that they had no possible means to discover that; they realised now that they had known him for three years now, during which, fragile and inviolable and undeviable and preceded for a mile or more by the strong sweet ringing of the horn, on his strong and tireless horse he would complete the bi-monthly trip from Nashville to the settlement and for the next three or four days would live among them, yet that they knew nothing whatever about him, and even now knew only that they dared not, simply dared not, take any chance, sitting for a while longer in the darkening room while old Alec still smoked, his back still squarely turned to them and their quandary too; then dispersing to their own cabins for the evening meal—with what appetite they could bring to it, since presently they had drifted back through the summer darkness when by ordinary they would have been already in bed, to the back room of Ratcliffe's store now, to sit again while Ratcliffe recapitulated in his mixture of bewilderment and alarm (and something else which they recognised was respect as they realised that he—Ratcliffe —was unshakably convinced that Pettigrew's aim was money; that Pettigrew had invented or evolved a scheme so richly rewarding that he—Ratcliffe—had not only been unable to forestall him and do it first, he—Ratcliff —couldn't even guess what it was after he had been given a hint) until Compson interrupted him.

"Hell," Compson said. "Everybody knows what's wrong with him. It's ethics. He's a damned moralist."

"Ethics?" Peabody said. He sounded almost startled. He said quickly: "That's bad. How can we corrupt an ethical man?"

"Who wants to corrupt him?" Compson said. "All we want him to do is stay on that damned horse and blow whatever extra wind he's got into that damned horn."

But Peabody was not even listening. He said, "Ethics," almost dreamily. He said, "Wait." They watched

him. He said suddenly to Ratcliffe: "I've heard it somewhere. If anybody here knows it, it'll be you. What's his
name?"

"His name?" Ratcliffe said. "Pettigrew's? Oh. His christian name." Ratcliffe told him. "Why?"

"Nothing," Peabody said. "I'm going home. Anybody
else coming?" He spoke directly to nobody and said and
would say no more, but that was enough: a straw perhaps, but at least a straw; enough anyway for the others
to watch and say nothing either as Compson got up too and
said to Ratcliffe:

"You coming?" and the three of them walked away together, beyond earshot then beyond sight too. Then
Compson said, "All right. What?"

"It may not work," Peabody said. "But you two will
have to back me up. When I speak for the whole settlement, you and Ratcliffe will have to make it stick. Will
you?"

Compson cursed. "But at least tell us a little of what
we're going to guarantee." So Peabody told them, some
of it, and the next morning entered the stall in the Holston
House stable where Pettigrew was grooming his ugly ham-
mer-headed ironmuscled horse.

"We decided not to charge that lock to old Mohataha,
after all," Peabody said.

"That so?" Pettigrew said. "Nobody in Washington
would ever catch it. Certainly not the ones that can read."

"We're going to pay for it ourselves," Peabody said. "In
fact, we're going to do a little more. We've got to repair
that jail wall anyhow; we've got to build one wall anyway. So by building three more, we will have another
room. We got to build one anyway, so that dont count. So
by building an extra three-wall room, we will have another four-wall house. That will be the courthouse." Pettigrew had been hissing gently between his teeth at each
stroke of the brush, like a professional Irish groom. Now

he stopped, the brush and his hand arrested in midstroke, and turned his head a little.

"Courthouse?"

"We're going to have a town," Peabody said. "We already got a church—that's Whitfield's cabin. And we're going to build a school too soon as we get around to it. But we're going to build the courthouse today; we've already got something to put in it to make it a courthouse: that iron box that's been in Ratcliffe's way in the store for the last ten years. Then we'll have a town. We've already even named her."

Now Pettigrew stood up, very slowly. They looked at one another. After a moment Pettigrew said, "So?"

"Ratcliffe says your name's Jefferson," Peabody said.

"That's right," Pettigrew said. "Thomas Jefferson Pettigrew. I'm from old Ferginny."

"Any kin?" Peabody said.

"No," Pettigrew said. "My ma named me for him, so I would have some of his luck."

"Luck?" Peabody said.

Pettigrew didn't smile. "That's right. She didn't mean luck. She never had any schooling. She didn't know the word she wanted to say."

"Have you had it?" Peabody said. Nor did Pettigrew smile now. "I'm sorry," Peabody said. "Try to forget it." He said: "We decided to name her Jefferson." Now Pettigrew didn't seem to breathe even. He just stood there, small, frail, less than boysize, childless and bachelor, incorrigibly kinless and tieless, looking at Peabody. Then he breathed, and raising the brush, he turned back to the horse and for an instant Peabody thought he was going back to the grooming. But instead of making the stroke, he laid the hand and the brush against the horse's flank and stood for a moment, his face turned away and his heat bent a little. Then he raised his head and turned his face back toward Peabody.

"You could call that lock 'axle grease' on that Indian account," he said.

"Fifty dollars' worth of axle grease?" Peabody said.

"To grease the wagons for Oklahoma," Pettigrew said.

"So we could," Peabody said. "Only her name's Jefferson now. We cant ever forget that any more now." And that was the courthouse—the courthouse which it had taken them almost thirty years not only to realise they didn't have, but to discover that they hadn't even needed, missed, lacked; and which, before they had owned it six months, they discovered was nowhere near enough. Because somewhere between the dark of that first day and the dawn of the next, something happened to them. They began that same day; they restored the jail wall and cut new logs and split out shakes and raised the little floorless lean-to against it and moved the iron chest from Ratcliffe's back room; it took only the two days and cost nothing but the labor and not much of that per capita since the whole settlement was involved to a man, not to mention the settlement's two slaves—Holston's man and the one belonging to the German blacksmith—; Ratcliffe too, all he had to do was put up the bar across the inside of his back door, since his entire patronage was countable in one glance sweating and cursing among the logs and shakes of the half dismantled jail across the way opposite—including Ikkemotubbe's Chickasaw, though these were neither sweating nor cursing: the grave dark men dressed in their Sunday clothes except for the trousers, pants, which they carried rolled neatly under their arms or perhaps tied by the two legs around their necks like capes or rather hussars' dolmans where they had forded the creek, squatting or lounging along the shade, courteous, interested, and reposed (even old Mohataha herself, the matriarch, barefoot in a purple silk gown and a plumed hat, sitting in a gilt brocade empire chair in a wagon behind two mules, under a silver-handled Paris parasol held by a female slave child)—because they (the other white men, his confreres, or—during this first day—his co-victims) had not yet remarked the thing—quality—something—esoteric, eccentric, in Ratcliffe's manner, attitude,—not an obstruction nor even an impediment, not even when on the second day they discovered what it was, because he was among them, busy too, sweating and cursing too, but rather like a single chip, infinitesimal, on an otherwise unbroken flood or tide, a single body or substance, alien and unreconciled, a single thin almost unheard voice crying thinly out of the roar of a mob: "Wait, look here, listen—"

Because they were too busy raging and sweating among the dismantled logs and felling the new ones in the adjacent woods and trimming and notching and dragging them out and mixing the tenuous clay mud to chink them together with; it was not until the second day that they learned what was troubling Ratcliffe, because now they had time, the work going no slower, no lessening of sweat but on the contrary, if anything the work going even a little faster because now there was a lightness in the speed and all that was abated was the rage and the outrage, because somewhere between the dark and the dawn of the first and the second day, something had happened to them —the men who had spent that first long hot endless July day sweating and raging about the wrecked jail, flinging indiscriminately and savagely aside the dismantled logs and the log-like laudanum-smitten inmates in order to rebuild the one, cursing old Holston and the lock and the four—three—bandits and the eleven militiamen who had arrested them, and Compson and Pettigrew and Peabody and the United States of America—the same men met at the project before sunrise on the next day which was already promising to be hot and endless too, but with the rage and the fury absent now, quiet, not grave so much as sobered, a little amazed, diffident, blinking a little perhaps, looking a little aside from one another, a little unfamiliar even to one another in the new jonquil-colored light, looking about them at the meagre huddle of crude cabins set without order and every one a little awry to every other and all dwarfed to doll-houses by the vast loom of the woods which enclosed them—the tiny clearing clawed punily not even into the flank of pathless wilderness but into the loin, the groin, the secret parts, which was the irrevocable cast die of their lives, fates, pasts and futures—not even speaking for a while yet since each one probably believed (a little shamefaced too) that the thought was solitarily his, until at last one spoke for all and then it was all right since it had taken one conjoined breath to shape that sound, the speaker speaking not loud, diffidently, tentatively, as you insert the first light tentative push of wind into the mouthpiece of a strange untried foxhorn: "By God. Jefferson."

"Jefferson, Mississippi," a second added.

"Jefferson, Yoknapatawpha County, Mississippi," a third corrected; who, which one, didn't matter this time either since it was still one conjoined breathing, one compound dream-state, mused and static, well capable of lasting on past sunrise too, though they probably knew better too since Compson was still there: the gnat, the thorn, the catalyst.

"It aint until we finish the goddamned thing," Compson said. "Come on. Let's get at it." So they finished it that day, working rapidly now, with speed and lightness too, concentrated yet inattentive, to get it done and that quickly, not to finish it but to get it out of the way, behind them; not to finish it quickly in order to own, possess it sooner, but to be able to obliterate, efface, it the sooner, as if they had also known in that first yellow light that it would not be near enough, would not even be the beginning; that the little lean-to room they were building would not even be a pattern and could not even be called practice, working on until noon, the hour to stop and eat, by which time Louis Grenier had arrived from Frenchman's Bend (his plantation: his manor, his kitchens and stables

and kennels and slave quarters and gardens and promenades and fields which a hundred years later will have
vanished, his name and his blood too, leaving nothing but
the name of his plantation and his own fading corrupted
legend like a thin layer of the native ephemeral yet inevictable dust on a section of country surrounding a little
lost paintless crossroads store) twenty miles away behind
a slave coachman and footman in his imported English
carriage and what was said to be the finest matched team
outside of Natchez or Nashville, and Compson said, "I
reckon that'll do"—all knowing what he meant: not aban-
donment: to complete it, of course, but so little remained
now that the two slaves could finish it. The four in fact,
since, although as soon as it was assumed that the two
Grenier Negroes would lend the two local ones a hand,
Compson demurred on the grounds that who would dare
violate the rigid protocol of bondage by ordering a stable-
servant, let alone a house-servant, to do manual labor, not
to mention having the temerity to approach old Louis
Grenier with the suggestion, Peabody nipped that at once.

"One of them can use my shadow," he said. "It never
blenched out there with a white doctor standing in it,"
and even offered to be emissary to old Grenier, except
that Grenier himself forestalled them. So they ate Holston's noon ordinary, while the Chickasaws, squatting unmoving still where the creep of shade had left them in the
full fierce glare of July noon about the wagon where old
Mohataha still sat under her slave-borne Paris parasol, ate
their lunches too which (Mohataha's and her personal
retinue's came out of a woven whiteoak withe fishbasket
in the wagonbed) they appeared to have carried in from
what, patterning the white people, they called their plantation too, under their arms inside the rolled-up trousers.
Then they moved back to the front gallery and—not the
settlement any more now: the town; it had been a town
for thirty-one hours now—watched the four slaves put up
the final log and pin down the final shake on the roof and

hang the door, and then, Ratcliffe leading something like the court chamberlain across a castle courtyard, cross back to the store and enter and emerge carrying the iron chest, the grave Chickasaws watching too the white man's slaves sweating the white man's ponderable dense inscrutable medicine into its new shrine. And now they had time to find out what was bothering Ratcliffe.

"That lock," Ratcliffe said.

"What?" somebody said.

"That Indian axle-grease," Ratcliffe said.

"What?" they said again. But they knew, understood, now. It was neither lock nor axle-grease; it was the fifteen dollars which could have been charged to the Indian Department on Ratcliffe's books and nobody would have ever found it, noticed it, missed it. It was not greed on Ratcliffe's part, and least of all was he advocating corruption. The idea was not even new to him; it did not need any casual man on a horse riding in to the settlement once every two or three weeks, to reveal to him that possibility; he had thought of that the first time he had charged the first sack of peppermint candy to the first one of old Mohataha's forty-year-old grandchildren and had refrained from adding two zeroes to the ten or fifteen cents for ten years now, wondering each time why he did refrain, amazed at his own virtue or at least his strength of will. It was a matter of principle. It was he—they: the settlement (town now)—who had thought of charging the lock to the United States as a provable lock, a communal risk, a concrete ineradicable object, win lose or draw, let the chips fall where they may, on that dim day when some Federal inspector might, just barely might, audit the Chickasaw affairs; it was the United States itself which had voluntarily offered to show them how to transmute the inevictable lock into proofless and ephemeral axle grease—the little scrawny childsized man, solitary unarmed impregnable and unalarmed, not even defying them, not even advocate and representative of the United

States, but *the* United States, as though the United States had said, "Please accept a gift of fifteen dollars," (the town had actually paid old Alec fifteen dollars for the lock; he would accept no more) and they had not even declined it but simply abolished it since, as soon as Pettigrew breathed it into sound, the United States had already forever lost it; as though Pettigrew had put the actual ponderable fifteen gold coins into—say, Compson's or Peabody's—hands and they had dropped them down a rathole or a well, doing no man any good, neither restoration to the ravaged nor emolument to the ravager, leaving in fact the whole race of man, as long as it endured, forever and irrevocably fifteen dollars deficit, fifteen dollars in the red;

That was Ratcliffe's trouble. But they didn't even listen. They heard him out of course, but they didn't even listen. Or perhaps they didn't even hear him either, sitting along the shade on Holston's gallery, looking, seeing, already a year away; it was barely the tenth of July; there was the long summer, the bright soft dry fall until the November rains, but they would require not two days this time but two years and maybe more, with a winter of planning and preparation before hand. They even had an instrument available and waiting, like providence almost: a man named Sutpen who had come into the settlement that same spring—a big gaunt friendless passion-worn untalkative man who walked in a fading aura of anonymity and violence like a man just entered a warm room or at least a shelter, out of a blizzard, bringing with him thirty-odd men slaves even wilder and more equivocal than the native wild men, the Chickasaws, to whom the settlement had become accustomed, who (the new Negroes) spoke no English but instead what Compson, who had visited New Orleans, said was the Carib-Spanish-French of the Sugar Islands, and who (Sutpen) had bought or proved on or anyway acquired a tract of land in the opposite direction and was apparently bent on establishing a place on an even more ambitious and grandiose scale than Grenier's; he had even brought with him a tame Parisian architect—or captive rather, since it was said in Ratcliffe's back room that the man slept at night in a kind of pit at the site of the chateau he was planning, tied wrist to wrist with one of his captor's Carib slaves; indeed, the settlement had only to see him once to know that he was no docile than his captor, any more than the weasel or rattlesnake is no less untame than the wolf or bear before which it gives way until completely and hopelessly cornered:—a man no larger than Pettigrew, with humorous sardonic undefeated eyes which had seen everything and believed none of it, in the broad expensive hat and brocaded waistcoat and ruffled wrists of a half-artist half-boulevardier; and they—Compson perhaps, Peabody certainly—could imagine him in his mudstained brier-slashed brocade and lace standing in a trackless wilderness dreaming colonnades and porticoes and fountains and promenades in the style of David, with just behind each elbow an identical giant half-naked Negro not even watching him, only breathing, moving each time he took a step or shifted like his shadow repeated in two and blown to gigantic size;

So they even had an architect. He listened to them for perhaps a minute in Ratcliffe's back room. Then he made an indescribable gesture and said, "Bah. You do not need advice. You are too poor. You have only your hands, and clay to make good brick. You dont have any money. You dont even have anything to copy: how can you go wrong?" But he taught them how to mold the brick; he designed and built the kiln to bake the brick in, plenty of them since they had probably known from that first yellow morning too that one edifice was not going to be enough. But although both were conceived in the same instant and planned simultaneously during the same winter and built in continuation during the next three years, the courthouse of course came first, and in March, with stakes and hanks of fishline, the architect laid out in a grove of oaks opposite the tavern and the store, the square and simple foundations, the irrevocable design not only of the courthouse but of the town too, telling them as much: "In fifty years you will be trying to change it in the name of what you will call progress. But you will fail; but you will never be able to get away from it." But they had already seen that, standing thigh-deep in wilderness also but with more than a vision to look at since they had at least the fishline and the stakes, perhaps less than fifty years, perhaps—who knew?—less than twenty-five even: a Square, the courthouse in its grove the center; quadrangular around it, the stores, two-storey, the offices of the lawyers and doctors and dentists, the lodge-rooms and auditoriums, above them; school and church and tavern and bank and jail each in its ordered place; the four broad diverging avenues straight as plumb-lines in the four directions, becoming the network of roads and by-roads until the whole county would be covered with it: the hands, the prehensile fingers clawing dragging lightward out of the disappearing wilderness year by year as up from the bottom of the receding sea, the broad rich fecund burgeoning fields, pushing thrusting each year further and further back the wilderness and its denizens— the wild bear and deer and turkey, and the wild men (or not so wild any more, familiar now, harmless now, just obsolete: anachronism out of an old dead time and a dead age; regrettable of course, even actually regretted by the old men, fiercely as old Doctor Habersham did, and with less fire but still as irreconcilable and stubborn as old Alec Holston and a few others were still doing, until in a few more years the last of them would have passed and vanished in their turn too, obsolescent too: because this was a white man's land; that was its fate, or not even fate but destiny, its high destiny in the roster of the earth)—the veins, arteries, life- and pulse-stream along which would flow the aggrandisement of harvest: the gold: the cotton and the grain;

But above all, the courthouse: the center, the focus, the hub; sitting looming in the center of the county's circumference like a single cloud in its ring of horizon, laying its vast shadow to the uttermost rim of horizon; musing, brooding, symbolic and ponderable, tall as cloud, solid as rock, dominating all: protector of the weak, judiciate and curb of the passions and lusts, repository and guardian of the aspirations and the hopes; rising course by brick course during that first summer, simply square, simplest Georgian colonial (this, by the Paris architect who was creating at Sutpen's Hundred something like a wing of Versailles glimpsed in a Lilliput's gothic nightmare—in revenge, Gavin Stevens would say a hundred years later, when Sutpen's own legend in the county would include the anecdote of the time the architect broke somehow out of his dungeon and tried to flee and Sutpen and his Negro head man and hunter ran him down with dogs in the swamp and brought him back) since, as the architect had told them, they had no money to buy bad taste with nor even anything from which to copy what bad taste might still have been within their compass; this one too still costing nothing but the labor and—the second year now—most of that was slave since there were still more slave owners in the settlement which had been a town and named for going on two years now, already a town and already named when the first ones waked up on that yellow morning two years back:—men other than Holston and the blacksmith (Compson was one now) who owned one or two or three Negroes, besides Grenier and Sutpen who had set up camps beside the creek in Compson's pasture for the two gangs of their Negroes to live in until the two buildings—the courthouse and the jail—should be completed. But not altogether slave, the boundmen, the unfree, because there were still the white men too, the same ones who on that hot July morning two and now three years ago had gathered in a kind of outraged unbelief to fling, hurl up in raging sweating impotent fury the little three-walled lean-to—the same men (with affairs of their own they might have been attending to or work of their own or for which they were being hired, paid, that they should have been doing) standing or lounging about the scaffolding and the stacks of brick and puddles of clay mortar for an hour or two hours or half a day, then putting aside one of the Negroes and taking his place with trowel or saw or adze, unbidden or unreproved either since there was none present with the right to order or deny; a stranger might have said probably for that reason, simply because now they didn't have to, except that it was more than that, working peacefully now that there was no outrage and fury, and twice as fast because there was no urgency since this was no more to be hurried by man or men than the burgeoning of a crop, working (this paradox too to anyone except men like Grenier and Compson and Peabody who had grown from infancy among slaves, breathed the same air and even suckled the same breast with the sons of Ham: black and white, free and unfree, shoulder to shoulder in the same tireless lift and rhythm as if they had the same aim and hope, which they did have as far as the Negro was capable, as even Ratcliffe, son of a long pure line of Anglo-Saxon mountain people and—destined—father of an equally long and pure line of white trash tenant farmers who never owned a slave and never would since each had and would imbibe with his mother's milk a personal violent antipathy not at all to slavery but to black skins, could have explained: the slave's simple child's mind had fired at once with the thought that he was helping to build not only the biggest edifice in the country, but probably the biggest he had ever seen; this was all but this was enough) as one because it was theirs, bigger than any because it was the

sum of all and, being the sum of all, it must raise all of
their hopes and aspirations level with its own aspirant and
soaring cupola, so that, sweating and tireless and unflagging, they would look about at one another a little shyly,
a little amazed, with something like humility too, as if they
were realising, or were for a moment at least capable of
believing, that men, all men, including themselves, were a
little better, purer maybe even, than they had thought,
expected, or even needed to be. Though they were still
having a little trouble with Ratcliffe: the money, the Holston lock-Chickasaw axle grease fifteen dollars; not trouble really because it had never been an obstruction even
three years ago when it was new, and now after three
years even the light impedeless chip was worn by familiarity and custom to less than a toothpick: merely present,
merely visible, or that is, audible: and no trouble *with*
Ratcliffe because he made one too contraposed the toothpick; more: he was its chief victim, sufferer, since where
with the others was mostly inattention, a little humor, now
and then a little fading annoyance and impatience, with
him was shame, bafflement, a little of anguish and despair
like a man struggling with a congenital vice, hopeless, indomitable, already defeated. It was not even the money
any more now, the fifteen dollars. It was the fact that they
had refused it and, refusing it, had maybe committed a
fatal and irremediable error. He would try to explain it:
"It's like Old Moster and the rest of them up there that
run the luck, would look down at us and say, Well well,
looks like them durn peckerwoods down there dont want
them fifteen dollars we was going to give them free-gratis-
for-nothing. So maybe they dont want nothing from us.
So maybe we better do like they seem to want, and let
them sweat and swivet and scrabble through the best
they can by themselves."

Which they—the town—did, though even then the courthouse was not finished for another six years. Not but

that they thought it was: complete: simple and square,
floored and roofed and windowed, with a central hallway
and the four offices—sheriff and tax assessor and circuit-
and chancery-clerk (which—the chancery-clerk's office—
would contain the ballot boxes and booths for voting)—
below, and the courtroom and jury-room and the judge's
chambers above—even to the pigeons and English sparrows, migrants too but not pioneers, inevictably urban in
fact, come all the way from the Atlantic coast as soon as
the town became a town with a name, taking possession of
the gutters and eave-boxes almost before the final hammer
was withdrawn, uxorious and interminable the one, garrulous and myriad the other. Then in the sixth year old
Alec Holston died and bequeathed back to the town the
fifteen dollars it had paid him for the lock; two years before, Louis Grenier had died and his heirs still held in
trust on demand the fifteen hundred dollars his will had
devised it, and now there was another newcomer in the
county, a man named John Sartoris, with slaves and gear
and money too like Grenier and Sutpen, but who was an
even better stalemate to Sutpen than Grenier had been
because it was apparent at once that he, Sartoris, was the
sort of man who could even cope with Sutpen in the
sense that a man with a sabre or even a small sword and
heart enough for it could cope with one with an axe; and
that summer (Sutpen's Paris architect had long since gone
back to whatever place he came from and to which he had
made his one abortive midnight try to return, but his
trickle, flow of bricks had never even faltered: his molds
and kilns had finished the jail and were now raising the
walls of two churches and by the half-century would have
completed what would be known through all north Mississippi and east Tennessee as *the* Academy, *the* Female
Institute) there was a committee: Compson and Sartoris
and Peabody (and *in absentia* Sutpen: nor would the
town ever know exactly how much of the additional cost
Sutpen and Sartoris made up): and the next year

the eight disjointed marble columns were landed from an Italian ship at New Orleans, into a steamboat up the Mississippi to Vicksburg, and into a smaller steamboat up the Yazoo and Sunflower and Tallahatchie, to Ikkemotubbe's old landing which Sutpen now owned, and thence the twelve miles by oxen into Jefferson: the two identical four-column porticoes, one on the north and one on the south, each with its balcony of wroughtiron New Orleans grillwork, on one of which—the south one—in 1861 Sartoris would stand in the first Confederate uniform the town had ever seen, while in the Square below the Richmond mustering officer enrolled and swore in the regiment which Sartoris as its colonel would take to Virginia as a part of Bee, to be Jackson's extreme left in front of the Henry house at First Manassas, and from both of which each May and November for a hundred years, bailiffs in their orderly appointive almost hereditary succession would cry without inflection or punctuation either "oyes oyes honorable circuit court of Yoknapatawpha County come all and ye shall be heard" and beneath which for that same length of time too except for the seven years between '63 and '70 which didn't really count a century afterward except to a few irreconcilable old ladies, the white male citizens of the county would pass to vote for county and state offices, because when in '63 a United States military force burned the Square and the business district, the courthouse survived. It didn't escape: it simply survived: harder than axes, tougher than fire, more fixed than dynamite; encircled by the tumbled and blackened ruins of lesser walls, it still stood, even the topless smoke-stained columns, gutted of course and roofless, but immune, not one hair even out of the Paris architect's almost forgotten plumb, so that all they had to do (it took nine years to build; they needed twenty-five to restore it) was put in new floors for the two storeys and a new roof, and this time with a cupola with a four-faced clock and a bell to strike the hours and ring alarms; by this time the Square, the banks and the stores and the lawyers' and doctors' and dentists' offices, had been restored, and the English sparrows were back too which had never really deserted— the garrulous noisy independent swarms which, as though concomitant with, inextricable from regularised and roted human quarreling, had appeared in possession of cornices and gutter-boxes almost before the last nail was driven—and now the pigeons also, interminably murmurous, nesting in, already usurping, the belfry even though they couldn't seem to get used to the bell, bursting out of the cupola at each stroke of the hour in frantic clouds, to sink and burst and whirl again at each succeeding stroke, until the last one: then vanishing back through the slatted louvers until nothing remained but the frantic and murmurous cooing like the fading echoes of the bell itself, the source of the alarm never recognised and even the alarm itself unremembered, as the actual stroke of the bell is no longer remembered by the vibration-fading air. Because they—the sparrows and the pigeons—endured, durable, a hundred years, the oldest things there except the courthouse centennial and serene above the town most of whose people now no longer even knew who Doctor Habersham and old Alec Holston and Louis Grenier were, had been; centennial and serene above the change: the electricity and gasoline, the neon and the crowded cacophonous air; even Negroes passing in beneath the balconies and into the chancery clerk's office to cast ballots too, voting for the same white-skinned rascals and demagogues and white supremacy champions that the white ones did—durable: every few years the county fathers, dreaming of bakshish, would instigate a movement to tear it down and erect a new modern one, but someone would at the last moment defeat them; they will try it again of course and be defeated perhaps once again or even maybe twice again, but no more than that. Because its fate is to stand in the hinterland of America: its doom is its longevity; like a man, its simple age is its own reproach, and after the hundred years, will become unbearable. But not for a little while yet; for a little while yet the sparrows and the pigeons: garrulous myriad and independent the one, the other uxorious and interminable, at once frantic and tranquil—until the clock strikes again which even after a hundred years, they still seem unable to get used to, bursting in one swirling explosion out of the belfry as though, the hour, instead of merely adding one puny infinitesimal more to the long weary increment since Genesis, had shattered the virgin pristine air with the first loud ding-dong of time and doom.

18—

Red Leaves

I

The two Indians crossed the plantation toward the slave quarters. Neat with whitewash, of baked soft brick, the two rows of houses in which lived the slaves belonging to the clan, faced one another across the mild shade of the lane marked and scored with naked feet and with a few homemade toys mute in the dust. There was no sign of life.

"I know what we will find," the first Indian said.

"What we will not find," the second said. Although it was noon, the lane was vacant, the doors of the cabins empty and quiet; no cooking smoke rose from any of the chinked and plastered chimneys.

"Yes. It happened like this when the father of him who is now the Man died."

"You mean, of him who was the Man."

"Yao."

The first Indian's name was Three Basket. He was perhaps sixty. They were both squat men, a little solid, burgherlike; paunchy, with big heads, big, broad, dust-colored faces of a certain blurred serenity like carved heads on a ruined wall in Siam or Sumatra, looming out of a mist. The sun had done it, the violent sun, the violent shade. Their hair looked like sedge grass on burnt-over land. Clamped through one ear Three Basket wore an enameled snuffbox.

"I have said all the time that this is not the good way. In the old days there were no quarters, no Negroes. A man's time was his own then. He had time. Now he must spend most of it finding work for them who prefer sweating to do."

"They are like horses and dogs."

"They are like nothing in this sensible world. Nothing contents them save sweat. They are worse than the white people."

"It is not as though the Man himself had to find work for them to do."

"You said it. I do not like slavery. It is not the good way. In the old days, there was the good way. But not now."

"You do not remember the old way either."

"I have listened to them who do. And I have tried this way. Man was not made to sweat."

"That's so. See what it has done to their flesh."

"Yes. Black. It has a bitter taste, too."

"You have eaten of it?"

"Once. I was young then, and more hardy in the appetite than now. Now it is different with me."

"Yes. They are too valuable to eat now."

"There is a bitter taste to the flesh which I do not like."

"They are too valuable to eat, anyway, when the white men will give horses for them."

They entered the lane. The mute, meager toys—the fetish-shaped objects made of wood and rags and feathers—lay in the dust about the patinaed doorsteps, among bones and broken gourd dishes. But there was no sound from any cabin, no face in any door; had not been since yesterday, when Issetibbeha died. But they already knew what they would find.

It was in the central cabin, a house a little larger than the others, where at certain phases of the moon the Negroes would gather to begin their ceremonies before removing after nightfall to the creek bottom, where they kept the drums. In this room they kept the minor accessories, the cryptic ornaments, the ceremonial records which consisted of sticks daubed with red clay in symbols. It had a hearth in the center of the floor, beneath a hole in the roof, with a few cold wood ashes and a suspended iron pot. The window shutters were closed; when the two Indians entered, after the abashless sunlight they could distinguish nothing with the eyes save a movement, shadow, out of which eyeballs rolled, so that the place appeared to be full of Negroes. The two Indians stood in the door.

"Yao," Basket said. "I said this is not the good way."

"I don't think I want to be here," the second said.

"That is black man's fear which you smell. It does not smell as ours does."

"I don't think I want to be here."

"Your fear has an odor too."

"Maybe it is Issetibbeha which we smell."

"Yao. He knows. He knows what we will find here. He knew when he died what we should find here today." Out of the rank twilight of the room the eyes, the smell, of Negroes rolled about them. "I am Three Basket, whom you know," Basket said into the room. "We are come from the Man. He whom we seek is gone?" The Negroes said nothing. The smell of them, of their bodies, seemed to ebb and flux in the still hot air. They seemed to be musing as one upon something remote, inscrutable. They were like a single octopus. They were like the roots of a huge tree uncovered, the earth broken momentarily upon the writhen, thick, fetid tangle of its lightless and outraged life. "Come," Basket said. "You know our errand. Is he whom we seek gone?"

"They are thinking something," the second said. "I do not want to be here."

"They are knowing something," Basket said.

"They are hiding him, you think?"

"No. He is gone. He has been gone since last night. It happened like this before, when the grandfather of him who is now the Man died. It took us three days to catch him. For three days Doom lay above the ground, saying, 'I see my horse and my dog. But I do not see my slave. What have you done with him that you will not permit me to lie quiet?'"

"They do not like to die."

"Yao. They cling. It makes trouble for us, always. A people without honor and without decorum. Always a trouble."

"I do not like it here."

"Nor do I. But then, they are savages; they cannot be expected to regard usage. That is why I say that this way is a bad way."

"Yao. They cling. They would even rather work in the sun than to enter the earth with a chief. But he is gone."

The Negroes had said nothing, made no sound. The white eyeballs rolled, wild, subdued; the smell was rank, violent. "Yes, they fear," the second said. "What shall we do now?"

"Let us go and talk with the Man."

"Will Moketubbe listen?"

"What can he do? He will not like to. But he is the Man now."

"Yao. He is the Man. He can wear the shoes with the red heels all the time now." They turned and went out. There was no door in the door frame. There were no doors in any of the cabins.

"He did that anyway," Basket said.

"Behind Issetibbeha's back. But now they are his shoes, since he is the Man."

"Yao. Issetibbeha did not like it. I have heard. I know that he said to Moketubbe: 'When you are the Man, the shoes will be yours. But until then, they are my shoes.' But now Moketubbe is the Man; he can wear them."

"Yao," the second said. "He is the Man now. He used

to wear the shoes behind Issetibbeha's back, and it was not known if Issetibbeha knew this or not. And then Issetibbeha became dead, who was not old, and the shoes are Moketubbe's, since he is the Man now. What do you think of that?"

"I don't think about it," Basket said. "Do you?"

"No," the second said.

"Good," Basket said. "You are wise."

II

The house sat on a knoll, surrounded by oak trees. The front of it was one story in height, composed of the deck house of a steamboat which had gone ashore and which Doom, Issetibbeha's father, had dismantled with his slaves and hauled on cypress rollers twelve miles home overland. It took them five months. His house consisted at the time of one brick wall. He set the steamboat broadside on to the wall, where now the chipped and flaked gliding of the rococo cornices arched in faint splendor above the gilt lettering of the stateroom names above the jalousied doors.

Doom had been born merely a subchief, a Mingo, one of three children on the mother's side of the family. He made a journey—he was a young man then and New Orleans was a European city—from north Mississippi to New Orlean by keel boat, where he met the Chevalier Sœur Blonde de Vitry, a man whose social position, on its face, was as equivocal as Doom's own. In New Orleans, among the gamblers and cutthroats of the river front, Doom, under the tutelage of his patron, passed as the chief, the Man, the hereditary owner of that land which belonged to the male side of the family; it was the Chevalier de Vitry who spoke of him as *l'Homme* or *de l'Homme,* and hence Doom.

They were seen everywhere together—the Indian, the squat man with a bold, inscrutable, underbred face, and

the Parisian, the expatriate, the friend, it was said, of
Carondelet and the intimate of General Wilkinson. Then
they disappeared, the two of them, vanishing from their
old equivocal haunts and leaving behind them the legend
of the sums which Doom was believed to have won, and
some tale about a young woman, daughter of a fairly well-
to-do West Indian family, the son and brother of whom
sought Doom with a pistol about his old haunts for some
time after his disappearance.

Six months later the young woman herself disappeared,
boarding the Saint Louis packet, which put in one night
at a wood landing on the north Mississippi side, where the
woman, accompanied by a Negro maid, got off. Four
Indians met her with a horse and wagon, and they traveled
for three days, slowly, since she was already big with
child, to the plantation, where she found that Doom was
now chief. He never told her how he accomplished it,
save that his uncle and his cousin had died suddenly. Before that time the house had consisted of a brick wall
built by shiftless slaves, against which was propped a
thatched lean-to divided into rooms and littered with
bones and refuse, set in the center of ten thousand acres
of matchless parklike forest where deer grazed like domes-
tic cattle. Doom and the woman were married there a
short time before Issetibbeha was born, by a combination
itinerant minister and slave trader who arrived on a mule,
to the saddle of which was lashed a cotton umbrella and a
three-gallon demijohn of whiskey. After that, Doom began
to acquire more slaves and to cultivate some of his land,
as the white people did. But he never had enough for
them to do. In utter idleness the majority of them led lives
transplanted whole out of African jungles, save on the
occasions when, entertaining guests, Doom coursed them
with dogs.

When Doom died, Issetibbeha, his son, was nineteen.
He became proprietor of the land and of the quin-
tupled herd of blacks for which he had no use at all.

Though the title of Man rested with him, there was a hierarchy of cousins and uncles who ruled the clan and who finally gathered in squatting conclave over the Negro question, squatting profoundly beneath the golden names above the doors of the steamboat.

"We cannot eat them," one said.

"Why not?"

"There are too many of them."

"That's true," a third said. "Once we started, we should have to eat them all. And that much flesh diet is not good for man."

"Perhaps they will be like deer flesh. That cannot hurt you."

"We might kill a few of them and not eat them," Issetibbeha said.

They looked at him for a while. "What for?" one said.

"That is true," a second said. "We cannot do that. They are too valuable; remember all the bother they have caused us, finding things for them to do. We must do as the white men do."

"How is that?" Issetibbeha said.

"Raise more Negroes by clearing more land to make corn to feed them, then sell them. We will clear the land and plant it with food and raise Negroes and sell them to the white men for money."

"But what will we do with this money?" a third said.

They thought for a while.

"We will see," the first said. They squatted, profound, grave.

"It means work," the third said.

"Let the Negroes do it," the first said.

"Yao. Let them. To sweat is bad. It is damp. It opens the pores."

"And then the night air enters."

"Yao. Let the Negroes do it. They appear to like sweating."

So they cleared the land with the Negroes and planted

it in grain. Up to that time the slaves had lived in a huge pen with a lean-to roof over one corner, like a pen for pigs. But now they began to build quarters, cabins, putting the young Negroes in the cabins in pairs to mate; five years later Issetibbeha sold forty head to a Memphis trader, and he took the money and went abroad upon it, his maternal uncle from New Orleans conducting the trip. At that time the Chevalier Sœur Blonde de Vitry was an old man in Paris, in a toupee and a corset and a careful, toothless old face fixed in a grimace quizzical and profoundly tragic. He borrowed three hundred dollars from Issetibbeha and in return he introduced him into certain circles; a year later Issetibbeha returned home with a gilt bed, a pair of girandoles by whose light it was said that Pompadour arranged her hair while Louis smirked at his mirrored face across her powdered shoulder, and a pair of slippers with red heels. They were too small for him, since he had not worn shoes at all until he reached New Orleans on his way abroad.

He brought the slippers home in tissue paper and kept them in the remaining pocket of a pair of saddlebags filled with cedar shavings, save when he took them out on occasion for his son, Moketubbe, to play with. At three years of age Moketubbe had a broad, flat, Mongolian face that appeared to exist in a complete and unfathomable lethargy, until confronted by the slippers.

Moketubbe's mother was a comely girl whom Issetibbeha had seen one day working in her shift in a melon patch. He stopped and watched her for a while—the broad, solid thighs, the sound back, the serene face. He was on his way to the creek to fish that day, but he didn't go any farther; perhaps while he stood there watching the unaware girl he may have remembered his own mother, the city woman, the fugitive with her fans and laces and her Negro blood, and all the tawdry shabbiness of that sorry affair. Within the year Moketubbe was born; even at three he could not get his feet into the slippers. Watching him in the still, hot afternoons as he struggled with the slippers with a certain monstrous repudiation of fact, Issetibbeha laughed quietly to himself. He laughed at Moketubbe's antics with the shoes for several years, because Moketubbe did not give up trying to put them on until he was sixteen. Then he quit. Or Issetibbeha thought he had. But he had merely quit trying in Issetibbeha's presence. Issetibbeha's newest wife told him that Moketubbe had stolen and hidden the shoes. Issetibbeha quit laughing then, and he sent the woman away, so that he was alone. "Yao," he said. "I too like being alive, it seems." He sent for Moketubbe. "I give them to you," he said.

Moketubbe was twenty-five then, unmarried. Issetibbeha was not tall, but he was taller by six inches than his son and almost a hundred pounds lighter. Moketubbe was already diseased with flesh, with a pale, broad, inert face and dropsical hands and feet. "They are yours now," Issetibbeha said, watching him. Moketubbe had looked at him once when he entered, a glance brief, discreet, veiled.

"Thanks," he said.

Issetibbeha looked at him. He could never tell if Moketubbe saw anything, looked at anything. "Why will it not be the same if I give the slippers to you?"

"Thanks," Moketubbe said. Issetibbeha was using snuff at the time; a white man had shown him how to put the powder into his lip and scour it against his teeth with a twig of gum or of alphea.

"Well," he said, "a man cannot live forever." He looked at his son, then his gaze went blank in turn, unseeing, and he mused for an instant. You could not tell what he was thinking, save that he said half aloud: "Yao. But Doom's uncle had no shoes with red heels." He looked at his son again, fat, inert. "Beneath all that, a man might think of doing anything and it not be known until too late." He sat in a splint chair hammocked with deer thongs. "He cannot even get them on; he and I are both frustrated by the same gross meat which he wears. He cannot even get them on. But is that my fault?"

He lived for five years longer, then he died. He was sick one night, and though the doctor came in a skunk-skin vest and burned sticks, Issetibbeha died before noon.

That was yesterday; the grave was dug, and for twelve hours now the People had been coming in wagons and carriages and on horseback and afoot, to eat the baked dog and the succotash and the yams cooked in ashes and to attend the funeral.

III

"It will be three days," Basket said, as he and the other Indian returned to the house. "It will be three days and the food will not be enough; I have seen it before."

The second Indian's name was Louis Berry. "He will smell too, in this weather."

"Yao. They are nothing but a trouble and a care."

"Maybe it will not take three days."

"They run far. Yao. We will smell this Man before he enters the earth. You watch and see if I am not right."

They approached the house.

"He can wear the shoes now," Berry said. "He can wear them now in man's sight."

"He cannot wear them for a while yet," Basket said. Berry looked at him. "He will lead the hunt."

"Moketubbe?" Berry said. "Do you think he will? A man to whom even talking is travail?"

"What else can he do? It is his own father who will soon begin to smell."

"That is true," Berry said. "There is even yet a price he must pay for the shoes. Yao. He has truly bought them. What do you think?"

"What do you think?"

"What do you think?"

"I think nothing."

"Nor do I. Issetibbeha will not need the shoes now. Let Moketubbe have them; Issetibbeha will not care."

"Yao. Man must die."

"Yao. Let him; there is still the Man."

The bark roof of the porch was supported by peeled cypress poles, high above the texas of the steamboat, shading an unfloored banquette where on the trodden earth mules and horses were tethered in bad weather. On the forward end of the steamboat's deck sat an old man and two women. One of the women was dressing a fowl, the other was shelling corn. The old man was talking. He was barefoot, in a long linen frock coat and a beaver hat.

"This world is going to the dogs," he said. "It is being ruined by white men. We got along fine for years and years, before the white men foisted their Negroes upon us. In the old days the old men sat in the shade and ate stewed deer's flesh and corn and smoked tobacco and talked of honor and grave affairs; now what do we do? Even the old wear themselves into the grave taking care of them that like sweating." When Basket and Berry crossed the deck he ceased and looked up at them. His eyes were querulous, bleared; his face was myriad with tiny wrinkles. "He is fled also," he said.

"Yes," Berry said, "he is gone."

"I knew it. I told them so. It will take three weeks, like when Doom died. You watch and see."

"It was three days, not three weeks," Berry said.

"Were you there?"

"No," Berry said. "But I have heard."

"Well, I was there," the old man said. "For three whole weeks, through the swamps and the briers—" They went on and left him talking.

What had been the saloon of the steamboat was now a shell. rotting slowly; the polished mahogany, the carving glinting momentarily and fading through the mold in figures cabalistic and profound; the gutted windows were like cataracted eyes. It contained a few sacks of seed or grain, and the fore part of the running gear of a barouche, to the axle of which two C-springs rusted in graceful curves, supporting nothing. In one corner a fox cub ran steadily and soundlessly up and down a willow cage; three scrawny gamecocks moved in the dust, and the place was pocked and marked with their dried droppings.

They passed through the brick wall and entered a big room of chinked logs. It contained the hinder part of the barouche, and the dismantled body lying on its side, the window slatted over with willow withes, through which protruded the heads, the still, beady, outraged eyes and frayed combs of still more game chickens. It was floored with packed clay; in one corner leaned a crude plow and two hand-hewn boat paddles. From the ceiling, suspended by four deer thongs, hung the gilt bed which Issetibbeha had fetched from Paris. It had neither mattress nor springs, the frame crisscrossed now by a neat hammocking of thongs.

Issetibbeha had tried to have his newest wife, the young one, sleep in the bed. He was congenitally short of breath himself, and he passed the nights half reclining in his splint chair. He would see her to bed and, later, wakeful, sleeping as he did but three or four hours a night, he would sit in the darkness and simulate slumber and listen to her sneak infinitesimally from the gilt and ribboned bed, to lie on a quilt pallet on the floor until just before daylight. Then she would enter the bed quietly again and in turn simulate slumber, while in the darkness beside her Issetibbeha quietly laughed and laughed.

The girandoles were lashed by thongs to two sticks propped in a corner where a ten-gallon whiskey keg lay also. There was a clay hearth; facing it, in the splint chair, Moketubbe sat. He was maybe an inch better than five feet tall, and he weighed two hundred and fifty pounds. He wore a broadcloth coat and no shirt, his round, smooth copper balloon of belly swelling above the bottom piece of a suit of linen underwear. On his feet were the slippers with the red heels. Behind his chair stood a stripling with a punkah-like fan made of fringed paper. Moketubbe sat motionless, with his broad, yellow face with its closed eyes and flat nostrils, his flipperlike arms extended. On his face was an expression profound, tragic, and inert. He did not open his eyes when Basket and Berry came in.

"He has worn them since daylight?" Basket said.

"Since daylight," the stripling said. The fan did not cease. "You can see."

"Yao," Basket said. "We can see." Moketubbe did not move. He looked like an effigy, like a Malay god in frock coat, drawers, naked chest, the trivial scarlet-heeled shoes.

"I wouldn't disturb him, if I were you," the stripling said.

"Not if I were you," Basket said. He and Berry squatted. The stripling moved the fan steadily. "O Man," Basket said, "listen." Moketubbe did not move. "He is gone," Basket said.

"I told you so," the stripling said. "I knew he would flee. I told you."

"Yao," Basket said. "You are not the first to tell us afterward what we should have known before. Why is it that some of you wise men took no steps yesterday to prevent this?"

"He does not wish to die," Berry said.

"Why should he not wish it?" Basket said.

"Because he must die some day is no reason," the stripling said. "That would not convince me either, old man."

"Hold your tongue," Berry said.

"For twenty years," Basket said, "while others of his race sweat in the fields, he served the Man in the shade. Why should he not wish to die, since he did not wish to sweat?"

"And it will be quick," Berry said. "It will not take long."

"Catch him and tell him that," the stripling said.

"Hush," Berry said. They squatted, watching Moke-tubbe's face. He might have been dead himself. It was as though he were cased so in flesh that even breathing took place too deep within him to show.

"Listen, O Man," Basket said. "Issetibbeha is dead. He waits. His dog and his horse we have. But his slave has fled. The one who held the pot for him, who ate of his food, from his dish, is fled. Issetibbeha waits."

"Yao," Berry said,

"This is not the first time," Basket said. "This happened when Doom, thy grandfather, lay waiting at the door of the earth. He lay waiting three days, saying, 'Where is my Negro?' And Issetibbeha, thy father, answered, 'I will find him. Rest; I will bring him to you so that you may begin the journey.'"

"Yao," Berry said.

Moketubbe had not moved, had not opened his eyes.

"For three days Issetibbeha hunted in the bottom," Basket said. "He did not even return home for food, until the Negro was with him; then he said to Doom, his father, 'Here is thy dog, thy horse, thy Negro; rest.' Issetibbeha, who is dead since yesterday, said it. And now Issetibbeha's Negro is fled. His horse and his dog wait with him, but his Negro is fled."

"Yao," Berry said.

Moketubbe had not moved. His eyes were closed; upon his supine monstrous shape there was a colossal inertia, something profoundly immobile, beyond and impervious to flesh. They watched his face, squatting.

"When thy father was newly the Man, this happened," Basket said. "And it was Issetibbeha who brought back the slave to where his father waited to enter the earth." Moketubbe's face had not moved, his eyes had not moved. After a while Basket said, "Remove the shoes."

The stripling removed the shoes. Moketubbe began to pant, his bare chest moving deep, as though he were rising from beyond his unfathomed flesh back into life, like up from the water, the sea. But his eyes had not opened yet.

Berry said, "He will lead the hunt."

"Yao," Basket said. "He is the Man. He will lead the hunt."

IV

All that day the Negro, Issetibbeha's body servant, hidden in the barn, watched Issetibbeha's dying. He was forty, a Guinea man. He had a flat nose, a close, small head; the inside corners of his eyes showed red a little, and his prominent gums were a pale bluish red above his square, broad teeth. He had been taken at fourteen by a trader off Kamerun, before his teeth had been filed. He had been Issetibbeha's body servant for twenty-three years.

On the day before, the day on which Issetibbeha lay sick, he returned to the quarters at dusk. In that unhurried hour the smoke of the cooking fires blew slowly across the street from door to door, carrying into the opposite one the smell of the identical meat and bread. The women tended them; the men were gathered at the head of the lane, watching him as he came down the slope from the house, putting his naked feet down carefully in a strange dusk. To the waiting men his eyeballs were a little luminous.

"Issetibbeha is not dead yet," the headman said.

"Not dead," the body servant said. "Who not dead?"

In the dusk they had faces like his, the different ages, the thoughts sealed inscrutable behind faces like the death masks of apes. The smell of the fires, the cooking, blew sharp and slow across the strange dusk, as from another world, above the lane and the pickaninnies naked in the dust.

"If he lives past sundown, he will live until daybreak," one said.

"Who says?"

"Talk says."

"Yao. Talk says. We know but one thing." They looked at the body servant as he stood among them, his eyeballs a little luminous. He was breathing slow and deep. His chest was bare; he was sweating a little. "He knows. He knows it."

"Let us let the drums talk."

"Yao. Let the drums tell it."

The drums began after dark. They kept them hidden in the creek bottom. They were made of hollowed cypress knees, and the Negroes kept them hidden; why, none knew. They were buried in the mud on the bank of a slough; a lad of fourteen guarded them. He was undersized, and a mute; he squatted in the mud there all day, clouded over with mosquitoes, naked save for the mud with which he coated himself against the mosquitoes, and about his neck a fiber bag containing a pig's rib to which black shreds of flesh still adhered, and two scaly barks on a wire. He slobbered onto his clutched knees, drooling; now and then Indians came noiselessly out of the bushes behind him and stood there and contemplated him for a while and went away, and he never knew it.

From the loft of the stable where he lay hidden until dark and after, the Negro could hear the drums. They were three miles away, but he could hear them as though they were in the barn itself below him, thudding and thudding. It was as though he could see the fire too, and the black limbs turning into and out of the flames in copper gleams. Only there would be no fire. There would be no more light there than where he lay in the dusty loft, with the whispering arpeggios of rat feet along the warm and immemorial ax-squared rafters. The only fire there would be the smudge against mosquitoes where the women with nursing children crouched, their heavy, sluggish breasts nippled full and smooth into the mouths of men children; contemplative, oblivious of the drumming, since a fire would signify life.

There was a fire in the steamboat, where Issetibbeha lay dying among his wives, beneath the lashed girandoles and the suspended bed. He could see the smoke, and just before sunset he saw the doctor come out, in a waistcoat made of skunk skins, and set fire to two clay-daubed sticks at the bows of the boat deck. "So he is not dead yet," the Negro said into the whispering gloom of the loft, answering himself; he could hear the two voices, himself and himself:

"Who not dead?"

"You are dead."

"Yao, I am dead," he said quietly. He wished to be where the drums were. He imagined himself springing out of the bushes, leaping among the drums on his bare, lean, greasy, invisible limbs. But he could not do that, because man leaped past life, into where death was; he dashed into death and did not die because when death took a man, it took him just this side of the end of living. It was when death overran him from behind, still in life. The thin whisper of rat feet died in fainting gusts along the rafters. Once he had eaten rat. He was a boy then, but just come to America. They had lived ninety days in a three-foot-high 'tween deck in tropic latitudes, hearing from topside the drunken New England captain intoning aloud from a book which he did not recognize for ten years afterward to be the Bible. Squatting in the stable so, he had watched the rat, civilized, by association with man reft of its inherent cunning of limb and eye; he had caught it without difficulty, with scarce a movement of his hand, and he ate it slowly, wondering how any of the rats had escaped so long. At that time he was still wearing the single white garment which the trader, a deacon in the Unitarian church, had given him, and he spoke then only his native tongue.

He was naked now, save for a pair of dungaree pants bought by Indians from white men, and an amulet slung on a thong about his hips. The amulet consisted of one half of a mother-of-pearl lorgnon which Issetibbeha had brought back from Paris, and the skull of a cottonmouth moccasin. He had killed the snake himself and eaten it, save the poison head. He lay in the loft, watching the house, the steamboat, listening to the drums, thinking of himself among the drums.

He lay there all night. The next morning he saw the doctor come out, in his skunk vest, and get on his mule and ride away, and he became quite still and watched the final dust from beneath the mule's delicate feet die away, and then he found that he was still breathing and it seemed strange to him that he still breathed air, still needed air. Then he lay and watched quietly, waiting to move, his eyeballs a little luminous, but with a quiet light, and his breathing light and regular, and saw Louis Berry come out and look at the sky. It was good light then, and already five Indians squatted in their Sunday clothes along the steamboat deck; by noon there were twenty-five there. That afternoon they dug the trench in which the meat would be baked, and the yams; by that time there were almost a hundred guests—decorous, quiet, patient in their stiff European finery—and he watched Berry lead Issetibbeha's mare from the stable and tie her to a tree, and then he watched Berry emerge from the house with the old hound which lay beside Issetibbeha's chair. He tied the hound to the tree too, and it sat there, looking gravely about at the faces. Then it began to howl. It was still howling at sundown, when the Negro climbed down the back wall of the barn and entered the spring branch, where it was already dusk. He began to run then. He could hear the hound howling behind him, and near the spring, already running, he passed another Negro. The two men, the one motionless and the other running, looked for an instant at each other as though across an actual boundary between two different worlds. He ran on into full darkness, mouth closed, fists doubled, his broad nostrils bellowing steadily.

He ran on in the darkness. He knew the country well, because he had hunted it often with Issetibbeha, following on his mule the course of the fox or the cat beside Issetibbeha's mare; he knew it as well as did the men who would pursue him. He saw them for the first time shortly before sunset of the second day. He had run thirty miles then, up the creek bottom, before doubling back; lying in a pawpaw thicket he saw the pursuit for the first time. There were two of them, in shirts and straw hats, carrying their neatly rolled trousers under their arms, and they had no weapons. They were middle-aged, paunchy, and they could not have moved very fast anyway; it would be twelve hours before they could return to where he lay watching them. "So I will have until midnight to rest," he said. He was near enough to the plantation to smell the cooking fires, and he thought how he ought to be hungry, since he had not eaten in thirty hours. "But it is more important to rest," he told himself. He continued to tell himself that, lying in the pawpaw thicket, because the effort of resting, the need and the haste to rest, made his heart thud the same as the running had done. It was as though he had forgot how to rest, as though the six hours were not long enough to do it in, to remember again how to do it.

As soon as dark came he moved again. He had thought to keep going steadily and quietly through the night, since there was nowhere for him to go, but as soon as he moved he began to run at top speed, breasting his panting chest, his broad-flaring nostrils through the choked and whipping darkness. He ran for an hour, lost by then, without direction, when suddenly he stopped, and after a time his thudding heart unraveled from the sound of the drums. By the sound they were not two miles away; he followed the sound until he could smell the smudge fire and taste the acrid smoke. When he stood among them the drums did not cease; only the headman came to him where he stood in the drifting smudge, panting, his nostrils flaring and pulsing, the hushed glare of his ceaseless eyeballs in his mud-daubed face as though they were worked from lungs.

"We have expected thee," the headman said. "Go, now."

"Go?"

"Eat, and go. The dead may not consort with the living; thou knowest that."

"Yao. I know that." They did not look at one another. The drums had not ceased.

"Wilt thou eat?" the headman said.

"I am not hungry. I caught a rabbit this afternoon, and ate while I lay hidden."

"Take some cooked meat with thee, then."

He accepted the cooked meat, wrapped in leaves, and entered the creek bottom again; after a while the sound of the drums ceased. He walked steadily until daybreak. "I have twelve hours," he said. "Maybe more, since the trail was followed by night." He squatted and ate the meat and wiped his hands on his thighs. Then he rose and removed the dungaree pants and squatted again beside a slough and coated himself with mud—face, arms, body and legs—and squatted again, clasping his knees, his head bowed. When it was light enough to see, he moved back into the swamp and squatted again and went to sleep so. He did not dream at all. It was well that he moved, for, waking suddenly in broad daylight and the high sun, he saw the two Indians. They still carried their neatly rolled trousers; they stood opposite the place where he lay hidden, paunchy, thick, soft-looking, a little ludicrous in their straw hats and shirt tails.

"This is wearying work," one said.

"I'd rather be at home in the shade myself," the other

said. "But there is the Man waiting at the door to the earth."

"Yao." They looked quietly about; stooping, one of them removed from his shirt tail a clot of cockleburs. "Damn that Negro," he said.

"Yao. When have they ever been anything but a trial and a care to us?"

In the early afternoon, from the top of a tree, the Negro looked down into the plantation. He could see Issetibbeha's body in a hammock between the two trees where the horse and the dog were tethered, and the concourse about the steamboat was filled with wagons and horses and mules, with carts and saddle-horses, while in bright clumps the women and the smaller children and the old men squatted about the long trench where the smoke from the barbecuing meat blew slow and thick. The men and the big boys would all be down there in the creek bottom behind him, on the trail, their Sunday clothes rolled carefully up and wedged into tree crotches. There was a clump of men near the door to the house, to the saloon of the steamboat, though, and he watched them, and after a while he saw them bring Moketubbe out in a litter made of buckskin and persimmon poles; high hidden in his leafed nook the Negro, the quarry, looked quietly down upon his irrevocable doom with an expression as profound as Moketubbe's own. "Yao," he said quietly. "He will go then. That man whose body has been dead for fifteen years, he will go also."

In the middle of the afternoon he came face to face with an Indian. They were both on a footlog across a slough—the Negro gaunt, lean, hard, tireless and desperate; the Indian thick, soft-looking, the apparent embodiment of the ultimate and the supreme reluctance and inertia. The Indian made no move, no sound; he stood on the log and watched the Negro plunge into the slough and swim ashore and crash away into the undergrowth.

Just before sunset he lay behind a down log. Up the log in slow procession moved a line of ants. He caught them and ate them slowly, with a kind of detachment, like that of a dinner guest eating salted nuts from a dish. They too had a salt taste, engendering a salivary reaction out of all proportion. He ate them slowly, watching the unbroken line move up the log and into oblivious doom with a steady and terrific undeviation. He had eaten nothing else all day; in his caked mud mask his eyes rolled in reddened rims. At sunset, creeping along the creek bank toward where he had spotted a frog, a cottonmouth moccasin slashed him suddenly across the forearm with a thick, sluggish blow. It struck clumsily, leaving two long slashes across his arm like two razor slashes, and half sprawled with its own momentum and rage, it appeared for the moment utterly helpless with its own awkwardness and choleric anger. "Olé, Grandfather," the Negro said. He touched its head and watched it slash him again across his arm, and again, with thick, raking, awkward blows. "It's that I do not wish to die," he said. Then he said it again—"It's that I do not wish to die"—in a quiet tone, of slow and low amaze, as though it were something that, until the words had said themselves, he found that he had not known, or had not known the depth and extent of his desire.

v

Moketubbe took the slippers with him. He could not wear them very long while in motion, not even in the litter where he was slung reclining, so they rested upon a square of fawnskin upon his lap—the cracked, frail slippers a little shapeless now, with their scaled patent-leather surface and buckleless tongues and scarlet heels, lying upon the supine, obese shape just barely alive, carried through swamp and brier by swinging relays of men who bore steadily all day long the crime and its object, on the business of the slain. To Moketubbe it must have been as though, himself immortal, he were being carried rapidly through hell by doomed spirits which, alive, had contemplated his disaster, and, dead, were oblivious partners to his damnation.

After resting for a while, the litter propped in the center of the squatting circle and Moketubbe motionless in it, with closed eyes and his face at once peaceful for the instant and filled with inescapable foreknowledge, he could wear the slippers for a while. The stripling put them on him, forcing his big, tender, dropsical feet into them; whereupon into his face came again that expression, tragic, passive, and profoundly attentive, which dyspeptics wear. Then they went on. He made no move, no sound, inert in the rhythmic litter out of some reserve of inertia, or maybe of some kingly virtue such as courage or fortitude. After a time they set the litter down and looked at him, at the yellow face like that of an idol, beaded over with sweat. Then Three Basket or Louis Berry would say: "Take them off. Honor has been served." They would remove the shoes. Moketubbe's face would not alter, but only then would his breathing become perceptible, going in and out of his pale lips with a faint ah-ah-ah sound, and they would squat again while the couriers and the runners came up.

"Not yet?"

"Not yet. He is going east. By sunset he will reach Mouth of Tippah. Then he will turn back. We may take him tomorrow."

"Let us hope so. It will not be too soon."

"Yao. It has been three days now."

"When Doom died, it took only three days."

"But that was an old man. This one is young."

"Yao. A good race. If he is taken tomorrow, I will win a horse."

"May you win it."

"Yao. This work is not pleasant."

That was the day on which the food gave out at the plantation. The guests returned home and came back the next day with more food, enough for a week longer. On that day Issetibbeha began to smell; they could smell him for a long way up and down the bottom when it got hot toward noon and the wind blew. But they didn't capture the Negro on that day, nor on the next. It was about dusk on the sixth day when the couriers came up to the litter; they had found blood. "He has injured himself."

"Not bad, I hope," Basket said. "We cannot send with Issetibbeha one who will be of no service to him."

"Nor whom Issetibbeha himself will have to nurse and care for," Berry said.

"We do not know," the courier said. "He has hidden himself. He has crept back into the swamp. We have left pickets."

They trotted with the litter now. The place where the Negro had crept into the swamp was an hour away. In the hurry and excitement they had forgotten that Moketubbe still wore the slippers; when they reached the place Moketubbe had fainted. They removed the slippers and brought him to.

With dark, they formed a circle about the swamp. They squatted, clouded over with gnats and mosquitoes; the evening star burned low and close down the west, and the constellations began to wheel overhead. "We will give him time," they said. "Tomorrow is just another name for today."

"Yao. Let him have time." Then they ceased, and gazed as one into the darkness where the swamp lay. After a while the noise ceased, and soon the courier came out of the darkness.

"He tried to break out."

"But you turned him back?"

"He turned back. We feared for a moment, the three of us. We could smell him creeping in the darkness, and we could smell something else, which we did not know. That was why we feared, until he told us. He said to slay him there, since it would be dark and he would not have to see the face when it came. But it was not that which we smelled; he told us what it was. A snake had struck him. That was two days ago. The arm swelled, and it smelled bad. But it was not that which we smelled then, because the swelling had gone down and his arm was no larger than that of a child. He showed us. We felt the arm, all of us did; it was no larger than that of a child. He said to give him a hatchet so he could chop the arm off. But tomorrow is today also."

"Yao. Tomorrow is today."

"We feared for a while. Then he went back into the swamp."

"That is good."

"Yao. We feared. Shall I tell the Man?"

"I will see," Basket said. He went away. The courier squatted, telling again about the Negro. Basket returned. "The Man says that it is good. Return to your post."

The courier crept away. They squatted about the litter; now and then they slept. Sometime after midnight the Negro waked them. He began to shout and talk to himself, his voice coming sharp and sudden out of the darkness, then he fell silent. Dawn came; a white crane flapped slowly across the jonquil sky. Basket was awake. "Let us go now," he said. "It is today."

Two Indians entered the swamp, their movements noisy. Before they reached the Negro they stopped, because he began to sing. They could see him, naked and mud-caked, sitting on a log, singing. They squatted silently a short distance away, until he finished. He was chanting something in his own language, his face lifted to the rising sun. His voice was clear, full, with a quality wild and sad. "Let him have time," the Indians said squatting, patient, waiting. He ceased and they approached. He looked back and up at them through the cracked mud mask. His eyes were bloodshot, his lips cracked upon his square short teeth. The mask of mud appeared to be loose on his face, as if he might have lost flesh since he put it there; he held his left arm close to his breast. From the elbow down it was caked and shapeless with black mud. They could smell him, a rank smell. He watched them quietly until one touched him on the arm. "Come," the Indian said. "You ran well. Do not be ashamed."

VI

As they neared the plantation in the tainted bright morning, the Negro's eyes began to roll a little, like those of a horse. The smoke from the cooking pit blew low along the earth and upon the squatting and waiting guests about the yard and upon the steamboat deck, in their bright, stiff, harsh finery; the women, the children, the old men. They had sent couriers along the bottom, and another on ahead, and Issetibbeha's body had already been removed to where the grave waited, along with the horse and the dog, though they could still smell him in death about the house where he had lived in life. The guests were beginning to move toward the grave when the bearers of Moketubbe's litter mounted the slope.

The Negro was the tallest there, his high, close, mud-caked head looming above them all. He was breathing hard, as though the desperate effort of the six suspended and desperate days had capitulated upon him at once; although they walked slowly, his naked scarred chest rose and fell above the close-clutched left arm. He looked this way and that continuously, as if he were not seeing, as though sight never quite caught up with the looking. His mouth was open a little upon his big white teeth; he began to pant. The already moving guests halted, pausing, looking back, some with pieces of meat in their hands, as the Negro looked about at their faces with his wild, restrained, unceasing eyes.

"Will you eat first?" Basket said. He had to say it twice.

"Yes," the Negro said. "That's it. I want to eat."

The throng had begun to press back toward the center; the word passed to the outermost: "He will eat first."

They reached the steamboat. "Sit down," Basket said. The Negro sat on the edge of the deck. He was still panting, his chest rising and falling, his head ceaseless with its white eyeballs, turning from side to side. It was as if the inability to see came from within, from hopelessness, not from absence of vision. They brought food and watched quietly as he tried to eat it. He put the food into his mouth and chewed it, but chewing, the half-masticated matter began to merge from the corners of his mouth and to drool down his chin, onto his chest, and after a while he stopped chewing and sat there, naked, covered with dried mud, the plate on his knees, and his mouth filled with a mass of chewed food, open, his eyes wide and unceasing, panting and panting. They watched him, patient, implacable, waiting.

"Come," Basket said at last.

"It's water I want," the Negro said. "I want water."

The well was a little way down the slope toward the quarters. The slope lay dappled with the shadows of noon, of that peaceful hour when, Issetibbeha napping in his chair and waiting for the noon meal and the long afternoon to sleep in, the Negro, the body servant, would be free. He would sit in the kitchen door then, talking with the women that prepared the food. Beyond the kitchen the lane between the quarters would be quiet, peaceful, with the women talking to one another across the lane and the smoke of the dinner fires blowing upon the pickaninnies like ebony toys in the dust.

"Come," Basket said.

The Negro walked among them, taller than any. The guests were moving on toward where Issetibbeha and the horse and the dog waited. The Negro walked with his high ceaseless head, his panting chest. "Come," Basket said. "You wanted water."

"Yes," the Negro said. "Yes." He looked back at the house, then down to the quarters, where today no fire burned, no face showed in any door, no pickaninny in the dust, panting. "It struck me here, raking me across this arm; once, twice, three times. I said, 'Olé, Grandfather.' "

"Come now," Basket said. The Negro was still going through the motion of walking, his knee action high, his head high, as though he were on a treadmill. His eyeballs had a wild, restrained glare, like those of a horse. "You wanted water," Basket said. "Here it is."

There was a gourd in the well. They dipped it full and gave it to the Negro, and they watched him try to drink. His eyes had not ceased rolling as he tilted the gourd slowly against his caked face. They could watch his throat working and the bright water cascading from either side of the gourd, down his chin and breast. Then the water stopped. "Come," Basket said.

"Wait," the Negro said. He dipped the gourd again and tilted it against his face, beneath his ceaseless eyes. Again they watched his throat working and the unswallowed water sheathing broken and myriad down his chin, channeling his caked chest. They waited, patient, grave, decorous, implacable; clansman and guest and kin. Then the water ceased, though still the empty gourd tilted higher and higher, and still his black throat aped the vain motion of his frustrated swallowing. A piece of water-loosened mud carried away from his chest and broke at his muddy feet, and in the empty gourd they could hear his breath: ah-ah-ah.

"Come," Basket said, taking the gourd from the Negro and hanging it back in the well.

1859

Was

I

When Cass Edmonds and Uncle Buck ran back to the house from discovering that Tomey's Turl had run again, they heard Uncle Buddy cursing and bellowing in the kitchen, then the fox and the dogs came out of the kitchen and crossed the hall into the dogs' room and they heard them run through the dogs' room into his and Uncle Buck's room, then they saw them cross the hall again into Uncle Buddy's room and heard them run through Uncle Buddy's room into the kitchen again and this time it sounded like the whole kitchen chimney had come down and Uncle Buddy bellowing like a steamboat blowing, and this time the fox and the dogs and five or six sticks of firewood all came out of the kitchen together with Uncle Buddy in the middle of them hitting at everything in sight with another stick. It was a good race.

When Cass and Uncle Buck ran into their room to get Uncle Buck's necktie, the fox had treed behind the clock on the mantel. Uncle Buck got the necktie from the drawer and kicked the dogs off and lifted the fox down by the scruff of the neck and shoved it back into the crate under the bed and they went to the kitchen, where Uncle Buddy was picking the breakfast up out of the ashes and wiping it off with his apron. "What in damn's hell do you mean," he said, "turning that damn fox out with the dogs all loose in the house?"

"Damn the fox," Uncle Buck said. "Tomey's Turl has broke out again. Give me and Cass some breakfast quick. We might just barely catch him before he gets there."

Because they knew exactly where Tomey's Turl had gone, he went there every time he could slip off, which was about twice a year. He was heading for Mr. Hubert Beauchamp's place just over the edge of the next county, that Mr. Hubert's sister, Miss Sophonsiba (Mr. Hubert was a bachelor too, like Uncle Buck and Uncle Buddy) was still trying to make people call Warwick after the place in England that she said Mr. Hubert was probably the true earl of only he never even had enough pride, not to mention energy, to take the trouble to establish his just rights. Tomey's Turl would go there to hang around Mr. Hubert's girl Tennie, until somebody came and got him. They couldn't keep him at home by buying Tennie from Mr. Hubert because Uncle Buck said he and Uncle Buddy had so many niggers already that they could hardly walk around on their own land for them, and they couldn't sell Tomey's Turl to Mr. Hubert because Mr. Hubert said he not only wouldn't buy Tomey's Turl, he wouldn't have that damn white half-McCaslin on his place even as a free gift, not even if Uncle Buck and Uncle Buddy were to pay board and keep for him. And if somebody didn't go and get Tomey's Turl right away, Mr. Hubert would fetch him back himself, bringing Miss Sophonsiba, and they would stay for a week or longer, Miss Sophonsiba living in Uncle Buddy's room and Uncle Buddy moved clean out of the house, sleeping in one of the cabins in the quarters where the niggers used to live in his great-grandfather's time until his great-grandfather died and Uncle Buck and Uncle Buddy moved all the niggers into the big house which his great-grandfather had not had time to finish, and not even doing the cooking while they were there and not even coming to the house any more except to sit on the front gallery after supper, sitting in the darkness between Mr. Hubert and Uncle Buck until after a

while even Mr. Hubert would give up telling how many
more head of niggers and acres of land he would add to
what he would give Miss Sophonsiba when she married,
and go to bed. And one midnight last summer Uncle
Buddy just happened by accident to be awake and hear
Mr. Hubert drive out of the lot and by the time he waked
them and they got Miss Sophonsiba up and dressed and
the team put to the wagon and caught Mr. Hubert, it was
almost daylight. So it was always he and Uncle Buck who
went to fetch Tomey's Turl because Uncle Buddy never
went anywhere, not even to town and not even to fetch
Tomey's Turl from Mr. Hubert's, even though they all
knew that Uncle Buddy could have risked it ten times as
much as Uncle Buck could have dared.

They ate breakfast fast. Uncle Buck put on his necktie
while they were running toward the lot to catch the
horses. The only time he wore the necktie was on Tomey's
Turl's account and he hadn't even had it out of the drawer
since that night last summer when Uncle Buddy had
waked them in the dark and said, "Get up out of that bed
and damn quick." Uncle Buddy didn't own a necktie at
all; Uncle Buck said Uncle Buddy wouldn't take that
chance even in a section like theirs, where ladies were
so damn seldom thank God that a man could ride for days
in a straight line without having to dodge a single one. His
grandmother (she was Uncle Buck's and Uncle Buddy's
sister; she had raised him following his mother's death.
That was where he had got his christian name: McCaslin,
Carothers McCaslin Edmonds) said that Uncle Buck and
Uncle Buddy both used the necktie just as another way of
daring people to say they looked like twins, because even
at sixty they would still fight anyone who claimed he
could not tell them apart; whereupon his father had answered that any man who ever played poker once with
Uncle Buddy would never mistake him again for Uncle
Buck or anybody else.

Jonas had the two horses saddled and waiting. Uncle

Buck didn't mount a horse like he was any sixty years old either, lean and active as a cat, with his round, close-cropped white head and his hard little gray eyes and his white-stubbled jaw, his foot in the iron and the horse already moving, already running at the open gate when Uncle Buck came into the seat. He scrabbled up too, onto the shorter pony, before Jonas could boost him up, clapping the pony with his heels into its own stiff, short-coupled canter, out the gate after Uncle Buck, when Uncle Buddy (he hadn't even noticed him) stepped out from the gate and caught the bit. "Watch him," Uncle Buddy said. "Watch Theophilus. The minute anything begins to look wrong, you ride to hell back here and get me. You hear?"

"Yes, sir," he said. "Lemme go now. I won't even ketch Uncle Buck, let alone Tomey's Turl——"

Uncle Buck was riding Black John, because if they could just catch sight of Tomey's Turl at least one mile from Mr. Hubert's gate, Black John would ride him down in two minutes. So when they came out on the long flat about three miles from Mr. Hubert's, sure enough, there was Tomey's Turl on the Jake mule about a mile ahead. Uncle Buck flung his arm out and back, reining in, crouched on the big horse, his little round head and his gnarled neck thrust forward like a cooter's. "Stole away!" he whispered. "You stay back where he won't see you and flush. I'll circle him through the woods and we will bay him at the creek ford."

He waited until Uncle Buck had vanished into the woods. Then he went on. But Tomey's Turl saw him. He closed in too fast; maybe he was afraid he wouldn't be there in time to see him when he treed. It was the best race he had ever seen. He had never seen old Jake go that fast, and nobody had ever known Tomey's Turl to go faster than his natural walk, even riding a mule. Uncle Buck whooped once from the woods, running on sight, then Black John came out of the trees, driving, soupled

out flat and level as a hawk, with Uncle Buck right up
behind his ears now and yelling so that they looked exactly like a big black hawk with a sparrow riding it, across
the field and over the ditch and across the next field, and
he was running too; the mare went out before he even
knew she was ready, and he was yelling too. Because, being a nigger, Tomey's Turl should have jumped down
and run for it afoot as soon as he saw them. But he didn't;
maybe Tomey's Turl had been running off from Uncle
Buck for so long that he had even got used to running
away like a white man would do it. And it was like he and
old Jake had added Tomey's Turl's natural walking speed
to the best that old Jake had ever done in his life, and it
was just exactly enough to beat Uncle Buck to the ford.
Because when he and the pony arrived, Black John was
blown and lathered and Uncle Buck was down, leading
him around in a circle to slow him down, and they could
already hear Mr. Hubert's dinner horn a mile away.

Only, for a while Tomey's Turl didn't seem to be at Mr.
Hubert's either. The boy was still sitting on the gatepost,
blowing the horn—there was no gate there; just two posts
and a nigger boy about his size sitting on one of them,
blowing a fox-horn; this was what Miss Sophonsiba was
still reminding people was named Warwick even when
they had already known for a long time that's what she
aimed to have it called, until when they wouldn't call it
Warwick she wouldn't even seem to know what they
were talking about and it would sound as if she and Mr.
Hubert owned two separate plantations covering the same
area of ground, one on top of the other. Mr. Hubert was
sitting in the springhouse with his boots off and his feet in
the water, drinking a toddy. But nobody there had seen
Tomey's Turl; for a time it looked like Mr. Hubert couldn't
even place who Uncle Buck was talking about. "Oh, that
nigger," he said at last. "We'll find him after dinner."

Only it didn't seem as if they were going to eat either.
Mr. Hubert and Uncle Buck had a toddy, then Mr. Hu-

bert finally sent to tell the boy on the gatepost he could quit blowing, and he and Uncle Buck had another toddy and Uncle Buck still saying, "I just want my nigger. Then we got to get on back toward home."

"After dinner," Mr. Hubert said. "If we don't start him somewhere around the kitchen, we'll put the dogs on him. They'll find him if it's in the power of mortal Walker dogs to do it."

But at last a hand began waving a handkerchief or something white through the broken place in an upstairs shutter. They went to the house, crossing the back gallery, Mr. Hubert warning them again, as he always did, to watch out for the rotted floor-board he hadn't got around to having fixed yet. Then they stood in the hall, until presently there was a jangling and swishing noise and they began to smell the perfume, and Miss Sophonsiba came down the stairs. Her hair was roached under a lace cap; she had on her Sunday dress and beads and a red ribbon around her throat and a little nigger girl carrying her fan and he stood quietly a step behind Uncle Buck, watching her lips until they opened and he could see the roan tooth. He had never known anyone before with a roan tooth and he remembered how one time his grandmother and his father were talking about Uncle Buddy and Uncle Buck and his grandmother said that Miss Sophonsiba had matured into a fine-looking woman once. Maybe she had. He didn't know. He wasn't but nine.

"Why, Mister Theophilus," she said. "And McCaslin," she said. She had never looked at him and she wasn't talking to him and he knew it, although he was prepared and balanced to drag his foot when Uncle Buck did. "Welcome to Warwick."

He and Uncle Buck dragged their foot. "I just come to get my nigger," Uncle Buck said. "Then we got to get on back home."

Then Miss Sophonsiba said something about a bumblebee, but he couldn't remember that. It was too fast and

there was too much of it, the earrings and beads clashing
and jingling like little trace chains on a toy mule trotting
and the perfume stronger too, like the earrings and beads
sprayed it out each time they moved and he watched the
roan-colored tooth flick and glint between her lips; something about Uncle Buck was a bee sipping from flower to
flower and not staying long anywhere and all that stored
sweetness to be wasted on Uncle Buddy's desert air, calling Uncle Buddy Mister Amodeus like she called Uncle
Buck Mister Theophilus, or maybe the honey was being
stored up against the advent of a queen and who was the
lucky queen and when? "Ma'am?" Uncle Buck said. Then
Mr. Hubert said:

"Hah. A buck bee. I reckon that nigger's going to think
he's a buck hornet, once he lays hands on him. But I
reckon what Buck's thinking about sipping right now is
some meat gravy and biscuit and a cup of coffee. And so
am I."

They went into the dining room and ate and Miss
Sophonsiba said how seriously now neighbors just a half
day's ride apart ought not to go so long as Uncle Buck did,
and Uncle Buck said Yessum, and Miss Sophonsiba said
Uncle Buck was just a confirmed roving bachelor from the
cradle born and this time Uncle Buck even quit chewing
and looked and said, Yes, ma'am, he sure was, and born
too late at it to ever change now but at least he could
thank God no lady would ever have to suffer the misery of
living with him and Uncle Buddy, and Miss Sophonsiba
said Ah, that maybe Uncle Buck just ain't met the woman
yet who would not only accept what Uncle Buck was
pleased to call misery, but who would make Uncle Buck
consider even his freedom a small price to pay, and Uncle
Buck said, "Nome. Not yet."

Then he and Mr. Hubert and Uncle Buck went out to
the front gallery and sat down. Mr. Hubert hadn't even
got done taking his shoes off again and inviting Uncle
Buck to take his off, when Miss Sophonsiba came out the

door carrying a tray with another toddy on it. "Damnit, Sibbey," Mr. Hubert said. "He's just et. He don't want to drink that now." But Miss Sophonsiba didn't seem to hear him at all. She stood there, the roan tooth not flicking now but fixed because she wasn't talking now, handing the toddy to Uncle Buck until after a while she said how her papa always said nothing sweetened a Missippi toddy like the hand of a Missippi lady and would Uncle Buck like to see how she use to sweeten her papa's toddy for him? She lifted the toddy and took a sip of it and handed it again to Uncle Buck and this time Uncle Buck took it. He dragged his foot again and drank the toddy and said if Mr. Hubert was going to lay down, he would lay down a while too, since from the way things looked Tomey's Turl was fixing to give them a long hard race unless Mr. Hubert's dogs were a considerable better than they used to be.

Mr. Hubert and Uncle Buck went into the house. After a while he got up too and went around to the back yard to wait for them. The first thing he saw was Tomey's Turl's head slipping along above the lane fence. But when he cut across the yard to turn him, Tomey's Turl wasn't even running. He was squatting behind a bush, watching the house, peering around the bush at the back door and the upstairs windows, not whispering exactly but not talking loud either: "Whut they doing now?"

"They're taking a nap now," he said. "But never mind that; they're going to put the dogs on you when they get up."

"Hah," Tomey's Turl said. "And nem you mind that neither. I got protection now. All I needs to do is to keep Old Buck from ketching me unto I gets the word."

"What word?" he said. "Word from who? Is Mr. Hubert going to buy you from Uncle Buck?"

"Huh," Tomey's Turl said again. "I got more protection than whut Mr. Hubert got even." He rose to his feet. 'I gonter tell you something to remember: anytime you wants to git something done, from hoeing out a crop to getting married, just get the womenfolks to working at it. Then all you needs to do is set down and wait. You member that."

Then Tomey's Turl was gone. And after a while he went back to the house. But there wasn't anything but the snoring coming out of the room where Uncle Buck and Mr. Hubert were, and some more light-sounding snoring coming from upstairs. He went to the springhouse and sat with his feet in the water as Mr. Hubert had been doing, because soon now it would be cool enough for a race. And sure enough, after a while Mr. Hubert and Uncle Buck came out onto the back gallery, with Miss Sophonsiba right behind them with the toddy tray only this time Uncle Buck drank his before Miss Sophonsiba had time to sweeten it, and Miss Sophonsiba told them to get back early, that all Uncle Buck knew of Warwick was just dogs and niggers and now that she had him, she wanted to show him her garden that Mr. Hubert and nobody else had any sayso in. "Yessum," Uncle Buck said. "I just want to catch my nigger. Then we got to get on back home."

Four or five niggers brought up the three horses. They could already hear the dogs waiting still coupled in the lane, and they mounted and went on down the lane, toward the quarters, with Uncle Buck already out in front of even the dogs. So he never did know just when and where they jumped Tomey's Turl, whether he flushed out of one of the cabins or not. Uncle Buck was away out in front on Black John and they hadn't even cast the dogs yet when Uncle Buck roared, "Gone away! I godfrey, he broke cover then!" and Black John's feet clapped four times like pistol shots while he was gathering to go out, then he and Uncle Buck vanished over the hill like they had run at the blank edge of the world itself. Mr. Hubert was roaring too: "Gone away! Cast them!" and they all piled over the crest of the hill just in time to see Tomey's Turl away out across the flat, almost to the woods, and the dogs streaking down the hill and out onto the flat. They just tongued once and when they came boiling up around Tomey's Turl it looked like they were trying to jump up and lick him in the face until even Tomey's Turl slowed down and he and the dogs all went into the woods together, walking, like they were going home from a rabbit hunt. And when they caught up with Uncle Buck in the woods, there was no Tomey's Turl and no dogs either, nothing but old Jake about a half an hour later, hitched in a clump of bushes with Tomey's Turl's coat tied on him for a saddle and near a half bushel of Mr. Hubert's oats scattered around on the ground that old Jake never even had enough appetite left to nuzzle up and spit back out again. It wasn't any race at all.

"We'll get him tonight though," Mr. Hubert said. "We'll bait for him. We'll throw a picquet of niggers and dogs around Tennie's house about midnight, and we'll get him."

"Tonight, hell," Uncle Buck said. "Me and Cass and that nigger all three are going to be half way home by dark. Ain't one of your niggers got a fyce or something that will trail them hounds?"

"And fool around here in the woods for half the night too?" Mr. Hubert said. "When I'll bet you five hundred dollars that all you got to do to catch that nigger is to walk up to Tennie's cabin after dark and call him?"

"Five hundred dollars?" Uncle Buck said. "Done! Because me and him neither one are going to be anywhere near Tennie's house by dark. Five hundred dollars!" He and Mr. Hubert glared at one another.

"Done!" Mr. Hubert said.

So they waited while Mr. Hubert sent one of the niggers back to the house on old Jake and in about a half an hour the nigger came back with a little bob-tailed black fyce and a new bottle of whiskey. Then he rode up to Uncle Buck and held something out to him wrapped in a piece of paper. "What?" Uncle Buck said.

"It's for you," the nigger said. Then Uncle Buck took it and unwrapped it. It was the piece of red ribbon that had been on Miss Sophonsiba's neck and Uncle Buck sat there on Black John, holding the ribbon like it was a little water moccasin only he wasn't going to let anybody see he was afraid of it, batting his eyes fast at the nigger. Then he stopped batting his eyes.

"What for?" he said.

"She just sont hit to you," the nigger said. "She say to tell you 'success.' "

"She said what?" Uncle Buck said.

"I don't know, sir," the nigger said. "She just say 'success.' "

"Oh," Uncle Buck said. And the fyce found the hounds. They heard them first, from a considerable distance. It was just before sundown and they were not trailing, they were making the noise dogs make when they want to get out of something. They found what that was too. It was a ten-foot-square cotton-house in a field about two miles from Mr. Hubert's house and all eleven of the dogs were inside it and the door wedged with a chunk of wood. They watched the dogs come boiling out when the nigger opened the door, Mr. Hubert sitting his horse and looking at the back of Uncle Buck's neck.

"Well, well," Mr. Hubert said. "That's something, anyway. You can use them again now. They don't seem to have no more trouble with your nigger than he seems to have with them."

"Not enough," Uncle Buck said. "That means both of them. I'll stick to the fyce."

"All right," Mr. Hubert said. Then he said, "Hell, 'Filus, come on. Let's go eat supper. I tell you, all you got to do to catch that nigger is———"

"Five hundred dollars," Uncle Buck said.

"What?" Mr. Hubert said. He and Uncle Buck looked at each other. They were not glaring now. They were not joking each other either. They sat there in the beginning of twilight, looking at each other, just blinking a little. "What five hundred dollars?" Mr. Hubert said. "That you won't catch that nigger in Tennie's cabin at midnight to-night?"

"That me or that nigger neither ain't going to be near nobody's house but mine at midnight tonight." Now they did glare at each other.

"Five hundred dollars," Mr. Hubert said. "Done."

"Done," Uncle Buck said.

"Done," Mr. Hubert said.

"Done," Uncle Buck said.

So Mr. Hubert took the dogs and some of the niggers and went back to the house. Then he and Uncle Buck and the nigger with the fyce went on, the nigger leading old Jake with one hand and holding the fyce's leash (it was a piece of gnawed plowline) with the other. Now Uncle Buck let the fyce smell Tomey's Turl's coat; it was like for the first time now the fyce found out what they were after and they would have let him off the leash and kept up with him on the horses, only about that time the nigger boy began blowing the fox-horn for supper at the house and they didn't dare risk it.

Then it was full dark. And then—he didn't know how much later nor where they were, how far from the house, except that it was a good piece and it had been dark for good while and they were still going on, with Uncle Buck leaning down from time to time to let the fyce have another smell of Tomey's Turl's coat while Uncle Buck took another drink from the whiskey bottle—they found that Tomey's Turl had doubled and was making a long swing back toward the house. "I godfrey, we've got him," Uncle Buck said. "He's going to earth. We'll cut back to the house and head him before he can den." So they left the nigger to cast the fyce and follow him on old Jake, and he and Uncle Buck rode for Mr. Hubert's, stopping on the hills to blow the horses and listen to the fyce down in the creek bottom where Tomey's Turl was still making his swing.

But they never caught him. They reached the dark quarters; they could see lights still burning in Mr. Hubert's house and somebody was blowing the fox-horn again and it wasn't any boy and he had never heard a fox-horn sound mad before either, and he and Uncle Buck scattered out on the slope below Tennie's cabin. Then they heard the fyce, not trailing now but yapping, about a mile away, then the nigger whooped and they knew the fyce had faulted. It was at the creek. They hunted the banks both ways for more than an hour, but they couldn't straighten Tomey's Turl out. At last even Uncle Buck gave up and they started back toward the house, the fyce riding too now, in front of the nigger on the mule. They were just coming up the lane to the quarters; they could see on along the ridge to where Mr. Hubert's house was all dark now, when all of a sudden the fyce gave a yelp and jumped down from old Jake and hit the ground running and yelling every jump, and Uncle Buck was down too and had snatched him off the pony almost before he could clear his feet from the irons, and they ran too, on past the dark cabins toward the one where the fyce had treed. "We got him!" Uncle Buck said. "Run around to the back. Don't holler; just grab up a stick and knock on the back door, loud."

Afterward, Uncle Buck admitted that it was his own mistake, that he had forgotten when even a little child should have known: not ever to stand right in front of or right behind a nigger when you scare him; but always to stand to one side of him. Uncle Buck forgot that. He was standing facing the front door and right in front of it, with the fyce right in front of him yelling fire and murder every time it could draw a new breath; he said the first he knew was when the fyce gave a shriek and whirled and Tomey's Turl was right behind it. Uncle Buck said he never even saw the door open; that the fyce just screamed once and ran between his legs and then Tomey's Turl ran right clean over him. He never even bobbled; he knocked Uncle Buck down and then caught him before he fell without even stopping, snatched him up under one arm, still running, and carried him along for about ten feet, saying, "Look out of here, old Buck. Look out of here, old Buck," before he threw him away and went on. By that time they couldn't even hear the fyce any more at all.

Uncle Buck wasn't hurt; it was only the wind knocked out of him where Tomey's Turl had thrown him down on his back. But he had been carrying the whiskey bottle in his back pocket, saving the last drink until Tomey's Turl was captured, and he refused to move until he knew for certain if it was just whiskey and not blood. So Uncle Buck laid over on his side easy, and he knelt behind him and raked the broken glass out of his pocket. Then they went on to the house. They walked. The nigger came up with the horses, but nobody said anything to Uncle Buck about riding again. They couldn't hear the fyce at all now. "He was going fast, all right," Uncle Buck said. "But I don't believe that even he will catch that fyce, I godfrey, what a night."

"We'll catch him tomorrow," he said.

"Tomorrow, hell," Uncle Buck said. "We'll be at home tomorrow. And the first time Hubert Beauchamp or that nigger either one set foot on my land, I'm going to have them arrested for trespass and vagrancy."

The house was dark. They could hear Mr. Hubert snoring good now, as if he had settled down to road-gaiting at it. But they couldn't hear anything from upstairs, even when they were inside the dark hall, at the foot of the stairs. "Likely hers will be at the back," Uncle Buck said. "Where she can holler down to the kitchen without having to get up. Besides, an unmarried lady will sholy have her door locked with strangers in the house." So Uncle

Buck eased himself down onto the bottom step, and he
knelt and drew Uncle Buck's boots off. Then he removed
his own and set them against the wall, and he and Uncle
Buck mounted the stairs, feeling their way up and into the
upper hall. It was dark too, and still there was no sound
anywhere except Mr. Hubert snoring below, so they felt
their way along the hall toward the front of the house,
until they felt a door. They could hear nothing beyond
the door, and when Uncle Buck tried the knob, it opened.
"All right," Uncle Buck whispered. "Be quiet." They
could see a little now, enough to see the shape of the bed
and the mosquito-bar. Uncle Buck threw down his suspenders and unbuttoned his trousers and went to the bed
and eased himself carefully down onto the edge of it, and
he knelt again and drew Uncle Buck's trousers off and he
was just removing his own when Uncle Buck lifted the
mosquito-bar and raised his feet and rolled into the bed.
That was when Miss Sophonsiba sat upon the other side
of Uncle Buck and gave the first scream.

II

When he reached home just before dinner time the
next day, he was just about worn out. He was too tired to
eat, even if Uncle Buddy had waited to eat dinner first;
he couldn't have stayed on the pony another mile without going to sleep. In fact, he must have gone to sleep
while he was telling Uncle Buddy, because the next thing
he knew it was late afternoon and he was lying on some
hay in the jolting wagon-bed, with Uncle Buddy sitting
on the seat above him exactly the same way he sat a
horse or sat in his rocking chair before the kitchen hearth
while he was cooking, holding the whip exactly as he
held the spoon or fork he stirred and tasted with. Uncle
Buddy had some cold bread and meat and a jug of butter-
milk wrapped in damp towsacks waiting when he waked
up. He ate, sitting in the wagon in almost the last of the
afternoon. They must have come fast, because they were

not more than two miles from Mr. Hubert's. Uncle Buddy waited for him to eat. Then he said, "Tell me again," and he told it again: how he and Uncle Buck finally found a room without anybody in it, and Uncle Buck sitting on the side of the bed saying, "O godfrey, Cass. O godfrey, Cass," and then they heard Mr. Hubert's feet on the stairs and watched the light come down the hall and Mr. Hubert came in, in his nightshirt, and walked over and set the candle on the table and stood looking at Uncle Buck.

"Well, 'Filus," he said. "She's got you at last."

"It was an accident," Uncle Buck said. "I swear to godfrey——"

"Hah," Mr. Hubert said. "Don't tell me. Tell her that."

"I did," Uncle Buck said. "I did tell her. I swear to God——"

"Sholy," Mr. Hubert said. "And just listen." They listened a minute. He had been hearing her all the time. She was nowhere near as loud as at first; she was just steady. "Don't you want to go back in there and tell her again it was an accident, that you never meant nothing and to just excuse you and forget about it? All right."

"All right what?" Uncle Buck said.

"Go back in there and tell her again," Mr. Hubert said. Uncle Buck looked at Mr. Hubert for a minute. He batted his eyes fast.

"Then what will I come back and tell you?" he said.

"To me?" Mr. Hubert said. "I would call that a horse of another color. Wouldn't you?"

Uncle Buck looked at Mr. Hubert. He batted his eyes fast again. Then he stopped again. "Wait," he said. "Be reasonable. Say I did walk into a lady's bedroom, even Miss Sophonsiba's; say, just for the sake of the argument, there wasn't no other lady in the world but her and so I walked into hers and tried to get in bed with her, would I have took a nine-year-old boy with me?"

"Reasonable is just what I'm being," Mr. Hubert said. "You come into bear-country of your own free will and accord. All right; you were a grown man and you knew it was bear-country and you knew the way back out like you knew the way in and you had your chance to take it. But no. You had to crawl into the den and lay down by the bear. And whether you did or didn't know the bear was in it don't make any difference. So if you got back out of that den without even a claw-mark on you, I would not only be unreasonable, I'd be a damned fool. After all, I'd like a little peace and quiet and freedom myself, now I got a chance for it. Yes, sir. She's got you, 'Filus, and you know it. You run a hard race and you run a good one, but you skun the henhouse one time too many."

"Yes," Uncle Buck said. He drew his breath in and let it out again, slow and not loud. But you could hear it. "Well," he said. "So I reckon I'll have to take the chance then."

"You already took it," Mr. Hubert said. "You did that when you came back here." Then he stopped too. Then he batted his eyes, but only about six times. Then he stopped and looked at Uncle Buck for more than a minute. "What chance?" he said.

"That five hundred dollars," Uncle Buck said.

"What five hundred dollars?" Mr. Hubert said. He and Uncle Buck looked at one another. Now it was Mr. Hubert that batted his eyes again and then stopped again. "I thought you said you found him in Tennie's cabin."

"I did," Uncle Buck said. "What you bet me was I would catch him there. If there had been ten of me standing in front of that door, we wouldn't have caught him." Mr. Hubert blinked at Uncle Buck, slow and steady.

"So you aim to hold me to that fool bet," he said.

"You took your chance too," Uncle Buck said. Mr. Hubert blinked at Uncle Buck. Then he stopped. Then he went and took the candle from the table and went out. They sat on the edge of the bed and watched the light go down the hall and heard Mr. Hubert's feet on the stairs. After a while they began to see the light again and they heard Mr. Hubert's feet coming back up the stairs. Then Mr. Hubert entered and went to the table and set the candle down and laid a deck of cards by it.

"One hand," he said. "Draw. You shuffle, I cut, this boy deals. Five hundred dollars against Sibbey. And we'll settle this nigger business once and for all too. If you win, you buy Tennie; if I win, I buy that boy of yours. The price will be the same for each one: three hundred dollars."

"Win?" Uncle Buck said. "The one that wins buys the niggers?"

"Wins Sibbey, damn it!" Mr. Hubert said. "Wins Sibbey! What the hell else are we setting up till midnight arguing about? The lowest hand wins Sibbey and buys the niggers."

"All right," Uncle Buck said. "I'll buy the damn girl then and we'll call the rest of this foolishness off."

"Hah," Mr. Hubert said again. "This is the most serious foolishness you ever took part in in your life. No. You said you wanted your chance, and now you've got it. Here it is, right here on this table, waiting on you."

So Uncle Buck shuffled the cards and Mr. Hubert cut them. Then he took up the deck and dealt in turn until Uncle Buck and Mr. Hubert had five. And Uncle Buck looked at his hand a long time and then said two cards and he gave them to him, and Mr. Hubert looked at his hand quick and said one card and he gave it to him and Mr. Hubert flipped his discard onto the two which Uncle Buck had discarded and slid the new card into his hand and opened it out and looked at it quick again and closed it and looked at Uncle Buck and said, "Well? Did you help them threes?"

"No," Uncle Buck said.

"Well I did," Mr. Hubert said. He shot his hand across the table so that the cards fell face-up in front of Uncle Buck and they were three kings and two fives, and said,

"By God, Buck McCaslin, you have met your match at last."

"And that was all?" Uncle Buddy said. It was late then, near sunset; they would be at Mr. Hubert's in another fifteen minutes.

"Yes, sir," he said, telling that too: how Uncle Buck waked him at daylight and he climbed out a window and got the pony and left, and how Uncle Buck said that if they pushed him too close in the meantime, he would climb down the gutter too and hide in the woods until Uncle Buddy arrived.

"Hah," Uncle Buddy said. "Was Tomey's Turl there?"

"Yes, sir," he said. "He was waiting in the stable when I got the pony. He said, 'Ain't they settled it yet?'"

"And what did you say?" Uncle Buddy said.

"I said, 'Uncle Buck looks like he's settled. But Uncle Buddy ain't got here yet.'"

"Hah," Uncle Buddy said.

And that was about all. They reached the house. Maybe Uncle Buck was watching them, but if he was, he never showed himself, never came out of the woods. Miss Sophonsiba was nowhere in sight either, so at least Uncle Buck hadn't quite given up; at least he hadn't asked her yet. And he and Uncle Buddy and Mr. Hubert ate supper and they came in from the kitchen and cleared the table, leaving only the lamp on it and the deck of cards.

Then it was just like it was the night before, except that Uncle Buddy had no necktie and Mr. Hubert wore clothes now instead of a nightshirt and it was a shaded lamp on the table instead of a candle, and Mr. Hubert sitting at his end of the table with the deck in his hands, riffling the edges with his thumb and looking at Uncle Buddy. Then he tapped the edges even and set the deck out in the middle of the table, under the lamp, and folded his arms on the edge of the table and leaned forward a little on the table, looking at Uncle Buddy, who was sitting at his end of the table with his hands in his lap, all one gray color, like an old gray rock or a stump with gray moss on it, that still, with his round white head like Uncle Buck's but he didn't blink like Uncle Buck and he was a little thicker than Uncle Buck, as if from sitting down so much watching food cook, as if the things he cooked had made him a little thicker than he would have been and the things he cooked with, the flour and such, had made him all one same quiet color.

"Little toddy before we start?" Mr. Hubert said.

"I don't drink," Uncle Buddy said.

"That's right," Mr. Hubert said. "I knew there was something else besides just being woman-weak that makes 'Filus seem human. But no matter." He batted his eyes twice at Uncle Buddy. "Buck McCaslin against the land and niggers you have heard me promise as Sophonsiba's dowry on the day she marries. If I beat you, 'Filus marries Sibbey without any dowry. If you beat me, you get 'Filus. But I still get the three hundred dollars 'Filus owes me for Tennie. Is that correct?"

"That's correct," Uncle Buddy said.

"Stud," Mr. Hubert said. "One hand. You to shuffle, me to cut, this boy to deal."

"No," Uncle Buddy said. "Not Cass. He's too young. I don't want him mixed up in any gambling."

"Hah," Mr. Hubert said. "It's said that a man playing cards with Amodeus McCaslin ain't gambling. But no matter." But he was still looking at Uncle Buddy; he never even turned his head when he spoke: "Go to the back door and holler. Bring the first creature that answers, animal mule or human, that can deal ten cards."

So he went to the back door. But he didn't have to call because Tomey's Turl was squatting against the wall just outside the door, and they returned to the dining-room where Mr. Hubert still sat with his arms folded on his side of the table and Uncle Buddy sat with his hands in his lap on his side and the deck of cards face-down under the

lamp between them. Neither of them even looked up
when he and Tomey's Turl entered. "Shuffle," Mr. Hubert said. Uncle Buddy shuffled and set the cards back
under the lamp and put his hands back into his lap and
Mr. Hubert cut the deck and folded his arms back onto
the table-edge. "Deal," he said. Still neither he nor Uncle
Buddy looked up. They just sat there while Tomey's
Turl's saddle-colored hands came into the light and took
up the deck and dealt, one card face-down to Mr. Hubert
and one face-down to Uncle Buddy, and one face-up to
Mr. Hubert and it was a king, and one face-up to Uncle
Buddy and it was a six.

"Buck McCaslin against Sibbey's dowry," Mr. Hubert
said. "Deal." And the hand dealt Mr. Hubert a card and it
was a three, and Uncle Buddy a card and it was a two.
Mr. Hubert looked at Uncle Buddy. Uncle Buddy rapped
once with his knuckles on the table.

"Deal," Mr. Hubert said. And the hand dealt Mr. Hubert a card and it was another three, and Uncle Buddy a
card and it was a four. Mr. Hubert looked at Uncle
Buddy's cards. Then he looked at Uncle Buddy and Uncle
Buddy rapped on the table again with his knuckles.

"Deal," Mr. Hubert said, and the hand dealt him an
ace and Uncle Buddy a five and now Mr. Hubert just sat
still. He didn't look at anything or move for a whole minute; he just sat there and watched Uncle Buddy put one
hand onto the table for the first time since he shuffled and
pinch up one corner of his face-down card and look at it
and then put his hand back into his lap. "Check," Mr.
Hubert said.

"I'll bet you them two niggers," Uncle Buddy said. He
didn't move either. He sat there just like he sat in the
wagon or on a horse or in the rocking chair he cooked
from.

"Against what?" Mr. Hubert said.

"Against the three hundred dollars Theophilus owes
you for Tennie, and the three hundred you and The-

ophilus agreed on for Tomey's Turl," Uncle Buddy said.

"Hah," Mr. Hubert said, only it wasn't loud at all this time, nor even short. Then he said "Hah. Hah. Hah" and not loud either. Then he said, "Well." Then he said, "Well, well." Then he said: "We'll check up for a minute. If I win, you take Sibbey without dowry and the two niggers, and I don't owe 'Filus anything. If you win——"

"—Theophilus is free. And you owe him the three hundred dollars for Tomey's Turl," Uncle Buddy said.

"That's just if I call you," Mr. Hubert said. "If I don't call you, 'Filus won't owe me nothing and I won't owe 'Filus nothing, unless I take that nigger which I have been trying to explain to you and him both for years that I won't have on my place. We will be right back where all this foolishness started from, except for that. So what it comes down to is, I either got to give a nigger away, or risk buying one that you done already admitted you can't keep at home." Then he stopped talking. For about a minute it was like he and Uncle Buddy had both gone to sleep. Then Mr. Hubert picked up his face-down card and turned it over. It was another three, and Mr. Hubert sat there without looking at anything at all, his fingers beating a tattoo, slow and steady and not very loud, on the table. "H'm," he said. "And you need a trey and there ain't but four of them and I already got three. And you just shuffled. And I cut afterward. And if I call you, I will have to buy that nigger. Who dealt these cards, Amodeus?" Only he didn't wait to be answered. He reached out and tilted the lamp-shade, the light moving up Tomey's Turl's arms that were supposed to be black but were not quite white, up his Sunday shirt that was supposed to be white but wasn't quite either, that he put on every time he ran away just as Uncle Buck put on the necktie each time he went to bring him back, and on to his face; and Mr. Hubert sat there, holding the lamp-shade and looking at Tomey's Turl. Then he tilted the shade back down and took up his cards and turned them face-down and pushed them toward the middle of the table. "I pass, Amodeus," he said.

III

He was still too worn out for sleep to sit on a horse, so this time he and Uncle Buddy and Tennie all three rode in the wagon, while Tomey's Turl led the pony from old Jake. And when they got home just after daylight, this time Uncle Buddy never even had time to get breakfast started and the fox never even got out of the crate, because the dogs were right there in the room. Old Moses went right into the crate with the fox, so that both of them went right on through the back end of it. That is, the fox went through, because when Uncle Buddy opened the door to come in, old Moses was still wearing most of the crate around his neck until Uncle Buddy kicked it off of him. So they just made one run, across the front gallery and around the house and they could hear the fox's claws when he went scrabbling up the lean-pole, onto the roof —a fine race while it lasted, but the tree was too quick.

"What in damn's hell do you mean," Uncle Buddy said, "casting that damn thing with all the dogs right in the same room?"

"Damn the fox," Uncle Buck said. "Go on and start breakfast. It seems to me I've been away from home a whole damn month."

2

THE UNVANQUISHED

Editor's Note

The Chickasaws moved westward to Oklahoma in President Jackson's time. Only a few of them adopted the white man's ways and stayed behind, as dependents of a half-French chieftain named François Vidal (or Frank Weddel), who turned the last of their land into a rich plantation. The Man remained with this branch of the tribe, losing his theocratic honors and becoming a sort of plantation overseer. There was only Sam Fathers—Had-Two-Fathers—living in the slave quarters, who was faithful to the old customs of the tribe.

Uncle Buck McCaslin married Miss Sophonsiba. When the war came, Uncle Buck and Uncle Buddy played three hands of poker to see which of them would enlist. Uncle Buck lost and stayed at home with his wife, while Uncle Buddy went off to Virginia, as a sergeant in the regiment raised and commanded by Colonel John Sartoris. In Virginia, the regiment held a new election of officers and Colonel Sartoris was demoted to major; Thomas Sutpen took over his command. Sartoris resigned from the regiment and came home to lead an irregular troop of cavalry attached to General Forrest's highly irregular army.

Of the three stories in this section, "Raid" and "An Odor of Verbena" are both taken from *The Unvanquished* (1938), the novel or connected series of stories that Faulkner devotes to the Sartoris clan in the Civil War and reconstruction. Faulkner always turns romantic when writing about the Sartorises. He says of the family name, in one of his most overwritten sentences, "There is death in the sound of it, and a glamorous fatality, like silver pennons downrushing at sunset or a dying fall of horns along the road to Roncevaux." And yet, in "An Odor of Verbena," he is pretty hard and unsentimental about the character of Colonel John Sartoris, who happens to be one of the few figures in his novels copied from a historical person. His prototype was Colonel William Falkner, the author's great-grandfather, who organized and for a time commanded the Second Mississippi Infantry, who built the first railroad in his section, who wrote several books (including one successful novel, *The White Rose of Memphis*), and who was killed in a duel.

"Wash," the second story in this section, describes the death of Colonel Sutpen. Its first book publication was in *Doctor Martino and Other Stories* (1934). At that time Faulkner was working on a whole cycle of stories about poor whites and backwoods farmers, in preparation for writing his novel *The Hamlet*; but he found that "Wash" didn't belong in the cycle. It seems to have been the germ out of which developed another novel, *Absalom, Absalom!*

1864

Raid

I

Granny Millard wrote the note with pokeberry juice. "Take it straight to Mrs. Compson and come straight back," she said to me and Ringo. "Don't you-all stop anywhere."

"You mean we got to walk?" Ringo said. "You gonter make us walk all them four miles to Jefferson and back, with them two horses standing in the lot doing nothing?"

"They are borrowed horses," Granny said. "I'm going to take care of them until I can return them."

"I reckon you calls starting out to be gone you don't know where and you don't know how long taking care of——" Ringo said.

Louvinia was standing there; she was Joby's wife and Ringo's grandmother. "Do you want me to whup you?" she said.

"Nome," Ringo said.

We walked to Jefferson and gave Mrs. Compson the note, and got the hat and the parasol and the hand mirror, and walked back home. That afternoon we greased the wagon, and that night after supper Granny got the pokeberry juice again and wrote on a scrap of paper, "Colonel Nathaniel G. Dick, ——th Ohio Cavalry," and folded it and pinned it inside her dress. "Now I won't forget it," she said.

"If you was to, I reckon these hellion boys can remind you," Louvinia said. "I reckon they ain't forgot him. Walking in that door just in time to keep them others from snatching them out from under your dress and nailing them to the barn door like two coon hides."

"Yes," Granny said. "Now we'll go to bed."

Now that the house was burned, we lived in Joby's cabin, with a red quilt nailed by one edge to a rafter and hanging down to make two rooms. Joby was waiting with the wagon when Granny came out with Mrs. Compson's hat on, and got into the wagon and told Ringo to open the parasol and took up the reins. Then we all stopped and watched Joby stick something into the wagon beneath the quilts; it was the barrel and the iron parts of the musket that Ringo and I found in the ashes of the house.

"What's that?" Granny said. Joby didn't look at her.

"Maybe if they just seed the end of hit they mought think hit was the whole gun," he said.

"Then what?" Granny said. Joby didn't look at anybody now.

"I was just doing what I could to help git the silver and the mules back," he said.

Louvinia didn't say anything either. She and Granny just looked at Joby. After a while he dug beneath the quilts again and took the musket barrel out of the wagon. Granny gathered up the reins.

"Take him with you," Louvinia said. "Leastways he can tend the horses."

"No," Granny said. "Don't you see I have got about all I can look after now?"

"Then you stay here and lemme go," Louvinia said. "I'll git um back."

"No," Granny said. "I'll be all right. I shall inquire until I find Colonel Dick, and then we will load the chest in the wagon and Loosh can lead the mules and we will come back home."

Louvinia stood there holding to the wagon wheel and

looked at Granny from under Father's old hat, and began
to holler.

"Don't you waste no time on colonels or nothing!" she
hollered. "You tell them niggers to send Loosh to you, and
you tell him to get that chest and them mules, and then
you whup him!" The wagon was moving now; she had
turned loose the wheel, and she walked along beside it,
hollering at Granny: "Take that pairsawl and wear hit out
on him!"

"All right," Granny said. The wagon went on; we
passed the ash pile and the chimneys standing up out of
it; Ringo and I found the insides of the big clock too. The
sun was just coming up, shining back on the chimneys; I
could still see Louvinia between them, standing in front of
the cabin, shading her eyes with her hand to watch us.
Joby was still standing behind her, holding the musket
barrel. They had broken the gates clean off; and then we
were in the road.

"Don't you want me to drive?" I said.

"I'll drive," Granny said. "These are borrowed horses."

"Case even Yankee could look at um and tell they
couldn't keep up with even a walking army," Ringo said.
"And I like to know how anybody can hurt this team
lessen he ain't got strength enough to keep um from laying
down in the road and getting run over with they own
wagon."

We drove until dark, and camped. By sunup we were
on the road again. "You better let me drive a while," I
said.

"I'll drive," Granny said. "I was the one who borrowed
them."

"You can tote this pairsawl a while, if you want something to do," Ringo said. "And give my arm a rest." I took
the parasol and he laid down in the wagon and put his hat
over his eyes. "Call me when we gitting nigh to Hawkhurst," he said, "so I can commence to look out for that
railroad you tells about."

That was how he travelled for the next six days—lying on his back in the wagon bed with his hat over his eyes, sleeping, or taking his turn holding the parasol over Granny and keeping me awake by talking of the railroad which he had never seen though I had seen it that Christmas we spent at Hawkhurst. That's how Ringo and I were. We were almost the same age, and Father always said that Ringo was a little smarter than I was, but that didn't count with us, any more than the difference in the color of our skins counted. What counted was, what one of us had done or seen that the other had not, and ever since that Christmas I had been ahead of Ringo because I had seen a railroad, a locomotive. Only I know now it was more than that with Ringo, though neither of us were to see the proof of my belief for some time yet and we were not to recognize it as such even then. It was as if Ringo felt it too and that the railroad, the rushing locomotive which he hoped to see symbolized it—the motion, the impulse to move which had already seethed to a head among his people, darker than themselves, reasonless, following and seeking a delusion, a dream, a bright shape which they could not know since there was nothing in their heritage, nothing in the memory even of the old men to tell the others, "This is what we will find"; he nor they could not have known what it was yet it was there—one of those impulses inexplicable yet invincible which appear among races of people at intervals and drive them to pick up and leave all security and familiarity of earth and home and start out, they don't know where, emptyhanded, blind to everything but a hope and a doom.

We went on; we didn't go fast. Or maybe it seemed slow because we had got into a country where nobody seemed to live at all; all that day we didn't even see a house. I didn't ask and Granny didn't say; she just sat there under the parasol with Mrs. Compson's hat on and the horses walking and even our own dust moving ahead of us; after a while even Ringo sat up and looked around.

"We on the wrong road," he said. "Ain't even nobody live here, let alone pass here."

But after a while the hills stopped, the road ran out flat and straight; and all of a sudden Ringo hollered, "Look out! Here they come again to git these uns!" We saw it, too, then—a cloud of dust away to the west, moving slow—too slow for men riding—and then the road we were on ran square into a big broad one running straight on into the east, as the railroad at Hawkhurst did when Granny and I were there that Christmas before the war; all of a sudden I remembered it.

"This is the road to Hawkhurst," I said. But Ringo was not listening; he was looking at the dust, and the wagon stopped now with the horses' heads hanging and our dust overtaking us again and the big dust cloud coming slow up in the west.

"Can't you see um coming?" Ringo hollered. "Git on away from here!"

"They ain't Yankees," Granny said. "The Yankees have already been here." Then we saw it, too—a burned house like ours, three chimneys standing above a mound of ashes, and then we saw a white woman and a child looking at us from a cabin behind them. Granny looked at the dust cloud, then she looked at the empty broad road going on into the east. "This is the way," she said.

We went on. It seemed like we went slower than ever now, with the dust cloud behind us and the burned houses and gins and thrown-down fences on either side, and the white women and children—we never saw a nigger at all—watching us from the nigger cabins where they lived now like we lived at home; we didn't stop. "Poor folks," Granny said. "I wish we had enough to share with them."

At sunset we drew off the road and camped; Ringo was looking back. "Whatever hit is, we done went off and left hit," he said. "I don't see no dust." We slept in the wagon this time, all three of us. I don't know what time it was, only that all of a sudden I was awake. Granny was already sitting up in the wagon. I could see her head against the branches and the stars. All of a sudden all three of us were sitting up in the wagon, listening. They were coming up the road. It sounded like about fifty of them; we could hear the feet hurrying, and a kind of panting murmur. It was not singing exactly; it was not that loud. It was just a sound, a breathing, a kind of gasping, murmuring chant and the feet whispering fast in the deep dust. I could hear women, too, and then all of a sudden I began to smell them.

"Niggers," I whispered. "Sh-h-h-h," I whispered.

We couldn't see them and they did not see us; maybe they didn't even look, just walking fast in the dark with that panting, hurrying murmuring, going on. And then the sun rose and we went on, too, along that big broad empty road between the burned houses and gins and fences. Before, it had been like passing through a country where nobody had ever lived; now it was like passing through one where everybody had died at the same moment. That night we waked up three times and sat up in the wagon in the dark and heard niggers pass in the road. The last time it was after dawn and we had already fed the horses. It was a big crowd of them this time, and they sounded like they were running, like they had to run to keep ahead of daylight. Then they were gone. Ringo and I had taken up the harness again when Granny said, "Wait. Hush." It was just one, we could hear her panting and sobbing, and then we heard another sound. Granny began to get down from the wagon. "She fell," she said. "You-all hitch up and come on."

When we turned into the road, the woman was kind of crouched beside it, holding something in her arms, and Granny standing beside her. It was a baby, a few months old; she held it like she thought maybe Granny was going to take it away from her. "I been sick and I couldn't keep up," she said. "They went off and left me."

"Is your husband with them?" Granny said.

"Yessum," the woman said. "They's all there."

"Who do you belong to?" Granny said. Then she didn't answer. She squatted there in the dust, crouched over the baby. "If I give you something to eat, will you turn around and go back home?" Granny said. Still she didn't answer. She just squatted there. "You see you can't keep up with them and they ain't going to wait for you," Granny said. "Do you want to die here in the road for buzzards to eat?" But she didn't even look at Granny; she just squatted there.

"Hit's Jordan we coming to," she said. "Jesus gonter see me that far."

"Get in the wagon," Granny said. She got in; she squatted again just like she had in the road, holding the baby and not looking at anything—just hunkered down and swaying on her hams as the wagon rocked and jolted. The sun was up; we went down a long hill and began to cross a creek bottom.

"I'll get out here," she said. Granny stopped the wagon and she got out. There was nothing at all but the thick gum and cypress and thick underbrush still full of shadow.

"You go back home, girl," Granny said. She just stood there. "Hand me the basket," Granny said. I handed it to her and she opened it and gave the woman a piece of bread and meat. We went on; we began to mount the hill. When I looked back she was still standing there, holding the baby and the bread and meat Granny had given her. She was not looking at us. "Were the others there in that bottom?" Granny asked Ringo.

"Yessum," Ringo said. "She done found um. Reckon she gonter lose um again tonight though."

We went on; we mounted the hill and crossed the crest of it. When I looked back this time the road was empty. That was the morning of the sixth day.

2

Late that afternoon we were descending again; we came around a curve in the late level shadows and our own quiet dust and I saw the graveyard on the knoll and the marble shaft at Uncle Dennison's grave; there was a dove somewhere in the cedars. Ringo was asleep again under his hat in the wagon bed but he waked as soon as I spoke, even though I didn't speak loud and didn't speak to him. "There's Hawkhurst," I said.

"Hawkhurst?" he said, sitting up. "Where's that railroad?" on his knees now and looking for something which he would have to find in order to catch up with me and which he would have to recognize only through hearsay when he saw it: "Where is it? Where?"

"You'll have to wait for it," I said.

"Seem like I been waiting on hit all my life," he said. "I reckon you'll tell me next the Yankees done moved hit too."

The sun was going down. Because suddenly I saw it shining level across the place where the house should have been and there was no house there. And I was not surprised; I remember that; I was just feeling sorry for Ringo, since (I was just fourteen then) if the house was gone, they would have taken the railroad too, since anybody would rather have a railroad than a house. We didn't stop; we just looked quietly at the same mound of ashes, the same four chimneys standing gaunt and blackened in the sun like the chimneys at home. When we reached the gate Cousin Denny was running down the drive toward us. He was ten; he ran up to the wagon with his eyes round and his mouth already open for hollering.

"Denny," Granny said, "do you know us?"

"Yessum," Cousin Denny said. He looked at me, hollering, "Come see——"

"Where's your mother?" Granny said.

"In Jingus' cabin," Cousin Denny said; he didn't even look at Granny. "They burnt the house!" he hollered. "Come see what they done to the railroad!"

We ran, all three of us. Granny hollered something and I turned and put the parasol back into the wagon and hollered "Yessum!" back at her, and ran on and caught up with Cousin Denny and Ringo in the road, and we ran on over the hill, and then it came in sight. When Granny and I were here before, Cousin Denny showed me the railroad, but he was so little then that Jingus had to carry him. It was the straightest thing I ever saw, running straight and empty and quiet through a long empty gash cut through the trees, and the ground, too, and full of sunlight like water in a river, only straighter than any river, with the crossties cut off even and smooth and neat, and the light shining on the rails like on two spider threads, running straight on to where you couldn't even see that far. It looked clean and neat, like the yard behind Louvinia's cabin after she had swept it on Saturday morning, with those two little threads that didn't look strong enough for anything to run on running straight and fast and light, like they were getting up speed to jump clean off the world.

Jingus knew when the train would come; he held my hand and carried Cousin Denny, and we stood between the rails and he showed us where it would come from, and then he showed us where the shadow of a dead pine would come to a stob he had driven in the ground, and then you would hear the whistle. And we got back and watched the shadow, and then we heard it; it whistled and then it got louder and louder fast, and Jingus went to the track and took his hat off and held it out with his face turned back toward us and his mouth hollering, "Watch now! Watch!" even after we couldn't hear him for the train; and then it passed. It came roaring up and went past; the river they had cut through the trees was all full of smoke and noise and sparks and jumping brass, and then empty again, and just Jingus' old hat bouncing and jumping along the empty track behind it like the hat was alive.

But this time what I saw was something that looked like piles of black straws heaped up every few yards, and we ran into the cut and we could see where they had dug the ties up and piled them and set them on fire. But Cousin Denny was still hollering, "Come see what they done to the rails!" he said.

They were back in the trees; it looked like four or five men had taken each rail and tied it around a tree like you knot a green cornstalk around a wagon stake, and Ringo was hollering, too, now.

"What's them?" he hollered. "What's them?"

"That's what it runs on!" Cousin Denny hollered.

"You mean hit have to come in here and run up and down around these here trees like a squirrel?" Ringo hollered. Then we all heard the horse at once; we just had time to look when Bobolink came up the road out of the trees and went across the railroad and into the trees again like a bird, with Cousin Drusilla riding astride like a man and sitting straight and light as a willow branch in the wind. They said she was the best woman rider in the country.

"There's Dru!" Cousin Denny hollered. "Come on! She's been up to the river to see them niggers! Come on!" He and Ringo ran again. When I passed the chimneys, they were just running into the stable. Cousin Drusilla had already unsaddled Bobolink, and she was rubbing him down with a crokersack when I came in. Cousin Denny was still hollering, "What did you see? What are they doing?"

"I'll tell about it at the house," Cousin Drusilla said. Then she saw me. She was not tall; it was the way she

stood and walked. She had on pants, like a man. She was
the best woman rider in the country. When Granny and I
were here that Christmas before the war and Gavin
Breckbridge had just given Bobolink to her, they looked
fine together; it didn't need Jingus to say that they were
the finest-looking couple in Alabama or Mississippi either.
But Gavin was killed at Shiloh and so they didn't marry.
She came and put her hand on my shoulder.

"Hello," she said. "Hello, John Sartoris." She looked at
Ringo. "Is this Ringo?" she said.

"That's what they tells me," Ringo said. "What about
that railroad?"

"How are you?" Cousin Drusilla said.

"I manages to stand hit," Ringo said. "What about that
railroad?"

"I'll tell you about that tonight too," Drusilla said.

"I'll finish Bobolink for you," I said.

"Will you?" she said. She went to Bobolink's head.
"Will you stand for Cousin Bayard, lad?" she said. "I'll see
you-all at the house, then," she said. She went out.

"Yawl sho must 'a' had this horse hid good when the
Yankees come," Ringo said.

"This horse?" Cousin Denny said. "Ain't no damn Yankee going to fool with Dru's horse no more." He didn't
holler now, but pretty soon he began again: "When they
come to burn the house, Dru grabbed the pistol and run
out here—she had on her Sunday dress—and them right
behind her. She run in here and she jumped on Bobolink
bareback, without even waiting for the bridle, and one of
them right there in the door hollering, 'Stop,' and Dru
said, 'Get away, or I'll ride you down,' and him hollering,
'Stop! Stop!' with his pistol out too"—Cousin Denny was
hollering good now—"and Dru leaned down to Bobolink's
ear and said, 'Kill him, Bob,' and the Yankee jumped back
just in time. The lot was full of them, too, and Dru
stopped Bobolink and jumped down in her Sunday dress
and put the pistol to Bobolink's ear and said, 'I can't shoot

you all, because I haven't enough bullets, and it wouldn't do any good anyway; but I won't need but one shot for the horse, and which shall it be?' So they burned the house and went away!" He was hollering good now, with Ringo staring at him so you could have raked Ringo's eyes off his face with a stick. "Come on!" Cousin Denny hollered. "Le's go hear about them niggers at the river!"

"I been having to hear about niggers all my life," Ringo said. "I got to hear about that railroad."

When we reached the house Cousin Drusilla was already talking, telling Granny mostly, though it was not about the railroad. Her hair was cut short; it looked like Father's would when he would tell Granny about him and the men cutting each other's hair with a bayonet. She was sunburned and her hands were hard and scratched like a man's that works. She was telling Granny mostly: "They began to pass in the road yonder while the house was still burning. We couldn't count them; men and women carrying children who couldn't walk and carrying old men and women who should have been at home waiting to die. They were singing, walking along the road singing, not even looking to either side. The dust didn't even settle for two days, because all that night they still passed; we sat up listening to them, and the next morning every few yards along the road would be the old ones who couldn't keep up any more, sitting or lying down and even crawling along, calling to the others to help them; and the others—the young strong ones—not stopping, not even looking at them. I don't think they even heard or saw them. 'Going to Jordan,' they told me. 'Going to cross Jordan.'"

"That was what Loosh said," Granny said. "That General Sherman was leading them all to Jordan."

"Yes," Cousin Drusilla said. "The river. They have stopped there; it's like a river itself, dammed up. The Yankees have thrown out a brigade of cavalry to hold them back while they build the bridge to cross the infantry and artillery; they are all right until they get up there and see or smell the water. That's when they go mad. Not fighting; it's like they can't even see the horses shoving them back and the scabbards beating them; it's like they can't see anything but the water and the other bank. They aren't angry, aren't fighting; just men, women and children singing and chanting and trying to get to that unfinished bridge or even down into the water itself, and the cavalry beating them back with sword scabbards. I don't know when they have eaten; nobody knows just how far some of them have come. They just pass here without food or anything, exactly as they rose up from whatever they were doing when the spirit or the voice or whatever it was told them to go. They stop during the day and rest in the woods; then, at night, they move again. We will hear them later—I'll wake you—marching on up the road until the cavalry stops them. There was an officer, a major, who finally took time to see I wasn't one of his men; he said, 'Can't you do anything with them? Promise them anything to go back home?' But it was like they couldn't see me or hear me speaking; it was only that water and that bank on the other side. But you will see for yourself tomorrow, when we go back."

"Drusilla," Aunt Louise said, "you're not going back tomorrow or any other time."

"They are going to mine the bridge and blow it up when the army has crossed," Cousin Drusilla said. "Nobody knows what they will do then."

"But we cannot be responsible," Aunt Louise said. "The Yankees brought it on themselves; let them pay the price."

"Those Negroes are not Yankees, Mother," Cousin Drusilla said. "At least there will be one person there who is not a Yankee either." She looked at Granny. "Four, counting Bayard and Ringo."

Aunt Louise looked at Granny. "Rosa, you shan't go. I forbid it. Brother John will thank me to do so."

"I reckon I will," Granny said. "I've got to get the silver anyway."

"And the mules," Ringo said; "don't forget them. And don't yawl worry about Granny. She 'cide what she want and then she kneel down about ten seconds and tell God what she aim to do, and then she git up and do hit. And them that don't like hit can git outen the way or git tromppled. But that railroad——"

"And now I reckon we better go to bed," Granny said. But we didn't go to bed then. I had to hear about the railroad too; possibly it was more the need to keep even with Ringo (or even ahead of him, since I had seen the railroad when it was a railroad, which he had not) than a boy's affinity for smoke and fury and thunder and speed. We sat there in that slave cabin partitioned, like Louvinia's cabin at home, into two rooms by that suspended quilt beyond which Aunt Louisa and Granny were already in bed and where Cousin Denny should have been too except for the evening's dispensation he had received, listening too who did not need to hear it again since he had been there to see it when it happened;——we sat there, Ringo and I, listening to Cousin Drusilla and staring at each other with the same amazed and incredulous question: *Where could we have been at that moment? What could we have been doing, even a hundred miles away, not to have sensed, felt this, paused to look at one another, aghast and uplifted, while it was happening?* Because this, to us, was it. Ringo and I had seen Yankees; we had shot at one; we had crouched like two rats and heard Granny, unarmed and not even rising from her chair, rout a whole regiment of them from the library. And we had heard about battles and fighting and seen those who had taken part in them, not only in the person of Father when once or twice each year and without warning he would appear on the strong gaunt horse, arrived from beyond that cloudbank region which Ringo believed was Tennessee, but in the persons of other men who returned home with actual arms and legs missing. But that was it: men had lost arms and legs in sawmills; old men had been telling young men and boys about wars and fighting before they discovered how to write it down: and what petty precisian to quibble about locations in space or in chronology, who to care or insist *Now come, old man, tell the truth: did you see this? were you really there?* Because wars are wars: the same exploding powder when there was powder, the same thrust and parry of iron when there was not—one tale, one telling, the same as the next or the one before. So we knew a war existed; we had to believe that, just as we had to believe that the name for the sort of life we had led for the last three years was hardship and suffering. Yet we had no proof of it. In fact, we had even less than no proof; we had had thrust into our faces the very shabby and unavoidable obverse of proof, who had seen Father (and the other men too) return home, afoot like tramps or on crowbait horses, in faded and patched (and at times obviously stolen) clothing, preceded by no flags nor drums and followed not even by two men to keep step with one another, in coats bearing no glitter of golden braid and with scabbards in which no sword reposed, actually almost sneaking home to spend two or three or seven days performing actions not only without glory (plowing land, repairing fences, killing meat for the smoke house) and in which they had no skill but the very necessity for which was the fruit of the absent occupations from which, returning, they bore no proof—actions in the clumsy performance of which Father's whole presence seemed (to us, Ringo and me) to emanate a kind of humility and apology, as if he were saying, "Believe me, boys; take my word for it: there's more to it than this, no matter what it looks like. I can't prove it, so you'll just have to believe me." And then to have it happen, where we could have been there to see it, and were not: and this no poste and riposte of sweat-reeking cavalry which all war-telling is full of, no galloping thunder of guns to wheel up and unlimber and crash and crash into the lurid grime-glare of their own demon-served inferno which even children would recognize, no ragged lines of gaunt and shrill-yelling infantry beneath a tattered flag which is a very part of that child's make-believe. Because this was it: an interval, a space, in which the toad-squatting guns, the panting men and the trembling horses paused, amphitheatric about the embattled land, beneath the fading fury of the smoke and the puny yelling, and permitted the sorry business which had dragged on for three years now to be congealed into an irrevocable instant and put to an irrevocable gambit, not by two regiments or two batteries or even two generals, but by two locomotives.

Cousin Drusilla told it while we sat there in the cabin which smelled of new whitewash and even (still faintly) of Negroes. She probably told us the reason for it (she must have known)—what point of strategy, what desperate gamble not for preservation, since hope of that was gone, but at least for prolongation, which it served. But that meant nothing to us. We didn't hear, we didn't even listen; we sat there in that cabin and waited and watched that railroad which no longer existed, which was now a few piles of charred ties among which green grass was already growing, a few threads of steel knotted and twisted about the trunks of trees and already annealing into the living bark, becoming one and indistinguishable with the jungle growth which had now accepted it, but which for us ran still pristine and intact and straight and narrow as the path to glory itself, as it ran for all of them who were there and saw when Ringo and I were not. Drusilla told about that too; "Atlanta" and "Chattanooga" were in it—the names, the beginning and the end—but they meant no more to us than they did to the other watchers—the black and the white, the old men, the children, the women who would not know for months yet if they were widows or childless or not—gathered, warned by grapevine, to see

the momentary flash and glare of indomitable spirit
starved by three years free of the impeding flesh. She told
it (and now Ringo and I began to see it; we were there
too)—the roundhouse in Atlanta where the engine
waited; we were there, we were of them who (they must
have) would slip into the roundhouse in the dark, to ca-
ress the wheels and pistons and iron flanks, to whisper to
it in the darkness like lover to mistress or rider to horse,
cajoling ruthlessly of her or it one supreme effort in return for making which she or it would receive annihilation
(and who would not pay that price), cajoling, whispering,
caressing her or it toward the one moment; we were of
them—the old men, the children, the women—gathered
to watch, drawn and warned by that grapevine of the
oppressed, deprived of everything now save the will and
the ability to deceive, turning inscrutable and impassive
secret faces to the blue enemies who lived among them.
Because they knew it was going to happen; Drusilla told
that too: how they seemed to know somehow the very
moment when the engine left Atlanta; it was as if the gray
generals themselves had send the word, had told them,
"You have suffered for three years; now we will give to
you and your children a glimpse of that for which you have
suffered and been denied." Because that's all it was. I know
that now. Even the successful passage of a hundred engines with trains of cars could not have changed the situation or its outcome; certainly not two free engines shrieking along a hundred yards apart up that drowsing solitude
of track which had seen no smoke and heard no bell in
more than a year. I don't think it was intended to do that.
It was like a meeting between two iron knights of the old
time, not for material gain but for principle—honor denied with honor, courage denied with courage—the deed
done not for the end but for the sake of the doing—put to
the ultimate test and proving nothing save the finality of
death and the vanity of all endeavor. We saw it, we were
there, as if Drusilla's voice had transported us to the wan-

dering light-ray in space in which was still held the furious
shadow—the brief section of track which existed inside
the scope of a single pair of eyes and nowhere else, coming from nowhere and having, needing, no destination,
the engine not coming into view but arrested in human
sight in thunderous yet dreamy fury, lonely, inviolate and
forlorn, wailing through its whistle precious steam which
could have meant seconds at the instant of passing and
miles at the end of its journey (and cheap at ten times
this price)—the flaring and streaming smoke stack, the
tossing bell, the starred Saint Andrew's cross nailed to the
cab roof, the wheels and the flashing driving rods on
which the brass fittings glinted like the golden spurs themselves—then gone, vanished. Only not gone or vanished
either, so long as there should be defeated or the descendants of defeated to tell it or listen to the telling.

"The other one, the Yankee one, was right behind it,"
Drusilla said. "But they never caught it. Then the next
day they came and tore the track up. They tore the track
up so we couldn't do it again; they could tear the track up
but they couldn't take back the fact that we had done it.
They couldn't take that from us."

We—Ringo and I—knew what she meant; we stood together just outside the door before Ringo went on to
Missy Lena's cabin, where he was to sleep. "I know what
you thinking," Ringo said. Father was right; he was
smarter than me. "But I heard good as you did. I heard
every word you heard."

"Only I saw the track before they tore it up. I saw
where it was going to happen."

"But you didn't know hit was fixing to happen when
you seed the track. So nemmine that. I heard. And I
reckon they ain't gonter git that away from me, neither."

He went on, then I went back into the house and behind the quilt where Denny was already asleep on the
pallet. Drusilla was not there only I didn't have time to
wonder where she was because I was thinking how I

probably wouldn't be able to go to sleep at all now though it was late. Then it was later still and Denny was shaking me and I remember how I thought then that he did not seem to need sleep either, that just by having been exposed for three or four seconds to war he had even at just ten acquired that quality which Father and the other men brought back from the front—the power to do without sleep and food both, needing only the opportunity to endure. "Dru says to come on out doors if you want to hear them passing," he whispered.

She was outside the cabin; she hadn't undressed even. I could see her in the starlight—her short jagged hair and the man's shirt and pants. "Hear them?" she said. We could hear it again, like we had in the wagon—the hurrying feet, the sound like they were singing in panting whispers, hurrying on past the gate and dying away up the road. "That's the third tonight," Cousin Drusilla said. "Two passed while I was down at the gate. You were tired, and so I didn't wake you before."

"I thought it was late," I said. "You haven't been to bed even. Have you?"

"No," she said. "I've quit sleeping."

"Quit sleeping?" I said. "Why?"

She looked at me. I was as tall as she was; we couldn't see each other's faces; it was just her head with the short jagged hair like she had cut it herself without bothering about a mirror, and her neck that had got thin and hard like her hands since Granny and I were here before. "I'm keeping a dog quiet," she said.

"A dog?" I said. "I haven't seen any dog."

"No. It's quiet now," she said. "It doesn't bother anybody any more now. I just have to show it the stick now and then." She was looking at me. "Why not stay awake now? Who wants to sleep now, with so much happening, so much to see? Living used to be dull, you see. Stupid. You lived in the same house your father was born in, and your father's sons and daughters had the sons and daughters of the same Negro slaves to nurse and coddle; and then you grew up and you fell in love with your acceptable young man, and in time you would marry him, in your mother's wedding gown, perhaps, and with the same silver for presents she had received; and then you settled down forevermore while you got children to feed and bathe and dress until they grew up, too; and then you and your husband died quietly and were buried together maybe on a summer afternoon just before suppertime. Stupid, you see. But now you can see for yourself how it is; it's fine now; you don't have to worry now about the house and the silver, because they get burned up and carried away; and you don't have to worry about the Negroes, because they tramp the roads all night waiting for a chance to drown in homemade Jordan; and you don't have to worry about getting children to bathe and feed and change, because the young men can ride away and get killed in the fine battles; and you don't even have to sleep alone, you don't even have to sleep at all; and so, all you have to do is show the stick to the dog now and then and say, 'Thank God for nothing.' You see? There. They've gone now. And you'd better get back to bed, so we can get an early start in the morning. It will take a long time to get through them."

"You're not coming in now?" I said.

"Not yet," she said. But we didn't move. And then she put her hand on my shoulder. "Listen," she said. "When you go back home and see Uncle John, ask him to let me come there and ride with his troop. Tell him I can ride, and maybe I can learn to shoot. Will you?"

"Yes," I said. "I'll tell him you are not afraid too."

"Aren't I?" she said. "I hadn't thought about it. It doesn't matter anyway. Just tell him I can ride and that I don't get tired." Her hand was on my shoulder; it felt thin and hard. "Will you do that for me? Ask him to let me come, Bayard."

"All right," I said. Then I said, "I hope he will let you."

"So do I," she said. "Now you go back to bed. Good night."

I went back to the pallet and then to sleep; again it was Denny shaking me awake; by sunup we were on the road again, Drusilla on Bobolink riding beside the wagon. But not for long.

We began to see the dust almost at once and I even believed that I could already smell them though the distance between us did not appreciably decrease, since they were travelling almost as fast as we were. We never did overtake them, just as you do not overtake a tide. You just keep moving, then suddenly you know that the set is about you, beneath you, overtaking you, as if the slow and ruthless power, become aware of your presence at last, had dropped back a tentacle, a feeler, to gather you in and sweep you remorselessly on. Singly, in couples, in groups and families they began to appear from the woods, ahead of us, alongside of us and behind; they covered and hid from sight the road exactly as an infiltration of flood water would have, hiding the road from sight and then the very wheels of the wagon in which we rode, our two horses as well as Bobolink breasting slowly on, enclosed by a mass of heads and shoulders—men and women carrying babies and dragging older children by the hand, old men and women on improvised sticks and crutches, and very old ones sitting beside the road and even calling to us when we passed; there was one old woman who even walked along beside the wagon, holding to the bed and begging Granny to at least let her see the river before she died.

But mostly they did not look at us. We might not have even been there. We did not even ask them to let us through because we could look at their faces and know they couldn't have heard us. They were not singing yet, they were just hurrying, while our horses pushed slow through them, among the blank eyes not looking at anything out of faces caked with dust and sweat, breasting slowly and terrifically through them as if we were driving in midstream up a creek full of floating logs and the dust and the smell of them everywhere and Granny in Mrs. Compson's hat sitting bolt upright under the parasol which Ringo held and looking sicker and sicker, and it already afternoon though we didn't know it anymore than we knew how many miles we had come. Then all of a sudden we reached the river, where the cavalry was holding them back from the bridge. It was just a sound at first, like wind, like it might be in the dust itself. We didn't even know what it was until we saw Drusilla holding Bobolink reined back, her face turned toward us wan and small above the dust and her mouth open and crying thinly: "Look out, Aunt Rosa! Oh, look out!"

It was like we all heard it at the same time—we in the wagon and on the horse, they all around us in the sweat-caking dust. They made a kind of long wailing sound, and then I felt the whole wagon lift clear of the ground and begin to rush forward. I saw our old rib-gaunted horses standing on their hind feet one minute and then turned sideways in the traces the next, and Drusilla leaning forward a little and taut as a pistol hammer holding Bobolink, and I saw men and women and children going down under the horses and we could feel the wagon going over them and we could hear them screaming. And we couldn't stop anymore than if the earth had tilted up and was sliding us all down toward the river.

It went fast, like that, like it did every time anybody named Sartoris or Millard came within sight, hearing or smell of Yankees, as if Yankees were not a people nor a belief nor even a form of behavior, but instead were a kind of gully, precipice, into which Granny and Ringo and I were sucked pell-mell every time we got close to them. It was sunset; now there was a high bright rosy glow quiet beyond the trees and shining on the river, and now we could see it plain—the tide of niggers dammed back from the entrance to the bridge by a detachment of

cavalry, the river like a sheet of rosy glass beneath the
delicate arch of the bridge which the tail of the Yankee
column was just crossing. They were in silhouette, running tiny and high above the placid water; I remember
the horses' and mules' heads all mixed up among the
bayonets, and the barrels of cannon tilted up and kind of
rushing slow across the high peaceful rosy air like split-
cane clothespins being jerked along a clothesline, and the
singing everywhere up and down the river bank, with the
voices of the women coming out of it thin and high:
"Glory! Glory! Hallelujah!"

They were fighting now, the horses rearing and shoving against them, the troopers beating at them with their
scabbards, holding them clear of the bridge while the last
of the infantry began to cross; all of a sudden there was
an officer beside the wagon, holding his scabbarded sword
by the little end like a stick and hanging onto the wagon
and screaming at us. I don't know where he came from,
how he ever got to us, but there he was with his little
white face with a stubble of beard and a long streak of
blood on it, bareheaded and with his mouth open. "Get
back!" he shrieked. "Get back! We're going to blow the
bridge!" screaming right into Granny's face while she
shouted back at him with Mrs. Compson's hat knocked to
one side of her head and hers and the Yankee's faces not
a yard apart:

"I want my silver! I'm John Sartoris' mother-in-law!
Send Colonel Dick to me!" Then the Yankee officer was
gone, right in the middle of shouting and beating at the
nigger heads with his sabre, with his little bloody
shrieking face and all. I don't know where he went any
more than I know where he came from; he just vanished
still holding onto the wagon and flailing about him with
the sabre, and then Cousin Drusilla was there on Bobolink; she had our nigh horse by the head-stall and was
trying to turn the wagon sideways. I started to jump
down to help. "Stay in the wagon," she said. She

didn't shout; she just said it. "Take the lines and turn
them." When we got the wagon turned sideways we
stopped. And then for a minute I thought we were going
backward, until I saw it was the niggers. Then I saw that
the cavalry had broken; I saw the whole mob of it—
horses and men and sabres and niggers—rolling on toward
the end of the bridge like when a dam breaks, for about
ten clear seconds behind the last of the infantry. And
then the bridge vanished. I was looking right at it; I
could see the clear gap between the infantry and the
wave of niggers and cavalry, with a little empty thread of
bridge joining them together in the air above the water,
and then there was a bright glare and I felt my insides
suck and a clap of wind hit me on the back of the head. I
didn't hear anything at all. I just sat there in the wagon
with a funny buzzing in my ears and a funny taste in my
mouth, and watched little toy men and horses and pieces
of plank floating along in the air above the water. But I
didn't hear anything at all; I couldn't even hear Cousin
Drusilla. She was right beside the wagon now, leaning
toward us, her mouth urgent and wide and no sound
coming out of it at all.

"What?" I said.

"Stay in the wagon!"

"I can't hear you!" I said. That's what I said, that's
what I was thinking; I didn't realize even then that the
wagon was moving again. But then I did; it was like the
whole long bank of the river had turned and risen under
us and was rushing us down toward the water, we sitting
in the wagon and rushing down toward the water on
another river of faces that couldn't see or hear either.
Cousin Drusilla had the nigh horse by the bridle again,
and I dragged at them, too, and Granny was standing up
in the wagon and beating at the faces with Mrs. Compson's
parasol, and then the whole rotten bridle came off in
Cousin Drusilla's hand.

"Get away!" I said. "The wagon will float!"

"Yes," she said, "it will float. Just stay in it. Watch Aunt Rosa and Ringo."

"Yes," I said. Then she was gone. We passed her; turned, and holding Bobolink like a rock again and leaning down talking to him and patting his cheek, she was gone. Then maybe the bank did cave. I don't know. I didn't even know we were in the river. It was just like the earth had fallen out from under the wagon and the faces and all, and we all rushed down slow, with the faces looking up and their eyes blind and their mouths open and their arms held up. High up in the air across the river I saw a cliff and a big fire on it running fast sideways; and then all of a sudden the wagon was moving fast sideways, and then a dead horse came shining up from out of the yelling faces and went down slow again, exactly like a fish feeding, with, hanging over his rump by one stirrup, a man in a black uniform, and then I realized that the uniform was blue, only it was wet. They were screaming then, and now I could feel the wagon bed tilt and slide as they caught at it. Granny was kneeling beside me now, hitting at the screaming faces with Mrs. Compson's parasol. Behind us they were still marching down the bank and into the river, singing.

III

A Yankee patrol helped Ringo and me cut the drowned horses out of the harness and drag the wagon ashore. We sprinkled water on Granny until she came to, and they rigged harness with ropes and hitched up two of their horses. There was a road on top of the bluff, and then we could see the fires along the bank. They were still singing on the other side of the river, but it was quieter now. But there were patrols still riding up and down the cliff on this side, and squads of infantry down at the water where the fires were. Then we began to pass between rows of tents, with Granny lying against me, and I could see her face then; it was white and still, and her eyes were shut. She looked old and tired; I hadn't realized how old and little she was. Then we began to pass big fires, with niggers in wet clothes crouching around them and soldiers going among them passing out food; then we came to a broad street, and stopped before a tent with a sentry at the door and a light inside. The soldiers looked at Granny.

"We better take her to the hospital," one of them said.

Granny opened her eyes; she tried to sit up. "No," she said. "Just take me to Colonel Dick. I will be all right then."

They carried her into the tent and put her in a chair. She hadn't moved; she was sitting there with her eyes closed and a strand of wet hair sticking to her face when Colonel Dick came in. I had never seen him before—only heard his voice while Ringo and I were squatting under Granny's skirt and holding our breath—but I knew him at once, with his bright beard and his hard bright eyes, stooping over Granny and saying, "Damn this war. Damn it. Damn it."

"They took the silver and the darkies and the mules," Granny said. "I have come to get them."

"Have them you shall," he said, "if they are anywhere in this corps. I'll see the general myself." He was looking at Ringo and me now. "Ha!" he said. "I believe we have met before also." Then he was gone again.

It was hot in the tent, and quiet, with three bugs swirling around the lantern, and outside the sound of the army like wind far away. Ringo was already asleep, sitting on the ground with his head on his knees, and I wasn't much better, because all of a sudden Colonel Dick was back and there was an orderly writing at the table, and Granny sitting again with her eyes closed in her white face.

"Maybe you can describe them," Colonel Dick said to me.

"I will do it," Granny said. She didn't open her eyes. "The chest of silver tied with hemp rope. The rope was new. Two darkies, Loosh and Philadelphy. The mules, Old Hundred and Tinney."

Colonel Dick turned and watched the orderly writing. "Have you got that?" he said.

The orderly looked at what he had written. "I guess the general will be glad to give them twice the silver and mules just for taking that many niggers," he said.

"Now I'll go see the general," Colonel Dick said.

Then we were moving again. I don't know how long it had been, because they had to wake me and Ringo both; we were in the wagon again, with two Army horses pulling it on down the long broad street, and there was another officer with us and Colonel Dick was gone. We came to a pile of chests and boxes that looked higher than a mountain. There was a rope pen behind it full of mules and then, standing to one side and waiting there, was what looked like a thousand niggers, men, women and children, with their wet clothes dried on them. And now it began to go fast again; there was Granny in the wagon with her eyes wide open now and the lieutenant reading from the paper and the soldiers jerking chests and trunks out of the pile. "Ten chests tied with hemp rope," the lieutenant read. "Got them? . . . A hundred and ten mules. It says from Philadelphia—that's in Mississippi. Get these Mississippi mules. They are to have rope and halters."

"We ain't got a hundred and ten Mississippi mules," the sergeant said.

"Get what we have got. Hurry." He turned to Granny. "And there are your niggers, madam."

Granny was looking at him with her eyes wide as Ringo's. She was drawn back a little, with her hand at her chest. "But they're not—they ain't——" she said.

"They ain't all yours?" the lieutenant said. "I know it. The general said to give you another hundred with his compliments."

"But that ain't—— We didn't——" Granny said.

"She wants the house back, too," the sergeant said. "We ain't got any houses, grandma," he said. "You'll just have to make out with trunks and niggers and mules. You wouldn't have room for it on the wagon, anyway."

We sat there while they loaded the ten trunks into the wagon. It just did hold them all. They got another set of trees and harness, and hitched four mules to it. "One of you darkies that can handle two span come here," the lieutenant said. One of the niggers came and got on the seat with Granny; none of us had ever seen him before. Behind us they were leading the mules out of the pen.

"You want to let some of the women ride?" the lieutenant said.

"Yes," Granny whispered.

"Come on," the lieutenant said. "Just one to a mule, now." Then he handed me the paper. "Here you are. There's a ford about twenty miles up the river; you can cross there. You better get on away from here before any more of these niggers decide to go with you."

We rode until daylight, with the ten chests in the wagon and the mules and our army of niggers behind. Granny had not moved, sitting there beside the strange nigger with Mrs. Compson's hat on and the parasol in her hand. But she was not asleep, because when it got light enough to see, she said, "Stop the wagon." The wagon stopped. She turned and looked at me. "Let me see that paper," she said.

We opened the paper and looked at it, at the neat writing:

> *Field Headquarters,*
> *——th Army Corps,*
> *Department of Tennessee,*
> *August 14, 1863.*

To all Brigade, Regimental and Other Commanders: You will see that bearer is repossessed in full of the following

*property, to wit: Ten (10) chests tied with hemp rope and
containing silver. One hundred ten (110) mules captured
loose near Philadelphia in Mississippi. One hundred ten
(110) Negroes of both sexes belonging to and having
strayed from the same locality.*

*You will further see that bearer is supplied with nec-
essary food and forage to expedite his passage to his
destination.*

By order of the General Commanding.

We looked at one another in the gray light. "I reckon
you gonter take um back now," Ringo said.

Granny looked at me. "We can get food and fodder
too," I said.

"Yes," Granny said. "I tried to tell them better. You and
Ringo heard me. It's the hand of God."

We stopped and slept until noon. That afternoon we
came to the ford. We had already started down the bluff
when we saw the troop of cavalry camped there. It
was too late to stop.

"They done found hit out and headed us off," Ringo
said. It was too late; already an officer and two men were
riding toward us.

"I will tell them the truth," Granny said. "We have done
nothing." She sat there, drawn back a little again, with
her hand already raised and holding the paper out in
the other when they rode up. The officer was a heavy-
built man with a red face; he looked at us and took the
paper and read it and began to swear. He sat there on his
horse swearing while we watched him.

"How many do you lack?" he said.

"How many do I what?" Granny said.

"Mules!" the officer shouted. "Mules! Mules! Do I look
like I had any chests of silver or niggers tied with hemp
rope?"

"Do we——" Granny said, with her hand to her chest,
looking at him; I reckon it was Ringo that knew first what
he meant.

"We like fifty," Ringo said.

"Fifty, hey?" the officer said. He cursed again; he turned to one of the men behind him and cursed him now. "Count 'em!" he said. "Do you think I'm going to take their word for it?"

The man counted the mules; we didn't move; I don't think we even breathed hardly. "Sixty-three," the man said.

The officer looked at us. "Sixty-three from a hundred and ten leaves forty-seven," he said. He cursed. "Get forty-seven mules! Hurry!" He looked at us again. "Think you can beat me out of three mules, hey?"

"Forty-seven will do," Ringo said. "Only I reckon maybe we better eat something, like the paper mention."

We crossed the ford. We didn't stop; we went on as soon as they brought up the other mules, and some more of the women got on them. We went on. It was after sundown then, but we didn't stop.

"Hah!" Ringo said. "Whose hand was that?"

We went on until midnight before we stopped. This time it was Ringo that Granny was looking at. "Ringo," she said.

"I never said nothing the paper never said," Ringo said. "Hit was the one that said it; hit wasn't me. All I done was to told him how much the hundred and ten liked; I never said we liked that many. 'Sides, hit ain't no use in praying about hit now; ain't no telling what we gonter run into 'fore we gits home. The main thing now is, whut we gonter do with all these niggers."

"Yes," Granny said. We cooked and ate the food the cavalry officer gave us; then Granny told all the niggers that lived in Alabama to come forward. It was about half of them. "I suppose you all want to cross some more rivers and run after the Yankee Army, don't you?" Granny said. They stood there, moving their feet in the dust. "What? Don't any of you want to?" They just stood there. "Then who are you going to mind from now on?"

After a while, one of them said, "You, missy."

"All right," Granny said. "Now listen to me. Go home. And if I ever hear of any of you straggling off like this again, I'll see to it. Now line up and come up here one at a time while we divide the food."

It took a long time until the last one was gone; when we started again, we had almost enough mules for everybody to ride, but not quite, and Ringo drove now. He didn't ask; he just got in and took the reins, with Granny on the seat by him; it was just once that she told him not to go so fast. So I rode in the back then, on one of the chests, and that afternoon I was asleep; it was the wagon stopping that woke me. We had just come down a hill onto a flat, and then I saw them beyond a field, about a dozen of them, cavalry in blue coats. They hadn't seen us yet, trotting along, while Granny and Ringo watched them.

"They ain't hardly worth fooling with," Ringo said. "Still, they's horses."

"We've already got a hundred and ten," Granny said. "That's all the paper calls for."

"All right," Ringo said. "You wanter go on?" Granny didn't answer, sitting there drawn back a little, with her hand at her breast again. "Well, what you wanter do?" Ringo said. "You got to 'cide quick, or they be gone." He looked at her; she didn't move. Ringo leaned out of the wagon. "Hey!" he hollered. They looked back quick and saw us and whirled about. "Granny say come here!" Ringo hollered.

"You, Ringo," Granny whispered.

"All right," Ringo said. "You want me to tell um to never mind?" She didn't answer; she was looking past Ringo at the two Yankees who were riding toward us across the field, with that kind of drawn-back look on her face and her hand holding the front of her dress. It was a lieutenant and a sergeant; the lieutenant didn't look much older than Ringo and me. He saw Granny and took off his hat. And then all of a sudden she took her hand away from her chest; it had the paper in it; she held it out to the lieutenant without saying a word. The lieutenant opened it, the sergeant looking over his shoulder. Then the sergeant looked at us.

"This says mules, not horses," he said.

"Just the first hundred was mules," Ringo said. "The extra twelve is horses."

"Damn it!" the lieutenant said. He sounded like a girl swearing. "I told Captain Bowen not to mount us with captured stock!"

"You mean you're going to give them the horses?" the sergeant said.

"What else can I do?" the lieutenan said. He looked like he was fixing to cry. "It's the general's signature!"

So then we had enough stock for all of them to ride except about fifteen or twenty. We went on. The soldiers stood under a tree by the road, with their saddles and bridles on the ground beside them—all but the lieutenant. When we started again, he ran along by the wagon; he looked like he was going to cry, trotting along by the wagon with his hat in his hand, looking at Granny.

"You'll meet some troops somewhere," he said. "I know you will. Will you tell them where we are and to send us something—mounts or wagons—anything we can ride in? You won't forget?"

"They's some of yawl about twenty or thirty miles back that claim to have three extry mules," Ringo said. "But when we sees any more of um, we'll tell um about yawl."

We went on. We came in sight of a town, but we went around it; Ringo didn't even want to stop and send the lieutenant's message in, but Granny made him stop and we sent the message in by one of the niggers.

"That's one more mouth to feed we got shed of," Ringo said.

We went on. We went fast now, changing the mules every few miles; a woman told us we were in Mississippi again, and then, in the afternoon, we came over the hill, and there our chimneys were, standing up into the sunlight, and the cabin behind them and Louvinia bending over a washtub and the clothes on the line, flapping bright and peaceful.

"Stop the wagon," Granny said.

We stopped—the wagon, the hundred and twenty-two mules and horses, and the niggers we never had had time to count.

Granny got out slow and turned to Ringo. "Get out," she said; then she looked at me. "You too," she said. "Because you said nothing at all." We got out of the wagon. She looked at us. "We have lied," she said.

"Hit was the paper that lied; hit wasn't us," Ringo said.

"The paper said a hundred and ten. We have a hundred and twenty-two," Granny said. "Kneel down."

"But they stole them 'fore we did," Ringo said.

"But we lied," Granny said. "Kneel down." She knelt first. Then we all three knelt by the road while she prayed. The washing blew soft and peaceful and bright on the clothesline. And then Louvinia saw us; she was already running across the pasture while Granny was praying.

1869

Wash

Sutpen stood above the pallet bed on which the mother and child lay. Between the shrunken planking of the wall the early sunlight fell in long pencil strokes, breaking upon his straddled legs and upon the riding whip in his hand, and lay across the still shape of the mother, who lay looking up at him from still, inscrutable, sullen eyes, the child at her side wrapped in a piece of dingy though clean cloth. Behind them an old Negro woman squatted beside the rough hearth where a meager fire smoldered.

"Well, Milly," Sutpen said, "too bad you're not a mare. Then I could give you a decent stall in the stable."

Still the girl on the pallet did not move. She merely continued to look up at him without expression, with a young, sullen, inscrutable face still pale from recent travail. Sutpen moved, bringing into the splintered pencils of sunlight the face of a man of sixty. He said quietly to the squatting Negress, "Griselda foaled this morning."

"Horse or mare?" the Negress said.

"A horse. A damned fine colt. . . . What's this?" He indicated the pallet with the hand which held the whip.

"That un's a mare, I reckon."

"Hah," Sutpen said. "A damned fine colt. Going to be the spit and image of old Rob Roy when I rode him North in '61. Do you remember?"

"Yes, Master."

144

"Hah." He glanced back towards the pallet. None could have said if the girl still watched him or not. Again his whip hand indicated the pallet. "Do whatever they need with whatever we've got to do it with." He went out, passing out the crazy doorway and stepping down into the rank weeds (there yet leaned rusting against the corner of the porch the scythe which Wash had borrowed from him three months ago to cut them with) where his horse waited, where Wash stood holding the reins.

When Colonel Sutpen rode away to fight the Yankees, Wash did not go. "I'm looking after the Kernel's place and niggers," he would tell all who asked him and some who had not asked—a gaunt, malaria-ridden man with pale, questioning eyes, who looked about thirty-five, though it was known that he had not only a daughter but an eight-year-old granddaughter as well. This was a lie, as most of them—the few remaining men between eighteen and fifty—to whom he told it, knew, though there were some who believed that he himself really believed it, though even these believed that he had better sense than to put it to the test with Mrs. Sutpen or the Sutpen slaves. Knew better or was just too lazy and shiftless to try it, they said, knowing that his sole connection with the Sutpen plantation lay in the fact that for years now Colonel Sutpen had allowed him to squat in a crazy shack on a slough in the river bottom on the Sutpen place, which Sutpen had built for a fishing lodge in his bachelor days and which had since fallen in dilapidation from disuse, so that now it looked like an aged or sick wild beast crawled terrifically there to drink in the act of dying.

The Sutpen slaves themselves heard of his statement. They laughed. It was not the first time they had laughed at him, calling him white trash behind his back. They began to ask him themselves, in groups, meeting him in the faint road which led up from the slough and the old fish camp, "Why ain't you at de war, white man?"

Pausing, he would look about the ring of black faces and white eyes and teeth behind which derision lurked. "Because I got a daughter and family to keep," he said. "Git out of my road, niggers."

"Niggers?" they repeated; "niggers?" laughing now. "Who him, calling us niggers?"

"Yes," he said. "I ain't got no niggers to look after my folks if I was gone."

"Nor nothing else but dat shack down yon dat Cunnel wouldn't *let* none of us live in."

Now he cursed them; sometimes he rushed at them, snatching up a stick from the ground while they scattered before him, yet seeming to surround him still with that black laughing, derisive, evasive, inescapable, leaving him panting and impotent and raging. Once it happened in the very back yard of the big house itself. This was after bitter news had come down from the Tennessee mountains and from Vicksburg, and Sherman had passed through the plantation, and most of the Negroes had followed him. Almost everything else had gone with the Federal troops, and Mrs. Sutpen had sent word to Wash that he could have the scuppernongs ripening in the arbor in the back yard. This time it was a house servant, one of the few Negroes who remained; this time the Negress had to retreat up the kitchen steps, where she turned. "Stop right dar, white man. Stop right whar you is. You ain't never crossed dese steps whilst Cunnel here, and you ain't ghy' do hit now."

This was true. But there was this of a kind of pride: he had never tried to enter the big house, even though he believed that if he had, Sutpen would have received him, permitted him. "But I ain't going to give no black nigger the chance to tell me I can't go nowhere," he said to himself. "I ain't even going to give Kernel the chance to have to cuss a nigger on my account." This, though he and Sutpen had spent more than one afternoon together on those rare Sundays when there would be no company in the house. Perhaps his mind knew that it was because Sutpen had nothing else to do, being a man who could not bear his own company. Yet the fact remained that the two of them would spend whole afternoons in the scuppernong arbor, Sutpen in the hammock and Wash squatting against a post, a pail of cistern water between them, taking drink for drink from the same demijohn. Meanwhile on weekdays he would see the fine figure of the man—they were the same age almost to a day, though neither of them (perhaps because Wash had a grandchild while Sutpen's son was a youth in school) ever thought of himself as being so—on the fine figure of the black stallion, galloping about the plantation. For that moment his heart would be quiet and proud. It would seem to him that that world in which Negroes, whom the Bible told him had been created and cursed by God to be brute and vassal to all men of white skin, were better found and housed and even clothed than he and his; that world in which he sensed always about him mocking echoes of black laughter was but a dream and an illusion, and that the actual world was this one across which his own lonely apotheosis seemed to gallop on the black thoroughbred, thinking how the Book said also that all men were created in the image of God and hence all men made the same image in God's eyes at least; so that he could say, as though speaking of himself, "A fine proud man. If God Himself was to come down and ride the natural earth, that's what He would aim to look like."

Sutpen returned in 1865, on the black stallion. He seemed to have aged ten years. His son had vanished the same winter in which his wife had died. He returned with his citation for gallantry from the hand of General Lee to a ruined plantation, where for a year now his daughter had subsisted partially on the meager bounty of the man to whom fifteen years ago he had granted permission to live in that tumbledown fishing camp whose very existence he had at the time forgotten. Wash was there to meet him, unchanged: still gaunt, still ageless, with his pale, questioning gaze, his air diffident, a little servile, a little familiar. "Well, Kernel," Wash said, "they kilt us but they ain't whupped us yit, air they?"

That was the tenor of their conversation for the next five years. It was inferior whiskey which they drank now together from a stoneware jug, and it was not in the scuppernong arbor. It was in the rear of the little store which Sutpen managed to set up on the highroad: a frame shelved room where, with Wash for clerk and porter, he dispensed kerosene and staple foodstuffs and stale gaudy candy and cheap beads and ribbons to Negroes or poor whites of Wash's own kind, who came afoot or on gaunt mules to haggle tediously for dimes and quarters with a man who at one time could gallop (the black stallion was still alive; the stable in which his jealous get lived was in better repair than the house where the master himself lived) for ten miles across his own fertile land and who had led troops gallantly in battle; until Sutpen in fury would empty the store, close and lock the doors from the inside. Then he and Wash would repair to the rear and the jug. But the talk would not be quiet now, as when Sutpen lay in the hammock, delivering an arrogant monologue while Wash squatted guffawing against his post. They both sat now, though Sutpen had the single chair while Wash used whatever box or keg was handy, and even this for just a little while, because soon Sutpen would reach that stage of impotent and furious undefeat in which he would rise, swaying and plunging, and declare again that he would take his pistol and the black stallion and ride single-handed into Washington and kill Lincoln, dead now, and Sherman, now a private citizen. "Kill them!" he would shout. "Shoot them down like the dogs they are—"

"Sho, Kernel; sho, Kernel," Wash would say, catching Sutpen as he fell. Then he would commandeer the first passing wagon or, lacking that, he would walk the mile to the nearest neighbor and borrow one and return and carry Sutpen home. He entered the house now. He had been doing so for a long time, taking Sutpen home in whatever borrowed wagon might be, talking him into locomotion with cajoling murmurs as though he were a horse, a stallion himself. The daughter would meet them and hold open the door without a word. He would carry his burden through the once white formal entrance, surmounted by a fanlight imported piece by piece from Europe and with a board now nailed over a missing pane, across a velvet carpet from which all nap was now gone, and up a formal stairs, now but a fading ghost of bare boards between two strips of fading paint, and into the bedroom. It would be dusk by now, and he would let his burden sprawl onto the bed and undress it and then he would sit quietly in a chair beside. After a time the daughter would come to the door. "We're all right now," he would tell her. "Don't you worry none, Miss Judith."

Then it would become dark, and after a while he would lie down on the floor beside the bed, though not to sleep, because after a time—sometimes before midnight—the man on the bed would stir and groan and then speak. "Wash?"

"Hyer I am, Kernel. You go back to sleep. We ain't whupped yit, air we? Me and you kin do hit."

Even then he had already seen the ribbon about his granddaughter's waist. She was now fifteen, already mature, after the early way of her kind. He knew where the ribbon came from; he had been seeing it and its kind daily for three years, even if she had lied about where she got it, which she did not, at once bold, sullen, and fearful.

"Sho now," he said. "Ef Kernel wants to give hit to you, I hope you minded to thank him."

His heart was quiet, even when he saw the dress, watching her secret, defiant, frightened face when she told him that Miss Judith, the daughter, had helped her to make it. But he was quite grave when he approached Sutpen after they closed the store that afternoon, following the other to the rear.

"Get the jug," Sutpen directed.

"Wait," Wash said. "Not yit for a minute."

Neither did Sutpen deny the dress. "What about it?" he said.

But Wash met his arrogant stare; he spoke quietly. "I've knowed you for going on twenty years. I ain't never yit denied to do what you told me to do. And I'm a man nigh sixty. And she ain't nothing but a fifteen-year-old gal."

"Meaning that I'd harm a girl? I, a man as old as you are?"

"If you was ara other man, I'd say you was as old as me. And old or no old, I wouldn't let her keep that dress nor nothing else that come from your hand. But you are different."

"How different?" But Wash merely looked at him with his pale, questioning, sober eyes. "So that's why you are afraid of me?"

Now Wash's gaze no longer questioned. It was tranquil, serene. "I ain't afraid. Because you air brave. It ain't that you were a brave man at one minute or day of your life and got a paper to show hit from General Lee. But you air brave, the same as you air alive and breathing. That's where hit's different. Hit don't need no ticket from nobody to tell me that. And I know that whatever you handle or tech, whether hit's a regiment of men or a ignorant gal or just a hound dog, that you will make hit right."

Now it was Sutpen who looked away, turning suddenly, brusquely. "Get the jug," he said sharply.

"Sho, Kernel," Wash said.

So on that Sunday dawn two years later, having watched the Negro midwife, whom he had walked three miles to fetch, enter the crazy door beyond which his granddaughter lay wailing, his heart was still quiet though concerned. He knew what they had been saying—the Negroes in cabins about the land, the white men who loafed all day long about the store, watching quietly the three of them: Sutpen, himself, his granddaughter with her air of brazen and shrinking defiance as her condition become daily more and more obvious, like three actors that came and went upon a stage. "I know what they say to one another," he thought. "I can almost hyear them: *Wash Jones has fixed old Sutpen at last. Hit taken him twenty years, but he has done hit at last.*"

It would be dawn after a while, though not yet. From the house, where the lamp shone dim beyond the warped door frame, his granddaughter's voice came steadily as though run by a clock, while thinking went slowly and terrifically, fumbling, involved somehow with a sound of galloping hooves, until there broke suddenly free in mid-gallop the fine proud figure of the man on the fine proud stallion, galloping; and then that at which thinking fumbled, broke free too and quite clear, not in justification nor even explanation, but as the apotheosis, lonely, explicable, beyond all fouling by human touch: "He is bigger than all them Yankees that kilt his son and his wife and taken his niggers and ruined his land, bigger than this hyer durn country that he fit for and that has denied him into keeping a little country store; bigger than the denial which hit helt to his lips like the bitter cup in the Book. And how could I have lived this nigh to him for twenty years without being teched and changed by him? Maybe I ain't as big as him and maybe I ain't done none of the galloping. But at least I done been drug along. Me and him kin do hit, if so be he will show me what he aims for me to do."

Then it was dawn. Suddenly he could see the house, and the old Negress in the door looking at him. Then he realized that his granddaughter's voice had ceased.

"It's a girl," the Negress said. "You can go tell him if you want to." She reëntered the house.

"A girl," he repeated; "a girl"; in astonishment, hearing the galloping hooves, seeing the proud galloping figure emerge again. He seemed to watch it pass, galloping through avatars which marked the accumulation of years, time, to the climax where it galloped beneath a brandished sabre and a shot-torn flag rushing down a sky in color like thunderous sulphur, thinking for the first time in his life that perhaps Sutpen was an old man like himself. "Gittin a gal," he thought in that astonishment; then he thought with the pleased surprise of a child: "Yes, sir. Be dawg if I ain't lived to be a great-grandpaw after all."

He entered the house. He moved clumsily, on tiptoe, as if he no longer lived there, as if the infant which had just drawn breath and cried in light had dispossessed him, be it of his own blood too though it might. But even above the pallet he could see little save the blur of his granddaughter's exhausted face. Then the Negress squatting at the hearth spoke, "You better gawn tell him if you going to. Hit's daylight now."

But this was not necessary. He had no more than turned the corner of the porch where the scythe leaned which he had borrowed three months ago to clear away the weeds through which he walked, when Sutpen himself rode up on the old stallion. He did not wonder how Sutpen had got the word. He took it for granted that this was what had brought the other out at this hour on Sunday morning, and he stood while the other dismounted, and he took the reins from Sutpen's hand, an expression on his gaunt face almost imbecile with a kind of weary triumph, saying, "Hit's a gal, Kernel. I be dawg if you ain't as old as I am——" until Sutpen passed him and entered the house. He stood there with the reins in his hand and heard Sutpen cross the floor to the pallet. He heard what Sutpen said, and something seemed to stop dead in him before going on.

The sun was now up, the swift sun of Mississippi latitudes, and it seemed to him that he stood beneath
a strange sky, in a strange scene, familiar only as things
are familiar in dream, like the dreams of falling to one
who has never climbed. "I kain't have heard what I
thought I heard," he thought quietly. "I know I kain't."
Yet the voice, the familiar voice which had said the words
was still speaking, talking now to the old Negress about a
colt foaled that morning. "That's why he was up so early,"
he thought. "That was hit. Hit ain't me and mine. Hit
ain't even hisn that got him outen bed."

Sutpen emerged. He descended into the weeds, moving
with that heavy deliberation which would have been
haste when he was younger. He had not yet looked full
at Wash. He said, "Dicey will stay and tend to her. You
better—" Then he seemed to see Wash facing him and
paused. "What?" he said.

"You said—" To his own ears Wash's voice sounded
flat and ducklike, like a deaf man's. "You said if she was
a mare, you could give her a good stall in the stable."

"Well?" Sutpen said. His eyes widened and narrowed,
almost like a man's fists flexing and shutting, as Wash began to advance towards him, stooping a little. Very astonishment kept Sutpen still for the moment, watching
that man whom in twenty years he had no more known to
make any motion save at command than he had the horse
which he rode. Again his eyes narrowed and widened;
without moving he seemed to rear suddenly upright.
"Stand back," he said suddenly and sharply. "Don't you
touch me."

"I'm going to tech you, Kernel," Wash said in that flat,
quiet, almost soft voice, advancing.

Sutpen raised the hand which held the riding whip;
the old Negress peered around the crazy door with her
black gargoyle face of a worn gnome. "Stand back, Wash,"
Sutpen said. Then he struck. The old Negress leaped down
into the weeds with the agility of a goat and fled. Sutpen

slashed Wash again across the face with the whip, striking him to his knees. When Wash rose and advanced once more he held in his hands the scythe which he had borrowed from Sutpen three months ago and which Sutpen would never need again.

When he reëntered the house his granddaughter stirred on the pallet bed and called his name fretfully. "What was that?" she said.

"What was what, honey?"

"That ere racket out there."

" 'Twarn't nothing," he said gently. He knelt and touched her hot forehead clumsily. "Do you want ara thing?"

"I want a sup of water," she said querulously. "I been laying here wanting a sup of water a long time, but don't nobody care enough to pay me no mind."

"Sho now," he said soothingly. He rose stiffly and fetched the dipper of water and raised her head to drink and laid her back and watched her turn to the child with an absolutely stonelike face. But a moment later he saw that she was crying quietly. "Now, now," he said, "I wouldn't do that. Old Dicey says hit's a right fine gal. Hit's all right now. Hit's all over now. Hit ain't no need to cry now."

But she continued to cry quietly, almost sullenly, and he rose again and stood uncomfortably above the pallet for a time, thinking as he had thought when his own wife lay so and then his daughter in turn: "Women. Hit's a mystry to me. They seem to want em, and yit when they git em they cry about hit. Hit's a mystry to me. To ara man." Then he moved away and drew a chair up to the window and sat down.

Through all that long, bright, sunny forenoon he sat at the window, waiting. Now and then he rose and tip-toed to the pallet. But his granddaughter slept now, her face sullen and calm and weary, the child in the crook of her arm. Then he returned to the chair and sat again, waiting, wondering why it took them so long, until he remembered that it was Sunday. He was sitting there at mid-afternoon when a half-grown white boy came around the corner of the house upon the body and gave a choked cry and looked up and glared for a mesmerized instant at Wash in the window before he turned and fled. Then Wash rose and tiptoed again to the pallet.

The granddaughter was awake now, wakened perhaps by the boy's cry without hearing it. "Milly," he said, "air you hungry?" She didn't answer, turning her face away. He built up the fire on the hearth and cooked the food which he had brought home the day before: fatback it was, and cold corn pone; he poured water into the stale coffee pot and heated it. But she would not eat when he carried the plate to her, so he ate himself, quietly, alone, and left the dishes as they were and returned to the window.

Now he seemed to sense, feel, the men who would be gathering with horses and guns and dogs—the curious, and the vengeful: men of Sutpen's own kind, who had made the company about Sutpen's table in the time when Wash himself had yet to approach nearer to the house than the scuppernong arbor—men who had also shown the lesser ones how to fight in battle, who maybe also had signed papers from the generals saying that they were among the first of the brave; who had also galloped in the old days arrogant and proud on the fine horses across the fine plantations—symbols also of admiration and hope; instruments too of despair and grief.

That was who they would expect him to run from. It seemed to him that he had no more to run from than he had to run to. If he ran, he would merely be fleeing one set of bragging and evil shadows for another just like them, since they were all of a kind throughout all the earth which he knew, and he was old, too old to flee far even if he were to flee. He could never escape them, no matter how much or how far he ran: a man going on sixty could not run that far. Not far enough to escape beyond the boundaries of earth where such men lived, set the order and the rule of living. It seemed to him that he now saw for the first time, after five years, how it was that Yankees or any other living armies had managed to whip them: the gallant, the proud, the brave; the acknowledged and chosen best among them all to carry courage and honor and pride. Maybe if he had gone to the war with them he would have discovered them sooner. But if he had discovered them sooner, what would he have done with his life since? How could he have borne to remember for five years what his life had been before?

Now it was getting toward sunset. The child had been crying; when he went to the pallet he saw his granddaughter nursing it, her face still bemused, sullen, inscrutable. "Air you hungry yit?" he said.

"I don't want nothing."

"You ought to eat."

This time she did not answer at all, looking down at the child. He returned to his chair and found that the sun had set. "Hit kain't be much longer," he thought. He could feel them quite near now, the curious and the vengeful. He could even seem to hear what they were saying about him, the undercurrent of believing beyond the immediate fury: *Old Wash Jones he come a tumble at last. He thought he had Sutpen, but Sutpen fooled him. He thought he had Kernel where he would have to marry the gal or pay up. And Kernel refused.* "But I never expected that, Kernel!" he cried aloud, catching himself at the sound of his own voice, glancing quickly back to find his granddaughter watching him.

"Who you talking to now?" she said.

"Hit ain't nothing. I was just thinking and talked out before I knowed hit."

Her face was becoming indistinct again, again a sullen blur in the twilight. "I reckon so. I reckon you'll have to holler louder than that before he'll hear you, up yonder at that house. And I reckon you'll need to do more than holler before you get him down here too."

"Sho now," he said. "Don't you worry none." But already thinking was going smoothly on: "You know I never. You know how I ain't never expected or asked nothing from ara living man but what I expected from you. And I never asked that. I didn't think hit would need. I said, *I don't need to. What need has a fellow like Wash Jones to question or doubt the man that General Lee himself says in a handwrote ticket that he was brave?* Brave," he thought. "Better if nara one of them had never rid back home in '65"; thinking *Better if his kind and mine too had never drawn the breath of life on this earth. Better that all who remain of us be blasted from the face of earth than that another Wash Jones should see his whole life shredded from him and shrivel away like a dried shuck thrown onto the fire.*

He ceased, became still. He heard the horses, suddenly and plainly; presently he saw the lantern and the movement of men, the glint of gun barrels, in its moving light. Yet he did not stir. It was quite dark now, and he listened to the voices and the sounds of underbrush as they surrounded the house. The lantern itself came on; its light fell upon the quiet body in the weeds and stopped, the horses tall and shadowy. A man descended and stooped in the lantern light, above the body. He held a pistol; he rose and faced the house. "Jones," he said.

"I'm here," Wash said quietly from the window "That you, Major?"

"Come out."

"Sho," he said quietly. "I just want to see to my granddaughter."

"We'll see to her. Come on out."

"Sho, Major. Just a minute."

"Show a light. Light your lamp."

"Sho. In just a minute." They could hear his voice retreat into the house, though they could not see him as he went swiftly to the crack in the chimney where he kept the butcher knife: the one thing in his slovenly life and house in which he took pride, since it was razor sharp. He approached the pallet, his granddaughter's voice:

"Who is it? Light the lamp, grandpaw."

"Hit won't need no light, honey. Hit won't take but a minute," he said, kneeling, fumbling toward her voice, whispering now. "Where air you?"

"Right here," she said fretfully. "Where would I be? What is. . . ." His hand touched her face. "What is. . . . Grandpaw! Grand. . . ."

"Jones!" the sheriff said. "Come out of there!"

"In just a minute, Major," he said. Now he rose and moved swiftly. He knew where in the dark the can of kerosene was, just as he knew that it was full, since it was not two days ago that he had filled it at the store and held it there until he got a ride home with it, since the five gallons were heavy. There were still coals on the hearth; besides the crazy building itself was like tinder: the coals, the hearth, the walls exploding in a single blue glare. Against it the waiting men saw him in a wild instant springing toward them with the lifted scythe before the horses reared and whirled. They checked the horses and turned them back toward the glare, yet still in wild relief against it the gaunt figure ran toward them with the lifted scythe.

"Jones!" the sheriff shouted. "Stop! Stop, or I'll shoot. Jones! *Jones!*" Yet still the gaunt, furious figure came on against the glare and roar of the flames. With the scythe lifted, it bore down upon them, upon the wild glaring eyes of the horses and the swinging glints of gun barrels, without any cry, any sound.

1874

An Odor of Verbena

I

It was just after supper. I had just opened my *Coke* on the
table beneath the lamp; I heard Professor Wilkins' feet
in the hall and then the instant of silence as he put his
hand to the doorknob, and I should have known. People
talk glibly of presentiment, but I had none. I heard his
feet on the stairs and then in the hall approaching and
there was nothing in the feet because although I had
lived in his house for three college years now and although
both he and Mrs. Wilkins called me Bayard in the house,
he would no more have entered my room without knocking
than I would have entered his—or hers. Then he flung the
door violently inward against the doorstop with one of
those gestures with or by which an almost painfully unflagging preceptory of youth ultimately aberrates, and
stood there saying, "Bayard. Bayard, my son, my dear
son."

I should have known; I should have been prepared. Or
maybe I was prepared because I remember how I closed
the book carefully, even marking the place, before I rose.
He (Professor Wilkins) was doing something, bustling at
something; it was my hat and cloak which he handed
me and which I took although I would not need the cloak,
unless even then I was thinking (although it was October,
the equinox had not occurred) that the rains and the cool
weather would arrive before I should see this room again

159

and so I would need the cloak anyway to return to it if I returned, thinking "God, if he had only done this last night, flung that door crashing and bouncing against the stop last night without knocking so I could have gotten there before it happened, been there when it did, beside him on whatever spot, wherever it was that he would have to fall and lie in the dust and dirt."

"Your boy is downstairs in the kitchen," he said. It was not until years later that he told me (someone did; it must have been Judge Wilkins) how Ringo had apparently flung the cook aside and come on into the house and into the library where he and Mrs. Wilkins were sitting and said without preamble and already turning to withdraw: "They shot Colonel Sartoris this morning. Tell him I be waiting in the kitchen," and was gone before either of them could move. "He has ridden forty miles yet he refuses to eat anything." We were moving toward the door now—the door on my side of which I had lived for three years now with what I knew, what I knew now I must have believed and expected, yet beyond which I had heard the approaching feet yet heard nothing in the feet. "If there was just anything I could do."

"Yes, sir," I said. "A fresh horse for my boy. He will want to go back with me."

"By all means take mine—Mrs. Wilkins'," he cried. His tone was no different yet he did cry it and I suppose that at the same moment we both realized that was funny—a short-legged, deep-barrelled mare who looked exactly like a spinster music teacher, which Mrs. Wilkins drove to a basket phaeton—which was good for me, like being doused with a pail of cold water would have been good for me.

"Thank you, sir," I said. "We won't need it. I will get a fresh horse for him at the livery stable when I get my mare." Good for me, because even before I finished speaking I knew that would not be necessary either, that Ringo would have stopped at the livery stable before he came

out to the college and attended to that and that the fresh
horse for him and my mare both would be saddled and
waiting now at the side fence and we would not have to
go through Oxford at all. Loosh would not have thought
of that if he had come for me, he would have come
straight to the college, to Professor Wilkins', and told his
news and then sat down and let me take charge from then
on. But not Ringo.

He followed me from the room. From now until Ringo
and I rode away into the hot, thick, dusty darkness, quick
and strained for the overdue equinox like a laboring de-
layed woman, he would be somewhere either just beside me or just behind me and I never to know exactly
nor care which. He was trying to find the words with
which to offer me his pistol too. I could almost hear him:
"Ah, this unhappy land, not ten years recovered from the
fever yet still men must kill one another, still we must pay
Cain's price in his own coin." But he did not actually say
it. He just followed me, somewhere beside or behind me
as we descended the stairs toward where Mrs. Wilkins
waited in the hall beneath the chandelier—a thin gray
woman who reminded me of Granny, not that she looked
like Granny probably but because she had known Granny
—a lifted, anxious, still face which was thinking *Who lives
by the sword shall die by it* just as Granny would have
thought, toward which I walked, had to walk not because
I was Granny's grandson and had lived in her house for
three college years and was about the age of her son when
he was killed in almost the last battle nine years ago, but
because I was now The Sartoris. (The Sartoris: that had
been one of the concomitant flashes, along with the *at last
it has happened* when Professor Wilkins opened my door.)
She didn't offer me a horse and pistol, not because she
liked me any less than Professor Wilkins but because she
was a woman and so wiser than any man, else the men
would not have gone on with the War for two years after
they knew they were whipped. She just put her hands (a

small woman, no bigger than Granny had been) on my shoulders and said, "Give my love to Drusilla and your Aunt Jenny. And come back when you can."

"Only I don't know when that will be," I said. "I don't know how many things I will have to attend to." Yes, I lied even to her; it had not been but a minute yet since he had flung that door bouncing into the stop yet already I was beginning to realize, to become aware of that which I still had no yardstick to measure save that one consisting of what, despite myself, despite my raising and background (or maybe because of them) I had for some time known I was becoming and had feared the test of it; I remember how I thought while her hands still rested on my shoulders: *At least this will be my chance to find out if I am what I think I am or if I just hope; if I am going to do what I have taught myself is right or if I am just going to wish I were.*

We went on to the kitchen, Professor Wilkins still somewhere beside or behind me and still offering me the pistol and horse in a dozen different ways. Ringo was waiting; I remember how I thought then that no matter what might happen to either of us, I would never be The Sartoris to him. He was twenty-four too, but in a way he had changed even less than I had since that day when we had nailed Grumby's body to the door of the old compress. Maybe it was because he had outgrown me, had changed so much that summer while he and Granny traded mules with the Yankees that since then I had had to do most of the changing just to catch up with him. He was sitting quietly in a chair beside the cold stove, spent-looking too who had ridden forty miles (at one time, either in Jefferson or when he was alone at last on the road somewhere, he had cried; dust was now caked and dried in the tear-channels on his face) and would ride forty more yet would not eat, looking up at me a little red-eyed with weariness (or maybe it was more than just weariness and so I would never catch up with him) then rising without a word and going on toward the door and I following and Professor Wilkins still offering the horse and the pistol without speaking the words and still thinking (I could feel that too) *Dies by the sword. Dies by the sword.*

Ringo had the two horses saddled at the side gate, as I had known he would—the fresh one for himself and my mare Father had given me three years ago, that could do a mile under two minutes any day and a mile every eight minutes all day long. He was already mounted when I realized that what Professor Wilkins wanted was to shake my hand. We shook hands; I knew he believed he was touching flesh which might not be alive tomorrow night, and I thought for a second how if I told him what I was going to do, since we had talked about it, about how if there was anything at all in the Book, anything of hope and peace for His blind and bewildered spawn which He had chosen above all others to offer immortality, *Thou shalt not kill* must be it, since maybe he even believed that he had taught it to me, except that he had not, nobody had, not even myself, since it went further than just having been learned. But I did not tell him. He was too old to be forced so, to condone even in principle such a decision; he was too old to have to stick to principle in the face of blood and raising and background, to be faced without warning and made to deliver like by a highwayman out of the dark: only the young could do that—one still young enough to have his youth supplied him gratis as a reason (not an excuse) for cowardice.

So I said nothing. I just shook his hand and mounted too, and Ringo and I rode on. We would not have to pass through Oxford now and so soon (there was a thin sickle of moon like the heel print of a boot in wet sand) the road to Jefferson lay before us, the road which I had travelled for the first time three years ago with Father and travelled twice at Christmas time and then in June and September and twice at Christmas time again and then June and September again each college term since alone on the mare,

not even knowing that this was peace; and now this time
and maybe last time who would not die (I knew that) but
who maybe forever after could never again hold up his
head. The horses took the gait which they would hold for
forty miles. My mare knew the long road ahead and
Ringo had a good beast too, had talked Hilliard at the
livery stable out of a good horse too. Maybe it was the
tears, the channels of dried mud across which his strain-
reddened eyes had looked at me, but I rather think it was
that same quality which used to enable him to replenish
his and Granny's supply of United States Army letterheads
during that time—some outrageous assurance gained
from too long and too close association with white people:
the one whom he called Granny, the other with whom he
had slept from the time we were born until Father rebuilt
the house. We spoke one time, then no more:

"We could bushwhack him," he said. "Like we done
Grumby that day. But I reckon that wouldn't suit that
white skin you walks around in."

"No," I said. We rode on; it was October; there was
plenty of time still for verbena although I would have to
reach home before I would realize there was a need for
it; plenty of time for verbena yet from the garden where
Aunt Jenny puttered beside old Joby, in a pair of Father's
old cavalry gauntlets, among the coaxed and ordered
beds, the quaint and odorous old names, for though it was
October no rain had come yet and hence no frost to bring
(or leave behind) the first half-warm half-chill nights of
Indian Summer—the drowsing air cool and empty for
geese yet languid still with the old hot dusty smell of fox
grape and sassafras—the nights when before I became a
man and went to college to learn law Ringo and I, with
lantern and axe and crokersack and six dogs (one to follow the trail and five more just for the tonguing, the music) would hunt possum in the pasture where, hidden, we
had seen our first Yankee that afternoon on the bright
horse, where for the last year now you could hear the

whistling of the trains which had no longer belonged to
Mr. Redmond for a long while now and which at some instant, some second during the morning Father too had relinquished along with the pipe which Ringo said he was
smoking, which slipped from his hand as he fell. We rode
on, toward the house where he would be lying in the parlor now, in his regimentals (sabre too) and where Drusilla
would be waiting for me beneath all the festive glitter of
the chandeliers, in the yellow ball gown and the sprig of
verbena in her hair, holding the two loaded pistols (I
could see that too, who had had no presentiment; I could
see her, in the formal brilliant room arranged formally for
obsequy, not tall, not slender as a woman is but as a youth,
a boy, is, motionless, in yellow, the face calm, almost
bemused, the head simple and severe, the balancing sprig
of verbena above each ear, the two arms bent at the elbows, the two hands shoulder high, the two identical
duelling pistols lying upon, not clutched in, one to each:
the Greek amphora priestess of a succinct and formal violence).

II

Drusilla said that he had a dream. I was twenty then
and she and I would walk in the garden in the summer
twilight while we waited for Father to ride in from the
railroad. I was just twenty then: that summer before I
entered the University to take the law degree which Father decided I should have and four years after the one,
the day, the evening when Father and Drusilla had kept
old Cash Benbow from becoming United States Marshal
and returned home still unmarried and Mrs. Habersham
herded them into her carriage and drove them back to
town and dug her husband out of his little dim hole in the
new bank and made him sign Father's peace bond for
killing the two carpet baggers, and took Father and Drusilla to the minister herself and saw that they were mar-

ried. And Father had rebuilt the house too, on the same blackened spot, over the same cellar, where the other had burned, only larger, much larger: Drusilla said that the house was the aura of Father's dream just as a bride's trousseau and veil is the aura of hers. And Aunt Jenny had come to live with us now so we had the garden (Drusilla would no more have bothered with flowers than Father himself would have, who even now, even four years after it was over, still seemed to exist, breathe, in that last year of it while she had ridden in man's clothes and with her hair cut short like any other member of Father's troop, across Georgia and both Carolinas in front of Sherman's army) for her to gather sprigs of verbena from to wear in her hair because she said verbena was the only scent you could smell above the smell of horses and courage and so it was the only one that was worth the wearing. The railroad was hardly begun then and Father and Mr. Redmond were not only still partners, they were still friends, which as George Wyatt said was easily a record for Father, and he would leave the house at daybreak on Jupiter, riding up and down the unfinished line with two saddlebags of gold coins borrowed on Friday to pay the men on Saturday, keeping just two cross-ties ahead of the sheriff as Aunt Jenny said. So we walked in the dusk, slowly between Aunt Jenny's flower beds while Drusilla (in a dress now, who still would have worn pants all the time if Father had let her) leaned lightly on my arm and I smelled the verbena in her hair as I had smelled the rain in it and in Father's beard that night four years ago when he and Drusilla and Uncle Buck McCaslin found Grumby and then came home and found Ringo and me more than just asleep: escaped into that oblivion which God or Nature or whoever it was had supplied us with for the time being, who had had to perform more than should be required of children because there should be some limit to the age, the youth at least below which one should not have to kill. This was just after the Saturday night when he re-

turned and I watched him clean the derringer and reload it and we learned that the dead man was almost a
neighbor, a hill man who had been in the first infantry
regiment when it voted Father out of command: and we
never to know if the man actually intended to rob Father
or not because Father had shot too quick, but only that he
had a wife and several children in a dirt-floored cabin in
the hills, to whom Father the next day sent some money
and she (the wife) walked into the house two days later
while we were sitting at the dinner table and flung the
money at Father's face.

"But nobody could have had more of a dream than
Colonel Sutpen," I said. He had been Father's second-in-
command in the first regiment and had been elected colonel when the regiment deposed Father after Second
Manassas, and it was Sutpen and not the regiment whom
father never forgave. He was underbred, a cold ruthless
man who had come into the country about thirty years before the War, nobody knew from where except Father
said you could look at him and know he would not dare to
tell. He had got some land and nobody knew how he did
that either, and he got money from somewhere—Father
said they all believed he robbed steamboats, either as a
card sharper or as an out-and-out highwayman—and built
a big house and married and set up as a gentleman. Then
he lost everything in the War like everybody else, all
hope of descendants too (his son killed his daughter's fiancé on the eve of the wedding and vanished), yet he
came back home and set out singlehanded to rebuild his
plantation. He had no friends to borrow from and he had
nobody to leave it to and he was past sixty years old, yet
he set out to rebuild his place like it used to be; they
told how he was too busy to bother with politics or anything; how when Father and the other men organized the
night riders to keep the carpet baggers from organizing
the Negroes into an insurrection, he refused to have anything to do with it. Father stopped hating him long enough

to ride out to see Sutpen himself and he (Sutpen) came to the door with a lamp and did not even invite them to come in and discuss it; Father said, "Are you with us or against us?" and he said, "I'm for my land. If every man of you would rehabilitate his own land, the country will take care of itself" and Father challenged him to bring the lamp out and set it on a stump where they could both see to shoot and Sutpen would not. "Nobody could have more of a dream than that."

"Yes. But his dream was just Sutpen. John's is not. He is thinking of this whole country which he is trying to raise by its bootstraps, so that all the people in it, not just his kind nor his old regiment, but all the people, black and white, the women and children back in the hills who don't even own shoes— Don't you see?"

"But how can they get any good from what he wants to do for them if they are—after he has———"

"Killed some of them? I suppose you include those two carpet baggers he had to kill to hold that first election, don't you?"

"They were men. Human beings."

"They were Northerners, foreigners who had no business here. They were pirates." We walked on, her weight hardly discernible on my arm, her head just reaching my shoulder. I had always been a little taller than she, even on that night at Hawkhurst while we listened to the niggers passing in the road, and she had changed but little since —the same boy-hard body, the close implacable head with its savagely cropped hair which I had watched from the wagon above the tide of crazed singing niggers as we went down into the river—the body not slender as women are but as boys are slender. "A dream is not a very safe thing to be near, Bayard. I know; I had one once. It's like a loaded pistol with a hair trigger: if it stays alive long enough, somebody is going to be hurt. But if it's a good dream, it's worth it. There are not many dreams in the world, but there are a lot of human lives. And one human life or two dozen——"

"Are not worth anything?"

"No. Not anything.—Listen. I hear Jupiter. I'll beat you to the house." She was already running, the skirts she did not like to wear lifted almost to her knees, her legs beneath it running as boys run just as she rode like men ride.

I was twenty then. But the next time I was twenty-four; I had been three years at the University and in another two weeks I would ride back to Oxford for the final year and my degree. It was just last summer, last August, and Father had just beat Redmond for the State legislature. The railroad was finished now and the partnership between Father and Redmond had been dissolved so long ago that most people would have forgotten they were ever partners if it hadn't been for the enmity between them. There had been a third partner but nobody hardly remembered his name now; he and his name both had vanished in the fury of the conflict which set up between Father and Redmond almost before they began to lay the rails, between Father's violent and ruthless dictatorialness and will to dominate (the idea was his; he did think of the railroad first and then took Redmond in) and that quality in Redmond (as George Wyatt said, he was not a coward or Father would never have teamed with him) which permitted him to stand as much as he did from Father, to bear and bear and bear until something (not his will nor his courage) broke in him. During the War Redmond had not been a soldier, he had had something to do with cotton for the Government; he could have made money himself out of it but he had not and everybody knew he had not, Father knew it, yet Father would even taunt him with not having smelled powder. He was wrong; he knew he was when it was too late for him to stop just as a drunkard reaches a point where it is too late for him to stop, where he promises himself that he will and maybe believes he will or can but it is too late. Finally they reached the point (they had both put everything they could mortgage or borrow into it for Father to ride up and down the line, paying the workmen and the waybills on the rails at the last possible instant) where even Father realized that one of them would have to get out. So (they were not speaking then; it was arranged by Judge Benbow) they met and agreed to buy or sell, naming a price which, in reference to what they had put into it, was ridiculously low but which each believed the other could not raise—at least Father claimed that Redmond did not believe he could raise it. So Redmond accepted the price, and found out that Father had the money. And according to Father, that's what started it, although Uncle Buck McCaslin said Father could not have owned a half interest in even one hog, let alone a railroad, and not dissolve the business either sworn enemy or death-pledged friend to his recent partner. So they parted and Father finished the road. By that time, seeing that he was going to finish it, some Northern people sold him a locomotive on credit which he named for Aunt Jenny, with a silver oil can in the cab with her name engraved on it; and last summer the first train ran into Jefferson, the engine decorated with flowers and Father in the cab blowing blast after blast on the whistle when he passed Redmond's house; and there were speeches at the station, with more flowers and a Confederate flag and girls in white dresses and red sashes and a band, and Father stood on the pilot of the engine and made a direct and absolutely needless allusion to Mr. Redmond. That was it. He wouldn't let him alone. George Wyatt came to me right afterward and told me. "Right or wrong," he said, "us boys and most of the other folks in this county know John's right. But he ought to let Redmond alone. I know what's wrong: he's had to kill too many folks, and that's bad for a man. We all know Colonel's brave as a lion, but Redmond ain't no coward either and there ain't any use in making a brave man that made one mistake eat crow all the time. Can't you talk to him?"

"I don't know," I said. "I'll try." But I had no chance. That is, I could have talked to him and he would have listened, but he could not have heard me because he had stepped straight from the pilot of that engine into the race for the Legislature. Maybe he knew that Redmond would have to oppose him to save his face even though he (Redmond) must have known that, after that train ran into Jefferson, he had no chance against Father, or maybe Redmond had already announced his candidacy and Father entered the race just because of that, I don't remember. Anyway they ran, a bitter contest in which Father continued to badger Redmond without reason or need, since they both knew it would be a landslide for Father. And it was, and we thought he was satisfied. Maybe he thought so himself, as the drunkard believes that he is done with drink; and it was that afternoon and Drusilla and I walked in the garden in the twilight and I said something about what George Wyatt had told me and she released my arm and turned me to face her and said, "This from you? You? Have you forgotten Grumby?"

"No," I said. "I never will forget him."

"You never will. I wouldn't let you. There are worse things than killing men, Bayard. There are worse things than being killed. Sometimes I think the finest thing that can happen to a man is to love something, a woman preferably, well, hard hard hard, then to die young because he believed what he could not help but believe and was what he could not (could not? would not) help but be." Now she was looking at me in a way she never had before. I did not know what it meant then and was not to know until tonight since neither of us knew then that two months later Father would be dead. I just knew that she was looking at me as she never had before and that the scent of the verbena in her hair seemed to have increased a hundred times, to have got a hundred times stronger, to

be everywhere in the dusk in which something was about
to happen which I had never dreamed of. Then she spoke.
"Kiss me, Bayard."

"No. You are Father's wife."

"And eight years older than you are. And your fourth
cousin, too. And I have black hair. Kiss me, Bayard."

"No."

"Kiss me, Bayard." So I leaned my face down to her.
But she didn't move, standing so, bent lightly back from
me from the waist, looking at me; now it was she who said,
"No." So I put my arms around her. Then she came to me,
melted as women will and can, the arms with the wrist-
and elbow-power to control horses about my shoulders,
using the wrists to hold my face to hers until there was no
longer need for the wrists; I thought then of the woman
of thirty, the symbol of the ancient and eternal Snake
and of the men who have written of her, and I realized
then the immitigable chasm between all life and all print
—that those who can, do, those who cannot and suffer
enough because they can't, write about it. Then I was
free, I could see her again, I saw her still watching me
with that dark inscrutable look, looking up at me now
across her down-slanted face; I watched her arms rise with
almost the exact gesture with which she had put them
around me as if she were repeating the empty and formal
gesture of all promise so that I should never forget it, the
elbows angling outward as she put her hands to the sprig
of verbena in her hair, I standing straight and rigid facing
the slightly bent head, the short jagged hair, the rigid curiously formal angle of the bare arms gleaming faintly in the
last of light as she removed the verbena sprig and put it
into my lapel, and I thought how the War had tried to
stamp all the women of her generation and class in the
South into a type and how it had failed—the suffering, the
identical experience (hers and Aunt Jenny's had been almost the same except that Aunt Jenny had spent a few
nights with her husband before they brought him back

home in an ammunition wagon while Gavin Breckbridge
was just Drusilla's fiancé) was there in the eyes, yet beyond that was the incorrigibly individual woman: not like
so many men who return from wars to live on Government
reservations like so many steers, emasculate and empty of
all save an identical experience which they cannot forget
and dare not, else they would cease to live at that moment, almost interchangeable save for the old habit of
answering to a given name.

"Now I must tell Father," I said.

"Yes," she said. "You must tell him. Kiss me." So again
it was like it had been before. No. Twice, a thousand times
and never like—the eternal and symbolical thirty to a
young man, a youth, each time both cumulative and retro-
active, immitigably unrepetitive, each wherein remembering excludes experience, each wherein experience
antedates remembering; the skill without weariness, the
knowledge virginal to surfeit, the cunning secret muscles
to guide and control just as within the wrists and elbows
lay slumbering the mastery of horses: she stood back, already turning, not looking at me when she spoke, never
having looked at me, already moving swiftly on in the
dusk: "Tell John. Tell him tonight."

I intended to. I went to the house and into the office at
once; I went to the center of the rug before the cold
hearth, I don't know why, and stood there rigid like soldiers stand, looking at eye level straight across the room
and above his head and said "Father" and then stopped.
Because he did not even hear me. He said, "Yes, Bayard?"
but he did not hear me although he was sitting behind the
desk doing nothing, immobile, as still as I was rigid, one
hand on the desk with a dead cigar in it, a bottle of brandy
and a filled and untasted glass beside his hand, clothed
quiet and bemused in whatever triumph it was he felt
since the last overwhelming return of votes had come in
late in the afternoon. So I waited until after supper. We
went to the dining-room and stood side by side until Aunt

Jenny entered and then Drusilla, in the yellow ball gown, who walked straight to me and gave me one fierce inscrutable look then went to her place and waited for me to draw her chair while Father drew Aunt Jenny's. He had roused by then, not to talk himself but rather to sit at the head of the table and reply to Drusilla as she talked with a sort of feverish and glittering volubility—to reply now and then to her with that courteous intolerant pride which had lately become a little forensic, as if merely being in a political contest filled with fierce and empty oratory had retroactively made a lawyer of him who was anything and everything except a lawyer. Then Drusilla and Aunt Jenny rose and left us and he said, "Wait" to me who had made no move to follow and directed Joby to bring one of the bottles of wine which he had fetched back from New Orleans when he went there last to borrow money to liquidate his first private railroad bonds. Then I stood again like soldiers stand, gazing at eye level above his head while he sat half-turned from the table, a little paunchy now though not much, a little grizzled too in the hair though his beard was as strong as ever, with that spurious forensic air of lawyers and the intolerant eyes which in the last two years had acquired that transparent film which the eyes of carnivorous animals have and from behind which they look at a world which no ruminant ever sees, perhaps dares to see, which I have seen before on the eyes of men who have killed too much, who have killed so much that never again as long as they live will they ever be alone. I said again, "Father," then I told him.

"Hah?" he said. "Sit down." I sat down, I looked at him, watched him fill both glasses and this time I knew it was worse with him than not hearing: it didn't even matter. "You are doing well in the law, Judge Wilkins tells me. I am pleased to hear that. I have not needed you in my affairs so far, but from now on I shall. I have now accomplished the active portion of my aims in which you could not have helped me; I acted as the land and the time de-

manded and you were too young for that, I wished to
shield you. But now the land and the time too are changing; what will follow will be a matter of consolidation, of
pettifogging and doubtless chicanery in which I would be
a babe in arms but in which you, trained in the law, can
hold your own—our own. Yes. I have accomplished my
aim, and now I shall do a little moral housecleaning. I am
tired of killing men, no matter what the necessity or the
end. Tomorrow, when I go to town and meet Ben Redmond, I shall be unarmed."

III

We reached home just before midnight; we didn't have
to pass through Jefferson either. Before we turned in the
gates I could see the lights, the chandeliers—hall, parlor,
and what Aunt Jenny (without any effort or perhaps even
design on her part) had taught even Ringo to call the
drawing room, the light falling outward across the portico,
past the columns. Then I saw the horses, the faint shine of
leather and buckle-glints on the black silhouettes and then
the men too—Wyatt and others of Father's old troop—
and I had forgot that they would be there. I had forgot
that they would be there; I remember how I thought,
since I was tired and spent with strain, *Now it will have to
begin tonight. I won't even have until tomorrow in which
to begin to resist.* They had a watchman, a picquet out,
I suppose, because they seemed to know at once that we
were in the drive. Wyatt met me, I halted the mare, I
could look down at him and at the others gathered a few
yards behind him with that curious vulture-like formality
which Southern men assume in such situations.

"Well, boy," George said.

"Was it—" I said. "Was he——"

"It was all right. It was in front. Redmond ain't no coward. John had the derringer inside his cuff like always, but
he never touched it, never made a move toward it." I

have seen him do it, he showed me once: the pistol (it was not four inches long) held flat inside his left wrist by a clip he made himself of wire and an old clock spring; he would raise both hands at the same time, cross them, fire the pistol from beneath his left hand almost as if he were hiding from his own vision what he was doing; when he killed one of the men he shot a hole through his own coat sleeve. "But you want to get on to the house," Wyatt said. He began to stand aside, then he spoke again: "We'll take this off your hands, any of us. Me." I hadn't moved the mare yet and I had made no move to speak, yet he continued quickly, as if he had already rehearsed all this, his speech and mine, and knew what I would say and only spoke himself as he would have removed his hat on entering a house or used "sir" in conversing with a stranger: "You're young, just a boy, you ain't had any experience in this kind of thing. Besides, you got them two ladies in the house to think about. He would understand, all right."

"I reckon I can attend to it," I said.

"Sure," he said; there was no surprise, nothing at all, in his voice because he had already rehearsed this: "I reckon we all knew that's what you would say." He stepped back then; almost it was as though he and not I bade the mare to move on. But they all followed, still with that unctuous and voracious formality. Then I saw Drusilla standing at the top of the front steps, in the light from the open door and the windows like a theatre scene, in the yellow ball gown and even from here I believed that I could smell the verbena in her hair, standing there motionless yet emanating something louder than the two shots must have been—something voracious too and passionate. Then, although I had dismounted and someone had taken the mare, I seemed to be still in the saddle and to watch myself enter that scene which she had postulated like another actor while in the background for chorus Wyatt and the others stood with the unctuous formality which the Southern man shows in the presence of death—that Roman holiday engendered by mist-born Protestantism grafted onto this land of violent sun, of violent alteration from snow to heat-stroke which has produced a race impervious to both. I mounted the steps toward the figure straight and yellow and immobile as a candle which moved only to extend one hand; we stood together and looked down at them where they stood clumped, the horses too gathered in a tight group beyond them at the rim of light from the brilliant door and windows. One of them stamped and blew his breath and jangled his gear.

"Thank you, gentlemen," I said. "My aunt and my— Drusilla thank you. There's no need for you to stay. Good night." They murmured, turning. George Wyatt paused, looking back at me.

"Tomorrow?" he said.

"Tomorrow." Then they went on, carrying their hats and tiptoeing, even on the ground, the quiet and resilient earth, as though anyone in that house awake would try to sleep, anyone already asleep in it whom they could have wakened. Then they were gone and Drusilla and I turned and crossed the portico, her hand lying light on my wrist yet discharging into me with a shock like electricity that dark and passionate voracity, the face at my shoulder— the jagged hair with a verbena sprig above each ear, the eyes staring at me with that fierce exaltation. We entered the hall and crossed it, her hand guiding me without pressure, and entered the parlor. Then for the first time I realized it—the alteration which is death—not that he was now just clay but that he was lying down. But I didn't look at him yet because I knew that when I did I would begin to pant; I went to Aunt Jenny who had just risen from a chair behind which Louvinia stood. She was Father's sister, taller than Drusilla but no older, whose husband had been killed at the very beginning of the War, by a shell from a Federal frigate at Fort Moultrie, come to us from Carolina six years ago. Ringo and I went to Tennessee Junction in the wagon to meet her. It was January, cold and clear and with ice in the ruts; we returned just before dark with Aunt Jenny on the seat beside me holding a lace parasol and Ringo in the wagon bed nursing a hamper basket containing two bottles of old sherry and the two jasmine cuttings which were bushes in the garden now, and the panes of colored glass which she had salvaged from the Carolina house where she and Father and Uncle Bayard were born and which Father had set in a fanlight about one of the drawing room windows for her—who came up the drive and Father (home now from the railroad) went down the steps and lifted her from the wagon and said, "Well, Jenny," and she said, "Well, Johnny," and began to cry. She stood too, looking at me as I approached—the same hair, the same high nose, the same eyes as Father's except that they were intent and very wise instead of intolerant. She said nothing at all, she just kissed me, her hands light on my shoulders. Then Drusilla spoke, as if she had been waiting with a sort of dreadful patience for the empty ceremony to be done, in a voice like a bell: clear, unsentient, on a single pitch, silvery and triumphant: "Come, Bayard."

"Hadn't you better go to bed now?" Aunt Jenny said.

"Yes," Drusilla said in that silvery ecstatic voice, "Oh yes. There will be plenty of time for sleep." I followed her, her hand again guiding me without pressure; now I looked at him. It was just as I had imagined it—sabre, plumes, and all—but with that alteration, that irrevocable difference which I had known to expect yet had not realized, as you can put food into your stomach which for a while the stomach declines to assimilate—the illimitable grief and regret as I looked down at the face which I knew—the nose, the hair, the eyelids closed over the intolerance—the face which I realized I now saw in repose for the first time in my life; the empty hands still now beneath the invisible stain of what had been (once, surely) needless blood, the hands now appearing clumsy in their very inertness, too clumsy to have performed the fatal ac-

tions which forever afterward he must have waked and
slept with and maybe was glad to lay down at last—those
curious appendages clumsily conceived to begin with yet
with which man has taught himself to do so much, so
much more than they were intended to do or could be forgiven for doing, which had now surrendered that life to
which his intolerant heart had fiercely held; and then I
knew that in a minute I would begin to pant. So Drusilla
must have spoken twice before I heard her and turned and
saw in the instant Aunt Jenny and Louvinia watching us,
hearing Drusilla now, the unsentient bell quality gone
now, her voice whispering into that quiet death-filled
room with a passionate and dying fall: "Bayard." She
faced me, she was quite near; again the scent of the verbena in her hair seemed to have increased a hundred times
as she stood holding out to me, one in either hand, the two
duelling pistols. "Take them, Bayard," she said, in the
same tone in which she had said "Kiss me" last summer,
already pressing them into my hands, watching me with
that passionate and voracious exaltation, speaking in a
voice fainting and passionate with promise: "Take them.
I have kept them for you. I give them to you. Oh you will
thank me, you will remember me who put into your hands
what they say is an attribute only of God's, who took what
belongs to heaven and gave it to you. Do you feel them?
the long true barrels true as justice, the triggers (you have
fired them) quick as retribution, the two of them slender
and invincible and fatal as the physical shape of love?"
Again I watched her arms angle out and upward as she
removed the two verbena sprigs from her hair in two motions faster than the eye could follow, already putting one
of them into my lapel and crushing the other in her other
hand while she still spoke in that rapid passionate voice
not much louder than a whisper: "There. One I give to
you to wear tomorrow (it will not fade), the other I cast
away, like this—" dropping the crushed bloom at her feet.
"I abjure it. I abjure verbena forever more; I have smelled

it above the odor of courage; that was all I wanted. Now let me look at you." She stood back, staring at me—the face tearless and exalted, the feverish eyes brilliant and voracious. "How beautiful you are: do you know it? How beautiful: young, to be permitted to kill, to be permitted vengeance, to take into your bare hands the fire of heaven that cast down Lucifer. No; I. I gave it to you; I put it into your hands; Oh you will thank me, you will remember me when I am dead and you are an old man saying to himself, 'I have tasted all things.'—It will be the right hand, won't it?" She moved; she had taken my right hand which still held one of the pistols before I knew what she was about to do; she had bent and kissed it before I comprehended why she took it. Then she stopped dead still, still stooping in that attitude of fierce exultant humility, her hot lips and her hot hands still touching my flesh, light on my flesh as dead leaves yet communicating to it that battery charge, dark, passionate, and damned forever of all peace. Because they are wise, women are—a touch, lips or fingers, and the knowledge, even clairvoyance, goes straight to the heart without bothering the laggard brain at all. She stood erect now, staring at me with intolerable and amazed incredulity which occupied her face alone for a whole minute while her eyes were completely empty; it seemed to me that I stood there for a full minute while Aunt Jenny and Louvinia watched us, waiting for her eyes to fill. There was no blood in her face at all, her mouth open a little and pale as one of those rubber rings women seal fruit jars with. Then her eyes filled with an expression of bitter and passionate betrayal. "Why, he's not—" she said. "He's not— And I kissed his hand," she said in an aghast whisper; *"I kissed his hand!"* beginning to laugh, the laughter rising, becoming a scream yet still remaining laughter, screaming with laughter, trying herself to deaden the sound by putting her hand over her mouth, the laughter spilling between her fingers like vomit, the incredulous betrayed eyes still watching me across the hand.

"Louvinia!" Aunt Jenny said. They both came to her. Louvinia touched and held her and Drusilla turned her face to Louvinia.

"I kissed his hand, Louvinia!" she cried. "Did you see it? *I kissed his hand!*" the laughter rising again, becoming the scream again yet still remaining laughter, she still trying to hold it back with her hand like a small child who has filled its mouth too full.

"Take her upstairs," Aunt Jenny said. But they were already moving toward the door, Louvinia half-carrying Drusilla, the laughter diminishing as they neared the door as though it waited for the larger space of the empty and brilliant hall to rise again. Then it was gone; Aunt Jenny and I stood there and I knew soon that I would begin to pant. I could feel it beginning like you feel regurgitation beginning, as though there were not enough air in the room, the house, not enough air anywhere under the heavy hot low sky where the equinox couldn't seem to accomplish, nothing in the air for breathing, for the lungs. Now it was Aunt Jenny who said, "Bayard," twice before I heard her. "You are not going to try to kill him. All right."

"All right?" I said.

"Yes. All right. Don't let it be Drusilla, a poor hysterical young woman. And don't let it be him, Bayard, because he's dead now. And don't let it be George Wyatt and those others who will be waiting for you tomorrow morning. I know you are not afraid."

"But what good will that do?" I said. "What good will that do?" It almost began then; I stopped it just in time. "I must live with myself, you see."

"Then it's not just Drusilla? Not just him? Not just George Wyatt and Jefferson?"

"No," I said.

"Will you promise to let me see you before you go to town tomorrow?" I looked at her; we looked at one another for a moment. Then she put her hands on my shoulders and kissed me and released me, all in one motion. "Good night, son," she said. Then she was gone too and now it could begin. I knew that in a minute I would look at him and it would begin and I did look at him, feeling the long-held breath, the hiatus before it started, thinking how maybe I should have said, "Good-bye, Father," but did not. Instead I crossed to the piano and laid the pistols carefully on it, still keeping the panting from getting too loud too soon. Then I was outside on the porch and (I don't know how long it had been) I looked in the window and saw Simon squatting on a stool beside him. Simon had been his body servant during the War and when they came home Simon had a uniform too—a Confederate private's coat with a Yankee brigadier's star on it and he had put it on now, too, like they had dressed Father, squatting on the stool beside him, not crying, not weeping the facile tears which are the white man's futile trait and which Negroes know nothing about but just sitting there, motionless, his lower lip slacked down a little; he raised his hand and touched the coffin, the black hand rigid and fragile-looking as a clutch of dead twigs, then dropped the hand; once he turned his head and I saw his eyes roll red and unwinking in his skull like those of a cornered fox. It had begun by that time; I panted, standing there, and this was it—the regret and grief, the despair out of which the tragic mute insensitive bones stand up that can bear anything, anything.

IV

After a while the whippoorwills stopped and I heard the first day bird, a mockingbird. It had sung all night too but now it was the day song, no longer the drowsy moony fluting. Then they all began—the sparrows from the stable, the thrush that lived in Aunt Jenny's garden, and I heard a quail too from the pasture and now there was light in the room. But I didn't move at once. I still lay on the bed (I hadn't undressed) with my hands under my head and the scent of Drusilla's verbena faint from where my coat lay on a chair, watching the light grow, watching it turn rosy with the sun. After a while I heard Louvinia come up across the back yard and go into the kitchen; I heard the door and then the long crash of her armful of stovewood into the box. Soon they would begin to arrive—the carriages and buggies in the drive— but not for a while yet because they too would wait first to see what I was going to do. So the house was quiet when I went down to the dining-room, no sound in it except Simon snoring in the parlor, probably still sitting on the stool though I didn't look in to see. Instead I stood at the dining-room window and drank the coffee which Louvinia brought me, then I went to the stable; I saw Joby watching me from the kitchen door as I crossed the yard and in the stable Loosh looked up at me across Betsy's head, a curry comb in his hand, though Ringo didn't look at me at all. We curried Jupiter then. I didn't know if we would be able to without trouble or not, since always Father would come in first and touch him and tell him to stand and he would stand like a marble horse (or pale bronze rather) while Loosh curried him. But he stood for me too, a little restive but he stood, then that was done and now it was almost nine o'clock and soon they would begin to arrive and I told Ringo to bring Betsy on to the house.

I went on to the house and into the hall. I had not had to pant in some time now but it was there, waiting, a part of the alteration, as though by being dead and no longer needing air he had taken all of it, all that he had compassed and claimed and postulated between the walls which he had built, along with him. Aunt Jenny must have been waiting; she came out of the dining-room at once, without a sound, dressed, the hair that was like Father's combed and smooth above the eyes that were different from Father's eyes because they were not intolerant but just intent and grave and (she was wise too) without pity. "Are you going now?" she said.

"Yes." I looked at her. Yes, thank God, without pity. "You see, I want to be thought well of."

"I do," she said. "Even if you spend the day hidden in the stable loft, I still do."

"Maybe if she knew that I was going. Was going to town anyway."

"No," she said. "No, Bayard." We looked at one another. Then she said quietly, "All right. She's awake." So I mounted the stairs. I mounted steadily, not fast because if I had gone fast the panting would have started again or I might have had to slow for a second at the turn or at the top and I would not have gone on. So I went slowly and steadily, across the hall to her door and knocked and opened it. She was sitting at the window, in something soft and loose for morning in her bedroom, only she never did look like morning in a bedroom because there was no hair to fall about her shoulders. She looked up, she sat there looking at me with her feverish brilliant eyes and I remembered I still had the verbena sprig in my lapel and suddenly she began to laugh again. It seemed to come not from her mouth but to burst out all over her face like sweat does and with a dreadful and painful convulsion as when you have vomited until it hurts you yet still you must vomit again—burst out all over her face except her eyes, the brilliant, incredulous eyes looking at me out of the laughter as if they belonged to somebody else, as if they were two inert fragments of tar or coal lying on the bottom of a receptacle filled with turmoil: "I kissed his hand! *I kissed his hand!*" Louvinia entered, Aunt Jenny must have sent her directly after me; again I walked slowly and steadily so it would not start yet, down the stairs where Aunt Jenny stood beneath the chandelier in the hall as Mrs. Wilkins had stood yesterday at the University. She had my hat in her hand. "Even if you hid all day in the stable, Bayard," she said. I took the hat; she said quietly, pleasantly, as if she were talking to a stranger, a guest: "I used to see a lot of blockade runners in Charleston. They were heroes in a way, you see—not heroes because they were helping to prolong the Confederacy but heroes in the sense that David Crockett or John Sevier would have been to small boys or fool young women. There was one of them, an Englishman. He had no business there; it was the money of course, as with all of them. But he was the Davy Crockett to us because by that time we had all forgot what money was, what you could do with it. He must have been a gentleman once or associated with gentlemen before he changed his name, and he had a vocabulary of seven words, though I must admit he got along quite well with them. The first four were, 'I'll have rum, thanks,' and then, when he had the rum, he would use the other three—across the champagne, to whatever ruffled bosom or low gown: 'No bloody moon.' No bloody moon, Bayard."

Ringo was waiting with Betsy at the front steps. Again he did not look at me, his face sullen, downcast even while he handed me the reins. But he said nothing, nor did I look back. And sure enough I was just in time; I passed the Compson carriage at the gates, General Compson lifted his hat as I did mine as we passed. It was four miles to town but I had not gone two of them when I heard the horse coming up behind me and I did not look back because I knew it was Ringo. I did not look back; he came up on one of the carriage horses, he rode up beside me and looked me full in the face for one moment, the sullen determined face, the eyes rolling at me defiant and momentary and red; we rode on. Now we were in town—the long shady street leading to the square, the new courthouse at the end of it; it was eleven o'clock now: long past breakfast and not yet noon so there were only women on the street, not to recognize me perhaps, or at least not the walking stopped sudden and dead in midwalking as if the legs contained the sudden eyes, the caught breath, that not to begin until we reached the square, and I thinking *If I could only be invisible until I reach the stairs to his office and begin to mount.* But I could not, I was not; we rode up to the Holston House and I saw the row of feet along the gallery rail come suddenly and quietly down and I did not look at them; I stopped Betsy and waited until Ringo was down; then I dismounted and gave him the reins. "Wait for me here," I said.

"I'm going with you," he said, not loud; we stood there under the still circumspect eyes and spoke quietly to one another like two conspirators. Then I saw the pistol, the outline of it inside his shirt, probably the one we had taken from Grumby that day we killed him.

"No you ain't," I said.

"Yes I am."

"No you ain't." So I walked on, along the street in the hot sun. It was almost noon now and I could smell nothing except the verbena in my coat, as if it had gathered all the sun, all the suspended fierce heat in which the equinox could not seem to occur and were distilling it, so that I moved in a cloud of verbena as I might have moved in a cloud of smoke from a cigar. Then George Wyatt was beside me (I don't know where he came from) and five or six others of Father's old troop a few yards behind, George's hand on my arm, drawing me into a doorway out of the avid eyes like caught breaths.

"Have you got that derringer?" George said.

"No," I said.

"Good," George said. "They are tricky things to fool with. Couldn't nobody but Colonel ever handle one right; I never could. So you take this. I tried it this morning and I know it's right. Here." He was already fumbling the pistol into my pocket, then the same thing seemed to happen to him that happened to Drusilla last night when she kissed my hand—something communicated by touch straight to the simple code by which he lived, without going through the brain at all: so that he too stood suddenly back, the pistol in his hand, staring at me with his pale outraged eyes and speaking in a whisper thin with fury: "Who are you? Is your name Sartoris? By God, if you don't kill him, I'm going to." Now it was not panting, it was a terrible desire to laugh, to laugh as Drusilla had, and say, "That's what Drusilla said." But I didn't. I said,

"I'm tending to this. You stay out of it. I don't need any help." Then his fierce eyes faded gradually, exactly as you turn a lamp down.

"Well," he said, putting the pistol back into his pocket. "You'll have to excuse me, son. I should have knowed you wouldn't do anything that would keep John from laying quiet. We'll follow you and wait at the foot of the steps. And remember: he's a brave man, but he's been sitting in that office by himself since yesterday morning waiting for you and his nerves are on edge."

"I'll remember," I said. "I don't need any help." I had started on when suddenly I said it without having any warning that I was going to: "No bloody moon."

"What?" he said. I didn't answer. I went on across the square itself now, in the hot sun, they following though not close so that I never saw them again until afterward, surrounded by the remote still eyes not following me yet either, just stopped where they were before the stores and about the door to the courthouse, waiting. I walked steadily on enclosed in the now fierce odor of the verbena sprig. Then shadow fell upon me; I did not pause, I looked once at the small faded sign nailed to the brick *B. J. Redmond. Atty at Law* and began to mount the stairs, the wooden steps scuffed by the heavy bewildered boots of countrymen approaching litigation and stained by tobacco spit, on down the dim corridor to the door which bore the name again, *B. J. Redmond* and knocked once and opened it. He sat behind the desk, not much taller than Father but thicker as a man gets who spends most of his time sitting and listening to people, freshly shaven and with fresh linen; a lawyer yet it was not a lawyer's face—a face much thinner than the body would indicate, strained (and yes, tragic; I know that now) and exhausted beneath the neat recent steady strokes of the razor, holding a pistol flat on the desk before him, loose beneath his hand and aimed at nothing. There was no smell of drink, not even of tobacco in the neat clean dingy room although I knew he smoked. I didn't pause. I walked steadily toward him. It was not twenty feet from door to desk yet I seemed to walk in a dreamlike state in which there was neither time nor distance, as though the mere act of walking was no more intended to encompass space than was his sitting. We didn't speak. It was as if we both knew what the passage of words would be and the futility of it; how he might have said, "Go out, Bayard. Go away, boy" and then, "Draw then. I will allow you to draw" and it would have been the same as if he had never said it. So we did not speak; I just walked steadily toward him as the pistol rose from the desk. I watched it, I could see the foreshortened slant of the barrel and I knew it would miss me though his hand did not tremble. I walked toward him, toward the pistol in the rocklike hand, I heard no bullet. Maybe I didn't even hear the explosion though I remember the sudden orange bloom and smoke as they appeared against his white shirt as they had appeared against Grumby's greasy Confederate coat; I still watched that foreshortened slant of barrel which I knew was not aimed at me and saw the second orange flash and smoke and heard no bullet that time either. Then I stopped; it was done then. I watched the pistol descend to the desk in short jerks; I saw him release it and sit back, both hands on the desk, I looked at his face and I knew too what it was to want air when there was nothing in the circumambience for the lungs. He rose, shoved the chair back with a convulsive motion and rose, with a queer ducking motion of his head; with his head still ducked aside and one arm extended as though he couldn't see and the other hand resting on the desk as if he couldn't stand alone, he turned and crossed to the wall and took his hat from the rack and with his head still ducked aside and one hand extended he blundered along the wall and passed me and reached the door and went through it. He was brave; no one denied that. He walked down those stairs and out onto the street where George Wyatt and the other six of Father's old troop waited and where the other men had begun to run now; he walked through the middle of them with his hat on and his head up (they told me how someone shouted at him: "Have you killed that boy too?"), saying no word, staring straight ahead and with his back to them, on to the station where the south-bound train was just in and got on it with no baggage, nothing, and went away from Jefferson and from Mississippi and never came back.

I heard their feet on the stairs then in the corridor then in the room, but for a while yet (it wasn't that long, of course) I still sat behind the desk as he had sat, the flat of the pistol still warm under my hand, my hand growing slowly numb between the pistol and my forehead. Then I raised my head; the little room was full of men. "My God!" George Wyatt cried. "You took the pistol away from him and then missed him, missed him *twice?*" Then he answered himself—that same rapport for violence which Drusilla had and which in George's case was actual character judgment: "No; wait. You walked in here without even a pocket knife and let him miss you twice. My God in heaven." He turned, shouting: "Get to hell out of here! You, White, ride out to Sartoris and tell his folks it's all over and he's all right. Ride!" So they departed, went away; presently only George was left, watching me with that pale bleak stare which was speculative yet not at all ratiocinative. "Well by God," he said. "—Do you want a drink?"

"No," I said. "I'm hungry. I didn't eat any breakfast."

"I reckon not, if you got up this morning aiming to do what you did. Come on. We'll go to the Holston House."

"No," I said. "No. Not there."

"Why not? You ain't done anything to be ashamed of. I wouldn't have done it that way, myself. I'd a shot at him once, anyway. But that's your way or you wouldn't have done it."

"Yes," I said. "I would do it again."

"Be damned if I would.—You want to come home with me? We'll have time to eat and then ride out there in time for the——" But I couldn't do that either.

"No," I said. "I'm not hungry after all. I think I'll go home."

"Don't you want to wait and ride out with me?"

"No. I'll go on."

"You don't want to stay here, anyway." He looked around the room again, where the smell of powder smoke still lingered a little, still lay somewhere on the hot dead air though invisible now, blinking a little with his fierce pale unintroverted eyes. "Well by God," he said again. "Maybe you're right, maybe there has been enough killing in your family without— Come on." We left the office. I waited at the foot of the stairs and soon Ringo came up with the horses. We crossed the square again. There were no feet on the Holston House railing now (it was twelve o'clock) but a group of men stood before the door who raised their hats and I raised mine and Ringo and I rode on.

We did not go fast. Soon it was one, maybe after; the carriages and buggies would begin to leave the square soon, so I turned from the road at the end of the pasture and I sat the mare, trying to open the gate without dismounting, until Ringo dismounted and opened it. We crossed the pasture in the hard fierce sun; I could have seen the house now but I didn't look. Then we were in the shade, the close thick airless shade of the creek bottom; the old rails still lay in the undergrowth where we had built the pen to hide the Yankee mules. Presently I heard the water, then I could see the sunny glints. We dismounted. I lay on my back, I thought *Now it can begin again if it wants to.* But it did not. I went to sleep. I went to sleep almost before I had stopped thinking. I slept for almost five hours and I didn't dream anything at all yet I waked myself up crying, crying too hard to stop it. Ringo was squatting beside me and the sun was gone though there was a bird of some sort still singing somewhere and the whistle of the north-bound evening train sounded and the short broken puffs of starting where it had evidently stopped at our flag station. After a while I began to stop and Ringo brought his hat full of water from the creek but instead I went down to the water myself and bathed my face.

There was still a good deal of light in the pasture, though the whippoorwills had begun, and when we reached the house there was a mockingbird singing in the magnolia, the night song now, the drowsy moony one, and again the moon like the rim print of a heel in wet sand. There was just one light in the hall now and so it was all over though I could still smell the flowers even above the verbena in my coat. I had not looked at him again. I had started to before I left the house but I did not, I did not see him again and all the pictures we had of him were bad ones because a picture could no more have held him dead than the house could have kept his body. But I didn't need to see him again because he was there, he would always be there; maybe what Drusilla meant by his dream was not something which he possessed but something which he had bequeathed us which we could never forget, which would even assume the corporeal shape of him whenever any of us, black or white, closed our eyes. I went into the house. There was no light in the drawing room except the last of the afterglow which came through the western window where Aunt Jenny's colored glass was; I was about to go on upstairs when I saw her sitting there beside the window. She didn't call me and I didn't speak Drusilla's name, I just went to the door and stood there. "She's gone," Aunt Jenny said. "She took the evening train. She has gone to Montgomery, to Dennison." Denny had been married about a year now; he was living in Montgomery, reading law.

"I see," I said. "Then she didn't——" But there wasn't any use in that either; Jed White must have got there before one o'clock and told them. And besides, Aunt Jenny didn't answer. She could have lied to me but she didn't, she said,

"Come here." I went to her chair. "Kneel down. I can't see you."

"Don't you want the lamp?"

"No. Kneel down." So I knelt beside the chair. "So you had a perfectly splendid Saturday afternoon, didn't you? Tell me about it." Then she put her hands on my shoulders. I watched them come up as though she were trying to stop them; I felt them on my shoulders as if they had a separate life of their own and were trying to do something which for my sake she was trying to restrain, prevent. Then she gave up or she was not strong enough because they came up and took my face between them, hard, and suddenly the tears sprang and streamed down her face like Drusilla's laughing had. "Oh, damn you Sartorises!" she said. "Damn you! Damn you!"

As I passed down the hall the light came up in the dining-room and I could hear Louvinia laying the table for supper. So the stairs were lighted quite well. But the upper hall was dark. I saw her open door (that unmistakable way in which an open door stands open when nobody lives in the room any more) and I realized I had not believed that she was really gone. So I didn't look into the room. I went on to mine and entered. And then for a long moment I thought it was the verbena in my lapel which I still smelled. I thought that until I had crossed the room and looked down at the pillow on which it lay—the single sprig of it (without looking she would pinch off a half dozen of them and they would be all of a size, almost all of a shape, as if a machine had stamped them out) filling the room, the dusk, the evening with that odor which she said you could smell alone above the smell of horses.

3

THE LAST WILDERNESS

Editor's Note

The county built a marble monument to Colonel Sartoris; it stands on the highest site in the Jefferson cemetery, overlooking the railroad he built. Drusilla disappeared from the family records. Young Bayard Sartoris lost control of his father's railroad, but he founded a bank in Jefferson and was its president during the rest of his long life. Years afterward, with the death of Major Cassius de Spain, he became the county's leading citizen.

Major de Spain, as a result of tax sales and mortgage foreclosures, had acquired most of the hundred square miles that Colonel Sutpen once owned. He remodeled the shack where Wash Jones had died into a hunting lodge; and there, late every fall, he used to entertain a group of his friends, including General Compson and McCaslin Edmonds and young Isaac McCaslin, the son of Uncle Buck and Miss Sophonsiba. Sam Fathers was their guide through the wild lands in the Tallahatchie River bottom. It was on the north bank of the river that Boon Hogganbeck, who also had Chickasaw ancestors, finally killed Old Ben, the enormous bear with the mutilated paw.

"The Bear" appeared as a chapter of *Go Down, Moses* after being reworked in a masterly fashion from two magazine stories. The chapter, here reprinted, is divided into five sections. Those who would like to read what is first of all a hunting story—or better, a story of the chase, with overtones that make it one of the greatest in the language —should confine themselves to the first three sections and the last, which are written in the author's simplest manner. It is the long fourth section that creates difficulties for the reader, partly because of its complicated style, but chiefly because it deals with the general theme of *Go Down, Moses*—which is the relation between the white and the black descendants of old Carothers McCaslin— rather than with the yearly pursuit of Old Ben. Faulkner himself omitted the section when he reprinted "The Bear" as part of his book about the wilderness—*Big Woods* (1955)—and the result was a more unified story. Strangely, however, it had lost some of the haunting power that it possesses in the longer version.

It is in the fourth section that Faulkner carries to an extreme his effort toward putting the whole world into one sentence, holding it suspended between one capital letter and one period. There is a sentence that occupies six pages of the present volume (259-265), with a two-page parenthesis in the middle. Containing several paragraphs, each of which begins with a small letter, and a quantity of quoted matter, it runs to more than eighteen hundred words, and it was quite probably—until Faulkner himself exceeded that length in a sentence of "The Jail" (1951)— the longest in American fiction. In all this section of "The Bear," the reader may have difficulty in fitting the subjects to the predicates and in disentangling the subordinate clauses—let alone in tracing the genealogy of the McCaslin family—and yet, if he perseveres, he will discover one of Faulkner's most impressive themes: the belief in Isaac McCaslin's heart that the land itself has been cursed by slavery, and that the only way for him to escape the curse is to relinquish the land.

1883

The Bear

I

There was a man and a dog too this time. Two beasts, counting Old Ben, the bear, and two men, counting Boon Hogganbeck, in whom some of the same blood ran which ran in Sam Fathers, even though Boon's was a plebeian strain of it and only Sam and Old Ben and the mongrel Lion were taintless and incorruptible.

Isaac McCaslin was sixteen. For six years now he had been a man's hunter. For six years now he had heard the best of all talking. It was of the wilderness, the big woods, bigger and older than any recorded document— of white man fatuous enough to believe he had bought any fragment of it, of Indian ruthless enough to pretend that any fragment of it had been his to convey; bigger than Major de Spain and the scrap he pretended to, knowing better; older than old Thomas Sutpen of whom Major de Spain had had it and who knew better; older even than old Ikkemotubbe, the Chickasaw chief, of whom old Sutpen had had it and who knew better in his turn. It was of the men, not white nor black nor red, but men, hunters, with the will and hardihood to endure and the humility and skill to survive, and the dogs and the bear and deer juxtaposed and reliefed against it, ordered and compelled by and within the wilderness in the ancient and unremitting contest according to the ancient and immitigable rules which voided all regrets and brooked no quarter;—the

best game of all, the best of all breathing and forever the
best of all listening, the voices quiet and weighty and deliberate for retrospection and recollection and exactitude
among the concrete trophies—the racked guns and the
heads and skins—in the libraries of town houses or the
offices of plantation houses or (and best of all) in the
camps themselves where the intact and still-warm meat
yet hung, the men who had slain it sitting before the burning logs on hearths, when there were houses and hearths,
or about the smoky blazing of piled wood in front of
stretched tarpaulins when there were not. There was always a bottle present, so that it would seem to him that
those fine fierce instants of heart and brain and courage
and wiliness and speed were concentrated and distilled
into that brown liquor which not women, not boys and
children, but only hunters drank, drinking not of the blood
they spilled but some condensation of the wild immortal
spirit, drinking it moderately, humbly even, not with the
pagan's base and baseless hope of acquiring thereby the
virtues of cunning and strength and speed but in salute to
them. Thus it seemed to him on this December morning
not only natural but actually fitting that this should have
begun with whiskey.

He realized later that it had begun long before that. It
had already begun on that day when he first wrote his age
in two ciphers and his cousin McCaslin brought him for
the first time to the camp, the big woods, to earn for himself from the wilderness the name and state of hunter provided he in his turn were humble and enduring enough.
He had already inherited then, without ever having seen
it, the big old bear with one trap-ruined foot that in an
area almost a hundred miles square had earned for himself a name, a definite designation like a living man:—the
long legend of corncribs broken down and rifled, of shoats
and grown pigs and even calves carried bodily into the
woods and devoured, and traps and deadfalls overthrown
and dogs mangled and slain, and shotgun and even rifle

shots delivered at point-blank range yet with no more effect than so many peas blown through a tube by a child —a corridor of wreckage and destruction beginning back before the boy was born, through which sped, not fast but rather with the ruthless and irresistible deliberation of a locomotive, the shaggy tremendous shape. It ran in his knowledge before he ever saw it. It loomed and towered in his dreams before he even saw the unaxed woods where it left its crooked print, shaggy, tremendous, red-eyed, not malevolent but just big, too big for the dogs which tried to bay it, for the horses which tried to ride it down, for the men and the bullets they fired into it; too big for the very country which was its constricting scope. It was as if the boy had already divined what his senses and intellect had not encompassed yet: that doomed wilderness whose edges were being constantly and punily gnawed at by men with plows and axes who feared it because it was wilderness, men myriad and nameless even to one another in the land where the old bear had earned a name, and through which ran not even a mortal beast but an anachronism indomitable and invincible out of an old, dead time, a phantom, epitome and apotheosis of the old, wild life which the little puny humans swarmed and hacked at in a fury of abhorrence and fear, like pygmies about the ankles of a drowsing elephant;—the old bear, solitary, indomitable, and alone; widowered, childless, and absolved of mortality—old Priam reft of his old wife and outlived all his sons.

Still a child, with three years, then two years, then one year yet before he too could make one of them, each November he would watch the wagon containing the dogs and the bedding and food and guns and his cousin Mc-Caslin and Tennie's Jim and Sam Fathers too, until Sam moved to the camp to live, depart for the Big Bottom, the big woods. To him, they were going not to hunt bear and deer but to keep yearly rendezvous with the bear which they did not even intend to kill. Two weeks later they would return, with no trophy, no skin. He had not expected it. He had not even feared that it might be in the wagon this time with the other skins and heads. He did not even tell himself that in three years or two years or one year more he would be present and that it might even be his gun. He believed that only after he had served his apprenticeship in the woods which would prove him worthy to be a hunter, would he even be permitted to distinguish the crooked print, and that even then for two November weeks he would merely make another minor one, along with his cousin and Major de Spain and General Compson and Walter Ewell and Boon and the dogs which feared to bay it, and the shotguns and rifles which failed even to bleed it, in the yearly pageant-rite of the old bear's furious immortality.

His day came at last. In the surrey with his cousin and Major de Spain and General Compson he saw the wilderness through a slow drizzle of November rain just above the ice point, as it seemed to him later he always saw it or at least always remembered it—the tall and endless wall of dense November woods under the dissolving afternoon and the year's death, sombre, impenetrable (he could not even discern yet how, at what point they could possibly hope to enter it even though he knew that Sam Fathers was waiting there with the wagon), the surrey moving through the skeleton stalks of cotton and corn in the last of open country, the last trace of man's puny gnawing at the immemorial flank, until, dwarfed by that perspective into an almost ridiculous diminishment, the surrey itself seemed to have ceased to move (this too to be completed later, years later, after he had grown to a man and had seen the sea) as a solitary small boat hangs in lonely immobility, merely tossing up and down, in the infinite waste of the ocean, while the water and then the apparently impenetrable land which it nears without appreciable progress, swings slowly and opens the widening inlet which is the anchorage. He entered it. Sam was waiting, wrapped in a quilt on the wagon seat behind the patient and steaming mules. He entered his novitiate to the true wilderness with Sam beside him as he had begun his apprenticeship in miniature to manhood after the rabbits and such with Sam beside him, the two of them wrapped in the damp, warm, Negro-rank quilt, while the wilderness closed behind his entrance as it had opened momentarily to accept him, opening before his advancement as it closed behind his progress, no fixed path the wagon followed but a channel nonexistent ten yards ahead of it and ceasing to exist ten yards after it had passed, the wagon progressing not by its own volition but by attrition of their intact yet fluid circumambience, drowsing, earless, almost lightless.

It seemed to him that at the age of ten he was witnessing his own birth. It was not even strange to him. He had experienced it all before, and not merely in dreams. He saw the camp—a paintless six-room bungalow set on piles above the spring high-water—and he knew already how it was going to look. He helped in the rapid orderly disorder of their establishment in it, and even his motions were familiar to him, foreknown. Then for two weeks he ate the coarse, rapid food—the shapeless sour bread, the wild strange meat, venison and bear and turkey and coon which he had never tasted before—which men ate, cooked by men who were hunters first and cooks afterward; he slept in harsh sheetless blankets as hunters slept. Each morning the gray of dawn found him and Sam Fathers on the stand, the crossing, which had been allotted him. It was the poorest one, the most barren. He had expected that; he had not dared yet to hope even to himself that he would even hear the running dogs this first time. But he did hear them. It was on the third morning—a murmur, sourceless, almost indistinguishable, yet he knew what it was although he had never before heard that many dogs running at once, the murmur swelling into separate and distinct voices until he could call the five dogs which his cousin owned from among the others. "Now," Sam said, "slant your gun up a little and draw back the hammers and then stand still."

But it was not for him, not yet. The humility was there; he had learned that. And he could learn the patience. He was only ten, only one week. The instant had passed. It seemed to him that he could actually see the deer, the buck, smoke-colored, elongated with speed, vanished, the woods, the gray solitude still ringing even when the voices of the dogs had died away; from far away across the sombre woods and the gray half-liquid morning there came two shots. "Now let your hammers down," Sam said.

He did so. "You knew it too," he said.

"Yes," Sam said. "I want you to learn how to do when you didn't shoot. It's after the chance for the bear or the deer has done already come and gone that men and dogs get killed."

"Anyway, it wasn't him," the boy said. "It wasn't even a bear. It was just a deer."

"Yes," Sam said, "it was just a deer."

Then one morning, it was in the second week, he heard the dogs again. This time before Sam even spoke he readied the too-long, too-heavy, man-size gun as Sam had taught him, even though this time he knew the dogs and the deer were coming less close than ever, hardly within hearing even. They didn't sound like any running dogs he had ever heard before even. Then he found that Sam, who had taught him first of all to cock the gun and take position where he could see best in all directions and then never to move again, had himself moved up beside him. "There," he said. "Listen." The boy listened, to no ringing chorus strong and fast on a free scent but, a moiling yapping an octave too high and with something more than indecision and even abjectness in it which he could not yet recognize, reluctant, not even moving very fast, taking a long time to pass out of hearing, leaving even then in the air that echo of thin and almost human hysteria, abject, almost humanly grieving, with this time nothing ahead of it, no sense of a fleeing unseen smoke-colored shape. He could hear Sam breathing at his shoulder. He saw the arched curve of the old man's inhaling nostrils.

"It's Old Ben!" he cried, whispering.

Sam didn't move save for the slow gradual turning of his head as the voices faded on and the faint steady rapid arch and collapse of his nostrils. "Hah," he said. "Not even running. Walking."

"But up here!" the boy cried. "Way up here!"

"He do it every year," Sam said. "Once. Ash and Boon say he comes up here to run the other little bears away. Tell them to get to hell out of here and stay out until the hunters are gone. Maybe." The boy no longer heard anything at all, yet still Sam's head continued to turn gradually and steadily until the back of it was toward him. Then it turned back and looked down at him—the same face, grave, familiar, expressionless until it smiled, the same old man's eyes from which as he watched there faded slowly a quality darkly and fiercely lambent, passionate and proud. "He don't care no more for bears than he does for dogs or men neither. He come to see who's here, who's new in camp this year, whether he can shoot or not, can stay or not. Whether we got the dog yet that can bay and hold him until a man gets there with a gun. Because he's the head bear. He's the man." It faded, was gone; again they were the eyes as he had known them all his life. "He'll let them follow him to the river. Then he'll send them home. We might as well go too; see how they look when they get back to camp."

The dogs were there first, ten of them huddled back under the kitchen, himself and Sam squatting to peer back into the obscurity where they crouched, quiet, the eyes rolling and luminous, vanishing, and no sound, only that effluvium which the boy could not quite place yet, of something more than dog, stronger than dog and not just animal, just beast even. Because there had been nothing in front of the abject and painful yapping except the solitude, the wilderness, so that when the eleventh hound got back about mid-afternoon and he and Tennie's Jim held the passive and still trembling bitch while Sam daubed her tattered ear and raked shoulder with turpentine and axle-grease, it was still no living creature but only the wilderness which, leaning for a moment, had patted lightly once her temerity. "Just like a man," Sam said. "Just like folks. Put off as long as she could having to be brave, knowing all the time that sooner or later she would have to be brave once so she could keep on calling herself a dog, and knowing beforehand what was going to happen when she done it."

He did not know just when Sam left. He only knew that he was gone. For the next three mornings he rose and ate breakfast and Sam was not waiting for him. He went to his stand alone; he found it without help now and stood on it as Sam had taught him. On the third morning he heard the dogs again, running strong and free on a true scent again, and he readied the gun as he had learned to do and heard the hunt sweep past on since he was not ready yet, had not deserved other yet in just one short period of two weeks as compared to all the long life which he had already dedicated to the wilderness with patience and humility; he heard the shot again, one shot, the single clapping report of Walter Ewell's rifle. By now he could not only find his stand and then return to camp without guidance, by using the compass his cousin had given him he reached Walter, waiting beside the buck and the moiling of dogs over the cast entrails, before any of the others except Major de Spain and Tennie's Jim on the horses, even before Uncle Ash arrived with the one-eyed wagon-mule which did not mind the smell of blood or even, so they said, of bear.

It was not Uncle Ash on the mule. It was Sam, returned. And Sam was waiting when he finished his dinner and, himself on the one-eyed mule and Sam on the other one of the wagon team, they rode for more than three hours through the rapid shortening sunless afternoon, following no path, no trail even that he could discern, into a section of country he had never seen before. Then he understood why Sam had made him ride the one-eyed mule which would not spook at the smell of blood, of wild animals. The other one, the sound one, stopped short and tried to whirl and bolt even as Sam got down, jerking and wrenching at the rein while Sam held it, coaxing it forward with his voice since he did not dare risk hitching it, drawing it forward while the boy dismounted from the marred one which would stand. Then, standing beside Sam in the thick great gloom of ancient woods and the winter's dying afternoon, he looked quietly down at the rotted log scored and gutted with claw-marks and, in the wet earth beside it, the print of the enormous warped two-toed foot. Now he knew what he had heard in the hounds' voices in the woods that morning and what he had smelled when he peered under the kitchen where they huddled. It was in him too, a little different because they were brute beasts and he was not, but only a little different—an eagerness, passive; an abjectness, a sense of his own fragility and impotence against the timeless woods, yet without doubt or dread; a flavor like brass in the sudden run of saliva in his mouth, a hard sharp constriction either in his brain or his stomach, he could not tell which and it did not matter; he knew only that for the first time he realized that the bear which had run in his listening and loomed in his dreams since before he could remember and which therefore must have existed in the listening and the dreams of his cousin and Major de Spain and even old General Compson before they began to remember in their turn, was a mortal animal and that they had departed for the camp each November with no actual intention of slaying it, not because it could not be slain but because so far they had no actual hope of being able to. "It will be tomorrow," he said.

"You mean we will try tomorrow," Sam said. "We ain't got the dog yet."

"We've got eleven," he said. "They ran him Monday."

"And you heard them," Sam said. "Saw them too. We ain't got the dog yet. It won't take but one. But he ain't there. Maybe he ain't nowhere. The only other way will be for him to run by accident over somebody that had a gun and knowed how to shoot it."

"That wouldn't be me," the boy said. "It would be Walter or Major or——"

"It might," Sam said. "You watch close tomorrow. Because he's smart. That's how come he has lived this long. If he gets hemmed up and has got to pick out somebody to run over, he will pick out you."

"How?" he said. "How will he know. . . ." He ceased. "You mean he already knows me, that I ain't never been to the big bottom before, ain't had time to find out yet whether I . . ." He ceased again, staring at Sam; he said humbly, not even amazed: "It was me he was watching. I don't reckon he did need to come but once."

"You watch tomorrow," Sam said. "I reckon we better start back. It'll be long after dark now before we get to camp."

The next morning they started three hours earlier than they had ever done. Even Uncle Ash went, the cook, who called himself by profession a camp cook and who did little else save cook for Major de Spain's hunting and camping parties, yet who had been marked by the wilderness from simple juxtaposition to it until he responded as they all did, even the boy who until two weeks ago had never even seen the wilderness, to a hound's ripped ear and shoulder and the print of a crooked foot in a patch of wet earth. They rode. It was too far to walk: the boy and Sam and Uncle Ash in the wagon with the dogs, his cousin and Major de Spain and General Compson and Boon and Walter and Tennie's Jim riding double on the horses; again the first gray light found him, as on that first morning two weeks ago, on the stand where Sam had placed and left him. With the gun which was too big for

him, the breech-loader which did not even belong to him
but to Major de Spain and which he had fired only once,
at a stump on the first day to learn the recoil and how to
reload it with the paper shells, he stood against a big gum
tree beside a little bayou whose black still water crept
without motion out of a cane-brake, across a small clearing and into the cane again, where, invisible, a bird, the
big woodpecker called Lord-to-God by Negroes, clattered
at a dead trunk. It was a stand like any other stand, dis-
similar only in incidentals to the one where he had stood
each morning for two weeks; a territory new to him yet
no less familiar than that other one which after two weeks
he had come to believe he knew a little—the same solitude, the same loneliness through which frail and timor-
ous man had merely passed without altering it, leaving no
mark nor scar, which looked exactly as it must have
looked when the first ancestor of Sam Fathers' Chickasaw
predecessors crept into it and looked about him, club or
stone axe or bone arrow drawn and ready, different only
because, squatting at the edge of the kitchen, he had
smelled the dogs huddled and cringing beneath it and
saw the raked ear and side of the bitch that, as Sam had
said, had to be brave once in order to keep on calling herself a dog, and saw yesterday in the earth beside the
gutted log, the print of the living foot. He heard no dogs
at all. He never did certainly hear them. He only heard
the drumming of the woodpecker stop short off, and knew
that the bear was looking at him. He never saw it. He did
not know whether it was facing him from the cane or behind him. He did not move, holding the useless gun which
he knew now he would never fire at it, now or ever, tasting in his saliva that taint of brass which he had smelled in
the huddled dogs when he peered under the kitchen.

Then it was gone. As abruptly as it had stopped, the
woodpecker's dry hammering set up again, and after a
while he believed he even heard the dogs—a murmur,
scarce a sound even, which he had probably been hear-

ing for a time, perhaps a minute or two, before he remarked it, drifting into hearing and then out again, dying
away. They came nowhere near him. If it was dogs he
heard, he could not have sworn to it; if it was a bear they
ran, it was another bear. It was Sam himself who emerged
from the cane and crossed the bayou, the injured bitch
following at heel as a bird dog is taught to walk. She came
and crouched against his leg, trembling. "I didn't see him,"
he said. "I didn't, Sam."

"I know it," Sam said. "He done the looking. You didn't
hear him neither, did you?"

"No," the boy said. "I——"

"He's smart," Sam said. "Too smart." Again the boy saw
in his eyes that quality of dark and brooding lambence as
Sam looked down at the bitch trembling faintly and steadily against the boy's leg. From her raked shoulder a few
drops of fresh blood clung like bright berries. "Too big.
We ain't got the dog yet. But maybe some day."

Because there would be a next time, after and after.
He was only ten. It seemed to him that he could see them,
the two of them, shadowy in the limbo from which time
emerged and became time: the old bear absolved of mortality and himself who shared a little of it. Because he
recognized now what he had smelled in the huddled dogs
and tasted in his own saliva, recognized fear as a boy, a
youth, recognizes the existence of love and passion and
experience which is his heritage but not yet his patrimony,
from entering by chance the presence or perhaps even
merely the bedroom of a woman who has loved and been
loved by many men. *So I will have to see him,* he thought,
without dread or even hope. *I will have to look at him.*
So it was in June of the next summer. They were at the
camp again, celebrating Major de Spain's and General
Compson's birthdays. Although the one had been born in
September and the other in the depth of winter and almost thirty years earlier, each June the two of them and
McCaslin and Boon and Walter Ewell (and the boy too

from now on) spent two weeks at the camp, fishing and shooting squirrels and turkey and running coons and wildcats with the dogs at night. That is, Boon and the Negroes (and the boy too now) fished and shot squirrels and ran the coons and cats, because the proven hunters, not only Major de Spain and old General Compson (who spent those two weeks sitting in a rocking chair before a tremendous iron pot of Brunswick stew, stirring and tasting, with Uncle Ash to quarrel with about how he was making it and Tennie's Jim to pour whiskey into the tin dipper from which he drank it), but even McCaslin and Walter Ewell who were still young enough, scorned such, other than shooting the wild gobblers with pistols for wagers or to test their marksmanship.

That is, his cousin McCaslin and the others thought he was hunting squirrels. Until the third evening he believed that Sam Fathers thought so too. Each morning he would leave the camp right after breakfast. He had his own gun now, a new breech-loader, a Christmas gift; he would own and shoot it for almost seventy years, through two new pairs of barrels and locks and one new stock, until all that remained of the original gun was the silver-inlaid triggerguard with his and McCaslin's engraved names and the date in 1878. He found the tree beside the little bayou where he had stood that morning. Using the compass he ranged from that point; he was teaching himself to be better than a fair woodsman without even knowing he was doing it. On the third day he even found the gutted log where he had first seen the print. It was almost completely crumbled now, healing with unbelievable speed, a passionate and almost visible relinquishment, back into the earth from which the tree had grown. He ranged the summer woods now, green with gloom, if anything actually dimmer than they had been in November's gray dissolution, where even at noon the sun fell only in windless dappling upon the earth which never completely dried and which crawled with snakes—moccasins and water-

snakes and rattlers, themselves the color of the dappled
gloom so that he would not always see them until they
moved; returning to camp later and later and later, first
day, second day, passing in the twilight of the third evening the little log pen enclosing the log barn where Sam
was putting up the stock for the night. "You ain't looked
right yet," Sam said.

He stopped. For a moment he didn't answer. Then he
said peacefully, in a peaceful rushing burst, as when a
boy's miniature dam in a little brook gives way: "All
right. Yes. But how? I went to the bayou. I even found
that log again. I——"

"I reckon that was all right. Likely he's been watching
you. You never saw his foot?"

"I . . ." the boy said. "I didn't . . . I never
thought . . ."

"It's the gun," Sam said. He stood beside the fence,
motionless, the old man, son of a Negro slave and a Chickasaw chief, in the battered and faded overalls and the
frayed five-cent straw hat which had been the badge of
the Negro's slavery and was now the regalia of his freedom. The camp—the clearing, the house, the barn and
its tiny lot with which Major de Spain in his turn had
scratched punily and evanescently at the wilderness—
faded in the dusk, back into the immemorial darkness of
the woods. *The gun*, the boy thought. *The gun*. "You will
have to choose," Sam said.

He left the next morning before light, without breakfast, long before Uncle Ash would wake in his quilts on
the kitchen floor and start the fire. He had only the compass and a stick for the snakes. He could go almost a mile
before he would need to see the compass. He sat on a log,
the invisible compass in his hand, while the secret night-
sounds which had ceased at his movements, scurried again
and then fell still for good and the owls ceased and gave
over to the waking day birds and there was light in the
gray wet woods and he could see the compass. He went

fast yet still quietly, becoming steadily better and better as a woodsman without yet having time to realize it; he jumped a doe and a fawn, walked them out of the bed, close enough to see them—the crash of undergrowth, the white scut, the fawn scudding along behind her, faster than he had known it could have run. He was hunting right, upwind, as Sam had taught him, but that didn't matter now. He had left the gun; by his own will and relinquishment he had accepted not a gambit, not a choice, but a condition in which not only the bear's heretofore inviolable anonymity but all the ancient rules and balances of hunter and hunted had been abrogated. He would not even be afraid, not even in the moment when the fear would take him completely: blood, skin, bowels, bones, memory from the long time before it even became his memory—all save that thin clear quenchless lucidity which alone differed him from this bear and from all the other bears and bucks he would follow during almost seventy years, to which Sam had said: "Be scared. You can't help that. But don't be afraid. Ain't nothing in the woods going to hurt you if you don't corner it or it don't smell that you are afraid. A bear or a deer has got to be scared of a coward the same as a brave man has got to be."

By noon he was far beyond the crossing on the little bayou, farther into the new and alien country than he had ever been, travelling now not only by the compass but by the old, heavy, biscuit-thick silver watch which had been his father's. He had left the camp nine hours ago; nine hours from now, dark would already have been an hour old. He stopped, for the first time since he had risen from the log when he could see the compass face at last, and looked about, mopping his sweating face on his sleeve. He had already relinquished, of his will, because of his need, in humility and peace and without regret, yet apparently that had not been enough, the leaving of the gun was not enough. He stood for a moment—a child, alien and lost in the green and soaring gloom of the markless wilderness.

Then he relinquished completely to it. It was the watch and the compass. He was still tainted. He removed the linked chain of the one and the looped thong of the other from his overalls and hung them on a bush and leaned the stick beside them and entered it.

When he realized he was lost, he did as Sam had coached and drilled him: made a cast to cross his back-track. He had not been going very fast for the last two or three hours, and he had gone even less fast since he left the compass and watch on the bush. So he went slower still now, since the tree could not be very far; in fact, he found it before he really expected to and turned and went to it. But there was no bush beneath it, no compass nor watch, so he did next as Sam had coached and drilled him: made this next circle in the opposite direction and much larger, so that the pattern of the two of them would bisect his track somewhere, but crossing no trace nor mark anywhere of his feet or any feet, and now he was going faster though still not panicked, his heart beating a little more rapidly but strong and steady enough, and this time it was not even the tree because there was a down log beside it which he had never seen before and beyond the log a little swamp, a seepage of moisture somewhere between earth and water, and he did what Sam had coached and drilled him as the next and the last, seeing as he sat down on the log the crooked print, the warped indentation in the wet ground which while he looked at it continued to fill with water until it was level full and the water began to overflow and the sides of the print began to dissolve away. Even as he looked up he saw the next one, and, moving, the one beyond it; moving, not hurrying, running, but merely keeping pace with them as they appeared before him as though they were being shaped out of thin air just one constant pace short of where he would lose them forever and be lost forever himself, tireless, eager, without doubt or dread, panting a little above the strong rapid little hammer of his heart, emerging suddenly into a little glade, and the wilderness coalesced. It rushed, soundless, and solidified—the tree, the bush, the compass and the watch glinting where a ray of sunlight touched them. Then he saw the bear. It did not emerge, appear: it was just there, immobile, fixed in the green and windless noon's hot dappling, not as big as he had dreamed it but as big as he had expected, bigger, dimensionless against the dappled obscurity, looking at him. Then it moved. It crossed the glade without haste, walking for an instant into the sun's full glare and out of it, and stopped again and looked back at him across one shoulder. Then it was gone. It didn't walk into the woods. It faded, sank back into the wilderness without motion as he had watched a fish, a huge old bass, sink back into the dark depths of its pool and vanish without even any movement of its fins.

II

So he should have hated and feared Lion. He was thirteen then. He had killed his buck and Sam Fathers had marked his face with the hot blood, and in the next November he killed a bear. But before that accolade he had become as competent in the woods as many grown men with the same experience. By now he was a better woodsman than most grown men with more. There was no territory within twenty-five miles of the camp that he did not know—bayou, ridge, landmark trees and path; he could have led anyone direct to any spot in it and brought him back. He knew game trails that even Sam Fathers had never seen; in the third fall he found a buck's bedding-place by himself and unbeknown to his cousin he borrowed Walter Ewell's rifle and lay in wait for the buck at dawn and killed it when it walked back to the bed as Sam had told him how the old Chickasaw fathers did.

By now he knew the old bear's footprint better than he did his own, and not only the crooked one. He could see any one of the three sound prints and distinguish it at once from any other, and not only because of its size. There were other bears within that fifty miles which left tracks almost as large, or at least so near that the one would have appeared larger only by juxtaposition. It was more than that. If Sam Fathers had been his mentor and the backyard rabbits and squirrels his kindergarten, then the wilderness the old bear ran was his college and the old male bear itself, so long unwifed and childless as to have become its own ungendered progenitor, was his alma mater.

He could find the crooked print now whenever he wished, ten miles or five miles or sometimes closer than that, to the camp. Twice while on stand during the next three years he heard the dogs strike its trail and once even jump it by chance, the voices high, abject, almost human in their hysteria. Once, still-hunting with Walter Ewell's rifle, he saw it cross a long corridor of down timber where a tornado had passed. It rushed through rather than across the tangle of trunks and branches as a locomotive would, faster than he had ever believed it could have moved, almost as fast as a deer even because the deer would have spent most of that distance in the air; he realized then why it would take a dog not only of abnormal courage but size and speed to ever to bring it to bay. He had a little dog at home, a mongrel, of the sort called fyce by Negroes, a ratter, itself not much bigger than a rat and possessing that sort of courage which had long since stopped being bravery and had become foolhardiness. He brought it with him one June and, timing them as if they were meeting an appointment with another human being, himself carrying the fyce with a sack over its head and Sam Fathers with a brace of the hounds on a rope leash, they lay downwind of the trail and actually ambushed the bear. They were so close that it turned at bay although he realized later this might have been from surprise and amazement at the shrill and frantic uproar of the fyce.

It turned at bay against the trunk of a big cypress, on its hind feet; it seemed to the boy that it would never stop rising, taller and taller, and even the two hounds seemed to have taken a kind of desperate and despairing courage from the fyce. Then he realized that the fyce was actually not going to stop. He flung the gun down and ran. When he overtook and grasped the shrill, frantically pinwheeling little dog, it seemed to him that he was directly under the bear. He could smell it, strong and hot and rank. Sprawling, he looked up where it loomed and towered over him like a thunderclap. It was quite familiar, until he remembered: this was the way he had used to dream about it.

Then it was gone. He didn't see it go. He knelt, holding the frantic fyce with both hands, hearing the abased wailing of the two hounds drawing further and further away, until Sam came up, carrying the gun. He laid it quietly down beside the boy and stood looking down at him. "You've done seed him twice now, with a gun in your hands," he said. "This time you couldn't have missed him."

The boy rose. He still held the fyce. Even in his arms it continued to yap frantically, surging and straining toward the fading sound of the hounds like a collection of live-wire springs. The boy was panting a little. "Neither could you," he said. "You had the gun. Why didn't you shoot him?"

Sam didn't seem to have heard. He put out his hand and touched the little dog in the boy's arms which still yapped and strained even though the two hounds were out of hearing now. "He's done gone," Sam said. "You can slack off and rest now, until next time." He stroked the little dog until it began to grow quiet under his hand. "You's almost the one we wants," he said. "You just ain't big enough. We ain't got that one yet. He will need to be just a little bigger than smart, and a little braver than either." He withdrew his hand from the fyce's head and stood looking into the woods where the bear and the hounds had vanished. "Somebody is going to, some day."

"I know it," the boy said. "That's why it must be one of us. So it won't be until the last day. When even he don't want it to last any longer."

So he should have hated and feared Lion. It was in the fourth summer, the fourth time he had made one in the celebration of Major de Spain's and General Compson's birthday. In the early spring Major de Spain's mare had foaled a horse colt. One evening when Sam brought the horses and mules up to stable them for the night, the colt was missing and it was all he could do to get the frantic mare into the lot. He had thought at first to let the mare lead him back to where she had become separated from the foal. But she would not do it. She would not even feint toward any particular part of the woods or even in any particular direction. She merely ran, as if she couldn't see, still frantic with terror. She whirled and ran at Sam once, as if to attack him in some ultimate desperation, as if she could not for the moment realize that he was a man and a long-familiar one. He got her into the lot at last. It was too dark by that time to back-track her, to unravel the erratic course she had doubtless pursued.

He came to the house and told Major de Spain. It was an animal, of course, a big one, and the colt was dead now, wherever it was. They all knew that. "It's a panther," General Compson said at once. "The same one. That doe and fawn last March." Sam had sent Major de Spain word of it when Boon Hogganbeck came to the camp on a routine visit to see how the stock had wintered—the doe's throat torn out, and the beast had run down the helpless fawn and killed it too.

"Sam never did say that was a panther," Major de Spain said. Sam said nothing now, standing behind Major de Spain where they sat at supper, inscrutable, as if he were just waiting for them to stop talking so he could go home.

He didn't even seem to be looking at anything. "A panther might jump a doe, and he wouldn't have much trouble catching the fawn afterward. But no panther would have jumped that colt with the dam right there with it. It was Old Ben," Major de Spain said. "I'm disappointed in him. He has broken the rules. I didn't think he would have done that. He has killed mine and McCaslin's dogs, but that was all right. We gambled the dogs against him; we gave each other warning. But now he has come into my house and destroyed my property, out of season too. He broke the rules. It was Old Ben, Sam." Still Sam said nothing, standing there until Major de Spain should stop talking. "We'll back-track her tomorrow and see," Major de Spain said.

Sam departed. He would not live in the camp; he had built himself a little hut something like Joe Baker's, only stouter, tighter, on the bayou a quarter-mile away, and a stout log crib where he stored a little corn for the shoat he raised each year. The next morning he was waiting when they waked. He had already found the colt. They did not even wait for breakfast. It was not far, not five hundred yards from the stable—the three-months' colt lying on its side, its throat torn out and the entrails and one ham partly eaten. It lay not as if it had been dropped but as if it had been struck and hurled, and no cat-mark, no claw-mark where a panther would have gripped it while finding its throat. They read the tracks where the frantic mare had circled and at last rushed in with that same ultimate desperation with which she had whirled on Sam Fathers yesterday evening, and the long tracks of dead and terrified running and those of the beast which had not even rushed at her when she advanced but had merely walked three or four paces toward her until she broke, and General Compson said, "Good God, what a wolf!"

Still Sam said nothing. The boy watched him while the men knelt, measuring the tracks. There was something in Sam's face now. It was neither exultation nor joy nor hope. Later, a man, the boy realized what it had been, and that Sam had known all the time what had made the tracks and what had torn the throat out of the doe in the spring and killed the fawn. It had been foreknowledge in Sam's face that morning. *And he was glad,* he told himself. *He was old. He had no children, no people, none of his blood anywhere above earth that he would ever meet again. And even if he were to, he could not have touched it, spoken to it, because for seventy years now he had had to be a Negro. It was almost over now and he was glad.*

They returned to camp and had breakfast and came back with guns and the hounds. Afterward the boy realized that they also should have known then what killed the colt as well as Sam Fathers did. But that was neither the first nor the last time he had seen men rationalize from and even act upon their misconceptions. After Boon, standing astride the colt, had whipped the dogs away from it with his belt, they snuffed at the tracks. One of them, a young dog hound without judgment yet, bayed once, and they ran for a few feet on what seemed to be a trail. Then they stopped, looking back at the men, eager enough, not baffled, merely questioning, as if they were asking "Now what?" Then they rushed back to the colt, where Boon, still astride it, slashed at them with the belt.

"I never knew a trail to get cold that quick," General Compson said.

"Maybe a single wolf big enough to kill a colt with the dam right there beside it don't leave scent," Major de Spain said.

"Maybe it was a hant," Walter Ewell said. He looked at Tennie's Jim. "Hah, Jim?"

Because the hounds would not run it, Major de Spain had Sam hunt out and find the tracks a hundred yards farther on and they put the dogs on it again and again the young one bayed and not one of them realized then that the hound was not baying like a dog striking game but was merely bellowing like a country dog whose yard has been invaded. General Compson spoke to the boy and Boon and Tennie's Jim: to the squirrel hunters. "You boys keep the dogs with you this morning. He's probably hanging around somewhere, waiting to get his breakfast off the colt. You might strike him."

But they did not. The boy remembered how Sam stood watching them as they went into the woods with the leashed hounds—the Indian face in which he had never seen anything until it smiled, except that faint arching of the nostrils on that first morning when the hounds had found Old Ben. They took the hounds with them on the next day, though when they reached the place where they hoped to strike a fresh trail, the carcass of the colt was gone. Then on the third morning Sam was waiting again, this time until they had finished breakfast. He said, "Come." He led them to his house, his little hut, to the corn-crib beyond it. He had removed the corn and had made a deadfall of the door, baiting it with the colt's carcass; peering between the logs, they saw an animal almost the color of a gun or pistol barrel, what little time they had to examine its color or shape. It was not crouched nor even standing. It was in motion, in the air, coming toward them—a heavy body crashing with tremendous force against the door so that the thick door jumped and clattered in its frame, the animal, whatever it was, hurling itself against the door again seemingly before it could have touched the floor and got a new purchase to spring from. "Come away," Sam said, "fore he break his neck." Even when they retreated the heavy and measured crashes continued, the stout door jumping and clattering each time, and still no sound from the beast itself—no snarl, no cry.

"What in hell's name is it?" Major de Spain said.

"It's a dog," Sam said, his nostrils arching and collapsing

faintly and steadily and that faint, fierce milkiness in his eyes again as on that first morning when the hounds had struck the old bear. "It's the dog."

"*The* dog?" Major de Spain said.

"That's gonter hold Old Ben."

"Dog the devil," Major de Spain said. "I'd rather have Old Ben himself in my pack than that brute. Shoot him."

"No," Sam said.

"You'll never tame him. How do you ever expect to make an animal like that afraid of you?"

"I don't want him tame," Sam said; again the boy watched his nostrils and the fierce milky light in his eyes. "But I almost rather he be tame than scared, of me or any man or any thing. But he won't be neither, of nothing."

"Then what are you going to do with it?"

"You can watch," Sam said.

Each morning through the second week they would go to Sam's crib. He had removed a few shingles from the roof and had put a rope on the colt's carcass and had drawn it out when the trap fell. Each morning they would watch him lower a pail of water into the crib while the dog hurled itself tirelessly against the door and dropped back and leaped again. It never made any sound and there was nothing frenzied in the act but only a cold and grim indomitable determination. Toward the end of the week it stopped jumping at the door. Yet it had not weakened appreciably and it was not as if it had rationalized the fact that the door was not going to give. It was as if for that time it simply disdained to jump any longer. It was not down. None of them had ever seen it down. It stood, and they could see it now—part mastiff, something of Airedale and something of a dozen other strains probably, better than thirty inches at the shoulders and weighing as they guessed almost ninety pounds, with cold yellow eyes and a tremendous chest and over all that strange color like a blued gun-barrel.

Then the two weeks were up. They prepared to break

camp. The boy begged to remain and his cousin let him. He moved into the little hut with Sam Fathers. Each morning he watched Sam lower the pail of water into the crib. By the end of that week the dog was down. It would rise and half stagger, half crawl to the water and drink and collapse again. One morning it could not even reach the water, could not raise its forequarters even from the floor. Sam took a short stick and prepared to enter the crib. "Wait," the boy said. "Let me get the gun——"

"No," Sam said. "He can't move now." Nor could it. It lay on its side while Sam touched it, its head and the gaunted body, the dog lying motionless, the yellow eyes open. They were not fierce and there was nothing of petty malevolence in them, but a cold and almost impersonal malignance like some natural force. It was not even looking at Sam nor at the boy peering at it between the logs.

Sam began to feed it again. The first time he had to raise its head so it could lap the broth. That night he left a bowl of broth containing lumps of meat where the dog could reach it. The next morning the bowl was empty and the dog was lying on its belly, its head up, the cold yellow eyes watching the door as Sam entered, no change whatever in the cold yellow eyes and still no sound from it even when it sprang, its aim and coordination still bad from weakness so that Sam had time to strike it down with the stick and leap from the crib and slam the door as the dog, still without having had time to get its feet under it to jump again seemingly, hurled itself against the door as if the two weeks of starving had never been.

At noon that day someone came whooping through the woods from the direction of the camp. It was Boon. He came and looked for a while between the logs, at the tremendous dog lying again on its belly, its head up, the yellow eyes blinking sleepily at nothing: the indomitable and unbroken spirit. "What we better do," Boon said, "is to let that sonofabitch go and catch Old Ben and run him on the dog." He turned to the boy his weather-reddened and beetling face. "Get your traps together. Cass says for you to come on home. You been in here fooling with that horse-eating varmint long enough."

Boon had a borrowed mule at the camp; the buggy was waiting at the edge of the bottom. He was at home that night. He told McCaslin about it. "Sam's going to starve him again until he can go in and touch him. Then he will feed him again. Then he will starve him again, if he has to."

"But why?" McCaslin said. "What for? Even Sam will never tame that brute."

"We don't want him tame. We want him like he is. We just want him to find out at last that the only way he can get out of that crib and stay out of it is to do what Sam or somebody tells him to do. He's the dog that's going to stop Old Ben and hold him. We've already named him. His name is Lion."

Then November came at last. They returned to the camp. With General Compson and Major de Spain and his cousin and Walter and Boon he stood in the yard among the guns and bedding and boxes of food and watched Sam Fathers and Lion come up the lane from the lot—the Indian, the old man in battered overalls and rubber boots and a worn sheepskin coat and a hat which had belonged to the boy's father; the tremendous dog pacing gravely beside him. The hounds rushed out to meet them and stopped, except the young one which still had but little of judgment. It ran up to Lion, fawning. Lion didn't snap at it. He didn't even pause. He struck it rolling and yelping for five or six feet with a blow of one paw as a bear would have done and came on into the yard and stood, blinking sleepily at nothing, looking at no one, while Boon said, "Jesus. Jesus.—Will he let me touch him?"

"You can touch him," Sam said. "He don't care. He don't care about nothing or nobody."

The boy watched that too. He watched it for the next

two years from that moment when Boon touched Lion's
head and then knelt beside him, feeling the bones and
muscles, the power. It was as if Lion were a woman—
or perhaps Boon was the woman. That was more like it—
the big, grave, sleepy-seeming dog which, as Sam Fathers
said, cared about no man and no thing; and the violent,
insensitive, hard-faced man with his touch of remote Indian blood and the mind almost of a child. He watched
Boon take over Lion's feeding from Sam and Uncle Ash
both. He would see Boon squatting in the cold rain beside the kitchen while Lion ate. Because Lion neither slept
nor ate with the other dogs though none of them knew
where he did sleep until in the second November, thinking
until then that Lion slept in his kennel beside Sam Fathers'
hut, when the boy's cousin McCaslin said something about
it to Sam by sheer chance and Sam told him. And that
night the boy and Major de Spain and McCaslin with a
lamp entered the back room where Boon slept—the
little, tight, airless room rank with the smell of Boon's un-
washed body and his wet hunting-clothes—where Boon,
snoring on his back, choked and waked and Lion raised
his head beside him and looked back at them from his
cold, slumbrous yellow eyes.

"Damn it, Boon," McCaslin said. "Get that dog out of
here. He's got to run Old Ben tomorrow morning. How
in hell do you expect him to smell anything fainter than
a skunk after breathing you all night?"

"The way I smell ain't hurt my nose none that I ever
noticed," Boon said.

"It wouldn't matter if it had," Major de Spain said.
"We're not depending on you to trail a bear. Put him outside. Put him under the house with the other dogs."

Boon began to get up. "He'll kill the first one that happens to yawn or sneeze in his face or touches him."

"I reckon not," Major de Spain said. "None of them
are going to risk yawning in his face or touching him
either, even asleep. Put him outside. I want his nose

right tomorrow. Old Ben fooled him last year. I don't think he will do it again."

Boon put on his shoes without lacing them; in his long soiled underwear, his hair still tousled from sleep, he and Lion went out. The others returned to the front room and the poker game where McCaslin's and Major de Spain's hands waited for them on the table. After a while McCaslin said, "Do you want me to go back and look again?"

"No," Major de Spain said. "I call," he said to Walter Ewell. He spoke to McCaslin again. "If you do, don't tell me. I am beginning to see the first sign of my increasing age: I don't like to know that my orders have been disobeyed, even when I knew when I gave them that they would be.—A small pair," he said to Walter Ewell.

"How small?" Walter said.

"Very small," Major de Spain said.

And the boy, lying beneath his piled quilts and blankets waiting for sleep, knew likewise that Lion was already back in Boon's bed, for the rest of that night and the next one and during all the nights of the next November and the next one. He thought then: *I wonder what Sam thinks. He could have Lion with him, even if Boon is a white man. He could ask Major or McCaslin either. And more than that. It was Sam's hand that touched Lion first and Lion knows it.* Then he became a man and he knew that too. It had been all right. That was the way it should have been. Sam was the chief, the prince; Boon, the plebeian, was his huntsman. Boon should have nursed the dogs.

On the first morning that Lion led the pack after Old Ben, seven strangers appeared in the camp. They were swampers: gaunt, malaria-ridden men appearing from nowhere, who ran trap-lines for coons or perhaps farmed little patches of cotton and corn along the edge of the bottom, in clothes but little better than Sam Fathers' and nowhere near as good as Tennie's Jim's, with worn shotguns

and rifles, already squatting patiently in the cold drizzle
in the side yard when day broke. They had a spokesman;
afterward Sam Fathers told Major de Spain how all during the past summer and fall they had drifted into the
camp singly or in pairs and threes, to look quietly at Lion
for a while and then go away: "Mawnin, Major. We heerd
you was aimin to put that ere blue dawg on that old two-
toed bear this mawnin. We figgered we'd come up and
watch, if you don't mind. We won't do no shooting, lessen
he runs over us."

"You are welcome," Major de Spain said. "You are welcome to shoot. He's more your bear than ours."

"I reckon that ain't no lie. I done fed him enough cawn
to have a sheer in him. Not to mention a shoat three years
ago."

"I reckon I got a sheer too," another said. "Only it ain't
in the bear." Major de Spain looked at him. He was chewing tobacco. He spat. "Hit was a heifer calf. Nice un too.
Last year. When I finally found her, I reckon she looked
about like that colt of yourn looked last June."

"Oh," Major de Spain said. "Be welcome. If you see
game in front of my dogs, shoot it."

Nobody shot Old Ben that day. No man saw him. The
dogs jumped him within a hundred yards of the glade
where the boy had seen him that day in the summer of
his eleventh year. The boy was less than a quarter-mile
away. He heard the jump but he could distinguish no voice
among the dogs that he did not know and therefore would
be Lion's, and he thought, believed, that Lion was not
among them. Even the fact that they were going much
faster than he had ever heard them run behind Old Ben
before and that the high thin note of hysteria was missing
now from their voices was not enough to disabuse him.
He didn't comprehend until that night, when Sam told
him that Lion would never cry on a trail. "He gonter growl
when he catches Old Ben's throat," Sam said. "But he
ain't gonter never holler, no more than he ever done when

he was jumping at that two-inch door. It's that blue dog in him. What you call it?"

"Airedale," the boy said.

Lion was there; the jump was just too close to the river. When Boon returned with Lion about eleven that night, he swore that Lion had stopped Old Ben once but that the hounds would not go in and Old Ben broke away and took to the river and swam for miles down it and he and Lion went down one bank for about ten miles and crossed and came up the other but it had begun to get dark before they struck any trail where Old Ben had come up out of the water, unless he was still in the water when he passed the ford where they crossed. Then he fell to cursing the hounds and ate the supper Uncle Ash had saved for him and went off to bed and after a while the boy opened the door of the little stale room thunderous with snoring and the great grave dog raised its head from Boon's pillow and blinked at him for a moment and lowered its head again.

When the next November came and the last day, the day which it was now becoming traditional to save for Old Ben, there were more than a dozen strangers waiting. They were not all swampers this time. Some of them were townsmen, from other county seats like Jefferson, who had heard about Lion and Old Ben and had come to watch the great blue dog keep his yearly rendezvous with the old two-toed bear. Some of them didn't even have guns and the hunting-clothes and boots they wore had been on a store shelf yesterday.

This time Lion jumped Old Ben more than five miles from the river and bayed and held him and this time the hounds went in, in a sort of desperate emulation. The boy heard them; he was that near. He heard Boon whooping; he heard the two shots when General Compson delivered both barrels, one containing five buckshot, the other a single ball, into the bear from as close as he could force his almost unmanageable horse. He heard the dogs when the bear broke free again. He was running now; panting, stumbling, his lungs bursting, he reached the place where General Compson had fired and where Old Ben had killed two of the hounds. He saw the blood from General Compson's shots, but he could go no further. He stopped, leaning against a tree for his breathing to ease and his heart to slow, hearing the sound of the dogs as it faded on and died away.

In camp that night—they had as guests five of the still terrified strangers in new hunting coats and boots who had been lost all day until Sam Fathers went out and got them—he heard the rest of it: how Lion had stopped and held the bear again but only the one-eyed mule which did not mind the smell of wild blood would approach and Boon was riding the mule and Boon had never been known to hit anything. He shot at the bear five times with his pump gun, touching nothing, and Old Ben killed another hound and broke free once more and reached the river and was gone. Again Boon and Lion hunted as far down one bank as they dared. Too far; they crossed in the first of dusk and dark overtook them within a mile. And this time Lion found the broken trail, the blood perhaps, in the darkness where Old Ben had come up out of the water, but Boon had him on a rope, luckily, and he got down from the mule and fought Lion hand-to-hand until he got him back to camp. This time Boon didn't even curse. He stood in the door, muddy, spent, his huge gargoyle's face tragic and still amazed. "I missed him," he said. "I was in twenty-five feet of him and I missed him five times."

"But we have drawn blood," Major de Spain said. "General Compson drew blood. We have never done that before."

"But I missed him," Boon said. "I missed him five times. With Lion looking right at me."

"Never mind," Major de Spain said. "It was a damned fine race. And we drew blood. Next year we'll let General Compson or Walter ride Katie, and we'll get him."

Then McCaslin said, "Where is Lion, Boon?"

"I left him at Sam's," Boon said. He was already turning away. 'I ain't fit to sleep with him."

So he should have hated and feared Lion. Yet he did not. It seemed to him that there was a fatality in it. It seemed to him that something, he didn't know what, was beginning; had already begun. It was like the last act on a set stage. It was the beginning of the end of something, he didn't know what except that he would not grieve. He would be humble and proud that he had been found worthy to be a part of it too or even just to see it too.

III

It was December. It was the coldest December he had ever remembered. They had been in camp four days over two weeks, waiting for the weather to soften so that Lion and Old Ben could run their yearly race. Then they would break camp and go home. Because of these unforeseen additional days which they had had to pass waiting on the weather, with nothing to do but play poker, the whiskey had given out and he and Boon were being sent to Memphis with a suitcase and a note from Major de Spain to Mr. Semmes, the distiller, to get more. That is, Major de Spain and McCaslin were sending Boon to get the whiskey and sending him to see that Boon got back with it or most of it or at least some of it.

Tennie's Jim waked him at three. He dressed rapidly, shivering, not so much from the cold because a fresh fire already boomed and roared on the hearth, but in that dead winter hour when the blood and the heart are slow and sleep is incomplete. He crossed the gap between house and kitchen, the gap of iron earth beneath the bril-

liant and rigid night where dawn would not begin for
three hours yet, tasting, tongue, palate, and to the very
bottom of his lungs, the searing dark, and entered
the kitchen, the lamp-lit warmth where the stove glowed,
fogging the windows, and where Boon already sat at the
table at breakfast, hunched over his plate, almost in his
plate, his working jaws blue with stubble and his face innocent of water and his coarse, horse-mane hair innocent
of comb—the quarter Indian, grandson of a Chickasaw
squaw, who on occasion resented with his hard and furious
fists the intimation of one single drop of alien blood and
on others, usually after whiskey, affirmed with the same
fists and the same fury that his father had been the full-
blood Chickasaw and even a chief and that even his
mother had been only half white. He was four inches
over six feet; he had the mind of a child, the heart of a
horse, and little hard shoe-button eyes without depth or
meanness or generosity or viciousness or gentleness or
anything else, in the ugliest face the boy had ever seen.
It looked like somebody had found a walnut a little larger
than a football and with a machinist's hammer had shaped
features into it and then painted it, mostly red; not Indian
red but a fine bright ruddy color which whiskey might
have had something to do with but which was mostly just
happy and violent out-of-doors, the wrinkles in it not the
residue of the forty years it had survived but from squint-
ing into the sun or into the gloom of cane-brakes where
game had run, baked into it by the camp fires before
which he had lain trying to sleep on the cold November or
December ground while waiting for daylight so he could
rise and hunt again, as though time were merely something he walked through as he did through air, aging him
no more than air did. He was brave, faithful, improvident
and unreliable; he had neither profession job nor trade
and owned one vice and one virtue: whiskey, and that
absolute and unquestioning fidelity to Major de Spain and
the boy's cousin McCaslin. "Sometimes I'd call them both

virtues," Major de Spain said once. "Or both vices," Mc-Caslin said.

He ate his breakfast, hearing the dogs under the kitchen, wakened by the smell of frying meat or perhaps by the feet overhead. He heard Lion once, short and peremptory, as the best hunter in any camp has only to speak once to all save the fools, and none other of Major de Spain's and McCaslin's dogs were Lion's equal in size and strength and perhaps even in courage, but they were not fools; Old Ben had killed the last fool among them last year.

Tennie's Jim came in as they finished. The wagon was outside. Ash decided he would drive them over to the log-line where they would flag the outbound log-train and let Tennie's Jim wash the dishes. The boy knew why. It would not be the first time he had listened to old Ash badgering Boon.

It was cold. The wagon wheels banged and clattered on the frozen ground; the sky was fixed and brilliant. He was not shivering, he was shaking, slow and steady and hard, the food he had just eaten still warm and solid inside him while his outside shook slow and steady around it as though his stomach floated loose. "They won't run this morning," he said. "No dog will have any nose today."

"Cep Lion," Ash said. "Lion don't need no nose. All he need is a bear." He had wrapped his feet in towsacks and he had a quilt from his pallet bed on the kitchen floor drawn over his head and wrapped around him until in the thin brilliant starlight he looked like nothing at all that the boy had ever seen before. "He run a bear through a thousand-acre ice-house. Catch him too. Them other dogs don't matter because they ain't going to keep up with Lion nohow, long as he got a bear in front of him."

"What's wrong with the other dogs?" Boon said. "What the hell do you know about it anyway? This is the first time you've had your tail out of that kitchen since we got here except to chop a little wood."

"Ain't nothing wrong with them," Ash said. "And long as it's left up to them, ain't nothing going to be. I just wish I had knowed all my life how to take care of my health good as them hounds knows."

"Well, they ain't going to run this morning," Boon said. His voice was harsh and positive. "Major promised they wouldn't until me and Ike get back."

"Weather gonter break today. Gonter soft up. Rain by night." Then Ash laughed, chuckled, somewhere inside the quilt which concealed even his face. "Hum up here, mules!" he said, jerking the reins so that the mules leaped forward and snatched the lurching and banging wagon for several feet before they slowed again into their quick, short-paced, rapid plodding. "Sides, I like to know why Major need to wait on you. It's Lion he aiming to use. I ain't never heard tell of you bringing no bear nor no other kind of meat into this camp."

Now Boon's going to curse Ash or maybe even hit him, the boy thought. But Boon never did, never had; the boy knew he never would even though four years ago Boon had shot five times with a borrowed pistol at a Negro on the street in Jefferson, with the same result as when he had shot five times at Old Ben last fall. "By God," Boon said, "he ain't going to put Lion or no other dog on nothing until I get back tonight. Because he promised me. Whip up them mules and keep them whipped up. Do you want me to freeze to death?"

They reached the log-line and built a fire. After a while the log-train came up out of the woods under the paling east and Boon flagged it. Then in the warm caboose the boy slept again while Boon and the conductor and brakeman talked about Lion and Old Ben as people later would talk about Sullivan and Kilrain and, later still, about Dempsey and Tunney. Dozing, swaying as the springless caboose lurched and clattered, he would hear them still talking, about the shoats and calves Old Ben had killed and the cribs he had rifled and the traps and deadfalls he had

wrecked and the lead he probably carried under his hide
—Old Ben, the two-toed bear in a land where bears with
trap-ruined feet had been called Two-Toe or Three-Toe
or Cripple-Foot for fifty years, only Old Ben was an extra
bear (the head bear, General Compson called him) and so
had earned a name such as a human man could have
worn and not been sorry.

They reached Hoke's at sunup. They emerged from the
warm caboose in their hunting clothes, the muddy boots
and stained khaki and Boon's blue unshaven jowls. But
that was all right. Hoke's was a sawmill and commissary
and two stores and a loading-chute on a sidetrack from
the main line, and all the men in it wore boots and khaki
too. Presently the Memphis train came. Boon bought three
packages of popcorn-and-molasses and a bottle of beer
from the news butch and the boy went to sleep again
to the sound of his chewing.

But in Memphis it was not all right. It was as if the high
buildings and the hard pavements, the fine carriages and
the horse cars and the men in starched collars and neck-
ties made their boots and khaki look a little rougher and a
little muddier and made Boon's beard look worse and
more unshaven and his face look more and more like he
should never have brought it out of the woods at all or at
least out of reach of Major de Spain or McCaslin or someone who knew it and could have said, "Don't be afraid.
He won't hurt you." He walked through the station, on
the slick floor, his face moving as he worked the popcorn
out of his teeth with his tongue, his legs spraddled and
stiff in the hips as if he were walking on buttered glass,
and that blue stubble on his face like the filings from a new
gunbarrel. They passed the first saloon. Even through the
closed doors the boy could seem to smell the sawdust and
the reek of old drink. Boon began to cough. He coughed
for something less than a minute. "Damn this cold," he
said. "I'd sure like to know where I got it."

"Back there in the station," the boy said.

Boon had started to cough again. He stopped. He looked at the boy. "What?" he said.

"You never had it when we left camp nor on the train either." Boon looked at him, blinking. Then he stopped blinking. He didn't cough again. He said quietly:

"Lend me a dollar. Come on. You've got it. If you ever had one, you've still got it. I don't mean you are tight with your money because you ain't. You just don't never seem to ever think of nothing you want. When I was sixteen a dollar bill melted off of me before I even had time to read the name of the bank that issued it." He said quietly: "Let me have a dollar, Ike."

"You promised Major. You promised McCaslin. Not till we get back to camp."

"All right," Boon said in that quiet and patient voice. "What can I do on just one dollar? You ain't going to lend me another."

"You're damn right I ain't," the boy said, his voice quiet too, cold with rage which was not at Boon, remembering: Boon snoring in a hard chair in the kitchen so he could watch the clock and wake him and McCaslin and drive them the seventeen miles in to Jefferson to catch the train to Memphis; the wild, never-bridled Texas paint pony which he had persuaded McCaslin to let him buy and which he and Boon had bought at auction for four dollars and seventy-five cents and fetched home wired between two gentle old mares with pieces of barbed wire and which had never even seen shelled corn before and didn't even know what it was unless the grains were bugs maybe, and at last (he was ten and Boon had been ten all his life) Boon said the pony was gentled and with a towsack over its head and four Negroes to hold it they backed it into an old two-wheeled cart and hooked up the gear and he and Boon got up and Boon said, "All right, boys. Let him go" and one of the Negroes—it was Tennie's Jim—snatched the towsack off and leaped for his life and they lost the first wheel against a post of the open gate only at that moment Boon caught him by the scruff of the neck and flung him into the roadside ditch so he only saw the rest of it in fragments: the other wheel as it slammed through the side gate and crossed the back yard and leaped up onto the gallery and scraps of the cart here and there along the road and Boon vanishing rapidly on his stomach in the leaping and spurting dust and still holding the reins until they broke too and two days later they finally caught the pony seven miles away still wearing the hames and the headstall of the bridle around its neck like a duchess with two necklaces at one time. He gave Boon the dollar.

"All right," Boon said. "Come on in out of the cold."

"I ain't cold," he said.

"You can have some lemonade."

"I don't want any lemonade."

The door closed behind him. The sun was well up now. It was a brilliant day, though Ash had said it would rain before night. Already it was warmer; they could run tomorrow. He felt the old lift of the heart, as pristine as ever, as on the first day; he would never lose it, no matter how old in hunting and pursuit: the best, the best of all breathing, the humility and the pride. He must stop thinking about it. Already it seemed to him that he was running, back to the station, to the tracks themselves: The first train going south; he must stop thinking about it. The street was busy. He watched the big Norman draft horses, the Percherons; the trim carriages from which the men in the fine overcoats and the ladies rosy in furs descended and entered the station. (They were still next door to it but one.) Twenty years ago his father had ridden into Memphis as a member of Colonel Sartoris' horse in Forrest's command, up Main street and (the tale told) into the lobby of the Gayoso Hotel where the Yankee officers sat in the leather chairs spitting into the tall bright cuspidors and then out again, scot-free——

The door opened behind him. Boon was wiping his

mouth on the back of his hand. "All right," he said. "Let's go tend to it and get the hell out of here."

They went and had the suitcase packed. He never knew where or when Boon got the other bottle. Doubtless Mr. Semmes gave it to him. When they reached Hoke's again at sundown, it was empty. They could get a return train to Hoke's in two hours; they went straight back to the station as Major de Spain and then McCaslin had told Boon to do and then ordered him to do and had sent the boy along to see that he did. Boon took the first drink from his bottle in the washroom. A man in a uniform cap came to tell him he couldn't drink there and looked at Boon's face once and said nothing. The next time he was pouring into his water glass beneath the edge of a table in the restaurant when the manager (she was a woman) did tell him he couldn't drink there and he went back to the washroom. He had been telling the Negro waiter and all the other people in the restaurant who couldn't help but hear him and who had never heard of Lion and didn't want to, about Lion and Old Ben. Then he happened to think of the zoo. He had found out that there was another train to Hoke's at three o'clock and so they would spend the time at the zoo and take the three o'clock train until he came back from the washroom for the third time. Then they would take the first train back to camp, get Lion and come back to the zoo where, he said, the bears were fed on ice cream and lady fingers and he would match Lion against them all.

So they missed the first train, the one they were supposed to take, but he got Boon onto the three o'clock train and they were all right again, with Boon not even going to the washroom now but drinking in the aisle and talking about Lion and the men he buttonholed no more daring to tell Boon he couldn't drink there than the man in the station had dared.

When they reached Hoke's at sundown, Boon was asleep. The boy waked him at last and got him and the suitcase off the train and he even persuaded him to eat some supper at the sawmill commissary. So he was all right when they got in the caboose of the log-train to go back into the woods, with the sun going down red and the sky already overcast and the ground would not freeze to-night. It was the boy who slept now, sitting behind the ruby stove while the springless caboose jumped and clattered and Boon and the brakeman and the conductor talked about Lion and Old Ben because they knew what Boon was talking about because this was home. "Over-cast and already thawing," Boon said. "Lion will get him tomorrow."

It would have to be Lion, or somebody. It would not be Boon. He had never hit anything bigger than a squir-rel that anybody ever knew, except the Negro woman that day when he was shooting at the Negro man. He was a big Negro and not ten feet away but Boon shot five times with the pistol he had borrowed from Major de Spain's Negro coachman and the Negro he was shooting at outed with a dollar-and-a-half mail-order pistol and would have burned Boon down with it only it never went off, it just went snicksnicksnicksnicksnick five times and Boon still blasting away and he broke a plate-glass win-dow that cost McCaslin forty-five dollars and hit a Negro woman who happened to be passing in the leg only Major de Spain paid for that; he and McCaslin cut cards, the plate-glass window against the Negro woman's leg. And the first day on stand this year, the first morning in camp, the buck ran right over Boon; he heard Boon's old pump gun go whow. whow. whow. whow. whow. and then his voice: "God damn, here he comes! Head him! Head him!" and when he got there the buck's tracks and the five ex-ploded shells were not twenty paces apart.

There were five guests in camp that night from Jeffer-son: Mr. Bayard Sartoris and his son and General Comp-son's son and two others. And the next morning he looked out the window, into the gray thin drizzle of daybreak which Ash had predicted, and there they were, standing and squatting beneath the thin rain, almost two dozen of them who had fed Old Ben corn and shoats and even calves for ten years, in their worn hats and hunting coats and overalls which any town Negro would have thrown away or burned and only the rubber boots strong and sound, and the worn and blueless guns, and some even without guns. While they ate breakfast a dozen more arrived, mounted and on foot: loggers from the camp thirteen miles below and sawmill men from Hoke's and the only gun among them that one which the log-train conductor carried: so that when they went into the woods this morning Major de Spain led a party almost as strong, excepting that some of them were not armed, as some he had led in the last darkening days of '64 and '65. The little yard would not hold them. They overflowed it, into the lane where Major de Spain sat his mare while Ash in his dirty apron thrust the greasy cartridges into his carbine and passed it up to him and the great grave blue dog stood at his stirrup not as a dog stands but as a horse stands, blinking his sleepy topaz eyes at nothing, deaf even to the yelling of the hounds which Boon and Tennie's Jim held on leash.

"We'll put General Compson on Katie this morning," Major de Spain said. "He drew blood last year; if he'd had a mule then that would have stood, he would have——"

"No," General Compson said. "I'm too old to go helling through the woods on a mule or a horse or anything else any more. Besides, I had my chance last year and missed it. I'm going on a stand this morning. I'm going to let that boy ride Katie."

"No, wait," McCaslin said. "Ike's got the rest of his life to hunt bears in. Let somebody else——"

"No," General Compson said. "I want Ike to ride Katie. He's already a better woodsman than you or me either and in another ten years he'll be as good as Walter."

At first he couldn't believe it, not until Major de Spain spoke to him. Then he was up, on the one-eyed mule which would not spook at wild blood, looking down at the dog motionless at Major de Spain's stirrup, looking in the gray streaming light bigger than a calf, bigger than he knew it actually was—the big head, the chest almost as big as his own, the blue hide beneath which the muscles flinched or quivered to no touch since the heart which drove blood to them loved no man and no thing, standing as a horse stands yet different from a horse which infers only weight and speed while Lion inferred not only courage and all else that went to make up the will and desire to pursue and kill, but endurance, the will and desire to endure beyond all imaginable limits of flesh in order to overtake and slay. Then the dog looked at him. It moved its head and looked at him across the trivial uproar of the hounds, out of the yellow eyes as depthless as Boon's, as free as Boon's of meanness or generosity or gentleness or viciousness. They were just cold and sleepy. Then it blinked, and he knew it was not looking at him and never had been, without even bothering to turn its head away.

That morning he heard the first cry. Lion had already vanished while Sam and Tennie's Jim were putting saddles on the mule and horse which had drawn the wagon and he watched the hounds as they crossed and cast, snuffing and whimpering, until they too disappeared. Then he and Major de Spain and Sam and Tennie's Jim rode after them and heard the first cry out of the wet and thawing woods not two hundred yards ahead, high, with that abject, almost human quality he had come to know, and the other hounds joining in until the gloomed woods rang and clamored. They rode then. It seemed to him that he could actually see the big blue dog boring on, silent, and the bear too: the thick, locomotive-like shape which he had seen that day four years ago crossing the blow-down, crashing on ahead of the dogs faster than he had believed it could have moved, drawing away even from the running mules. He heard a shotgun, once. The woods had opened, they were going fast, the clamor faint and fading on ahead; they passed the man who had fired —a swamper, a pointing arm, a gaunt face, the small black orifice of his yelling studded with rotten teeth.

He heard the changed note in the hounds' uproar and two hundred yards ahead he saw them. The bear had turned. He saw Lion drive in without pausing and saw the bear strike him aside and lunge into the yelling hounds and kill one of them almost in its tracks and whirl and run again. Then they were in a streaming tide of dogs. He heard Major de Spain and Tennie's Jim shouting and the pistol sound of Tennie's Jim's leather thong as he tried to turn them. Then he and Sam Fathers were riding alone. One of the hounds had kept on with Lion though. He recognized its voice. It was the young hound which even a year ago had had no judgment and which, by the lights of the other hounds anyway, still had none. *Maybe that's what courage is,* he thought. "Right," Sam said behind him. "Right. We got to turn him from the river if we can."

Now they were in cane: a brake. He knew the path through it as well as Sam did. They came out of the undergrowth and struck the entrance almost exactly. It would traverse the brake and come out onto a high open ridge above the river. He heard the flat clap of Walter Ewell's rifle, then two more. "No," Sam said. "I can hear the hound. Go on."

They emerged from the narrow roofless tunnel of snapping and hissing cane, still galloping, onto the open ridge below which the thick yellow river, reflectionless in the gray and streaming light, seemed not to move. Now he could hear the hound too. It was not running. The cry was a high frantic yapping and Boon was running along the edge of the bluff, his old gun leaping and jouncing against his back on its sling made of a piece of cotton plowline. He whirled and ran up to them, wild-faced, and flung himself onto the mule behind the boy. "That damn boat!" he cried. "It's on the other side! He went straight across! Lion was too close to him! That little hound too! Lion was so close I couldn't shoot! Go on!" he cried, beating his heels into the mule's flanks. "Go on!"

They plunged down the bank, slipping and sliding in the thawed earth, crashing through the willows and into the water. He felt no shock, no cold, he on one side of the swimming mule, grasping the pommel with one hand and holding his gun above the water with the other, Boon opposite him. Sam was behind them somewhere, and then the river, the water about them, was full of dogs. They swam faster than the mules; they were scrabbling up the bank before the mules touched bottom. Major de Spain was whooping from the bank they had just left and, looking back, he saw Tennie's Jim and the horse as they went into the water.

Now the woods ahead of them and the rain-heavy air were one uproar. It rang and clamored; it echoed and broke against the bank behind them and reformed and clamored and rang until it seemed to the boy that all the hounds which had ever bayed game in this land were yelling down at him. He got his leg over the mule as it came up out of the water. Boon didn't try to mount again. He grasped one stirrup as they went up the bank and crashed through the undergrowth which fringed the bluff and saw the bear, on its hind feet, its back against a tree while the bellowing hounds swirled around it and once more Lion drove in, leaping clear of the ground.

This time the bear didn't strike him down. It caught the dog in both arms, almost loverlike, and they both went down. He was off the mule now. He drew back both hammers of the gun but he could see nothing but moiling spotted houndbodies until the bear surged up again. Boon was yelling something, he could not tell what; he could see Lion still clinging to the bear's throat and he saw the bear, half erect, strike one of the hounds with one paw and hurl it five or six feet and then, rising and rising as though it would never stop, stand erect again and begin to rake at Lion's belly with its forepaws. Then Boon was running. The boy saw the gleam of the blade in his hand and watched him leap among the hounds, hurdling them, kicking them aside as he ran, and fling himself astride the bear as he had hurled himself onto the mule, his legs locked around the bear's belly, his left arm under the bear's throat where Lion clung, and the glint of the knife as it rose and fell.

It fell just once. For an instant they almost resembled a piece of statuary: the clinging dog, the bear, the man astride its back, working and probing the buried blade. Then they went down, pulled over backward by Boon's weight, Boon underneath. It was the bear's back which reappeared first but at once Boon was astride it again. He had never released the knife and again the boy saw the almost infinitesimal movement of his arm and shoulder as he probed and sought; then the bear surged erect, raising with it the man and the dog too, and turned and still carrying the man and the dog it took two or three steps toward the woods on its hind feet as a man would have walked and crashed down. It didn't collapse, crumple. It fell all of a piece, as a tree falls, so that all three of them, man dog and bear, seemed to bounce once.

He and Tennie's Jim ran forward. Boon was kneeling at the bear's head. His left ear was shredded, his left coat sleeve was completely gone, his right boot had been ripped from knee to instep; the bright blood thinned in the thin rain down his leg and hand and arm and down the side of his face which was no longer wild but was quite calm. Together they prized Lion's jaws from the bear's throat. "Easy, goddamn it," Boon said. "Can't you see his guts are all out of him?" He began to remove his coat. He spoke to Tennie's Jim in that calm voice: "Bring the boat up. It's about a hundred yards down the bank there. I saw it." Tennie's Jim rose and went away. Then, and he could not remember if it had been a call or an exclamation from Tennie's Jim or if he had glanced up by chance, he saw Tennie's Jim stooping and saw Sam Fathers lying motionless on his face in the trampled mud.

The mule had not thrown him. He remembered that Sam was down too even before Boon began to run. There was no mark on him whatever and when he and Boon turned him over, his eyes were open and he said something in that tongue which he and Joe Baker had used to speak together. But he couldn't move. Tennie's Jim brought the skiff up; they could hear him shouting to Major de Spain across the river. Boon wrapped Lion in his hunting coat and carried him down to the skiff and they carried Sam down and returned and hitched the bear to the one-eyed mule's saddle-bow with Tennie's Jim's leash-thong and dragged him down to the skiff and got him into it and left Tennie's Jim to swim the horse and the two mules back across. Major de Spain caught the bow of the skiff as Boon jumped out and past him before it touched the bank. He looked at Old Ben and said quietly: "Well." Then he walked into the water and leaned down and touched Sam and Sam looked up at him and said something in that old tongue he and Joe Baker spoke. "You don't know what happened?" Major de Spain said.

"No, sir," the boy said. "It wasn't the mule. It wasn't anything. He was off the mule when Boon ran in on the bear. Then we looked up and he was lying on the ground." Boon was shouting at Tennie's Jim, still in the middle of the river.

"Come on, goddamn it!" he said. "Bring me that mule!"

"What do you want with a mule?" Major de Spain said.

Boon didn't even look at him. "I'm going to Hoke's to get the doctor," he said in that calm voice, his face quite calm beneath the steady thinning of the bright blood.

"You need a doctor yourself," Major de Spain said. "Tennie's Jim——"

"Damn that," Boon said. He turned on Major de Spain.

His face was still calm, only his voice was a pitch higher. "Can't you see his goddamn guts are all out of him?"

"Boon!" Major de Spain said. They looked at one another. Boon was a good head taller than Major de Spain; even the boy was taller now than Major de Spain.

"I've got to get the doctor," Boon said. "His goddamn guts——"

"All right," Major de Spain said. Tennie's Jim came up out of the water. The horse and the sound mule had already scented Old Ben; they surged and plunged all the way up to the top of the bluff, dragging Tennie's Jim with them, before he could stop them and tie them and come back. Major de Spain unlooped the leather thong of his compass from his buttonhole and gave it to Tennie's Jim. "Go straight to Hoke's," he said. "Bring Doctor Crawford back with you. Tell him there are two men to be looked at. Take my mare. Can you find the road from here?"

"Yes, sir," Tennie's Jim said.

"All right," Major de Spain said. "Go on." He turned to the boy. "Take the mules and the horse and go back and get the wagon. We'll go on down the river in the boat to Coon bridge. Meet us there. Can you find it again?"

"Yes, sir," the boy said.

"All right. Get started."

He went back to the wagon. He realized then how far they had run. It was already afternoon when he put the mules into the traces and tied the horse's lead-rope to the tail-gate. He reached Coon bridge at dusk. The skiff was already there. Before he could see it and almost before he could see the water he had to leap from the tilting wagon, still holding the reins, and work around to where he could grasp the bit and then the ear of the plunging sound mule and dig his heels and hold it until Boon came up the bank. The rope of the led horse had already snapped and it had already disappeared up the road toward camp. They turned the wagon around and took the mules out and he led the sound mule a hundred

yards up the road and tied it. Boon had already brought
Lion up to the wagon and Sam was sitting up in the skiff
now and when they raised him he tried to walk, up the
bank and to the wagon and he tried to climb into the
wagon but Boon did not wait; he picked Sam up bodily
and set him on the seat. Then they hitched Old Ben to
the one-eyed mule's saddle again and dragged him up
the bank and set two skid-poles into the open tail-
gate and got him into the wagon and he went and got the
sound mule and Boon fought it into the traces, striking it
across its hard hollow-sounding face until it came into
position and stood trembling. Then the rain came down,
as though it had held off all day waiting on them.

They returned to camp through it, through the streaming and sightless dark, hearing long before they saw any
light the horn and the spaced shots to guide them. When
they came to Sam's dark little hut he tried to stand up.
He spoke again in the tongue of the old fathers; then he
said clearly: "Let me out. Let me out."

"He hasn't got any fire," Major said. "Go on!" he said
sharply.

But Sam was struggling now, trying to stand up. "Let
me out, master," he said. "Let me go home."

So he stopped the wagon and Boon got down and lifted
Sam out. He did not wait to let Sam try to walk this time.
He carried him into the hut and Major de Spain got light
on a paper spill from the buried embers on the hearth and
lit the lamp and Boon put Sam on his bunk and drew off
his boots and Major de Spain covered him and the boy
was not there, he was holding the mules, the sound one
which was trying again to bolt since when the wagon
stopped Old Ben's scent drifted forward again along the
streaming blackness of air, but Sam's eyes were probably
open again on that profound look which saw further than
them or the hut, further than the death of a bear and the
dying of a dog. Then they went on, toward the long
wailing of the horn and the shots which seemed each

to linger intact somewhere in the thick streaming air until the next spaced report joined and blended with it, to the lighted house, the bright streaming windows, the quiet faces as Boon entered, bloody and quite calm, carrying the bundled coat. He laid Lion, blood coat and all, on his stale sheetless pallet bed which not even Ash, as deft in the house as a woman, could ever make smooth.

The sawmill doctor from Hoke's was already there. Boon would not let the doctor touch him until he had seen to Lion. He wouldn't risk giving Lion chloroform. He put the entrails back and sewed him up without it while Major de Spain held his head and Boon his feet. But he never tried to move. He lay there, the yellow eyes open upon nothing while the quiet men in the new hunting clothes and in the old ones crowded into the little airless room rank with the smell of Boon's body and garments, and watched. Then the doctor cleaned and disinfected Boon's face and arm and leg and bandaged them and, the boy in front with a lantern and the doctor and Mc-Caslin and Major de Spain and General Compson following, they went to Sam Fathers' hut. Tennie's Jim had built up the fire; he squatted before it, dozing. Sam had not moved since Boon had put him in the bunk and Major de Spain had covered him with the blankets, yet he opened his eyes and looked from one to another of the faces and when McCaslin touched his shoulder and said, "Sam. The doctor wants to look at you," he even drew his hands out of the blanket and began to fumble at his shirt buttons until McCaslin said, "Wait. We'll do it." They undressed him. He lay there—the copper-brown, almost hairless body, the old man's body, the old man, the wild man not even one generation from the woods, child-less, kinless, peopleless—motionless, his eyes open but no longer looking at any of them, while the doctor examined him and drew the blankets up and put the stethoscope back into his bag and snapped the bag and only the boy knew that Sam too was going to die.

"Exhaustion," the doctor said. "Shock maybe. A man his age swimming rivers in December. He'll be all right. Just make him stay in bed for a day or two. Will there be somebody here with him?"

"There will be sombody here," Major de Spain said.

They went back to the house, to the rank little room where Boon still sat on the pallet bed with Lion's head under his hand while the men, the ones who had hunted behind Lion and the ones who had never seen him before today, came quietly in to look at him and went away. Then it was dawn and they all went out into the yard to look at Old Ben, with his eyes open too and his lips snarled back from his worn teeth and his mutilated foot and the little hard lumps under his skin which were the old bullets (there were fifty-two of them, buckshot rifle and ball) and the single almost invisible slit under his left shoulder where Boon's blade had finally found his life. Then Ash began to beat on the bottom of the dishpan with a heavy spoon to call them to breakfast and it was the first time he could remember hearing no sound from the dogs under the kitchen while they were eating. It was as if the old bear, even dead there in the yard, was a more potent terror still than they could face without Lion between them.

The rain had stopped during the night. By midmorning the thin sun appeared, rapidly burning away mist and cloud, warming the air and the earth; it would be one of those windless Mississippi December days which are a sort of Indian summer's Indian summer. They moved Lion out to the front gallery, into the sun. It was Boon's idea. "Goddamn it," he said, "he never did want to stay in the house until I made him. You know that." He took a crowbar and loosened the floor boards under his pallet bed so it could be raised, mattress and all, without disturbing Lion's position, and they carried him out to the gallery and put him down facing the woods.

Then he and the doctor and McCaslin and Major de

Spain went to Sam's hut. This time Sam didn't open his eyes and his breathing was so quiet, so peaceful that they could hardly see that he breathed. The doctor didn't even take out his stethoscope nor even touch him. "He's all right," the doctor said. "He didn't even catch cold. He just quit."

"Quit?" McCaslin said.

"Yes. Old people do that sometimes. Then they get a good night's sleep or maybe it's just a drink of whiskey, and they change their minds."

They returned to the house. And then they began to arrive—the swamp-dwellers, the gaunt men who ran traplines and lived on quinine and coons and river water, the farmers of little corn- and cotton-patches along the bottom's edge whose fields and cribs and pig-pens the old bear had rifled, the loggers from the camp, and the sawmill men from Hoke's, and the town men from further away than that, whose hounds the old bear had slain and whose traps and deadfalls he had wrecked and whose lead he carried. They came up mounted and on foot and in wagons, to enter the yard and look at him and then go on to the front where Lion lay, filling the little yard and overflowing it until there were almost a hundred of them squatting and standing in the warm and drowsing sunlight, talking quietly of hunting, of the game and the dogs which ran it, of hounds and bear and deer and men of yesterday vanished from the earth, while from time to time the great blue dog would open his eyes, not as if he were listening to them but as though to look at the woods for a moment before closing his eyes again, to remember the woods or to see that they were still there. He died at sundown.

Major de Spain broke camp that night. They carried Lion into the woods, or Boon carried him that is, wrapped in a quilt from his bed, just as he had refused to let anyone else touch Lion yesterday until the doctor got there; Boon carrying Lion, and the boy and General Compson and Walter and still almost fifty of them following with lanterns and lighted pine-knots—men from Hoke's and even further, who would have to ride out of the bottom in the dark, and swampers and trappers who would have to walk even, scattering toward the little hidden huts where they lived. And Boon would let nobody else dig the grave either and lay Lion in it and cover him, and then General Compson stood at the head of it while the blaze and smoke of the pine-knots streamed away among the winter branches and spoke as he would have spoken over a man. Then they returned to camp. Major de Spain and McCaslin and Ash had rolled and tied all the bedding. The mules were hitched to the wagon and pointed out of the bottom and the wagon was already loaded and the stove in the kitchen was cold and the table was set with scraps of cold food and bread and only the coffee was hot when the boy ran into the kitchen where Major de Spain and McCaslin had already eaten. "What?" he cried. "What? I'm not going."

"Yes," McCaslin said, "we're going out tonight. Major wants to get on back home."

"No!" he said. "I'm going to stay."

"You've got to be back in school Monday. You've already missed a week more than I intended. It will take you from now until Monday to catch up. Sam's all right. You heard Doctor Crawford. I'm going to leave Boon and Tennie's Jim both to stay with him until he feels like getting up."

He was panting. The others had come in. He looked rapidly and almost frantically around at the other faces. Boon had a fresh bottle. He upended it and started the cork by striking the bottom of the bottle with the heel of his hand and drew the cork with his teeth and spat it out and drank. "You're damn right you're going back to school," Boon said. "Or I'll burn the tail off of you myself if Cass don't, whether you are sixteen or sixty. Where in hell do you expect to get without education? Where

would Cass be? Where in hell would I be if I hadn't
never went to school?"

He looked at McCaslin again. He could feel his breath
coming shorter and shorter and shallower and shallower,
as if there were not enough air in the kitchen for that
many to breathe. "This is just Thursday. I'll come home
Sunday night on one of the horses. I'll come home Sunday,
then. I'll make up the time I lost studying Sunday night,
McCaslin," he said, without even despair.

"No, I tell you," McCaslin said. "Sit down here and
eat your supper. We're going out to——"

"Hold up, Cass," General Compson said. The boy did
not know General Compson had moved until he put his
hand on his shoulder. "What is it, bud?" he said.

"I've got to stay," he said. "I've got to."

"All right," General Compson said. "You can stay. If
missing an extra week of school is going to throw you so
far behind you'll have to sweat to find out what some
hired pedagogue put between the covers of a book, you
better quit altogether.—And you shut up, Cass," he said,
though McCaslin had not spoken. "You've got one foot
straddled into a farm and the other foot straddled into a
bank; you ain't even got a good hand-hold where this
boy was already an old man long before you damned
Sartorises and Edmondses invented farms and banks to
keep yourselves from having to find out what this boy
was born knowing, and fearing too maybe, but without
being afraid, that could go ten miles on a compass because
he wanted to look at a bear none of us had ever got near
enough to put a bullet in and looked at the bear and
came the ten miles back on the compass in the dark;
maybe by God that's the why and the wherefore of
farms and banks.—I reckon you still ain't going to tell
what it is?"

But still he could not. "I've got to stay," he said.

"All right," General Compson said. "There's plenty of

grub left. And you'll come home Sunday, like you promised McCaslin? Not Sunday night: Sunday."

"Yes, sir," he said.

"All right," General Compson said. "Sit down and eat, boys," he said. "Let's get started. It's going to be cold before we get home."

They ate. The wagon was already loaded and ready to depart; all they had to do was to get into it. Boon would drive them out to the road, to the farmer's stable where the surrey had been left. He stood beside the wagon, in silhouette on the sky, turbaned like a Paythan and taller than any there, the bottle tilted. Then he flung the bottle from his lips without even lowering it, spinning and glinting in the faint starlight, empty. "Them that's going," he said, "get in the goddamn wagon. Them that ain't, get out of the goddamn way." The others got in. Boon mounted to the seat beside General Compson and the wagon moved, on into the obscurity until the boy could no longer see it, even the moving density of it amid the greater night. But he could still hear it, for a long while: the slow, deliberate banging of the wooden frame as it lurched from rut to rut. And he could hear Boon even when he could no longer hear the wagon. He was singing, harsh, tuneless, loud.

That was Thursday. On Saturday morning Tennie's Jim left on McCaslin's woods-horse which had not been out of the bottom one time now in six years, and late that afternoon rode through the gate on the spent horse and on to the commissary where McCaslin was rationing the tenants and the wage-hands for the coming week, and this time McCaslin forestalled any necessity or risk of having to wait while Major de Spain's surrey was being horsed and harnessed. He took their own, and with Tennie's Jim already asleep in the back seat he drove in to Jefferson and waited while Major de Spain changed to boots and put on his overcoat, and they drove the thirty miles in the dark of that night and at daybreak on Sunday morning they swapped to the waiting mare and mule and as the sun rose they rode out of the jungle and onto the low ridge where they had buried Lion: the low mound of unannealed earth where Boon's spade-marks still showed, and beyond the grave the platform of freshly cut saplings bound between four posts and the blanket-wrapped bundle upon the platform and Boon and the boy squatting between the platform and the grave until Boon, the bandage removed, ripped from his head so that the long scoriations of Old Ben's claws resembled crusted tar in the sunlight, sprang up and threw down upon them with the old gun with which he had never been known to hit anything although McCaslin was already off the mule, kicked both feet free of the irons and vaulted down before the mule had stopped, walking toward Boon.

"Stand back," Boon said. "By God, you won't touch him. Stand back, McCaslin." Still McCaslin came on, fast yet without haste.

"Cass!" Major de Spain said. Then he said, "Boon! You, Boon!" and he was down too and the boy rose too, quickly, and still McCaslin came on not fast but steady and walked up to the grave and reached his hand steadily out, quickly yet still not fast, and took hold the gun by the middle so that he and Boon faced one another across Lion's grave, both holding the gun, Boon's spent indomitable amazed and frantic face almost a head higher than McCaslin's beneath the black scoriations of beast's claws and then Boon's chest began to heave as though there were not enough air in all the woods, in all the wilderness, for all of them, for him and anyone else, even for him alone.

"Turn it loose, Boon," McCaslin said.

"You damn little spindling—" Boon said. "Don't you know I can take it away from you? Don't you know I can tie it around your neck like a damn cravat?"

"Yes," McCaslin said. "Turn it loose, Boon."

"This is the way he wanted it. He told us. He told us

exactly how to do it. And by God you ain't going to move him. So we did it like he said, and I been sitting here ever since to keep the damn wildcats and varmints away from him and by God—" Then McCaslin had the gun, down-slanted while he pumped the slide, the five shells snicking out of it so fast that the last one was almost out before the first one touched the ground and McCaslin dropped the gun behind him without once having taken his eyes from Boon's.

"Did you kill him, Boon?" he said. Then Boon moved. He turned, he moved like he was still drunk and then for a moment blind too, one hand out as he blundered toward the big tree and seemed to stop walking before he reached the tree so that he plunged, fell toward it, flinging up both hands and catching himself against the tree and turning until his back was against it, backing with the tree's trunk his wild spent scoriated face and the tremendous heave and collapse of his chest, McCaslin following, facing him again, never once having moved his eyes from Boon's eyes. "Did you kill him, Boon?"

"No!" Boon said. "No!"

"Tell the truth," McCaslin said. "I would have done it if he had asked me to." Then the boy moved. He was between them, facing McCaslin; the water felt as if it had burst and sprung not from his eyes alone but from his whole face, like sweat.

"Leave him alone!" he cried. "Goddamn it! Leave him alone!"

IV

then he was twenty-one. He could say it, himself and his cousin juxtaposed not against the wilderness but against the tamed land which was to have been his heritage, the land which old Carothers McCaslin, his grandfather, had bought with white man's money from the wild men whose grandfathers without guns hunted it, and tamed and ordered, or believed he had tamed and ordered it, for the reason that the human beings he held in bondage and in the power of life and death had removed the forest from it and in their sweat scratched the surface of it to a depth of perhaps fourteen inches in order to grow something out of it which had not been there before, and which could be translated back into the money he who believed he had bought it had had to pay to get it and hold it, and a reasonable profit too: and for which reason old Carothers McCaslin, knowing better, could raise his children, his descendants and heirs, to believe the land was his to hold and bequeath, since the strong and ruthless man has a cynical foreknowledge of his own vanity and pride and strength and a contempt for all his get: just as, knowing better, Major de Spain had his fragment of that wilderness which was bigger and older than any recorded deed: just as, knowing better, old Thomas Sutpen, from whom Major de Spain had had his fragment for money: just as Ikkemotubbe, the Chickasaw chief, from whom Thomas Sutpen had had the fragment for money or rum or whatever it was, knew in his turn that not even a fragment of it had been his to relinquish or sell

not against the wilderness but against the land, not in pursuit and lust but in relinquishment; and in the commissary as it should have been, not the heart perhaps but certainly the solar-plexus of the repudiated and relinquished: the square, galleried, wooden building squatting like a portent above the fields whose laborers it still held in thrall, '65 or no, and placarded over with advertisements for snuff and cures for chills and salves and potions manufactured and sold by white men to bleach the pigment and straighten the hair of Negroes that they might resemble the very race which for two hundred years had held them in bondage and from which for another hundred years not even a bloody civil war would have set them completely free

himself and his cousin amid the old smells of cheese

and salt meat and kerosene and harness, the ranked shelves of tobacco and overalls and bottled medicine and thread and plow-bolts, the barrels and kegs of flour and meal and molasses and nails, the wall pegs dependant with plowlines and plow-collars and hames and trace-chains, and the desk and the shelf above it on which rested the ledgers in which McCaslin recorded the slow outward trickle of food and supplies and equipment which returned each fall as cotton made and ginned and sold (two threads frail as truth and impalpable as equators yet cable-strong to bind for life them who made the cotton to the land their sweat fell on), and the older ledgers, clumsy and archaic in size and shape, on the yellowed pages of which were recorded in the faded hand of his father Theophilus and his uncle Amodeus during the two decades before the Civil War the manumission, in title at least, of Carothers McCaslin's slaves:

'Relinquish,' McCaslin said. 'Relinquish. You, the direct male descendant of him who saw the opportunity and took it, bought the land, took the land, got the land no matter how, held it to bequeath, no matter how, out of the old grant, the first patent, when it was a wilderness of wild beasts and wilder men, and cleared it, translated it into something to bequeath to his children, worthy of bequeathment for his descendants' ease and security and pride, and to perpetuate his name and accomplishments. Not only the male descendant but the only and last descendant in the male line and in the third generation, while I am not only four generations from old Carothers, I derived through a woman and the very McCaslin in my name is mine only by sufferance and courtesy and my grandmother's pride in what that man accomplished, whose legacy and monument you think you can repudiate.' and he

'I can't repudiate it. It was never mine to repudiate. It was never Father's and Uncle Buddy's to bequeath me to repudiate, because it was never Grandfather's to bequeath them to bequeath me to repudiate, because it was

never old Ikkemotubbe's to sell to Grandfather for bequeathment and repudiation. Because it was never Ikkemotubbe's fathers' fathers' to bequeath Ikkemotubbe
to sell to Grandfather or any man because on the instant
when Ikkemotubbe discovered, realized, that he could sell
it for money, on that instant it ceased ever to have been
his forever, father to father to father, and the man who
bought it bought nothing.'

'Bought nothing?' and he

'Bought nothing. Because He told in the Book how He
created the earth, made it and looked at it and said it was
all right, and then He made man. He made the earth first
and peopled it with dumb creatures, and then He created
man to be His overseer on the earth and to hold suzerainty
over the earth and the animals on it in His name, not to
hold for himself and his descendants inviolable title forever, generation after generation, to the oblongs and
squares of the earth, but to hold the earth mutual and intact in the communal anonymity of brotherhood, and all
the fee He asked was pity and humility and sufferance and
endurance and the sweat of his face for bread. And I know
what you are going to say,' he said: 'That nevertheless
Grandfather—' and McCaslin

'—did own it. And not the first. Not alone and not the
first since, as your Authority states, man was dispossessed
of Eden. Nor yet the second and still not alone, on down
through the tedious and shabby chronicle of His chosen
sprung from Abraham; and of the sons of them who dispossessed Abraham, and of the five hundred years during
which half the known world and all it contained was chattel to one city, as this plantation and all the life it contained
was chattel and revokeless thrall to this commissary store
and those ledgers yonder during your grandfather's life;
and the next thousand years while men fought over the
fragments of that collapse until at last even the fragments
were exhausted and men snarled over the gnawed bones
of the old world's worthless evening until an accidental

egg discovered to them a new hemisphere. So let me say it: That nevertheless and notwithstanding old Carothers did own it. Bought it, got it, no matter; kept it, held it, no matter; bequeathed it: else why do you stand here relinquishing and repudiating? Held it, kept it for fifty years until you could repudiate it, while He—this Arbiter, this Architect, this Umpire—condoned—or did He? looked down and saw—or did He? Or at least did nothing: saw, and could not, or did not see; saw, and would not, or perhaps He would not see—perverse, impotent, or blind: which?' and he

'Dispossessed.' and McCaslin

'What?' and he

'Dispossessed. Not impotent: He didn't condone; not blind, because He watched it. And let me say it. Dispossessed of Eden. Dispossessed of Canaan, and those who dispossessed him dispossessed him dispossessed, and the five hundred years of absentee landlords in the Roman bagnios, and the thousand years of wild men from the northern woods who dispossessed them and devoured their ravished substance ravished in turn again and then snarled in what you call the old world's worthless twilight over the old world's gnawed bones, blasphemous in His name until He used a simple egg to discover to them a new world where a nation of people could be founded in humility and pity and sufferance and pride of one to another. And Grandfather did own the land nevertheless and notwithstanding because He permitted it, not impotent and not condoning and not blind, because He ordered and watched it. He saw the land already accursed even as Ikkemotubbe and Ikkemotubbe's father old Issetibbeha and old Issetibbeha's fathers too held it, already tainted even before any white man owned it by what Grandfather and his kind, his fathers, had brought into the new land which He had vouchsafed them out of pity and sufferance, on condition of pity and humility and sufferance, on condition of pity and humility and sufferance and endurance, from that old world's corrupt and worthless twilight as though in the sailfuls of the old world's tainted wind which drove the ships—' and McCaslin

'Ah.'

'—and no hope for the land anywhere so long as Ikkemotubbe and Ikkemotubbe's descendants held it in unbroken succession. Maybe He saw that only by voiding the land for a time of Ikkemotubbe's blood and substituting for it another blood, could He accomplish His purpose. Maybe He knew already what that other blood would be, maybe it was more than justice that only the white man's blood was available and capable to raise the white man's curse, more than vengeance when—' and McCaslin

'Ah.'

'—when He used the blood which had brought in the evil to destroy the evil as doctors use fever to burn up fever, poison to slay poison. Maybe He chose Grandfather out of all of them He might have picked. Maybe He knew that Grandfather himself would not serve His purpose because Grandfather was born too soon too, but that Grandfather would have descendants, the right descendants; maybe He had foreseen already the descendants Grandfather would have, maybe He saw already in Grandfather the seed progenitive of the three generations He saw it would take to set at least some of His lowly people free—' and McCaslin

'The sons of Ham. You who quote the Book: the sons of Ham.' and he

'There are some things He said in the Book, and some things reported of Him that He did not say. And I know what you will say now: That if truth is one thing to me and another thing to you, how will we choose which is truth? You don't need to choose. The heart already knows. He didn't have His Book written to be read by what must elect and choose, but by the heart, not by the wise of the earth because maybe they don't need it or maybe the wise no longer have any heart, but by the doomed and lowly of the earth who have nothing else to read with but the heart. Because the men who wrote His Book for Him were writing about truth and there is only one truth and it covers all things that touch the heart.' and McCaslin

'So these men who transcribed His Book for Him were sometime liars.' and he

'Yes. Because they were human men. They were trying to write down the heart's truth out of the heart's driving complexity, for all the complex and troubled hearts which would beat after them. What they were trying to tell, what He wanted said, was too simple. Those for whom they transcribed His words could not have believed them. It had to be expounded in the everyday terms which they were familiar with and could comprehend, not only those who listened but those who told it too, because if they who were that near to Him as to have been elected from among all who breathed and spoke language to transcribe and relay His words, could comprehend truth only through the complexity of passion and lust and hate and fear which drives the heart, what distance back to truth must they traverse whom truth could only reach by word-of-mouth?' and McCaslin

'I might answer that, since you have taken to proving your points and disproving mine by the same text, I don't know. But I don't say that, because you have answered yourself: No time at all if, as you say, the heart knows truth, the infallible and unerring heart. And perhaps you are right, since although you admitted three generations from old Carothers to you, there were not three. There were not even completely two. Uncle Buck and Uncle Buddy. And they not the first and not alone. A thousand other Bucks and Buddies in less than two generations and sometimes less than one in this land which so you claim God created and man himself cursed and tainted. Not to mention 1865.' and he

'Yes. More men than Father and Uncle Buddy,' not even glancing toward the shelf above the desk, nor did

McCaslin. They did not need to. To him it was as though the ledgers in their scarred cracked leather bindings were being lifted down one by one in their fading sequence and spread open on the desk or perhaps upon some apocryphal Bench, or even Altar, or perhaps before the Throne Itself for a last perusal and contemplation and refreshment of the Allknowledgeable, before the yellowed pages and the brown thin ink in which was recorded the injustice and a little at least of its amelioration and restitution faded back forever into the anonymous communal original dust

the yellowed pages scrawled in fading ink by the hand first of his grandfather and then of his father and uncle, bachelors up to and past fifty and then sixty, the one who ran the plantation and the farming of it, and the other who did the housework and the cooking and continued to do it even after his twin married and the boy himself was born

the two brothers who as soon as their father was buried moved out of the tremendously-conceived, the almost barnlike edifice which he had not even completed, into a one-room log cabin which the two of them built themselves and added other rooms to while they lived in it, refusing to allow any slave to touch any timber of it other than the actual raising into place the logs which two men alone could not handle, and domiciled all the slaves in the big house some of the windows of which were still merely boarded up with odds and ends of plank or with the skins of bear and deer nailed over the empty frames: each sundown the brother who superintended the farming would parade the Negroes as a first sergeant dismisses a company, and herd them willynilly, man woman and child, without question protest or recourse, into the tremendous abortive edifice scarcely yet out of embryo, as if even old Carothers McCaslin had paused aghast at the concrete indication of his own vanity's boundless conceiving: he would call his mental roll and herd them in and with a hand-wrought nail as long as a flenching-knife and suspended from a short deer-hide thong attached to the door-jamb for that purpose, he would nail to the door of that house which lacked half its windows and had no hinged back door at all, so that presently, and for fifty years afterward, when the boy himself was big to hear and remember it, there was in the land a sort of folk-tale: of the countryside all night long full of skulking McCaslin slaves dodging the moonlit roads and the Patrol-riders to visit other plantations, and of the unspoken gentlemen's agreement between the two white men and the two dozen black ones that, after the white man had counted them and driven the home-made nail into the front door at sundown, neither of the white men would go around behind the house and look at the back door, provided that all the Negroes were behind the front one when the brother who drove it drew out the nail again at daybreak

the twins who were identical even in their handwriting, unless you had specimens side by side to compare, and even when both hands appeared on the same page (as often happened, as if, long since past any oral intercourse, they had used the diurnally advancing pages to conduct the unavoidable business of the compulsion which had traversed all the waste wilderness of North Mississippi in 1830 and '40 and singled them out to drive) they both looked as though they had been written by the same perfectly normal ten-year-old boy, even to the spelling, except that the spelling did not improve as one by one the slaves which Carothers McCaslin had inherited and purchased— Roscius and Phoebe and Thucydides and Eunice and their descendants, and Sam Fathers and his mother for both of whom he had swapped an underbred trotting gelding to old Ikkemotubbe, the Chickasaw chief, from whom he had likewise bought the land, and Tennie Beauchamp whom the twin Amodeus had won from a neighbor in a poker-game, and the anomaly calling itself Percival Brownlee which the twin Theophilus had purchased, nei-

ther he nor his brother ever knew why apparently, from
Bedford Forrest while he was still only a slave-dealer and
not yet a general (It was a single page, not long and covering less than a year, not seven months in fact, begun in the
hand which the boy had learned to distinguish as that of
his father:

> *Percavil Brownly 26yr Old. cleark @ Bookepper.
> bought from N.B.Forest at Cold Water 3 Mar 1856
> $265. dolars*

and beneath that, in the same hand:

> *5 mar 1856 No bookepper any way Cant read. Can
> write his Name but I already put that down My self
> Says he can Plough but dont look like it to Me. sent
> to Feild to day Mar 5 1856*

and the same hand:

> *6 Mar 1856 Cant plough either Says he aims to be a
> Precher so may be he can lead live stock to Crick to
> Drink*

and this time it was the other, the hand which he now
recognized as his uncle's when he could see them both on
the same page:

> *Mar 23th 1856 Cant do that either Except one at a
> Time Get shut of him*

then the first again:

> *24 Mar 1856 Who in hell would buy him*

then the second:

> *19th of Apr 1856 Nobody You put yourself out of
> Market at Cold Water two months ago I never said
> sell him Free him*

the first:

> *22 Apr 1856 Ill get it out of him*

the second:

> *Jun 13th 1856 How $1 per yr 265$ 265 yrs Wholl sign his Free paper*

then the first again:

> *1 Oct 1856 Mule josephine Broke Leg @ shot Wrong stall wrong niger wrong everything $100. dolars*

and the same:

> *2 Oct 1856 Freed Debit McCaslin @ McCaslin $265. dolars*

then the second again:

> *Oct 3th Debit Theophilus McCaslin Niger 265$ Mule 100$ 365$ He hasnt gone yet Father should be here*

then the first:

> *3 Oct 1856 Son of a bitch wont leave What would father done*

the second:

> *29th of Oct 1856 Renamed him*

the first:

> *31 Oct 1856 Renamed him what*

the second:

> *Chrstms 1856 Spintrius*

) took substance and even a sort of shadowy life with their passions and complexities too, as page followed page and year year; all there, not only the general and condoned injustice and its slow amortization but the specific tragedy which had not been condoned and could never be amortized; the new page and the new ledger, the hand which he could now recognize at first glance as his father's:

Father dide Lucius Quintus Carothers McCaslin, Callina 1772 Missippy 1837. Dide and burid 27 June 1837

Roskus. rased by Granfather in Callina Dont know how old. Freed 27 June 1837 Dont want to leave. Dide and Burid 12 Jan 1841

Fibby Roskus Wife. bought by granfather in Callina says Fifty Freed 27 June 1837 Dont want to leave. Dide and burd 1 Aug 1849

Thucydus Roskus @ Fibby Son born in Callina 1779. Refused 10acre peace fathers Will 28 Jun 1837 Refused Cash offer $200. dolars from A. @ T. McCaslin 28 Jun 1837 Wants to stay and work it out

and beneath this and covering the next five pages and almost that many years, the slow, day-by-day accrument of the wages allowed him and the food and clothing—the molasses and meat and meal, the cheap durable shirts and jeans and shoes, and now and then a coat against rain and cold—charged against the slowly yet steadily mounting sum of balance (and it would seem to the boy that he could actually see the black man, the slave whom his white owner had forever manumitted by the very act from which the black man could never be free so long as memory lasted, entering the commissary, asking permission perhaps of the white man's son to see the ledger-page which he could not even read, not even asking for the white man's word, which he would have had to accept for the reason that there was absolutely no way under the sun for him to test it, as to how the account stood, how much longer before he could go and never return, even if only as far as Jefferson seventeen miles away), on to the double pen-stroke closing the final entry:

3 Nov 1841 By Cash to Thucydus McCaslin $200. dolars Set Up blaksmith in J. Dec 1841 Dide and burid in J. 17 feb. 1854

Eunice Bought by Father in New Orleans 1807 $650. dolars. Marrid to Thucydus 1809 Drownd in Crick Cristmas Day 1832 and then the other hand appeared, the first time he had seen it in the ledger to distinguish it as his uncle's, the cook and housekeeper whom even McCaslin, who had known him and the boy's father for sixteen years before the boy was born, remembered as sitting all day long in the rocking chair from which he cooked the food, before the kitchen fire on which he cooked it:

June 21th 1833 Drownd herself

and the first:

23 Jun 1833 Who in hell ever heard of a niger drownding him self

and the second, unhurried, with a complete finality; the two identical entries might have been made with a rubber stamp save for the date:

Aug 13th 1833 Drownd herself

and he thought *But why? But why?* He was sixteen then. It was neither the first time he had been alone in the commissary nor the first time he had taken down the old ledgers familiar on their shelf above the desk ever since he could remember. As a child and even after nine and ten and eleven, when he had learned to read, he would look up at the scarred and cracked backs and ends but with no particular desire to open them, and though he intended to examine them someday because he realized that they probably contained a chronological and much more comprehensive though doubtless tedious record than he would ever get from any other source, not alone of his own flesh and blood but of all his people, not only the whites but the black ones too, who were as much a part of his ancestry as his white progenitors, and of the land which they had all held and used in common and fed from and on and would continue to use in common without regard to color or titular ownership, it would only be on some idle day when he was old and perhaps even bored a little, since what the old books contained would be after all these years fixed immutably, finished, unalterable, harmless. Then he was sixteen. He knew what he was going to find before he found it. He got the commissary key from McCaslin's room after midnight while McCaslin was asleep and with the commissary door shut and locked behind him and the forgotten lantern stinking anew the rank dead icy air, he leaned above the yellowed page and thought not Why drowned herself, but thinking what he believed his father had thought when he found his brother's first comment: Why did Uncle Buddy think she had drowned herself? finding, beginning to find on the next succeeding page what he knew he would find, only this was still not it because he already knew this:

> *Tomasina called Tomy Daughter of Thucydus @ Eunice Born 1810 dide in Child bed June 1833 and Burd. Yr stars fell*

nor the next:

> *Turl Son of Thucydus @ Eunice Tomy born Jun 1833 yr stars fell Fathers will*

and nothing more, no tedious recording filling this page of wages, day by day, and food and clothing charged against them, no entry of his death and burial because he had outlived his white half-brothers and the books which McCaslin kept did not include obituaries: just *Fathers will* and he had seen that too: old Carothers' bold cramped hand far less legible than his sons' even and not much better in spelling, who while capitalizing almost every noun and verb, made no effort to punctuate or construct whatever, just as he made no effort either to explain or obfuscate the thousand-dollar legacy to the son of an unmarried slave-girl, to be paid only at the child's coming-of-age, bearing the consequence of the act of which there was still no definite incontrovertible proof that he acknowledged, not out of his own substance, but penalizing his sons with it, charging them a cash forfeit on the accident of their own paternity; not even a bribe for silence toward his own fame since his fame would suffer only after he was no longer present to defend it, flinging almost contemptuously, as he might a cast-off hat or pair of shoes, the thousand dollars which could have had no more reality to him under those conditions than it would have to the Negro, the slave who would not even see it until he came of age, twenty-one years too late to begin to learn what money was. *So I reckon that was cheaper than saying My son to a nigger,* he thought. *Even if My son wasn't but just two words. But there must have been love,* he thought. *Some sort of love. Even what he would have called love: not just an afternoon's or a night's spittoon.* There was the old man, old, within five years of his life's end, long a widower and, since his sons were not only bachelors but were approaching middleage, lonely in the house and doubtless even bored, since his plantation was established now and functioning and there was enough money now, too much of it probably for a man whose vices even apparently remained below his means; there was the girl, husbandless and young, only twenty-three when the child was born: perhaps he had sent for her at first out of loneliness, to have a young voice and movement in the house, summoned her, bade her mother send her each morning to sweep the floors and make the beds and the mother acquiescing since that was probably already understood, already planned: the only child of a couple who were not field hands and who held themselves something above the other slaves, not alone for that reason but because the husband and his father and mother too had been inherited by the white man from his father, and the white man himself had travelled three hundred miles and better to New Orleans in a day when men travelled by horseback or steamboat, and bought the girl's mother as a wife for him and that was all. The old frail pages seemed to turn of their own accord even while he thought, *His own daughter His own daughter. No. No Not even him,* back to that one where the white man (not even a widower then) who never went anywhere, any more than his sons in their time ever did, and who did not need another slave, had gone all the way to New Orleans and bought one. And Tomey's Terrel was still alive when the boy was ten years old and he knew from his own observation and memory that there had already been some white in Tomey's Terrel's blood before his father gave him the rest of it; and looking down at the yellowed page spread beneath the yellow glow of the lantern smoking and stinking in that rank chill midnight room fifty years later, he seemed to see her actually walking into the icy creek on that Christmas day six months before her daughter's and her lover's (*Her first lover's,* he thought. *Her first*) child was born, solitary, inflexible, griefless, ceremonial, in formal and succinct repudiation of grief and despair, who had already had to repudiate belief and hope

that was all. He would never need look at the ledgers again nor did he; the yellowed pages in their fading and implacable succession were as much a part of his consciousness and would remain so forever, as the fact of his own nativity:

> *Tennie Beauchamp 21yrs Won by Amodeus McCaslin from Hubert Beauchamp Esqre Possible Strait against three Treys in sigt Not called 1859 Marrid to Tomys Turl 1859*

and no date of freedom because her freedom, as well as that of her first surviving child, derived not from Buck and Buddy McCaslin in the commissary but from a stranger in Washington, and no date of death and burial, not only because McCaslin kept no obituaries in his books, but because in this year 1883 she was still alive and would remain so to see a grandson by her last surviving child:

> *Amodeus McCaslin Beauchamp Son of tomys Turl*
> *@ Tennie Beauchamp 1859 dide 1859*

then his uncle's hand entire, because his father was now a
member of the cavalry command of that man whose name
as a slave-dealer he could not even spell: and not even a
page and not even a full line:

> *Dauter Tomes Turl and tenny 1862*

and not even a line and not even a sex and no cause given
though the boy could guess it because McCaslin was thirteen then and he remembered how there was not always
enough to eat in more places than Vicksburg:

> *Child of tomes Turl and Tenny 1863*

and the same hand again and this one lived, as though
Tennie's perseverance and the fading and diluted ghost of
old Carothers' ruthlessness had at last conquered even
starvation: and clearer, fuller, more carefully written and
spelled than the boy had yet seen it, as if the old man,
who should have been a woman to begin with, trying to
run what was left of the plantation in his brother's absence
in the intervals of cooking and caring for himself and the
fourteen-year-old orphan, had taken as an omen for renewed hope the fact that this nameless inheritor of slaves
was at least remaining alive long enough to receive a
name:

> *James Thucydus Beauchamp Son of Tomes Turl and*
> *Tenny Beauchamp Born 29th december 1864 and*
> *both Well Wanted to call him Theophilus but Tride*
> *Amodeus McCaslin and Callina McCaslin and both*
> *dide so Disswaded Them Born at Two clock A,m,*
> *both Well*

but no more, nothing; it would be another two years yet
before the boy, almost a man now, would return from the
abortive trip into Tennessee with the still-intact third of
old Carothers' legacy to his Negro son and his descendants,

which as the three surviving children established at last
one by one their apparent intention of surviving, their
white half-uncles had increased to a thousand dollars
each, conditions permitting, as they came of age, and completed the page himself as far as it would even be completed when that day was long passed beyond which a
man born in 1864 (or 1867 either, when he himself saw
light) could have expected or himself hoped or even
wanted to be still alive; his own hand now, queerly enough
resembling neither his father's nor his uncle's nor even
McCaslin's, but like that of his grandfather's save for the
spelling:

> *Vanished sometime on night of his twenty-first birth-
> day Dec 29 1885. Traced by Isaac McCaslin to
> Jackson Tenn. and there lost. His third of legacy
> $1000.00 returned to McCaslin Edmonds Trustee this
> day Jan 12 1886*

but not yet: that would be two years yet, and now his father's again, whose old commander was now quit of sol-
diering and slave-trading both; once more in the ledger
and then not again, and more illegible than ever, almost
indecipherable at all from the rheumatism which now
crippled him, and almost completely innocent now even of
any sort of spelling as well as punctuation, as if the four
years during which he had followed the sword of the only
man ever breathing who ever sold him a Negro, let alone
beat him in a trade, had convinced him not only of the
vanity of faith and hope, but of orthography too:

> *Miss sophonsiba b dtr t t @ t 1869*

but not of belief and will because it was there, written, as
McCaslin had told him, with the left hand, but there in
the ledger one time more and then not again, for the boy
himself was a year old, and when Lucas was born six years
later, his father and uncle had been dead inside the same

twelve-months almost five years; his own hand again, who was there and saw it, 1886, she was just seventeen, two years younger than himself, and he was in the commissary when McCaslin entered out of the first of dusk and said, 'He wants to marry Fonsiba,' like that: and he looked past McCaslin and saw the man, the stranger, taller than Mc-Caslin and wearing better clothes than McCaslin and most of the other white men the boy knew habitually wore, who entered the room like a white man and stood in it like a white man, as though he had let McCaslin precede him into it not because McCaslin's skin was white but simply because McCaslin lived there and knew the way, and who talked like a white man too, looking at him past Mc-Caslin's shoulder rapidly and keenly once and then no more, without further interest, as a mature and contained white man not impatient but just pressed for time might have looked. 'Marry Fonsiba?' he cried. 'Marry Fonsiba?' and then no more either, just watching and listening while McCaslin and the Negro talked:

'To live in Arkansas, I believe you said.'

'Yes. I have property there. A farm.'

'Property? A farm? You own it?'

'Yes.'

'You don't say Sir, do you?'

'To my elders, yes.'

'I see. You are from the North.'

'Yes. Since a child.'

'Then your father was a slave.'

'Yes. Once.'

'Then how do you own a farm in Arkansas?'

'I have a grant. It was my father's. From the United States. For military service.'

'I see,' McCaslin said. 'The Yankee army.'

'The United States army,' the stranger said; and then himself again, crying it at McCaslin's back:

'Call aunt Tennie! I'll go get her! I'll—' But McCaslin was not even including him; the stranger did not even glance back toward his voice, the two of them speaking to one another again as if he were not even there:

'Since you seem to have it all settled,' McCaslin said, 'why have you bothered to consult my authority at all?'

'I don't,' the stranger said. 'I acknowledge your authority only so far as you admit your responsibility toward her as a female member of the family of which you are the head. I don't ask your permission. I——'

'That will do!' McCaslin said. But the stranger did not falter. It was neither as if he were ignoring McCaslin nor as if he had failed to hear him. It was as though he were making, not at all an excuse and not exactly a justification, but simply a statement which the situation absolutely required and demanded should be made in McCaslin's hearing whether McCaslin listened to it or not. It was as if he were talking to himself, for himself to hear the words spoken aloud. They faced one another, not close yet at slightly less than foils' distance, erect, their voices not raised, not impactive, just succinct:

'——I inform you, notify you in advance as chief of her family. No man of honor could do less. Besides, you have, in your way, according to your lights and upbringing——'

'That's enough, I said,' McCaslin said. 'Be off this place by full dark. Go.' But for another moment the other did not move, contemplating McCaslin with that detached and heatless look, as if he were watching reflected in McCaslin's pupils the tiny image of the figure he was sustaining.

'Yes,' he said. 'After all, this is your house. And in your fashion you have. . . . But no matter. You are right. This is enough.' He turned back toward the door; he paused again but only for a second, already moving while he spoke: 'Be easy. I will be good to her.' Then he was gone.

'But how did she ever know him?' the boy cried. 'I never even heard of him before! And Fonsiba, that's never been off this place except to go to church since she was born——'

'Ha,' McCaslin said. 'Even their parents don't know until too late how seventeen-year-old girls ever met the men who marry them too, if they are lucky.' And the next morning they were both gone, Fonsiba too. McCaslin never saw her again, nor did he, because the woman he found at last, five months later, was no one he had ever known. He carried a third of the three-thousand-dollar fund in gold in a money-belt, as when he had vainly traced Tennie's Jim into Tennessee a year ago. They—the man—had left an address of some sort with Tennie, and three months later a letter came, written by the man although McCaslin's wife, Alice, had taught Fonsiba to read and write too a little. But it bore a different postmark from the address the man had left with Tennie, and he travelled by rail as far as he could and then by contracted stage and then by a hired livery rig and then by rail again for a distance: an experienced traveller by now and an experienced bloodhound too, and a successful one this time because he would have to be; as the slow interminable empty muddy December miles crawled and crawled and night followed night in hotels, in roadside taverns of rough logs and containing little else but a bar, and in the cabins of strangers, and the hay of lonely barns, in none of which he dared undress because of his secret golden girdle like that of a disguised one of the Magi travelling incognito and not even hope to draw him, but only determination and desperation, he would tell himself: *I will have to find her. I will have to. We have already lost one of them. I will have to find her this time.* He did. Hunched in the slow and icy rain, on a spent hired horse splashed to the chest and higher, he saw it—a single log edifice with a clay chimney, which seemed in process of being flattened by the rain to a nameless and valueless rubble of dissolution in that roadless and even pathless waste of unfenced fallow and wilderness jungle—no barn, no stable, not so much as a hen-coop: just a log cabin built by hand and no clever hand either, a meagre pile of clumsily-cut

firewood sufficient for about one day and not even a gaunt
hound to come bellowing out from under the house when
he rode up—a farm only in embryo, perhaps a good farm,
maybe even a plantation someday, but not now, not for
years yet and only then with labor, hard and enduring
and unflagging work and sacrifice; he shoved open the
crazy kitchen door in its awry frame and entered an icy
gloom where not even a fire for cooking burned, and after
another moment saw, crouched into the wall's angle behind a crude table, the coffee-colored face which he had
known all his life but knew no more, the body which had
been born within a hundred yards of the room that he was
born in and in which some of his own blood ran, but which
was now completely inheritor of generation after generation to whom an unannounced white man on a horse was a
white man's hired Patroller wearing a pistol sometimes and
a blacksnake whip always; he entered the next room, the
only other room the cabin owned, and found, sitting in a
rocking chair before the hearth, the man himself, reading
—sitting there in the only chair in the house, before that
miserable fire for which there was not wood sufficient to
last twenty-four hours, in the same ministerial clothing in
which he had entered the commissary five months ago and
a pair of gold-framed spectacles which, when he looked
up and then rose to his feet, the boy saw did not even contain lenses, reading a book in the midst of that desolation,
that muddy waste, fenceless and even pathless and without even a walled shed for stock to stand beneath: and
over all, permeant, clinging to the man's very clothing and
exuding from his skin itself, that rank stink of baseless and
imbecile delusion, that boundless rapacity and folly, of the
carpet-bagger followers of victorious armies.

'Don't you see?' he cried. 'Don't you see? This whole
land, the whole South, is cursed, and all of us who derive
from it, whom it ever suckled, white and black both, lie
under the curse? Granted that my people brought the
curse onto the land: maybe for that reason their descend-

ants alone can—not resist it, not combat it—maybe just endure and outlast it until the curse is lifted. Then your peoples' turn will come because we have forfeited ours. But not now. Not yet. Don't you see?'

The other stood now, the unfrayed garments still ministerial even if not quite so fine, the book closed upon one finger to keep the place, the lenseless spectacles held like a music master's wand in the other workless hand while the owner of it spoke his measured and sonorous imbecility of the boundless folly and the baseless hope: 'You're wrong. The curse you whites brought into this land has been lifted. It has been voided and discharged. We are seeing a new era, an era dedicated, as our founders intended it, to freedom, liberty and equality for all, to which this country will be the new Canaan——'

'Freedom from what? From work? Canaan?' He jerked his arm, comprehensive, almost violent: whereupon it all seemed to stand there about them, intact and complete and visible in the drafty, damp, heatless, Negro-stale Negro-rank sorry room—the empty fields without plow or seed to work them, fenceless against the stock which did not exist within or without the walled stable which likewise was not there. 'What corner of Canaan is this?'

'You are seeing it at a bad time. This is winter. No man farms this time of year.'

'I see. And of course her need for food and clothing will stand still while the land lies fallow.'

'I have a pension,' the other said. He said it as a man might say *I have grace* or *I own a gold mine.* 'I have my father's pension too. It will arrive on the first of the month. What day is this?'

'The eleventh,' he said. 'Twenty days more. And until then?'

'I have a few groceries in the house from my credit account with the merchant in Midnight who banks my pension check for me. I have executed to him a power of attorney to handle it for me as a matter of mutual—'

'I see. And if the groceries don't last the twenty days?'

'I still have one more hog.'

'Where?'

'Outside,' the other said. 'It is customary in this country to allow stock to range free during the winter for food. It comes up from time to time. But no matter if it doesn't; I can probably trace its footprints when the need——'

'Yes!' he cried. 'Because no matter: you still have the pension check. And the man in Midnight will cash it and pay himself out of it for what you have already eaten and if there is any left over, it is yours. And the hog will be eaten by then or you still can't catch it, and then what will you do?'

'It will be almost spring then,' the other said. 'I am planning in the spring——'

'It will be January,' he said. 'And then February. And then more than half of March——' and when he stopped again in the kitchen she had not moved, she did not even seem to breathe or to be alive except her eyes watching him; when he took a step toward her it was still not movement because she could have retreated no further: only the tremendous, fathomless, ink-colored eyes in the narrow, thin, too thin, coffee-colored face watching him without alarm, without recognition, without hope. 'Fonsiba,' he said. 'Fonsiba. Are you all right?'

'I'm free,' she said. Midnight was a tavern, a livery stable, a big store (that would be where the pension check banked itself as a matter of mutual elimination of bother and fret, he thought) and a little one, a saloon and a blacksmith shop. But there was a bank there too. The president (the owner, for all practical purposes) of it was a translated Mississippian who had been one of Forrest's men too: and his body lightened of the golden belt for the first time since he left home eight days ago, with pencil and paper he multiplied three dollars by twelve months and divided it into one thousand dollars; it would stretch that way over almost twenty-eight years and for twenty-eight years at least she would not starve, the banker promising to send the three dollars himself by a trusty messenger on the fifteenth of each month and put it into her actual hand, and he returned home and that was all because in 1874 his father and his uncle were both dead and the old ledgers never again came down from the shelf above the desk to which his father had returned them for the last time that day in 1869. But he could have completed it:

> *Lucas Quintus Carothers McCaslin Beauchamp. Last surviving son and child of Tomey's Terrel and Tennie Beauchamp. March 17, 1874*

except that there was no need: not *Lucius Quintus* @c @c @c, but *Lucas Quintus,* not refusing to be called Lucius, because he simply eliminated that word from the name; not denying, declining the name itself, because he used three quarters of it; but simply taking the name and changing, altering it, making it no longer the white man's but his own, by himself composed, himself selfprogenitive and nominate, by himself ancestored, as, for all the old ledgers recorded to the contrary, old Carothers himself was

and that was all: 1874 the boy; 1888 the man, repudiated denied and free; 1895 and husband but no father, unwidowered but without a wife, and found long since that no man is ever free and probably could not bear it if he were; married then and living in Jefferson in the little new jerrybuilt bungalow which his wife's father had given them: and one morning Lucas stood suddenly in the doorway of the room where he was reading the Memphis paper and he looked at the paper's dateline and thought *It's his birthday. He's twenty-one today* and Lucas said: 'Whar's the rest of that money old Carothers left? I wants it. All of it.'

that was all: and McCaslin

'More men than that one Buck and Buddy to fumble-heed that truth so mazed for them that spoke it and so confused for them that heard yet still there was 1865:' and he

'But not enough. Not enough of even Father and Uncle Buddy to fumble-heed in even three generations not even three generations fathered by Grandfather not even if there had been nowhere beneath His sight any but Grandfather and so He would not even have needed to elect and choose. But He tried and I know what you will say. That having Himself created them He could have known no more of hope than He could have pride and grief, but He didn't hope He just waited because He had made them: not just because He had set them alive and in motion but because He had already worried with them so long: worried with them so long because He had seen how in individual cases they were capable of anything, any height or depth remembered in mazed incomprehension out of heaven where hell was created too, and so He must admit them or else admit his equal somewhere and so be no longer God and therefore must accept responsibility for what He Himself had done in order to live with Himself in His lonely and paramount heaven. And He probably knew it was vain but He had created them and knew them capable of all things because He had shaped them out of the primal Absolute which contained all and had watched them since in their individual exaltation and baseness, and they themselves not knowing why nor how nor even when: until at last He saw that they were all Grandfather all of them and that even from them the elected and chosen the best the very best He could expect (not hope mind: not hope) would be Bucks and Buddies and not even enough of them and in the third generation not even Bucks and Buddies but—' and McCaslin

'Ah:' and he

'Yes. If He could see Father and Uncle Buddy in Grandfather He must have seen me too. —an Isaac born into a later life than Abraham's and repudiating immolation: fatherless and therefore safe declining the altar because maybe this time the exasperated Hand might not supply the kid—' and McCaslin

'Escape:' and he

'All right. Escape.—Until one day He said what you told Fonsiba's husband that afternoon here in this room: *This will do. This is enough:* not in exasperation or rage or even just sick to death as you were sick that day: just *This is enough* and looked about for one last time, for one time more since He had created them, upon this land this South for which He had done so much with woods for game and streams for fish and deep rich soil for seed and lush springs to sprout it and long summers to mature it and serene falls to harvest it and short mild winters for men and animals, and saw no hope anywhere and looked beyond it where hope should have been, where to East North and West lay illimitable that whole hopeful continent dedicated as a refuge and sanctuary of liberty and freedom from what you called the old world's worthless evening, and saw the rich descendants of slavers, females of both sexes, to whom the black they shrieked of was another specimen another example like the Brazilian macaw brought home in a cage by a traveller, passing resolutions about horror and outrage in warm and air-proof halls: and the thundering cannonade of politicians earning votes and the medicine-shows of pulpiteers earning Chautauqua fees, to whom the outrage and the injustice were as much abstractions as Tariff or Silver or Immortality and who employed the very shackles of its servitude and the sorry rags of its regalia as they did the other beer and banners and mottoes, redfire and brimstone and sleight-of-hand and musical handsaws: and the whirling wheels which manufactured for a profit the pristine replacements of the shackles and shoddy garments as they wore out, and spun the cotton and made the gins which ginned it and the cars and ships which hauled it, and the men who ran the wheels for that profit and established and collected the taxes it

was taxed with and the rates for hauling it and the com-
missions for selling it: and He could have repudiated them
since they were His creation now and forever more
throughout all their generations, until not only that old
world from which He had rescued them but this new one
too which He had revealed and led them to as a sanctuary
and refuge were become the same worthless tideless rock
cooling in the last crimson evening, except that out of all
that empty sound and bootless fury one silence, among
that loud and moiling all of them just one simple enough
to believe that horror and outrage were first and last simply horror and outrage and crude enough to act upon that,
illiterate and had no words for talking or perhaps was just
busy and had no time to, one out of them all who did not
bother Him with cajolery and adjuration then pleading
then threat, and had not even bothered to inform Him in
advance what he was about so that a lesser than He might
have even missed the simple act of lifting the long an-
cestral musket down from the deerhorns above the door,
whereupon He said *My name is Brown too* and the other
So is mine and He *Then mine or yours can't be because I
am against it* and the other *So am I* and He triumphantly
Then where are you going with that gun? and the other
told him in one sentence one word and He: amazed:
Who knew neither hope nor pride nor grief *But your Association, your Committee, your Officers. Where are your
Minutes, your Motions, your Parliamentary Procedures?*
and the other *I ain't against them. They are all right I
reckon for them that have the time. I am just against the
weak because they are niggers being held in bondage by
the strong just because they are white.* So He turned once
more to this land which He still intended to save because
He had done so much for it—' and McCaslin

'What?' and he

'—to these people He was still committed to because
they were his creations—' and McCaslin

'Turned back to us? His face to us?' and he

'—whose wives and daughters at least made soups and jellies for them when they were sick, and carried the trays through the mud and the winter too into the stinking cabins, and sat in the stinking cabins and kept fires going until crises came and passed, but that was not enough: and when they were very sick had them carried into the big house itself into the company room itself maybe and nursed them there, which the white man would have done too for any other of his cattle that was sick but at least the man who hired one from a livery wouldn't have, and still that was not enough: so that He said and not in grief either, Who had made them and so could know no more of grief than He could of pride or hope: *Apparently they can learn nothing save through suffering, remember nothing save when underlined in blood*—' and McCaslin

'Ashby on an afternoon's ride, to call on some remote maiden cousins of his mother or maybe just acquaintances of hers, comes by chance upon a minor engagement of outposts and dismounts and with his crimson-lined cloak for target leads a handful of troops he never saw before against an entrenched position of backwoods-trained riflemen. Lee's battle-order, wrapped maybe about a handful of cigars and doubtless thrown away when the last cigar was smoked, found by a Yankee Intelligence officer on the floor of a saloon behind the Yankee lines after Lee had already divided his forces before Sharpsburg. Jackson on the Plank Road, already rolled up the flank which Hooker believed could not be turned and, waiting only for night to pass to continue the brutal and incessant slogging which would fling that whole wing back into Hooker's lap where he sat on a front gallery in Chancellorsville drinking rum toddies and telegraphing Lincoln that he had defeated Lee, is shot from among a whole covey of minor officers and in the blind night by one of his own patrols, leaving as next by seniority Stuart, that gallant man born apparently already horsed and sabred and already knowing all there was to know about war except the slogging and brutal stupidity of it: and that same Stuart off raiding Pennsylvania hen-roosts when Lee should have known of all of Meade just where Hancock was on Cemetery Ridge: and Longstreet too at Gettysburg and that same Longstreet shot out of saddle by his own men in the dark by mistake just as Jackson was. His face to us? His face to us?' and he

'How else have made them fight? Who else but Jacksons and Stuarts and Ashbys and Morgans and Forrests?—the farmers of the central and middle-west, holding land by the acre instead of the tens or maybe even the hundreds, farming it themselves and to no single crop of cotton or tobacco or cane, owning no slaves and needing and wanting none, and already looking toward the Pacific coast, not always as long as two generations there and having stopped where they did stop only through the fortuitous mischance that an ox died or a wagon-axle broke. And the New England mechanics who didn't even own land and measured all things by the weight of water and the cost of turning wheels, and the narrow fringe of traders and ship-owners still looking backward across the Atlantic and attached to the continent only by their counting-houses. And those who should have had the alertness to see: the wild-cat manipulators of mythical wilderness townsites; and the astuteness to rationalize: the bankers who held the mortgages on the land which the first were only waiting to abandon, and on the railroads and steamboats to carry them still further west, and on the factories and the wheels and the rented tenements those who ran them lived in; and the leisure and scope to comprehend and fear in time and even anticipate: the Boston-bred (even when not born in Boston) spinster, descendants of long lines of similarly-bred and likewise spinster aunts and uncles whose hands knew no callus except that of the indicting pen, to whom the wilderness itself began at the top of tide and who looked, if at anything other than Beacon Hill, only toward heaven—not to mention all the loud rabble of the camp-followers of pioneers: the bellowing of politicians, the mellifluous choiring of self-styled men of God, the—' and McCaslin

'Here, here. Wait a minute:' And he

'Let me talk now. I'm trying to explain to the head of my family something which I have got to do which I don't quite understand myself, not in justification of it but to explain it if I can. I could say I don't know why I must do it but that I do know I have got to because I have got myself to have to live with for the rest of my life and all I want is peace to do it in. But you are the head of my family. More. I knew a long time ago that I would never have to miss my father, even if you are just finding out that you have missed your son—the drawers of bills and the shavers of notes and the schoolmasters and the self-ordained to teach and lead and all that horde of the semi-literate with a white shirt but no change for it, with one eye on themselves and watching each other with the other one. Who else could have made them fight: could have struck them so aghast with fear and dread as to turn shoulder to shoulder and face one way and even stop talking for a while and even after two years of it keep them still so wrung with terror that some among them would seriously propose moving their very capital into a foreign country lest it be ravaged and pillaged by a people whose entire white male population would have little more than filled any one of their larger cities: except Jackson in the Valley and three separate armies trying to catch him and none of them ever knowing whether they were just retreating from a battle or just running into one, and Stuart riding his whole command entirely around the biggest single armed force this continent ever saw in order to see what it looked like from behind, and Morgan leading a cavalry charge against a stranded man-of-war. Who else could have declared a war against a power with ten times the area and a hundred times the men and a thousand times the resources, except men who could believe that all necessary

to conduct a successful war was not acumen nor shrewd-
ness nor politics nor diplomacy nor money nor even integrity and simple arithmetic, but just love of land and courage———'

'And an unblemished and gallant ancestry and the
ability to ride a horse,' McCaslin said. 'Don't leave that
out.' It was evening now, the tranquil sunset of October
mazy with windless woodsmoke. The cotton was long since
picked and ginned, and all day now the wagons loaded
with gathered corn moved between field and crib, pro-
cessional across the enduring land. 'Well, maybe that's
what He wanted. At least, that's what He got.' This time
there was no yellowed procession of fading and harmless
ledger-pages. This was chronicled in a harsher book, and
McCaslin, fourteen and fifteen and sixteen, had seen it
and the boy himself had inherited it as Noah's grandchildren had inherited the Flood although they had not
been there to see the deluge: that dark corrupt and bloody
time while three separate peoples had tried to adjust not
only to one another but to the new land which they had
created and inherited too and must live in for the reason
that those who had lost it were no less free to quit it than
those who had gained it were:—those upon whom freedom and equality had been dumped overnight and without warning or preparation or any training in how to em-
ploy it or even just endure it and who misused it, not as
children would nor yet because they had been so long in
bondage and then so suddenly freed, but misused it as
human beings always misuse freedom, so that he thought
*Apparently there is a wisdom beyond even that learned
through suffering necessary for a man to distinguish between liberty and license;* those who had fought for four
years and lost to preserve a condition under which that
franchisement was anomaly and paradox, not because they
were opposed to freedom as freedom but for the old reasons for which man (not the generals and politicians but
man) has always fought and died in wars: to preserve a

status quo or to establish a better future one to endure for his children; and lastly, as if that were not enough for bitterness and hatred and fear, that third race even more alien to the people whom they resembled in pigment and in whom even the same blood ran, than to the people whom they did not,—that race threefold in one and alien even among themselves save for a single fierce will for rapine and pillage, composed of the sons of middleaged Quartermaster lieutenants and Army sutlers and contractors in military blankets and shoes and transport mules, who followed the battles they themselves had not fought and inherited the conquest they themselves had not helped to gain, sanctioned and protected even if not blessed, and left their bones and in another generation would be engaged in a fierce economic competition of small sloven farms with the black men they were supposed to have freed and the white descendants of fathers who had owned no slaves anyway whom they were supposed to have disinherited, and in the third generation would be back once more in the little lost county seats as barbers and garage mechanics and deputy sheriffs and mill- and gin-hands and power-plant firemen, leading, first in mufti then later in an actual formalized regalia of hooded sheets and passwords and fiery Christian symbols, lynching mobs against the race their ancestors had come to save: and of all that other nameless horde of speculators in human misery, manipulators of money and politics and land, who follow catastrophe and are their own protection as grasshoppers are and need no blessing and sweat no plow or axe-helve and batten and vanish and leave no bones, just as they derived apparently from no ancestry, no mortal flesh, no act even of passion or even of lust: and the Jew who came without protection too, since after two thousand years he had got out of the habit of being or needing it, and solitary, without even the solidarity of the locusts, and in this a sort of courage since he had come thinking not in terms of simple pillage but in

terms of his great-grandchildren, seeking yet some place
to establish them to endure even though forever alien:
and unblessed: a pariah about the face of the Western
earth which twenty centuries later was still taking revenge on him for the fairy tale with which he had conquered it. McCaslin had actually seen it, and the boy even
at almost eighty would never be able to distinguish certainly between what he had seen and what had been told
him: a lightless and gutted and empty land where women
crouched with the huddled children behind locked doors
and men armed in sheets and masks rode the silent roads
and the bodies of white and black both, victims not so
much of hate as of desperation and despair, swung from
lonely limbs: and men shot dead in polling-booths with
the still wet pen in one hand and the unblotted ballot in
the other: and a United States marshal in Jefferson who
signed his official papers with a crude cross, an ex-slave
called Sickymo, not at all because his ex-owner was a doctor and apothecary but because, still a slave, he would
steal his master's grain alcohol and dilute it with water and
peddle it in pint bottles from a cache beneath the roots of
a big sycamore tree behind the drug store, who had attained his high office because his half-white sister was the
concubine of the Federal A.P.M.: and this time McCaslin
did not even say Look but merely lifted one hand, not
even pointing, not even specifically toward the shelf of
ledgers but toward the desk, toward the corner where
it sat beside the scuffed patch on the floor where two
decades of heavy shoes had stood while the white man at
the desk added and multiplied and subtracted. And again
he did not need to look because he had seen this himself
and, twenty-three years after the Surrender and twenty-
four after the Proclamation, was still watching it: the
ledgers, new ones now and filled rapidly, succeeding one
another rapidly and containing more names than old
Carothers or even his father and Uncle Buddy had ever
dreamed of; new names and new faces to go with them,

among which the old names and faces that even his father and uncle would have recognized, were lost, vanished—Tomey's Terrel dead, and even the tragic and
miscast Percival Brownlee, who couldn't keep books and
couldn't farm either, found his true niche at last, reappeared in 1862 during the boy's father's absence and had
apparently been living on the plantation for at least a
month before his uncle found out about it, conducting im-
promptu revival meetings among Negroes, preaching and
leading the singing also in his high sweet true soprano
voice and disappeared again on foot and at top speed,
not behind but ahead of a body of raiding Federal horse
and reappeared for the third and last time in the entou-
rage of a travelling Army paymaster, the two of them
passing through Jefferson in a surrey at the exact moment
when the boy's father (it was 1866) also happened to be
crossing the Square, the surrey and its occupants traversing rapidly that quiet and bucolic scene and even in that
fleeting moment, and to others beside the boy's father, giving an illusion of flight and illicit holiday like a man on an
excursion during his wife's absence with his wife's personal maid, until Brownlee glanced up and saw his late co-
master and gave him one defiant female glance and then
broke again, leaped from the surrey and disappeared this
time for good, and it was only by chance that McCaslin,
twenty years later, heard of him again, an old man now
and quite fat, as the well-to-do proprietor of a select New
Orleans brothel; and Tennie's Jim gone, nobody knew
where, and Fonsiba in Arkansas with her three dollars
each month and the scholar-husband with his lensless
spectacles and frock coat and his plans for the spring; and
only Lucas was left, the baby, the last save himself of old
Carothers' doomed and fatal blood which in the male
derivation seemed to destroy all it touched, and even he
was repudiating and at least hoping to escape it;—Lucas,
the boy of fourteen whose name would not even appear
for six years yet among those rapid pages in the bindings

new and dustless too since McCaslin lifted them down daily now to write into them the continuation of that record which two hundred years had not been enough to complete, and another hundred would not be enough to discharge; that chronicle which was a whole land in miniature, which multiplied and compounded was the entire South, twenty-three years after surrender and twenty-four from emancipation—that slow trickle of molasses and meal and meat, of shoes and straw hats and overalls, of plowlines and collars and heel-bolts and buckheads and clevises, which returned each fall as cotton—the two threads frail as truth and impalpable as equators yet cable-strong to bind for life them who made the cotton to the land their sweat fell on: and he

'Yes. Binding them for a while yet, a little while yet. Through and beyond that life and maybe through and beyond the life of that life's sons and maybe even through and beyond that of the sons of those sons. But not always, because they will endure. They will outlast us because they are—' it was not a pause, barely a falter even, possibly appreciable only to himself, as if he couldn't speak even to McCaslin, even to explain his repudiation, that which to him too, even in the act of escaping (and maybe this was the reality and the truth of his need to escape), was heresy: so that even in escaping he was taking with him more of that evil and unregenerate old man who could summon, because she was his property, a human being because she was old enough and female, to his widower's house and get a child on her and then dismiss her because she was of an inferior race, and then bequeath a thousand dollars to the infant because he would be dead then and wouldn't have to pay it, than even he had feared. 'Yes. He didn't want to. He had to. Because they will endure. They are better than we are. Stronger than we are. Their vices are vices aped from white men or that white men and bondage have taught them: improvidence and intemperance and evasion—not laziness: evasion: of what white men had set them to, not for their aggrandizement or even comfort but his own—' and McCaslin

'All right. Go on: Promiscuity. Violence. Instability and lack of control. Inability to distinguish between mine and thine—' and he

'How distinguish, when for two hundred years mine did not even exist for them?' and McCaslin

'All right. Go on. And their virtues—' and he

'Yes. Their own. Endurance—' and McCaslin

'So have mules:' and he

'—and pity and tolerance and forbearance and fidelity and love of children—' and McCaslin

'So have dogs:' and he

'—whether their own or not or black or not. And more: what they got not only not from white people but not even despite white people because they had it already from the old free fathers a longer time free than us because we have never been free—' and it was in McCaslin's eyes too, he had only to look at McCaslin's eyes and it was there, that summer twilight seven years ago, almost a week after they had returned from the camp before he discovered that Sam Fathers had told McCaslin: an old bear, fierce and ruthless not just to stay alive but ruthless with the fierce pride of liberty and freedom, jealous and proud enough of liberty and freedom to see it threatened not with fear nor even alarm but almost with joy, seeming deliberately to put it into jeopardy in order to savor it and keep his old strong bones and flesh supple and quick to defend and preserve it; an old man, son of a Negro slave and an Indian king, inheritor on the one hand of the long chronicle of a people who had learned humility through suffering and learned pride through the endurance which survived the suffering, and on the other side the chronicle of a people even longer in the land than the first, yet who now existed there only in the solitary brotherhood of an old and childless Negro's alien blood and the wild and invincible spirit of an old bear; a boy who wished to learn

humility and pride in order to become skillful and worthy
in the woods but found himself becoming so skillful so
fast that he feared he would never become worthy, because he had not learned humility and pride though he
had tried, until one day an old man, who could not have
defined either, led him as though by the hand to where
an old bear and a little mongrel dog showed him that, by
possessing one thing other, he would possess them both;
and a little dog, nameless and mongrel and many-fathered,
grown yet weighing less than six pounds, who couldn't be
dangerous because there was nothing anywhere much
smaller, not fierce because that would have been called
just noise, not humble because it was already too near the
ground to genuflect, and not proud because it would not
have been close enough for anyone to discern what was
casting that shadow, and which didn't even know it was
not going to heaven since they had already decided it had
no immortal soul, so that all it could be was brave, even
though they would probably call that too just noise. 'And
you didn't shoot,' McCaslin said. 'How close were you?'

'I don't know,' he said. 'There was a big wood tick just
inside his off hind leg. I saw that. But I didn't have the
gun then.'

'But you didn't shoot when you had the gun,' McCaslin
said. 'Why?' But McCaslin didn't wait, rising and crossing
the room, across the pelt of the bear he had killed two
years ago and the bigger one McCaslin had killed before
he was born, to the bookcase beneath the mounted head
of his first buck, and returned with the book and sat down
again and opened it. 'Listen,' he said. He read the five
stanzas aloud and closed the book on his finger and looked
up. 'All right,' he said. 'Listen,' and read again, but only
one stanza this time and closed the book and laid it on the
table. 'She cannot fade, though thou hast not thy bliss,'
McCaslin said: 'Forever wilt thou love, and she be fair.'

'He's talking about a girl,' he said.

'He had to talk about something,' McCaslin said. Then

he said, 'He was talking about truth. Truth is one. It doesn't change. It covers all things which touch the heart —honor and pride and pity and justice and courage and love. Do you see now?' He didn't know. Somehow it had seemed simpler than that, simpler than somebody talking in a book about a young man and a girl he would never need to grieve over because he could never approach any nearer and would never have to get any further away. He had heard about an old bear and finally got big enough to hunt it and he hunted it four years and at last met it with a gun in his hands and he didn't shoot. Because a little dog—But he could have shot long before the fyce covered the twenty yards to where the bear waited, and Sam Fathers could have shot at any time during the interminable minute while Old Ben stood on his hind legs over them. . . . He ceased. McCaslin watched him, still speaking, the voice, the words as quiet as the twilight itself was: 'Courage and honor and pride, and pity and love of justice and of liberty. They all touch the heart, and what the heart holds to becomes truth, as far as we know truth. Do you see now?'

and he could still hear them, intact in this twilight as in that one seven years ago, no louder still because they did not need to be because they would endure: and he had only to look at McCaslin's eyes beyond the thin and bitter smiling, the faint lip-lift which would have had to be called smiling;—his kinsman, his father almost, who had been born too late into the old time and too soon for the new, the two of them juxtaposed and alien now to each other against their ravaged patrimony, the dark and ravaged fatherland still prone and panting from its etherless operation:

'Habet then.—So this land is, indubitably, of and by itself cursed:' and he

'Cursed:' and again McCaslin merely lifted one hand, not even speaking and not even toward the ledgers: so that, as the stereopticon condenses into one instantaneous

field the myriad minutiae of its scope, so did that slight
and rapid gesture establish in the small cramped and cluttered twilit room not only the ledgers but the whole plantation in its mazed and intricate entirety—the land, the
fields and what they represented in terms of cotton ginned
and sold, the men and women whom they fed and clothed
and even paid a little cash money at Christmas-time in return for the labor which planted and raised and picked and
ginned the cotton, the machinery and mules and gear with
which they raised it and their cost and upkeep and re-
placement—that whole edifice intricate and complex and
founded upon injustice and erected by ruthless rapacity
and carried on even yet with at times downright savagery
not only to the human beings but the valuable animals
too, yet solvent and efficient and, more than that: not only
still intact but enlarged, increased; brought still intact by
McCaslin, himself little more than a child then, through
and out of the debacle and chaos of twenty years ago
where hardly one in ten survived, and enlarged and increased and would continue so, solvent and efficient and
intact and still increasing so long as McCaslin and his Mc-
Caslin successors lasted, even though their surnames might
not even be Edmonds then: and he

'Habet too. Because that's it: not the land, but us. Not
only the blood, but the name too; not only its color but its
designation: Edmonds, white, but, a female line, could
have no other but the name his father bore; Beauchamp,
the elder line and the male one, but, black, could have had
any name he liked and no man would have cared, except
the name his father bore who had no name—' and Mc-
Caslin

'And since I know too what you know I will say now,
once more let me say it: And one other, and in the third
generation too, and the male, the eldest, the direct and
sole and white and still McCaslin even, father to son to
son—' and he

'I am free:' and this time McCaslin did not even gesture,

no inference of fading pages, no postulation of the stereoptic whole, but the frail and iron thread strong as truth and impervious as evil and longer than life itself and reaching beyond record and patrimony both to join him with the lusts and passions, the hopes and dreams and griefs, of bones whose names while still fleshed and capable even old Carothers' grandfather had never heard: and he:

'And of that too:' and McCaslin

'Chosen, I suppose (I will concede it) out of all your time by Him, as you say Buck and Buddy were from theirs. And it took Him a bear and an old man and four years just for you. And it took you fourteen years to reach that point and about that many, maybe more, for Old Ben, and more than seventy for Sam Fathers. And you are just one. How long then? How long?' and he

'It will be long. I have never said otherwise. But it will be all right because they will endure—' and McCaslin

'And anyway, you will be free.—No, not now nor ever, we from them nor they from us. So I repudiate too. I would deny even if I knew it were true. I would have to. Even you can see that I could do no else. I am what I am; I will be always what I was born and have always been. And more than me. More than me, just as there were more than Buck and Buddy in what you called His first plan which failed:' and he

'And more than me:' and McCaslin

'No. Not even you. Because mark. You said how on that instant when Ikkemotubbe realized that he could sell the land to Grandfather, it ceased forever to have been his. All right; go on: Then it belonged to Sam Fathers, old Ikkemotubbe's son. And who inherited from Sam Fathers, if not you? co-heir perhaps with Boon, if not of his life maybe, at least of his quitting it?' and he

'Yes. Sam Fathers set me free.'

and Isaac McCaslin, not yet Uncle Ike, a long time yet before he would be uncle to half a county and still father

to none, living in one small cramped fireless rented room
in a Jefferson boardinghouse where petit juries were domiciled during court terms and itinerant horse- and muletraders stayed, with his kit of brand-new carpenter's tools
and the shotgun McCaslin had given him with his name
engraved in silver and old General Compson's compass
(and, when the General died, his silver-mounted horn too)
and the iron cot and mattress and the blankets which he
would take each fall into the woods for more than sixty
years and the bright tin coffee-pot

there had been a legacy, from his Uncle Hubert Beauchamp, his godfather, that bluff burly roaring childlike
man from whom Uncle Buddy had won Tomey's Terrel's
wife Tennie in the poker-game in 1859—'possible strait
against three Treys in sigt Not called'—; no pale sentence
or paragraph scrawled in cringing fear of death by a weak
and trembling hand as a last desperate sop flung backward
at retribution, but a Legacy, a Thing, possessing weight to
the hand and bulk to the eye and even audible: a silver
cup filled with gold pieces and wrapped in burlap and
sealed with his godfather's ring in the hot wax, which
(intact still) even before his Uncle Hubert's death and
long before his own majority, when it would be his, had
become not only a legend but one of the family lares. After
his father's and his Uncle Hubert's sister's marriage they
moved back into the big house, the tremendous cavern
which old Carothers had started and never finished,
cleared the remaining Negroes out of it and with his
mother's dowry completed it, at least the rest of the windows and doors and moved into it, all of them save Uncle
Buddy who declined to leave the cabin he and his twin
had built, the move being the bride's notion and more
than just a notion, and none ever to know if she really
wanted to live in the big house or if she knew beforehand
that Uncle Buddy would refuse to move: and two weeks
after his birth in 1867, the first time he and his mother
came down stairs one night, and the silver cup sitting on

the cleared dining-room table beneath the bright lamp, and while his mother and his father and McCaslin and Tennie (his nurse: carrying him)—all of them again but Uncle Buddy—watched, his Uncle Hubert rang one by one into the cup the bright and glinting mintage and wrapped it into the burlap envelope and heated the wax and sealed it and carried it back home with him where he lived alone now without even his sister either to hold him down as McCaslin said or to try to raise him up as Uncle Buddy said, and (dark times then in Mississippi) Uncle Buddy said most of the niggers gone and the ones that didn't go even Hub Beauchamp could not have wanted: but the dogs remained and Uncle Buddy said Beauchamp fiddled while Nero fox-hunted

they would go and see it there; at last his mother would prevail and they would depart in the surrey, once more all save Uncle Buddy and McCaslin to keep Uncle Buddy company, until one winter Uncle Buddy began to fail and from then on it was himself, beginning to remember now, and his mother and Tennie and Tomey's Terrel to drive: the twenty-two miles into the next county, the twin gate-posts on one of which McCaslin could remember the half-grown boy blowing a fox-horn at breakfast, dinner, and supper-time and jumping down to open to any passer who happened to hear it, but where there were no gates at all now, the shabby and overgrown entrance to what his mother still insisted that people call Warwick because her brother was, if truth but triumphed and justice but prevailed, the rightful earl of it, the paintless house which outwardly did not change but which on the inside seemed each time larger because he was too little to realize then that there was less and less in it of the fine furnishings, the rosewood and mahogany and walnut, which for him had never existed anywhere anyway save in his mother's tearful lamentations, and the occasional piece small enough to be roped somehow onto the rear or the top of the carriage on their return (And he remembered this, he had seen it: an instant, a flash, his mother's soprano 'Even my dress! Even my dress!' loud and outraged in the barren unswept hall; a face young and female and even lighter in color than Tomey's Terrel's for an instant in a closing door; a swirl, a glimpse of the silk gown and the flick and glint of an ear-ring: an apparition rapid and tawdry and illicit, yet somehow even to the child, the infant still almost, breathless and exciting and evocative: as though, like two limpid and pellucid streams meeting, the child which he still was had made serene and absolute and perfect rapport and contact through that glimpsed nameless illicit hybrid female flesh with the boy which had existed at that stage of inviolable and immortal adolescence in his uncle for almost sixty years; the dress, the face, the ear-rings gone in that same aghast flash and his uncle's voice: 'She's my cook! She's my new cook! I had to have a cook, didn't I?' then the uncle himself, the face alarmed and aghast too yet still innocently and somehow even indomitably of a boy, they retreating in their turn now, back to the front gallery, and his uncle again, pained and still amazed, in a sort of desperate resurgence if not of courage at least of self-assertion: 'They're free now; They're folks too just like we are!' and his mother: 'That's why! That's why! My mother's house! Defiled! Defiled!' and his uncle: 'Damn it, Sibbey, at least give her time to pack her grip:' then over, finished, the loud uproar and all, himself and Tennie and he remembered Tennie's inscrutable face at the broken shutterless window of the bare room which had once been the parlor while they watched, hurrying down the lane at a stumbling trot, the routed compounder of his uncle's uxory: the back, the nameless face which he had seen only for a moment, the once-hooped dress ballooning and flapping below a man's overcoat, the worn heavy carpet-bag jouncing and banging against her knee, routed and in retreat true enough and in the empty lane, solitary, young-looking, and forlorn, yet withal still exciting and evocative and wearing still the silken banner captured inside the very citadel of respectability, and unforgettable.)

the cup, the sealed inscrutable burlap, sitting on the shelf in the locked closet, Uncle Hubert unlocking the door and lifting it down and passing it from hand to hand: his mother, his father, McCaslin and even Tennie, insisting that each take it in turn and heft it for weight and shake it again to prove the sound, Uncle Hubert himself standing spraddled before the cold unswept hearth in which the very bricks themselves were crumbling into a litter of soot and dust and mortar and the droppings of chimney-sweeps, still roaring and still innocent and still indomitable: and for a long time he believed nobody but himself had noticed that his uncle now put the cup only into his hands, unlocked the door and lifted it down and put it into his hands and stood over him until he had shaken it obediently until it sounded then took it from him and locked it back into the closet before anyone else could have offered to touch it, and even later, when competent not only to remember but to rationalize, he could not say what it was or even if it had been anything because the parcel was still heavy and still rattled, not even when, Uncle Buddy dead and his father, at last and after almost seventy-five years in bed after the sun rose, said: 'Go get that damn cup. Bring that damn Hub Beauchamp too if you have to:' because it still rattled though his uncle no longer put it even into his hands now but carried it himself from one to the other, his mother, McCaslin, Tennie, shaking it before each in turn, saying: 'Hear it? Hear it?' his face still innocent, not quite baffled but only amazed and not very amazed and still indomitable:

and, his father and Uncle Buddy both gone now, one day without reason or any warning the almost completely empty house in which his uncle and Tennie's ancient and quarrelsome great-grandfather (who claimed to have seen Lafayette and McCaslin said in another ten years would be remembering God) lived, cooked and slept in one single room, burst into peaceful conflagration, a tranquil instan-

taneous sourceless unanimity of combustion, walls floors
and roof: at sunup it stood where his uncle's father had
built it sixty years ago, at sundown the four blackened and
smokeless chimneys rose from a light white powder of
ashes and a few charred ends of planks which did not even
appear to have been very hot: and out of the last of evening, the last one of the twenty-two miles, on the old
white mare which was the last of that stable which McCaslin remembered, the two old men riding double up to the
sister's door, the one wearing his fox-horn on its braided
deerhide thong and the other carrying the burlap parcel
wrapped in a shirt, the tawny wax-daubed shapeless lump
sitting again and on an almost identical shelf and his uncle
holding the half-opened door now, his hand not only on
the knob but one foot against it and the key waiting in
the other hand, the face urgent and still not baffled but
still and even indomitably not very amazed and himself
standing in the half-opened door looking quietly up at the
burlap shape, become almost three times its original height
and a good half less than its original thickness, and turning
away, and he would remember not his mother's look this
time nor yet Tennie's inscrutable expression but McCaslin's dark and aquiline face grave insufferable and bemused:

then one night they waked him and fetched him still
half-asleep into the lamp light, the smell of medicine
which was familiar by now in that room and the smell of
something else which he had not smelled before and knew
at once and would never forget, the pillow, the worn and
ravaged face from which looked out still the boy innocent
and immortal and amazed and urgent, looking at him and
trying to tell him until McCaslin moved and leaned over
the bed and drew from the top of the night shirt the big
iron key on the greasy cord which suspended it, the eyes
saying Yes Yes Yes now, and cut the cord and unlocked
the closet and brought the parcel to the bed, the eyes still
trying to tell him even when he took the parcel so that was

still not it, the hands still clinging to the parcel even while
relinquishing it, the eyes more urgent than ever trying to
tell him but they never did; and he was ten and his mother
was dead too and McCaslin said, 'You are almost halfway now. You might as well open it:' and he: 'No. He said
twenty-one:' and he was twenty-one and McCaslin shifted
the bright lamp to the center of the cleared dining-room
table and set the parcel beside it and laid his open knife
beside the parcel and stood back with that expression of
old grave intolerant and repudiating and he lifted it, the
burlap lump which fifteen years ago had changed its shape
completely overnight, which shaken gave forth a thin
weightless not-quite-musical curiously muffled clatter, the
bright knife-blade hunting amid the mazed intricacy of
string, the knobby gouts of wax bearing his uncle's Beauchamp seal rattling onto the table's polished top and,
standing amid the collapse of burlap folds, the unstained
tin coffee-pot still brand new, the handful of copper coins
and now he knew what had given them the muffled
sound: a collection of minutely folded scraps of paper
sufficient almost for a rat's nest, of good linen bond, of the
crude ruled paper such as Negroes use, of raggedly-torn
ledger-pages and the margins of newspapers and once the
paper label from a new pair of overalls, all dated and all
signed, beginning with the first one not six months after
they had watched him seal the silver cup into the burlap
on this same table in this same room by the light even of
this same lamp almost twenty-one years ago:

> *I owe my Nephew Isaac Beauchamp McCaslin five
> (5) pieces Gold which I,O.U constitutes My note of
> hand with Interest at 5 percent.*
> > *Hubert Fitz-Hubert Beauchamp*
> *at Warwick 27 Nov 1867*

and he: 'Anyway he called it Warwick:' once at least,
even if no more. But there was more:

Isaac 24 Dec 1867 I.O.U. 2 pieces Gold H.Fh.B.
I.O.U. Isaac 1 piece Gold 1 Jan 1868 H.Fh.B.

then five again then three then one then one then a long
time and what dream, what dreamed splendid recoup, not
of any injury or betrayal of trust because it had been
merely a loan: nay, a partnership:

> *I.O.U. Beauchamp McCaslin or his heirs twenty-five*
> *(25) pieces Gold This & All preceeding constituting*
> *My notes of hand at twenty (20) percentum com-*
> *pounded annually. This date of 19th January 1873*
>
>   *Beauchamp*

no location save that in time and signed by the single not
name but word as the old proud earl himself might have
scrawled Nevile: and that made forty-three and he could
not remember himself of course but the legend had it at
fifty, which balanced: one: then one: then one: then one
and then the last three and then the last chit, dated after
he came to live in the house with them and written in the
shaky hand not of a beaten old man because he had never
been beaten to know it but of a tired old man maybe and
even at that tired only on the outside and still indomitable,
the simplicity of the last one the simplicity not of resignation but merely of amazement, like a simple comment or
remark, and not very much of that:

> *One silver cup. Hubert Beauchamp*

and McCaslin: 'So you have plenty of coppers anyway.
But they are still not old enough yet to be either rarities
or heirlooms. So you will have to take the money:' except
that he didn't hear McCaslin, standing quietly beside the
table and looking peacefully at the coffee-pot and the pot
sitting one night later on the mantel above what was not
even a fireplace in the little cramped ice-like room in Jefferson as McCaslin tossed the folded banknotes onto the

bed and, still standing (there was nowhere to sit save on the bed) did not even remove his hat and overcoat: and he

'As a loan. From you. This one:' and McCaslin

'You can't. I have no money that I can lend to you. And you will have to go to the bank and get it next month because I won't bring it to you:' and he could not hear McCaslin now either, looking peacefully at McCaslin, his kinsman, his father almost yet no kin now as, at the last, even fathers and sons are no kin: and he

'It's seventeen miles, horseback and in the cold. We could both sleep here:' and McCaslin

'Why should I sleep here in my house when you won't sleep yonder in yours?' and gone, and he looking at the bright rustless unstained tin and thinking, and not for the first time, how much it takes to compound a man (Isaac McCaslin for instance) and of the devious intricate choosing yet unerring path that man's (Isaac McCaslin's for instance) spirit takes among all that mass to make him at last what he is to be, not only to the astonishment of them (the ones who sired the McCaslin who sired his father and Uncle Buddy and their sister, and the ones who sired the Beauchamp who sired his Uncle Hubert and his Uncle Hubert's sister) who believed they had shaped him, but to Isaac McCaslin too

as a loan and used it though he would not have had to: Major de Spain offered him a room in his house as long as he wanted it and asked nor would ever ask any question, and old General Compson more than that, to take him into his own room, to sleep in half of his own bed and more than Major de Spain because he told him baldly why: 'You sleep with me and before this winter is out, I'll know the reason. You'll tell me. Because I don't believe you just quit. It looks like you just quit but I have watched you in the woods too much and I don't believe you just quit even if it does look damn like it:' using it as a loan, paid his board and rent for a month and bought the tools, not simply because he was good with his hands because he had intended to use his hands and it could have been with horses, and not in mere static and hopeful emulation of the Nazarene, as the young gambler buys a spotted shirt because the old gambler won in one yesterday, but (without the arrogance of false humility and without the false humbleness of pride, who intended to earn his bread, didn't especially want to earn it but had to earn it and for more than just bread) because if the Nazarene had found carpentering good for the life and ends He had assumed and elected to serve, it would be all right too for Isaac McCaslin even though Isaac McCaslin's ends, although simple enough in their apparent motivation, were and would be always incomprehensible to him, and his life, invincible enough in its needs, if he could have helped himself, not being the Nazarene, he would not have chosen it: and paid it back. He had forgotten the thirty dollars which McCaslin put into the bank in his name each month, fetched it in to him and flung it onto the bed that first one time but no more; he had a partner now or rather he was the partner: a blasphemous profane clever old dipsomaniac who had built blockade-runners in Charleston in '62 and '63 and had been a ship's carpenter since and appeared in Jefferson two years ago, nobody knew from where nor why, and spent a good part of his time since recovering from delirium tremens in the jail; they had put a new roof on the stable of the bank's president and (the old man in jail again still celebrating that job) he went to the bank to collect for it and the president said, 'I should borrow from you instead of paying you:' and it had been seven months now and he remembered for the first time, two-hundred-and-ten dollars, and this was the first job of any size and when he left the bank the account stood at two-twenty, two-forty to balance, only twenty dollars more to go, then it did balance though by then the total had increased to three hundred and thirty and he said, 'I will transfer it now:' and the president said, 'I can't do that. McCaslin told me not to. Haven't you got another initial you could use and open another account?' but that was all right, the coins the silver and the bills as they accumulated knotted into a handkerchief and the coffee-pot wrapped in an old shirt as when Tennie's great-grandfather had fetched it from Warwick eighteen years ago, in the bottom of the iron-bound trunk which old Carothers had brought from Carolina and his landlady said, 'Not even a lock! And you don't even lock your door, not even when you leave!' and himself looking at her as peacefully as he had looked at McCaslin that first night in this same room, no kin to him at all yet more than kin as those who serve you even for pay are your kin and those who injure you are more than brother or wife

and he had the wife now; got the old man out of jail and fetched him to the rented room and sobered him by superior strength, did not even remove his own shoes for twenty-four hours, got him up and got food into him and they built the barn this time from the ground up and he married her: an only child, a small girl yet curiously bigger than she seemed at first, solider perhaps, with dark eyes and a passionate heart-shaped face, who had time even on that farm to watch most of the day while he sawed timbers to the old man's measurements: and she: 'Papa told me about you. That farm is really yours, isn't it?' and he

'And McCaslin's:' and she

'Was there a will leaving half of it to him?' and he

'There didn't need to be a will. His grandmother was my father's sister. We were the same as brothers:' and she

'You are the same as second cousins and that's all you ever will be. But I don't suppose it matters:' and they were married, they were married and it was the new country, his heritage too as it was the heritage of all, out of the earth, beyond the earth yet of the earth because his too was of the earth's long chronicle, his too because each must share with another in order to come into it, and in the sharing they become one: for that while, one: for that little while at least, one: indivisible, that while at least irrevocable and unrecoverable, living in a rented room still but for just a little while and that room wall-less and topless and floorless in glory for him to leave each morning and return to at night; her father already owned the lot in town and furnished the material and he and his partner would build it, her dowry from one: her wedding-present from three, she not to know it until the bungalow was finished and ready to be moved into and he never know who told her, not her father and not his partner and not even in drink though for a while he believed that, himself coming home from work and just time to wash and rest a moment before going down to supper, entering no rented cubicle since it would still partake of glory even after they would have grown old and lost it: and he saw her face then, just before she spoke: 'Sit down:' the two of them sitting on the bed's edge, not even touching yet, her face strained and terrible, her voice a passionate and expiring whisper of immeasurable promise: 'I love you. You know I love you. When are we going to move?' and he

'I didn't—I didn't know—Who told you—' the hot fierce palm clapped over his mouth, crushing his lips into his teeth, the fierce curve of fingers digging into his cheek and only the palm slacked off enough for him to answer:

'The farm. Our farm. Your farm:' and he

'I——' then the hand again, finger and palm, the whole enveloping weight of her although she still was not touching him save the hand, the voice: 'No! No!' and the fingers themselves seeming to follow through the cheek the impulse to speech as it died in his mouth, then the whisper, the breath again, of love and of incredible promise, the palm slackening again to let him answer:

'When?' and he

'I——' then she was gone, the hand too, standing, her

back to him and her head bent, the voice so calm now
that for an instant it seemed no voice of hers that he ever
remembered: 'Stand up and turn your back and shut your
eyes:' and repeated before he understood and stood himself with his eyes shut and heard the bell ring for supper
below stairs, and the calm voice again: 'Lock the door:'
and he did so and leaned his forehead against the cold
wood, his eyes closed, hearing his heart and the sound
he had begun to hear before he moved until it ceased and
the bell rang again below stairs and he knew it was for
them this time, and he heard the bed and turned and he
had never seen her naked before, he had asked her to
once, and why: that he wanted to see her naked because
he loved her and he wanted to see her looking at him
naked because he loved her, but after that he never
mentioned it again, even turning his face when she put
the nightgown on over her dress to undress at night and
putting the dress on over the gown to remove it in the
morning and she would not let him get into bed beside her
until the lamp was out and even in the heat of summer
she would draw the sheet up over them both before she
would let him turn to her: and the landlady came up the
stairs up the hall and rapped on the door and then called
their names but she didn't move, lying still on the bed
outside the covers, her face turned away on the pillow,
listening to nothing, thinking of nothing, not of him anyway he thought: then the landlady went away and she
said, 'Take off your clothes:' her head still turned away,
looking at nothing, thinking of nothing, waiting for nothing, not even him, her hand moving as though with volition and vision of its own, catching his wrist at the exact
moment when he paused beside the bed so that he never
paused but merely changed the direction of moving,
downward now, the hand drawing him and she moved
at last, shifted, a movement one single complete inherent
not practiced and one time older than man, looking at
him now, drawing him still downward with the one hand

down and down and he neither saw nor felt it shift, palm flat against his chest now and holding him away with the same apparent lack of any effort or any need for strength, and not looking at him now, she didn't need to, the chaste woman, the wife, already looked upon all the men who ever rutted and now her whole body had changed, altered, he had never seen it but once and now it was not even the one he had seen but composite of all woman-flesh since man that ever of its own will reclined on its back and opened, and out of it somewhere, without any movement of lips even, the dying and invincible whisper: 'Promise:' and he

'Promise?'

'The farm.' He moved. He had moved, the hand shifting from his chest once more to his wrist, grasping it, the arm still lax and only the light increasing pressure of the fingers as though arm and hand were a piece of wire cable with one looped end, only the hand tightening as he pulled against it. 'No,' he said. 'No:' and she was not looking at him still but not like the other, but still the hand: 'No, I tell you. I won't. I can't. Never:' and still the hand and he said, for the last time, he tried to speak clearly and he knew it was still gently and he thought, *She already knows more than I with all the man-listening in camps where there was nothing to read ever even heard of. They are born already bored with what a boy approaches only at fourteen and fifteen with blundering and aghast trembling:* 'I can't. Not ever. Remember:' and still the steady and invincible hand and he said 'Yes' and he thought, *She is lost. She was born lost. We were all born lost* then he stopped thinking and even saying Yes, it was like nothing he had ever dreamed, let alone heard in mere man-talking until after a no-time he returned and lay spent on the insatiate immemorial beach and again with a movement one time more older than man she turned and freed herself and on their wedding night she had cried and he thought she was crying now at first, into the

tossed and wadded pillow, the voice coming from somewhere between the pillow and the cachinnation: 'And
that's all. That's all from me. If this don't get you that son
you talk about, it won't be mine:' lying on her side, her
back to the empty rented room, laughing and laughing

v

He went back to the camp one more time before the
lumber company moved in and began to cut the timber.
Major de Spain himself never saw it again. But he made
them welcome to use the house and hunt the land
whenever they liked, and in the winter following the last
hunt when Sam Fathers and Lion died, General Compson
and Walter Ewell invented a plan to corporate
themselves, the old group, into a club and lease the camp
and the hunting privileges of the woods—an invention
doubtless of the somewhat childish old General but actually worthy of Boon Hogganbeck himself. Even the boy,
listening, recognized it for the subterfuge it was: to change
the leopard's spots when they could not alter the leopard,
a baseless and illusory hope to which even McCaslin
seemed to subscribe for a while, that once they had persuaded Major de Spain to return to the camp he might
revoke himself, which even the boy knew he would not
do. And he did not. The boy never knew what occurred
when Major de Spain declined. He was not present when
the subject was broached and McCaslin never told him.
But when June came and the time for the double birthday
celebration there was no mention of it and when November came no one spoke of using Major de Spain's house
and he never knew whether or not Major de Spain knew
they were going on the hunt though without doubt old
Ash probably told him: he and McCaslin and General
Compson (and that one was the General's last hunt too)
and Walter and Boon and Tennie's Jim and old Ash loaded
two wagons and drove two days and almost forty miles

beyond any country the boy had ever seen before and lived in tents for the two weeks. And the next spring they heard (not from Major de Spain) that he had sold the timber-rights to a Memphis lumber company and in June the boy came to town with McCaslin one Saturday and went to Major de Spain's office—the big, airy, booklined, second-storey room with windows at one end opening upon the shabby hinder purlieus of stores and at the other a door giving onto the railed balcony above the Square, with its curtained alcove where sat a cedar water-bucket and a sugar-bowl and spoon and tumbler and a wicker-covered demijohn of whiskey, and the bamboo-and-paper punkah swinging back and forth above the desk while old Ash in a tilted chair beside the entrance pulled the cord.

"Of course," Major de Spain said. "Ash will probably like to get off in the woods himself for a while, where he won't have to eat Daisy's cooking. Complain about it, anyway. Are you going to take anybody with you?"

"No sir," he said. "I thought that maybe Boon—" For six months now Boon had been town-marshal at Hoke's; Major de Spain had compounded with the lumber company—or perhaps compromised was closer, since it was the lumber company who had decided that Boon might be better as a town-marshal than head of a logging gang.

"Yes," Major de Spain said. "I'll wire him today. He can meet you at Hoke's. I'll send Ash on by the train and they can take some food in and all you will have to do will be to mount your horse and ride over."

"Yes sir," he said. "Thank you." And he heard his voice again. He didn't know he was going to say it yet he did not, he had known it all the time: "Maybe if you . . ." His voice died. It was stopped, he never knew how because Major de Spain did not speak and it was not until his voice ceased that Major de Spain moved, turned back to the desk and the papers spread on it and even that without moving because he was sitting at the desk with a paper in his hand when the boy entered, the boy standing there looking down at the short plumpish gray-haired man in sober fine broadcloth and an immaculate glazed shirt whom he was used to seeing in boots and muddy corduroy, unshaven, sitting the shaggy powerful long-hocked mare with the worn Winchester carbine across the saddlebow and the great blue dog standing motionless as bronze at the stirrup, the two of them in that last year and to the boy anyway coming to resemble one another somehow as two people competent for love or for business who have been in love or in business together for a long time sometimes do. Major de Spain did not look up again.

"No. I will be too busy. But good luck to you. If you have it, you might bring me a young squirrel."

"Yes sir," he said. "I will."

He rode his mare, the three-year-old filly he had bred and raised and broken himself. He left home a little after midnight and six hours later, without even having sweated her, he rode into Hoke's, the tiny log-line junction which he had always thought of as Major de Spain's property too although Major de Spain had merely sold the company (and that many years ago) the land on which the sidetracks and loading-platforms and the commissary store stood, and looked about in shocked and grieved amazement even though he had had forewarning and had believed himself prepared: a new planing-mill already half completed which would cover two or three acres and what looked like miles and miles of stacked steel rails red with the light bright rust of newness and of piled crossties sharp with creosote, and wire corrals and feeding-troughs for two hundred mules at least and the tents for the men who drove them; so that he arranged for the care and stabling of his mare as rapidly as he could and did not look any more, mounted into the log-train caboose with his gun and climbed into the cupola and looked no more save toward the wall of wilderness ahead within which he would be able to hide himself from it once more anyway.

Then the little locomotive shrieked and began to move: a rapid churning of exhaust, a lethargic deliberate clashing of slack couplings travelling backward along the train, the exhaust changing to the deep slow clapping bites of power as the caboose too began to move and from the cupola he watched the train's head complete the first and only curve in the entire line's length and vanish into the wilderness, dragging its length of train behind it so that it resembled a small dingy harmless snake vanishing into weeds, drawing him with it too until soon it ran once more at its maximum clattering speed between the twin walls of unaxed wilderness as of old. It had been harmless once. Not five years ago Walter Ewell had shot a six-point buck from this same moving caboose, and there was the story of the half-grown bear: the train's first trip in to the cutting thirty miles away, the bear between the rails, its rear end elevated like that of a playing puppy while it dug to see what sort of ants or bugs they might contain or perhaps just to examine the curious symmetrical squared barkless logs which had appeared apparently from nowhere in one endless mathematical line overnight, still digging until the driver on the braked engine not fifty feet away blew the whistle at it, whereupon it broke frantically and took the first tree it came to: an ash sapling not much bigger than a man's thigh and climbed as high as it could and clung there, its head ducked between its arms as a man (a woman perhaps) might have done while the brakeman threw chunks of ballast at it, and when the engine returned three hours later with the first load of outbound logs the bear was halfway down the tree and once more scrambled back up as high as it could and clung again while the train passed and was still there when the engine went in again in the afternoon and still there when it came back out at dusk; and Boon had been in Hoke's with the wagon after a barrel of flour that noon when the train-crew told about it and Boon and Ash, both twenty years younger then, sat under the tree all that night to keep anybody from shooting it and the next morning Major de Spain had the log-train held at Hoke's and just before sundown on the second day, with not only Boon and Ash but Major de Spain and General Compson and Walter and McCaslin, twelve then, watching, it came down the tree after almost thirty-six hours without even water and McCaslin told him how for a minute they thought it was going to stop right there at the barrow-pit where they were standing and drink, how it looked at the water and paused and looked at them and at the water again, but did not, gone, running, as bears run, the two sets of feet, front and back, tracking two separate though parallel courses.

It had been harmless then. They would hear the passing log-train sometimes from the camp; sometimes, because nobody bothered to listen for it or not. They would hear it going in, running light and fast, the light clatter of the trucks, the exhaust of the diminutive locomotive and its shrill peanut-parcher whistle flung for one petty moment and absorbed by the brooding and inattentive wilderness without even an echo. They would hear it going out, loaded, not quite so fast now yet giving its frantic and toylike illusion of crawling speed, not whistling now to conserve steam, flinging its bitten laboring miniature puffing into the immemorial woodsface with frantic and bootless vainglory, empty and noisy and puerile, carrying to no destination or purpose sticks which left nowhere any scar or stump, as the child's toy loads and transports and unloads its dead sand and rushes back for more, tireless and unceasing and rapid yet never quite so fast as the Hand which plays with it moves the toy burden back to load the toy again. But it was different now. It was the same train, engine cars and caboose, even the same enginemen brakeman and conductor to whom Boon, drunk then sober then drunk again then fairly sober once more all in the space of fourteen hours, had bragged that day two years ago about what they were going to do to Old Ben tomorrow, running with its same illusion of frantic rapidity between the same twin walls of impenetrable and impervious woods, passing the old landmarks, the old game crossings over which he had trailed bucks wounded and not wounded and more than once seen them, anything but wounded, bot out of the woods and up and across the embankment which bore the rails and ties then down and into the woods again as the earth-bound supposedly move but crossing as arrows travel, groundless, elongated, three times its actual length and even paler, different in color, as if there were a point between immobility and absolute motion where even mass chemically altered, changing without pain or agony not only in bulk and shape but in color too, approaching the color of wind, yet this time it was as though the train (and not only the train but himself, not only his vision which had seen it and his memory which remembered it but his clothes too, as garments carry back into the clean edgeless blowing of air the lingering effluvium of a sick-room or of death) had brought with it into the doomed wilderness, even before the actual axe, the shadow and portent of the new mill not even finished yet and the rails and ties which were not even laid; and he knew now what he had known as soon as he saw Hoke's this morning but had not yet thought into words: why Major de Spain had not come back, and that after this time he himself, who had had to see it one time other, would return no more.

Now they were near. He knew it before the engine-driver whistled to warn him. Then he saw Ash and the wagon, the reins without doubt wrapped once more about the brake-lever as within the boy's own memory Major de Spain had been forbidding him for eight years to do, the train slowing, the slackened couplings jolting and clashing again from car to car, the caboose slowing past the wagon as he swung down with his gun, the conductor leaning out above him to signal the engine, the caboose still slowing, creeping, although the engine's exhaust was already slatting in mounting tempo against the unechoing wilderness, the crashing of drawbars once more travelling backward along the train, the caboose picking up speed at last. Then it was gone. It had not been. He could no longer hear it. The wilderness soared, musing, inattentive, myriad, eternal, green; older than any mill-shed, longer than any spur-line. "Mr. Boon here yet?" he said.

"He beat me in," Ash said. "Had the wagon loaded and ready for me at Hoke's yistiddy when I got there and set-ting on the front steps at camp last night when I got in. He already been in the wools since fo daylight this morn-ing. Said he gwine up to the Gum Tree and for you to hunt up that way and meet him." He knew where that was: a single big sweet-gum just outside the woods, in an old clearing; if you crept up to it very quietly this time of year and then ran suddenly into the clearing, sometimes you caught as many as a dozen squirrels in it, trapped, since there was no other tree near they could jump to. So he didn't get into the wagon at all.

"I will," he said.

"I figured you would," Ash said, "I fotch you a box of shells." He passed the shells down and began to un-wrap the lines from the brake-pole.

"How many times up to now do you reckon Major has told you not to do that?" the boy said.

"Do which?" Ash said. Then he said: "And tell Boon Hogganbeck dinner gonter be on the table in a hour and if yawl want any to come on and eat it."

"In an hour?" he said. "It ain't nine o'clock yet." He drew out his watch and extended it face-toward Ash. "Look." Ash didn't even look at the watch.

"That's town time. You ain't in town now. You in the woods."

"Look at the sun then."

"Nemmine the sun too," Ash said. "If you and Boon

Hogganbeck want any dinner, you better come on in and get it when I tole you. I aim to get done in that kitchen because I got my wood to chop. And watch your feet. They're crawling."

"I will," he said.

Then he was in the woods, not alone but solitary; the solitude closed about him, green with summer. They did not change, and, timeless, would not, any more than would the green of summer and the fire and rain of fall and the iron cold and sometimes even snow

the day, the morning when he killed the buck and Sam marked his face with its hot blood, they returned to camp and he remembered old Ash's blinking and disgruntled and even outraged disbelief until at last McCaslin had had to affirm the fact that he had really killed it: and that night Ash sat snarling and unapproachable behind the stove so that Tennie's Jim had to serve the supper and waked them with breakfast already on the table the next morning and it was only half-past one o'clock and at last out of Major de Spain's angry cursing and Ash's snarling and sullen rejoinders the fact emerged that Ash not only wanted to go into the woods and shoot a deer also but he intended to and Major de Spain said, 'By God, if we don't let him we will probably have to do the cooking from now on:' and Walter Ewell said, 'Or get up at midnight to eat what Ash cooks:' and since he had already killed his buck for this hunt and was not to shoot again unless they needed meat, he offered his gun to Ash until Major de Spain took command and allotted that gun to Boon for the day and gave Boon's unpredictable pump gun to Ash, with two buckshot shells but Ash said, 'I got shells:' and showed them, four: one buck, one of number three shot for rabbits, two of bird-shot and told one by one their history and their origin and he remembered not Ash's face alone but Major de Spain's and Walter's and General Compson's too, and Ash's voice: 'Shoot? In course they'll shoot! Genl Cawmpson guv me this un'—the buckshot—

'right outen the same gun he kilt that big buck with eight years ago. And this un'—it was the rabbit shell: triumphantly—'is oldern thisyer boy!' And that morning he loaded the gun himself, reversing the order: the birdshot, the rabbit, then the buck so that the buckshot would feed first into the chamber, and himself without a gun, he and Ash walked beside Major de Spain's and Tennie's Jim's horses and the dogs (that was the snow) until they cast and struck, the sweet strong cries ringing away into the muffled falling air and gone almost immediately, as if the constant and unmurmuring flakes had already buried even the unformed echoes beneath their myriad and weightless falling, Major de Spain and Tennie's Jim gone too, whooping on into the woods; and then it was all right, he knew as plainly as if Ash had told him that Ash had now hunted his deer and that even his tender years had been forgiven for having killed one, and they turned back toward home through the falling snow—that is, Ash said, 'Now whut?' and he said, 'This way'—himself in front because, although they were less than a mile from camp, he knew that Ash, who had spent two weeks of his life in the camp each year for the last twenty, had no idea whatever where they were, until quite soon the manner in which Ash carried Boon's gun was making him a good deal more than just nervous and he made Ash walk in front, striding on, talking now, an old man's garrulous monologue beginning with where he was at the moment then of the woods and of camping in the woods and of eating in camps then of eating then of cooking it and of his wife's cooking then briefly of his old wife and almost at once and at length of a new light-colored woman who nursed next door to Major de Spain's and if she didn't watch out who she was switching her tail at he would show her how old was an old man or not if his wife just didn't watch him all the time, the two of them in a game trail through a dense brake of cane and brier which would bring them out within a quarter-mile of camp, approach-

ing a big fallen tree-trunk lying athwart the path and just as Ash, still talking, was about to step over it the bear, the yearling, rose suddenly beyond the log, sitting up, its forearms against its chest and its wrists limply arrested as if it had been surprised in the act of covering its face to pray: and after a certain time Ash's gun yawed jerkily up and he said, 'You haven't got a shell in the barrel yet. Pump it:' but the gun already snicked and he said, 'Pump it. You haven't got a shell in the barrel yet:' and Ash pumped the action and in a certain time the gun steadied again and snicked and he said, 'Pump it:' and watched the buckshot shell jerk, spinning heavily, into the cane. This is the rabbit shot: he thought and the gun snicked and he thought: The next is bird-shot: and he didn't have to say Pump it; he cried, 'Don't shoot! Don't shoot!' but that was already too late too, the light dry vicious snick! before he could speak and the bear turned and dropped to all-fours and then was gone and there was only the log, the cane, the velvet and constant snow and Ash said, 'Now whut?' and he said, 'This way. Come on:' and began to back away down the path and Ash said, 'I got to find my shells:' and he said, 'Goddamn it, goddamn it, come on:' but Ash leaned the gun against the log and returned and stooped and fumbled among the cane roots until he came back and stooped and found the shells and they rose and at that moment the gun, untouched, leaning against the log six feet away and for that while even forgotten by both of them, roared, bellowed and flamed, and ceased: and he carried it now, pumped out the last mummified shell and gave that one also to Ash and, the action still open, himself carried the gun until he stood it in the corner behind Boon's bed at the camp

—; summer, and fall, and snow, and wet and sap-rife spring in their ordered immortal sequence, the deathless and immemorial phases of the mother who had shaped him if any had toward the man he almost was, mother and father both to the old man born of a Negro slave and a Chickasaw chief who had been his spirit's father if any had, whom he had revered and harkened to and loved and lost and grieved: and he would marry someday and they too would own for their brief while that brief unsubstanced glory which inherently of itself cannot last and hence why glory: and they would, might, carry even the remembrance of it into the time when flesh no longer talks to flesh because memory at least does last: but still the woods would be his mistress and his wife.

He was not going toward the Gum Tree. Actually he was getting farther from it. Time was and not so long ago either when he would not have been allowed here without someone with him, and a little later, when he had begun to learn how much he did not know, he would not have dared be here without someone with him, and later still, beginning to ascertain, even if only dimly, the limits of what he did not know, he could have attempted and carried it through with a compass, not because of any increased belief in himself but because McCaslin and Major de Spain and Walter and General Compson too had taught him at last to believe the compass regardless of what it seemed to state. Now he did not even use the compass but merely the sun and that only subconsciously, yet he could have taken a scaled map and plotted at any time to within a hundred feet of where he actually was; and sure enough, at almost the exact moment when he expected it, the earth began to rise faintly, he passed one of the four concrete markers set down by the lumber company's surveyor to establish the four corners of the plot which Major de Spain had reserved out of the sale, then he stood on the crest of the knoll itself, the four corner-markers all visible now, blanched still even beneath the winter's weathering, lifeless and shockingly alien in that place where dissolution itself was a seething turmoil of ejaculation tumescence conception and birth, and death did not even exist. After two winters' blanketings of leaves and the flood-waters of two springs, there was no trace of the two graves any more at all. But those who would have come this far to find them would not need head-stones but would have found them as Sam Fathers him-self had taught him to find such: by bearings on trees: and did, almost the first thrust of the hunting knife find-ing (but only to see if it was still there) the round tin box manufactured for axle-grease and containing now Old Ben's dried mutilated paw, resting above Lion's bones.

He didn't disturb it. He didn't even look for the other grave where he and McCaslin and Major de Spain and Boon had laid Sam's body, along with his hunting horn and his knife and his tobacco-pipe, that Sunday morning two years ago; he didn't have to. He had stepped over it, perhaps on it. But that was all right. *He probably knew I was in the woods this morning long before I got here,* he thought, going on to the tree which had supported one end of the platform where Sam lay when McCaslin and Major de Spain found them—the tree, the other axle-grease tin nailed to the trunk, but weathered, rusted, alien too yet healed already into the wilderness' concord-ant generality, raising no tuneless note, and empty, long since empty of the food and tobacco he had put into it that day, as empty of that as it would presently be of this which he drew from his pocket—the twist of tobacco, the new bandanna handkerchief, the small paper sack of the peppermint candy which Sam had used to love; that gone too, almost before he had turned his back, not vanished but merely translated into the myriad life which printed the dark mold of these secret and sunless places with deli-cate fairy tracks, which, breathing and biding and immo-bile, watched him from beyond every twig and leaf until he moved, moving again, walking on; he had not stopped, he had only paused, quitting the knoll which was no abode of the dead because there was no death, not Lion and not Sam: not held fast in earth but free in earth and not in earth but of earth, myriad yet undiffused of every myriad part, leaf and twig and particle, air and sun and rain and dew and night, acorn oak and leaf and acorn again, dark and dawn and dark and dawn again in their immutable progression, and, being myriad, one: and Old Ben too. Old Ben too; they would give him his paw back even, certainly they would give him his paw back: then the long challenge and the long chase, no heart to be driven and outraged, no flesh to be mauled and bled— Even as he froze himself, he seemed to hear Ash's parting admonition. He could even hear the voice as he froze, immobile, one foot just taking his weight, the toe of the other just lifted behind him, not breathing, feeling again and as always the sharp shocking inrush from when Isaac McCaslin long yet was not, and so it was fear all right but not fright as he looked down at it. It had not coiled yet and the buzzer had not sounded either, only one thick rapid contraction, one loop cast sideways as though merely for purchase from which the raised head might start slightly backward, not in fright either, not in threat quite yet, more than six feet of it, the head raised higher than his knee and less than his knee's length away, and old, the once-bright markings of its youth dulled now to a monotone concordant too with the wilderness it crawled and lurked: the old one, the ancient and accursed about the earth, fatal and solitary and he could smell it now: the thin sick smell of rotting cucumbers and something else which had no name, evocative of all knowledge and an old weariness and of pariah-hood and of death. At last it moved. Not the head. The elevation of the head did not change as it began to glide away from him, moving erect yet off the perpendicular as if the head and that elevated third were complete and all: an entity walking on two feet and free of all laws of mass and balance, and should have been because even now he could not quite believe that all that shift and flow of shadow behind that walking head could have been one snake: going and then gone; he put the other foot down at last and didn't know it, standing with one hand raised as Sam

had stood that afternoon six years ago when Sam led him
into the wilderness and showed him and he ceased to be
a child, speaking the old tongue which Sam had spoken
that day without premeditation either: "Chief," he said:
"Grandfather."

He couldn't tell when he first began to hear the sound,
because when he became aware of it, it seemed to him
that he had been already hearing it for several seconds—
a sound as though someone were hammering a gun-barrel
against a piece of railroad iron, a sound loud and heavy
and not rapid yet with something frenzied about it, as the
hammerer were not only a strong man and an earnest one
but a little hysterical too. Yet it couldn't be on the logline
because, although the track lay in that direction, it was
at least two miles from him and this sound was not three
hundred yards away. But even as he thought that, he
realized where the sound must be coming from: whoever
the man was and whatever he was doing, he was somewhere near the edge of the clearing where the Gum Tree
was and where he was to meet Boon. So far, he had been
hunting as he advanced, moving slowly and quietly and
watching the ground and the trees both. Now he went
on, his gun unloaded and the barrel slanted up and back
to facilitate its passage through brier and undergrowth,
approaching as it grew louder and louder that steady savage somehow queerly hysterical beating of metal on
metal, emerging from the woods, into the old clearing,
with the solitary gum tree directly before him. At first
glance the tree seemed to be alive with frantic squirrels.
There appeared to be forty or fifty of them leaping and
darting from branch to branch until the whole tree had
become one green maelstrom of mad leaves, while from
time to time, singly or in twos and threes, squirrels would
dart down the trunk then whirl without stopping and rush
back up again as though sucked violently back by the
vacuum of their fellows' frenzied vortex. Then he saw
Boon, sitting, his back against the trunk, his head bent,

hammering furiously at something on his lap. What he hammered with was the barrel of his dismembered gun, what he hammered at was the breech of it. The rest of the gun lay scattered about him in a half-dozen pieces while he bent over the piece on his lap his scarlet and streaming walnut face, hammering the disjointed barrel against the gun-breech with the frantic abandon of a madman. He didn't even look up to see who it was. Still hammering, he merely shouted back at the boy in a hoarse strangled voice:

"Get out of here! Don't touch them! Don't touch a one of them! They're mine!"

4

THE PEASANTS

Editor's Note

Thirty or forty years after the Civil War, Flem Snopes appeared in the little community of Frenchman's Bend, in the southeastern corner of Faulkner's county. Flem was the son of a Civil War bushwhacker and horse thief. A lumpish and silent young man, with eyes the color of stagnant water, he never drank or smoked, but he sometimes chewed a nickel's worth of tobacco until the suption was out of it. "Flem Snopes don't even tell himself what he is up to," one of his neighbors said. "Not if he was laying in bed with himself in the dark of the moon."

In his dark-of-the-moon fashion, Flem managed to get control of the general store, the cotton gin, and the blacksmith shop, the only three money-making enterprises in Frenchman's Bend; and one by one he introduced a horde of his relatives to take charge of them. Lump Snopes, the storekeeper; I. O. Snopes, the schoolmaster; Mink Snopes, the killer; Ike Snopes, the idiot boy who fell in love with a cow; Eck Snopes, the stupid and good-natured blacksmith: all together they descended on the community like field mice, devouring everything, cheating everybody, cheating one another; and when Flem had cheated even Ratliff, the sewing-machine agent, known as the shrewdest man in the county, they all moved on to Jefferson, like mice into an untouched field of grain.

That is the story told in *The Hamlet* (1940), first volume in the Snopes trilogy, which is a book that took Faulkner a dozen years to write. When he first began working on the idea, it produced one story, "Spotted Horses," but went no further. About two years later, he wrote two other stories with the same background, "The Hound" and "Lizards in Jamshyd's Courtyard." "I wrote them mainly," he said in a letter, "because 'Spotted Horses' had created a character I fell in love with: the itinerant sewing-machine agent named Suratt. Later a man of that name turned up at home, so I changed my man to Ratliff. . . . Meanwhile my book had created Snopes and his clan, who produced stories in their saga which are to fall in later volumes: 'Mule in the Yard,' 'Brass,' etc. This over about ten years, until one day I decided I had better start on the first volume or I'd never get it down."

The later volumes are *The Town* (1957) and *The Mansion* (1959), which complete the Snopes trilogy. They contain many impressive episodes, but nothing so wildly funny as "Spotted Horses." The version of that story used in *The Hamlet,* and reprinted here, is nearly three times as long as the magazine version printed ten years earlier in *Scribner's,* as well as being three times as good. To me it seems the culminating example of American backwoods humor, a long tradition that goes back to the Davy Crockett almanacs and that reached an early flowering in Mark Twain.

1908

Spotted Horses

I

A little while before sundown the men lounging about the gallery of the store saw, coming up the road from the south, a covered wagon drawn by mules and followed by a considerable string of obviously alive objects which in the levelling sun resembled vari-sized and -colored tatters torn at random from large billboards—circus posters, say —attached to the rear of the wagon and inherent with its own separate and collective motion, like the tail of a kite.

"What in the hell is that?" one said.

"It's a circus," Quick said. They began to rise, watching the wagon. Now they could see that the animals behind the wagon were horses. Two men rode in the wagon.

"Hell fire," the first man—his name was Freeman— said. "It's Flem Snopes." They were all standing when the wagon came up and stopped and Snopes got down and approached the steps. He might have departed only this morning. He wore the same cloth cap, the minute bow tie against the white shirt, the same gray trousers. He mounted the steps.

"Howdy, Flem," Quick said. The other looked briefly at all of them and none of them, mounting the steps. "Starting you a circus?"

"Gentlemen," he said. He crossed the gallery; they made way for him. Then they descended the steps and approached the wagon, at the tail of which the horses stood in a restive clump, larger than rabbits and gaudy as parrots and shackled to one another and to the wagon itself with sections of barbed wire. Calico-coated, small-bodied, with delicate legs and pink faces in which their mismatched eyes rolled wild and subdued, they huddled, gaudy, motionless, and alert, wild as deer, deadly as rattlesnakes, quiet as doves. The men stood at a respectful distance, looking at them. At that moment Jody Varner came through the group, shouldering himself to the front of it.

"Watch yourself, doc," a voice said from the rear. But it was already too late. The nearest animal rose on its hind legs with lightning rapidity and struck twice with its forefeet at Varner's face, faster than a boxer, the movement of its surge against the wire which held it travelling backward among the rest of the band in a wave of thuds and lunges. "Hup, you broom-tailed, hay-burning sidewinders," the same voice said. This was the second man who had arrived in the wagon. He was a stranger. He wore a heavy, densely black moustache, a wide pale hat. When he thrust himself through and turned to herd them back from the horses they saw, thrust into the hip pockets of his tight jeans pants, the butt of a heavy pearl-handled pistol and a florid carton such as small cakes come in. "Keep away from them, boys," he said. "They've got kind of skittish, they ain't been rode in so long."

"Since when have they been rode?" Quick said. The stranger looked at Quick. He had a broad, quite cold, wind-gnawed face and bleak, cold eyes. His belly fitted neat and smooth as a peg into the tight trousers.

"I reckon that was when they were rode on the ferry to get across the Mississippi River," Varner said. The stranger looked at him. "My name's Varner," Jody said.

"Hipps," the other said. "Call me Buck." Across the left side of his head, obliterating the tip of that ear, was a savage and recent gash gummed over with a blackish substance like axle-grease. They looked at the scar. Then they watched him remove the carton from his pocket and tilt a gingersnap into his hand and put the gingersnap into his mouth, beneath the moustache.

"You and Flem have some trouble back yonder?" Quick said. The stranger ceased chewing. When he looked directly at anyone, his eyes became like two pieces of flint turned suddenly up in dug earth.

"Back where?" he said.

"Your nigh ear," Quick said.

"Oh," the other said. "That." He touched his ear. "That was my mistake. I was absent-minded one night when I was staking them out. Studying about something else and forgot how long the wire was." He chewed. They looked at his ear. "Happen to any man careless around a horse. Put a little axle-dope on it and you won't notice it to-morrow though. They're pretty lively now, lazing along all day doing nothing. It'll work out of them in a couple of days." He put another gingersnap into his mouth, chewing, "Don't you believe they'll gentle?" No one answered. They looked at the ponies, grave and noncommittal. Jody turned and went back into the store. "Them's good, gentle ponies," the stranger said. "Watch now." He put the carton back into his pocket and approached the horses, his hand extended. The nearest one was standing on three legs now. It appeared to be asleep. Its eyelid drooped over the cerulean eye; its head was shaped like an ironing-board. Without even raising the eyelid it flicked its head, the yellow teeth cropped. For an instant it and the man appeared to be inextricable in one violence. Then they became motionless, the stranger's high heels dug into the earth, one hand gripping the animal's nostrils, holding the horse's head wrenched half around while it breathed in hoarse, smothered groans. "See?" the stranger said in a panting voice, the veins standing white and rigid in his neck and along his jaw. "See? All you got to do is handle them a little and work hell out of them for a couple of days. Now look out. Give me room back there." They gave back a little. The stranger gathered himself then sprang away. As he did so, a second horse slashed at his back, severing his vest from collar to hem down the back exactly as the trick swordsman severs a floating veil with one stroke.

"Sho now," Quick said. "But suppose a man don't happen to own a vest."

At that moment Jody Varner, followed by the blacksmith, thrust through them again. "All right, Buck," he said. "Better get them on into the lot. Eck here will help you." The stranger, the severed halves of the vest swinging from either shoulder, mounted to the wagon seat, the blacksmith following.

"Get up, you transmogrified hallucinations of Job and Jezebel," the stranger said. The wagon moved on, the tethered ponies coming gaudily into motion behind it, behind which in turn the men followed at a respectful distance, on up the road and into the lane and so to the lot gate behind Mrs. Littlejohn's. Eck got down and opened the gate. The wagon passed through but when the ponies saw the fence the herd surged backward against the wire which attached it to the wagon, standing on its collective hind legs and then trying to turn within itself, so that the wagon moved backward for a few feet until the Texan, cursing, managed to saw the mules about and so lock the wheels. The men following had already fallen rapidly back. "Here, Eck," the Texan said. "Get up here and take the reins." The blacksmith got back in the wagon and took the reins. Then they watched the Texan descend, carrying a looped-up blacksnake whip, and go around to the rear of the herd and drive it through the gate, the whip snaking about the harlequin rumps in methodical and pistol-like reports. Then the watchers hurried across Mrs. Littlejohn's yard and mounted to the veranda, one end of which overlooked the lot.

"How you reckon he ever got them tied together?" Freeman said.

"I'd a heap rather watch how he aims to turn them

loose," Quick said. The Texan had climbed back into the halted wagon. Presently he and Eck both appeared at the rear end of the open hood. The Texan grasped the wire and began to draw the first horse up to the wagon, the animal plunging and surging back against the wire as though trying to hang itself, the contagion passing back through the herd from animal to animal until they were rearing and plunging again against the wire.

"Come on, grab a holt," the Texan said. Eck grasped the wire also. The horses laid back against it, the pink faces tossing above the back-surging mass. "Pull him up, pull him up," the Texan said sharply. "They couldn't get up here in the wagon even if they wanted to." The wagon moved gradually backward until the head of the first horse was snubbed up to the tail-gate. The Texan took a turn of the wire quickly about one of the wagon stakes. "Keep the slack out of it," he said. He vanished and re-appeared, almost in the same second, with a pair of heavy wire-cutters. "Hold them like that," he said, and leaped. He vanished, broad hat, flapping vest, wire-cutters and all, into a kaleidoscopic maelstrom of long teeth and wild eyes and slashing feet, from which presently the horses began to burst one by one like partridges flushing, each wearing a necklace of barbed wire. The first one crossed the lot at top speed, on a straight line. It galloped into the fence without any diminution whatever. The wire gave, recovered, and slammed the horse to earth where it lay for a moment, glaring, its legs still galloping in air. It scrambled up without having ceased to gallop and crossed the lot and galloped into the opposite fence and was slammed again to earth. The others were now freed. They whipped and whirled about the lot like dizzy fish in a bowl. It had seemed like a big lot until now, but now the very idea that all that fury and motion should be trans-piring inside any one fence was something to be repudi-ated with contempt, like a mirror trick. From the ultimate dust the stranger, carrying the wire-cutters and his vest completely gone now, emerged. He was not running, he merely moved with a light-poised and watchful celerity, weaving among the calico rushes of the animals, feinting and dodging like a boxer until he reached the gate and crossed the yard and mounted to the veranda. One sleeve of his shirt hung only at one point from his shoulder. He ripped it off and wiped his face with it and threw it away and took out the paper carton and shook a gingersnap into his hand. He was breathing only a little heavily. "Pretty lively now," he said. "But it'll work out of them in a couple of days." The ponies still streaked back and forth through the growing dusk like hysterical fish, but not so violently now.

"What'll you give a man to reduce them odds a little for you?" Quick said. The Texan looked at him, the eyes bleak, pleasant and hard above the chewing jaw, the heavy moustache. "To take one of them off your hands?" Quick said.

At that moment the little periwinkle-eyed boy came along the veranda, saying, "Papa, papa; where's papa?"

"Who you looking for, sonny?" one said.

"It's Eck's boy," Quick said. "He's still out yonder in the wagon. Helping Mr. Buck here." The boy went on to the end of the veranda, in diminutive overalls—a miniature replica of the men themselves.

"Papa," he said. "Papa." The blacksmith was still leaning from the rear of the wagon, still holding the end of the severed wire. The ponies, bunched for the moment, now slid past the wagon, flowing, stringing out again so that they appeared to have doubled in number, rushing on; the hard, rapid, light patter of unshod hooves came out of the dust. "Mamma says to come on to supper," the boy said.

The moon was almost full then. When supper was over and they had gathered again along the veranda the alteration was hardly one of visibility even. It was merely a translation from the lapidary-dimensional of day to the treacherous and silver receptivity in which the horses huddled in mazy camouflage, or singly or in pairs rushed, fluid, phantom, and unceasing, to huddle again in mirage-like clumps from which came high, abrupt squeals and the vicious thudding of hooves.

Ratliff was among them now. He had returned just before supper. He had not dared to take his team into the lot at all. They were now in Bookwright's stable a half mile from the store. "So Flem has come home again," he said. "Well, well, well. Will Varner paid to get him to Texas, so I reckon it ain't no more than fair for you fellows to pay the freight on him back." From the lot there came a high, thin squeal. One of the animals emerged. It seemed not to gallop but to flow, bodiless, without dimension. Yet there was the rapid light beat of hard hooves on the packed earth.

"He ain't said they was his yet," Quick said.

"He ain't said they ain't neither," Freeman said.

"I see," Ratliff said. "That's what you are holding back on. Until he tells you whether they are his or not. Or maybe you can wait until the auction's over and split up and some can follow Flem and some can follow that Texas fellow and watch to see which one spends the money. But then, when a man's done got trimmed, I don't reckon he cares who's got the money."

"Maybe if Ratliff would leave here tonight, they wouldn't make him buy one of them ponies tomorrow," a third said.

"That's fact," Ratliff said. "A fellow can dodge a Snopes if he just starts lively enough. In fact, I don't believe he would have to pass more than two folks before he would have another victim intervened betwixt them. You folks ain't going to buy them things sho enough, are you?" Nobody answered. They sat on the steps, their backs against the veranda posts, or on the railing itself. Only Ratliff and Quick sat in chairs, so that to them the others were black silhouettes against the dreaming lambence of the moonlight beyond the veranda. The pear tree across the road opposite was now in full and frosty bloom, the twigs and branches springing not outward from the limbs but standing motionless and perpendicular above the horizontal boughs like the separate and upstreaming hair of a drowned woman sleeping upon the uttermost floor of the windless and tideless sea.

"Anse McCallum brought two of them horses back from Texas once," one of the men on the steps said. He did not move to speak. He was not speaking to anyone. "It was a good team. A little light. He worked it for ten years. Light work, it was."

"I mind it," another said. "Anse claimed he traded fourteen rifle cartridges for both of them, didn't he?"

"It was the rifle too, I heard," a third said.

"No, it was just the shells," the first said. "The fellow wanted to swap him four more for the rifle too, but Anse said he never needed them. Cost too much to get six of them back to Mississippi."

"Sho," the second said. "When a man don't have to invest so much into a horse or a team, he don't need to expect so much from it." The three of them were not talking any louder, they were merely talking among themselves, to one another, as if they sat there alone. Ratliff, invisible in the shadow against the wall, made a sound, harsh, sardonic, not loud.

"Ratliff's laughing," a fourth said.

"Don't mind me," Ratliff said. The three speakers had not moved. They did not move now, yet there seemed to gather about the three silhouettes something stubborn, convinced, and passive, like children who have been chidden. A bird, a shadow, fleet and dark and swift, curved across the moonlight, upward into the pear tree and began to sing; a mockingbird.

"First one I've noticed this year," Freeman said.

"You can hear them along Whiteleaf every night," the

first man said. "I heard one in February. In that snow. Singing in a gum."

"Gum is the first tree to put out," the third said. "That was why. It made it feel like singing, fixing to put out that way. That was why it taken a gum."

"Gum first to put out?" Quick said. "What about willow?"

"Willow ain't a tree," Freeman said. "It's a weed."

"Well, I don't know what it is," the fourth said. "But it ain't no weed. Because you can grub up a weed and you are done with it. I been grubbing up a clump of willows outen my spring pasture for fifteen years. They are the same size every year. Only difference is, it's just two or three more trees every time."

"And if I was you," Ratliff said, "that's just exactly where I would be come sunup tomorrow. Which of course you ain't going to do. I reckon there ain't nothing under the sun or in Frenchman's Bend neither that can keep you folks from giving Flem Snopes and that Texas man your money. But I'd sholy like to know just exactly who I was giving my money to. Seems like Eck here would tell you. Seems like he'd do that for his neighbors, don't it? Besides being Flem's cousin, him and that boy of his, Wallstreet, helped that Texas man tote water for them tonight and Eck's going to help him feed them in the morning too. Why, maybe Eck will be the one that will catch them and lead them up one at a time for you folks to bid on them. Ain't that right, Eck?"

The other man sitting on the steps with his back against the post was the blacksmith. "I don't know," he said.

"Boys," Ratliff said, "Eck knows all about them horses. Flem's told him, how much they cost and how much him and that Texas man aim to get for them, make off of them. Come on, Eck. Tell us." The other did not move, sitting on the top step, not quite facing them, sitting there beneath the successive layers of their quiet and intent concentrated listening and waiting.

"I don't know," he said. Ratliff began to laugh. He sat in the chair, laughing while the others sat or lounged upon the steps and the railing, sitting beneath his laughing as Eck had sat beneath their listening and waiting. Ratliff ceased laughing. He rose. He yawned, quite loud.

"All right. You folks can buy them critters if you want to. But me, I'd just as soon buy a tiger or a rattlesnake. And if Flem Snopes offered me either one of them, I would be afraid to touch it for fear it would turn out to be a painted dog or a piece of garden hose when I went up to take possession of it. I bid you one and all goodnight." He entered the house. They did not look after him, though after a while they all shifted a little and looked down into the lot, upon the splotchy, sporadic surge and flow of the horses, from among which from time to time came an abrupt squeal, a thudding blow. In the pear tree the mockingbird's idiot reiteration pulsed and purled.

"Anse McCallum made a good team outen them two of hisn," the first man said. "They was a little light. That was all."

When the sun rose the next morning a wagon and three saddled mules stood in Mrs. Littlejohn's lane and six men and Eck Snopes' son were already leaning on the fence, looking at the horses which huddled in a quiet clump before the barn door, watching the men in their turn. A second wagon came up the road and into the lane and stopped, and then there were eight men beside the boy standing at the fence, beyond which the horses stood, their blue-and-brown eyeballs rolling alertly in their gaudy faces. "So this here is the Snopes circus, is it?" one of the newcomers said. He glanced at the faces, then he went to the end of the row and stood beside the black-smith and the little boy. "Are them Flem's horses?" he said to the blacksmith.

"Eck don't know who them horses belong to any more than we do," one of the others said. "He knows that Flem come here on the same wagon with them, because he saw him. But that's all."

"And all he will know," a second said. "His own kin will be the last man in the world to find out anything about Flem Snopes' business."

"No," the first said. "He wouldn't even be that. The first man Flem would tell his business to would be the man that was left after the last man died. Flem Snopes don't even tell himself what he is up to. Not if he was laying in bed with himself in a empty house in the dark of the moon."

"That's a fact," a third said. "Flem would trim Eck or any other of his kin quick as he would us. Ain't that right, Eck?"

"I don't know," Eck said. They were watching the horses, which at that moment broke into a high-eared, stiff-kneed swirl and flowed in a patchwork wave across the lot and brought up again, facing the men along the fence, so they did not hear the Texan until he was among them. He wore a new shirt and another vest a little too small for him and he was just putting the paper carton back into his hip pocket.

"Morning, morning," he said. "Come to get an early pick, have you? Want to make me an offer for one or two before the bidding starts and runs the prices up?" They had not looked at the stranger long. They were not looking at him now, but at the horses in the lot, which had lowered their heads, snuffing into the dust.

"I reckon we'll look a while first," one said.

"You are in time to look at them eating breakfast, anyhow," the Texan said. "Which is more than they done without they staid up all night." He opened the gate and entered it. At once the horses jerked their heads up, watching him. "Here, Eck," the Texan said over his shoulder, "two or three of you boys help me drive them into the barn." After a moment Eck and two others approached the gate, the little boy at his father's heels, though the other did not see him until he turned to shut the gate.

"You stay out of here," Eck said. "One of them things will snap your head off same as a acorn before you even know it." He shut the gate and went on after the others, whom the Texan had now waved fanwise outward as he approached the horses which now drew into a restive huddle, beginning to mill slightly, watching the men. Mrs. Littlejohn came out of the kitchen and crossed the yard to the woodpile, watching the lot. She picked up two or three sticks of wood and paused, watching the lot again. Now there were two more men standing at the fence.

"Come on, come on," the Texan said. "They won't hurt you. They just ain't never been in under a roof before."

"I just as lief let them stay out here, if that's what they want to do," Eck said.

"Get yourself a stick—there's a bunch of wagon stakes against the fence yonder—and when one of them tries to rush you, bust him over the head so he will understand what you mean." One of the men went to the fence and got three of the stakes and returned and distributed them. Mrs. Littlejohn, her armful of wood complete now, paused again halfway back to the house, looking into the lot. The little boy was directly behind his father again, though this time the father had not discovered him yet. The men advanced toward the horses, the huddle of which began to break into gaudy units turning inward upon themselves. The Texan was cursing them in a loud steady cheerful voice. "Get in there, you banjo-faced jack rabbits. Don't hurry them, now. Let them take their time. Hi! Get in there. What do you think that barn is—a law court maybe? Or maybe a church and somebody is going to take up a collection on you?" The animals fell slowly back. Now and then one feinted to break from the huddle, the Texan driving it back each time with skillfully thrown bits of dirt. Then one at the rear saw the barn door just behind it but before the herd could break the Texan snatched the wagon stake from Eck and, followed by one of the other men, rushed at the horses and began to lay about the heads and shoulders, choosing by unerring instinct the point animal and striking it first square in the face then on the withers as it turned and then on the rump as it turned further, so that when the break came it was reversed and the entire herd rushed into the long open hallway and brought up against the further wall with a hollow, thunderous sound like that of a collapsing mine-shaft. "Seems to have held all right," the Texan said. He and the other man slammed the half-length doors and looked over them into the tunnel of the barn, at the far end of which the ponies were now a splotchy, phantom moiling punctuated by crackings of wooden partitions and the dry reports of hooves which gradually died away. "Yep, it held all right," the Texan said. The other two came to the doors and looked over them. The little boy came up beside his father now, trying to see through a crack, and Eck saw him.

"Didn't I tell you to stay out of here?" Eck said. "Don't you know them things will kill you quicker than you can say scat? You go and get outside of that fence and stay there."

"Why don't you get your paw to buy you one of them, Wall?" one of the men said.

"Me buy one of them things?" Eck said. "When I can go to the river anytime and catch me a snapping turtle or a moccasin for nothing? You go on, now. Get out of here and stay out." The Texan had entered the barn. One of the men closed the doors after him and put the bar up again and over the top of the doors they watched the Texan go on down the hallway, toward the ponies which now huddled like gaudy phantoms in the gloom, quiet now and already beginning to snuff experimentally into the long lip-worn trough fastened against the rear wall. The little boy had merely gone around behind his father, to the other side, where he stood peering now through a knot-hole in a plank. The Texan opened a smaller door in the wall and entered it, though almost immediately he reappeared.

"I don't see nothing but shelled corn in here," he said. "Snopes said he would send some hay up here last night."

"Won't they eat corn either?" one of the men said.

"I don't know," the Texan said. "They ain't never seen any that I know of. We'll find out in a minute though." He disappeared, though they could still hear him in the crib. Then he emerged once more, carrying a big double-ended feed-basket, and retreated into the gloom where the parti-colored rumps of the horses were now ranged quietly along the feeding-trough. Mrs. Littlejohn appeared once more, on the veranda this time, carrying a big brass dinner bell. She raised it to make the first stroke. A small commotion set up among the ponies as the Texan approached but he began to speak to them at once, in a brisk loud unemphatic mixture of cursing and cajolery, disappearing among them. The men at the door heard the dry rattling of the corn-pellets into the trough, a sound broken by a single snort of amazed horror. A plank cracked with a loud report; before their eyes the depths of the hallway dissolved in loud fury, and while they stared over the doors, unable yet to begin to move, the entire interior exploded into mad tossing shapes like a downrush of flames.

"Hell fire," one of them said. "Jump!" he shouted. The three turned and ran frantically for the wagon, Eck last. Several voices from the fence were now shouting something but Eck did not even hear them until, in the act of scrambling madly at the tail-gate, he looked behind him and saw the little boy still leaning to the knot-hole in the door which in the next instant vanished into matchwood, the knot-hole itself exploding from his eye and leaving him, motionless in the diminutive overalls and still leaning forward a little until he vanished utterly beneath the towering parti-colored wave full of feet and glaring eyes and wild teeth which, overtopping, burst into scattering units, revealing at last the gaping orifice and the little boy still standing in it, unscratched, his eye still leaned to the vanished knot-hole.

"Wall!" Eck roared. The little boy turned and ran for the wagon. The horses were whipping back and forth across the lot, as if while in the barn they had once more doubled their number; two of them rushed up quattering and galloped all over the boy again without touching him as he ran, earnest and diminutive and seemingly without progress, though he reached the wagon at last, from which Eck, his sunburned skin now a sickly white, reached down and snatched the boy into the wagon by the straps of his overalls and slammed him face down across his knees and caught up a coiled itching-rope from the bed of the wagon.

"Didn't I tell you to get out of here?" Eck said in a shaking voice. "Didn't I tell you?"

"If you're going to whip him, you better whip the rest of us too and then one of us can frail hell out of you," one of the others said.

"Or better still, take the rope and hang that durn fellow yonder," the second said. The Texan was now standing in the wrecked door of the barn, taking the gingersnap carton from his hip pocket. "Before he kills the rest of Frenchman's Bend too."

"You mean Flem Snopes," the first said. The Texan tilted the carton above his other open palm. The horses still rushed and swirled back and forth but they were beginning to slow now, trotting on high, stiff legs, although their eyes were still rolling whitely and various.

"I misdoubted that damn shell corn all along," the Texan said. "But at least they have seen what it looks like. They can't claim they ain't got nothing out of this trip." He shook the carton over his open hand. Nothing came out of it. Mrs. Littlejohn on the veranda made the first stroke with the dinner bell; at the sound the horses rushed again, the earth of the lot becoming vibrant with the light dry clatter of hooves. The Texan crumpled the carton and threw it aside. "Chuck wagon," he said. There were three more wagons in the lane now and there were twenty or more men at the fence when the Texan, followed by his three assistants and the little boy, passed through the gate. The bright cloudless early sun gleamed upon the pearl butt of the pistol in his hip pocket and upon the bell which Mrs. Littlejohn still rang, peremptory, strong, and loud.

When the Texan, picking his teeth with a splintered kitchen match, emerged from the house twenty minutes later, the tethered wagons and riding horses and mules extended from the lot gate to Varner's store, and there were more than fifty men now standing along the fence beside the gate, watching him quietly, a little covertly, as he approached, rolling a little, slightly bowlegged, the high heels of his carved boots printing neatly into the dust. "Morning, gents," he said. "Here, Bud," he said to the little boy, who stood slightly behind him, looking at the protruding butt of the pistol. He took a coin from his pocket and gave it to the boy. "Run to the store and get me a box of gingersnaps." He looked about at the quiet faces, protuberant, sucking his teeth. He rolled the match from one side of his mouth to the other without touching it. "You boys done made your picks, have you? Ready to start her off, hah?" They did not answer. They were not looking at him now. That is, he began to have the feeling that each face had stopped looking at him the second before his gaze reached it. After a moment Freeman said:

"Ain't you going to wait for Flem?"

"Why?" the Texan said. Then Freeman stopped looking at him too. There was nothing in Freeman's face either. There was nothing, no alteration, in the Texan's voice. "Eck, you done already picked out yours. So we can start her off when you are ready."

"I reckon not," Eck said. "I wouldn't buy nothing I was afraid to walk up and touch."

"Them little ponies?" the Texan said. "You helped water and feed them. I bet that boy of yours could walk up to any one oi them."

"He better not let me catch him," Eck said. The Texan looked about at the quiet faces, his gaze at once abstract and alert, with an impenetrable surface quality like flint, as though the surface were impervious or perhaps there was nothing behind it.

"Them ponies is gentle as a dove, boys. The man that buys them will get the best piece of horseflesh he ever forked or druv for the money. Naturally they got spirit; I ain't selling crowbait. Besides, who'd want Texas crow-bait anyway, with Mississippi full of it?" His stare was still absent and unwinking; there was no mirth or humor in his voice and there was neither mirth nor humor in the single guffaw which came from the rear of the group. Two wagons were now drawing out of the road at the same time, up to the fence. The men got down from them and tied them to the fence and approached. "Come up, boys," the Texan said. "You're just in time to buy a good gentle horse cheap."

"How about that one that cut your vest off last night?" a voice said. This time three or four guffawed. The Texan looked toward the sound, bleak and unwinking.

"What about it?" he said. The laughter, if it had been laughter, ceased. The Texan turned to the nearest gate-post and climbed to the top of it, his alternate thighs deliberate and bulging in the tight trousers, the butt of the pistol catching and losing the sun in pearly gleams. Sitting on the post, he looked down at the faces along the fence which were attentive, grave, reserved and not looking at him. "All right," he said. "Who's going to start her off with a bid? Step right up; take your pick and make your bid, and when the last one is sold, walk in that lot and put your rope on the best piece of horseflesh you ever forked or druv for the money. There ain't a pony there that ain't worth fifteen dollars. Young, sound, good for saddle or work stock, guaranteed to outlast four ordinary horses; you couldn't kill one of them with a axle-tree—" There was a small violent commotion at the rear of the group. The little boy appeared, burrowing among the motionless overalls. He approached the post, the new and unbroken paper carton lifted. The Texan leaned down and took it and tore the end from it and shook three or four of the cakes into the boy's hand, a hand as small and almost as black as that of a coon. He held the carton in his hand while he talked, pointing out the horses with it as he indicated them. "Look at that one with the three stocking-feet and the frost-bit ear; watch him now when they pass again. Look at that shoulder-action; that horse is worth twenty dollars of any man's money. Who'll make me a bid on him to start her off?" His voice was harsh, ready, forensic. Along the fence below him the men stood with, buttoned close in their overalls, the tobacco-sacks and worn purses the sparse silver and frayed bills hoarded a coin at a time in the cracks of chimneys or chinked into the logs of walls. From time to time the horses broke and rushed with purposeless violence and huddled again, watching the faces along the fence with wild mismatched eyes. The lane was full of wagons now. As the others arrived they would have to stop in the road beyond it and the occupants came up the lane on foot. Mrs. Littlejohn came out of her kitchen. She crossed the yard, looking toward the lot gate. There was a blackened wash pot set on four bricks in the corner of the yard. She built a fire beneath the pot and came to the fence and stood there for a time, her hands on her hips and the smoke from the fire drifting blue and slow behind her. Then she turned and went back into the house. "Come on, boys," the Texan said. "Who'll make me a bid?"

"Four bits," a voice said. The Texan did not even glance toward it.

"Or, if he don't suit you, how about that fiddle-head horse without no mane to speak of? For a saddle pony, I'd rather have him than that stocking-foot. I heard somebody say fifty cents just now. I reckon he meant five dollars, didn't he? Do I hear five dollars?"

"Four bits for the lot," the same voice said. This time there were no guffaws. It was the Texan who laughed, harshly, with only his lower face, as if he were reciting a multiplication table.

"Fifty cents for the dried mud offen them, he means," he said. "Who'll give a dollar more for the genuine Texas cockle-burrs?" Mrs. Littlejohn came out of the kitchen, carrying the sawn half of a wooden hogshead which she set on a stump beside the smoking pot, and stood with her hands on her hips, looking into the lot for a while without coming to the fence this time. Then she went back into the house. "What's the matter with you boys?" the Texan said. "Here, Eck, you been helping me and you know them horses. How about making me a bid on that wall-eyed one you picked out last night? Here. Wait a minute." He thrust the paper carton into his other hip pocket and swung his feet inward and dropped, cat-light, into the lot. The ponies, huddled, watched him. Then they broke before him and slid stiffly along the fence. He turned them and they whirled and rushed back across the lot; whereupon, as though he had been waiting his chance when they should have turned their backs on him, the Texan began to run too, so that when they reached the opposite side of the lot and turned, slowing to huddle again, he was almost upon them. The earth became thunderous; dust arose, out of which the animals began to burst like flushed quail and into which, with that apparently unflagging faith in his own invulnerability, the Texan rushed. For an instant the watchers could see them in the dust—the pony backed into the angle of the fence and the stable, the man facing it, reaching toward his hip. Then the beast rushed at him in a sort of fatal and hopeless desperation and he struck it between the eyes with the pistol-butt and felled it and leaped onto its prone head. The pony recovered almost at once and pawed itself to its knees and heaved at its prisoned head and fought itself up, dragging the man with it; for an instant in the dust the watchers saw the man free of the earth and in violent lateral motion like a rag attached to the horse's head. Then the Texan's feet came back to earth and the dust blew aside and revealed them, motionless, the Texan's sharp heels braced into the ground, one hand gripping the pony's forelock and the other its nostrils, the long evil muzzle wrung backward over its scarred shoulder while it breathed in labored and hollow groans. Mrs. Littlejohn was in the yard again. No one had seen her emerge this time. She carried an armful of clothing and a metal-ridged washboard and she was standing motionless at the kitchen steps, looking into the lot. Then she moved across the yard, still looking into the lot, and dumped the garments into the tub, still looking into the lot. "Look him over, boys," the Texan panted, turning his own suffused face and the protuberant glare of his eyes toward the fence. "Look him over quick. Them shoulders and—" He had relaxed for an instant apparently. The animal exploded again; again for an instant the Texan was free of the earth, though he was still talking: "—and legs you whoa I'll tear your face right look him over quick boys worth fifteen dollars of let me get a holt of who'll make me a bid whoa you blare-eyed jack rabbit, whoa!" They were moving now—a kaleidoscope of inextricable and incredible violence on the periphery of which the metal clasps of the Texan's suspenders sun-glinted in ceaseless orbit, with terrific slowness across the lot. Then the broad clay-colored hat soared deliberately outward; an instant later the Texan followed it, though still on his feet, and the pony shot free in mad, staglike bounds. The Texan picked up the hat and struck the dust from it against his leg, and returned to the fence and mounted the post again. He was breathing heavily. Still the faces did not look at him as he took the carton from his hip and shook a cake from it and put the cake into his mouth, chewing, breathing harshly. Mrs. Littlejohn turned away and began to bail water from the pot into the tub, though after each bucketful she turned her head and looked into the lot again. "Now, boys," the Texan said. "Who says that pony ain't worth fifteen dollars? You couldn't buy that much dynamite for just fifteen dollars. There ain't one of them can't do a mile in three minutes; turn them into pasture and they will board themselves; work them like hell all day and every time you think about it, lay them over the head with a single-tree and after a couple of days every jack rabbit one of them will be so tame you will have to put them out of the house at night like a cat." He shook another cake from the carton and ate it. "Come on, Eck," he said. "Start her off. How about ten dollars for that horse, Eck?"

"What need I got for a horse I would need a bear-trap to catch?" Eck said.

"Didn't you just see me catch him?"

"I seen you," Eck said. "And I don't want nothing as big as a horse if I got to wrastle with it every time it finds me on the same side of a fence it's on."

"All right," the Texan said. He was still breathing harshly, but now there was nothing of fatigue or breathlessness in it. He shook another cake into his palm and inserted it beneath his moustache. "All right. I want to get this auction started. I ain't come here to live, no matter how good a country you folks claim you got. I'm going to give you that horse." For a moment there was no sound, not even that of breathing except the Texan's.

"You going to give it to me?" Eck said.

"Yes. Provided you will start the bidding on the next one." Again there was no sound save the Texan's breathing, and then the clash of Mrs. Littlejohn's pail against the rim of the pot.

"I just start the bidding," Eck said. "I don't have to buy it lessen I ain't over-topped." Another wagon had come up the lane. It was battered and paintless. One wheel had been repaired by crossed planks bound to the spokes with baling wire and the two underfed mules wore a battered harness patched with bits of cotton rope; the reins were ordinary cotton plowlines, not new. It contained a woman in a shapeless gray garment and a faded sunbonnet, and a man in faded and patched though clean overalls. There was not room for the wagon to draw out of the lane so the man left it standing where it was and got down and came forward—a thin man, not large, with something about his eyes, something strained and washed-out, at once vague and intense, who shoved into the crowd at the rear, saying,

"What? What's that? Did he give him that horse?"

"All right," the Texan said. "That wall-eyed horse with the scarred neck belongs to you. Now. That one that looks like he's had his head in a flour barrel. What do you say? Ten dollars?"

"Did he give him that horse?" the newcomer said.

"A dollar," Eck said. The Texan's mouth was still open for speech; for an instant his face died so behind the hard eyes.

"A dollar?" he said. "One dollar? Did I actually hear that?"

"Durn it," Eck said. "Two dollars then. But I ain't——"

"Wait," the newcomer said. "You, up there on the post." The Texan looked at him. When the others turned, they saw that the woman had left the wagon too, though they had not known she was there since they had not seen the wagon drive up. She came among them behind the man, gaunt in the gray shapeless garment and the sunbonnet, wearing stained canvas gymnasium shoes. She overtook the man but she did not touch him, standing just behind him, her hands rolled before her into the gray dress.

"Henry," she said in a flat voice. The man looked over his shoulder.

"Get back to that wagon," he said.

"Here, missus," the Texan said. "Henry's going to get the bargain of his life in about a minute. Here, boys, let the missus come up close where she can see. Henry's going to pick out that saddle-horse the missus has been wanting. Who says ten——"

"Henry," the woman said. She did not raise her voice. She had not once looked at the Texan. She touched the man's arm. He turned and struck her hand down.

"Get back to that wagon like I told you." The woman stood behind him, her hands rolled again into her dress. She was not looking at anything, speaking to anyone.

"He ain't no more despair than to buy one of them things," she said. "And us not but five dollars away from the poorhouse, he ain't no more despair." The man turned upon her with that curious air of leashed, of dreamlike fury. The others lounged along the fence in attitudes gravely inattentive, almost oblivious. Mrs. Littlejohn had been washing for some time now, pumping rhythmically up and down above the washboard in the sud-foamed tub. She now stood erect again, her soap-raw hands on her hips, looking into the lot.

"Shut your mouth and get back in that wagon," the man said. "Do you want me to take a wagon stake to you?" He turned and looked up at the Texan. "Did you give him that horse?" he said. The Texan was looking at the woman. Then he looked at the man; still watching him, he tilted the paper carton over his open palm. A single cake came out of it.

"Yes," he said.

"Is the fellow that bids in this next horse going to get that first one too?"

"No," the Texan said.

"All right," the other said. "Are you going to give a horse to the man that makes the first bid on the next one?"

"No," the Texan said.

"Then if you were just starting the auction off by giving away a horse, why didn't you wait till we were all

here?" The Texan stopped looking at the other. He raised
the empty carton and squinted carefully into it, as if it
might contain a precious jewel or perhaps a deadly insect.
Then he crumpled it and dropped it carefully beside the
post on which he sat.

"Eck bids two dollars," he said. "I believe he still thinks
he's bidding on them scraps of bob-wire they come here
in instead of on one of the horses. But I got to accept it.
But are you boys——"

"So Eck's going to get two horses at a dollar a head,"
the newcomer said. "Three dollars." The woman touched
him again. He flung her hand off without turning and she
stood again, her hands rolled into her dress across her flat
stomach, not looking at anything.

"Misters," she said, "we got chaps in the house that
never had shoes last winter. We ain't got corn to feed the
stock. We got five dollars I earned weaving by firelight
after dark. And he ain't no more despair."

"Henry bids three dollars," the Texan said. "Raise him
a dollar, Eck, and the horse is yours." Beyond the fence
the horses rushed suddenly and for no reason and as suddenly stopped, staring at the faces along the fence.

"Henry," the woman said. The man was watching
Eck. His stained and broken teeth showed a little beneath
his lip. His wrists dangled into fists below the faded
sleeves of his shirt too short from many washings.

"Four dollars," Eck said.

"Five dollars!" the husband said, raising one clenched
hand. He shouldered himself forward toward the gate-
post. The woman did not follow him. She now looked at
the Texan for the first time. Her eyes were a washed gray
also, as though they had faded too like the dress and the
sunbonnet.

"Mister," she said, "if you take that five dollars I earned
my chaps a-weaving for one of them things, it'll be a curse
on you and yours during all the time of man."

"Five dollars!" the husband shouted. He thrust himself

up to the post, his clenched hand on a level with the Texan's knees. He opened it upon a wad of frayed bank-notes and silver "Five dollars! And the man that raises it will have to beat my head off or I'll beat hisn."

"All right," the Texan said. "Five dollars is bid. But don't you shake your hand at me."

At five o'clock that afternoon the Texan crumpled the third paper carton and dropped it to the earth beneath him. In the copper slant of the levelling sun which fell also upon the line of limp garments in Mrs. Littlejohn's back-yard and which cast his shadow and that of the post on which he sat long across the lot where now and then the ponies still rushed in purposeless and tireless surges, the Texan straightened his leg and thrust his hand into his pocket and took out a coin and leaned down to the little boy. His voice was now hoarse, spent. "Here, bud," he said. "Run to the store and get me a box of gingersnaps." The men still stood along the fence, tireless, in their over-alls and faded shirts. Flem Snopes was there now, ap-peared suddenly from nowhere, standing beside the fence with a space the width of three or four men on either side of him, standing there in his small yet definite isolation, chewing tobacco, in the same gray trousers and minute bow tie in which he had departed last summer but in a new cap, gray too like the other, but new, and overlaid with a bright golfer's plaid, looking also at the horses in the lot. All of them save two had been sold for sums rang-ing from three dollars and a half to eleven and twelve dol-lars. The purchasers, as they had bid them in, had gath-ered as though by instinct into a separate group on the other side of the gate, where they stood with their hands lying upon the top strand of the fence, watching with a still more sober intensity the animals which some of them had owned for seven and eight hours now but had not yet laid hands upon. The husband, Henry, stood beside the post on which the Texan sat. The wife had gone back to the wagon, where she sat gray in the gray garment, motionless, looking at nothing, still, she might have been something inanimate which he had loaded into the wagon to move it somewhere, waiting now in the wagon until he should be ready to go on again, patient, insensate, timeless.

"I bought a horse and I paid cash for it," he said. His voice was harsh and spent too, the mad look in his eyes had a quality glazed now and even sightless. "And yet you expect me to stand around here till they are all sold before I can get my horse. Well, you can do all the expecting you want. I'm going to take my horse out of there and go home." The Texan looked down at him. The Texan's shirt was blotched with sweat. His big face was cold and still, his voice level.

"Take your horse then." After a moment Henry looked away. He stood with his head bent a little, swallowing from time to time.

"Ain't you going to catch him for me?"

"It ain't my horse," the Texan said in that flat still voice. After a while Henry raised his head. He did not look at the Texan.

"Who'll help me catch my horse?" he said. Nobody answered. They stood along the fence, looking quietly into the lot where the ponies huddled, already beginning to fade a little where the long shadow of the house lay upon them, deepening. From Mrs. Littlejohn's kitchen the smell of frying ham came. A noisy cloud of sparrows swept across the lot and into a chinaberry tree beside the house, and in the high soft vague blue swallows stooped and whirled in erratic indecision, their cries like strings plucked at random. Without looking back, Henry raised his voice: "Bring that ere plowline." After a time the wife moved. She got down from the wagon and took a coil of new cotton rope from it and moved toward the gate. The Texan began to descend from the post, stiffly, as Henry put his hand on the latch. "Come on here," he said. The wife had stopped when he took the rope from her. She moved again, obediently, her hands rolled into the dress across her stomach, passing the Texan without looking at him.

"Don't go in there, missus," he said. She stopped, not looking at him, not looking at anything. The husband opened the gate and entered the lot and turned, holding the gate open but without raising his eyes.

"Come on here," he said.

"Don't you go in there, missus," the Texan said. The wife stood motionless between them, her face almost concealed by the sunbonnet, her hands folded across her stomach.

"I reckon I better," she said. The other men did not look at her at all, at her or Henry either. They stood along the fence, grave and quiet and inattentive, almost bemused. Then the wife passed through the gate; the husband shut it behind them and turned and began to move toward the huddled ponies, the wife following in the gray and shapeless garment within which she moved without inference of locomotion, like something on a moving platform, a float. The horses were watching them. They clotted and blended and shifted among themselves, on the point of breaking though not breaking yet. The husband shouted at them. He began to curse them, advancing, the wife following. Then the huddle broke, the animals moving with high, stiff knees, circling the two people who turned and followed again as the herd flowed and huddled again at the opposite side of the lot.

"There he is," the husband said. "Get him into that corner." The herd divided; the horse which the husband had bought jolted on stiff legs. The wife shouted at it; it spun and poised, plunging, then the husband struck it across the face with the coiled rope and it whirled and slammed into the corner of the fence. "Keep him there now," the husband said. He shook out the rope, advancing. The horse watched him with wild, glaring eyes; it rushed again, straight toward the wife. She shouted at it and waved her arms but it soared past her in a long bound and rushed

again into the huddle of its fellows. They followed and
hemmed it again into another corner; again the wife failed
to stop its rush for freedom and the husband turned and
struck her with the coiled rope. "Why didn't you head
him?" he said. "Why didn't you?" He struck her again;
she did not move, not even to fend the rope with a raised
arm. The men along the fence stood quietly, their faces
lowered as though brooding upon the earth at their feet.
Only Flem Snopes was still watching—if he ever had been
looking into the lot at all, standing in his little island of isolation, chewing with his characteristic faint sidewise thrust
beneath the new plaid cap.

The Texan said something, not loud, harsh and short.
He entered the lot and went to the husband and jerked
the uplifted rope from his hand. The husband whirled as
though he were about to spring at the Texan, crouched
slightly, his knees bent and his arms held slightly away
from his sides, though his gaze never mounted higher
than the Texan's carved and dusty boots. Then the Texan
took the husband by the arm and led him back toward the
gate, the wife following, and through the gate which he
held open for the woman and then closed. He took a wad
of banknotes from his trousers and removed a bill from it
and put it into the woman's hand. "Get him into the
wagon and get him on home," he said.

"What's that for?" Flem Snopes said. He had approached. He now stood beside the post on which the
Texan had been sitting. The Texan did not look at him.

"Thinks he bought one of them ponies," the Texan said.
He spoke in a flat still voice, like that of a man after a sharp
run. "Get him on away, missus."

"Give him back that money," the husband said, in his
lifeless, spent tone. "I bought that horse and I aim to have
him if I got to shoot him before I can put a rope on him."
The Texan did not even look at him.

"Get him on away from here, missus," he said.

"You take your money and I take my horse," the husband said. He was shaking slowly and steadily now, as though he were cold. His hands open and shut below the frayed cuffs of his shirt. "Give it back to him," he said.

"You don't own no horse of mine," the Texan said. "Get him on home, missus." The husband raised his spent face, his mad glazed eyes. He reached out his hand. The woman held the banknote in her folded hands across her stomach. For a while the husband's shaking hand merely fumbled at it. Then he drew the banknote free.

"It's my horse," he said. "I bought it. These fellows saw me. I paid for it. It's my horse. Here." He turned and extended the banknote toward Snopes. "You got something to do with these horses. I bought one. Here's the money for it. I bought one. Ask him." Snopes took the banknote. The others stood, gravely inattentive, in relaxed attitudes along the fence. The sun had gone now; there was nothing save violet shadow upon them and upon the lot where once more and for no reason the ponies rushed and flowed. At that moment the little boy came up, tireless and indefatigable still, with the new paper carton. The Texan took it, though he did not open it at once. He had dropped the rope and now the husband stooped for it, fumbling at it for some time before he lifted it from the ground. Then he stood with his head bent, his knuckles whitening on the rope. The woman had not moved. Twilight was coming fast now; there was a last mazy swirl of swallows against the high and changing azure. Then the Texan tore the end from the carton and tilted one of the cakes into his hand; he seemed to be watching the hand as it shut slowly upon the cake until a fine powder of snuff-colored dust began to rain from his fingers. He rubbed the hand carefully on his thigh and raised his head and glanced about until he saw the little boy and handed the carton back to him.

"Here, Bud," he said. Then he looked at the woman, his voice flat, quiet again. "Mr. Snopes will have your money for you tomorrow. Better get him in the wagon and get him on home. He don't own no horse. You can get your money tomorrow from Mr. Snopes." The wife turned and went back to the wagon and got into it. No one watched her, nor the husband who still stood, his head bent, passing the rope from one hand to the other. They leaned along the fence, grave and quiet, as though the fence were in another land, another time.

"How many you got left?" Snopes said. The Texan roused; they all seemed to rouse then, returning, listening again.

"Got three now," the Texan said. "Swap all three of them for a buggy or a——"

"It's out in the road," Snopes said, a little shortly, a little quickly, turning away. "Get your mules." He went on up the lane. They watched the Texan enter the lot and cross it, the horses flowing before him but without the old irrational violence, as if they too were spent, vitiated with the long day, and enter the barn and then emerge, leading the two harnessed mules. The wagon had been backed under the shed beside the barn. The Texan entered this and came out a moment later, carrying a bedding-roll and his coat, and led the mules back toward the gate, the ponies huddled again and watching him with their various unmatching eyes, quietly now, as if they too realized there was not only an armistice between them at last but that they would never look upon each other again in both their lives. Someone opened the gate. The Texan led the mules through it and they followed in a body, leaving the husband standing beside the closed gate, his head still bent and the coiled rope in his hand. They passed the wagon in which the wife sat, her gray garment fading into the dusk, almost the same color and as still, looking at nothing; they passed the clothesline with its limp and unwinded drying garments, walking through the hot vivid smell of ham from Mrs. Littlejohn's kitchen. When they reached the end of the lane they could see the moon, almost full, tremendous and pale and still lightless in the sky from which

day had not quite gone. Snopes was standing at the end of
the lane beside an empty buggy. It was the one with the
glittering wheels and the fringed parasol top in which he
and Will Varner had used to drive. The Texan was motionless too, looking at it.

"Well well well," he said. "So this is it."

"If it don't suit you, you can ride one of the mules
back to Texas," Snopes said.

"You bet," the Texan said. "Only I ought to have a
powder puff or at least a mandolin to ride it with." He
backed the mules onto the tongue and lifted the breast-
yoke. Two of them came forward and fastened the traces
for him. Then they watched him get into the buggy and
raise the reins.

"Where you heading for?" one said. "Back to Texas?"

"In this?" the Texan said. "I wouldn't get past the first
Texas saloon without starting the vigilance committee.
Besides, I ain't going to waste all this here lace-trimmed
top and these spindle wheels just on Texas. Long as I am
this far, I reckon I'll go on a day or two and look-see them
Northern towns. Washington and New York and Balti-
more. What's the short way to New York from here?"
They didn't know. But they told him how to reach Jefferson.

"You're already headed right," Freeman said. "Just
keep right on up the road past the schoolhouse."

"All right," the Texan said. "Well, remember about
busting them ponies over the head now and then until
they get used to you. You won't have any trouble with
them then." He lifted the reins again. As he did so Snopes
stepped forward and got into the buggy.

"I'll ride as far as Varner's with you," he said.

"I didn't know I was going past Varner's," the Texan
said.

"You can go to town that way," Snopes said. "Drive on."
The Texan shook the reins. Then he said,

"Whoa." He straightened his leg and put his hand into

his pocket. "Here, Bud," he said to the little boy, "run to the store and— Never mind. I'll stop and get it myself, long as I am going back that way. Well, boys," he said. "Take care of yourselves." He swung the team around. The buggy went on. They looked after it.

"I reckon he aims to kind of come up on Jefferson from behind," Quick said.

"He'll be lighter when he gets there," Freeman said. "He can come up to it easy from any side he wants."

"Yes," Bookwright said. "His pockets won't rattle." They went back to the lot; they passed on through the narrow way between the two lines of patient and motionless wagons, which at the end was completely closed by the one in which the woman sat. The husband was still standing beside the gate with his coiled rope, and now night had completely come. The light itself had not changed so much; if anything, it was brighter but with that other-worldly quality of moonlight, so that when they stood once more looking into the lot, the splotchy bodies of the ponies had a distinctness, almost a brilliance, but without individual shape and without depth—no longer horses, no longer flesh and bone directed by a principle capable of calculated violence, no longer inherent with the capacity to hurt and harm.

"Well, what are we waiting for?" Freeman said. "For them to go to roost?"

"We better all get our ropes first," Quick said. "Get your ropes everybody." Some of them did not have ropes. When they left home that morning, they had not heard about the horses, the auction. They had merely happened through the village by chance and learned of it and stopped.

"Go to the store and get some then," Freeman said.

"The store will be closed now," Quick said.

"No it won't," Freeman said. "If it was closed, Lump Snopes would a been up here." So while the ones who had come prepared got their ropes from the wagons, the others went down to the store. The clerk was just closing it.

"You all ain't started catching them yet, have you?" he said. "Good; I was afraid I wouldn't get there in time." He opened the door again and amid the old strong sunless smells of cheese and leather and molasses he measured and cut off sections of plow-line for them and in a body and the clerk in the center and still talking, voluble and unlistened to, they returned up the road. The pear tree before Mrs. Littlejohn's was like drowned silver now in the moon. The mockingbird of last night, or another one, was already singing in it, and they now saw, tied to the fence, Ratliff's buckboard and team.

"I thought something was wrong all day," one said. "Ratliff wasn't there to give nobody advice." When they passed down the lane, Mrs. Littlejohn was in her backyard, gathering the garments from the clothesline; they could still smell the ham. The others were waiting at the gate, beyond which the ponies, huddled again, were like phantom fish, suspended apparently without legs now in the brilliant treachery of the moon.

"I reckon the best way will be for us all to take and catch them one at a time," Freeman said.

"One at a time," the husband, Henry, said. Apparently he had not moved since the Texan had led his mules through the gate, save to lift his hands to the top of the gate, one of them still clutching the coiled rope. "One at a time," he said. He began to curse in a harsh, spent monotone. "After I've stood around here all day, waiting for that—" He cursed. He began to jerk at the gate, shaking it with spent violence until one of the others slid the latch back and it swung open and Henry entered it, the others following, the little boy pressing close behind his father until Eck became aware of him and turned.

"Here," he said. "Give me that rope. You stay out of here."

"Aw, paw," the boy said.

"No sir. Them things will kill you. They almost done it this morning. You stay out of here."

"But we got two to catch." For a moment Eck stood looking down at the boy.

"That's right," he said. "We got two. But you stay close to me now. And when I holler run, you run. You hear me?"

"Spread out, boys," Freeman said. "Keep them in front of us." They began to advance across the lot in a ragged crescent-shaped line, each one with his rope. The ponies were now at the far side of the lot. One of them snorted; the mass shifted within itself but without breaking. Freeman, glancing back, saw the little boy. "Get that boy out of here," he said.

"I reckon you better," Eck said to the boy. "You go and get in the wagon yonder. You can see us catch them from there." The little boy turned and trotted toward the shed beneath which the wagon stood. The line of men advanced, Henry a little in front.

"Watch them close now," Freeman said. "Maybe we better try to get them into the barn first—" At that moment the huddle broke. It parted and flowed in both directions along the fence. The men at the ends of the line began to run, waving their arms and shouting. "Head them," Freeman said tensely. "Turn them back." They turned them, driving them back upon themselves again; the animals merged and spun in short, huddling rushes, phantom and inextricable. "Hold them now," Freeman said. "Don't let them get by us." The line advanced again. Eck turned; he did not know why—whether a sound, what. The little boy was just behind him again.

"Didn't I tell you to get in that wagon and stay there?" Eck said.

"Watch out, paw!" the boy said. "There he is! There's ourn!" It was the one the Texan had given Eck. "Catch him, paw!"

"Get out of my way," Eck said. "Get back to that wagon." The line was still advancing. The ponies milled, clotting, forced gradually backward toward the open door of the barn. Henry was still slightly in front, crouched slightly, his thin figure, even in the mazy moonlight, emanating something of that spent fury. The splotchy huddle of animals seemed to be moving before the advancing line of men like a snowball which they might have been pushing before them by some invisible means, gradually nearer and nearer to the black yawn of the barn door. Later it was obvious that the ponies were so intent upon the men that they did not realize the barn was even behind them until they backed into the shadow of it. Then an indescribable sound, a movement desperate and despairing, arose among them; for an instant of static horror men and animals faced one another, then the men whirled and ran before a gaudy vomit of long wild faces and splotched chests which overtook and scattered them and flung them sprawling aside and completely obliterated from sight Henry and the little boy, neither of whom had moved though Henry had flung up both arms, still holding his coiled rope, the herd sweeping on across the lot, to crash through the gate which the last man through it had neglected to close, leaving it slightly ajar, carrying all of the gate save the upright to which the hinges were nailed with them, and so among the teams and wagons which choked the lane, the teams springing and lunging too, snapping hitch-reins and tongues. Then the whole inextricable mass crashed among the wagons and eddied and divided about the one in which the woman sat, and rushed on down the lane and into the road, dividing, one half going one way and one half the other.

The men in the lot, except Henry, got to their feet and ran toward the gate. The little boy once more had not been touched, not even thrown off his feet; for a while his father held him clear of the ground in one hand, shaking him like a rag doll. "Didn't I tell you to stay in that wagon?" Eck cried. "Didn't I tell you?"

"Look out, paw!" the boy chattered out of the violent shaking, "there's ourn! There he goes!" It was the horse the Texan had given them again. It was as if they owned no other, the other one did not exist; as if by some absolute and instantaneous rapport of blood they had relegated to oblivion the one for which they had paid money. They ran to the gate and down the lane where the other men had disappeared. They saw the horse the Texan had given them whirl and dash back and rush through the gate into Mrs. Littlejohn's yard and run up the front steps and crash once on the wooden veranda and vanish through the front door. Eck and the boy ran up onto the veranda. A lamp sat on a table just inside the door. In its mellow light they saw the horse fill the long hallway like a pinwheel, gaudy, furious and thunderous. A little further down the hall there was a varnished yellow melodeon. The horse crashed into it; it produced a single note, almost a chord, in bass, resonant and grave, of deep and sober astonishment; the horse with its monstrous and antic shadow whirled again and vanished through another door. It was a bedroom; Ratliff, in his underclothes and one sock and with the other sock in his hand and his back to the door, was leaning out the open window facing the lane, the lot. He looked back over his shoulder. For an instant he and the horse glared at one another. Then he sprang through the window as the horse backed out of the room and into the hall again and whirled and saw Eck and the little boy just entering the front door, Eck still carrying his rope. It whirled again and rushed on down the hall and onto the back porch just as Mrs. Littlejohn, carrying an armful of clothes from the line and the washboard, mounted the steps.

"Get out of here, you son of a bitch," she said. She struck with the washboard; it divided neatly on the long mad face and the horse whirled and rushed back up the hall, where Eck and the boy now stood.

"Get to hell out of here, Wall!" Eck roared. He dropped to the floor, covering his head with his arms. The boy did not move, and for the third time the horse soared above the unwinking eyes and the unbowed and untouched head and onto the front veranda again just as Ratliff, still carrying the sock, ran around the corner of the house and up the steps. The horse whirled without breaking or pausing. It galloped to the end of the veranda and took the railing and soared outward, hobgoblin and floating, in the moon. It landed in the lot still running and crossed the lot and galloped through the wrecked gate and among the overturned wagons and the still intact one in which Henry's wife still sat, and on down the lane and into the road.

A quarter of a mile further on, the road gashed pallid and moony between the moony shadows of the bordering trees, the horse still galloping, galloping its shadow into the dust, the road descending now toward the creek and the bridge. It was of wood, just wide enough for a single vehicle. When the horse reached it, it was occupied by a wagon coming from the opposite direction and drawn by two mules already asleep in the harness and the soporific motion. On the seat was Tull and his wife, in splint chairs in the wagon behind them sat their four daughters, all returning belated from an all-day visit with some of Mrs. Tull's kin. The horse neither checked nor swerved. It crashed once on the wooden bridge and rushed between the two mules which waked lunging in opposite directions in the traces, the horse now apparently scrambling along the wagon-tongue itself like a mad squirrel and scrabbling at the end-gate of the wagon with its forefeet as if it intended to climb into the wagon while Tull shouted at it and struck at its face with his whip. The mules were now trying to turn the wagon around in the middle of the bridge. It slewed and tilted, the bridge-rail cracked with a sharp report above the shrieks of the women; the horse scrambled at last across the back of one of the mules and Tull stood up in the wagon and kicked at its face. Then the front end of the wagon rose, flinging Tull, the reins now wrapped several times about his wrist, backward into the wagon bed among the overturned chairs and the exposed stockings and undergarments of his women. The pony scrambled free and crashed again on the wooden planking, galloping again. The wagon lurched again; the mules had finally turned it on the bridge where there was not room for it to turn and were now kicking themselves free of the traces. When they came free, they snatched Tull bodily out of the wagon. He struck the bridge on his face and was dragged for several feet before the wrist-wrapped reins broke. Far up the road now, distancing the frantic mules, the pony faded on. While the five women still shrieked above Tull's unconscious body, Eck and the little boy came up, trotting, Eck still carrying his rope. He was panting. "Which way'd he go?" he said.

In the now empty and moon-drenched lot, his wife and Mrs. Littlejohn and Ratliff and Lump Snopes, the clerk, and three other men raised Henry out of the trampled dust and carried him into Mrs. Littlejohn's back yard. His face was blanched and stony, his eyes were closed, the weight of his head tautened his throat across the protruding larynx; his teeth glinted dully beneath his lifted lip. They carried him on toward the house, through the dappled shade of the chinaberry trees. Across the dreaming and silver night a faint sound like remote thunder came and ceased. "There's one of them on the creek bridge," one of the men said.

"It's that one of Eck Snopes's," another said. "The one that was in the house." Mrs. Littlejohn had preceded them into the hall. When they entered with Henry, she had already taken the lamp from the table and she stood beside an open door, holding the lamp high.

"Bring him in here," she said. She entered the room first and set the lamp on the dresser. They followed with clumsy scufflings and pantings and laid Henry on the bed and Mrs. Littlejohn came to the bed and stood looking down at Henry's peaceful and bloodless face. "I'll declare," she said. "You men." They had drawn back a little, clumped, shifting from one foot to another, not looking at her nor at his wife either, who stood at the foot of the bed, motionless, her hands folded into her dress. "You all get out of here, V. K.," she said to Ratliff. "Go outside. See if you can't find something else to play with that will kill some more of you."

"All right," Ratliff said. "Come on, boys. Ain't no more horses to catch in here." They followed him toward the door, on tiptoe, their shoes scuffling, their shadows monstrous on the wall.

"Go get Will Varner," Mrs. Littlejohn said. "I reckon you can tell him it's still a mule." They went out; they didn't look back. They tiptoed up the hall and crossed the veranda and descended into the moonlight. Now that they could pay attention to it, the silver air seemed to be filled with faint and sourceless sounds—shouts, thin and distant, again a brief thunder of hooves on a wooden bridge, more shouts faint and thin and earnest and clear as bells; once they even distinguished the words: "Whooey. Head him."

"He went through that house quick," Ratliff said. "He must have found another woman at home." Then Henry screamed in the house behind them. They looked back into the dark hall where a square of light fell through the bedroom door, listening while the scream sank into a harsh respiration: "Ah. Ah. Ah" on a rising note about to become screaming again. "Come on," Ratliff said. "We better get Varner." They went up the road in a body, treading the moon-blanched dust in the tremulous April night murmurous with the moving of sap and the wet busting of burgeoning leaf and bud and constant with the thin and urgent cries and the brief and fading bursts of galloping hooves. Varner's house was dark, blank and without depth in the moonlight. They stood, clumped darkly in the silver yard and called up at the blank windows until suddenly someone was standing in one of them. It was Flem Snopes' wife. She was in a white garment; the heavy braided club of her hair looked almost black against it. She did not lean out, she merely stood there, full in the moon, apparently blank-eyed or certainly not looking downward at them—the heavy gold hair, the mask not tragic and perhaps not even doomed: just damned, the strong faint lift of breasts beneath marblelike fall of the garment; to those below what Brunhilde, what Rhine-maiden on what spurious river-rock of papier-mache, what Helen returned to what topless and shoddy Argos, waiting for no one. "Evening, Mrs. Snopes," Ratliff said. "We want Uncle Will. Henry Armstid is hurt at Mrs. Littlejohn's." She vanished from the window. They waited in the moonlight, listening to the faint remote shouts and cries, until Varner emerged, sooner than they had actually expected, hunching into his coat and buttoning his trousers over the tail of his nightshirt, his suspenders still dangling in twin loops below the coat. He was carrying the battered bag which contained the plumber-like tools with which he drenched and wormed and blistered and floated or drew the teeth of horses and mules; he came down the steps, lean and loosejointed, his shrewd ruthless head cocked a little as he listened also to the faint bell-like cries and shouts with which the silver air was full.

"Are they still trying to catch them rabbits?" he said.

"All of them except Henry Armstid," Ratliff said. "He caught his."

"Hah," Varner said. "That you, V. K.? How many did you buy?"

"I was too late," Ratliff said. "I never got back in time."

"Hah," Varner said. They moved on to the gate and into the road again. "Well, it's a good bright cool night for running them." The moon was now high overhead, a pearled and mazy yawn in the soft sky, the ultimate ends of which rolled onward, whorl on whorl, beyond the pale stars and by pale stars surrounded. They walked in a close clump, tramping their shadows into the road's mild dust, blotting the shadows of the burgeoning trees which soared, trunk branch and twig against the pale sky, delicate and finely thinned. They passed the dark store. Then the pear tree came in sight. It rose in mazed and silver immobility like exploding snow; the mockingbird still sang in it. "Look at that tree," Varner said. "It ought to make this year, sho."

"Corn'll make this year too," one said.

"A moon like this is good for every growing thing outen earth," Varner said. "I mind when me and Mrs. Varner was expecting Eula. Already had a mess of children and maybe we ought to quit then. But I wanted some more gals. Others had done married and moved away, and a passel of boys, soon as they get big enough to be worth anything, they ain't got time to work. Got to set around the store and talk. But a gal will stay home and work until she does get married. So there was a old woman told my mammy once that if a woman showed her belly to the full moon after she had done caught, it would be a gal. So Mrs. Varner taken and laid every night with the moon on her nekid belly, until it fulled and after. I could lay my ear to her belly and hear Eula kicking and scrouging like all get-out, feeling the moon."

"You mean it actually worked sho enough, Uncle Will?" the other said.

"Hah," Varner said. "You might try it. You get enough women showing their nekid bellies to the moon or the sun either or even just to your hand fumbling around often enough and more than likely after a while there will be something in it you can lay your ear and listen to, provided something come up and you ain't got away by that time. Hah, V. K.?" Someone guffawed.

"Don't ask me," Ratliff said. "I can't even get nowhere in time to buy a cheap horse." Two or three guffawed this time. Then they began to hear Henry's respirations from the house: "Ah. Ah. Ah" and they ceased abruptly, as if they had not been aware of their closeness to it. Varner walked on in front, lean, shambling, yet moving quite rapidly, though his head was still slanted with listening as the faint, urgent, indomitable cries murmured in the silver lambence, sourceless, at times almost musical, like fading bell-notes; again there was a brief rapid thunder of hooves on wooden planking.

"There's another one on the creek bridge," one said.

"They are going to come out even on them things, after all," Varner said. "They'll get the money back in exercise and relaxation. You take a man that ain't got no other relaxation all year long except dodging mule-dung up and down a field furrow. And a night like this one, when a man ain't old enough yet to lay still and sleep, and yet he ain't young enough anymore to be tomcatting in and out of other folks' back windows, something like this is good for him. It'll make him sleep tomorrow night anyhow, provided he gets back home by then. If we had just knowed about this in time, we could have trained up a pack of horse-dogs. Then we could have held one of these field trials."

"That's one way to look at it, I reckon," Ratliff said. "In fact, it might be a considerable comfort to Bookwright and Quick and Freeman and Eck Snopes and them other new horse-owners if that side of it could be brought to their attention, because the chances are ain't none of them thought to look at it in that light yet. Probably there ain't a one of them that believes now there's any cure a tall for that Texas disease Flem Snopes and that Dead-eye Dick brought here."

"Hah," Varner said. He opened Mrs. Littlejohn's gate. The dim light still fell outward across the hall from the bedroom door; beyond it, Armstid was saying "Ah. Ah.

Ah" steadily. "There's a pill for every ill but the last one."

"Even if there was always time to take it," Ratliff said.

"Hah," Varner said again. He glanced back at Ratliff for an instant, pausing. But the little hard bright eyes were invisible now; it was only the bushy overhang of the brows which seemed to concentrate downward toward him in writhen immobility, not frowning but with a sort of fierce risibility. "Even if there was time to take it. Breathing is a sight-draft dated yesterday."

II

At nine o'clock on the second morning after that, five men were sitting or squatting along the gallery of the store. The sixth was Ratliff. He was standing up, and talking: "Maybe there wasn't but one of them things in Mrs. Littlejohn's house that night, like Eck says. But it was the biggest drove of just one horse I ever seen. It was in my rooms and it was on the front porch and I could hear Mrs. Littlejohn hitting it over the head with that washboard in the back yard all at the same time. And still it was missing everybody everytime. I reckon that's what that Texas man meant by calling them bargains: that a man would need to be powerful unlucky to ever get close enough to one of them to get hurt." They laughed, all except Eck himself. He and the little boy were eating. When they mounted the steps, Eck had gone on into the store and emerged with a paper sack, from which he took a segment of cheese and with his pocket knife divided it carefully into two exact halves and gave one to the boy and took a handful of crackers from the sack and gave them to the boy, and now they squatted against the wall, side by side and, save for the difference in size, identical, eating.

"I wonder what that horse thought Ratliff was," one said. He held a spray of peach bloom between his teeth. It bore four blossoms like miniature ballet skirts of pink tulle. "Jumping out windows and running indoors in his shirt-tail? I wonder how many Ratliffs that horse thought he saw."

"I don't know," Ratliff said. "But if he saw just half as many of me as I saw of him, he was sholy surrounded. Everytime I turned my head, that thing was just running over me or just swirling to run back over that boy again. And that boy there, he stayed right under it one time to my certain knowledge for a full one-and-one-half minutes without ducking his head or even batting his eyes. Yes sir, when I looked around and seen that varmint in the door behind me blaring its eyes at me, I'd a made sho Flem Snopes had brought a tiger back from Texas except I knowed that couldn't no just one tiger completely fill a entire room." They laughed again, quietly. Lump Snopes, the clerk, sitting in the only chair tilted back against the door-facing and partly blocking the entrance, cackled suddenly.

"If Flem had knowed how quick you fellows was going to snap them horses up, he'd a probably brought some tigers," he said. "Monkeys too."

"So they was Flem's horses," Ratliff said. The laughter stopped. The other three had open knives in their hands, with which they had been trimming idly at chips and slivers of wood. Now they sat apparently absorbed in the delicate and almost tedious movements of the knife-blades. The clerk had looked quickly up and found Ratliff watching him. His constant expression of incorrigible and mirthful disbelief had left him now; only the empty wrinkles of it remained about his mouth and eyes.

"Has Flem ever said they was?" he said. "But you town fellows are smarter than us country folks. Likely you done already read Flem's mind." But Ratliff was not looking at him now.

"And I reckon we'd a bought them," he said. He stood above them again, easy, intelligent, perhaps a little sombre but still perfectly impenetrable. "Eck here, for instance. With a wife and family to support. He owns two of them, though to be sho he never had to pay money for but one. I heard folks chasing them things up until midnight last night, but Eck and that boy ain't been home at all in two days." They laughed again, except Eck. He pared off a bit of cheese and speared it on the knife-point and put it into his mouth.

"Eck caught one of hisn," the second man said.

"That so?" Ratliff said. "Which one was it, Eck? The one he give you or the one you bought?"

"The one he give me," Eck said, chewing.

"Well, well," Ratliff said. "I hadn't heard about that. But Eck's still one horse short. And the one he had to pay money for. Which is pure proof enough that them horses wasn't Flem's because wouldn't no man even give his own blood kin something he couldn't even catch." They laughed again, but they stopped when the clerk spoke. There was no mirth in his voice at all.

"Listen," he said. "All right. We done all admitted you are too smart for anybody to get ahead of. You never bought no horse from Flem or nobody else, so maybe it ain't none of your business and maybe you better just leave it at that."

"Sholy," Ratliff said. "It's done already been left at that two nights ago. The fellow that forgot to shut that lot gate done that. With the exception of Eck's horse. And we know that wasn't Flem's, because that horse was give to Eck for nothing."

"There's others besides Eck that ain't got back home yet," the man with the peach spray said. "Bookwright and Quick are still chasing theirs. They was reported three miles west of Burtsboro Old Town at eight o'clock last night. They ain't got close enough to it yet to tell which one it belongs to."

"Sholy," Ratliff said. "The only new horse-owner in this country that could a been found without bloodhounds since whoever it was left that gate open two nights ago, is Henry Armstid. He's laying right there in Mrs. Littlejohn's bedroom where he can watch the lot so that any time the one he bought happens to run back into it, all he's got to do is to holler at his wife to run out with the rope and catch it—" He ceased, though he said, "Morning, Flem," so immediately afterward and with no change whatever in tone, that the pause was not even discernible. With the exception of the clerk, who sprang up, vacated the chair with a sort of servile alacrity, and Eck and the little boy who continued to eat, they watched above their stilled hands as Snopes in the gray trousers and the minute tie and the new cap with its bright overplaid mounted the steps. He was chewing; he already carried a piece of white pine board; he jerked his head at them, looking at nobody, and took the vacated chair and opened his knife and began to whittle. The clerk now leaned in the opposite side of the door, rubbing his back against the facing. The expression of merry and invincible disbelief had returned to his face, with a quality watchful and secret.

"You're just in time," he said. "Ratliff here seems to be in a considerable sweat about who actually owned them horses." Snopes drew his knife-blade neatly along the board, the neat, surgeon-like sliver curling before it. The others were whittling again, looking carefully at nothing, except Eck and the boy, who were still eating, and the clerk rubbing his back against the door-facing and watching Snopes with that secret and alert intensity. "Maybe you could put his mind at rest." Snopes turned his head slightly and spat, across the gallery and the steps and into the dust beyond them. He drew the knife back and began another curling sliver.

"He was there too," Snopes said. "He knows as much as anybody else." This time the clerk guffawed, chortling, his features gathering toward the center of his face as though plucked there by a hand. He slapped his leg, cackling.

"You might as well to quit," he said. "You can't beat him."

"I reckon not," Ratliff said. He stood above them, not looking at any of them, his gaze fixed apparently on the empty road beyond Mrs. Littlejohn's house, impenetrable, brooding even. A hulking, half-grown boy in overalls too small for him, appeared suddenly from nowhere in particular. He stood for a while in the road, just beyond spitting-range of the gallery, with the air of having come from nowhere in particular and of not knowing where he would go next when he should move again and of not being troubled by that fact. He was looking at nothing, certainly not toward the gallery, and no one on the gallery so much as looked at him except the little boy, who now watched the boy in the road, his periwinkle eyes grave and steady above the bitten cracker in his halted hand. The boy in the road moved on, thickly undulant in the tight overalls, and vanished beyond the corner of the store, the round head and the unwinking eyes of the little boy on the gallery turning steadily to watch him out of sight. Then the little boy bit the cracker again, chewing. "Of course there's Mrs. Tull," Ratliff said. "But that's Eck she's going to sue for damaging Tull against that bridge. And as for Henry Armstid——"

"If a man ain't got gumption enough to protect himself, it's his own look-out," the clerk said.

"Sholy," Ratliff said, still in that dreamy, abstracted tone, actually speaking over his shoulder even. "And Henry Armstid, that's all right because from what I hear of the conversation that taken place, Henry had already stopped owning that horse he thought was his before that Texas man left. And as for that broke leg, that won't put him out none because his wife can make his crop." The clerk had ceased to rub his back against the door. He watched the back of Ratliff's head, unwinking too, sober and intent; he glanced at Snopes who, chewing, was watching another sliver curl away from the advancing knife-blade, then he watched the back of Ratliff's head again.

"It won't be the first time she has made their crop," the man with the peach spray said. Ratliff glanced at him.

"You ought to know. This won't be the first time I ever saw you in their field, doing plowing Henry never got around to. How many days have you already given them this year?" The man with the peach spray removed it and spat carefully and put the spray back between his teeth.

"She can run a furrow straight as I can," the second said.

"They're unlucky," the third said. "When you are unlucky, it don't matter much what you do."

"Sholy," Ratliff said. "I've heard laziness called bad luck so much that maybe it is."

"He ain't lazy," the third said. "When their mule died three or four years ago, him and her broke their land working time about in the traces with the other mule. They ain't lazy."

"So that's all right," Ratliff said, gazing up the empty road again. "Likely she will begin right away to finish the plowing; the oldest gal is pretty near big enough to work with a mule, ain't she? or at least to hold the plow steady while Mrs. Armstid helps the mule?" He glanced again toward the man with the peach spray as though for an answer, but he was not looking at the other and he went on talking without any pause. The clerk stood with his rump and back pressed against the door-facing as if he had paused in the act of scratching, watching Ratliff quite hard now, unwinking. If Ratliff had looked at Flem Snopes, he would have seen nothing below the down-slanted peak of the cap save the steady motion of his jaws. Another sliver was curling with neat deliberation before the moving knife. "Plenty of time now because all she's got to do after she finishes washing Mrs. Littlejohn's dishes and sweeping out the house to pay hers and Henry's board, is to go out home and milk and cook up enough vittles to last the children until tomorrow and feed them and get the littlest ones to sleep and wait outside the door until that biggest gal gets the bar up and gets into bed herself with the axe——"

"The axe?" the man with the peach spray said.

"She takes it to bed with her. She's just twelve, and what with this country still more or less full of them uncaught horses that never belonged to Flem Snopes, likely she feels maybe she can't swing a mere washboard like Mrs. Littlejohn can—and then come back and wash up the supper dishes. And after that, not nothing to do until morning except to stay close enough where Henry can call her until it's light enough to chop the wood to cook breakfast and then help Mrs. Littlejohn wash the dishes and make the beds and sweep while watching the road. Because likely any time now Flem Snopes will get back from wherever he has been since the auction, which of course is to town naturally to see about his cousin that's got into a little legal trouble, and so get that five dollars. 'Only maybe he won't give it back to me,' she says, and maybe that's what Mrs. Littlejohn thought too, because she never said nothing. I could hear her——"

"And where did you happen to be during all this?" the clerk said.

"Listening," Ratliff said. He glanced back at the clerk, then he was looking away again, almost standing with his back to them. "—could hear her dumping the dishes into the pan like she was throwing them at it. 'Do you reckon he will give it back to me?' Mrs. Armstid says. 'That Texas man give it to him and said he would. All the folks there saw him give Mr. Snopes the money and heard him say I could get it from Mr. Snopes tomorrow.' Mrs. Littlejohn was washing the dishes now, washing them like a man would, like they was made out of iron. 'No,' she says. 'But asking him won't do no hurt.'— 'If he wouldn't give it back, it ain't no use to ask,' Mrs. Armstid says.—'Suit yourself,' Mrs. Littlejohn says. 'It's your money.' Then I couldn't hear nothing but the dishes for a while. 'Do you reckon he might give it back to me?'

Mrs. Armstid says. 'That Texas man said he would. They all heard him say it.'—'Then go and ask him for it,' Mrs. Littlejohn says. Then I couldn't hear nothing but the dishes again. 'He won't give it back to me,' Mrs. Armstid says.—'All right,' Mrs. Littlejohn says. 'Don't ask him, then.' Then I just heard the dishes. They would have two pans, both washing. 'You don't reckon he would, do you?' Mrs. Armstid says. Mrs. Littlejohn never said nothing. It sounded like she was throwing the dishes at one another. 'Maybe I better go and talk to Henry,' Mrs. Armstid says. —'I would,' Mrs. Littlejohn says. And I be dog if it didn't sound exactly like she had two plates in her hands, beating them together like these here brass bucket-lids in a band. 'Then Henry can buy another five-dollar horse with it. Maybe he'll buy one next time that will out and out kill him. If I just thought he would, I'd give him back that money, myself.'—'I reckon I better talk to him first,' Mrs. Armstid says. And then it sounded just like Mrs. Littlejohn taken up the dishes and pans and all and throwed the whole business at the cookstove—" Ratliff ceased. Behind him the clerk was hissing "Psst! Psst! Flem. Flem!" Then he stopped, and all of them watched Mrs. Armstid approach and mount the steps, gaunt in the shapeless gray garment, the stained tennis shoes hissing faintly on the boards. She came among them and stood, facing Snopes but not looking at anyone, her hands rolled into her apron.

"He said that day he wouldn't sell Henry that horse," she said in a flat toneless voice. "He said you had the money and I could get it from you." Snopes raised his head and turned it slightly again and spat neatly past the woman, across the gallery and into the road.

"He took all the money with him when he left," he said. Motionless, the gray garment hanging in rigid, almost formal folds like drapery in bronze, Mrs. Armstid appeared to be watching something near Snopes' feet, as though she had not heard him, or as if she had quitted her body as soon as she finished speaking and although her body, hearing, had received the words, they would have no life nor meaning until she returned. The clerk was rubbing his back steadily against the door-facing again, watching her. The little boy was watching her too with his unwinking ineffable gaze, but nobody else was. The man with the peach spray removed it and spat and put the twig back into his mouth.

"He said Henry hadn't bought no horse," she said. "He said I could get the money from you."

"I reckon he forgot it," Snopes said. "He took all the money away with him when he left." He watched her a moment longer, then he trimmed again at the stick. The clerk rubbed his back gently against the door, watching her. After a time Mrs. Armstid raised her head and looked up the road where it went on, mild with spring dust, past Mrs. Littlejohn's, beginning to rise, on past the not-yet-bloomed (that would be in June) locust grove across the way, on past the schoolhouse, the weathered roof of which, rising beyond an orchard of peach and pear trees, resembled a hive swarmed about by a cloud of pink-and-white bees, ascending, mounting toward the crest of the hill where the church stood among its sparse gleam of marble headstones in the sombre cedar grove where during the long afternoons of summer the constant mourning doves called back and forth. She moved; once more the rubber soles hissed on the gnawed boards.

"I reckon it's about time to get dinner started," she said.

"How's Henry this morning, Mrs. Armstid?" Ratliff said. She looked at him, pausing, the blank eyes waking for an instant.

"He's resting, I thank you kindly," she said. Then the eyes died again and she moved again. Snopes rose from the chair, closing his knife with his thumb and brushing a litter of minute shavings from his lap.

"Wait a minute," he said. Mrs. Armstid paused again, half-turning, though still not looking at Snopes nor at any of them. Because she can't possibly actually believe it,

Ratliff told himself, any more than I do. Snopes entered the store, the clerk, motionless again, his back and rump pressed against the door-facing as though waiting to start rubbing again, watched him enter, his head turning as the other passed him like the head of an owl, the little eyes blinking rapidly now. Jody Varner came up the road on his horse. He did not pass but instead turned in beside the store, toward the mulberry tree behind it where he was in the habit of hitching his horse. A wagon came up the road, creaking past. The man driving it lifted his hand; one or two of the men on the gallery lifted theirs in response. The wagon went on. Mrs. Armstid looked after it. Snopes came out of the door, carrying a small striped paper bag and approached Mrs. Armstid. "Here," he said. Her hand turned just enough to receive it. "A little sweetening for the chaps," he said. His other hand was already in his pocket, and as he turned back to the chair, he drew something from his pocket and handed it to the clerk, who took it. It was a five-cent piece. He sat down in the chair and tilted it back against the door again. He now had the knife in his hand again, already open. He turned his head slightly and spat again, neatly past the gray garment, into the road. The little boy was watching the sack in Mrs. Armstid's hand. Then she seemed to discover it also, rousing.

"You're right kind," she said. She rolled the sack into the apron, the little boy's unwinking gaze fixed upon the lump her hands made beneath the cloth. She moved again. "I reckon I better get on and help with dinner," she said. She descended the steps, though as soon as she reached the level earth and began to retreat, the gray folds of the garment once more lost all inference and intimation of locomotion, so that she seemed to progress without motion like a figure on a retreating and diminishing float; a gray and blasted tree-trunk moving, somehow intact and upright, upon an unhurried flood. The clerk in the doorway cackled suddenly, explosively, chortling. He slapped his thigh.

"By God," he said, "You can't beat him."

Jody Varner, entering the store from the rear, paused in midstride like a pointing bird-dog. Then, on tiptoe, in complete silence and with astonishing speed, he darted behind the counter and sped up the gloomy tunnel, at the end of which a hulking, bear-shaped figure stooped, its entire head and shoulders wedged into the glass case which contained the needles and thread and snuff and tobacco and the stale gaudy candy. He snatched the boy savagely and viciously out; the boy gave a choked cry and struggled flabbily, cramming a final handful of something into his mouth, chewing. But he ceased to struggle almost at once and became slack and inert save for his jaws. Varner dragged him around the counter as the clerk entered, seemed to bounce suddenly into the store with a sort of alert concern. "You, Saint Elmo!" he said.

"Ain't I told you and told you to keep him out of here?" Varner demanded, shaking the boy. "He's damn near eaten that candy-case clean. Stand up!" The boy hung like a half-filled sack from Varner's hand, chewing with a kind of fatalistic desperation, the eyes shut tight in the vast flaccid colorless face, the ears moving steadily and faintly to the chewing. Save for the jaw and the ears, he appeared to have gone to sleep chewing.

"You, Saint Elmo!" the clerk said. "Stand up!" The boy assumed his own weight, though he did not open his eyes yet nor cease to chew. Varner released him. "Git on home," the clerk said. The boy turned obediently to re-enter the store. Varner jerked him about again.

"Not that way," he said. The boy crossed the gallery and descended the steps, the tight overalls undulant and reluctant across his flabby thighs. Before he reached the ground, his hand rose from his pocket to his mouth; again his ears moved faintly to the motion of chewing.

"He's worse than a rat, ain't he?" the clerk said.

"Rat, hell," Varner said, breathing harshly. "He's worse than a goat. First thing I know, he'll graze on back and work through that lace leather and them hame-strings and lap-links and ring-bolts and eat me and you and him all three clean out the back door. And then be damned if I wouldn't be afraid to turn my back for fear he would cross the road and start in on the gin and the blacksmith shop. Now you mind what I say. If I catch him hanging around here one more time, I'm going to set a bear-trap for him."

He went out onto the gallery, the clerk following. "Well, Eck," he said, "I hear you caught one of your horses."

"That's right," Eck said. He and the little boy had finished the crackers and cheese and he had sat for some time now, holding the empty bag.

"It was the one he give you, wasn't it?" Varner said.

"That's right," Eck said.

"Give the other one to me, paw," the little boy said.

"What happened?" Varner said.

"He broke his neck," Eck said.

"I know," Varner said. "But how?" Eck did not move. Watching him, they could almost see him visibly gathering and arranging words, speech. Varner, looking down at him, began to laugh steadily and harshly, sucking his teeth. "I'll tell you what happened. Eck and that boy finally run it into that blind lane of Freeman's, after a chase of about twenty-four hours. They figured it couldn't possibly climb them eight-foot fences of Freeman's so him and the boy tied their rope across the end of the lane, about three feet off the ground. And sho enough, soon as the horse come to the end of the lane and seen Freeman's barn, it whirled just like Eck figured it would and come helling back up that lane like a scared hen-hawk. It probably never even seen the rope at all. Mrs. Freeman was watching from where she had run up onto the porch. She said that when it hit that rope, it looked just like one

of these here great big Christmas pinwheels. But the one
you bought got clean away, didn't it?"

"That's right," Eck said. "I never had time to see which
way the other one went."

"Give him to me, paw," the little boy said.

"You wait till we catch him," Eck said. "We'll see about
it then."

III

The two actions of Armstid pl. vs. Snopes, and Tull pl.
vs. Eckrum Snopes (and anyone else named Snopes or
Varner either which Tull's irate wife could contrive to
involve, as the village well knew) were accorded a change
of venue by mutual agreement and arrangement among
the litigants. Three of the parties did, that is, because
Flem Snopes flatly refused to recognise the existence of
the suit against himself, stating once and without heat and
first turning his head slightly aside to spit, "They wasn't
none of my horses," then fell to whittling again while the
baffled and helpless bailiff stood before the tilted chair
with the papers he was trying to serve.

So the Varner surrey was not among the wagons, the
buggies, and the saddled horses and mules which moved
out of the village on that May Saturday morning, to con-
verge upon Whiteleaf store eight miles away, coming not
only from Frenchman's Bend but from other directions
too, since by that time what Ratliff had called 'that
Texas sickness,' that spotted corruption of frantic and
uncatchable horses, had spread as far as twenty and thirty
miles. By the time the Frenchman's Bend people began to
arrive, there were two dozen wagons, the teams reversed
and eased of harness and tied to the rear wheels in order
to pass the day, and twice that many saddled animals already standing about the locust grove beside the store and
the site of the hearing had already been transferred from
the store to an adjacent shed where in the fall cotton would

be stored. But by nine o'clock it was seen that even the shed would not hold them all, so the palladium was moved again, from the shed to the grove itself. The horses and mules and wagons were cleared from it; the single chair, the gnawed table bearing a thick Bible which had the appearance of loving and constant use of a piece of old and perfectly-kept machinery and an almanac and a copy of Mississippi Reports dated 1881 and bearing along its opening edge a single thread-thin line of soilure, as if during all the time of his possession its owner (or user) had opened it at only one page though that quite often, were fetched from the shed to the grove; a wagon and four men were dispatched and returned presently from the church a mile away with four wooden pews for the litigants and their clansmen and witnesses; behind these in turn the spectators stood—the men, the women, the children, sober, attentive, and neat, not in their Sunday clothes to be sure, but in the clean working garments donned that morning for the Saturday's diversion of sitting about the country stores or trips into the county seat, and in which they would return to the field on Monday morning and would wear all that week until Friday night came round again.

The Justice of the Peace was a neat, small, plump old man resembling a tender caricature of all grandfathers who ever breathed, in a beautifully laundered though collarless white shirt with immaculate starch-gleaming cuffs and bosom, and steel-framed spectacles and neat, faintly curling white hair. He sat behind the table and looked at them—at the gray woman in the gray sunbonnet and dress, her clasped and motionless hands on her lap resembling a gnarl of pallid and drowned roots from a drained swamp; at Tull in his faded but absolutely clean shirt and the overalls which his womenfolks not only kept immaculately washed but starched and ironed also, and not creased through the legs but flat across them from seam to seam, so that on each Saturday morning they resembled the short pants of a small boy, and the sedate and innocent blue of

his eyes above the month-old corn-silk beard which concealed most of his abraded face and which gave him an air
of incredible and paradoxical dissoluteness, not as though at
last and without warning he had appeared in the sight of
his fellowmen in his true character, but as if an old Italian
portrait of a child saint had been defaced by a vicious
and idle boy; at Mrs. Tull, a strong, full-bosomed though
slightly dumpy woman with an expression of grim and
seething outrage which the elapsed four weeks had apparently neither increased nor diminished but had merely
set, an outrage which curiously and almost at once began
to give the impression of being directed not at any Snopes
or at any other man in particular but at all men, all males,
and of which Tull himself was not at all the victim but the
subject, who sat on one side of her husband while the biggest of the four daughters sat on the other as if they
(or Mrs. Tull at least) were not so much convinced that
Tull might leap up and flee, as determined that he would
not; and at Eck and the little boy, identical save for size,
and Lump, the clerk, in a gray cap which someone actually recognized as being the one which Flem Snopes
had worn when he went to Texas last year, who between
spells of rapid blinking would sit staring at the Justice with
the lidless intensity of a rat—and into the lens-distorted
and irisless old-man's eyes of the Justice there grew an
expression not only of amazement and bewilderment but,
as in Ratliff's eyes while he stood on the store gallery four
weeks ago, something very like terror.

"This—" he said. "I didn't expect—I didn't look to
see—. I'm going to pray," he said. "I ain't going to pray
aloud. But I hope—" He looked at them. "I wish. . . .
Maybe some of you all anyway had better do the same."
He bowed his head. They watched him, quiet and grave,
while he sat motionless behind the table, the light morning wind moving faintly in his thin hair and the shadow-
stipple of windy leaves gliding and flowing across the
starched bulge of bosom and the gleaming bone-buttoned

cuffs, as rigid and almost as large as sections of six-inch stovepipe, at his joined hands. He raised his head. "Armstid against Snopes," he said. Mrs. Armstid spoke. She did not move, she looked at nothing, her hands clasped in her lap, speaking in that flat, toneless and hopeless voice:

"That Texan man said——"

"Wait," the Justice said. He looked about at the faces, the blurred eyes fleeing behind the thick lenses. "Where is the defendant? I don't see him."

"He wouldn't come," the bailiff said.

"Wouldn't come?" the Justice said. "Didn't you serve the papers on him?"

"He wouldn't take them," the bailiff said. "He said——"

"Then he is in contempt!" the Justice cried.

"What for?" Lump Snopes said. "Ain't nobody proved yet they was his horses." The Justice looked at him.

"Are you representing the defendant?" he said. Snopes blinked at him for a moment.

"What's that mean?" he said. "That you aim for me to pay whatever fine you think you can clap onto him?"

"So he refuses to defend himself," the Justice said. "Don't he know that I can find against him for that reason, even if pure justice and decency ain't enough?"

"It'll be pure something," Snopes said. "It don't take no mind-reader to see how your mind is——"

"Shut up, Snopes," the bailiff said. "If you ain't in this case, you keep out of it." He turned back to the Justice. "What you want me to do: go over to the Bend and fetch Snopes here anyway? I reckon I can do it."

"No," the Justice said. "Wait." He looked about at the sober faces again with that bafflement, that dread. "Does anybody here know for sho who them horses belonged to? Anybody?" They looked back at him, sober, attentive—at the neat immaculate old man sitting with his hands locked together on the table before him to still the trembling. "All right, Mrs. Armstid," he said. "Tell the court what happened." She told it, unmoving, in the flat, inflectionless voice, looking at nothing, while they listened quietly, coming to the end and ceasing without even any fall of voice, as though the tale mattered nothing and came to nothing. The Justice was looking down at his hands. When she ceased, he looked up at her. "But you haven't showed yet that Snopes owned the horses. The one you want to sue is that Texas man. And he's gone. If you got a judgment against him, you couldn't collect the money. Don't you see?"

"Mr. Snopes brought him here," Mrs. Armstid said. "Likely that Texas man wouldn't have knowed where Frenchman's Bend was if Mr. Snopes hadn't showed him."

"But it was the Texas man that sold the horses and collected the money for them." The Justice looked about again at the faces. "Is that right? You, Bookwright, is that what happened?"

"Yes," Bookwright said. The Justice looked at Mrs. Armstid again, with that pity and grief. As the morning increased the wind had risen, so that from time to time gusts of it ran through the branches overhead, bringing a faint snow of petals, prematurely bloomed as the spring itself had condensed with spendthrift speed after the hard winter, and the heavy and drowsing scent of them, about the motionless heads.

"He give Mr. Snopes Henry's money. He said Henry hadn't bought no horse. He said I could get the money from Mr. Snopes tomorrow."

"And you have witnesses that saw and heard him?"

"Yes, sir. The other men that was there saw him give Mr. Snopes the money and say that I could get it——"

"And you asked Snopes for the money?"

"Yes, sir. He said that Texas man taken it away with him when he left. But I would. . . ." She ceased again, perhaps looking down at her hands also. Certainly she was not looking at anyone.

"Yes?" the Justice said. "You would what?"

"I would know them five dollars. I earned them myself, weaving at night after Henry and the chaps was asleep. Some of the ladies in Jefferson would save up string and such and give it to me and I would weave things and sell them. I earned that money a little at a time and I would know it when I saw it because I would take the can outen the chimney and count it now and then while it was making up to enough to buy my chaps some shoes for next winter. I would know it if I was to see it again. If Mr. Snopes would just let——"

"Suppose there was somebody seen Flem give that money back to that Texas fellow," Lump Snopes said suddenly.

"Did anybody here see that?" the Justice said.

"Yes," Snopes said, harshly and violently. "Eck here did." He looked at Eck. "Go on. Tell him." The Justice looked at Eck; the four Tull girls turned their heads as one head and looked at him, and Mrs. Tull leaned forward to look past her husband, her face cold, furious, and contemptuous, and those standing shifted to look past one another's heads at Eck sitting motionless on the bench.

"Did you see Snopes give Armstid's money back to the Texas man, Eck?" the Justice said. Still Eck did not answer nor move, Lump Snopes made a gross violent sound through the side of his mouth.

"By God, I ain't afraid to say it if Eck is. I seen him do it."

"Will you swear that as testimony?" Snopes looked at the Justice. He did not blink now.

"So you won't take my word," he said.

"I want the truth," the Justice said. "If I can't find that, I got to have sworn evidence of what I will have to accept as truth." He lifted the Bible from the two other books.

"All right," the bailiff said. "Step up here." Snopes rose from the bench and approached. They watched him, though now there was no shifting nor craning, no movement at all among the faces, the still eyes. Snopes at the table looked back at them once, his gaze traversing swiftly the crescent-shaped rank; he looked at the Justice again. The bailiff grasped the Bible; though the Justice did not release it yet.

"You are ready to swear you saw Snopes give that Texas man back the money he took from Henry Armstid for that horse?" he said.

"I said I was didn't I?" Snopes said. The Justice released the Bible.

"Swear him," he said.

"Put your left hand on the Book raise your right hand you solemnly swear and affirm—" the bailiff said rapidly. But Snopes had already done so, his left hand raised and his head turned away as once more his gaze went rapidly along the circle of expressionless and intent faces, saying in that harsh and snarling voice:

"Yes. I saw Flem Snopes give back to that Texas man whatever money Henry Armstid or anybody else thinks Henry Armstid or anybody else paid Flem for any of them horses. Does that suit you?"

"Yes," the Justice said. Then there was no movement, no sound anywhere among them. The bailiff placed the Bible quietly on the table beside the Justice's locked hands, and there was no movement save the flow and recover of the windy shadows and the drift of the locust petals. Then Mrs. Armstid rose; she stood once more (or still) looking at nothing, her hands clasped across her middle.

"I reckon I can go now, can't I?" she said.

"Yes," the Justice said, rousing. "Unless you would like——"

"I better get started," she said. "It's a right far piece." She had not come in the wagon, but on one of the gaunt and underfed mules. One of the men followed her across the grove and untied the mule for her and led it up to a wagon, from one hub of which she mounted. Then they looked at the Justice again. He sat behind the table, his hands still joined before him, though his head was not bowed now. Yet he did not move until the bailiff leaned and spoke to him, when he roused, came suddenly awake without starting, as an old man wakes from an old man's light sleep. He removed his hands from the table and, looking down, he spoke exactly as if he were reading from a paper:

"Tull against Snopes. Assault and——"

"Yes!" Mrs. Tull said. "I'm going to say a word before you start." She leaned, looking past Tull at Lump Snopes again. "If you think you are going to lie and perjure Flem and Eck Snopes out of——"

"Now, mamma," Tull said. Now she spoke to Tull, without changing her position or her tone or even any break or pause in her speech:

"Don't you say hush to me! You'll let Eck Snopes or Flem Snopes or that whole Varner tribe snatch you out of the wagon and beat you half to death against a wooden bridge. But when it comes to suing them for your just rights and a punishment, oh no. Because that wouldn't be neighborly. What's neighborly got to do with you lying flat on your back in the middle of planting time while we pick splinters out of your face?" By this time the bailiff was shouting,

"Order! Order! This here's a law court!" Mrs. Tull ceased. She sat back, breathing hard, staring at the Justice, who sat and spoke again as if he were reading aloud:

"——assault and battery on the person of Vernon Tull, through the agency and instrument of one horse, unnamed, belonging to Eckrum Snopes. Evidence of physical detriment and suffering, defendant himself. Witnesses, Mrs. Tull and daughters——"

"Eck Snopes saw it too," Mrs. Tull said, though with less violence now. "He was there. He got there in plenty of time to see it. Let him deny it. Let him look me in the face and deny it if he——"

"If you please, ma'am," the Justice said. He said it so quietly that Mrs. Tull hushed and became quite calm, almost a rational and composed being. "The injury to your husband ain't disputed. And the agency of the horse ain't disputed. The law says that when a man owns a creature which he knows to be dangerous and if that creature is restrained and restricted from the public commons by a pen or enclosure capable of restraining and restricting it, if a man enter that pen or enclosure, whether he knows the creature in it is dangerous or not dangerous, then that man has committed trespass and the owner of that creature is not liable. But if that creature known to him to be dangerous ceases to be restrained by that suitable pen or enclosure, either by accident or design and either with or without the owner's knowledge, then that owner is liable. That's the law. All necessary now is to establish first, the ownership of the horse, and second, that the horse was a dangerous creature within the definition of the law as provided."

"Hah," Mrs. Tull said. She said it exactly as Bookwright would have. "Dangerous. Ask Vernon Tull. Ask Henry Armstid if them things was pets."

"If you please, ma'am," the Justice said. He was looking at Eck. "What is the defendant's position? Denial of ownership?"

"What?" Eck said.

"Was that your horse that ran over Mr. Tull?"

"Yes," Eck said. "It was mine. How much do I have to p——"

"Hah," Mrs. Tull said again. "Denial of ownership. When there were at least forty men—fools too, or they wouldn't have been there. But even a fool's word is good about what he saw and heard—at least forty men heard that Texas murderer give that horse to Eck Snopes. Not sell it to him, mind; give it to him."

"What?" the Justice said. "Gave it to him?"

"Yes," Eck said. "He give it to me. I'm sorry Tull happened to be using that bridge too at the same time. How much do I——"

"Wait," the Justice said. "What did you give him? a note? a swap of some kind?"

"No," Eck said. "He just pointed to it in the lot and told me it belonged to me."

"And he didn't give you a bill of sale or a deed or anything in writing?"

"I reckon he never had time," Eck said. "And after Lon Quick forgot and left that gate open, never nobody had time to do no writing even if we had a thought of it."

"What's all this?" Mrs. Tull said. "Eck Snopes has just told you he owned that horse. And if you won't take his word, there were forty men standing at that gate all day long doing nothing, that heard that murdering card-playing whiskey-drinking anti-christ—" This time the Justice raised one hand, in its enormous pristine cuff, toward her. He did not look at her.

"Wait," he said. "Then what did he do?" he said to Eck. "Just lead the horse up and put the rope in your hand?"

"No," Eck said. "Him nor nobody else never got no ropes on none of them. He just pointed to the horse in the lot and said it was mine and auctioned off the rest of them and got into the buggy and said good-bye and druv off. And we got our ropes and went into the lot, only Lon Quick forgot to shut the gate. I'm sorry it made Tull's mules snatch him outen the wagon. How much do I owe him?" Then he stopped, because the Justice was no longer looking at him and, as he realized a moment later, no longer listening either. Instead, he was sitting back in the chair, actually leaning back in it for the first time, his head bent slightly and his hands resting on the table before him, the fingers lightly overlapped. They watched him quietly for almost a half-minute before anyone realized that he was looking quietly and steadily at Mrs. Tull.

"Well, Mrs. Tull," he said, "by your own testimony, Eck never owned that horse."

"What?" Mrs. Tull said. It was not loud at all. "What did you say?"

"In the law, ownership can't be conferred or invested by word-of-mouth. It must be established either by recorded or authentic document, or by possession or occupation. By your testimony and his both, he never gave that Texan anything in exchange for that horse, and by his testimony the Texas man never gave him any paper to prove he owned it, and by his testimony and by what I know myself from these last four weeks, nobody yet has ever laid hand or rope either on any one of them. So that horse never came into Eck's possession at all. That Texas man could have given that same horse to a dozen other men standing around that gate that day, without even needing to tell Eck he had done it; and Eck himself could have transferred all his title and equity in it to Mr. Tull right there while Mr. Tull was lying unconscious on that bridge just by thinking it to himself, and Mr. Tull's title would be just as legal as Eck's."

"So I get nothing," Mrs. Tull said. Her voice was still calm, quiet, though probably no one but Tull realized that it was too calm and quiet. "My team is made to run away by a wild spotted mad dog, my wagon is wrecked; my husband is jerked out of it and knocked unconscious and unable to work for a whole week with less than half of our seed in the ground, and I get nothing."

"Wait," the Justice said. "The law——"

"The law," Mrs. Tull said. She stood suddenly up—a short, broad, strong woman, balanced on the balls of her planted feet.

"Now, mamma," Tull said.

"Yes, ma'am," the Justice said. "Your damages are fixed by statute. The law says that when a suit for damages is brought against the owner of an animal which has committed damage or injury, if the owner of the animal either can't or won't assume liability, the injured or damaged party shall find recompense in the body of the animal. And since Eck Snopes never owned that horse at all, and since you just heard a case here this morning that failed to prove that Flem Snopes had any equity in any of them, that horse still belongs to that Texas man. Or did belong. Because now that horse that made your team run away and snatch your husband out of the wagon, belongs to you and Mr. Tull."

"Now, mamma!" Tull said. He rose quickly. But Mrs. Tull was still quiet, only quite rigid and breathing hard, until Tull spoke. Then she turned on him, not screaming: shouting; presently the bailiff was banging the table-top with his hand-polished hickory cane and roaring "Order! Order!" while the neat old man, thrust backward in his chair as though about to dodge and trembling with an old man's palsy, looked on with amazed unbelief.

"The horse!" Mrs. Tull shouted. "We see it for five seconds, while it is climbing into the wagon with us and then out again. Then it's gone, God don't know where and thank the Lord He don't! And the mules gone with it and the wagon wrecked and you laying there on the bridge with your face full of kindling-wood and bleeding like a hog and dead for all we knew. And he gives us the horse! Don't hush me! Get on to that wagon, fool that would sit there behind a pair of young mules with reins tied around his wrist! Get on to that wagon, all of you!"

"I can't stand no more!" the old Justice cried. "I won't! This court's adjourned! Adjourned!"

5

THE END OF AN ORDER

Editor's Note

A recurring theme in Faulkner's novels is that the old South was defeated from within. After four years of fighting against hopeless odds, the landowners of Yoknapatawpha County had remained "the unvanquished," and they all had tried, as did Colonel Sutpen, to restore their houses, their plantations, and their social order to the image of what they had been before the war. Moreover, they achieved a partial success. There were years in Jefferson when the prewar standards prevailed; when a Sartoris was mayor, a Benbow was county judge, and Major de Spain was the local magnate. But the heirs of the men who had withstood the Northern armies and defeated the carpetbaggers were driven from their posts of influence by Southern renegades, or rather by a coalition between Northern business and a new class of Southerners descended in part from the bushwhackers of Civil War days. Jefferson itself was overrun, infested by the tribe of Snopes: for a time there were Snopeses in the bank, in the power company, in politics, Snopeses everywhere gnawing like rats at the standards by which the South had lived.

The Snopeses and their allies are the destructive element in Faulkner's novels. The Negroes are an element of stability: they endured. Faulkner's favorite characters are the Negro cooks and matriarchs who hold a white family together: Elnora and Clytie and Dilsey and Aunt Mollie Beauchamp. After the Compson family has gone to pieces, in *The Sound and the Fury*, it is Dilsey the cook who is left behind to mourn. Looking up at the square unpainted house with its rotting portico, she thinks, "Ise seed de first en de last"; and later in the kitchen she says, looking at the cold stove, "I seed de first en de last."

Of the four stories in this section, "That Evening Sun," with its black heroine, is one of Faulkner's very best; it belongs to a cycle dealing with the Compson children. "Ad Astra" is part of another cycle recounting the adventures of Bayard Sartoris' twin grandsons in the Royal Air Force: John was killed, and Bayard, named for his grandfather, came home (in *Sartoris*, 1929) feeling that he too had died on the night of the Armistice. In "A Rose for Emily," often anthologized, Faulkner has found one of his most effective symbols for the decay of the old order. These three stories were included in *These 13* (1931) and reprinted in *Collected Stories of William Faulkner* (1950). "Dilsey" comes from the last part of *The Sound and the Fury* (1929), which describes the going to pieces of the Compson family and which remained Faulkner's favorite among his novels. For the earlier histroy of the Compsons and the fate of the survivors, see "Appendix: The Compsons," printed in the last part of this volume.

1902

That Evening Sun

Monday is no different from any other weekday in Jefferson now. The streets are paved now, and the telephone and electric companies are cutting down more and more of the shade trees—the water oaks, the maples and locusts and elms—to make room for iron poles bearing clusters of bloated and ghostly and bloodless grapes, and we have a city laundry which makes the rounds on Monday morning, gathering the bundles of clothes into bright-colored, specially made motorcars: the soiled wearing of a whole week now flees apparitionlike behind alert and irritable electric horns, with a long diminishing noise of rubber and asphalt like tearing silk, and even the Negro women who still take in white people's washing after the old custom, fetch and deliver it in automobiles.

But fifteen years ago, on Monday morning the quiet, dusty, shady streets would be full of Negro women with, balanced on their steady, turbaned heads, bundles of clothes tied up in sheets, almost as large as cotton bales, carried so without touch of hand between the kitchen door of the white house and the blackened washpot beside a cabin door in Negro Hollow.

Nancy would set her bundle on the top of her head, then upon the bundle in turn she would set the black straw sailor hat which she wore winter and summer. She was tall, with a high, sad face sunken a little where her teeth were missing. Sometimes we would go a part of the way down the lane and across the pasture with her, to watch the balanced bundle and the hat that never bobbed nor wavered, even when she walked down in the ditch and up the other side and stooped through the fence. She would go down on her hands and knees and crawl through the gap, her head rigid, uptilted, the bundle steady as a rock or a balloon, and rise to her feet again and go on.

Sometimes the husbands of the washing women would fetch and deliver the clothes, but Jesus never did that for Nancy, even before Father told him to stay away from our house, even when Dilsey was sick and Nancy would come to cook for us.

And then about half the time we'd have to go down the lane to Nancy's cabin and tell her to come on and cook breakfast. We would stop at the ditch, because Father told us to not have anything to do with Jesus—he was a short black man, with a razor scar down his face—and we would throw rocks at Nancy's house until she came to the door, leaning her head around it without any clothes on.

"What yawl mean, chunking my house?" Nancy said. "What you little devils mean?"

"Father says for you to come on and get breakfast," Caddy said. "Father says it's over a half an hour now, and you've got to come this minute."

"I ain't studying no breakfast," Nancy said. "I going to get my sleep out."

"I bet you're drunk," Jason said. "Father says you're drunk. Are you drunk, Nancy?"

"Who says I is?" Nancy said. "I got to get my sleep out. I ain't studying no breakfast."

So after a while we quit chunking the cabin and went back home. When she finally came, it was too late for me to go to school. So we thought it was whiskey until that day they arrested her again and they were taking her to jail and they passed Mr. Stovall. He was the cashier in the bank and a deacon in the Baptist church, and Nancy began to say:

"When you going to pay me, white man? When you going to pay me, white man? It's been three times now since you paid me a cent—" Mr. Stovall knocked her down, but she kept on saying, "When you going to pay me, white man? It's been three times now since—" until Mr. Stovall kicked her in the mouth with his heel and the marshal caught Mr. Stovall back, and Nancy lying in the street, laughing. She turned her head and spat out some blood and teeth and said, "It's been three times now since he paid me a cent."

That was how she lost her teeth, and all that day they told about Nancy and Mr. Stovall, and all that night the ones that passed the jail could hear Nancy singing and yelling. They could see her hands holding to the window bars, and a lot of them stopped along the fence, listening to her and to the jailer trying to make her stop. She didn't shut up until almost daylight, when the jailer began to hear a bumping and scraping upstairs and he went up there and found Nancy hanging from the window bar. He said that it was cocaine and not whiskey, because no nigger would try to commit suicide unless he was full of cocaine, because a nigger full of cocaine wasn't a nigger any longer.

The jailer cut her down and revived her; then he beat her, whipped her. She had hung herself with her dress. She had fixed it all right, but when they arrested her she didn't have on anything except a dress and so she didn't have anything to tie her hands with and she couldn't make her hands let go of the window ledge. So the jailer heard the noise and ran up there and found Nancy hanging from the window, stark naked, her belly already swelling out a little, like a little balloon.

When Dilsey was sick in her cabin and Nancy was cooking for us, we could see her apron swelling out; that was before father told Jesus to stay away from the house. Jesus was in the kitchen, sitting behind the stove, with his razor scar on his black face like a piece of dirty string. He said it was a watermelon that Nancy had under her dress.

"It never come off of your vine, though," Nancy said.

"Off of what vine?" Caddy said.

"I can cut down the vine it did come off of," Jesus said.

"What makes you want to talk like that before these chillen?" Nancy said. "Whyn't you go on to work? You done et. You want Mr. Jason to catch you hanging around his kitchen, talking that way before these chillen?"

"Talking what way?" Caddy said. "What vine?"

"I can't hang around white man's kitchen," Jesus said. "But white man can hang around mine. White man can come in my house, but I can't stop him. When white man want to come in my house, I ain't got no house. I can't stop him, but he can't kick me outen it. He can't do that."

Dilsey was still sick in her cabin. Father told Jesus to stay off our place. Dilsey was still sick. It was a long time. We were in the library after supper.

"Isn't Nancy through in the kitchen yet?" Mother said. "It seems to me that she has had plenty of time to have finished the dishes."

"Let Quentin go and see," Father said. "Go and see if Nancy is through, Quentin. Tell her she can go on home."

I went to the kitchen. Nancy was through. The dishes were put away and the fire was out. Nancy was sitting in a chair, close to the cold stove. She looked at me.

"Mother wants to know if you are through," I said.

"Yes," Nancy said. She looked at me. "I done finished." She looked at me.

"What is it?" I said. "What is it?"

"I ain't nothing but a nigger," Nancy said. "It ain't none of my fault."

She looked at me, sitting in the chair before the cold stove, the sailor hat on her head. I went back to the library. It was the cold stove and all, when you think of a kitchen being warm and busy and cheerful. And with a cold stove and the dishes all put away, and nobody wanting to eat at that hour.

"Is she through?" Mother said.

"Yessum," I said.

"What is she doing?" Mother said.

"She's not doing anything. She's through."

"I'll go and see," Father said.

"Maybe she's waiting for Jesus to come and take her home," Caddy said.

"Jesus is gone," I said. Nancy told us how one morning she woke up and Jesus was gone.

"He quit me," Nancy said. "Done gone to Memphis, I reckon. Dodging them city *po*-lice for a while, I reckon."

"And a good riddance," Father said. "I hope he stays there."

"Nancy's scaired of the dark," Jason said.

"So are you," Caddy said.

"I'm not," Jason said.

"Scairy cat," Caddy said.

"I'm not," Jason said.

"You, Candace!" Mother said. Father came back.

"I am going to walk down the lane with Nancy," he said. "She says that Jesus is back."

"Has she seen him?" Mother said.

"No. Some Negro sent her word that he was back in town. I won't be long."

"You'll leave me alone, to take Nancy home?" Mother said. "Is her safety more precious to you than mine?"

"I won't be long," Father said.

"You'll leave these children unprotected, with that Negro about?"

"I'm going too," Caddy said. "Let me go, Father."

"What would he do with them, if he were unfortunate enough to have them?" Father said.

"I want to go, too," Jason said.

"Jason!" Mother said. She was speaking to Father. You

could tell that by the way she said the name. Like she believed that all day Father had been trying to think of doing the thing she wouldn't like the most, and that she knew all the time that after a while he would think of it. I stayed quiet, because Father and I both knew that Mother would want him to make me stay with her if she just thought of it in time. So Father didn't look at me. I was the oldest. I was nine and Caddy was seven and Jason was five.

"Nonsense," Father said. "We won't be long."

Nancy had her hat on. We came to the lane. "Jesus always been good to me," Nancy said. "Whenever he had two dollars, one of them was mine." We walked in the lane. "If I can just get through the lane," Nancy said, "I be all right then."

The lane was always dark. "This is where Jason got scaired on Hallowe'en," Caddy said.

"I didn't," Jason said.

"Can't Aunt Rachel do anything with him?" Father said. Aunt Rachel was old. She lived in a cabin beyond Nancy's, by herself. She had white hair and she smoked a pipe in the door, all day long; she didn't work any more. They said she was Jesus' mother. Sometimes she said she was and sometimes she said she wasn't any kin to Jesus.

"Yes you did," Caddy said. "You were scairder than Frony. You were scairder than T.P. even. Scairder than niggers."

"Can't nobody do nothing with him," Nancy said. "He say I done woke up the devil in him and ain't but one thing going to lay it down again."

"Well, he's gone now," Father said. "There's nothing for you to be afraid of now. And if you'd just let white men alone."

"Let what white men alone?" Caddy said. "How let them alone?"

"He ain't gone nowhere," Nancy said. "I can feel him. I can feel him now, in this lane. He hearing us talk, every word, hid somewhere, waiting. I ain't seen him, and I ain't going to see him again but once more, with that razor in his mouth. That razor on that string down his back, inside his shirt. And then I ain't going to be even surprised."

"I wasn't scaired," Jason said.

"If you'd behave yourself, you'd have kept out of this," Father said. "But it's all right now. He's probably in Saint Louis now. Probably got another wife by now and forgot all about you."

"If he has, I better not find out about it," Nancy said. "I'd stand there right over them, and every time he wropped her, I'd cut that arm off. I'd cut his head off and I'd slit her belly and I'd shove—"

"Hush," Father said.

"Slit whose belly, Nancy?" Caddy said.

"I wasn't scaired," Jason said. "I'd walk right down this lane by myself."

"Yah," Caddy said. "You wouldn't dare to put your foot down in it if we were not here too."

II

Dilsey was still sick, so we took Nancy home every night until Mother said, "How much longer is this going on? I to be left alone in this big house while you take home a frightened Negro?"

We fixed a pallet in the kitchen for Nancy. One night we waked up, hearing the sound. It was not singing and it was not crying, coming up the dark stairs. There was a light in Mother's room and we heard Father going down the hall, down the back stairs, and Caddy and I went into the hall. The floor was cold. Our toes curled away from it while we listened to the sound. It was like singing and it wasn't like singing, like the sounds that Negroes make.

Then it stopped and we heard Father going down the back stairs, and we went to the head of the stairs. Then the sound began again, in the stairway, not loud, and we could see Nancy's eyes halfway up the stairs, against the wall. They looked like cat's eyes do, like a big cat against the wall, watching us. When we came down the steps to where she was, she quit making the sound again, and we stood there until Father came back up from the kitchen, with his pistol in his hand. He went back down with Nancy and they came back with Nancy's pallet.

We spread the pallet in our room. After the light in Mother's room went off, we could see Nancy's eyes again. "Nancy," Caddy whispered, "are you asleep, Nancy?"

Nancy whispered something. It was oh or no, I don't know which. Like nobody had made it, like it came from nowhere and went nowhere, until it was like Nancy was not there at all; that I had looked so hard at her eyes on the stairs that they had got printed on my eyeballs, like the sun does when you have closed your eyes and there is no sun. "Jesus," Nancy whispered. "Jesus."

"Was it Jesus?" Caddy said. "Did he try to come into the kitchen?"

"Jesus," Nancy said. Like this: Jeeeeeeeeeeeeeeeeesus, until the sound went out, like a match or a candle does.

"It's the other Jesus she means," I said.

"Can you see us, Nancy?" Caddy whispered. "Can you see our eyes too?"

"I ain't nothing but a nigger," Nancy said. "God knows. God knows."

"What did you see down there in the kitchen?" Caddy whispered. "What tried to get in?"

"God knows," Nancy said. We could see her eyes. "God knows."

Dilsey got well. She cooked dinner. "You'd better stay in bed a day or two longer," Father said.

"What for?" Dilsey said. "If I had been a day later, this place would be to rack and ruin. Get on out of here now, and let me get my kitchen straight again."

Dilsey cooked supper too. And that night, just before dark, Nancy came into the kitchen.

"How do you know he's back?" Dilsey said. "You ain't seen him."

"Jesus is a nigger," Jason said.

"I can feel him," Nancy said. "I can feel him laying yonder in the ditch."

"Tonight?" Dilsey said. "Is he there tonight?"

"Dilsey's a nigger too," Jason said.

"You try to eat something," Dilsey said.

"I don't want nothing," Nancy said.

"I ain't a nigger," Jason said.

"Drink some coffee," Dilsey said. She poured a cup of coffee for Nancy. "Do you know he's out there tonight? How come you know it's tonight?"

"I know," Nancy said. "He's there, waiting. I know. I done lived with him too long. I know what he is fixing to do fore he know it himself."

"Drink some coffee," Dilsey said. Nancy held the cup to her mouth and blew into the cup. Her mouth pursed out like a spreading adder's, like a rubber mouth, like she had blown all the color out of her lips with blowing the coffee.

"I ain't a nigger," Jason said. "Are you a nigger, Nancy?"

"I hellborn, child," Nancy said. "I won't be nothing soon. I going back where I come from soon."

III

She began to drink the coffee. While she was drinking, holding the cup in both hands, she began to make the sound again. She made the sound into the cup and the coffee sploshed out onto her hands and her dress. Her eyes looked at us and she sat there, her elbows on her knees, holding the cup in both hands, looking at us across the wet cup, making the sound.

"Look at Nancy," Jason said. "Nancy can't cook for us now. Dilsey's got well now."

"You hush up," Dilsey said. Nancy held the cup in both

hands, looking at us, making the sound, like there were two of them: one looking at us and the other making the sound. "Whyn't you let Mr. Jason telefoam the marshal?" Dilsey said. Nancy stopped then, holding the cup in her long brown hands. She tried to drink some coffee again, but it sploshed out of the cup, onto her hands and her dress, and she put the cup down. Jason watched her.

"I can't swallow it," Nancy said. "I swallows but it won't go down me."

"You go down to the cabin," Dilsey said. "Frony will fix you a pallet and I'll be there soon."

"Won't no nigger stop him," Nancy said.

"I ain't a nigger," Jason said. "Am I, Dilsey?"

"I reckon not," Dilsey said. She looked at Nancy. "I don't reckon so. What you going to do, then?"

Nancy looked at us. Her eyes went fast, like she was afraid there wasn't time to look, without hardly moving at all. She looked at us, at all three of us at one time. "You member that night I stayed in yawls' room?" she said. She told about how we waked up early the next morning, and played. We had to play quiet, on her pallet, until Father woke up and it was time to get breakfast. "Go and ask your maw to let me stay here tonight," Nancy said. "I won't need no pallet. We can play some more."

Caddy asked Mother. Jason went too. "I can't have Negroes sleeping in the bedrooms," Mother said. Jason cried. He cried until Mother said he couldn't have any dessert for three days if he didn't stop. Then Jason said he would stop if Dilsey would make a chocolate cake. Father was there.

"Why don't you do something about it?" Mother said. "What do we have officers for?"

"Why is Nancy afraid of Jesus?" Caddy said. "Are you afraid of Father, Mother?"

"What could the officers do?" Father said. "If Nancy hasn't seen him, how could the officers find him?"

"Then why is she afraid?" Mother said.

"She says he is there. She says she knows he is there tonight."

"Yet we pay taxes," Mother said. "I must wait here alone in this big house while you take a Negro woman home."

"You know that I am not lying outside with a razor," Father said.

"I'll stop if Dilsey will make a chocolate cake," Jason said. Mother told us to go out and Father said he didn't know if Jason would get a chocolate cake or not, but he knew what Jason was going to get in about a minute. We went back to the kitchen and told Nancy.

"Father said for you to go home and lock the door, and you'll be all right," Caddy said. "All right from what, Nancy? Is Jesus mad at you?" Nancy was holding the coffee cup in her hands again, her elbows on her knees and her hands holding the cup between her knees. She was looking into the cup. "What have you done that made Jesus mad?" Caddy said. Nancy let the cup go. It didn't break on the floor, but the coffee spilled out, and Nancy sat there with her hands still making the shape of the cup. She began to make the sound again, not loud. Not singing and not unsinging. We watched her.

"Here," Dilsey said. "You quit that, now. You get aholt of yourself. You wait here. I going to get Versh to walk home with you." Dilsey went out.

We looked at Nancy. Her shoulders kept shaking, but she quit making the sound. We stood and watched her.

"What's Jesus going to do to you?" Caddy said. "He went away."

Nancy looked at us. "We had fun that night I stayed in yawls' room, didn't we?"

"I didn't," Jason said. "I didn't have any fun."

"You were asleep in Mother's room," Caddy said. "You were not there."

"Let's go down to my house and have some more fun," Nancy said.

"Mother won't let us," I said. "It's too late now."

"Don't bother her," Nancy said. "We can tell her in the morning. She won't mind."

"She wouldn't let us," I said.

"Don't ask her now," Nancy said. "Don't bother her now."

"She didn't say we couldn't go," Caddy said.

"We didn't ask," I said.

"If you go, I'll tell," Jason said.

"We'll have fun," Nancy said. "They won't mind, just to my house. I been working for yawl a long time. They won't mind."

"I'm not afraid to go," Caddy said. "Jason is the one that's afraid. He'll tell."

"I'm not," Jason said.

"Yes, you are," Caddy said. "You'll tell."

"I won't tell," Jason said. "I'm not afraid."

"Jason ain't afraid to go with me," Nancy said. "Is you, Jason?"

"Jason is going to tell," Caddy said. The lane was dark. We passed the pasture gate. "I bet if something was to jump out from behind that gate, Jason would holler."

"I wouldn't," Jason said. We walked down the lane. Nancy was talking loud.

"What are you talking so loud for, Nancy?" Caddy said.

"Who, me?" Nancy said. "Listen at Quentin and Caddy and Jason saying I'm talking loud."

"You talk like there was five of us here," Caddy said. "You talk like Father was here too."

"Who; me talking loud, Mr. Jason?" Nancy said.

"Nancy called Jason 'Mister,' " Caddy said.

"Listen how Caddy and Quentin and Jason talk," Nancy said.

"We're not talking loud," Caddy said. "You're the one that's talking like Father—"

"Hush," Nancy said; "hush, Mr. Jason."

"Nancy called Jason 'Mister' aguh—"

"Hush," Nancy said. She was talking loud when we crossed the ditch and stooped through the fence where she used to stoop through with the clothes on her head. Then we came to her house. We were going fast then. She opened the door. The smell of the house was like the lamp and the smell of Nancy was like the wick, like they were waiting for one another to begin to smell. She lit the lamp and closed the door and put the bar up. Then she quit talking loud, looking at us.

"What're we going to do?" Caddy said.

"What do yawl want to do?" Nancy said.

"You said we would have some fun," Caddy said.

There was something about Nancy's house; something you could smell besides Nancy and the house. Jason smelled it, even. "I don't want to stay here," he said. "I want to go home."

"Go home, then," Caddy said.

"I don't want to go by myself," Jason said.

"We're going to have some fun," Nancy said.

"How?" Caddy said.

Nancy stood by the door. She was looking at us, only it was like she had emptied her eyes, like she had quit using them. "What do you want to do?" she said.

"Tell us a story," Caddy said. "Can you tell a story?"

"Yes," Nancy said.

"Tell it," Caddy said. We looked at Nancy. "You don't know any stories."

"Yes," Nancy said. "Yes I do."

She came and sat in a chair before the hearth. There was a little fire there. Nancy built it up, when it was already hot inside. She built a good blaze. She told a story. She talked like her eyes looked, like her eyes watching us and her voice talking to us did not belong to her. Like she was living somewhere else, waiting somewhere else. She was outside the cabin. Her voice was inside and the shape of her, the Nancy that could stoop under a barbed wire fence with a bundle of clothes balanced on her head as though without weight, like a balloon, was there. But that was all. "And so this here queen come walking up to the ditch, where that bad man was hiding. She was walking up to the ditch, and she say, 'If I can just get past this here ditch,' was what she say . . ."

"What ditch?" Caddy said. "A ditch like that one out there? Why did a queen want to go into a ditch?"

"To get to her house," Nancy said. She looked at us. "She had to cross the ditch to get into her house quick and bar the door."

"Why did she want to go home and bar the door?" Caddy said.

I V

Nancy looked at us. She quit talking. She looked at us. Jason's legs stuck straight out of his pants where he sat on Nancy's lap. "I don't think that's a good story," he said. "I want to go home."

"Maybe we had better," Caddy said. She got up from the floor. "I bet they are looking for us right now." She went toward the door.

"No," Nancy said. "Don't open it." She got up quick and passed Caddy. She didn't touch the door, the wooden bar.

"Why not?" Caddy said.

"Come back to the lamp," Nancy said. "We'll have fun. You don't have to go."

"We ought to go," Caddy said. "Unless we have a lot of fun." She and Nancy came back to the fire, the lamp.

"I want to go home," Jason said. "I'm going to tell."

"I know another story," Nancy said. She stood close to the lamp. She looked at Caddy, like when your eyes look up at a stick balanced on your nose. She had to look down to see Caddy, but her eyes looked like that, like when you are balancing a stick.

"I won't listen to it," Jason said. "I'll bang on the floor."

"It's a good one," Nancy said. "It's better than the other one."

"What's it about?" Caddy said. Nancy was standing by the lamp. Her hand was on the lamp, against the light, long and brown.

"Your hand is on that hot globe," Caddy said. "Don't it feel hot to your hand?"

Nancy looked at her hand on the lamp chimney. She took her hand away, slow. She stood there, looking at Caddy, wringing her long hand as though it were tied to her wrist with a string.

"Let's do something else," Caddy said.

"I want to go home," Jason said.

"I got some popcorn," Nancy said. She looked at Caddy and then at Jason and then at me and then at Caddy again. "I got some popcorn."

"I don't like popcorn," Jason said. "I'd rather have candy."

Nancy looked at Jason. "You can hold the popper." She was still wringing her hand; it was long and limp and brown.

"All right," Jason said. "I'll stay a while if I can do that. Caddy can't hold it. I'll want to go home again if Caddy holds the popper."

Nancy built up the fire. "Look at Nancy putting her hands in the fire," Caddy said. "What's the matter with you, Nancy?"

"I got popcorn," Nancy said. "I got some." She took the popper from under the bed. It was broken. Jason began to cry.

"Now we can't have any popcorn," he said.

"We ought to go home, anyway," Caddy said. "Come on, Quentin."

"Wait," Nancy said; "wait. I can fix it. Don't you want to help me fix it?"

"I don't think I want any," Caddy said. "It's too late now."

"You help me, Jason," Nancy said. "Don't you want to help me?"

"No," Jason said. "I want to go home."

"Hush," Nancy said; "hush. Watch. Watch me. I can fix it so Jason can hold it and pop the corn." She got a piece of wire and fixed the popper.

"It won't hold good," Caddy said.

"Yes it will," Nancy said. "Yawl watch. Yawl help me shell some corn."

The popcorn was under the bed too. We shelled it into the popper and Nancy helped Jason hold the popper over the fire.

"It's not popping," Jason said. "I want to go home."

"You wait," Nancy said. "It'll begin to pop. We'll have fun then."

She was sitting close to the fire. The lamp was turned up so high it was beginning to smoke. "Why don't you turn it down some?" I said.

"It's all right," Nancy said. "I'll clean it. Yawl wait. The popcorn will start in a minute."

"I don't believe it's going to start," Caddy said. "We ought to start home, anyway. They'll be worried."

"No," Nancy said. "It's going to pop. Dilsey will tell um yawl with me. I been working for yawl long time. They won't mind if yawl at my house. You wait, now. It'll start popping any minute now."

Then Jason got some smoke in his eyes and he began to cry. He dropped the popper into the fire. Nancy got a wet rag and wiped Jason's face, but he didn't stop crying.

"Hush," she said. "Hush." But he didn't hush. Caddy took the popper out of the fire.

"It's burned up," she said. "You'll have to get some more popcorn, Nancy."

"Did you put all of it in?" Nancy said.

"Yes," Caddy said. Nancy looked at Caddy. Then she took the popper and opened it and poured the cinders into her apron and began to sort the grains, her hands long and brown, and we watching her.

"Haven't you got any more?" Caddy said.

"Yes," Nancy said; "yes. Look. This here ain't burnt. All we need to do is—"

"I want to go home," Jason said. "I'm going to tell."

"Hush," Caddy said. We all listened. Nancy's head was already turned toward the barred door, her eyes filled with red lamplight. "Somebody is coming," Caddy said.

Then Nancy began to make that sound again, not loud, sitting there above the fire, her long hands dangling between her knees; all of a sudden water began to come out on her face in big drops, running down her face, carrying in each one a little turning ball of firelight like a spark until it dropped off her chin. "She's not crying," I said.

"I ain't crying," Nancy said. Her eyes were closed. "I ain't crying. Who is it?"

"I don't know," Caddy said. She went to the door and looked out. "We've got to go now," she said. "Here comes Father."

"I'm going to tell," Jason said. "Yawl made me come."

The water still ran down Nancy's face. She turned in her chair. "Listen. Tell him. Tell him we going to have fun. Tell him I take good care of yawl until in the morning. Tell him to let me come home with yawl and sleep on the floor. Tell him I won't need no pallet. We'll have fun. You member last time how we had so much fun?"

"I didn't have fun," Jason said. "You hurt me. You put smoke in my eyes. I'm going to tell."

V

Father came in. He looked at us. Nancy did not get up. "Tell him," she said.

"Caddy made us come down here," Jason said. "I didn't want to."

Father came to the fire. Nancy looked up at him. "Can't you go to Aunt Rachel's and stay?" he said. Nancy looked up at Father, her hands between her knees. "He's not here," Father said. "I would have seen him. There's not a soul in sight."

"He in the ditch," Nancy said. "He waiting in the ditch yonder."

"Nonsense," Father said. He looked at Nancy. "Do you know he's there?"

"I got the sign," Nancy said.

"What sign?"

"I got it. It was on the table when I come in. It was a hogbone, with blood meat still on it, laying by the lamp. He's out there. When yawl walk out that door, I gone."

"Gone where, Nancy?" Caddy said.

"I'm not a tattletale," Jason said.

"Nonsense," Father said.

"He out there," Nancy said. "He looking through that window this minute, waiting for yawl to go. Then I gone."

"Nonsense," Father said. "Lock up your house and we'll take you on to Aunt Rachel's."

" 'Twon't do no good," Nancy said. She didn't look at Father now, but he looked down at her, at her long, limp, moving hands. "Putting it off won't do no good."

"Then what do you want to do?" Father said.

"I don't know," Nancy said. "I can't do nothing. Just put it off. And that don't do no good. I reckon it belong to me. I reckon what I going to get ain't no more than mine."

"Get what?" Caddy said. "What's yours?"

"Nothing," Father said. "You all must get to bed."

"Caddy made me come," Jason said.

"Go on to Aunt Rachel's," Father said.

"It won't do no good," Nancy said. She sat before the fire, her elbows on her knees, her long hands between her knees. "When even your own kitchen wouldn't do no good. When even if I was sleeping on the floor in the room with your chillen, and the next morning there I am, and blood—"

"Hush," Father said. "Lock the door and put out the lamp and go to bed."

"I scaired of the dark," Nancy said. "I scaired for it to happen in the dark."

"You mean you're going to sit right here with the lamp lighted?" Father said. Then Nancy began to make the sound again, sitting before the fire, her long hands between her knees. "Ah, damnation," Father said. "Come along, chillen. It's past bedtime."

"When yawl go home, I gone," Nancy said. She talked quieter now, and her face looked quiet, like her hands. "Anyway, I got my coffin money saved up with Mr. Lovelady." Mr. Lovelady was a short, dirty man who collected the Negro insurance, coming around to the cabins or the kitchens every Saturday morning, to collect fifteen cents. He and his wife lived at the hotel. One morning his wife committed suicide. They had a child, a little girl. He and the child went away. After a week or two he came back alone. We would see him going along the lanes and the back streets on Saturday mornings.

"Nonsense," Father said. "You'll be the first thing I'll see in the kitchen tomorrow morning."

"You'll see what you'll see, I reckon," Nancy said. "But it will take the Lord to say what that will be."

VI

We left her sitting before the fire.

"Come and put the bar up," Father said. But she didn't move. She didn't look at us again, sitting quietly there between the lamp and the fire. From some distance down the lane we could look back and see her through the open door.

"What, Father?" Caddy said. "What's going to happen?"

"Nothing," Father said. Jason was on Father's back, so Jason was the tallest of all of us. We went down into the ditch. I looked at it, quiet. I couldn't see much where the moonlight and the shadows tangled.

"If Jesus *is* hid here, he can see us, can't he?" Caddy said.

"He's not there," Father said. "He went away a long time ago."

"You made me come," Jason said, high; against the sky it looked like Father had two heads, a little one and a big one. "I didn't want to."

We went up out of the ditch. We could still see Nancy's house and the open door, but we couldn't see Nancy now, sitting before the fire with the door open, because she was tired. "I just done got tired," she said. "I just a nigger. It ain't no fault of mine."

But we could hear her, because she began just after we came up out of the ditch, the sound that was not singing and not unsinging. "Who will do our washing now, Father?" I said.

"I'm not a nigger," Jason said, high and close above Father's head.

"You're worse," Caddy said, "you are a tattletale. If something was to jump out, you'd be scairder than a nigger."

"I wouldn't," Jason said.

"You'd cry," Caddy said.

"Caddy," Father said.

"I wouldn't!" Jason said.

"Scairy cat," Caddy said.

"Candace!" Father said.

1918

Ad Astra

I don't know what we were. With the exception of Comyn, we had started out Americans, but after three years, in our British tunics and British wings and here and there a ribbon, I don't suppose we had even bothered in three years to wonder what we were, to think or to remember.

And on that day, that evening, we were even less than that, or more than that: either beneath or beyond the knowledge that we had not even wondered in three years. The subadar—after a while he was there, in his turban and his trick major's pips—said that we were like men trying to move in water. "But soon it will clear away," he said. "The effluvium of hatred and of words. We are like men trying to move in water, with held breath watching our terrific and infinitesimal limbs, watching one another's terrific stasis without touch, without contact, robbed of all save the impotence and the need."

We were in the car then, going to Amiens, Sartoris driving and Comyn sitting half a head above him in the front seat like a tackling dummy, the subadar, Bland and I in back, each with a bottle or two in his pockets. Except the subadar, that is. He was squat, small and thick, yet his sobriety was colossal. In that maelstrom of alcohol where the rest of us had fled our inescapable selves he was like a rock, talking quietly in a grave bass four sizes too big for him: "In my country I was prince. But all men are brothers."

But after twelve years I think of us as bugs in the surface of the water, isolant and aimless and unflagging. Not on the surface; in it, within that line of demarcation not air and not water, sometimes submerged, sometimes not. You have watched an unbreaking groundswell in a cove, the water shallow, the cove quiet, a little sinister with satiate familiarity, while beyond the darkling horizon the dying storm has raged on. That was the water, we the flotsam. Even after twelve years it is no clearer than that. It had no beginning and no ending. Out of nothing we howled, unwitting the storm which we had escaped and the foreign strand which we could not escape; that in the interval between two surges of the swell we died who had been too young to have ever lived.

We stopped in the middle of the road to drink again. The land was dark and empty. And quiet: that was what you noticed, remarked. You could hear the earth breathe, like coming out of ether, like it did not yet know, believe, that it was awake. "But now it is peace," the subadar said. "All men are brothers."

"You spoke before the Union once," Bland said. He was blond and tall. When he passed through a room where women were he left a sighing wake like a ferry boat entering the slip. He was a Southerner, too, like Sartoris; but unlike Sartoris, in the five months he had been out, no one had ever found a bullet hole in his machine. But he had transferred out of an Oxford battalion—he was a Rhodes scholar—with a barnacle and wound-stripe. When he was tight he would talk about his wife, though we all knew that he was not married.

He took the bottle from Sartoris and drank. "I've got the sweetest little wife," he said. "Let me tell you about her."

"Don't tell us," Sartoris said. "Give her to Comyn. He wants a girl."

"All right," Bland said. "You can have her, Comyn."

"Is she blonde?" Comyn said.

"I don't know," Bland said. He turned back to the subadar. "You spoke before the Union once. I remember you."

"Ah," the subadar said. "Oxford. Yes."

"He can attend their schools among the gentleborn, the bleach-skinned," Bland said. "But he cannot hold their commission, because gentility is a matter of color and not lineage or behavior."

"Fighting is more important than truth," the subadar said. "So we must restrict the prestige and privileges of it to the few so that it will not lose popularity with the many who have to die."

"Why more important?" I said. "I thought this one was being fought to end war forevermore."

The subadar made a brief gesture, dark, deprecatory, tranquil. "I was a white man also for that moment. It is more important for the Caucasian because he is only what he can do; it is the sum of him."

"So you see further than we see?"

"A man sees further looking out of the dark upon the light than a man does in the light and looking out upon the light. That is the principle of the spyglass. The lens is only to tease him with that which the sense that suffers and desires can never affirm."

"What do you see, then?" Bland said.

"I see girls," Comyn said. "I see acres and acres of the yellow hair of them like wheat and me among the wheat. Have ye ever watched a hidden dog quartering a wheat field, any of yez?"

"Not hunting bitches," Bland said.

Comyn turned in the seat, thick and huge. He was big as all outdoors. To watch two mechanics shoehorning him into the cockpit of a Dolphin like two chambermaids putting an emergency bolster into a case too small for it, was a sight to see. "I will beat the head off ye for a shilling," he said.

"So you believe in the rightness of man?" I said.

"I will beat the heads off yez all for a shilling," Comyn said.

"I believe in the pitiableness of man," the subadar said. "That is better."

"I will give yez the shilling, then," Comyn said.

"All right," Sartoris said. "Did you ever try a little whiskey for the night air, any of you all?"

Comyn took the bottle and drank. "Acres and acres of them," he said, "with their little round white woman parts gleaming among the moiling wheat."

So we drank again, on the lonely road between two beet fields, in the dark quiet, and the turn of the inebriation began to make. It came back from wherever it had gone, rolling down upon us and upon the grave sober rock of the subadar until his voice sounded remote and tranquil and dreamlike, saying that we were brothers. Monaghan was there then, standing beside our car in the full glare of the headlights of his car, in a R.F.C. cap and an American tunic with both shoulder straps flapping loose, drinking from Comyn's bottle. Beside him stood a second man, also in a tunic shorter and trimmer than ours, with a bandage about his head.

"I'll fight you," Comyn told Monaghan. "I'll give you the shilling."

"All right," Monaghan said. He drank again.

"We are all brothers," the subadar said. "Sometimes we pause at the wrong inn. We think it is night and we stop, when it is not night. That is all."

"I'll give you a sovereign," Comyn told Monaghan.

"All right," Monaghan said. He extended the bottle to the other man, the one with the bandaged head.

"I thangk you," the man said. "I haf plenty yet."

"I'll fight him," Comyn said.

"It is because we can do only within the heart," the subadar said. "While we see beyond the heart."

"I'll be damned if you will," Monaghan said. "He's

mine." He turned to the man with the bandaged head. "Aren't you mine? Here; drink."

"I haf plenty, I thangk you, gentlemen," the other said. But I don't think any of us paid much attention to him until we were inside the Cloche-Clos. It was crowded, full of noise and smoke. When we entered all the noise ceased, like a string cut in two, the end raveling back into a sort of shocked consternation of pivoting faces, and the waiter —an old man in a dirty apron—falling back before us, slack-jawed, with an expression of outraged unbelief, like an atheist confronted with either Christ or the devil. We crossed the room, the waiter retreating before us, paced by the turning outraged faces, to a table adjacent to one where three French officers sat watching us with that same expression of astonishment and then outrage and then anger. As one they rose; the whole room, the silence, became staccato with voices, like machine guns. That was when I turned and looked at Monaghan's companion for the first time, in his green tunic and his black snug breeks and his black boots and his bandage. He had cut himself recently shaving, and with his bandaged head and his face polite and dazed and bloodless and sick, he looked like Monaghan had been using him pretty hard. Roundfaced, not old, with his immaculately turned bandage which served only to emphasize the generations of difference between him and the turbaned subadar, flanked by Monaghan with his wild face and wild tunic and surrounded by the French people's shocked and outraged faces, he appeared to contemplate with a polite and alert concern his own struggle against the inebriation which Monaghan was forcing upon him. There was something Anthony-like about him: rigid, soldierly, with every button in place, with his unblemished bandage and his fresh razor cuts, he appeared to muse furiously upon a clear flame of a certain conviction of individual behavior above a violent and inexplicable chaos. Then I remarked

Monaghan's second companion: an American military policeman. He was not drinking. He sat beside the German, rolling cigarettes from a cloth sack.

On the German's other side Monaghan was filling his glass. "I brought him down this morning," he said. "I'm going to take him home with me."

"Why?" Bland said. "What do you want with him?"

"Because he belongs to me," Monaghan said. He set the full glass before the German. "Here; drink."

"I once thought about taking one home to my wife," Bland said. "So I could prove to her that I have only been to a war. But I never could find a good one. A whole one, I mean."

"Come on," Monaghan said. "Drink."

"I haf plenty," the German said. "All day I haf plenty."

"Do you want to go to America with him?" Bland said.

"Yes. I would ligk it. Thanks."

"Sure you'll like it," Monaghan said. "I'll make a man of you. Drink."

The German raised the glass, but he merely held it in his hand. His face was strained, deprecatory, yet with a kind of sereneness, like that of a man who has conquered himself. I imagine some of the old martyrs must have looked at the lions with that expression. He was sick, too. Not from the liquor: from his head. "I haf in Bayreuth a wife and a little wohn. Mine son. I haf not him yet seen."

"Ah," the subadar said. "Bayreuth. I was there one spring."

"Ah," the German said. He looked quickly at the subadar. "So? The music?"

"Yes," the subadar said. "In your music a few of you have felt, tasted, lived, the true brotherhood. The rest of us can only look beyond the heart. But we can follow them for a little while in the music."

"And then we must return," the German said. "That iss not good. Why must we yet return always?"

"It is not the time for that yet," the subadar said. "But soon . . . It is not as far as it once was. Not now."

"Yes," the German said. "Defeat will be good for us. Defeat iss good for art; victory, it iss not good."

"So you admit you were whipped," Comyn said. He was sweating again, and Sartoris' nostrils were quite white. I thought of what the subadar had said about men in water. Only our water was drunkenness: that isolation of alcoholism which drives men to shout and laugh and fight, not with one another but with their unbearable selves which, drunk, they are even more fain and still less fell to escape. Loud and overloud, unwitting the black thunderhead of outraged France (steadily the other tables were being emptied; the other customers were now clotted about the high desk where the *patronne,* an old woman in steel spectacles, sat, a wad of knitting on the ledge before her), we shouted at one another, speaking in foreign tongues out of our inescapable isolations, reiterant, unlistened to by one another; while submerged by us and more foreign still, the German and the subadar talked quietly of music, art, the victory born of defeat. And outside in the chill November darkness was the suspension, the not-quite-believing, not-quite-awakened nightmare, the breathing spell of the old verbiaged lusts and the buntinged and panoplied greeds.

"By God, I'm shanty Irish," Monaghan said. "That's what I am."

"What about it?" Sartoris said, his nostrils like chalk against his high-colored face. His twin brother had been killed in July. He was in a Camel squadron below us, and Sartoris was down there when it happened. For a week after that, as soon as he came in from patrol he would fill his tanks and drums and go out again, alone. One day somebody saw him, roosting about five thousand feet above an old Ak.W. I suppose the other guy who was with his brother that morning had seen the markings on the Hun patrol leader's crate; anyway, that's what Sartoris was doing, using the Ak.W. for bait. Where he got it and who he got to fly it, we didn't know. But he got three Huns that week, catching them dead when they dived on the Ak.W., and on the eighth day he didn't go out again. "He must have got him," Hume said. But we didn't know. He never told us. But after that, he was all right again. He never did talk much; just did his patrols and maybe once a week he'd sit and drink his nostrils white in a quiet sort of way.

Bland was filling his glass, a drop at a time almost, with a catlike indolence. I could see why men didn't like him and why women did. Comyn, his arms crossed on the table, his cuff in a pool of spilt liquor, was staring at the German. His eyes were bloodshot, a little protuberant. Beneath his downcrushed monkey cap the American M.P. smoked his meager cigarettes, his face quite blank. The steel chain of his whistle looped into his breast pocket, his pistol was hunched forward onto his lap. Beyond, the French people, the soldiers, the waiter, the *patronne*, clotted at the desk. I could hear their voices like from a distance, like crickets in September grass, the shadows of their hands jerking up the wall and flicking away.

"I'm not a soldier," Monaghan said. "I'm not a gentleman. I'm not anything." At the base of each flapping shoulder strap there was a small rip; there were two longer ones parallel above his left pocket where his wings and ribbon had been. "I don't know what I am. I have been in this damn war for three years and all I know is, I'm not dead. I—"

"How do you know you're not dead?" Bland said.

Monaghan looked at Bland, his mouth open upon his uncompleted word.

"I'll kill you for a shilling," Comyn said. "I don't like your bloody face, Lootenant. Bloody lootenant."

"I'm shanty Irish," Monaghan said. "That's what I am. My father was shanty Irish, by God. And I don't know what my grandfather was. I don't know if I had one. My father don't remember one. Likely it could have been one of several. So he didn't even have to be a gentleman. He never had to be. That's why he could make a million dollars digging sewers in the ground. So he could look up at the tall glittering windows and say—I've heard him, and him smoking the pipe would gas the puking guts out of you damn, niggling, puny—"

"Are you bragging about your father's money or about his sewers?" Bland said.

"—would look up at them and he'd say to me, he'd say, 'When you're with your fine friends, the fathers and mothers and sisters of them you met at Yale, ye might just remind them that every man is the slave of his own refuse and so your old dad they would be sending around to the forty-storey back doors of their kitchens is the king of them all—' What did you say?" He looked at Bland.

"Look here, buddy," the M.P. said. "This is about enough of this. I've got to report this prisoner."

"Wait," Monaghan said. He did not cease to look at Bland. "What did you say?"

"Are you bragging about your father's money or about his sewers?" Bland said.

"No," Monaghan said. "Why should I? Any more than I would brag about the thirteen Huns I got, or the two ribbons, one of which his damned king—" he jerked his head at Comyn—"gave me."

"Don't call him my damned king," Comyn said, his cuff soaking slowly in the spilt liquor.

"Look," Monaghan said. He jerked his hand at the rips on his flapping shoulder straps, at the two parallel rips on his breast. "That's what I think of it. Of all your goddamn twaddle about glory and gentlemen. I was young; I thought you had to be. Then I was in it and there wasn't time to stop even when I found it didn't count. But now it's over; finished now. Now I can be what I am. Shanty Irish; son of an immigrant that knew naught but shovel and pick until youth and the time for pleasuring was wore out of him before his time. Out of a peat bog he came, and his son went to their gentlemen's school and returned across the water to swank it with any of them that owned the peat bogs and the bitter sweat of them that mired it, and the king said him well."

"I will give yez the shilling and I will beat the head off yez," Comyn said.

"But why do you want to take him back with you?" Bland said. Monaghan just looked at Bland. There was something of the crucified about Monaghan, too: furious, inarticulate not with stupidity but at it, like into him more than any of us had distilled the ceased drums of the old lust and greed waking at last aghast at its own impotence and accrued despair. Bland sat on his spine, legs extended, his hands in his slacks, his handsome face calmly insufferable. "What stringed pick would he bow? maybe a shovel strung with the gut of an alley-cat? he will create perhaps in music the flushed toilets of Manhattan to play for your father after supper of an evening?" Monaghan just looked at Bland with that wild, rapt expression. Bland turned his lazy face a little to the German.

"Look here," the M.P. said.

"You have a wife, Herr Leutnant?" Bland said.

The German looked up. He glanced swiftly from face to face. "Yes, thank you," he said. He still had not touched his full glass save to hold it in his hand. But he was no nearer sober than before, the liquor become the hurting of his head, his head the pulse and beat of alcohol in him. "My people are of Prussia little barons. There are four brothers: the second for the Army, the third who did nothing in Berlin, the little one a cadet of dragoons; I, the eldest, in the University. There I learned. There wass a time then. It wass as though we, young from the quiet land, were brought together, chosen and worthy to witness a period quick like a woman with a high destiny of the earth and of man. It iss as though the old trash, the old litter of man's blundering iss to be swept away for a new race that

will in the heroic simplicity of olden time to walk the new
earth. You knew that time, not? when the eye sparkled,
the blut ran quick?" He looked about at our faces. "No?
Well, in America perhaps not. America iss new; in a new
house it iss not the litter so much as in old." He looked at
his glass for a moment, his face tranquil. "I return home;
I say to my father, in the University I haf learned it iss
not good; baron I will not be. He cannot believe. He talks
of Germany, the fatherland; I say to him, It iss there; so.
You say fatherland; I, brotherland. I say, ṫhe word *father*
iss that barbarism which will be first swept away; it iss the
symbol of that hierarchy which hass stained the history of
man with injustice of arbitrary instead of moral; force instead of love.

"From Berlin they send for that one; from the Army
that one comes. I still say baron I will not be, for it iss not
good. We are in the little hall where my ancestors on the
walls hang; I stand before them like courtmartial; I say
that Franz must be baron, for I will not be. My father says
you can; you will; it iss for Germany. Then I say, For Germany then will my wife be baroness? And like a courtmartial I tell them I haf married the daughter of a musi-
cian who wass peasant.

"So it iss that. That one of Berlin iss to be baron. He and
Franz are twin, but Franz iss captain already, and the
most humble of the Army may eat meat with our kaiser; he
does not need to be baron. So I am in Bayreuth with my
wife and my music. It iss as though I am dead. I do not
get letter until to say my father iss dead and I haf killed
him, and that one iss now home from Berlin to be baron.
But he does not stay at home. In 1912 he iss in Berlin
newspaper dead of a lady's husband and so Franz iss baron
after all.

"Then it iss war. But I am in Bayreuth with my wife
and my music, because we think that it will not be long,
since it was not long before. The fatherland in its pride
needed us of the schools, but when it needed us it did not

know it. And when it did realize that it needed us it wass too late and any peasant who would be hard to die would do. And so—"

"Why did you go, then?" Bland said. "Did the women make you? throw eggs at you, maybe?"

The German looked at Bland. "I am German; that iss beyond the I, the I am. Not for baron and kaiser." Then he quit looking at Bland without moving his eyes. "There wass a Germany before there wass barons," he said. "And after, there will be."

"Even after this?"

"More so. Then it was pride, a word in the mouth. Now it is a—how you call it? . . ."

"A nation vanquishes its banners," the subadar said. "A man conquers himself."

"Or a woman a child bears," the German said.

"Out of the lust, the travail," the subadar said; "out of the travail, the affirmation, the godhead; truth."

The M.P. was rolling another cigarette. He watched the subadar, upon his face an expression savage, restrained, and cold. He licked the cigarette and looked at me.

"When I came to this goddamn country," he said, "I thought niggers were niggers. But now I'll be damned if I know what they are. What's he? snake-charmer?"

"Yes," I said. "Snake-charmer."

"Then he better get his snake out and beat it. I've got to report this prisoner. Look at those frogs yonder." As I turned and looked three of the Frenchmen were leaving the room, insult and outrage in the shapes of their backs. The German was talking again.

"I hear by the newspapers how Franz is colonel and then general, and how the cadet, who wass still the roundheaded boy part of a gun always when I last saw him, iss now ace with iron cross by the Kaiser's own hand. Then it iss 1916. I see by the paper how the cadet iss killed by your Bishop—" he bowed slightly to Comyn—"that good man. So now I am cadet myself. It iss as though I know. It iss as though I see what iss to be. So I transfer to be aviator, and yet though I know now that Franz iss general of staff and though to myself each night I say, 'You have again returned,' I know that it iss no good.

"That, until our Kaiser fled. Then I learn that Franz iss now in Berlin; I believe that there iss a truth, that we haf not forfeited all in pride, because we know it will not be much longer now, and Franz in Berlin safe, the fighting away from.

"Then it iss this morning. Then comes the letter in my mother's hand that I haf not seen in seven years, addressed to me as baron. Franz iss shot from his horse by German soldier in Berlin street. It iss as though all had been forgotten, because women can forget all that quick, since to them nothing iss real—truth, justice, all—nothing that cannot be held in the hands or cannot die. So I burn all my papers, the picture of my wife and my son that I haf not yet seen, destroy my identity disk and remove all insignia from my tunic—" he gestured toward his collar.

"You mean," Bland said, "that you had no intention of coming back? Why didn't you take a pistol to yourself and save your government an aeroplane?"

"Suicide iss just for the body," the German said. "The body settles nothing. It iss of no importance. It iss just to be kept clean when possible."

"It is merely a room in the inn," the subadar said. "It is just where we hide for a little while."

"The lavatory," Bland said; "the toilet."

The M.P. rose. He tapped the German on the shoulder. Comyn was staring at the German.

"So you admit you were whipped," he said.

"Yes," the German said. "It was our time first, because we were the sickest. It will be your England's next. Then she too will be well."

"Don't say my England," Comyn said. "I am of the Irish nation." He turned to Monaghan. "You said, my damned king. Don't say my damned king. Ireland has had no king since the Ur Neill, God bless the red-haired stern of him."

Rigid, controlled, the German made a faint gesture. "You see?" he said to no one at all.

"The victorious lose that which the vanquished gain," the subadar said.

"And what will you do now?" Bland said.

The German did not answer. He sat bolt upright with his sick face and his immaculate bandage.

"What will you do?" the subadar said to Bland. "What will any of us do? All this generation which fought in the war are dead tonight. But we do not yet know it."

We looked at the subadar: Comyn with his bloodshot pig's eyes, Sartoris with his white nostrils, Bland slumped in his chair, indolent, insufferable, with his air of a spoiled woman. Above the German the M.P. stood.

"It seems to worry you a hell of a lot," Bland said.

"You do not believe?" the subadar said. "Wait. You will see."

"Wait?" Bland said. "I don't think I've done anything in the last three years to have acquired that habit. In the last twenty-six years. Before that I don't remember. I may have."

"Then you will see sooner than waiting," the subadar said. "You will see." He looked about at us, gravely serene. "Those who have been four years rotting out yonder—" he waved his short thick arm—"are not more dead than we."

Again the M.P. touched the German's shoulder. "Hell," he said. "Come along, buddy." Then he turned his head and we all looked up at the two Frenchmen, an officer and a sergeant, standing beside the table. For a while we just remained so. It was like all the little bugs had suddenly found that their orbits had coincided and they wouldn't even have to be aimless any more or even to keep on moving. Beneath the alcohol I could feel that hard, hot ball beginning in my stomach, like in combat, like when you know something is about to happen; that instant when you think Now. Now I can dump everything overboard and just be. Now. Now. It is quite pleasant.

"Why is that here, monsieur?" the officer said. Monaghan looked up at him, thrust backward and sideways in his chair, poised on the balls of his thighs as though they were feet, his arm lying upon the table. "Why do you make desagreeable for France, monsieur, eh?" the officer said.

Someone grasped Monaghan as he rose; it was the M.P. behind him, holding him half risen. "Wa-a-a-i-daminute," the M.P. said; "wa-a-a-i-daminute." The cigarette bobbed on his lower lip as he talked, his hands on Monaghan's shoulders, the brassard on his arm lifted into bold relief. "What's it to you, Frog?" he said. Behind the officer and the sergeant the other French people stood, and the old woman. She was trying to push through the circle. "This is my prisoner," the M.P. said. "I'll take him anywhere I please and keep him there as long as I like. What do you think about that?"

"By which authority, monsieur?" the officer said. He was tall, with a gaunt tragic face. I saw then that one of his eyes was glass. It was motionless, rigid in a face that looked even deader than the spurious eye.

The M.P. glanced toward his brassard, then instead he looked at the officer again and tapped the pistol swinging low now against his flank. "I'll take him all over your goddamn lousy country. I'll take him into your goddamn senate and kick your president up for a chair for him and you can suck your chin until I come back to wipe the latrine off your feet again."

"Ah," the officer said, "a devil-dog, I see." He said "dehvil-dahg" between his teeth, with no motion of his dead face, in itself insult. Behind him the *patronne* began to shriek in French:

"Boche! Boche! Broken! Broken! Every cup, every saucer, glass, plate—all all! I will show you! I have kept them for this day. Eight months since the shelling I have kept them in a box against this day: plates, cups, saucers, glasses, all that I have had since thirty years, all gone, broken at one time! And it costing me fifty centimes the glass for such that I shame myself to have my patrons—"

There is an unbearable point, a climax, in weariness. Even alcohol cannot approach it. Mobs are motivated by it, by a sheer attenuation of sameness become unbearable. As Monaghan rose, the M.P. flung him back. Then it was as though we all flung everything overboard at once, facing unabashed and without shame the specter which for four years we had been decking out in high words, leaping forward with concerted and orderly promptitude each time the bunting slipped. I saw the M.P. spring at the officer, then Comyn rose and met him. I saw the M.P. hit Comyn three times on the point of the jaw with his fist before Comyn picked him up bodily and threw him clean over the crowd, where he vanished, horizontal in mid-air, tugging at his pistol. I saw three poilus on Monaghan's back and the officer trying to hit him with a bottle, and Sartoris leaping upon the officer from behind. Comyn was gone; through the gap which he had made the *patronne* emerged, shrieking. Two men caught at her and she strove forward, trying to spit on the German. "Boche! Boche!" she shrieked, spitting and slobbering, her gray hair broken loose about her face; she turned and spat full at me. "Thou, too!" she shrieked, "it was not England that was devastated! Thou, too, come to pick the bones of France. Jackal! Vulture! Animal! Broken, broken! All! All! All!" And beneath it all, unmoved, unmoving, alert, watchful and contained, the German and the subadar sat, the German with his high sick face, the subadar tranquil as a squat idol, the both of them turbaned like prophets in the Old Testament.

It didn't take long. There was no time in it. Or rather, we were outside of time; within, not on, that surface, that demarcation between the old where we knew we had not died and the new where the subadar said that we were dead. Beyond the brandished bottles, the blue sleeves and the grimed hands, the faces like masks grimaced into rigid and soundless shouts to frighten children, I saw Comyn again. He came plowing up like a laden ship in a chop sea; beneath his arm was the ancient waiter, to his lips he held the M.P.'s whistle. Then Sartoris swung a chair at the single light.

It was cold in the street, a cold that penetrated the clothing, the alcohol-distended pores, and murmured to the skeleton itself. The plaza was empty, the lights infrequent and remote. So quiet it was that I could hear the faint water in the fountain. From some distance away came sound, remote too under the thick low sky—shouting, far-heard, on a thin female note like all shouting, even a mob of men, broken now and then by the sound of a band. In the shadow of the wall Monaghan and Comyn held the German on his feet. He was unconscious; the three of them invisible save for the faint blur of the bandage, inaudible save for the steady monotone of Monaghan's cursing.

"There should never have been an alliance between Frenchmen and Englishmen," the subadar said. He spoke without effort; invisible, his effortless voice had an organ quality, out of all proportion to his size. "Different nations should never join forces to fight for the same object. Let each fight for something different; ends that do not conflict, each in his own way." Sartoris passed us, returning from the fountain, carrying his bulging cap carefully before him, bottom-up. We could hear the water dripping from it between his footsteps. He became one of the blob of thicker shadow where the bandage gleamed and where Monaghan cursed steadily and quietly. "And each after his own tradition," the subadar said. "My people. The English gave them rifles. They looked at them and came to me: 'This spear is too short and too heavy: how can a man slay a swift enemy with a spear of this size and weight?' They gave them tunics with buttons to be kept buttoned; I have passed a whole trench of them squatting, motionless, buried to the ears in blankets, straw, empty sand bags, their faces gray with cold; I have lifted the blankets away from patient torsos clad only in a shirt.

"The English officers would say to them, 'Go there and do thus'; they would not stir. Then one day at fall noon the whole battalion, catching movement beyond a crater, sprang from the trench, carrying me and an officer with it. We carried the trench without firing a shot; what was left of us—the officer, I, and seventeen others—lived three days in a traverse of the enemy's front line; it required a whole brigade to extricate us. 'Why didn't you shoot?' the officer said. 'You let them pick you off like driven pheasant.' They did not look at him. Like children they stood, murmurous, alert, without shame. I said to the headman, 'Were the rifles loaded, O Das?' Like children they stood, diffident, without shame. 'O Son of many kings,' Das said. 'Speak the truth of thy knowing to the sahib,' I said. 'They were not loaded, sahib,' Das said."

Again the band came, remote, thudding in the thick air. They were giving the German drink from a bottle. Monaghan said: "Now. Feel better now?"

"It iss mine head," the German said. They spoke quietly, like they were discussing wallpaper.

Monaghan cursed again. "I'm going back. By God, I—"

"No, no," the German said. "I will not permit. You haf already obligated—"

We stood in the shadow beneath the wall and drank. We had one bottle left. Comyn crashed it, empty, against the wall.

"Now what?" Bland said.

"Girls," Comyn said. "Would ye watch Comyn of the Irish nation among the yellow hair of them like a dog among the wheat?"

We stood there, hearing the far band, the far shouting. "You sure you feel all right?" Monaghan said.

"Thanks," the German said. "I feel goot."

"Come on, then," Comyn said.

"You going to take him with you?" Bland said.

"Yes," Monaghan said. "What of it?"

"Why not take him on to the A.P.M.? He's sick."

"Do you want me to bash your bloody face in?" Monaghan said.

"All right," Bland said.

"Come on," Comyn said. "What fool would rather fight than fush? All men are brothers, and all their wives are sisters. So come along, yez midnight fusileers."

"Look here," Bland said to the German, "do you want to go with them?" With his bandaged head, he and the subadar alone were visible, like two injured men among five spirits.

"Hold him up a minute," Monaghan told Comyn. Monaghan approached Bland. He cursed Bland. "I like fighting," he said, in that same monotone. "I even like being whipped."

"Wait," the German said. "Again I will not permit." Monaghan halted, he and Bland not a foot apart. "I haf wife and son in Bayreuth," the German said. He was speaking to me. He gave me the address, twice, carefully.

"I'll write to her," I said. "What shall I tell her?"

"Tell her it iss nothing. You will know."

"Yes. I'll tell her you are all right."

"Tell her this life iss nothing."

Comyn and Monaghan took his arms again, one on either side. They turned and went on, almost carrying him. Comyn looked back once. "Peace be with you," he said.

"And with you, peace," the subadar said. They went on. We watched them come into silhouette in the mouth of an alley where a light was. There was an arch there, and the faint cold pale light on the arch and on the walls so that it was like a gate and they entering the gate, holding the German up between them.

"What will they do with him?" Bland said. "Prop him in the corner and turn the light off? Or do French brothels have he-beds too?"

"Who the hell's business is that?" I said.

The sound of the band came, thudding; it was cold. Each time my flesh jerked with alcohol and cold I believed that I could hear it rasp on the bones.

"Since seven years now I have been in this climate," the subadar said. "But still I do not like the cold." His voice was deep, quiet, like he might be six feet tall. It was like when they made him they said among themselves, "We'll give him something to carry his message around with." "Why? Who'll listen to his message?" "He will. So we'll give him something to hear it with."

"Why don't you go back to India, then?" Bland said.

"Ah," the subadar said. "I am like him; I too will not be baron."

"So you clear out and let foreigners who will treat the people like oxen or rabbits come in and take it."

"By removing myself I undid in one day what it took two thousand years to do. Is not that something?"

We shook with the cold. Now the cold was the band, the shouting, murmuring with cold hands to the skeleton, not the ears.

"Well," Bland said, "I suppose the English government is doing more to free your people than you could."

The subadar touched Bland on the chest, lightly. "You are wise, my friend. Let England be glad that all Englishmen are not so wise."

"So you will be an exile for the rest of your days, eh?"

The subadar jerked his short, thick arm toward the empty arch where Comyn and the German and Monaghan had disappeared. "Did you not hear what he said? This life is nothing."

"You can think so," Bland said. "But, by God, I'd hate

to think that what I saved out of the last three years is nothing."

"You saved a dead man," the subadar said serenely. "You will see."

"I saved my destiny," Bland said. "You nor nobody else knows what that will be."

"What is your destiny except to be dead? It is unfortunate that your generation had to be the one. It is unfortunate that for the better part of your days you will walk the earth a spirit. But that was your destiny." From far away came the shouting, on that sustained note, feminine and childlike all at once, and then the band again, brassy, thudding, like the voices, forlornly gay, hysteric, but most of all forlorn. The arch in the cold glow of the light yawned empty, profound, silent, like the gate to another city, another world. Suddenly Sartoris left us. He walked steadily to the wall and leaned against it on his propped arms, vomiting.

"Hell," Bland said. "I want a drink." He turned to me. "Where's your bottle?"

"It's gone."

"Gone where? You had two."

"I haven't got one now, though. Drink water."

"Water?" he said. "Who the hell drinks water?"

Then the hot hard ball came into my stomach again, pleasant, unbearable, real; again that instant when you say Now. Now I can dump everything. "You will, you goddamn son," I said.

Bland was not looking at me. "Twice," he said in a quiet, detached tone. "Twice in an hour. How's that for high?" He turned and went toward the fountain. Sartoris came back, walking steadily erect. The band blent with the cold along the bones.

"What time is it?" I said.

Sartoris peered at his wrist. "Twelfth."

"It's later than midnight," I said. "It must be."

"I said it was the twelfth," Sartoris said.

Bland was stooping at the fountain. There was a little light there. As we reached him he stood up, mopping at his face. The light was on his face and I thought for some time that he must have had his whole head under to be mopping that high up his face before I saw that he was crying. He stood there, mopping at his face, crying hard but quiet.

"My poor little wife," he said. "My poor little wife."

1924

A Rose for Emily

I

When Miss Emily Grierson died, our whole town went to her funeral: the men through a sort of respectful affection for a fallen monument, the women mostly out of curiosity to see the inside of her house, which no one save an old manservant—a combined gardener and cook—had seen in at least ten years.

It was a big, squarish frame house that had once been white, decorated with cupolas and spires and scrolled balconies in the heavily lightsome style of the seventies, set on what had once been our most select street. But garages and cotton gins had encroached and obliterated even the august names of that neighborhood; only Miss Emily's house was left, lifting its stubborn and coquettish decay above the cotton wagons and the gasoline pumps—an eyesore among eyesores. And now Miss Emily had gone to join the representatives of those august names where they lay in the cedar-bemused cemetery among the ranked and anonymous graves of Union and Confederate soldiers who fell at the battle of Jefferson.

Alive, Miss Emily had been a tradition, a duty, and a care; a sort of hereditary obligation upon the town, dating from that day in 1894 when Colonel Sartoris, the mayor—he who fathered the edict that no Negro woman should appear on the streets without an apron—remitted her taxes, the dispensation dating from the death of her father on into perpetuity. Not that Miss Emily would have accepted charity. Colonel Sartoris invented an involved tale to the effect that Miss Emily's father had loaned money to the town, which the town, as a matter of business, preferred this way of repaying. Only a man of Colonel Sartoris' generation and thought could have invented it, and only a woman could have believed it.

When the next generation, with its more modern ideas, became mayors and aldermen, this arrangement created some little dissatisfaction. On the first of the year they mailed her a tax notice. February came, and there was no reply. They wrote her a formal letter, asking her to call at the sheriff's office at her convenience. A week later the mayor wrote her himself, offering to call or to send his car for her, and received in reply a note on paper of an archaic shape, in a thin, flowing calligraphy in faded ink, to the effect that she no longer went out at all. The tax notice was also enclosed, without comment.

They called a special meeting of the Board of Aldermen. A deputation waited upon her, knocked at the door through which no visitor had passed since she ceased giving china-painting lessons eight or ten years earlier. They were admitted by the old Negro into a dim hall from which a stairway mounted into still more shadow. It smelled of dust and disuse—a close, dank smell. The Negro led them into the parlor. It was furnished in heavy, leather-covered furniture. When the Negro opened the blinds of one window, they could see that the leather was cracked; and when they sat down, a faint dust rose sluggishly about their thighs, spinning with slow motes in the single sunray. On a tarnished gilt easel before the fireplace stood a crayon portrait of Miss Emily's father.

They rose when she entered—a small, fat woman in black, with a thin gold chain descending to her waist and vanishing into her belt, leaning on an ebony cane with a tarnished gold head. Her skeleton was small and spare; perhaps that was why what would have been merely plumpness in another was obesity in her. She looked bloated, like a body long submerged in motionless water, and of that pallid hue. Her eyes, lost in the fatty ridges of her face, looked like two small pieces of coal pressed into a lump of dough as they moved from one face to another while the visitors stated their errand.

She did not ask them to sit. She just stood in the door and listened quietly until the spokesman came to a stumbling halt. Then they could hear the invisible watch ticking at the end of the gold chain.

Her voice was dry and cold. "I have no taxes in Jefferson. Colonel Sartoris explained it to me. Perhaps one of you can gain access to the city records and satisfy yourselves."

"But we have. We are the city authorities, Miss Emily. Didn't you get a notice from the sheriff, signed by him?"

"I received a paper, yes," Miss Emily said. "Perhaps he considers himself the sheriff . . . I have no taxes in Jefferson."

"But there is nothing on the books to show that, you see. We must go by the—"

"See Colonel Sartoris. I have no taxes in Jefferson."

"But, Miss Emily—"

"See Colonel Sartoris." (Colonel Sartoris had been dead almost ten years.) "I have no taxes in Jefferson. Tobe!" The Negro appeared. "Show these gentlemen out."

I I

So she vanquished them, horse and foot, just as she had vanquished their fathers thirty years before about the smell. That was two years after her father's death and a short time after her sweetheart—the one we believed would marry her—had deserted her. After her father's death she went out very little; after her sweetheart went away, people hardly saw her at all. A few of the ladies had the temerity to call, but were not received, and the only sign of life about the place was the Negro man—a young man then—going in and out with a market basket.

"Just as if a man—any man—could keep a kitchen properly," the ladies said; so they were not surprised when the smell developed. It was another link between the gross, teeming world and the high and mighty Griersons.

A neighbor, a woman, complained to the mayor, Judge Stevens, eighty years old.

"But what will you have me do about it, madam?" he said.

"Why, send her word to stop it," the woman said. "Isn't there a law?"

"I'm sure that won't be necessary," Judge Stevens said. "It's probably just a snake or a rat that nigger of hers killed in the yard. I'll speak to him about it."

The next day he received two more complaints, one from a man who came in diffident deprecation. "We really must do something about it, Judge. I'd be the last one in the world to bother Miss Emily, but we've got to do something." That night the Board of Aldermen met—three graybeards and one younger man, a member of the rising generation.

"It's simple enough," he said. "Send her word to have her place cleaned up. Give her a certain time to do it in, and if she don't . . ."

"Dammit, sir," Judge Stevens said, "will you accuse a lady to her face of smelling bad?"

So the next night, after midnight, four men crossed Miss Emily's lawn and slunk about the house like burglars, sniffing along the base of the brickwork and at the cellar openings while one of them performed a regular sowing motion with his hand out of a sack slung from his shoulder. They broke open the cellar door and sprinkled lime there, and in all the outbuildings. As they recrossed the lawn, a window that had been dark was lighted and Miss Emily sat in it, the light behind her, and her upright torso motionless as that of an idol. They crept quietly across the lawn and into the shadow of the locusts that lined the street. After a week or two the smell went away.

That was when people had begun to feel really sorry for her. People in our town, remembering how old lady Wyatt, her great-aunt, had gone completely crazy at last, believed that the Griersons held themselves a little too high for what they really were. None of the young men were quite good enough to Miss Emily and such. We had long thought of them as a tableau; Miss Emily a slender figure in white in the background, her father a spraddled silhouette in the foreground, his back to her and clutching a horsewhip, the two of them framed by the back-flung front door. So when she got to be thirty and was still single, we were not pleased exactly, but vindicated; even with insanity in the family she wouldn't have turned down all of her chances if they had really materialized.

When her father died, it got about that the house was all that was left to her; and in a way, people were glad. At last they could pity Miss Emily. Being left alone, and a pauper, she had become humanized. Now she too would know the old thrill and the old despair of a penny more or less.

The day after his death all the ladies prepared to call at the house and offer condolence and aid, as is our custom. Miss Emily met them at the door, dressed as usual and with no trace of grief on her face. She told them that her father was not dead. She did that for three days, with the ministers calling on her, and the doctors, trying to persuade her to let them dispose of the body. Just as they were about to resort to law and force, she broke down, and they buried her father quickly.

We did not say she was crazy then. We believed she had to do that. We remembered all the young men her father had driven away, and we knew that with nothing left, she would have to cling to that which had robbed her, as people will.

III

She was sick for a long time. When we saw her again, her hair was cut short, making her look like a girl, with a vague resemblance to those angels in colored church windows—sort of tragic and serene.

The town had just let the contracts for paving the sidewalks, and in the summer after her father's death they began the work. The construction company came with niggers and mules and machinery, and a foreman named Homer Barron, a Yankee—a big, dark, ready man, with a big voice and eyes lighter than his face. The little boys would follow in groups to hear him cuss the niggers, and the niggers singing in time to the rise and fall of picks. Pretty soon he knew everybody in town. Whenever you heard a lot of laughing anywhere about the square, Homer Barron would be in the center of the group. Presently we began to see him and Miss Emily on Sunday afternoons driving in the yellow-wheeled buggy and the matched team of bays from the livery stable.

At first we were glad that Miss Emily would have an interest, because the ladies all said, "Of course a Grierson would not think seriously of a Northerner, a day laborer." But there were still others, older people, who said that even grief could not cause a real lady to forget *noblesse oblige*—without calling it *noblesse oblige*. They just said, "Poor Emily. Her kinsfolk should come to her." She had some kin in Alabama; but years ago her father had fallen out with them over the estate of old lady Wyatt, the crazy woman, and there was no communication between the two families. They had not even been represented at the funeral.

And as soon as the old people said, "Poor Emily," the whispering began. "Do you suppose it's really so?" they said to one another. "Of course it is. What else could . . ." This behind their hands; rustling of craned silk and satin behind jalousies closed upon the sun of Sunday afternoon as the thin, swift clop-clop-clop of the matched team passed: "Poor Emily."

She carried her head high enough—even when we believed that she was fallen. It was as if she demanded more than ever the recognition of her dignity as the last Grierson; as if it had wanted that touch of earthiness to reaffirm her imperviousness. Like when she bought the rat poison, the arsenic. That was over a year after they had begun to say "Poor Emily," and while the two female cousins were visiting her.

"I want some poison," she said to the druggist. She was over thirty then, still a slight woman, though thinner than usual, with cold, haughty black eyes in a face the flesh of which was strained across the temples and about the eye-sockets as you imagine a lighthouse-keeper's face ought to look. "I want some poison," she said.

"Yes, Miss Emily. What kind? For rats and such? I'd recom—"

"I want the best you have. I don't care what kind."

The druggist named several. "They'll kill anything up to an elephant. But what you want is—"

"Arsenic," Miss Emily said. "Is that a good one?"

"Is . . . arsenic? Yes, ma'am. But what you want—"

"I want arsenic."

The druggist looked down at her. She looked back at him, erect, her face like a strained flag. "Why, of course," the druggist said. "If that's what you want. But the law requires you to tell what you are going to use it for."

Miss Emily just stared at him, her head tilted back in order to look him eye for eye, until he looked away and went and got the arsenic and wrapped it up. The Negro delivery boy brought her the package; the druggist didn't come back. When she opened the package at home there was written on the box, under the skull and bones: "For rats."

IV

So the next day we all said, "She will kill herself"; and we said it would be the best thing. When she had first begun to be seen with Homer Barron, we had said, "She will marry him." Then we said, "She will persuade him yet," because Homer himself had remarked—he liked men, and it was known that he drank with the younger men in the Elks' Club—that he was not a marrying man. Later we said, "Poor Emily" behind the jalousies as they passed on Sunday afternoon in the glittering buggy, Miss Emily with her head high and Homer Barron with his hat cocked and a cigar in his teeth, reins and whip in a yellow glove.

Then some of the ladies began to say that it was a disgrace to the town and a bad example to the young people. The men did not want to interfere, but at last the ladies forced the Baptist minister—Miss Emily's people were Episcopal—to call upon her. He would never divulge what happened during that interview, but he refused to go back again. The next Sunday they again drove about the streets, and the following day the minister's wife wrote to Miss Emily's relations in Alabama.

So she had blood-kin under her roof again and we sat back to watch developments. At first nothing happened. Then we were sure that they were to be married. We learned that Miss Emily had been to the jeweler's and ordered a man's toilet set in silver, with the letters H. B. on each piece. Two days later we learned that she had bought a complete outfit of men's clothing, including a nightshirt, and we said, "They are married." We were really glad. We were glad because the two female cousins were even more Grierson than Miss Emily had ever been.

So we were not surprised when Homer Barron—the streets had been finished some time since—was gone. We were a little disappointed that there was not a public

blowing-off, but we believed that he had gone on to prepare for Miss Emily's coming, or to give her a chance to
get rid of the cousins. (By that time it was a cabal, and
we were all Miss Emily's allies to help circumvent the
cousins.) Sure enough, after another week they departed.
And, as we had expected all along, within three days
Homer Barron was back in town. A neighbor saw the Negro man admit him at the kitchen door at dusk one evening.

And that was the last we saw of Homer Barron. And
of Miss Emily for some time. The Negro man went in and
out with the market basket, but the front door remained
closed. Now and then we would see her at a window for
a moment, as the men did that night when they sprinkled
the lime, but for almost six months she did not appear
on the streets. Then we knew that this was to be expected
too; as if that quality of her father which had thwarted
her woman's life so many times had been too virulent and
too furious to die.

When we next saw Miss Emily, she had grown fat and
her hair was turning gray. During the next few years it
grew grayer and grayer until it attained an even pepper-
and-salt iron-gray, when it ceased turning. Up to the day
of her death at seventy-four it was still that vigorous iron-
gray, like the hair of an active man.

From that time on her front door remained closed, save
for a period of six or seven years, when she was about
forty, during which she gave lessons in china-painting.
She fitted up a studio in one of the downstairs rooms,
where the daughters and granddaughters of Colonel
Sartoris' contemporaries were sent to her with the same
regularity and in the same spirit that they were sent to
church on Sundays with a twenty-five cent piece for the
collection plate. Meanwhile her taxes had been remitted.

Then the newer generation became the backbone and
the spirit of the town, and the painting pupils grew up
and fell away and did not send their children to her with

boxes of color and tedious brushes and pictures cut from the ladies' magazines. The front door closed upon the last one and remained closed for good. When the town got free postal delivery, Miss Emily alone refused to let them fasten the metal numbers above her door and attach a mailbox to it. She would not listen to them.

Daily, monthly, yearly we watched the Negro grow grayer and more stooped, going in and out with the market basket. Each December we sent her a tax notice, which would be returned by the post office a week later, unclaimed. Now and then we would see her in one of the downstairs windows—she had evidently shut up the top floor of the house—like the carven torso of an idol in a niche, looking or not looking at us, we could never tell which. Thus she passed from generation to generation— dear, inescapable, impervious, tranquil, and perverse.

And so she died. Fell ill in the house filled with dust and shadows, with only a doddering Negro man to wait on her. We did not even know she was sick; we had long since given up trying to get any information from the Negro. He talked to no one, probably not even to her, for his voice had grown harsh and rusty, as if from disuse.

She died in one of the downstairs rooms, in a heavy walnut bed with a curtain, her gray head propped on a pillow yellow and moldy with age and lack of sunlight.

v

The Negro met the first of the ladies at the front door and let them in, with their hushed, sibilant voices and their quick, curious glances, and then he disappeared. He walked right through the house and out the back and was not seen again.

The two female cousins came at once. They held the funeral on the second day, with the town coming to look at Miss Emily beneath a mass of bought flowers, with the crayon face of her father musing profoundly above the bier and the ladies sibilant and macabre; and the very old men—some in their brushed Confederate uniforms— on the porch and the lawn, talking of Miss Emily as if she had been a contemporary of theirs, believing that they had danced with her and courted her perhaps, confusing time with its mathematical progression, as the old do, to whom all the past is not a diminishing road but, instead, a huge meadow which no winter ever quite touches, divided from them now by the narrow bottle-neck of the most recent decade of years.

Already we knew that there was one room in that region above stairs which no one had seen in forty years, and which would have to be forced. They waited until Miss Emily was decently in the ground before they opened it.

The violence of breaking down the door seemed to fill this room with pervading dust. A thin, acrid pall as of the tomb seemed to lie everywhere upon this room decked and furnished as for a bridal: upon the valence curtains of faded rose color, upon the rose-shaded lights, upon the dressing table, upon the delicate array of crystal and the man's toilet things backed with tarnished silver, silver so tarnished that the monogram was obscured. Among them lay a collar and tie, as if they had just been removed, which, lifted, left upon the surface a pale crescent in the dust. Upon a chair hung the suit, carefully folded; beneath it the two mute shoes and the discarded socks.

The man himself lay in the bed.

For a long while we just stood there, looking down at the profound and fleshless grin. The body had apparently once lain in the attitude of an embrace, but now the long sleep that outlasts love, that conquers even the grimace of love, had cuckolded him. What was left of him, rotted beneath what was left of the nightshirt, had become inextricable from the bed in which he lay; and upon him and upon the pillow beside him lay that even coating of the patient and biding dust.

Then we noticed that in the second pillow was the indentation of a head. One of us lifted something from it, and leaning forward, that faint and invisible dust dry and acrid in the nostrils, we saw a long strand of iron-gray hair.

1928

Dilsey

The day dawned bleak and chill, a moving wall of gray light out of the northeast which, instead of dissolving into moisture, seemed to disintegrate into minute and venomous particles like dust that, when Dilsey opened the door of the cabin and emerged, needled laterally into her flesh, precipitating not so much a moisture as a substance partaking of the quality of thin, not quite congealed oil. She wore a stiff black straw hat perched upon her turban, and a maroon velvet cape with a border of mangy and anonymous fur above a dress of purple silk, and she stood in the door for a while with her myriad and sunken face lifted to the weather, and one gaunt hand flac-soled as the belly of a fish, then she moved the cape aside and examined the bosom of her gown.

The gown fell gauntly from her shoulders, across her fallen breasts, then tightened upon her paunch and fell again, ballooning a little above the nether garments which she would remove layer by layer as the spring accomplished and the warm days, in color regal and moribund. She had been a big woman once but now her skeleton rose, draped loosely in unpadded skin that tightened again upon a paunch almost dropsical, as though muscle and tissue had been courage or fortitude which the days or the years had consumed until only the indomitable skeleton was left rising like a ruin or a landmark above the somnolent and impervious guts, and above that the collapsed face that gave the impression of the bones themselves being outside the flesh, lifted into the driving day with an expression at once fatalistic and of a child's astonished disappointment, until she turned and entered the house again and closed the door.

The earth immediately about the door was bare. It had a patina, as though from the soles of bare feet in generations, like old silver or the walls of Mexican houses which have been plastered by hand. Beside the house, shading it in summer, stood three mulberry trees, the fledged leaves that would later be broad and placid as the palms of hands steaming flatly undulant upon the driving air. A pair of jaybirds came up from nowhere, whirled up on the blast like gaudy scraps of cloth or paper and lodged in the mulberries, where they swung in raucous tilt and recover, screaming into the wind that ripped their harsh cries onward and away like scraps of paper or of cloth in turn. Then three more joined them and they swung and tilted in the wrung branches for a time, screaming. The door of the cabin opened and Dilsey emerged once more, this time in a man's felt hat and an army overcoat, beneath the frayed skirts of which her blue gingham dress fell in uneven balloonings, streaming too about her as she crossed the yard and mounted the steps to the kitchen door.

A moment later she emerged, carrying an open umbrella now, which she slanted ahead into the wind, and crossed to the woodpile and laid the umbrella down, still open. Immediately she caught at it and arrested it and held to it for a while, looking about her. Then she closed it and laid it down and stacked stovewood into her crooked arm, against her breast, and picked up the umbrella and got it open at last and returned to the steps and held the wood precariously balanced while she contrived to close the umbrella, which she propped in the corner just within the door. She dumped the wood into the box behind the stove. Then she removed the overcoat and hat and took a soiled apron down from the wall and put it on and built a fire in the stove. While she was doing so, rattling the grate bars and clattering the lids, Mrs. Compson began to call her from the head of the stairs.

She wore a dressing gown of quilted black satin, holding it close under her chin. In the other hand she held a red rubber hot water bottle and she stood at the head of the back stairway, calling, "Dilsey," at steady and inflectionless intervals into the quiet stairwell that descended into complete darkness, then opened again where a gray window fell across it. "Dilsey," she called, without inflection or emphasis or haste, as though she were not listening for a reply at all. "Dilsey."

Dilsey answered and ceased clattering the stove, but before she could cross the kitchen Mrs. Compson called her again, and before she crossed the dining room and brought her head into relief against the gray splash of the window, still again.

"All right," Dilsey said, "all right, here I is. I'll fill hit soon ez I git some hot water." She gathered up her skirts and mounted the stairs, wholly blotting the gray light. "Put hit down dar en g'awn back to bed."

"I couldn't understand what was the matter," Mrs. Compson said. "I've been lying awake for an hour at least, without hearing a sound from the kitchen."

"You put hit down and g'awn back to bed," Dilsey said. She toiled painfully up the steps, shapeless, breathing heavily. "I'll have de fire gwine in a minute, en de water hot in two mo."

"I've been lying there for an hour, at least," Mrs. Compson said. "I thought maybe you were waiting for me to come down and start the fire."

Dilsey reached the top of the stairs and took the water bottle. "I'll fix hit in a minute," she said. "Luster overslep' dis mawnin, up half de night at dat show. I gwine build de fire myself. Go on now, so you won't wake de others twell I ready."

"If you permit Luster to do things that interfere with his work, you'll have to suffer for it yourself," Mrs. Compson said. "Jason won't like this if he hears about it. You know he won't."

"Twusn't none of Jason's money he went on," Dilsey said. "Dat's one thing sho." She went on down the stairs. Mrs. Compson returned to her room. As she got into bed again she could hear Dilsey yet descending the stairs with a sort of painful and terrific slowness that would have become maddening had it not presently ceased beyond the flapping diminishment of the pantry door.

She entered the kitchen and built up the fire and began to prepare breakfast. In the midst of this she ceased and went to the window and looked out toward her cabin, then she went to the door and opened it and shouted into the driving weather.

"Luster!" she shouted, standing to listen, tilting her face from the wind. "You, Luster?" She listened, then as she prepared to shout again Luster appeared around the corner of the kitchen.

"Ma'am?" he said innocently, so innocently that Dilsey looked down at him, for a moment motionless, with something more than mere surprise.

"Whar you at?" she said.

"Nowhere," he said. "Jes in de cellar."

"Whut you doin' in de cellar?" she said. "Don't stand dar in de rain, fool," she said.

"Ain't doin' nothin'," he said. He came up the steps.

"Don't you dare come in dis do' widout a armful of wood," she said. "Here I done had to tote yo wood en build yo fire bofe. Didn't I tole you not to leave dis place last night befo' dat woodbox was full to de top?"

"I did," Luster said. "I filled hit."

"Whar hit gone to, den?"

"I don't know'm. I ain't teched hit."

"Well, you git hit full up now," she said. "And git on up den en see 'bout Benjy."

She shut the door. Luster went to the woodpile. The five jaybirds whirled over the house, screaming, and into the mulberries again. He watched them. He picked up a rock and threw it. "Whoo," he said, "git on back to hell, whar you belong at. 'Tain't Monday yit."

He loaded himself mountainously with stove wood. He could not see over it, and he staggered to the steps and up them and blundered crashing against the door, shedding billets. Then Dilsey came and opened the door for him and he blundered across the kitchen. "You, Luster!" she shouted, but he had already hurled the wood into the box with a thunderous crash. "Hah!" he said.

"Is you tryin' to wake up de whole house?" Dilsey said. She hit him on the back of his head with the flat of her hand. "Go on up dar and git Benjy dressed, now."

"Yessum," he said. He went toward the outer door.

"Whar you gwine?" Dilsey said.

"I thought I better go round de house en in by de front, so I won't wake up Miss Cahline en dem."

"You go on up dem back stairs like I tole you en git Benjy's clothes on him," Dilsey said. "Go on, now."

"Yessum," Luster said. He returned and left by the dining-room door. After a while it ceased to flap. Dilsey prepared to make biscuit. As she ground the sifter steadily above the breadboard, she sang, to herself at first, something without particular tune or words, repetitive, mournful and plaintive, austere, as she ground a faint, steady snowing of flour onto the breadboard. The stove had begun to heat the room and to fill it with murmurous minors of the fire, and presently she was singing louder, as if her voice too had been thawed out by the growing warmth, and then Mrs. Compson called her name again from within the house. Dilsey raised her face as if her eyes could and did penetrate the walls and ceiling and saw the old woman in her quilted dressing gown at the head of the stairs, calling her name with machine-like regularity.

"Oh, Lawd," Dilsey said. She set the sifter down and swept up the hem of her apron and wiped her hands and caught up the bottle from the chair on which she had laid it and gathered her apron about the handle of the kettle which was now jetting faintly. "Jes a minute," she called. "De water jes dis minute got hot."

It was not the bottle which Mrs. Compson wanted, however, and clutching it by the neck like a dead hen Dilsey went to the foot of the stairs and looked upward.

"Ain't Luster up dar wid him?" she said.

"Luster hasn't been in the house. I've been lying here listening for him. I knew he would be late, but I did hope he'd come in time to keep Benjamin from disturbing Jason on Jason's one day in the week to sleep in the morning."

"I don't see how you expect anybody to sleep, wid you standin' in de hall, holl'in at folks fum de crack of dawn," Dilsey said. She began to mount the stairs, toiling heavily. "I sont dat boy up dar half hour ago."

Mrs. Compson watched her, holding the dressing gown under her chin. "What are you going to do?" she said.

"Gwine git Benjy dressed en bring him down to de kitchen, whar he won't wake Jason en Quentin," Dilsey said.

"Haven't you started breakfast yet?"

"I'll tend to dat too," Dilsey said. "You better git back in bed twell Luster make yo fire. Hit cold dis mawnin."

"I know it," Mrs. Compson said. "My feet are like ice. They were so cold they waked me up." She watched Dilsey mount the stairs. It took her a long while. "You know how it frets Jason when breakfast is late," Mrs. Compson said.

"I can't do but one thing at a time," Dilsey said. "You git on back to bed, fo I has you on my hands dis mawnin too."

"If you're going to drop everything to dress Benjamin, I'd better come down and get breakfast. You know as well as I do how Jason acts when it's late."

"En who gwine eat yo messin'?" Dilsey said. "Tell me dat. Go on now," she said, toiling upward. Mrs. Compson stood watching her as she mounted, steadying herself against the wall with one hand, holding her skirts up with the other.

"Are you going to wake him up just to dress him?" she said.

Dilsey stopped. With her foot lifted to the next step she stood there, her hand against the wall and the gray splash of the window behind her, motionless and shapeless she looked.

"He ain't awake den?" she said.

"He wasn't when I looked in," Mrs. Compson said. "But it's past his time. He never does sleep after half past seven. You know he doesn't."

Dilsey said nothing. She made no further move, but though she could not see her save as a blobby shape without depth, Mrs. Compson knew that she had lowered her face a little and that she stood now like a cow in the rain, as she held the empty water bottle by its neck.

"You're not the one who has to bear it," Mrs. Compson said. "It's not your responsibility. You can go away. You don't have to bear the brunt of it day in and day out. You owe nothing to them, to Mr. Compson's memory. I know you have never had any tenderness for Jason. You've never tried to conceal it."

Dilsey said nothing. She turned slowly and descended, lowering her body from step to step, as a small child does, her hand against the wall. "You go on and let him alone," she said. "Don't go in dar no mo', now. I'll send Luster up soon as I find him. Let him alone, now."

She returned to the kitchen. She looked into the stove, then she drew her apron over her head and donned the overcoat and opened the outer door and looked up and down the yard. The weather drove upon her flesh, harsh and minute, but the scene was empty of all else that moved. She descended the steps, gingerly, as if for silence, and went around the corner of the kitchen. As she did so Luster emerged quickly and innocently from the cellar door.

Dilsey stopped. "What you up to?" she said.

"Nothin'," Luster said. "Mr. Jason say fer me to find out whar dat water leak in de cellar fum."

"En when was hit he say fer you to do dat?" Dilsey said. "Last New Year's day, wasn't hit?"

"I thought I jes be lookin whiles dey sleep," Luster said. Dilsey went to the cellar door. He stood aside and she peered down into the obscurity odorous of dank earth and mold and rubber.

"Huh," Dilsey said. She looked at Luster again. He met her gaze blandly, innocent and open. "I don't know what you up to, but you ain't got no business doin' hit. You jes trying me too dis mawnin cause de others is, ain't you? You git on up dar en see to Benjy, you hear?"

"Yessum," Luster said. He went on toward the kitchen steps, swiftly.

"Here," Dilsey said, "you git me another armful of wood while I got you."

"Yessum," he said. He passed her on the steps and went to the woodpile. When he blundered again at the door a moment later, again invisible and blind within and beyond his wooden avatar, Dilsey opened the door and guided him across the kitchen with a firm hand.

"Jes thow hit at dat box again, " she said, "Jes thow hit."

"I got to," Luster said, panting, "I can't put hit down no other way."

"Den you stand dar en hold hit a while," Dilsey said. She unloaded him a stick at a time. "Whut got into you dis mawnin? Here I sont you fer wood en you ain't never brought mo'n six sticks at a time to save yo life twell today. Whut you fixin to ax me kin you do now? Ain't dat show left town yit?"

"Yessum. Hit done gone."

She put the last stick into the box. "Now you go on up dar wid Benjy, like I tole you befo," she said. "And I don't want nobody else yellin' down dem stairs at me twell I rings de bell. You hear me."

"Yessum," Luster said. He vanished through the swing door. Dilsey put some more wood in the stove and returned to the breadboard. Presently she began to sing again.

The room grew warmer. Soon Dilsey's skin had taken on a rich, lustrous quality as compared with that as of a faint dusting of wood ashes which both it and Luster's had worn, as she moved about the kitchen, gathering about her the raw materials of food, coördinating the meal. On the wall above a cupboard, invisible save at night, by lamplight and even then evincing an enigmatic profundity because it had but one hand, a cabinet clock ticked, then with a preliminary sound as if it had cleared its throat, struck five times.

"Eight o'clock," Dilsey said. She ceased and tilted her head upward, listening. But there was no sound save the clock and the fire. She opened the oven and looked at the pan of bread, then stooping she paused while someone descended the stairs. She heard the feet cross the dining-room, then the swing door opened and Luster entered, followed by a big man who appeared to have been shaped of some substance whose particles would not or did not cohere to one another or to the frame which supported it. His skin was dead looking and hairless; dropsical too, he moved with a shambling gait like a trained bear. His hair was pale and fine. It had been brushed smoothly down upon his brow like that of children in daguerreotypes. His eyes were clear, of the pale sweet blue of cornflowers, his thick mouth hung open, drooling a little.

"Is he cold?" Dilsey said. She wiped her hands on her apron and touched his hand.

"Ef he ain't, I is," Luster said. "Always cold Easter. Ain't never seen hit fail. Miss Cahline say ef you ain't got time to fix her hot water bottle to never mind about hit."

"Oh, Lawd," Dilsey said. She drew a chair into the corner between the woodbox and the stove. The man went obediently and sat in it. "Look in de dinin' room and see whar I laid dat bottle down," Dilsey said. Luster fetched the bottle from the dining-room and Dilsey filled it and gave it to him. "Hurry up, now," she said. "See ef Jason 'wake now. Tell em hit's all ready."

Luster went out. Ben sat beside the stove. He sat loosely, utterly motionless save for his head, which made a continual bobbing sort of movement as he watched Dilsey with his sweet vague gaze as she moved about. Luster returned.

"He up," he said, "Miss Cahline say put hit on de table." He came to the stove and spread his hands palm down above the firebox. "He up, too," he said. "Gwine hit wid bofe feet dis mawnin'."

"Whut's de matter now?" Dilsey said. "Git away fum dar. How kin I do anything wid you standing over de stove?"

"I cold," Luster said.

"You ought to thought about dat whiles you wus down dar in dat cellar," Dilsey said. "Whut de matter wid Jason?"

"Sayin' me en Benjy broke dat winder in his room."

"Is dey one broke?" Dilsey said.

"Dat's whut he sayin'," Luster said. "Say I broke hit."

"How could you, when he keep hit locked all day en night?"

"Say I broke hit chunkin' rocks at hit," Luster said.

"En did you?"

"Nome," Luster said.

"Don't lie to me, boy," Dilsey said.

"I never done hit," Luster said. "Ask Benjy ef I did. I ain't stud'in' dat winder."

"Who could a broke hit, den?" Dilsey said. "He jes tryin hisself, to wake Quentin up," she said, taking the pan of biscuits out of the stove.

"Reckin so," Luster said. "Dese is funny folks. Glad I ain't none of em."

"Ain't none of who?" Dilsey said. "Lemme tell you somethin', nigger boy, you got jes es much Compson devilment in you es any of em. Is you right sho you never broke dat window?"

"Whut I want to break hit fur?"

"Whut you do any of yo devilment fur?" Dilsey said. "Watch him now, so he can't burn his hand again twell I git de table set."

She went to the dining-room, where they heard her moving about, then she returned and set a plate at the kitchen table and set food there. Ben watched her, slobbering, making a faint, eager sound.

"All right, honey," she said. "Here yo breakfast. Bring his chair, Luster." Luster moved the chair up and Ben sat down, whimpering and slobbering. Dilsey tied a cloth about his neck and wiped his mouth with the end of it. "And see kin you kep fum messin' up his clothes one time," she said, handing Luster a spoon.

Ben ceased whimpering. He watched the spoon as it rose to his mouth. It was as if even eagerness were muscle-bound in him too, and hunger itself inarticulate, not knowing it is hunger. Luster fed him with skill and detachment. Now and then his attention would return long enough to enable him to feint the spoon and cause Ben to close his mouth upon the empty air, but it was apparent that Luster's mind was elsewhere. His other hand lay on the back of the chair and upon that dead surface it moved tentatively, delicately, as if he were picking an inaudible tune out of the dead void, and once he even forgot to tease Ben with the spoon while his fingers teased out of the slain wood a soundless and involved arpeggio until Ben recalled him by whimpering again.

In the dining-room Dilsey moved back and forth. Presently she rang a small clear bell, then in the kitchen Luster heard Mrs. Compson and Jason descending, and Jason's voice, and he rolled his eyes whitely with listening.

"Sure, I know they didn't break it," Jason said. "Sure, I know that. Maybe the change of weather broke it."

"I don't see how it could have," Mrs. Compson said. "Your room stays locked all day long, just as you leave it when you go to town. None of us ever go in there except Sunday, to clean it. I don't want you to think that I would go where I'm not wanted, or that I would permit anyone else to."

"I never said you broke it, did I?" Jason said.

"I don't want to go in your room," Mrs. Compson said. "I respect anybody's private affairs. I wouldn't put my foot over the threshold, even if I had a key."

"Yes," Jason said, "I know your keys won't fit. That's why I had the lock changed. What I want to know is, how that window got broken."

"Luster say he didn't do hit," Dilsey said.

"I knew that without asking him," Jason said. "Where's Quentin?" he said.

"Where she is ev'y Sunday mawnin," Dilsey said. "Whut got into you de last few days, anyhow?"

"Well, we're going to change all that," Jason said. "Go up and tell her breakfast is ready."

"You leave her alone now, Jason," Dilsey said. "She gits up fer breakfast ev'y week mawnin, en Cahline lets her stay in bed ev'y Sunday. You knows dat."

"I can't keep a kitchen full of niggers to wait on her pleasure, much as I'd like to," Jason said. "Go and tell her to come down to breakfast."

"Ain't nobody have to wait on her," Dilsey said. "I puts her breakfast in de warmer en she—"

"Did you hear me?" Jason said.

"I hears you," Dilsey said. "All I been hearin', when you in de house. Ef hit ain't Quentin er yo maw, hit's Luster en Benjy. Whut you let him go on dat way fer, Miss Cahline?"

"You'd better do as he says," Mrs. Compson said. "He's head of the house now. It's his right to require us to respect his wishes. I try to do it, and if I can, you can too."

" 'Tain't no sense in him bein' so bad tempered he got to make Quentin git up jes to suit him," Dilsey said. "Maybe you think she broke dat window."

"She would, if she happened to think of it," Jason said. "You go and do what I told you."

"En I wouldn't blame her none ef she did," Dilsey said, going toward the stairs. "Wid you naggin' at her all de blessed time you in de house."

"Hush, Dilsey," Mrs. Compson said. "It's neither your place nor mine to tell Jason what to do. Sometimes I think he is wrong, but I try to obey his wishes for you all's sakes. If I'm strong enough to come to the table, Quentin can too."

Dilsey went out. They heard her mounting the stairs. They heard her a long while on the stairs.

"You've got a prize set of servants," Jason said. He helped his mother and himself to food. "Did you ever have one that was worth killing? You must have had some before I was big enough to remember."

"I have to humor them," Mrs. Compson said. "I have to depend on them so completely. It's not as if I were strong. I wish I were. I wish I could do all the housework myself. I could at least take that much off your shoulders."

"And a fine pigsty we'd live in, too," Jason said. "Hurry up, Dilsey," he shouted.

"I know you blame me," Mrs. Compson said, "for letting them off to go to church today."

"Go where?" Jason said. "Hasn't that damn show left yet?"

"To church," Mrs. Compson said. "The darkies are

having a special Easter service. I promised Dilsey two weeks ago that they could get off."

"Which means we'll eat cold dinner," Jason said, "or none at all."

"I know it's my fault," Mrs. Compson said. "I know you blame me."

"For what?" Jason said. "You never resurrected Christ, did you?"

They heard Dilsey mount the final stair, then her slow feet overhead.

"Quentin," she said. When she called the first time Jason laid his knife and fork down and he and his mother appeared to wait across the table from one another, in identical attitudes; the one cold and shrewd, with close-thatched brown hair curled into two stubborn hooks, one on either side of his forehead like a bartender in carica-ture, and hazel eyes with black-ringed irises like marbles, the other cold and querulous, with perfectly white hair and eyes pouched and baffled and so dark as to appear to be all pupil or all iris.

"Quentin," Dilsey said, "get up, honey. Dey waitin breakfast on you."

"I can't understand how that window got broken," Mrs. Compson said. "Are you sure it was done yesterday? It could have been like that a long time, with the warm weather. The upper sash, behind the shade like that."

"I've told you for the last time that it happened yes-terday," Jason said. "Don't you reckon I know the room I live in? Do you reckon I could have lived in it a week with a hole in the window you could stick your hand—" his voice ceased, ebbed, left him staring at his mother with eyes that for an instant were quite empty of any-thing. It was as though his eyes were holding their breath, while his mother looked at him, her face flaccid and quer-ulous, interminable, clairvoyant yet obtuse. As they sat so Dilsey said,

"Quentin. Don't play wid me, honey. Come on to breakfast, honey. Dey waitin' fer you."

"I can't understand it," Mrs. Compson said. "It's just as if somebody had tried to break into the house—" Jason sprang up. His chair crashed over backward. "What—" Mrs. Compson said, staring at him as he ran past her and went jumping up the stairs, where he met Dilsey. His face was now in shadow, and Dilsey said,

"She sullin. Yo ma ain't unlocked—" But Jason ran on past her and along the corridor to a door. He didn't call. He grasped the knob and tried it, then he stood with the knob in his hand and his head bent a little, as if he were listening to something much further away than the dimensioned room beyond the door, and which he already heard. His attitude was that of one who goes through the motions of listening in order to deceive himself as to what he already hears. Behind him Mrs. Compson mounted the stairs, calling his name. Then she saw Dilsey and she quit calling him and began to call Dilsey instead.

"I told you she ain't unlocked dat do' yit," Dilsey said.

When she spoke he turned and ran toward her, but his voice was quiet, matter of fact. "She carry the key with her?" he said. "Has she got it now, I mean, or will she have—"

"Dilsey," Mrs. Compson said on the stairs.

"Is which?" Dilsey said. "Whyn't you let—"

"The key," Jason said, "to that room. Does she carry it with her all the time. Mother." Then he saw Mrs. Compson and he went down the stairs and met her. "Give me the key," he said. He fell to pawing at the pockets of the rusty black dressing sacque she wore. She resisted.

"Jason," she said, "Jason! Are you and Dilsey trying to put me to bed again?" she said, trying to fend him off. "Can't you even let me have Sunday in peace?"

"The key," Jason said, pawing at her. "Give it here." He looked back at the door, as if he expected it to fly open before he could get back to it with the key he did not yet have.

"You, Dilsey!" Mrs. Compson said, clutching her sacque about her.

"Give me the key, you old fool!" Jason cried suddenly. From her pocket he tugged a huge bunch of rusted keys on an iron ring like a medieval jailer's and ran back up the hall with the two women behind him.

"You, Jason!" Mrs. Compson said. "He will never find the right one," she said. "You know I never let anyone take my keys, Dilsey," she said. She began to wail.

"Hush," Dilsey said. "He ain't gwine do nothin' to her. I ain't gwine let him."

"But on Sunday morning, in my own house," Mrs. Compson said. "When I've tried so hard to raise them Christians. Let me find the right key, Jason," she said. She put her hand on his arm. Then she began to struggle with him, but he flung her aside with a motion of his elbow and looked around at her for a moment, his eyes cold and harried, then he turned to the door again and the unwieldy keys.

"Hush," Dilsey said. "You, Jason!"

"Something terrible has happened," Mrs. Compson said, wailing again. "I know it has. You, Jason," she said, grasping at him again. "He won't even let me find the key to a room in my own house!"

"Now, now," Dilsey said, "whut kin happen? I right here. I ain't gwine let him hurt her. Quentin," she said, raising her voice, "don't you be skeered, honey, I'se right here."

The door opened, swung inward. He stood in it for a moment, hiding the room, then he stepped aside. "Go in," he said in a thick, light voice. They went in. It was not a girl's room. It was not anybody's room, and the faint scent of cheap cosmetics and the few feminine objects and the other evidences of crude and hopeless efforts to feminize it but added to its anonymity, giving it that dead and ster-

eotyped transience of rooms in assignation houses. The
bed had not been disturbed. On the floor lay a soiled undergarment of cheap silk a little too pink; from a half-open
bureau drawer dangled a single stocking.

The window was open. A pear tree grew there, close
against the house. It was in bloom and the branches
scraped and rasped against the house and the myriad air,
driving in the window, brought into the room the forlorn
scent of the blossoms.

"Dar now," Dilsey said, "didn't I told you she all
right?"

"All right?" Mrs. Compson said. Dilsey followed her
into the room and touched her.

"You come on and lay down, now," she said. "I find
her in ten minutes."

Mrs. Compson shook her off. "Find the note," she said.
"Quentin left a note when he did it."

"All right," Dilsey said, "I'll find hit. You come on to
yo room, now."

"I knew the minute they named her Quentin this would
happen," Mrs. Compson said. She went to the bureau and
began to turn over the scattered objects there—scent bottles, a box of powder, a chewed pencil, a pair of scissors
with one broken blade lying upon a darned scarf dusted with
powder and stained with rouge. "Find the note," she said.

"I is," Dilsey said. "You come on, now. Me and Jason'll
find hit. You come on to yo' room."

"Jason," Mrs. Compson said, "where is he?" She went
to the door. Dilsey followed her on down the hall, to another door. It was closed. "Jason," she called through the
door. There was no answer. She tried the knob, then she
called him again. But there was still no answer, for he
was hurling things backward out of the closet: garments,
shoes, a suitcase. Then he emerged carrying a sawn section of tongue-and-groove planking and laid it down and
entered the closet again and emerged with a metal box.
He set it on the bed and stood looking at the broken lock

while he dug a key ring from his pocket and selected a key, and for a time longer he stood with the selected key, in his hand, looking at the broken lock, then he put the keys back in his pocket and carefully tilted the contents of the box out upon the bed. Still carefully he sorted the papers, taking them up one at a time and shaking them. Then he upended the box and shook it too and slowly replaced the papers and stood again, looking at the broken lock, with the box in his hands and his head bent. Outside the window he heard some jaybirds swirl shrieking past, and away, their cries whipping away along the wind, and an automobile passed somewhere and died away also. His mother spoke his name again beyond the door, but he didn't move. He heard Dilsey lead her away up the hall, and then a door closed. Then he replaced the box in the closet and flung the garments back into it and went downstairs to the telephone. While he stood there with the receiver to his ear, waiting, Dilsey came down the stairs. She looked at him, without stopping, and went on.

The wire opened. "This is Jason Compson," he said, his voice so harsh and thick that he had to repeat himself. "Jason Compson," he said, controlling his voice. "Have a car ready, with a deputy, if you can't go, in ten minutes. I'll be there— What?—Robbery. My house. I know who it— Robbery, I say. Have a car read— What? Aren't you a paid law enforcement— Yes, I'll be there in five minutes. Have that car ready to leave at once. If you don't, I'll report it to the governor."

He clapped the receiver back and crossed the diningroom, where the scarce-broken meal now lay cold on the table, and entered the kitchen. Dilsey was filling the hot water bottle. Ben sat, tranquil and empty. Beside him Luster looked like a fyce dog, brightly watchful. He was eating something. Jason went on across the kitchen.

"Ain't you going to eat no breakfast?" Dilsey said. He paid her no attention. "Go on and eat yo breakfast, Jason."

He went on. The outer door banged behind him. Luster rose and went to the window and looked out.

"Whoo," he said, "whut happenin' up dar? He been beatin' Miss Quentin?"

"You hush yo mouf," Dilsey said. "You git Benjy started now en I beat yo head off. You keep him quiet es you kin twell I get back, now." She screwed the cap on the bottle and went out. They heard her go up the stairs, then they heard Jason pass the house in his car. Then there was no sound in the kitchen save the simmering murmur of the kettle and the clock.

"You know whut I bet?" Luster said. "I bet he beat her. I bet he knock her in de head en now he gone fer de doctor. Dat's whut I bet." The clock ticktocked, solemn and profound. It might have been the dry pulse of the decaying house itself; after a while it whirred and cleared its throat and struck six times. Ben looked up at it, then he looked at the bullet-like silhouette of Luster's head in the window and he began to bob his head again, drooling. He whimpered.

"Hush up, loony," Luster said without turning. "Look like we ain't gwine git to go to no church today." But Ben sat in the chair, his big soft hands dangling between his knees, moaning faintly. Suddenly he wept, a slow bellowing sound, meaningless and sustained. "Hush," Luster said. He turned and lifted his hand. "You want me to whup you?" But Ben looked at him, bellowing slowly with each expiration. Luster came and shook him. "You hush dis minute!" he shouted. "Here," he said. He hauled Ben out of the chair and dragged the chair around facing the stove and opened the door to the firebox and shoved Ben into the chair. They looked like a tug nudging at a clumsy tanker in a narrow dock. Ben sat down again facing the rosy door. He hushed. Then they heard the clock again, and Dilsey slow on the stairs. When she entered he began to whimper again. Then he lifted his voice.

"Whut you done to him?" Dilsey said. "Why can't you let him 'lone dis mawnin, of all times?"

"I ain't doin' nothin' to him," Luster said. "Mr. Jason skeered him, dat's whut hit is. He ain't kilt Miss Quentin, is he?"

"Hush, Benjy," Dilsey said. He hushed. She went to the window and looked out. "Is it quit rainin'?" she said.

"Yessum," Luster said. "Quit long time ago."

"Den y'all go out do's awhile," she said. "I jes got Miss Cahline quiet now."

"Is we gwine to church?" Luster said.

"I let you know bout dat when de time come. You keep him away fum de house twell I calls you."

"Kin we go to de pastuh?" Luster said.

"All right. Only you keep him away fum de house. I done stood all I kin."

"Yessum," Luster said. "Whar Mr. Jason gone, mammy?"

"Dat's some mo' of yo' business, ain't it?" Dilsey said. She began to clear the table. "Hush, Benjy. Luster gwine take you out to play."

"Whut he done to Miss Quentin, mammy?" Luster said.

"Ain't done nothin' to her. You all git on outen here?"

"I bet she ain't here," Luster said.

Dilsey looked at him. "How you know she ain't here?"

"Me and Benjy seed her clamb out de window last night. Didn't us, Benjy?"

"You did?" Dilsey said, looking at him.

"We sees her doin' hit ev'y night," Luster said. "Clamb right down dat pear tree."

"Don't you lie to me, nigger boy," Dilsey said.

"I ain't lyin'. Ask Benjy ef I is."

"Whyn't you say somethin' about it, den?"

" 'Twarn't none o' my business," Luster said. "I ain't gwine git mixed up in white folks business. Come on here, Benjy, les go out do's."

They went out. Dilsey stood for a while at the table,

then she went and cleared the breakfast things from the dining-room and ate her breakfast and cleaned up the kitchen. Then she removed her apron and hung it up and went to the foot of the stairs and listened for a moment. There was no sound. She donned the overcoat and the hat and went across to her cabin.

The rain had stopped. The air now drove out of the southeast, broken overhead into blue patches. Upon the crest of a hill beyond the trees and roofs and spires of town sunlight lay like a pale scrap of cloth, was blotted away. Upon the air a bell came, then as if at a signal, other bells took up the sound and repeated it.

The cabin door opened and Dilsey emerged, again in the maroon cape and the purple gown, and wearing soiled white elbow-length gloves and minus her headcloth now. She came into the yard and called Luster. She waited a while, then she went to the house and around it to the cellar door, moving close to the wall, and looked into the door. Ben sat on the steps. Before him Luster squatted on the damp floor. He held a saw in his left hand, the blade sprung a little by pressure of his hand, and he was in the act of striking the blade with the worn wooden mallet with which she had been making beaten biscuit for more than thirty years. The saw gave forth a single sluggish twang that ceased with lifeless alacrity, leaving the blade in a thin clean curve between Luster's hand and the floor. Still, inscrutable, it bellied.

"Dat's de way he done hit," Luster said. "I jes ain't foun' de right thing to hit it wid."

"Dat's whut you doin', is it?" Dilsey said. "Bring me dat mallet," she said.

"I ain't hurt hit," Luster said.

"Bring hit here," Dilsey said. "Put dat saw whar you got hit first."

He put the saw away and brought the mallet to her. Then Ben wailed again, hopeless and prolonged. It was nothing. Just sound. It might have been all time and in-

justice and sorrow become vocal for an instant by a conjunction of planets.

"Listen at him," Luster said. "He been gwine on dat
way ev'y since you sont us outen de house. I don't know
whut got into him dis mawnin."

"Bring him here," Dilsey said.

"Come on, Benjy," Luster said. He went back down
the steps and took Ben's arm. He came obediently, wailing, that slow hoarse sound that ships make, that seems
to begin before the sound itself has started, seems to
cease before the sound itself has stopped.

"Run and git his cap," Dilsey said. "Don't make no
noise Miss Cahline kin hear. Hurry, now. We already
late."

"She gwine hear him anyhow, ef you don't stop him,"
Luster said.

"He stop when we git off de place," Dilsey said. "He
smellin' hit. Dat's whut hit is."

"Smell whut, mammy?" Luster said.

"You go git dat cap," Dilsey said. Luster went on. They
stood in the cellar door, Ben one step below her. The sky
was broken now into scudding patches that dragged their
swift shadows up out of the shabby garden, over the
broken fence and across the yard. Dilsey stroked Ben's
head, slowly and steadily, smoothing the bang upon his
brow. He wailed quietly, unhurriedly. "Hush," Dilsey
said. "Hush, now. We be gone in a minute. Hush, now."
He wailed quietly and steadily.

Luster returned, wearing a stiff new straw hat with a
colored band and carrying a cloth cap. The hat seemed
to isolate Luster's skull, in the beholder's eye as a spot-
light would, in all its individual planes and angles. So pe-
culiarly individual was its shape that at first glance the
hat appeared to be on the head of someone standing immediately behind Luster. Dilsey looked at the hat.

"Whyn't you wear yo' old hat?" she said.

"Couldn't find hit," Luster said.

"I bet you couldn't. I bet you fixed hit last night so you couldn't find hit. You fixin' to ruin dat un."

"Aw, mammy," Luster said, "hit ain't gwine rain."

"How you know? You go git dat old hat en put dat new un away."

"Aw, mammy."

"Den you go git de umbreller."

"Aw, mammy."

"Take yo choice," Dilsey said. "Git yo old hat, er de umbreller. I don't keer which."

Luster went to the cabin. Ben wailed quietly.

"Come on," Dilsey said, "dey kin ketch up wid us. We gwine to hear de singin'." They went around the house, toward the gate. "Hush," Dilsey said from time to time as they went down the drive. They reached the gate. Dilsey opened it. Luster was coming down the drive behind them, carrying the umbrella. A woman was with him. "Here dey come," Dilsey said. They passed out the gate. "Now, den," she said. Ben ceased. Luster and his mother overtook them. Frony wore a dress of bright blue silk and a flowered hat. She was a thin woman, with a flat, pleasant face.

"You got six weeks' work right dar on yo back," Dilsey said. "Whut you gwine do ef hit rain?"

"Git wet, I reckon," Frony said. "I ain't never stopped no rain yit."

"Mammy always talkin' bout hit gwine rain," Luster said.

"Ef I don't worry bout y'all, I don't know who is," Dilsey said. "Come on, we already late."

"Rev'un Shegog gwine preach today," Frony said.

"Is?" Dilsey said. "Who him?"

"He fum Saint Looey," Frony said. "Dat big preacher."

"Huh," Dilsey said. "Whut dey needs is a man kin put de fear of God into dese here triflin' young niggers."

"Rev'un Shegog gwine preach today," Frony said. "So dey tells."

They went on along the street. Along its quiet length white people in bright clumps moved churchward, under the windy bells, walking now and then in the random and tentative sun. The wind was gusty, out of the southeast, chill and raw after the warm days.

"I wish you wouldn't keep on bringin' him to church, mammy," Frony said. "Folks talkin."

"Whut folks?" Dilsey said.

"I hears em," Frony said.

"And I knows whut kind of folks," Dilsey said. "Trash white folks. Dat's who it is. Thinks he ain't good enough fer white church, but nigger church ain't good enough fer him."

"Dey talks, jes de same," Frony said.

"Den you send um to me," Dilsey said. "Tell um de good Lawd don't keer whether he smart er not. Don't nobody but white trash keer dat."

A street turned off at right angles, descending, and became a dirt road. On either hand the land dropped more sharply; a broad flat dotted with small cabins whose weathered roofs were on a level with the crown of the road. They were set in small grassless plots littered with broken things, bricks, planks, crockery, things of a once utilitarian value. What growth there was consisted of rank weeds and the trees were mulberries and locusts and sycamores—trees that partook also of the foul desiccation which surrounded the houses; trees whose very burgeoning seemed to be the sad and stubborn remnant of September, as if even spring had passed them by, leaving them to feed upon the rich and unmistakable smell of Negroes in which they grew.

From the doors Negroes spoke to them as they passed, to Dilsey usually:

"Sis' Gibson! How you dis mawnin?"

"I'm well. Is you well?"

"I'm right well, I thank you."

They emerged from the cabins and struggled up the

shading levee to the road—men in staid, hard brown or
black, with gold watch chains and now and then a stick;
young men in cheap, violent blues or stripes and swaggering hats; women a little stiffly sibilant, and children in
garments bought second hand of white people, who
looked at Ben with the covertness of nocturnal animals:

"I bet you won't go up en tech him."

"How come I won't?"

"I bet you won't. I bet you skeered to."

"He won't hurt folks. He des a loony."

"How come a loony won't hurt folks?"

"Dat un won't. I teched him."

"I bet you won't now."

"Case Miss Dilsey lookin'."

"You won't no ways."

"He don't hurt folks. He des a loony."

And steadily the older people speaking to Dilsey,
though, unless they were quite old, Dilsey permitted
Frony to respond.

"Mammy ain't feelin' well dis mawnin."

"Dat's too bad. But Rev'un Shegog'll cure dat. He'll
give her de comfort en de unburdenin'."

The road rose again, to a scene like a painted backdrop. Notched into a cut of red clay crowned with oaks
the road appeared to stop short off, like a cut ribbon. Beside it a weathered church lifted its crazy steeple like a
painted church, and the whole scene was as flat and without perspective as a painted cardboard set upon the ultimate edge of the flat earth, against the windy sunlight
of space and April and a midmorning filled with bells. Toward the church they thronged with slow sabbath deliberation. The women and children went on in, the men
stopped outside and talked in quiet groups until the bell
ceased ringing. Then they too entered.

The church had been decorated, with sparse flowers
from kitchen gardens and hedgerows, and with streamers
of colored crepe paper. Above the pulpit hung a battered

Christmas bell, the accordion sort that collapses. The pul·
pit was empty, though the choir was already in place,
fanning themselves although it was not warm.

Most of the women were gathered on one side of the
room. They were talking. Then the bell struck one time
and they dispersed to their seats and the congregation sat
for an instant, expectant. The bell struck again one time.
The choir rose and began to sing and the congregation
turned its head as one, as six small children—four girls
with tight pigtails bound with small scraps of cloth like
butterflies, and two boys with close-napped heads—entered and marched up the aisle, strung together in a harness of white ribbons and flowers, and followed by two
men in single file. The second man was huge, of a light
coffee color, imposing in a frock coat and white tie. His
head was magisterial and profound, his neck rolled above
his collar in rich folds. But he was familiar to them, and
so the heads were still reverted when he had passed,
and it was not until the choir ceased singing that they
realized that the visiting clergyman had already entered,
and when they saw the man who had preceded their minister enter the pulpit still ahead of him an indescribable
sound went up, a sigh, a sound of astonishment and disappointment.

The visitor was undersized, in a shabby alpaca coat.
He had a wizened, black face like a small, aged monkey.
And all the while that the choir sang again and while the
six children rose and sang in thin, frightened, tuneless
whispers, they watched the insignificant-looking man sitting dwarfed and countrified by the minister's imposing
bulk, with something like consternation. They were still
looking at him with consternation and unbelief when the
minister rose and introduced him in rich, rolling tones
whose very unction served to increase the visitor's insignificance.

"En dey brung dat all de way fum Saint Looey," Frony
whispered.

"I've knowed de Lawd to use cuiser tools dan dat," Dilsey said. "Hush, now," she said to Ben. "Dey fixin' to sing again in a minute."

When the visitor rose to speak he sounded like a white man. His voice was level and cold. It sounded too big to have come from him and they listened at first through curiosity, as they would have to a monkey talking. They began to watch him as they would a man on a tightrope. They even forgot his insignificant appearance in the virtuosity with which he ran and poised and swooped upon the cold inflectionless wire of his voice, so that at last, when with a sort of swooping glide he came to rest again beside the reading desk with one arm resting upon it at shoulder height and his monkey body as reft of all motion as a mummy or an emptied vessel, the congregation sighed as if it waked from a collective dream and moved a little in its seats. Behind the pulpit the choir fanned steadily. Dilsey whispered, "Hush, now. Dey fixin' to sing in a minute."

Then a voice said, "Brethren."

The preacher had not moved. His arm lay yet across the desk, and he still held that pose while the voice died in sonorous echoes between the walls. It was as different as day and dark from his former tone, with a sad, timbrous quality like an alto horn, sinking into their hearts and speaking there again when it had ceased in fading and cumulate echoes.

"Brethren and sisteren," it said again. The preacher removed his arm and he began to walk back and forth before the desk, his hands clasped behind him, a meagre figure, hunched over upon itself like that of one long immured in striving with the implacable earth, "I got the recollection and the blood of the Lamb!" He tramped steadily back and forth beneath the twisted paper and the Christmas bell, hunched, his hands clasped behind him. He was like a worn, small rock whelmed by the successive waves of his voice. With his body he seemed to feed the voice that, succubus like, had fleshed its teeth in him. And the congregation seemed to watch with its own eyes while the voice consumed him, until he was nothing and they were nothing and there was not even a voice, but instead their hearts were speaking to one another in chanting measures beyond the need for words, so that when he came to rest against the reading desk, his monkey face lifted and his whole attitude that of a serene, tortured crucifix that transcended its shabbiness and insignificance and made it of no moment, a long, moaning expulsion of breath rose from them, and a woman's single soprano: "Yes, Jesus!"

As the scudding day passed overhead the dingy windows glowed and faded in ghostly retrograde. A car passed along the road outside, laboring in the sand, died away. Dilsey sat bolt upright, her hand on Ben's knee. Two tears slid down her fallen cheeks, in and out of the myriad coruscations of immolation and abnegation and time.

"Brethren," the minister said in a harsh whisper, without moving.

"Yes, Jesus!" the woman's voice said, hushed yet.

"Breddren en sistuhn!" His voice rang again, with the horns. He removed his arm and stood erect and raised his hands. "I got de ricklickshun en de blood of de Lamb!" They did not mark just when his intonation, his pronunciation, became Negroid, they just sat swaying a little in their seats as the voice took them into itself.

"When de long, cold— Oh, I tells you, breddren, when de long, cold—I sees de light en I sees de word, po' sinner! Dey passed away in Egypt, de swingin' chariots; de generations passed away. Wus a rich man: whar he now, O breddren? Wus a po' man: whar he now, O sistuhn? Oh I tells you, ef you ain't got de milk en de dew of de old salvation when de long, cold years rolls away!"

"Yes, Jesus!"

"I tells you, breddren, en I tells you, sistuhn, dey'll

come a time. Po' sinner saying Let me lay down wid de Lawd, lemme lay down my load. Den whut Jesus gwine say, O breddren? O sistuhn? Is you got de ricklickshun en de blood of de Lamb? Case I ain't gwine load down heaven!"

He fumbled in his coat and took out a handkerchief and mopped his face. A low, concerted sound rose from the congregation: Mmmmmmmmmmmmmm! The woman's voice said, "Yes, Jesus! Jesus!"

"Breddren! Look at dem little chillen settin dar. Jesus wus like dat once. He mammy suffered de glory en de pangs. Sometime maybe she helt him at de nightfall, whilst de angels singin' him to sleep; maybe she look out de do' en see de Roman po-lice passin'." He tramped back and forth, mopping his face. "Listen breddren! I sees de day. Ma'y settin in de do' wid Jesus on her lap, de little Jesus. Like dem chillen dar, de little Jesus. I hears de angels singin' de peaceful songs en de glory; I sees de closin' eyes; sees Mary jump up, sees de sojer face: We gwine to kill! We gwine to kill! We gwine to kill yo little Jesus! I hears de weepin' en de lamentation of de po' mammy widout de salvation en de word of God!"

"Mmmmmmmmmmmmmmmmmm! Jesus! Little Jesus!" and another voice, rising:

"I sees, O Jesus! Oh I sees!" and still another, without words, like bubbles rising in water.

"I sees hit, breddren! I sees hit! Sees de blastin', blindin' sight! I sees Calvary, wid de sacred trees, sees de thief en de murderer en de least of dese; I hears de boastin' en de braggin': Ef you be Jesus, lif up yo' tree en walk! I hears de wailin' of women en de evenin' lamentations; I hears de weepin' en de cryin' en de turnt-away face of God: dey done kilt Jesus; dey done kilt my Son!"

"Mmmmmmmmmmmmmmm. Jesus! I sees, O Jesus!"

"O blind sinner! Breddren, I tells you; sistuhn, I says to you, when de Lawd did turn His mighty face, say, Ain't gwine overload heaven! I can see de widowed God

shet His do'; I sees de whelmin' flood roll between; I sees
de darkness en de death everlastin' upon de generations.
Den, lo! Breddren! Yes, breddren! Whut I see? Whut I
see, O sinner? I sees de resurrection en de light; sees de
meek Jesus sayin' Dey kilt Me dat ye shall live again; I
died dat dem whut sees en believes shall never die. Breddren, O breddren! I sees de doom crack en hears de
golden horns shoutin' down de glory, en de arisen dead
whut got de blood en de ricklickshun of de Lamb!"

In the midst of the voices and the hands Ben sat, rapt
in his sweet blue gaze. Dilsey sat bolt upright beside, crying rigidly and quietly in the annealment and the blood
of the remembered Lamb.

As they walked through the bright noon, up the sandy
road with the dispersing congregation talking, easily
again, group to group, she continued to weep, unmindful
of the talk.

"He sho a preacher, mon! He didn't look like much at
first, but hush!"

"He seed de power en de glory."

"Yes, suh. He seed hit. Face to face he seed hit."

Dilsey made no sound, her face did not quiver as the
tears took their sunken and devious courses, walking with
her head up, making no effort to dry them away even.

"Whyn't you quit dat, mammy?" Frony said. "Wid all
dese people lookin'. We be passin' white folks soon."

"I've seed de first en de last," Dilsey said. "Never you
mind me."

"First en last whut?" Frony said.

"Never you mind," Dilsey said. "I seed de beginnin',
en now I sees de endin'."

Before they reached the street, though, she stopped
and lifted her skirt and dried her eyes on the hem of her
topmost underskirt. Then they went on. Ben shambled
along beside Dilsey, watching Luster who anticked along
ahead, the umbrella in his hand and his new straw hat

slanted viciously in the sunlight, like a big foolish dog watching a small clever one. They reached the gate and entered. Immediately Ben began to whimper again, and for a while all of them looked up the drive at the square, paintless house with its rotting portico.

"Whut's gwine on up dar today?" Frony said. "Somethin' is."

"Nothin'," Dilsey said. "You tend to yo business en let de white folks tend to deir'n."

"Somethin' is," Frony said. "I heard him first thing dis mawnin. 'Taint none of my busines, dough."

"En I knows whut, too," Luster said.

"You knows mo dan you got any use fer," Dilsey said. "Ain't you jes heard Frony say hit ain't none of yo business? You take Benjy on to de back and keep him quiet twell I put dinner on."

"I knows whar Miss Quentin is," Luster said.

"Den jes keep hit," Dilsey said. "Soon es Quentin need any of yo' egvice, I'll let you know. Y'all g'awn en play in de back, now."

"You know whut gwine happen soon es dey start playin' dat ball over yonder," Luster said.

"Dey won't start fer a while yit. By dat time T.P. be here to tak him ridin'. Here, you gimme dat new hat."

Luster gave her the hat and he and Ben went on across the back yard. Ben was still whimpering, though not loud. Dilsey and Frony went to the cabin. After a while Dilsey emerged, again in the faded calico dress, and went to the kitchen. The fire had died down. There was no sound in the house. She put on the apron and went upstairs. There was no sound anywhere. Quentin's room was as they had left it. She entered and picked up the undergarment and put the stocking back in the drawer and closed it. Mrs. Compson's door was closed. Dilsey stood beside it for a moment, listening. Then she opened it and entered, entered a pervading reek of camphor. The shades were drawn, the room in half-light, and the bed, so that at first she thought Mrs. Compson was asleep and was about to close the door when the other spoke.

"Well?" she said. "What is it?"

"Hit's me," Dilsey said. "You want anything?"

Mrs. Compson didn't answer. After a while, without moving her head at all, she said: "Where's Jason?"

"He ain't come back yit," Dilsey said. "Whut you want?"

Mrs. Compson said nothing. Like so many cold, weak people, when faced at last by the incontrovertible disaster she exhumed from somewhere a sort of fortitude, strength. In her case it was an unshakable conviction regarding the yet unplumbed event. "Well," she said presently, "did you find it?"

"Find whut? Whut you talkin' about?"

"The note. At least she would have enough consideration to leave a note. Even Quentin did that."

"Whut you talkin' about?" Dilsey said. "Don't you know she all right? I bet she be walkin' right in dis do' befo' dark."

"Fiddlesticks," Mrs. Compson said. "It's in the blood. Like uncle, like niece. Or mother. I don't know which would be worse. I don't seem to care."

"Whut you keep on talkin' that way fur?" Dilsey said. "Whut she want to do anything like that fur?"

"I don't know. What reason did Quentin have? Under God's heaven what reason did he have? It can't be simply to flout and hurt me. Whoever God is, He would not permit that. I'm a lady. You might not believe that from my offspring, but I am."

"You des wait en see," Dilsey said. "She be here by night, right dar in her bed." Mrs. Compson said nothing. The camphor-soaked cloth lay upon her brow. The black robe lay across the foot of the bed. Dilsey stood with her hand on the doorknob.

"Well," Mrs. Compson said. "What do you want? Are

you going to fix some dinner for Jason and Benjamin, or not?"

"Jason ain't come yit," Dilsey said. "I gwine fix somethin.' You sho you don't want nothin? Yo' bottle still hot enough?"

"You might hand me my Bible."

"I give hit to you dis mawnin, befo' I left."

"You laid it on the edge of the bed. How long did you expect it to stay there?"

Dilsey crossed to the bed and groped among the shadows beneath the edge of it and found the Bible, face down. She smoothed the bent pages and laid the book on the bed again. Mrs. Compson didn't open her eyes. Her hair and the pillow were the same color, beneath the wimple of the medicated cloth she looked like an old nun praying. "Don't put it there again," she said, without opening her eyes. "That's where you put it before. Do you want me to have to get out of bed to pick it up?"

Dilsey reached the book across her and laid it on the broad side of the bed. "You can't see to read, noways," she said. "You want me to raise de shade a little?"

"No. Let them alone. Go on and fix Jason something to eat."

Dilsey went out. She closed the door and returned to the kitchen. The stove was almost cold. While she stood there the clock above the cupboard struck ten times. "One o'clock," she said aloud. "Jason ain't comin' home. Ise seed de first en de last," she said, looking at the cold stove. "I seed de first en de last."

6

MISSISSIPPI FLOOD

Editor's Note

Early in April 1927, the big river overflowed its banks, and the entire population of the state prison farm at Parchman, Mississippi, was set to work on a threatened levee. One tall convict was ordered out in a rowboat to look for a woman in a cypress snag and a man on the ridge-pole of a cottonhouse. The water continued to rise. It was the worst flood in the history of the river: for six weeks more than 20,000 square miles were under water, including the whole of the rich Delta, and 600,000 persons were driven from their homes. Several hundreds were drowned, in addition to 25,000 horses, 50,000 cattle, 148,000 hogs, 1300 sheep, and 1,300,000 chickens; 400,000 acres of crops were destroyed and hundreds of miles of levees. A few weeks after the river had returned to its bed, the tall convict rowed back to the state prison farm. "Yonder's your boat," he said, "and here's the woman. But I never did find that bastard on the cotton-house."

The tall convict was born in the pine hills southeast of Frenchman's Bend, but otherwise "Old Man"—of course the title refers to the River—stands apart from the Yoknapatawpha County saga. It is, as it were, a connection between Yoknapatawpha and the rest of the South: our horizons widen as the convict drifts down the Mississippi. Originally the story formed half of a novel published in

1939. The other half was a completely separate story called "The Wild Palms," which is also the title of the novel as a whole. Faulkner had made an experiment with the aim of keeping the work at a high pitch of intensity.

When I reached the end of what is now the first section of *The Wild Palms* [he told Jean Stein when she interviewed him for *Paris Review*], I realized suddenly that something was missing, it needed emphasis, something to lift it like counterpoint in music. So I wrote on the "Old Man" story until "The Wild Palms" story rose back to pitch. Then I stopped the "Old Man" story at what is now its first section, and took up "The Wild Palms" story until it began again to sag. Then I raised it to pitch again with another section of its antithesis. . . .

Besides keeping his pitch, Faulkner also gained an effect of contrast or counterpoint: in "The Wild Palms," a man sacrifices everything for freedom and love, and loses them both; in "Old Man," the convict sacrifices everything to escape from freedom and love and to regain the womanless security of the state prison farm. The second story, however, is more effective than the first, and I think it gains by standing alone, as in the present volume. It isn't as good as *Huckleberry Finn,* by some distance, but it is the only other story of the Mississippi that can be set beside *Huckleberry Finn* without shriveling under the comparison; it is the only other story in American literature that gives the same impression of the power and legendary sweep of the River.

1927

Old Man

I

Once (it was in Mississippi, in May, in the flood year 1927) there were two convicts. One of them was about twenty-five, tall, lean, flat-stomached, with a sunburned face and Indian-black hair and pale, china-colored, outraged eyes—an outrage directed not at the men who had foiled his crime, not even at the lawyers and judges who had sent him here, but at the writers, the uncorporeal names attached to the stories, the paper novels—the Diamond Dicks and Jesse Jameses and such—whom he believed had led him into his present predicament through their own ignorance and gullibility regarding the medium in which they dealt and took money for, in accepting information on which they placed the stamp of verisimilitude and authenticity (this so much the more criminal since there was no sworn notarized statement attached and hence so much the quicker would the information be accepted by one who expected the same unspoken good faith, demanding, asking, expecting no certification, which he extended along with the dime or fifteen cents to pay for it) and retailed for money and which, on actual application, proved to be impractical and (to the convict) criminally false; there would be times when he would halt his mule and plow in midfurrow (there is no walled penitentiary in Mississippi; it is a cotton plantation which the convicts work under the rifles and shotguns of guards

481

and trusties) and muse with a kind of enraged impotence, fumbling among the rubbish left him by his one and only experience with courts and law, fumbling until the meaningless and verbose shibboleth took form at last (himself seeking justice at the same blind font where he had met justice and been hurled back and down): Using the mails to defraud: who felt that he had been defrauded by the third-class mail system not of crass and stupid money which he did not particularly want anyway, but of liberty and honor and pride.

He was in for fifteen years (he had arrived shortly after his nineteenth birthday) for attempted train robbery. He had laid his plans in advance, he had followed his printed (and false) authority to the letter; he had saved the paper-backs for two years, reading and rereading them, memorizing them, comparing and weighing story and method against story and method, taking the good from each and discarding the dross as his workable plan emerged, keeping his mind open to make the subtle last-minute changes, without haste and without impatience, as the newer pamphlets appeared on their appointed days, as a conscientious dressmaker makes the subtle alterations in a court presentation costume as the newer bulletins appear. And then when the day came, he did not even have a chance to go through the coaches and collect the watches and the rings, the brooches and the hidden money-belts, because he had been captured as soon as he entered the express car where the safe and the gold would be. He had shot no one because the pistol which they took away from him was not that kind of a pistol although it was loaded; later he admitted to the District Attorney that he had got it, as well as the dark lantern in which a candle burned and the black handkerchief to wear over the face, by peddling among his pinehill neighbors subscriptions to the *Detectives' Gazette*. So now from time to time (he had ample leisure for it) he mused with that raging impotence, because there was something else he could not tell them at the trial, did not know how to tell them. It was not the money he had wanted. It was not riches, not the crass loot; that would have been merely a bangle to wear upon the breast of his pride like the Olympic runner's amateur medal—a symbol, a badge to show that he too was the best at his chosen gambit in the living and fluid world of his time. So that at times as he trod the richly shearing black earth behind his plow or with a hoe thinned the sprouting cotton and corn or lay on his sullen back in his bunk after supper, he cursed in a harsh steady unrepetitive stream, not at the living men who had put him where he was but at what he did not even know were pen-names, did not even know were not actual men but merely the designations of shades who had written about shades.

The second convict was short and plump. Almost hairless, he was quite white. He looked like something exposed to light by turning over rotting logs or planks and he too carried (though not in his eyes like the first convict) a sense of burning and impotent outrage. So it did not show on him and hence none knew it was there. But then nobody knew very much about him, including the people who had sent him here. His outrage was directed at no printed word but at the paradoxical fact that he had been forced to come here of his own free choice and will. He had been forced to choose between the Mississippi State penal farm and the Federal Penitentiary at Atlanta, and the fact that he, who resembled a hairless and pallid slug, had chosen the out-of-doors and the sunlight was merely another manifestation of the close-guarded and solitary enigma of his character, as something recognizable roils momentarily into view from beneath stagnant and opaque water, then sinks again. None of his fellow prisoners knew what his crime had been, save that he was in for a hundred and ninety-nine years—this incredible and impossible period of punishment or restraint itself carrying a vicious and fabulous quality which indicated that his reason for being here was such that the very men, the paladins and pillars of justice and equity who had sent him here had during that moment become blind apostles not of mere justice but of all human decency, blind instruments not of equity but of all human outrage and vengeance, acting in a savage personal concert, judge, lawyer and jury, which certainly abrogated justice and possibly even law.

Possibly only the Federal and State's Attorneys knew what the crime actually was. There had been a woman in it, and a stolen automobile transported across a State line, a filling station robbed and the attendant shot to death. There had been a second man in the car at the time and anyone could have looked once at the convict (as the two attorneys did) and known he would not even have had the synthetic courage of alcohol to pull trigger on anyone. But he and the woman and the stolen car had been captured while the second man, doubtless the actual murderer, had escaped, so that, brought to bay at last in the State's Attorney's office, harried, dishevelled, and snarling, the two grimly implacable and viciously gleeful attorneys in his front and the now raging woman held by two policemen in the anteroom in his rear, he was given his choice. He could be tried in Federal Court under the Mann Act and for the automobile, that is, by electing to pass through the anteroom where the woman raged he could take his chances on the lesser crime in Federal Court, or by accepting a sentence for manslaughter in the State Court he would be permitted to quit the room by a back entrance, without having to pass the woman. He had chosen; he stood at the bar and heard a judge (who looked down at him as if the District Attorney actually had turned over a rotten plank with his toe and exposed him) sentence him to a hundred and ninety-nine years at the State Farm. Thus (he had ample leisure too; they had tried to teach him to plow and had failed, they had put him in the blacksmith shop and the foreman trusty himself had asked to have him removed: so that now, in a long apron like a woman, he cooked and swept and dusted in the deputy wardens' barracks) he too mused at times with that sense of impotence and outrage though it did not show on him as on the first convict since he leaned on no halted broom to do it and so none knew it was there.

It was this second convict who, toward the end of April, began to read aloud to the others from the daily newspapers when, chained ankle to ankle and herded by armed guards, they had come up from the fields and had eaten supper and were gathered in the bunkhouse. It was the Memphis newspaper which the deputy wardens had read at breakfast; the convict read aloud from it to his companions who could have had but little active interest in the outside world, some of whom could not have read it for themselves at all and did not even know where the Ohio and Missouri river basins were, some of whom had never even seen the Mississippi River, although for past periods ranging from a few days to ten and twenty and thirty years (and for future periods ranging from a few months to life) they had plowed and planted and eaten and slept beneath the shadow of the levee itself, knowing only that there was water beyond it from hearsay and because now and then they heard the whistles of steamboats from beyond it and, during the last week or so had seen the stacks and pilot houses moving along the sky sixty feet above their heads.

But they listened, and soon even those who, like the taller convict, had probably never before seen more water than a horse pond would hold, knew what thirty feet on a river gauge at Cairo or Memphis meant and could (and did) talk glibly of sandboils. Perhaps what actually moved them were the accounts of the conscripted levee gangs, mixed blacks and whites working in double shifts against the steadily rising water; stories of men, even though they were Negroes, being forced like themselves to do work for which they received no other pay than coarse food and a place in a mudfloored tent to sleep on —stories, pictures, which emerged from the shorter convict's reading voice: the mudsplashed white men with the inevitable shot-guns, the antlike lines of Negroes carrying sandbags, slipping and crawling up the steep face of the revetment to hurl their futile ammunition into the face of a flood and return for more. Or perhaps it was more than this. Perhaps they watched the approach of the disaster with that same amazed and incredulous hope of the slaves—the lions and bears and elephants, the grooms and bathmen and pastrycooks—who watched the mounting flames of Rome from Ahenobarbus' gardens. But listen they did and presently it was May and the wardens' newspaper began to talk in headlines two inches tall—those black staccato slashes of ink which, it would almost seem, even the illiterate should be able to read: *Crest Passes Memphis at Midnight 4000 Homeless in White River Basin Governor Calls out National Guard Martial Law Declared in Following Counties Red Cross Train with President Hoover Leaves Washington Tonight;* then, three evenings later (It had been raining all day—not the vivid brief thunderous downpours of April and May, but the slow steady gray rain of November and December before a cold north wind. The men had not gone to the fields at all during the day, and the very second-hand optimism of the almost twenty-four-hour-old news seemed to contain its own refutation.): *Crest Now Below Memphis 22,000 Refugees Safe at Vicksburg Army Engineers Say Levees Will Hold.*

"I reckon that means it will bust tonight," one convict said.

"Well, maybe this rain will hold on until the water gets here," a second said. They all agreed to this because what they meant, the living unspoken thought among them, was that if the weather cleared, even though the levees broke and the flood moved in upon the Farm itself, they would have to return to the fields and work, which they would have had to do. There was nothing paradoxical in this, although they could not have expressed the reason for it which they instinctively perceived: that the land they farmed and the substance they produced from it belonged neither to them who worked it nor to those who forced them at guns' point to do so, that as far as either— convicts or guards—were concerned, it could have been pebbles they put into the ground and papier-mâché cotton- and corn-sprouts which they thinned. So it was that, what between the sudden wild hoping and the idle day and the evening's headlines, they were sleeping restlessly beneath the sound of the rain on the tin roof when at midnight the sudden glare of the electric bulbs and the guards' voices waked them and they heard the throbbing of the waiting trucks.

"Turn out of there!" the deputy shouted. He was fully dressed—rubber boots, slicker and shotgun. "The levee went out at Mound's Landing an hour ago. Get up out of it!"

II

When the belated and streaming dawn broke the two convicts, along with twenty others, were in a truck. A trusty drove, two armed guards sat in the cab with him. Inside the high, stall-like, topless body the convicts stood, packed like matches in an upright box or like the pencil-shaped ranks of cordite in a shell, shackled by the ankles to a single chain which wove among the motionless feet and swaying legs and a clutter of picks and shovels among which they stood, and was riveted by both ends to the steel body of the truck.

Then and without warning, they saw the flood about which the plump convict had been reading and they listening for two weeks or more. The road ran south. It was built on a raised levee, known locally as a dump, about eight feet above the flat surrounding land, bordered on both sides by the barrow pits from which the earth of the levee had been excavated. These barrow pits had held water all winter from the fall rains, not to speak of the rain of yesterday, but now they saw that the pit on either side of the road had vanished and instead there lay a flat still sheet of brown water which extended into the fields beyond the pits, ravelled out into long motionless shreds in the bottom of the plow furrows and gleamed faintly in the gray light like the bars of a prone and enormous grating. And then (the truck was moving at good speed) as they watched quietly (they had not been talking much anyway but now they were all silent and quite grave, shifting and craning as one to look soberly off to the west side of the road) the crests of the furrows vanished too, and they now looked at a single perfectly flat and motionless steel-colored sheet in which the telephone poles and the straight hedgerows which marked section lines seemed to be fixed and rigid as though set in concrete.

It was perfectly motionless, perfectly flat. It looked, not innocent, but bland. It looked almost demure. It looked as if you could walk on it. It looked so still that they did not realize it possessed motion until they came to the first bridge. There was a ditch under the bridge, a small stream, but ditch and stream were both invisible now, indicated only by the rows of cypress and bramble which marked its course. Here they both saw and heard movement—the slow profound eastward and upstream ("It's running backward," one convict said quietly) set of the still rigid surface, from beneath which came a deep faint subaquean rumble which (though none in the truck could have made the comparison) sounded like a subway train passing far beneath the street, and which suggested a terrific and secret speed. It was as if the water itself were in three strata, separate and distinct, the bland and unhurried surface bearing a frothy scum and a miniature flotsam of twigs and screening, as though by vicious calculation, the rush and fury of the flood itself, and beneath this in turn the original stream trickle, murmuring along in the opposite direction, following undisturbed and unaware of its appointed course and serving its Lilliputian end, like a thread of ants between the rails on which an express train passes, they (the ants) as unaware of the power and fury as if it were a cyclone crossing Saturn.

Now there was water on both sides of the road and now, as if once they had become aware of movement in the water it had given over deception and concealment, they seemed to be able to watch it rising up the flanks of the dump; trees which a few miles back had stood on tall trunks above the water now seemed to burst from the surface at the level of the lower branches like decorative shrubs on barbered lawns. The truck passed a Negro cabin. The water was up to the window ledges. A woman clutching two children squatted on the ridgepole, a man and a halfgrown youth, standing waist-deep, were hoisting a squealing pig onto the slanting roof of a barn, on the ridgepole of which sat a row of chickens and a turkey. Near the barn was a haystack on which a cow stood tied by a rope to the center pole and bawling steadily; a yelling Negro boy on a saddleless mule which he flogged steadily, his legs clutching the mule's barrel and his body leaned to the drag of a rope attached to a second mule, approached the haystack, splashing and floundering. The woman on the housetop began to shriek at the passing truck, her voice carrying faint and melodious across the brown water, becoming fainter and fainter as the truck passed and went on, ceasing at last, whether because of distance or because she had stopped screaming those in the truck did not know.

Then the road vanished. There was no perceptible slant to it yet it had slipped abruptly beneath the brown surface with no ripple, no ridgy demarcation, like a flat thin blade slipped obliquely into flesh by a delicate hand, annealed into the water without disturbance, as if it had ex-

isted so for years, had been built that way. The truck
stopped. The trusty descended from the cab and came
back and dragged two shovels from among their feet, the
blades clashing against the serpentining of the chain
about their ankles. "What is it?" one said. "What are you
fixing to do?" The trusty didn't answer. He returned to
the cab, from which one of the guards had descended,
without his shotgun. He and the trusty, both in hip boots
and each carrying a shovel, advanced into the water, gingerly, probing and feeling ahead with the shovel handles.
The same convict spoke again. He was a middle-aged
man with a wild thatch of iron-gray hair and a slightly
mad face. "What the hell are they doing?" he said. Again
nobody answered him. The truck moved, on into the water, behind the guard and the trusty, beginning to push
ahead of itself a thick slow viscid ridge of chocolate water. Then the gray-haired convict began to scream. "God
damn it, unlock the chain!" He began to struggle, thrashing violently about him, striking at the men nearest him
until he reached the cab, the roof of which he now hammered on with his fists, screaming. "God damn it, unlock
us! Unlock us! Son of a bitch!" he screamed, addressing
no one. "They're going to drown us! Unlock the chain!"
But for all the answer he got the men within radius of
his voice might have been dead. The truck crawled on,
the guard and the trusty feeling out the road ahead with
the reversed shovels, the second guard at the wheel, the
twenty-two convicts packed like sardines into the truck
bed and padlocked by the ankles to the body of the truck
itself. They crossed another bridge—two delicate and
paradoxical iron railings slanting out of the water, travelling parallel to it for a distance, then slanting down into
it again with an outrageous quality almost significant yet
apparently meaningless like something in a dream not
quite nightmare. The truck crawled on.

Along toward noon they came to a town, their destination. The streets were paved; now the wheels of the truck

made a sound like tearing silk. Moving faster now, the guard and the trusty in the cab again, the truck even had a slight bone in its teeth, its bow-wave spreading beyond the submerged sidewalks and across the adjacent lawns, lapping against the stoops and porches of houses where people stood among piles of furniture. They passed through the business district; a man in hip boots emerged knee-deep in water from a store, dragging a flat-bottomed skiff containing a steel safe.

At last they reached the railroad. It crossed the street at right angles, cutting the town in two. It was on a dump, a levee, also, eight or ten feet above the town itself; the street ran blankly into it and turned at right angles beside a cotton compress and a loading platform on stilts at the level of a freight-car door. On this platform was a khaki army tent and a uniformed National Guard sentry with a rifle and bandolier.

The truck turned and crawled out of the water and up the ramp which cotton wagons used and where trucks and private cars filled with household goods came and unloaded onto the platform. They were unlocked from the chain in the truck and, shackled ankle to ankle in pairs, they mounted the platform and into an apparently inextricable jumble of beds and trunks, gas and electric stoves, radios and tables and chairs and framed pictures, which a chain of Negroes under the eye of an unshaven white man in muddy corduroy and hip boots carried piece by piece into the compress, at the door of which another guardsman stood with his rifle, they (the convicts) not stopping here but herded on by the two guards with their shotguns into the dim and cavernous building where, among the piled heterogeneous furniture, the ends of cotton bales and the mirrors on dressers and sideboards gleamed with an identical mute and unreflecting concentration of pallid light.

They passed on through, onto the loading platform where the army tent and the first sentry were. They waited here. Nobody told them for what nor why. While the two guards talked with the sentry before the tent, the convicts sat in a line along the edge of the platform like buzzards on a fence, their shackled feet dangling above the brown motionless flood out of which the railroad embankment rose, pristine and intact, in a kind of paradoxical denial and repudiation of change and portent; not talking, just looking quietly across the track to where the other half of the amputated town seemed to float, house, shrub, and tree, ordered and pageant-like and without motion, upon the limitless liquid plain beneath the thick gray sky.

After a while the other four trucks from the Farm arrived. They came up, bunched closely, radiator to tail light, with their four separate sounds of tearing silk and vanished beyond the compress. Presently the ones on the platform heard the feet, the mute clashing of the shackles. The first truckload emerged from the compress, the second, the third; there were more than a hundred of them now in their bed-ticking overalls and jumpers and fifteen or twenty guards with rifles and shotguns. The first lot rose and they mingled, paired, twinned by their clanking and clashing umbilicals; then it began to rain, a slow steady gray drizzle like November instead of May. Yet not one of them made any move toward the open door of the compress. They did not even look toward it, with longing or hope or without it. If they thought at all, they doubtless knew that the available space in it would be needed for furniture, even if it were not already filled. Or perhaps they knew that, even if there were room in it, it would not be for them, not that the guards would wish them to get wet but that the guards would not think about getting them out of the rain. So they just stopped talking and, with their jumper collars turned up and shackled in braces like dogs at a field trial, they stood, immobile, patient, almost ruminant, their backs turned to the rain as sheep and cattle do.

After another while they became aware that the number of soldiers had increased to a dozen or more, warm and dry beneath rubberized ponchos, there was an officer with a pistol at his belt, then and without making any move toward it, they began to smell food and, turning to look, saw an army field kitchen set up just inside the compress door. But they made no move, they waited until they were herded into line, they inched forward, their heads lowered and patient in the rain, and received each a bowl of stew, a mug of coffee, two slices of bread. They ate this in the rain. They did not sit down because the platform was wet, they squatted on their heels as country men do, hunching forward, trying to shield the bowls and mugs into which nevertheless the rain splashed steadily as into miniature ponds and soaked, invisible and soundless, into the bread.

After they had stood on the platform for three hours, a train came for them. Those nearest the edge saw it, watched it—a passenger coach apparently running under its own power and trailing a cloud of smoke from no visible stack, a cloud which did not rise but instead shifted slowly and heavily aside and lay upon the surface of the aqueous earth with a quality at once weightless and completely spent. It came up and stopped, a single old-fashioned open-ended wooden car coupled to the nose of a pushing switch engine considerably smaller. They were herded into it, crowding forward to the other end where there was a small cast-iron stove. There was no fire in it, nevertheless they crowded about it—the cold and voiceless lump of iron stained with fading tobacco and hovered about by the ghosts of a thousand Sunday excursions to Memphis or Moorhead and return—the peanuts, the bananas, the soiled garments of infants—huddling, shoving for places near it. "Come on, come on," one of the guards shouted. "Sit down, now." At last three of the guards, laying aside their guns, came among them and broke up the huddle, driving them back and into seats.

There were not enough seats for all. The others stood in the aisle, they stood braced, they heard the air hiss out of the released brakes, the engine whistled four blasts, the car came into motion with a snapping jerk; the platform, the compress fled violently as the train seemed to transpose from immobility to full speed with that same quality of unreality with which it had appeared, running backward now though with the engine in front where before it had moved forward but with the engine behind.

When the railroad in its turn ran beneath the surface of the water, the convicts did not even know it. They felt the train stop, they heard the engine blow a long blast which wailed away unechoed across the waste, wild and forlorn, and they were not even curious; they sat or stood behind the rain-streaming windows as the train crawled on again, feeling its way as the truck had while the brown water swirled between the tracks and among the spokes of the driving wheels and lapped in cloudy steam against the dragging fire-filled belly of the engine; again it blew four short harsh blasts filled with the wild triumph and defiance yet also with repudiation and even farewell, as if the articulated steel itself knew it did not dare stop and would not be able to return. Two hours later in the twilight they saw through the streaming windows a burning plantation house. Juxtaposed to nowhere and neighbored by nothing it stood, a clear steady pyre-like flame rigidly fleeing its own reflection, burning in the dusk above the watery desolation with a quality paradoxical, outrageous and bizarre.

Sometime after dark the train stopped. The convicts did not know where they were. They did not ask. They would no more have thought of asking where they were than they would have asked why and what for. They couldn't even see, since the car was unlighted and the windows fogged on the outside by rain and on the inside by the engendered heat of the packed bodies. All they could see was a milky and sourceless flick and glare of flashlights. They could hear shouts and commands, then the guards inside the car began to shout; they were herded to their feet and toward the exit, the ankle chains clashing and clanking. They descended into a fierce hissing of steam, through ragged whisps of it blowing past the car. Laid-to alongside the train and resembling a train itself was a thick blunt motor launch to which was attached a string of skiffs and flat boats. There were more soldiers; the flashlights played on the rifle barrels and bandolier buckles and flicked and glinted on the ankle chains of the convicts as they stepped gingerly down into knee-deep water and entered the boats; now car and engine both vanished completely in steam as the crew began dumping the fire from the firebox.

After another hour they began to see lights ahead—a faint wavering row of red pin-pricks extending along the horizon and apparently hanging low in the sky. But it took almost another hour to reach them while the convicts squatted in the skiffs, huddled into the soaked garments (they no longer felt the rain any more at all as separate drops) and watched the lights draw nearer and nearer until at last the crest of the levee defined itself; now they could discern a row of army tents stretching along it and people squatting about the fires, the wavering reflections from which, stretching across the water, revealed an involved mass of other skiffs tied against the flank of the levee which now stood high and dark overhead. Flashlights glared and winked along the base, among the tethered skiffs; the launch, silent now, drifted in.

When they reached the top of the levee they could see the long line of khaki tents, interspersed with fires about which people—men, women and children, Negro and white—crouched or stood among shapeless bales of clothing, their heads turning, their eyeballs glinting in the firelight as they looked quietly at the striped garments and the chains; further down the levee, huddled together too though untethered, was a drove of mules and two or three cows. Then the taller convict became conscious of another sound. He did not begin to hear it all at once, he suddenly became aware that he had been hearing it all the time, a sound so much beyond all his experience and his powers of assimilation that up to this point he had been as oblivious of it as an ant or a flea might be of the sound of the avalanche on which it rides; he had been travelling upon water since early afternoon and for seven years now he had run his plow and harrow and planter within the very shadow of the levee on which he now stood, but this profound deep whisper which came from the further side of it he did not at once recognize. He stopped. The line of convicts behind jolted into him like a line of freight cars stopping, with an iron clashing like cars. "Get on!" a guard shouted.

"What's that?" the convict said. A Negro man squatting before the nearest fire answered him:

"Dat's him. Dat's de Ole Man."

"The old man?" the convict said.

"Get on! Get on up there!" the guard shouted. They went on; they passed another huddle of mules, the eyeballs rolling too, the long morose faces turning into and out of the firelight; they passed them and reached a section of empty tents, the light pup tents of a military campaign, made to hold two men. The guards herded the convicts into them, three brace of shackled men to each tent.

They crawled in on all fours, like dogs into cramped kennels, and settled down. Presently the tent became warm from their bodies. Then they became quiet and then all of them could hear it, they lay listening to the bass whisper deep, strong, and powerful. "The old man?" the train-robber convict said.

"Yah," another said. "He don't have to brag."

At dawn the guards waked them by kicking the soles of the projecting feet. Opposite the muddy landing and the huddle of skiffs an army field kitchen was set up, already they could smell the coffee. But the taller convict at least, even though he had had but one meal yesterday and that at noon in the rain, did not move at once toward the food. Instead and for the first time he looked at the River within whose shadow he had spent the last seven years of his life but had never seen before; he stood in quiet and amazed surmise and looked at the rigid steel-colored surface not broken into waves but merely slightly undulant. It stretched from the levee on which he stood, further than he could see—a slowly and heavily roiling chocolate-frothy expanse broken only by a thin line a mile away as fragile in appearance as a single hair, which after a moment he recognized. *It's another levee,* he thought quietly. *That's what we look like from there. That's what I am standing on looks like from there.* He was prodded from the rear; a guard's voice carried forward: "Go on! Go on! You'll have plenty of time to look at that!"

They received the same stew and coffee and bread as the day before; they squatted again with their bowls and mugs as yesterday, though it was not raining yet. During the night an intact wooden barn had floated up. It now lay jammed by the current against the levee while a crowd of Negroes swarmed over it, ripping off the shingles and planks and carrying them up the bank; eating steadily and without haste, the taller convict watched the barn dissolve rapidly down to the very water-line exactly as a dead fly vanished beneath the moiling industry of a swarm of ants.

They finished eating. Then it began to rain again, as upon a signal, while they stood or squatted in their harsh garments which had not dried out during the night but had merely become slightly warmer than the air. Presently they were haled to their feet and told off into two groups, one of which was armed from a stack of mud-clogged picks and shovels nearby, and marched away up the levee. A little later the motor launch with its train of skiffs came up across what was, fifteen feet beneath its

keel, probably a cotton field, the skiffs loaded to the gunwales with Negroes and a scattering of white people nursing bundles on their laps. When the engine shut off the
faint plinking of a guitar came across the water. The skiffs
warped in and unloaded; the convicts watched the men
and women and children struggle up the muddy slope,
carrying heavy towsacks and bundles wrapped in quilts.
The sound of the guitar had not ceased and now the convicts saw him—a young, black, lean-hipped man, the
guitar slung by a piece of cotton plow line about his neck.
He mounted the levee, still picking it. He carried nothing
else, no food, no change of clothes, not even a coat.

The taller convict was so busy watching this that he did
not hear the guard until the guard stood directly beside
him shouting his name. "Wake up!" the guard shouted.
"Can you fellows paddle a boat?"

"Paddle a boat where?" the taller convict said.

"In the water," the guard said. "Where in hell do you
think?"

"I ain't going to paddle no boat nowhere out yonder,"
the tall convict said, jerking his head toward the invisible
river beyond the levee behind him.

"No, it's on this side," the guard said. He stooped
swiftly and unlocked the chain which joined the tall convict and the plump hairless one. "It's just down the road
a piece." He rose. The two convicts followed him down
to the boats. "Follow them telephone poles until you
come to a filling station. You can tell it, the roof is still
above water. It's on a bayou and you can tell the bayou
because the tops of the trees are sticking up. Follow the
bayou until you come to a cypress snag with a woman in
it. Pick her up and then cut straight back west until you
come to a cottonhouse with a fellow sitting on the ridge-
pole—" He turned, looking at the two convicts, who stood
perfectly still, looking first at the skiff and then at the water with intense sobriety. "Well? What are you waiting
for?"

"I can't row a boat," the plump convict said.

"Then it's high time you learned," the guard said. "Get in."

The tall convict shoved the other forward. "Get in," he said. "That water ain't going to hurt you. Ain't nobody going to make you take a bath."

As, the plump one in the bow and the other in the stern, they shoved away from the levee, they saw other pairs being unshackled and manning the other skiffs. "I wonder how many more of them fellows are seeing this much water for the first time in their lives too," the tall convict said. The other did not answer. He knelt in the bottom of the skiff, pecking gingerly at the water now and then with his paddle. The very shape of his thick soft back seemed to wear that expression of wary and tense concern.

Some time after midnight a rescue boat filled to the guard rail with homeless men and women and children docked at Vicksburg. It was a steamer, shallow of draft; all day long it had poked up and down cypress- and gum-choked bayous and across cotton fields (where at times instead of swimming it waded) gathering its sorry cargo from the tops of houses and barns and even out of trees, and now it warped into that mushroom city of the forlorn and despairing, where kerosene flares smoked in the drizzle and hurriedly strung electrics glared upon the bayonets of martial policemen and the Red-Cross brassards of doctors and nurses and canteen-workers. The bluff overhead was almost solid with tents, yet still there were more people than shelter for them; they sat or lay, single and by whole families, under what shelter they could find, or sometimes under the rain itself, in the little death of profound exhaustion while the doctors and the nurses and the soldiers stepped over and around and among them.

Among the first to disembark was one of the penitentiary deputy wardens, followed closely by the plump convict and another white man—a small man with a gaunt unshaven wan face still wearing an expression of incredulous outrage. The deputy warden seemed to know exactly where he wished to go. Followed closely by his two companions he threaded his way swiftly among the piled furniture and the sleeping bodies and stood presently in a fiercely lighted and hastily established temporary office, almost a military post of command in fact, where the Warden of the Penitentiary sat with two army officers wearing majors' leaves. The deputy warden spoke without preamble. "We lost a man," he said. He called the tall convict's name.

"Lost him?" the Warden said.

"Yah. Drowned." Without turning his head he spoke to the plump convict. "Tell him," he said.

"He was the one that said he could row a boat," the plump convict said. "I never. I told him myself—" he indicated the deputy warden with a jerk of his head "—I couldn't. So when we got to the bayou—"

"What's this?" the Warden said.

"The launch brought word in," the deputy warden said. "Woman in a cypress snag on the bayou, then this fellow—" he indicated the third man; the Warden and the two officers looked at the third man "—on a cottonhouse. Never had room in the launch to pick them up. Go on."

"So we come to where the bayou was," the plump convict continued in a voice perfectly flat, without any inflection whatever. "Then the boat got away from him. I don't know what happened. I was just sitting there because he was so positive he could row a boat. I never saw any current. Just all of a sudden the boat whirled clean around and begun to run fast backward like it was hitched to a train and it whirled around again and I happened to look up and there was a limb right over my head and I grabbed it just in time and that boat was snatched out from under me like you'd snatch off a sock and I saw it one time more upside down and that fellow that said he knew all about rowing holding to it with one hand and still holding the paddle in the other—" He ceased. There was no dying fall to his voice, it just ceased and the convict stood looking quietly at a half-full quart of whiskey sitting on the table.

"How do you know he's drowned?" the Warden said to the deputy. "How do you know he didn't just see his chance to escape, and took it?"

"Escape where?" the other said. "The whole Delta's flooded. There's fifteen foot of water for fifty miles, clean back to the hills. And that boat was upside down."

"That fellow's drowned," the plump convict said. "You don't need to worry about him. He's got his pardon; it won't cramp nobody's hand signing it, neither."

"And nobody else saw him?" the Warden said. "What about the woman in the tree?"

"I don't know," the deputy said. "I ain't found her yet. I reckon some other boat picked her up. But this is the fellow on the cotton house."

Again the Warden and the two officers looked at the third man, at the gaunt, unshaven wild face in which an old terror, an old blending of fear and impotence and rage still lingered. "He never came for you?" the Warden said. "You never saw him?"

"Never nobody came for me," the refugee said. He began to tremble though at first he spoke quietly enough. "I set there on that sonabitching cotton house, expecting hit to go any minute. I saw that launch and them boats come up and they never had no room for me. Full of bastard niggers and one of them setting there playing a guitar but there wasn't no room for me. A guitar!" he cried; now he began to scream, trembling, slavering, his face twitching and jerking. "Room for a bastard nigger guitar but not for me—"

"Steady now," the Warden said. "Steady now."

"Give him a drink," one of the officers said. The Warden poured the drink. The deputy handed it to the refugee, who took the glass in both jerking hands and tried to raise it to his mouth. They watched him for perhaps twenty seconds, then the deputy took the glass from him and held it to his lips while he gulped, though even then a thin trickle ran from each corner of his mouth, into the stubble on his chin.

"So we picked him and—" the deputy called the plump convict's name now "—both up just before dark and come on in. But that other fellow is gone."

"Yes," the Warden said. "Well. Here I haven't lost a prisoner in ten years, and now, like this—I'm sending you back to the Farm tomorrow. Have his family notified, and his discharge papers filled out at once."

"All right," the deputy said. "And listen, chief. He wasn't a bad fellow and maybe he never had no business in that boat. Only he did say he could paddle one. Listen. Suppose I write on his discharge, Drowned while trying to save lives in the great flood of nineteen twenty-seven, and send it down for the Governor to sign it. It will be something nice for his folks to have, to hang on the wall when neighbors come in or something. Maybe they will even give his folks a cash bonus because after all they sent him to the Farm to raise cotton, not to fool around in a boat in a flood."

"All right," the Warden said. "I'll see about it. The main thing is to get his name off the books as dead before some politician tries to collect his food allowance."

"All right," the deputy said. He turned and herded his companions out. In the drizzling darkness again he said to the plump convict: "Well, your partner beat you. He's free. He's done served his time out but you've got a right far piece to go yet."

"Yah," the plump convict said. "Free. He can have it."

III

As the short convict had testified, the tall one, when he returned to the surface, still retained what the short one called the paddle. He clung to it, not instinctively against the time when he would be back inside the boat and would need it, because for a time he did not believe he would ever regain the skiff or anything else that would support him, but because he did not have time to think about turning it loose. Things had moved too fast for him. He had not been warned, he had felt the first snatching tug of the current, he had seen the skiff begin to spin and his companion vanish violently upward like in a translation out of Isaiah, then he himself was in the water, struggling against the drag of the paddle which he did not know he still held each time he fought back to the surface and grasped at the spinning skiff which at one instant was ten feet away and the next poised above his head as though about to brain him, until at last he grasped the stern, the drag of his body becoming a rudder to the skiff, the two of them, man and boat and with the paddle perpendicular above them like a jackstaff, vanishing from the view of the short convict (who had vanished from that of the tall one with the same celerity though in a vertical direction) like a tableau snatched offstage intact with violent and incredible speed.

He was now in the channel of a slough, a bayou, in which until today no current had run probably since the old subterranean outrage which had created the country. There was plenty of current in it now though; from his trough behind the stern he seemed to see the trees and sky rushing past with vertiginous speed, looking down at him between the gouts of cold yellow in lugubrious and mournful amazement. But they were fixed and secure in something; he thought of that, he remembered in an instant of despairing rage the firm earth fixed and founded strong and cemented fast and stable forever by the generations of laborious sweat, somewhere beneath him, beyond the reach of his feet, when, and again without warning, the stern of the skiff struck him a stunning blow across the bridge of his nose. The instinct which had caused him to cling to it now caused him to fling the paddle into the boat in order to grasp the gunwale with both hands just as the skiff pivoted and spun away again. With both hands free he now dragged himself over the stern and lay prone on his face, streaming with blood and water and panting, not with exhaustion but with that furious rage which is terror's aftermath.

But he had to get up at once because he believed he had come much faster (and so further) than he had. So he rose, out of the watery scarlet puddle in which he had lain, streaming, the soaked denim heavy as iron on his limbs, the black hair plastered to his skull, the blood-infused water streaking his jumper, and dragged his forearm gingerly and hurriedly across his lower face and glanced at it then grasped the paddle and began to try to swing the skiff back upstream. It did not even occur to him that he did not know where his companion was, in which tree among all which he had passed or might pass. He did not even speculate on that for the reason that he knew so incontestably that the other was upstream from him, and after his recent experience the mere connotation of the term upstream carried a sense of such violence and force and speed that the conception of it as other than a straight line was something which the intelligence, reason, simply refused to harbor, like the notion of a rifle bullet the width of a cotton field.

The bow began to swing back upstream. It turned readily, it outpaced the aghast and outraged instant in which he realized it was swinging far too easily, it had swung on over the arc and lay broadside to the current and began again that vicious spinning while he sat, his teeth bared in his bloody streaming face while his spent arms flailed the impotent paddle at the water, that inno-cent-appearing medium which at one time had held him in ironlike and shifting convolutions like an anaconda yet which now seemed to offer no more resistance to the thrust of his urge and need than so much air, like air; the boat which had threatened him and at last actually struck him in the face with the shocking violence of a mule's hoof now seemed to poise weightless upon it like a thistle bloom, spinning like a wind vane while he flailed at the water and thought of, envisioned, his companion safe, inactive, and at ease in the tree with nothing to do but wait, musing with impotent and terrified fury upon that arbitrariness of human affairs which had abrogated to the one the secure tree and to the other the hysterical and unmanageable boat for the very reason that it knew that he alone of the two of them would make any attempt to return and rescue his companion.

The skiff had paid off and now ran with the current again. It seemed again to spring from immobility into incredible speed, and he thought he must already be miles away from where his companion had quitted him, though actually he had merely described a big circle since getting back into the skiff, and the object (a clump of cypress trees choked by floating logs and debris) which the skiff was now about to strike was the same one it had careened into before when the stern had struck him. He didn't know this because he had not yet ever looked higher than the bow of the boat. He didn't look higher now, he just saw that he was going to strike; he seemed to feel run through the very insentient fabric of the skiff a current of eager gleeful vicious incorrigible wilfulness; and he who had never ceased to flail at the bland treacherous water with what he had believed to be the limit of his strength now from somewhere, some ultimate absolute reserve, produced a final measure of endurance, will to endure, which adumbrated mere muscle and nerves, continuing to flail the paddle right up to the instant of striking, completing one last reach, thrust and recover out of pure desperate reflex, as a man slipping on ice reaches for his hat and money-pocket, as the skiff struck and hurled him once more flat on his face in the bottom of it.

This time he did not get up at once. He lay flat on his

face, slightly spread-eagled and in an attitude almost peaceful, a kind of abject meditation. He would have to get up sometime, he knew that, just as all life consists of having to get up sooner or later and then having to lie down again sooner or later after a while. And he was not exactly exhausted and he was not particularly without hope and he did not especially dread getting up. It merely seemed to him that he had accidentally been caught in a situation in which time and environment, not himself, were mesmerized; he was being toyed with by a current of water going nowhere, beneath a day which would wane toward no evening; when it was done with him it would spew him back into the comparatively safe world he had been snatched violently out of, and in the meantime it did not much matter just what he did or did not do. So he lay on his face, now not only feeling but hearing the strong quiet rustling of the current on the underside of the planks, for a while longer. Then he raised his head and this time touched his palm gingerly to his face and looked at the blood again, then he sat up onto his heels and leaning over the gunwale he pinched his nostrils between thumb and finger and expelled a gout of blood and was in the act of wiping his fingers on his thigh when a voice slightly above his line of sight said quietly, "It's taken you a while," and he who up to this moment had had neither reason nor time to raise his eyes higher than the bows looked up and saw, sitting in a tree and looking at him, a woman. She was not ten feet away. She sat on the lowest limb of one of the trees holding the jam he had grounded on, in a calico wrapper and an army private's tunic and a sunbonnet, a woman whom he did not even bother to examine since that first startled glance had been ample to reveal to him all the generations of her life and background, who could have been his sister if he had a sister, his wife if he had not entered the penitentiary at an age scarcely out of adolescence and some years younger than that at which even his prolific

and monogamous kind married—a woman who sat clutching the trunk of the tree, her stockingless feet in a pair of
man's unlaced brogans less than a yard from the water,
who was very probably somebody's sister and quite certainly (or certainly should have been) somebody's wife,
though this too he had entered the penitentiary too
young to have had more than mere theoretical female experience to discover yet. "I thought for a minute you
wasn't aiming to come back."

"Come back?"

"After the first time. After you run into this brush pile
the first time and got into the boat and went on." He
looked about, touching his face tenderly again; it could
very well be the same place where the boat had hit him
in the face.

"Yah," he said. "I'm here now though."

"Could you maybe get the boat a little closer? I taken
a right sharp strain getting up here; maybe I better . . ."
He was not listening; he had just discovered that the paddle was gone; this time when the skiff hurled him forward
he had flung the paddle not into it but beyond it. "It's
right there in them brush tops," the woman said. "You
can get it. Here. Catch a holt of this." It was a grapevine.
It had grown up into the tree and the flood had torn the
roots loose. She had taken a turn with it about her upper
body; she now loosed it and swung it out until he could
grasp it. Holding to the end of the vine he warped the
skiff around the end of the jam, picking up the paddle,
and warped the skiff on beneath the limb and held it and
now he watched her move, gather herself heavily and
carefully to descend—that heaviness which was not painful but just excruciatingly careful, that profound and almost lethargic awkwardness which added nothing to the
sum of that first aghast amazement which had served already for the catafalque of invincible dream since even in
durance he had continued (and even with the old avid-
ity, even though they had caused his downfall) to con-

sume the impossible pulp-printed fables carefully cen-
sored and as carefully smuggled into the penitentiary;
and who to say what Helen, what living Garbo, he had
not dreamed of rescuing from what craggy pinnacle or
dragoned keep when he and his companion embarked in
the skiff. He watched her, he made no further effort to
help her beyond holding the skiff savagely steady while
she lowered herself from the limb—the entire body, the
deformed swell of belly bulging the calico, suspended by
its arms, thinking, *And this is what I get. This, out of all
the female meat that walks, is what I have to be caught
in a runaway boat with.*

"Where's that cottonhouse?" he said.

"Cottonhouse?"

"With that fellow on it. The other one."

"I don't know. It's a right smart of cottonhouses around
here. With folks on them too, I reckon." She was examining him. "You're bloody as a hog," she said. "You look
like a convict."

"Yah," he said, snarled. "I feel like I done already been
hung. Well, I got to pick up my pardner and then find
that cottonhouse." He cast off. That is, he released his
hold on the vine. That was all he had to do, for even while
the bow of the skiff hung high on the log jam and even
while he held it by the vine in the comparatively dead
water behind the jam, he felt steadily and constantly the
whisper, the strong purring power of the water just one
inch beyond the frail planks on which he squatted and
which, as soon as he released the vine, took charge of the
skiff not with one powerful clutch but in a series of
touches light, tentative, and catlike; he realized now that
he had entertained a sort of foundationless hope that
the added weight might make the skiff more controllable.
During the first moment or two he had a wild (and still
foundationless) belief that it had; he had got the head
upstream and managed to hold it so by terrific exertion
continued even after he discovered that they were travel-

ling straight enough but stern-first and continued somehow even after the bow began to wear away and swing:
the old irresistible movement which he knew well by now,
too well to fight against it, so that he let the bow swing
on downstream with the hope of utilizing the skiff's
own momentum to bring it through the full circle and so
upstream again, the skiff travelling broadside then bow-
first then broadside again, diagonally across the channel,
toward the other wall of submerged trees; it began to flee
beneath him with terrific speed, they were in an eddy but
did not know it; he had no time to draw conclusions or
even wonder; he crouched, his teeth bared in his blood-
caked and swollen face, his lungs bursting, flailing at the
water while the trees stooped hugely down at him. The
skiff struck, spun, struck again; the woman half lay in the
bow, clutching the gunwales, as if she were trying to
crouch behind her own pregnancy; he banged now not
at the water but at the living sapblooded wood with the
paddle, his desire now not to go anywhere, reach any destination, but just to keep the skiff from beating itself to
fragments against the tree trunks. Then something ex-
ploded, this time against the back of his head, and stooping trees and dizzy water, the woman's face and all,
fled together and vanished in bright soundless flash and
glare.

An hour later the skiff came slowly up an old logging
road and so out of the bottom, the forest, and into (or
onto) a cottonfield—a gray and limitless desolation now
free of turmoil, broken only by a thin line of telephone
poles like a wading millipede. The woman was now paddling, steadily and deliberately, with that curious lethargic care, while the convict squatted, his head between
his knees, trying to stanch the fresh and apparently inexhaustible flow of blood from his nose with handfuls of
water. The woman ceased paddling, the skiff drifted on,
slowing, while she looked about. "We're done out," she
said.

The convict raised his head and also looked about. "Out where?"

"I thought maybe you might know."

"I don't even know where I used to be. Even if I knowed which way was north, I wouldn't know if that was where I wanted to go." He cupped another handful of water to his face and lowered his hand and regarded the resulting crimson marbling on his palm, not with dejection, not with concern, but with a kind of sardonic and vicious bemusement. The woman watched the back of his head.

"We got to get somewhere."

"Don't I know it? A fellow on a cottonhouse. Another in a tree. And now that thing in your lap."

"It wasn't due yet. Maybe it was having to climb that tree quick yesterday, and having to set in it all night. I'm doing the best I can. But we better get somewhere soon."

"Yah," the convict said. "I thought I wanted to get somewhere too and I ain't had no luck at it. You pick out a place to get to now and we'll try yours. Gimme that oar." The woman passed him the paddle. The boat was a double-ender; he had only to turn around.

"Which way you fixing to go?" the woman said.

"Never you mind that. You just keep on holding on." He began to paddle, on across the cottonfield. It began to rain again, though not hard at first. "Yah," he said. "Ask the boat. I been in it since breakfast and I ain't never knowed, where I aimed to go or where I was going either."

That was about one o'clock. Toward the end of the afternoon the skiff (they were in a channel of some sort again, they had been in it for some time; they had got into it before they knew it and too late to get out again, granted there had been any reason to get out, as, to the convict anyway, there was certainly none and the fact that their speed had increased again was reason enough to stay in it) shot out upon a broad expanse of debris-filled water which the convict recognized as a river and, from its size, the Yazoo River, though it was little enough he had seen of this country which he had not quitted for so much as one single day in the last seven years of his life. What he did not know was that it was now running backward. So as soon as the drift of the skiff indicated the set of the current, he began to paddle in that direction which he believed to be downstream, where he knew there were towns—Yazoo City, and as a last resort, Vicksburg, if his luck was that bad, if not, smaller towns whose names he did not know but where there would be people, houses, something, anything he might reach and surrender his charge to and turn his back on her forever, on all pregnant and female life forever and return to that monastic existence of shotguns and shackles where he would be secure from it. Now, with the imminence of habitations, release from her, he did not even hate her. When he looked upon the swelling and unmanageable body before him it seemed to him that it was not the woman at all but rather a separate demanding threatening inert yet living mass of which both he and she were equally victims; thinking, as he had been for the last three or four hours, of that minute's—nay, second's—aberration of eye or hand which would suffice to precipitate her into the water to be dragged down to death by that senseless millstone which, in its turn, would not even have to feel agony, he no longer felt any glow of revenge toward her as its custodian, he felt sorry for her as he would for the living timber in a barn which had to be burned to rid itself of vermin.

He paddled on, helping the current, steadily and strongly, with a calculated husbandry of effort, toward what he believed was downstream, towns, people, something to stand upon, while from time to time the woman raised herself to bail the accumulated rain from the skiff. It was raining steadily now though still not hard, still without passion, the sky, the day itself dissolving without grief; the skiff moved in a nimbus, an aura of gray gauze which merged almost without demarcation with the roiling spittle-frothed debris-choked water. Now the day, the light, definitely began to end and the convict permitted himself an extra notch or two of effort because it suddenly seemed to him that the speed of the skiff had lessened. This was actually the case though the convict did not know it. He merely took it as a phenomenon of the increasing obfuscation, or at most as a result of the long day's continuous effort with no food, complicated by the ebbing and fluxing phases of anxiety and impotent rage at his absolutely gratuitous predicament. So he stepped up his stroke a beat or so, not from alarm but on the contrary, since he too had received that lift from the mere presence of a known stream, a river known by its ineradicable name to generations of men who had been drawn to live beside it as man always has been drawn to dwell beside water, even before he had a name for water and fire, drawn to the living water, the course of his destiny and his actual physical appearance rigidly coerced and postulated by it. So he was not alarmed. He paddled on, upstream without knowing it, unaware that all the water which for forty hours now had been pouring through the levee break to the north was somewhere ahead of him, on its way back to the River.

It was full dark now. That is, night had completely come, the gray dissolving sky had vanished, yet as though in perverse ratio surface visibility had sharpened, as though the light which the rain of the afternoon had washed out of the air had gathered upon the water as the rain itself had done, so that the yellow flood spread on before him now with a quality almost phosphorescent, right up to the instant where vision ceased. The darkness in fact had its advantages; he could now stop seeing the rain. He and his garments had been wet for more than twenty-four hours now so he had long since stopped feeling it, and now that he could no longer see it either it had in a certain sense ceased for him. Also, he now had to make no effort even not to see the swell of his passenger's belly. So he was paddling on, strongly and steadily, not alarmed and not concerned but just exasperated because he had not yet begun to see any reflection on the clouds which would indicate the city or cities which he believed he was approaching but which were actually now miles behind him, when he heard a sound. He did not know what it was because he had never heard it before and he would never be expected to hear such again, since it is not given to every man to hear such at all and to none to hear it more than once in his life. And he was not alarmed now either because there was not time, for although the visibility ahead, for all its clarity, did not extend very far, yet in the next instant to the hearing he was also seeing something such as he had never seen before. This was that the sharp line where the phosphorescent water met the darkness was now about ten feet higher than it had been an instant before and that it was curled forward upon itself like a sheet of dough being rolled out for a pudding. It reared, stooping; the crest of it swirled like the mane of a galloping horse and, phosphorescent too, fretted and flickered like fire. And while the woman huddled in the bows, aware or not aware the convict did not know which, he (the convict), his swollen and blood-streaked face gaped in an expression of aghast and incredulous amazement, continued to paddle directly into it. Again he simply had not had time to order his rhythm-hypnotized muscles to cease. He continued to paddle though the skiff had ceased to move forward at all but seemed to be hanging in space, while the paddle still reached, thrust, recovered and reached again; now instead of space the skiff became abruptly surrounded by a welter of fleeing debris—planks, small buildings, the bodies of drowned yet antic animals, entire trees leaping and diving like porpoises, above which the skiff seemed to hover in weightless and airy indecision like a bird above a fleeing countryside, undecided where to light or whether to light at all, while the convict squatted in it still going through the motions of paddling, waiting for an opportunity to scream. He never found it. For an instant the skiff seemed to stand erect on its stern and then shoot scrabbling and scrambling up the curling wall of water like a cat, and soared on above the licking crest itself and hung cradled into the high actual air in the limbs of a tree, from which bower of new-leafed boughs and branches the convict, like a bird in its nest and still waiting his chance to scream and still going through the motions of paddling though he no longer even had the paddle now, looked down upon a world turned to furious motion and in incredible retrograde.

Some time about midnight, accompanied by a rolling cannonade of thunder and lightning like a battery going into action, as though some forty hours' constipation of the elements, the firmament itself, were discharging in clapping and glaring salute to the ultimate acquiescence to desperate and furious motion, and still leading its charging welter of dead cows and mules and outhouses and cabins and hencoops, the skiff passed Vicksburg. The convict didn't know it. He wasn't looking high enough above the water; he still squatted, clutching the gunwales and glaring at the yellow turmoil about him, out of which entire trees, the sharp gables of houses, the long mournful heads of mules which he fended off with a splintered length of plank snatched from he knew not where in passing (and which seemed to glare reproachfully back at him with sightless eyes, in limber-lipped and incredulous amazement) rolled up and then down again, the skiff now travelling forward, now sideways, now sternward, sometimes in the water, sometimes riding for yards upon the roofs of houses and trees and even upon the backs of the mules as though even in death they were not to escape that burden-bearing doom with which their eunuch race was cursed. But he didn't see Vicksburg; the skiff, travel-

ling at express speed, was in a seething gut between soaring and dizzy banks with a glare of light above them but
he did not see it; he saw the flotsam ahead of him divide
violently and begin to climb upon itself, mounting, and he
was sucked through the resulting gap too fast to recognize it as the trestling of a railroad bridge; for a horrible
moment the skiff seemed to hang in static indecision before the looming flank of a steamboat as though undecided whether to climb over it or dive under it, then a
hard icy wind filled with the smell and taste and sense of
wet and boundless desolation blew upon him; the skiff
made one long bounding lunge as the convict's native
state, in a final paroxysm, regurgitated him onto the wild
bosom of the Father of Waters.

This is how he told about it seven weeks later, sitting
in new bedticking garments, shaved and with his hair cut
again, on his bunk in the barracks:

During the next three or four hours after the thunder
and lightning had spent itself, the skiff ran in pitch
streaming darkness upon a roiling expanse which, even
if he could have seen, apparently had no boundaries. Wild
and invisible, it tossed and heaved about and beneath the
boat, ridged with dirty phosphorescent foam and filled
with a debris of destruction—objects nameless and enormous and invisible, which struck and slashed at the skiff
and whirled on. He did not know he was now upon the
River. At that time he would have refused to believe it,
even if he had known. Yesterday he had known he was
in a channel by the regularity of the spacing between the
bordering trees. Now, since even by daylight he could
have seen no boundaries, the last place under the sun (or
the streaming sky rather) he would have suspected himself to be would have been a river; if he had pondered at
all about his present whereabouts, about the geography
beneath him, he would merely have taken himself to be
travelling at dizzy and inexplicable speed above the largest cottonfield in the world; if he who yesterday had

known he was in a river, had accepted that fact in good faith and earnest, then had seen that river turn without warning and rush back upon him with furious and deadly intent like a frenzied stallion in a lane—if he had suspected for one second that the wild and limitless expanse on which he now found himself was a river, consciousness would simply have refused; he would have fainted.

When daylight—a gray and ragged dawn filled with driving scud between icy rain-squalls—came and he could see again, he knew he was in no cottonfield. He knew that the wild water on which the skiff tossed and fled flowed above no soil tamely trod by man, behind the straining and surging buttocks of a mule. That was when it occurred to him that its present condition was no phenomenon of a decade, but that the intervening years during which it consented to bear upon its placid and sleepy bosom the frail mechanicals of man's clumsy contriving was the phenomenon and this the norm and the River was now doing what it liked to do, had waited patiently the ten years in order to do, as a mule will work for you ten years for the privilege of kicking you once. And he also learned something else about fear too, something he had even failed to discover on that other occasion when he was really afraid—that three or four seconds of that night in his youth while he looked down the twice-flashing pistol barrel of the terrified mail clerk before the clerk could be persuaded that his (the convict's) pistol would not shoot: that if you just held on long enough a time would come in fear after which it would no longer be agony at all but merely a kind of horrible outrageous itching, as after you have been burned bad.

He did not have to paddle now, he just steered (who had been without food for twenty-four hours now and without any sleep to speak of for fifty) while the skiff sped on across that boiling desolation where he had long since begun to not dare believe he could possibly be where he could not doubt he was, trying with his frag-

ment of splintered plank merely to keep the skiff intact
and afloat among the houses and trees and dead animals
(the entire towns, stores, residences, parks and farmyards,
which leaped and played about him like fish), not trying
to reach any destination, just trying to keep the skiff afloat
until he did. He wanted so little. He wanted nothing for
himself. He just wanted to get rid of the woman, the belly,
and he was trying to do that in the right way, not for himself, but for her. He could have put her back into another
tree at any time—

"Or you could have jumped out of the boat and let her
and it drown," the plump convict said. "Then they could
have given you the ten years for escaping and then hung
you for the murder and charged the boat to your folks."

"Yah," the tall convict said.—But he had not done that.
He wanted to do it the right way, find somebody, anybody he could surrender her to, something solid he
could set her down on and then jump back into the river,
if that would please anyone. That was all he wanted—
just to come to something, anything. That didn't seem
like a great deal to ask. And he couldn't do it. He told
how the skiff fled on—

"Didn't you pass nobody?" the plump convict said.
"No steamboat, nothing?"

"I don't know," the tall one said.—while he tried
merely to keep it afloat, until the darkness thinned and
lifted and revealed—

"Darkness?" the plump convict said. "I thought you
said it was already daylight."

"Yah," the tall one said. He was rolling a cigarette,
pouring the tobacco carefully from a new sack, into the
creased paper. "This was another one. They had several
while I was gone."—the skiff to be moving still rapidly up
a winding corridor bordered by drowned trees which the
convict recognized again to be a river running again in
the direction that, until two days ago, had been upstream.
He was not exactly warned through instinct that this one,

like that of two days ago, was in reverse. He would not
say that he now believed himself to be in the same river,
though he would not have been surprised to find that he
did believe this, existing now, as he did and had and apparently was to continue for an unnamed period, in a
state in which he was toy and pawn on a vicious and inflammable geography. He merely realized that he was in
a river again, with all the subsequent inferences of a com-
prehensible, even if not familiar, portion of the earth's
surface. Now he believed that all he had to do would be
to paddle far enough and he would come to something
horizontal and above water even if not dry and perhaps
even populated; and, if fast enough, in time, and that his
only other crying urgency was to refrain from looking at
the woman who, as vision, the incontrovertible and apparently inescapable presence of his passenger, returned
with dawn, had ceased to be a human being and (you
could add twenty-four more hours to the first twenty-four
and the first fifty now, even counting the hen. It was dead,
drowned, caught by one wing under a shingle on a roof
which had rolled momentarily up beside the skiff yesterday and he had eaten some of it raw though the woman
would not) had become instead one single inert monstrous
sentient womb from which, he now believed, if he could
only turn his gaze away and keep it away, would disappear, and if he could only keep his gaze from pausing
again at the spot it had occupied, would not return. That's
what he was doing this time when he discovered the
wave was coming.

He didn't know how he discovered it was coming back.
He heard no sound, it was nothing felt nor seen. He did
not even believe that finding the skiff to be now in slack
water—that is, that the motion of the current which,
whether right or wrong, had at least been horizontal, had
now stopped that and assumed a vertical direction—was
sufficient to warn him. Perhaps it was just an invincible
and almost fanatic faith in the inventiveness and innate

viciousness of that medium on which his destiny was now cast, apparently forever; a sudden conviction far beyond either horror or surprise that now was none too soon for it to prepare to do whatever it was it intended doing. So he whirled the skiff, spun it on its heel like a running horse, whereupon, reversed, he could not even distinguish the very channel he had come up. He did not know whether he simply could not see it or if it had vanished some time ago and he not aware at the time; whether the river had become lost in a drowned world or if the world had become drowned in one limitless river. So now he could not tell if he were running directly before the wave or quartering across its line of charge; all he could do was keep that sense of swiftly accumulating ferocity behind him and paddle as fast as his spent and now numb muscles could be driven, and try not to look at the woman, to wrench his gaze from her and keep it away until he reached something flat and above water. So, gaunt, hollow-eyed, striving and wrenching almost physically at his eyes as if they were two of those suction-tipped rubber arrows shot from the toy gun of a child, his spent muscles obeying not will now, but that attenuation beyond mere exhaustion which, mesmeric, can continue easier than cease, he once more drove the skiff full tilt into something it could not pass and, once more hurled violently forward onto his hands and knees, crouching, he glared with his wild swollen face up at the man with the shotgun and said in a harsh, croaking voice: "Vicksburg? Where's Vicksburg?"

Even when he tried to tell it, even after the seven weeks and he safe, secure, riveted warranted and doubly guaranteed by the ten years they had added to his sentence for attempted escape, something of the old hysteric incredulous outrage came back into his face, his voice, his speech. He never did even get on the other boat. He told how he clung to a strake (it was a dirty unpainted shanty boat with a drunken rake of tin stove pipe, it had been moving when he struck it and apparently it had not even changed course even though the three people on it must have been watching him all the while—a second man, barefoot and with matted hair and beard also at the steering sweep, and then—he did not know how long— a woman leaning in the door, in a filthy assortment of men's garments, watching him too with the same cold speculation) being dragged violently along, trying to state and explain his simple (and to him at least) reasonable desire and need; telling it, trying to tell it, he could feel again the old unforgettable affronting like an ague fit as he watched the abortive tobacco rain steadily and faintly from between his shaking hands and then the paper itself part with a thin dry snapping report:

"Burn my clothes?" the convict cried. "Burn them?"

"How in hell do you expect to escape in them billboards?" the man with the shotgun said. He (the convict) tried to tell it, tried to explain as he had tried to explain not to the three people on the boat alone but to the entire circumambience—desolate water and forlorn trees and sky—not for justification because he needed none and knew that his hearers, the other convicts, required none from him, but rather as, on the point of exhaustion, he might have picked dreamily and incredulously at a suffocation. He told the man with the gun how he and his partner had been given the boat and told to pick up a man and a woman, how he had lost his partner and failed to find the man, and now all in the world he wanted was something flat to leave the woman on until he could find an officer, a sheriff. He thought of home, the place where he had lived almost since childhood, his friends of years whose ways he knew and who knew his ways, the familiar fields where he did work he had learned to do well and to like, the mules with characters he knew and respected as he knew and respected the characters of certain men; he thought of the barracks at night, with screens against the bugs in summer and good stoves in winter and someone to supply the fuel and the food too; the Sunday ball games and the picture shows—things which, with the exception of the ball games, he had never known before. But most of all, his own character (Two years ago they had offered to make a trusty of him. He would no longer need to plow or feed stock, he would only follow those who did with a loaded gun, but he declined. "I reckon I'll stick to plowing," he said, absolutely without humor. "I done already tried to use a gun one time too many.") his good name, his responsibility not only toward those who were responsible toward him but to himself, his own honor in the doing of what was asked of him, his pride in being able to do it, no matter what it was. He thought of this and listened to the man with the gun talking about escape and it seemed to him that, hanging there, being dragged violently along (It was here he said that he first noticed the goats' beards of moss in the trees, though it could have been there for several days so far as he knew. It just happened that he first noticed it here.) that he would simply burst.

"Can't you get it into your head that the last thing I want to do is run away?" he cried. "You can set there with that gun and watch me; I give you fair lief. All I want is to put this woman—"

"And I told you she could come aboard," the man with the gun said in his level voice. "But there ain't no room on no boat of mine for nobody hunting a sheriff in no kind of clothes, let alone a penitentiary suit."

"When he steps aboard, knock him in the head with the gun barrel," the man at the sweep said. "He's drunk."

"He ain't coming aboard," the man with the gun said. "He's crazy."

Then the woman spoke. She didn't move, leaning in the door, in a pair of faded and patched and filthy overalls like the two men: "Give them some grub and tell them to get out of here." She moved, she crossed the deck and looked down at the convict's companion with her cold sullen face. "How much more time have you got?"

"It wasn't due till next month," the woman in the boat said. "But I—" The woman in overalls turned to the man with the gun.

"Give them some grub," she said. But the man with the gun was still looking down at the woman in the boat.

"Come on," he said to the convict. "Put her aboard, and beat it."

"And what'll happen to you," the woman in overalls said, "when you try to turn her over to an officer. When you lay alongside a sheriff and the sheriff asks you who you are?" Still the man with the gun didn't even look at her. He hardly even shifted the gun across his arm as he struck the woman across the face with the back of his other hand, hard. "You son of a bitch," she said. Still the man with the gun did not even look at her.

"Well?" he said to the convict.

"Don't you see I can't?" the convict cried. "Can't you see that?"

Now, he said, he gave up. He was doomed. That is, he knew now that he had been doomed from the very start never to get rid of her, just as the ones who sent him out with the skiff knew that he never would actually give up; when he recognized one of the objects which the woman in overalls was hurling into the skiff to be a can of condensed milk, he believed it to be a presage, gratuitous and irrevocable as a death-notice over the telegraph, that he was not even to find a flat stationary surface in time for the child to be born on it. So he told how he held the skiff alongside the shanty-boat while the first tentative toying of the second wave made up beneath him, while the woman in overalls passed back and forth between house and rail, flinging the food—the hunk of salt meat, the ragged and filthy quilt, the scorched lumps of cold bread which she poured into the skiff from a heaped dishpan like so much garbage—while he clung to the strake against the mounting pull of the current, the new wave

which for the moment he had forgotten because he was
still trying to state the incredible simplicity of his desire
and need until the man with the gun (the only one of the
three who wore shoes) began to stamp at his hands, he
snatching his hands away one at a time to avoid the heavy
shoes, then grasping the rail again until the man with the
gun kicked at his face, he flinging himself sideways to
avoid the shoe and so breaking his hold on the rail, his
weight canting the skiff off at a tangent on the increasing
current so that it began to leave the shanty boat behind
and he paddling again now, violently, as a man hurries
toward the precipice for which he knows at last he is
doomed, looking back at the other boat, the three faces
sullen, derisive, and grim and rapidly diminishing across
the widening water and at last, apoplectic, suffocating
with the intolerable fact not that he had been refused but
that he had been refused so little, had wanted so little,
asked for so little, yet there had been demanded of him
in return the one price out of all breath which (they
must have known) if he could have paid it, he would not
have been where he was, asking what he asked, raising
the paddle and shaking it and screaming curses back at
them even after the shotgun flashed and the charge went
scuttering past along the water to one side.

So he hung there, he said, shaking the paddle and
howling, when suddenly he remembered that other wave,
the second wall of water full of houses and dead mules
building up behind him back in the swamp. So he quit
yelling then and went back to paddling. He was not trying to outrun it. He just knew from experience that when
it overtook him, he would have to travel in the same direction it was moving in anyway, whether he wanted to
or not, and when it did overtake him, he would begin to
move too fast to stop, no matter what places he might
come to where he could leave the woman, land her in
time. Time: that was his itch now, so his only chance was
to stay ahead of it as long as he could and hope to reach

something before it struck. So he went on, driving the skiff with muscles which had been too tired so long they had quit feeling it, as when a man has had bad luck for so long that he ceases to believe it is even bad, let alone luck. Even when he ate—the scorched lumps the size of baseballs and the weight and durability of cannel coal even after having lain in the skiff's bilge where the shanty boat woman had thrown them—the iron-like lead-heavy objects which no man would have called bread outside of the crusted and scorched pan in which they had cooked—it was with one hand, begrudging even that from the paddle.

He tried to tell that too—that day while the skiff fled on among the bearded trees while every now and then small quiet tentative exploratory feelers would come up from the wave behind and toy for a moment at the skiff, light and curious, then go on with a faint hissing sighing, almost a chuckling, sound, the skiff going on, driving on with nothing to see but trees and water and solitude: until after a while it no longer seemed to him that he was trying to put space and distance behind him or shorten space and distance ahead but that both he and the wave were now hanging suspended simultaneous and unprogressing in pure time, upon a dreamy desolation in which he paddled on not from any hope even to reach anything at all but merely to keep intact what little of distance the length of the skiff provided between himself and the inert and inescapable mass of female meat before him; then night and the skiff rushing on, fast since any speed over anything unknown and invisible is too fast, with nothing before him, and behind him the outrageous idea of a volume of moving water toppling forward, its crest frothed and shredded like fangs, and then dawn again (another of those dreamlike alterations day to dark then back to day again with that quality truncated, anachronic, and unreal as the waxing and waning of lights in a theatre scene) and the skiff emerging now with the woman no longer supine beneath the shrunken soaked private's coat but sitting bolt upright, gripping the gunwales with both hands, her eyes closed and her lower lip caught between her teeth and he driving the splintered board furiously now, glaring at her out of his wild swollen sleepless face and crying, croaking, "Hold on! For God's sake hold on!"

"I'm trying to," she said. "But hurry! Hurry!" He told it, the unbelievable: hurry, hasten: the man falling from a cliff being told to catch onto something and save himself; the very telling of it emerging shadowy and burlesque, ludicrous, comic, and mad, from the ague of unbearable forgetting with a quality more dreamily furious than any fable behind proscenium lights:

He was in a basin now— "A basin?" the plump convict said. "That's what you wash in."

"All right," the tall one said, harshly, above his hands. "I did." With a supreme effort he stilled them long enough to release the two bits of cigarette paper and watched them waft in light fluttering indecision to the floor between his feet, holding his hands motionless even for a moment longer—a basin, a broad peaceful yellow sea which had an abruptly and curiously ordered air, giving him, even at that moment, the impression that it was accustomed to water even if not total submersion; he even remembered the name of it, told to him two or three weeks later by someone: Atchafalaya—

"Louisiana?" the plump convict said. "You mean you were clean out of Mississippi? Hell fire." He stared at the tall one. "Shucks," he said. "That ain't but just across from Vicksburg."

"They never named any Vicksburg across from where I was," the tall one said. "It was Baton Rouge they named." And now he began to talk about a town, a little neat white portrait town nestling among enormous very green trees, appearing suddenly in the telling as it probably appeared in actuality, abrupt and airy and mirage-like and incredibly serene before him, behind a scattering of boats moored to a line of freight cars standing flush to the doors in water. And now he tried to tell that too: how he stood waist-deep in water for a moment looking back and down at the skiff in which the woman half lay, her eyes still closed, her knuckles white on the gunwales and a tiny thread of blood creeping down her chin from her chewed lip, and he looking down at her in a kind of furious desperation.

"How far will I have to walk?" she said.

"I don't know, I tell you!" he cried. "But it's land somewhere yonder! It's land, houses."

"If I try to move, it won't even be born inside a boat," she said. "You'll have to get closer."

"Yes," he cried, wild, desperate, incredulous. "Wait. I'll go and surrender, then they will have—" He didn't finish, wait to finish; he told that too: himself splashing, stumbling, trying to run, sobbing and gasping; now he saw it—another loading platform standing above the yellow flood, the khaki figures on it as before, identical, the same; he said how the intervening days since that first innocent morning telescoped, vanished as if they had never been, the two contiguous succeeding instants (succeeding? simultaneous) and he transported across no intervening space but merely turned in his own footsteps, plunging, splashing, his arms raised, croaking harshly. He heard the startled shout, "There's one of them!", the command, the clash of equipment, the alarmed cry: "There he goes! There he goes!"

"Yes!" he cried, running, plunging, "here I am! Here! Here!" running on, into the first scattered volley, stopping among the bullets, waving his arms, shrieking, "I want to surrender! I want to surrender!" watching not in terror but in amazed and absolutely unbearable outrage as a squatting clump of the khaki figures parted and he saw the machine gun, the blunt thick muzzle slant and drop and probe toward him and he still screaming in his hoarse crow's voice, "I want to surrender! Can't you hear me?" continuing to scream even as he whirled and plunged splashing, ducking, went completely under and heard the bullets going thuck-thuck-thuck on the water above him and he scrabbling still on the bottom, still trying to scream even before he regained his feet and still all submerged save his plunging unmistakable buttocks, the outraged screaming bubbling from his mouth and about his face since he merely wanted to surrender. Then he was comparatively screened, out of range, though not for long. That is (he didn't tell how nor where) there was a moment in which he paused, breathed for a second before running again, the course back to the skiff open for the time being though he could still hear the shouts behind him and now and then a shot, and he panting, sobbing, a long savage tear in the flesh of one hand, got when and how he did not know, and he wasting precious breath, speaking to no one now any more than the scream of the dying rabbit is addressed to any mortal ear but rather an indictment of all breath and its folly and suffering, its infinite capacity for folly and pain, which seems to be its only immortality: "All in the world I want is just to surrender."

He returned to the skiff and got in and took up his splintered plank. And now when he told this, despite the fury of element which climaxed it, it (the telling) became quite simple; he now even creased another cigarette paper between fingers which did not tremble at all and filled the paper from the tobacco sack without spilling a flake, as though he had passed from the machine-gun's barrage into a bourne beyond any more amazement: so that the subsequent part of his narrative seemed to reach his listeners as though from beyond a sheet of slightly milky though still transparent glass, as something not heard but seen—a series of shadows, edgeless yet distinct, and smoothly flowing, logical and unfrantic and making no sound: They were in the skiff, in the center of the broad placid trough which had no boundaries and down which the tiny forlorn skiff flew to the irresistible coercion of a current going once more he knew not where, the neat small liveoak-bowered towns unattainable and miragelike and apparently attached to nothing upon the airy and unchanging horizon. He did not believe them, they did not matter, he was doomed; they were less than the figments of smoke or of delirium, and he driving his unceasing paddle without destination or even hope now, looking now and then at the woman sitting with her knees drawn up and locked and her entire body one terrific clench while the threads of bloody saliva crept from her teeth-clenched lower lip. He was going nowhere and fleeing from nothing, he merely continued to paddle because he had paddled so long now that he believed if he stopped his muscles would scream in agony. So when it happened he was not surprised. He heard the sound which he knew well (he had heard it but once before, true enough, but no man needed hear it but once) and he had been expecting it; he looked back, still driving the paddle, and saw it, curled, crested with its strawlike flotsam of trees and debris and dead beasts and he glared over his shoulder at it for a full minute out of that attenuation far beyond the point of outragement where even suffering, the capability of being further affronted, had ceased, from which he now contemplated with savage and invulnerable curiosity the further extent to which his now anesthetized nerves could bear, what next could be invented for them to bear, until the wave actually began to rear above his head into its thunderous climax. Then only did he turn his head. His stroke did not falter, it neither slowed nor increased; still paddling with that spent hypnotic steadiness, he saw the swimming deer. He did not know what it was nor that he had altered the skiff's course to follow it, he just watched the swimming head before him as the wave boiled down and the skiff rose bodily in the old familiar fashion on a welter of tossing trees and houses and bridges and fences, he still paddling even while the

paddle found no purchase save air and still paddled even
as he and the deer shot forward side by side at arm's
length, he watching the deer now, watching the deer
begin to rise out of the water bodily until it was actually
running along upon the surface, rising still, soaring clear
of the water altogether, vanishing upward in a dying crescendo of splashings and snapping branches, its damp scut
flashing upward, the entire animal vanishing upward as
smoke vanishes. And now the skiff struck and canted and
he was out of it too, standing knee-deep, springing out
and falling to his knees, scrambling up, glaring after the
vanished deer. "Land!" he croaked. "Land! Hold on! Just
hold on!" He caught the woman beneath the arms, dragging her out of the boat, plunging and panting after the
vanished deer. Now earth actually appeared—an acclivity
smooth and swift and steep, bizarre, solid, and unbelievable; an Indian mound, and he plunging at the muddy
slope, slipping back, the woman struggling in his muddy
hands.

"Let me down!" she cried. "Let me down!" But he held
her, panting, sobbing, and rushed again at the muddy
slope; he had almost reached the flat crest with his now
violently unmanageable burden when a stick under his
foot gathered itself with thick convulsive speed. *It was a
snake*, he thought as his feet fled beneath him and with
the indubitable last of his strength he half pushed and
half flung the woman up the bank as he shot feet first and
face down back into that medium upon which he had
lived for more days and nights than he could remember
and from which he himself had never completely
emerged, as if his own failed and spent flesh were attempt-
ing to carry out his furious unflagging will for severance
at any price, even that of drowning, from the burden
with which, unwitting and without choice, he had been
doomed. Later it seemed to him that he had carried back
beneath the surface with him the sound of the infant's first
mewling cry.

IV

When the woman asked him if he had a knife, standing there in the streaming bedticking garments which had got him shot at, the second time by a machine gun, on the two occasions when he had seen any human life after leaving the levee four days ago, the convict felt exactly as he had in the fleeing skiff when the woman suggested that they had better hurry. He felt the same outrageous affronting of a condition purely moral, the same raging impotence to find any answer to it; so that, standing above her, spent suffocating and inarticulate, it was a full minute before he comprehended that she was now crying, "The can! The can in the boat!" He did not anticipate what she could want with it; he did not even wonder nor stop to ask. He turned running; this time he thought, *It's another moccasin* as the thick body truncated in that awkward reflex which had nothing of alarm in it but only alertness, he not even shifting his stride though he knew his running foot would fall within a yard of the flat head. The bow of the skiff was well up the slope now where the wave had set it and there was another snake just crawling over the stern into it and as he stooped for the bailing can he saw something else swimming toward the mound, he didn't know what—a head, a face at the apex of a vee of ripples. He snatched up the can; by pure juxtaposition of it and water he scooped it full, already turning. He saw the deer again, or another one. That is, he saw a deer —a side glance, the light smoke-colored phantom in a cypress vista then gone, vanished, he not pausing to look after it, galloping back to the woman and kneeling with the can to her lips until she told him better.

It had contained a pint of beans or tomatoes, something, hermetically sealed and opened by four blows of an axe heel, the metal flap turned back, the jagged edges razor-sharp. She told him how, and he used this in lieu of a knife, he removed one of his shoelaces and cut it in two with the sharp tin. Then she wanted warm water—"If I just had a little hot water," she said in a weak serene voice without particular hope; only when he thought of matches it was again a good deal like when she had asked him if he had a knife, until she fumbled in the pocket of the shrunken tunic (it had a darker double vee on one cuff and a darker blotch on the shoulder where service stripes and a divisional emblem had been ripped off but this meant nothing to him) and produced a match-box contrived by telescoping two shotgun shells. So he drew her back a little from the water and went to hunt wood dry enough to burn, thinking this time, *It's just another snake,* only, he said, he should have thought *ten thousand other snakes:* and now he knew it was not the same deer because he saw three at one time, does or bucks, he did not know which since they were all antlerless in May, and besides he had never seen one of any kind anywhere before except on a Christmas card; and then the rabbit, drowned, dead anyway, already torn open, the bird, the hawk, standing upon it—the erected crest, the hard vicious patrician nose, the intolerant omnivorous yellow eye— and he kicking at it, kicking it lurching and broad-winged into the actual air.

When he returned with the wood and the dead rabbit, the baby, wrapped in the tunic, lay wedged between two cypress-knees and the woman was not in sight, though while the convict knelt in the mud, blowing and nursing his meagre flame, she came slowly and weakly from the direction of the water. Then, the water heated at last and there, produced from somewhere he was never to know, she herself perhaps never to know until the need comes, no woman perhaps ever to know, only no woman will even wonder, that square of something somewhere between sackcloth and silk—squatting, his own wet garments steaming in the fire's heat, he watched her bathe the child with a savage curiosity and interest that became amazed unbelief, so that at last he stood above them both, looking down at the tiny terra-cotta colored creature resembling nothing, and thought, *And this is all. This is what severed me violently from all I ever knew and did not wish to leave and cast me upon a medium I was born to fear, to fetch up at last in a place I never saw before and where I do not even know where I am.*

Then he returned to the water and refilled the bailing can. It was drawing toward sunset now (or what would have been sunset save for the high prevailing overcast) of this day whose beginning he could not even remember. When he returned to where the fire burned in the interlaced gloom of the cypresses, even after this short absence, evening had definitely come, as though darkness too had taken refuge upon that quarter-acre mound, that earthen Ark out of Genesis, that dim wet cypress-choked life-teeming constricted desolation, in what direction and how far from what and where he had no more idea than of the day of the month, and had now with the setting of the sun crept forth again to spread upon the waters. He stewed the rabbit in sections while the fire burned redder and redder in the darkness where the shy wild eyes of small animals—once the tall mild almost plate-sized stare of one of the deer—glowed and vanished and glowed again, the broth hot and rank after the four days; he seemed to hear the roar of his own saliva as he watched the woman sip the first canful. Then he drank too; they ate the other fragments which had been charring and scorching on willow twigs; it was full night now. "You and him better sleep in the boat," the convict said. "We want to get an early start tomorrow." He shoved the bow of the skiff off the land so it would lie level, he lengthened the painter with a piece of grapevine and returned to the fire and tied the grapevine about his wrist and lay down. It was mud he lay upon, but it was solid underneath, it was earth, it did not move; if you fell upon it you broke your bones against its incontrovertible passivity sometimes, but it did not accept you substance-less and enveloping and suffocating, down and down and down; it was hard at times to drive a plow through, it sent you spent, weary, and cursing its light-long insatiable demands, back to your bunk at sunset at times, but it did not snatch you violently out of all familiar knowing and sweep you, thrall and impotent, for days against any returning. *I don't know where I am and I don't reckon I know the way back to where I want to go,* he thought. *But at least the boat has stopped long enough to give me a chance to turn it around.*

He waked at dawn, the light faint, the sky jonquil-colored; the day would be fine. The fire had burned out; on the opposite side of the cold ashes lay three snakes motionless and parallel as underscoring, and in the swiftly making light others seemed to materialize: earth which an instant before had been mere earth broke up into motionless coils and loops, branches which a moment before had been mere branches now become immobile ophidian festoons, even as the convict stood thinking about food, about something hot before they started. But he decided against this, against wasting this much time, since there still remained in the skiff quite a few of the rocklike objects which the shanty woman had flung into it, besides (thinking this) no matter how fast nor successfully he hunted, he would never be able to lay up enough food to get them back to where they wanted to go. So he returned to the skiff, paying himself back to it by his vine-spliced painter, back to the water on which a low mist, thick as cotton batting (though apparently not very tall, deep), lay, into which the stern of the skiff was already beginning to disappear, although it lay with its prow almost touching the mound. The woman waked, stirred. "We fixing to start now?" she said.

"Yah," the convict said. "You ain't aiming to have another one this morning, are you?" He got in and shoved the skiff clear of the land, which immediately began to dissolve into the mist. "Hand me the oar," he said over his shoulder, not turning yet.

"The oar?"

He turned his head. "The oar. You're laying on it." But she was not, and for an instant during which the mound, the island continued to fade slowly into the mist which seemed to enclose the skiff in weightless and impalpable wool like a precious or fragile bauble or jewel, the convict squatted not in dismay but in that frantic and astonished outrage of a man who, having just escaped a falling safe, is struck by the following two-ounce paper weight which was sitting on it: this the more unbearable because he knew that never in his life had he less time to give way to it. He did not hesitate. Grasping the grape-vine end he sprang into the water, vanishing in the violent action of climbing and reappeared still climbing and (who had never learned to swim) plunged and threshed on toward the almost-vanished mound, moving through the water then upon it as the deer had done yesterday and scrabbled up the muddy slope and lay gasping and panting, still clutching the grapevine end.

Now the first thing he did was to choose what he believed to be the most suitable tree (for an instant in which he knew he was insane he thought of trying to saw it down with the flange of the bailing can) and build a fire against the butt of it. Then he went to seek food. He spent the next six days seeking it while the tree burned through and fell and burned through again at the proper length and he nursing little constant cunning flames along the flanks of the log to make it paddle-shaped, nursing them at night too while the woman and baby (it was eating, nursing now, he turning his back or even returning into the woods each time she prepared to open the faded tunic) slept in the skiff. He learned to watch for stooping hawks and so found more rabbits, and twice possums; they ate some drowned fish which gave them both a rash and then a violent flux and one snake which the woman thought was turtle and which did them no harm, and one night it rained and he got up and dragged brush, shaking the snakes (he no longer thought, *It ain't nothing but another moccasin,* he just stepped aside for them as they, when there was time, telescoped sullenly aside for him) out of it with the old former feeling of personal invulnerability and built a shelter and the rain stopped at once and did not recommence and the woman went back to the skiff.

Then one night—the slow tedious charring log was almost a paddle now—one night and he was in bed, in his bed in the bunkhouse, and it was cold, he was trying to pull the covers up only his mule wouldn't let him, prodding and bumping heavily at him, trying to get into the narrow bed with him, and now the bed was cold too and wet and he was trying to get out of it only the mule would not let him, holding him by his belt in its teeth, jerking and bumping him back into the cold wet bed and, leaning, gave him a long swipe across the face with its cold limber musculated tongue, and he waked to no fire, no coal even beneath where the almost-finished paddle had been charring, and something else prolonged and coldly limber passed swiftly across his body where he lay in four inches of water while the nose of the skiff alternately tugged at the grapevine tied about his waist and bumped and shoved him back into the water again. Then something else came up and began to nudge at his ankle (the log, the oar, it was) even as he groped frantically for the skiff, hearing the swift rustling going to and fro inside the hull as the woman began to thrash about and scream. "Rats!" she cried. "It's full of rats!"

"Lay still!" he cried. "It's just snakes. Can't you hold still long enough for me to find the boat?" Then he found it, he got into it with the unfinished paddle; again the thick muscular body convulsed under his foot; it did not strike; he would not have cared, glaring astern where he could see a little—the faint outer luminosity of the open water. He poled toward it, thrusting aside the snake-looped branches, the bottom of the skiff resounding faintly to thick solid plops, the woman shrieking steadily. Then the skiff was clear of the trees, the mound, and now he could feel the bodies whipping about his ankles and hear the rasp of them as they went over the gunwale. He drew the log in and scooped it forward along the bottom of the boat and up and out; against the pallid water he could see three more of them in lashing convolutions before they vanished. "Shut up!" he cried. "Hush! I wish I was a snake so I could get out too!"

When once more the pale and heatless wafer disc of the early sun stared down at the skiff (whether they were moving or not the convict did not know) in its nimbus of fine cotton batting, the convict was hearing again that sound which he had heard twice before and would never forget—that sound of deliberate and irresistible and monstrously disturbed water. But this time he could not tell from what direction it came. It seemed to be everywhere, waxing and fading; it was like a phantom behind the mist, at one instant miles away, the next on the point of overwhelming the skiff within the next second; suddenly, in the instant he would believe (his whole weary body would spring and scream) that he was about to drive the skiff point-blank into it and with the unfinished paddle of the color and texture of sooty bricks, like something gnawed out of an old chimney by beavers and weighing twenty-five pounds, he would whirl the skiff frantically and find the sound dead ahead of him again. Then something bellowed tremendously above his head, he heard human voices, a bell jangled and the sound ceased and the mist vanished as when you draw your hand across a frosted pane, and the skiff now lay upon a sunny glitter of brown water flank to flank with, and about thirty yards away from, a steamboat. The decks were crowded and packed with men, women, and children sitting or standing beside and among a homely conglomeration of hurried furniture, who looked mournfully and silently down into the skiff while the convict and the man with a megaphone in the pilot house talked to each other in alternate puny shouts and roars above the chuffing of the reversed engines:

"What in hell are you trying to do? Commit suicide?"

"Which is the way to Vicksburg?"

"Vicksburg? Vicksburg? Lay alongside and come aboard."

"Will you take the boat too?"

"Boat? Boat?" Now the megaphone cursed, the roaring waves of blasphemy and biological supposition empty cavernous and bodiless in turn, as if the water, the air, the mist had spoken it, roaring the words then taking them back to itself and no harm done, no scar, no insult left anywhere. "If I took aboard every floating sardine can you sonabitchin mushrats want me to I wouldn't even have room forrard for a leadsman. Come aboard! Do you expect me to hang here on stern engines till hell freezes?"

"I ain't coming without the boat," the convict said. Now another voice spoke, so calm and mild and sensible that for a moment it sounded more foreign and out of place than even the megaphone's bellowing and bodiless profanity:

"Where is it you are trying to go?"

"I ain't trying," the convict said. "I'm going. Parchman." The man who had spoken last turned and appeared to converse with a third man in the pilot house. Then he looked down at the skiff again.

"Carnarvon?"

"What?" the convict said. "Parchman?"

"All right. We're going that way. We'll put you off where you can get home. Come aboard."

"The boat too?"

"Yes, yes. Come along. We're burning coal just to talk to you." So the convict came alongside then and watched them help the woman and baby over the rail and he came aboard himself, though he still held to the end of the vine-spliced painter until the skiff was hoisted onto the boiler deck. "My God," the man, the gentle one, said, "is that what you have been using for a paddle?"

"Yah," the convict said. "I lost the plank."

"The plank," the mild man (the convict told how he seemed to whisper it), "the plank. Well. Come along and get something to eat. Your boat is all right now."

"I reckon I'll wait here," the convict said. Because now, he told them, he began to notice for the first time that the other people, the other refugees who crowded the deck, who had gathered in a quiet circle about the upturned skiff on which he and the woman sat, the grapevine painter wrapped several times about his wrist and clutched in his hand, staring at him and the woman with queer hot mournful intensity, were not white people—

"You mean niggers?" the plump convict said.

"No. Not Americans."

"Not Americans? You was clean out of *America* even?"

"I don't know," the tall one said. "They called it Atcha-falaya."—Because after a while he said, "What?" to the man and the man did it again, gobble-gobble—

"Gobble-gobble?" the plump convict said.

"That's the way they talked," the tall one said. "Gob-ble-gobble, whang, caw-caw-to-to."—And he sat there and watched them gobbling at one another and then look-ing at him again, then they fell back and the mild man (he wore a Red-Cross brassard) entered, followed by a waiter with a tray of food. The mild man carried two glasses of whiskey.

"Drink this," the mild man said. "This will warm you." The woman took hers and drank it but the convict told how he looked at his and thought, *I ain't tasted whiskey in seven years.* He had not tasted it but once before that; it was at the still itself back in a pine hollow; he was seventeen, he had gone there with four companions, two of whom were grown men, one of twenty-two or -three,

the other about forty; he remembered it. That is, he remembered perhaps a third of that evening—a fierce turmoil in the hell-colored firelight, the shock and shock of
blows about his head (and likewise of his own fists on
other hard bone), then the waking to a splitting and blind-
ing sun in a place, a cowshed, he had never seen before
and which later turned out to be twenty miles from his
home. He said he thought of this and he looked about at
the faces watching him and he said,

"I reckon not."

"Come, come," the mild man said. "Drink it."

"I don't want it."

"Nonsense," the mild man said. "I'm a doctor. Here.
Then you can eat." So he took the glass and even then he
hesitated but again the mild man said, "Come along, down
with it; you're still holding us up," in that voice still calm
and sensible but a little sharp too—the voice of a man
who could keep calm and affable because he wasn't used
to being crossed—and he drank the whiskey and even in
the second between the sweet full fire in his belly and
when it began to happen he was trying to say, "I tried to
tell you! I tried to!" But it was too late now in the pallid
sun-glare of the tenth day of terror and hopelessness and
despair and impotence and rage and outrage and it was
himself and the mule, his mule (they had let him name it
—John Henry) which no man save he had plowed for
five years now and whose ways and habits he knew and
respected and who knew his ways and habits so well that
each of them could anticipate the other's very movements
and intentions; it was himself and the mule, the little
gobbling faces flying before them, the familiar hard skull-
bones shocking against his fists, his voice shouting, "Come
on, John Henry! Plow them down! Gobble them down,
boy!" even as the bright hot red wave turned back, meeting it joyously, happily, lifted, poised, then hurling
through space, triumphant and yelling, then again the old
shocking blow at the back of his head: he lay on the deck,

flat on his back and pinned arm and leg and cold sober
again, his nostrils gushing again, the mild man stooping
over him with behind the thin rimless glasses the coldest
eyes the convict had ever seen—eyes which the convict
said were not looking at him but at the gushing blood with
nothing in the world in them but complete impersonal
interest.

"Good man," the mild man said. "Plenty of life in the
old carcass yet, eh? Plenty of good red blood too. Did anyone ever suggest to you that you were hemophilic?"

—"What?" the plump convict said. "Hemophilic? You
know what that means?" The tall convict had his cigarette
going now, his body jackknifed backward into the coffin-
like space between the upper and lower bunks, lean,
clean, motionless, the blue smoke wreathing across his
lean dark aquiline shaven face. "That's a calf that's a bull
and a cow at the same time."

"No, it ain't," a third convict said. "It's a calf or a colt
that ain't neither one."

"Hell fire," the plump one said. "He's got to be one or
the other to keep from drounding." He had never ceased
to look at the tall one in the bunk; now he spoke to him
again: "You let him call you that?"—The tall one had
done so. He did not answer the doctor (this was where
he stopped thinking of him as the mild man) at all. He
could not move either, though he felt fine, he felt better
than he had in ten days. So they helped him to his feet
and steadied him over and lowered him onto the upturned
skiff beside the woman, where he sat bent forward, elbows on knees in the immemorial attitude, watching his
own bright crimson staining the mud-trodden deck, until the doctor's clean clipped hand appeared under his
nose with a phial.

"Smell," the doctor said. "Deep." The convict inhaled,
the sharp ammoniac sensation burned up his nostrils and
into his throat. "Again," the doctor said. The convict inhaled obediently. This time he choked and spat a gout

of blood, his nose now had no more feeling than a toenail, other than it felt about the size of a ten-inch shovel, and as cold.

"I ask you to excuse me," he said. "I never meant—"

"Why?" the doctor said. "You put up as pretty a scrap against forty or fifty men as I ever saw. You lasted a good two seconds. Now you can eat something. Or do you think that will send you haywire again?"

They both ate, sitting on the skiff, the gobbling faces no longer watching them now, the convict gnawing slowly and painfully at the thick sandwich, hunched, his face laid sideways to the food and parallel to the earth as a dog chews; the steamboat went on. At noon there were bowls of hot soup and bread and more coffee; they ate this too, sitting side by side on the skiff, the grapevine still wrapped about the convict's wrist. The baby waked and nursed and slept again and they talked quietly:

"Was it Parchman he said he was going to take us?"

"That's where I told him I wanted to go."

"It never sounded exactly like Parchman to me. It sounded like he said something else." The convict had thought that too. He had been thinking about that fairly soberly ever since they boarded the steamboat and soberly indeed ever since he had remarked the nature of the other passengers, those men and women definitely a little shorter than he and with skin a little different in pigmentation from any sunburn, even though the eyes were sometimes blue or gray, who talked to one another in a tongue he had never heard before and who apparently did not understand his own, people the like of whom he had never seen about Parchman nor anywhere else and whom he did not believe were going there or beyond there either. But after his hill-billy country fashion and kind he would not ask, because, to his raising, asking information was asking a favor and you did not ask favors of strangers; if they offered them perhaps you accepted and you expressed gratitude almost tediously recapitulant, but you did not ask. So he would watch and wait, as he had done before, and do or try to do to the best of his ability what the best of his judgment dictated.

So he waited, and in midafternoon the steamboat chuffed and thrust through a willow-choked gorge and emerged from it, and now the convict knew it was the River. He could believe it now—the tremendous reach, yellow and sleepy in the afternoon—"Because it's too big," he told them soberly. "Ain't no flood in the world big enough to make it do more than stand a little higher so it can look back and see just where the flea is, just exactly where to scratch. It's the little ones, the little piddling creeks, that run backward one day and forward the next and come busting down on a man full of dead mules and hen houses."—and the steamboat moving up this now (*like a ant crossing a plate,* the convict thought, sitting beside the woman on the upturned skiff, the baby nursing again, apparently looking too out across the water where, a mile away on either hand, the twin lines of levee resembled parallel unbroken floating thread) and then it was nearing sunset and he began to hear, to notice, the voices of the doctor and of the man who had first bawled at him through the megaphone now bawling again from the pilot house overhead:

"Stop? Stop? Am I running a street car?"

"Stop for the novelty then," the doctor's pleasant voice said. "I don't know how many trips back and forth you have made in yonder nor how many of what you call mushrats you have fetched out. But this is the first time you ever had two people—no, three—who not only knew the name of some place they wished to go to but were actually trying to go there." So the convict waited while the sun slanted more and more and the steamboat-ant crawled steadily on across its vacant and gigantic plate turning more and more to copper. But he did not ask, he just waited. *Maybe it was Carrollton he said,* he thought. *It begun with a C.* But he did not believe that either. He did not know where he was, but he did know that this was not anywhere near the Carrollton he remembered from that day seven years ago when, shackled wrist to wrist with the deputy sheriff, he had passed through it on the train—the slow spaced repeated shattering banging of trucks where two railroads crossed, a random scattering of white houses tranquil among trees on green hills lush with summer, a pointing spire, the finger of the hand of God. But there was no river there. *And you ain't never close to this river without knowing it,* he thought. *I don't care who you are nor where you have been all your life.* Then the head of the steamboat began to swing across the stream, its shadow swinging too, travelling long before it across the water, toward the vacant ridge of willow-massed earth empty of all life. There was nothing there at all, the convict could not even see either earth or water beyond it; it was as though the steamboat were about to crash slowly through the thin low frail willow barrier and embark into space, or lacking this, slow and back and fill and disembark him into space, granted it was about to disembark him, granted this was that place which was not near Parchman and was not Carrollton either, even though it did begin with C. Then he turned his head and saw the doctor stooping over the woman, pushing the baby's eyelid up with his forefinger, peering at it.

"Who else was there when he came?" the doctor said.

"Nobody," the convict said.

"Did it all yourselves, eh?"

"Yes," the convict said. Now the doctor stood up and looked at the convict.

"This is Carnarvon," he said.

"Carnarvon?" the convict said. "That ain't—" Then he stopped, ceased. And now he told about that—the intent eyes as dispassionate as ice behind the rimless glasses, the clipped quick-tempered face that was not accustomed to being crossed or lied to either.—"Yes," the plump convict said. "That's what I was aiming to ask. Them clothes.

Anybody would know them. How if this doctor was as smart as you claim he was—"

"I had slept in them for ten nights, mostly in the mud," the tall one said. "I had been rowing since midnight with that sapling oar I had tried to burn out that I never had time to scrape the soot off. But it's being scared and worried and then scared and then worried again in clothes for days and days and days that changes the way they look. I don't mean just your pants." He did not laugh. "Your face too. That doctor knowed."

"All right," the plump one said. "Go on."—

"I know it," the doctor said. "I discovered that while you were lying on the deck yonder sobering up again. Now don't lie to me. I don't like lying. This boat is going to New Orleans."

"No," the convict said immediately, quietly, with absolute finality. He could hear them again—the thuck-thuck-thuck on the water where an instant before he had been. But he was not thinking of the bullets. He had forgotten them, forgiven them. He was thinking of himself crouching, sobbing, panting before running again—the voice, the indictment, the cry of final and irrevocable repudiation of the old primal faithless Manipulator of all the lust and folly and injustice: *All in the world I wanted was just to surrender;* thinking of it, remembering it but without heat now, without passion now and briefer than an epitaph: *No. I tried that once. They shot at me.*

"So you don't want to go to New Orleans. And you didn't exactly plan to go to Carnarvon. But you will take Carnarvon in preference to New Orleans." The convict said nothing. The doctor looked at him, the magnified pupils like the heads of two bridge nails. "What were you in for? Hit him harder than you thought, eh?"

"No. I tried to rob a train."

"Say that again." The convict said it again. "Well? Go on. You don't say that in the year 1927 and just stop, man." So the convict told it, dispassionately too—about the magazines, the pistol which would not shoot, the mask and the dark lantern in which no draft had been arranged to keep the candle burning so that it died almost with the match but even then left the metal too hot to carry, won with subscriptions. *Only it ain't my eyes or my mouth either he's watching,* he thought. *It's like he is watching the way my hair grows on my head.* "I see," the doctor said. "But something went wrong. But you've had plenty of time to think about it since. To decide what was wrong, what you failed to do."

"Yes," the convict said. "I've thought about it a right smart since."

"So next time you are not going to make that mistake."

"I don't know," the convict said. 'There ain't going to be a next time."

"Why? If you know what you did wrong, they won't catch you next time."

The convict looked at the doctor steadily. They looked at each other steadily; the two sets of eyes were not so different after all. "I reckon I see what you mean," the convict said presently. "I was eighteen then. I'm twenty-five now."

"Oh," the doctor said. Now (the convict tried to tell it) the doctor did not move, he just simply quit looking at the convict. He produced a pack of cheap cigarettes from his coat. "Smoke?" he said.

"I wouldn't care for none," the convict said.

"Quite," the doctor said in that affable clipped voice. He put the cigarettes away. "There has been conferred upon my race (the Medical race) also the power to bind and to loose, if not by Jehovah perhaps, certainly by the American Medical Association—on which incidentally, in this day of Our Lord, I would put my money, at any odds, at any amount, at any time. I don't know just how far out of bounds I am on this specific occasion but I think we'll put it to the touch." He cupped his hands to his mouth, toward the pilot house overhead. "Captain!" he

shouted. "We'll put these three passengers ashore here."
He turned to the convict again. "Yes," he said, "I think
I shall let your native State lick its own vomit. Here."
Again his hand emerged from his pocket, this time with
a bill in it.

"No," the convict said.

"Come, come; I don't like to be disputed either."

"No," the convict said. "I ain't got any way to pay it
back."

"Did I ask you to pay it back?"

"No," the convict said. "I never asked to borrow it either."

So once more he stood on dry land, who had already
been toyed with twice by that risible and concentrated
power of water, once more than should have fallen to the
lot of any one man, any one lifetime, yet for whom there
was reserved still another unbelievable recapitulation, he
and the woman standing on the empty levee, the sleeping child wrapped in the faded tunic and the grapevine
painter still wrapped about the convict's wrist, watching
the steamboat back away and turn and once more crawl
onward up the platter-like reach of vacant water burnished
more and more to copper, its trailing smoke roiling in
slow copper-edged gouts, thinning out along the water,
fading, stinking, away across the vast serene desolation,
the boat growing smaller and smaller until it did not seem
to crawl at all but to hang stationary in the airy substance-
less sunset, dissolving into nothing like a pellet of floating
mud.

Then he turned and for the first time looked about him.
behind him, recoiling, not through fear but through pure
reflex and not physically but the soul, the spirit, that profound sober alert attentiveness of the hillman who will
not ask anything of strangers, not even information, thinking quietly, *No. This ain't Carrollton neither.* Because he
now looked down the almost perpendicular landward
slope of the levee through sixty feet of absolute space,

upon a surface, a terrain flat as a waffle and of the color
of a waffle, or perhaps of the summer coat of a claybank
horse, and possessing that same piled density of a rug or
peltry, spreading away without undulation yet with that
curious appearance of imponderable solidity like fluid,
broken here and there by thick humps of arsenical green
which nevertheless still seemed to possess no height and
by writhen veins of the color of ink which he began to
suspect to be actual water but with judgment reserved,
with judgment still reserved even when presently he was
walking in it. That's what he said, told: So they went on.
He didn't tell how he got the skiff singlehanded up the
revetment and across the crown and down the opposite
sixty foot drop, he just said he went on, in a swirling cloud
of mosquitoes like hot cinders, thrusting and plunging
through the saw-edged grass which grew taller than his
head and which whipped back at his arms and face like
limber knives, dragging by the vine-spliced painter the
skiff in which the woman sat, slogging and stumbling
knee-deep in something less of earth than water, along
one of those black winding channels less of water than
earth: and then (he was in the skiff too now, paddling
with the charred log, what footing there had been having given away beneath him without warning thirty minutes ago, leaving only the air-filled bubble of his jumper-
back ballooning lightly on the twilit water until he rose
to the surface and scrambled into the skiff) the house,
the cabin a little larger than a horse-box, of cypress boards
and an iron roof, rising on ten-foot stilts slender as spi-
ders' legs, like a shabby and death-stricken (and probably
poisonous) wading creature which had got that far into
that flat waste and died with nothing nowhere in reach
or sight to lie down upon, a pirogue tied to the foot of a
crude ladder, a man standing in the open door holding a
lantern (it was that dark now) above his head, gobbling
down at them.

He told it—of the next eight or nine or ten days, he

did not remember which, while the four of them—himself and the woman and baby and the little wiry man with rotting teeth and soft wild bright eyes like a rat or a chipmunk, whose language neither of them could understand —lived in the room and a half. He did not tell it that way, just as he apparently did not consider it worth the breath to tell how he had got the hundred-and-sixty-pound skiff singlehanded up and across and down the sixty-foot levee. He just said, "After a while we come to a house and we stayed there eight or nine days then they blew up the levee with dynamite so we had to leave." That was all. But he remembered it, but quietly now, with the cigar now, the good one the Warden had given him (though not lighted yet) in his peaceful and steadfast hand, remembering that first morning when he waked on the thin pallet beside his host (the woman and baby had the one bed) with the fierce sun already latticed through the warped rough planking of the wall, and stood on the rickety porch looking out upon that flat fecund waste, neither earth nor water, where even the senses doubted which was which, which rich and massy air and which mazy and impalpable vegetation, and thought quietly, *He must do something here to eat and live. But I don't know what. And until I can go on again, until I can find where I am and how to pass that town without them seeing me I will have to help him do it so we can eat and live too, and I don't know what.* And he had a change of clothing too, almost at once on that first morning, not telling any more than he had about the skiff and the levee how he had begged borrowed or bought from the man whom he had not laid eyes on twelve hours ago and with whom on the day he saw him for the last time he still could exchange no word, the pair of dungaree pants which even the Cajun had discarded as no longer wearable, filthy, buttonless, the legs slashed and frayed into fringe like that on an 1890 hammock, in which he stood naked from the waist up and holding out to her the mud-caked and

soot-stained jumper and overall when the woman waked
on that first morning in the crude bunk nailed into one
corner and filled with dried grass, saying, "Wash them.
Good. I want all them stains out. All of them."

"But the jumper," she said. "Ain't he got ere old shirt
too? That sun and them mosquitoes—" But he did not
even answer, and she said no more either, though when
he and the Cajun returned at dark the garments were
clean, stained a little still with the old mud and soot, but
clean, resembling again what they were supposed to resemble as (his arms and back already a fiery red which
would be blisters by tomorrow) he spread the garments
out and examined them and then rolled them up carefully
in a six-months-old New Orleans paper and thrust the
bundle behind a rafter, where it remained while day followed day and the blisters on his back broke and sup-
purated and he would sit with his face expressionless as
a wooden mask beneath the sweat while the Cajun doped
his back with something on a filthy rag from a filthy saucer,
she still saying nothing since she too doubtless knew what
his reason was, not from that rapport of the wedded conferred upon her by the two weeks during which they had
jointly suffered all the crises, emotional social economic
and even moral, which do not always occur even in the
ordinary fifty married years (the old married: you have
seen them, the electroplate reproductions, the thousand
identical coupled faces with only a collarless stud or a
fichu out of Louisa Alcott to denote the sex, looking in
pairs like the winning braces of dogs after a field trial, out
from among the packed columns of disaster and alarm
and baseless assurance and hope and incredible insensi-
tivity and insulation from tomorrow, propped by a thousand morning sugar bowls or coffee urns; or singly, rocking on porches or sitting in the sun beneath the tobacco-
stained porticoes of a thousand county courthouses, as
though with the death of the other having inherited a
sort of rejuvenescence, immortality; relict, they take a

new lease on breath and seem to live forever, as though
that flesh which the old ceremony or ritual had morally
purified and made legally one had actually become so with
long tedious habit and he or she who entered the ground
first took all of it with him or her, leaving only the old
permanent enduring bone, free and trammelless)—not because of this but because she too had stemmed at some
point from the same dim hill-bred Abraham.

So the bundle remained behind the rafter and day followed day while he and his partner (he was in partnership now with his host, hunting alligators on shares, on
the halvers he called it—"Halvers?" the plump convict
said. "How could you make a business agreement with a
man you claim you couldn't even talk to?"

"I never had to talk to him," the tall one said. "Money
ain't got but one language."—departed at dawn each day,
at first together in the pirogue but later singly, the one in
the pirogue and the other in the skiff, the one with the
battered and pitted rifle, the other with the knife and a
piece of knotted rope and a lightwood club the size and
weight and shape of a Thuringian mace, stalking their
pleistocene nightmares up and down the secret inky channels which writhed the flat brass-colored land. He remembered that too: that first morning when turning in the sunrise from the rickety platform he saw the hide nailed
drying to the wall and stopped dead, looking at it quietly,
thinking quietly and soberly, *So that's it. That's what he
does in order to eat and live,* knowing it was a hide, a skin,
but from what animal, by association, ratiocination, or
even memory of any picture out of his dead youth, he did
not know, but knowing that it was the reason, the explanation, for the little lost spider-legged house (which
had already begun to die, to rot from the legs upward almost before the roof was nailed on) set in that teeming
and myriad desolation, enclosed and lost within the furious embrace of flowing mare earth and stallion sun, divining through pure rapport of kind for kind, hill-billy and

bayou-rat, the two one and identical because of the same grudged dispensation and niggard fate of hard and unceasing travail not to gain future security, a balance in the bank or even in a buried soda can for slothful and easy old age, but just permission to endure and endure to buy air to feel and sun to drink for each's little while, thinking (the convict), *Well, anyway I am going to find out what it is sooner than I expected to,* and did so, re-entered the house where the woman was just waking in the one sorry built-in straw-filled bunk which the Cajun had surrendered to her, and ate the breakfast (the rice, a semiliquid mess violent with pepper and mostly fish considerably high, the chicory-thickened coffee) and, shirtless, followed the little scuttling bobbing bright-eyed rotten-toothed man down the crude ladder and into the pirogue. He had never seen a pirogue either and he believed that it would not remain upright—not that it was light and precariously balanced with its open side upward but that there was inherent in the wood, the very log, some dynamic and unsleeping natural law, almost will, which its present position outraged and violated—yet accepting this too as he had the fact that that hide had belonged to something larger than any calf or hog, and that anything which looked like that on the outside would be more than likely to have teeth and claws too, accepting this, squatting in the pirogue, clutching both gunwales, rigidly immobile as though he had an egg filled with nitroglycerin in his mouth and scarcely breathing, thinking, *If that's it, then I can do it too and even if he can't tell me how I reckon I can watch him and find out.* And he did this too, he remembered it, quietly even yet, thinking, *I thought that was how to do it and I reckon I would still think that even if I had it to do again now for the first time*—the brazen day already fierce upon his naked back, the crooked channel like a voluted thread of ink, the pirogue moving steadily to the paddle which both entered and left the water without a sound; then the sudden cessation of the paddle behind him and the fierce hissing gobble of the Cajun at his back, and he squatting bate-breathed and with that intense immobility of complete sobriety of a blind man listening, while the frail wooden shell stole on at the dying apex of its own parted water. Afterward he remembered the rifle too—the rust-pitted single-shot weapon with a clumsily wired stock and a muzzle you could have driven a whiskey cork into, which the Cajun had brought into the boat—but not now; now he just squatted, crouched, immobile, breathing with infinitesimal care, his sober unceasing gaze going here and there constantly as he thought, *What? What? I not only don't know what I am looking for, I don't even know where to look for it.* Then he felt the motion of the pirogue as the Cajun moved and then the tense gobbling hissing actually, hot rapid and repressed, against his neck and ear, and glancing downward saw projecting between his own arm and body from behind the Cajun's hand holding the knife, and glaring up again saw the flat thick spit of mud, which as he looked at it divided and became a thick mud-colored log which in turn seemed, still immobile, to leap suddenly against his retinae in three—no, four—dimensions: volume, solidity, shape, and another: not fear but pure and intense speculation and he looking at the scaled motionless shape, thinking not, *It looks dangerous* but *It looks big*, thinking, *Well, maybe a mule standing in a lot looks big to a man that never walked up to one with a halter before*, thinking, *Only if he could just tell me what to do it would save time*, the pirogue drawing nearer now, creeping now, with no ripple now even, and it seemed to him that he could even hear his companion's held breath, and he taking the knife from the other's hand now and not even thinking this since it was too fast, a flash; it was not a surrender, not a resignation, it was too calm, it was a part of him, he had drunk it with his mother's milk and lived with it all his life: *After all a man can't only do what he has to do, with what he*

*has to do with, with what he has learned, to the best of
his judgment. And I reckon a hog is still a hog, no matter
what it looks like. So here goes,* sitting still for an instant
longer until the bow of the pirogue grounded lighter
than the falling of a leaf and stepped out of it and paused
just for one instant while the words *It does look big* stood
for just a second, unemphatic and trivial, somewhere
where some fragment of his attention could see them and
vanished, and stooped straddling, the knife driving even
as he grasped the near foreleg, this all in the same instant
when the lashing tail struck him a terrific blow upon the
back. But the knife was home, he knew that even on his
back in the mud, the weight of the thrashing beast long-
wise upon him, its ridged back clutched to his stomach,
his arm about its throat, the hissing head clamped against
his jaw, the furious tail lashing and flailing, the knife in
his other hand probing for the life and finding it, the hot
fierce gush: and now sitting beside the profound up-bel-
lied carcass, his head again between his knees in the old
attitude while his own blood freshened the other which
drenched him, thinking, *It's my durn nose again.*

So he sat there, his head, his streaming face, bowed between his knees in an attitude not of dejection but profoundly bemused, contemplative, while the shrill voice
of the Cajun seemed to buzz at him from an enormous
distance; after a time he even looked up at the antic wiry
figure bouncing hysterically about him, the face wild and
grimacing, the voice gobbling and high; while the convict, holding his face carefully slanted so the blood would
run free, looked at him with the cold intentness of a cura-
tor or custodian paused before one of his own glass cases,
the Cajun threw up the rifle, cried "Boom-boom-boom!"
flung it down and in pantomime re-enacted the recent
scene then whirled his hands again, crying "Magnifique!
Magnifique! Cent d'argent! mille d'argent! Tout l'argent
sous le ciel de Dieu!" But the convict was already looking
down again, cupping the coffee-colored water to his face,

watching the constant bright carmine marble it, thinking, *It's a little late to be telling me that now,* and not even thinking this long because presently they were in the pirogue again, the convict squatting again with that un-breathing rigidity as though he were trying by holding his breath to decrease his very weight, the bloody skin in the bows before him and he looking at it, thinking, *And I can't even ask him how much my half will be.*

But this not for long either, because as he was to tell the plump convict later, money has but one language. He remembered that too (they were at home now, the skin spread on the platform, where for the woman's bene-fit now the Cajun once more went through the pantomime —the gun which was not used, the hand-to-hand battle; for the second time the invisible alligator was slain amid cries, the victor rose and found this time that not even the woman was watching him. She was looking at the once more swollen and inflamed face of the convict. "You mean it kicked you right in the face?" she said.

"Nah," the convict said harshly, savagely. "It never had to. I done seem to got to where if that boy was to shoot me in the tail with a bean blower my nose would bleed.")—remembered that too but he did not try to tell it. Perhaps he could not have—how two people who could not even talk to one another made an agreement which both not only understood but which each knew the other would hold true and protect (perhaps for this reason) better than any written and witnessed contract. They even discussed and agreed somehow that they should hunt separately, each in his own vessel, to double the chances of finding prey. But this was easy: the con-vict could almost understand the words in which the Cajun said, "You do not need me and the rifle; we will only hinder you, be in your way." And more than this, they even agreed about the second rifle: that there was someone, it did not matter who—friend, neighbor, per-haps one in business in that line—from whom they could

rent a second rifle; in their two patois, the one bastard
English, the other bastard French—the one volatile, with
his wild bright eyes and his voluble mouth full of stumps
of teeth, the other sober, almost grim, swollen-faced and
with his naked back blistered and scoriated like so much
beef—they discussed this, squatting on either side of the
pegged-out hide like two members of a corporation facing
each other across a mahogany board table, and decided
against it, the convict deciding: "I reckon not," he said.
"I reckon if I had knowed enough to wait to start out with
a gun, I still would. But since I done already started out
without one, I don't reckon I'll change." Because it was
a question of the money in terms of time, days. (Strange
to say, that was the one thing which the Cajun could not
tell him: how much the half would be. But the convict
knew it was half.) He had so little of them. He would
have to move on soon, thinking (the convict), *All this
durn foolishness will stop soon and I can get on back,* and
then suddenly he found that he was thinking, *Will have
to get on back,* and he became quite still and looked
about at the rich strange desert which surrounded him,
in which he was temporarily lost in peace and hope and
into which the last seven years had sunk like so many
trivial pebbles into a pool, leaving no ripple, and he
thought quietly, with a kind of bemused amazement, *Yes.
I reckon I had done forgot how good making money was.
Being let to make it.*

So he used no gun, his the knotted rope and the Thuringian mace, and each morning he and the Cajun took
their separate ways in the two boats to comb and creep
the secret channels about the lost land from (or out of)
which now and then still other pint-sized dark men appeared gobbling, abruptly and as though by magic from
nowhere, in other hollowed logs, to follow quietly and
watch him at his single combats—men named Tine and
Toto and Theule, who were not much larger than and
looked a good deal like the muskrats which the Cajun

(the host did this too, supplied the kitchen too; he expressed this too like the rifle business, in his own tongue,
the convict comprehending this too as though it had been
English: "Do not concern yourself about food, O Hercules.
Catch alligators; I will supply the pot.") took now and
then from traps as you take a shoat pig at need from a pen,
and varied the eternal rice and fish (the convict did tell
this: how at night, in the cabin, the door and one sashless
window battened against mosquitoes—a form, a ritual, as
empty as crossing the fingers or knocking on wood—sitting beside the bug-swirled lantern on the plank table in
a temperature close to blood heat he would look down at
the swimming segment of meat on his sweating plate and
think, *It must be Theule. He was the fat one.*)—day following day, unemphatic and identical, each like the one
before and the one which would follow while his theoretical half of a sum to be reckoned in pennies, dollars, or
tens of dollars he did not know, mounted—the mornings
when he set forth to find waiting for him like the *matador*
his *aficionados* the small clump of constant and deferential
pirogues, the hard noons when ringed half about by little
motionless shells he fought his solitary combats, the evenings, the return, the pirogues departing one by one into
inlets and passages which during the first few days he
could not even distinguish, then the platform in the twilight where before the static woman and the usually nursing infant and the one or two bloody hides of the day's
take the Cajun would perform his ritualistic victorious
pantomime before the two growing rows of knifemarks
in one of the boards of the wall; then the nights when,
the woman and child in the single bunk and the Cajun already snoring on the pallet and the reeking lantern set
close, he (the convict) would sit on his naked heels,
sweating steadily, his face worn and calm, immersed and
indomitable, his bowed back raw and savage as beef beneath the suppurant old blisters and the fierce welts of

tails, and scrape and chip at the charred sapling which was almost a paddle now, pausing now and then to raise his head while the cloud of mosquitoes about it whined and whirled, to stare at the wall before him until after a while the crude boards themselves must have dissolved away and let his blank unseeing gaze go on and on unhampered, through the rich oblivious darkness, beyond it even perhaps, even perhaps beyond the seven wasted years during which, so he had just realized, he had been permitted to toil but not to work. Then he would retire himself, he would take a last look at the rolled bundle behind the rafter and blow out the lantern and lie down as he was beside his snoring partner, to lie sweating (on his stomach, he could not bear the touch of anything to his back) in the whining oven-like darkness filled with the forlorn bellowing of alligators, thinking not, *They never gave me time to learn* but *I had forgot how good it is to work.*

Then on the tenth day it happened. It happened for the third time. At first he refused to believe it, not that he felt that now he had served out and discharged his apprenticeship to mischance, had with the birth of the child reached and crossed the crest of his Golgotha and would now be, possibly not permitted so much as ignored, to descend the opposite slope free-wheeling. That was not his feeling at all. What he declined to accept was the fact that a power, a force such as that which had been consistent enough to concentrate upon him with deadly undeviation for weeks, should with all the wealth of cosmic violence and disaster to draw from, have been so barren of invention and imagination, so lacking in pride of artistry and craftmanship, as to repeat itself twice. Once he had accepted, twice he even forgave, but three times he simply declined to believe, particularly when he was at last persuaded to realize that this third time was to be instigated not by the blind potency of volume and motion but by human direction and hands: that now the cosmic joker, foiled twice, had stooped in its vindictive concentration to the employing of dynamite.

He did not tell that. Doubtless he did not know himself how it happened, what was happening. But he doubtless remembered it (but quietly above the thick, rich-colored, pristine cigar in his clean, steady hand), what he knew, divined of it. It would be evening, the ninth evening, he and the woman on either side of their host's empty place at the evening meal, he hearing the voices from without but not ceasing to eat, still chewing steadily, because it would be the same as though he were seeing them anyway—the two or three or four pirogues floating on the dark water beneath the platform on which the host stood, the voices gobbling and jabbering, incomprehensible and filled not with alarm and not exactly with rage or ever perhaps absolute surprise but rather just cacophony like those of disturbed marsh fowl, he (the convict) not ceasing to chew but just looking up quietly and maybe without a great deal of interrogation or surprise too as the Cajun burst in and stood before them, wild-faced, glaring, his blackened teeth gaped against the inky orifice of his distended mouth, watching (the convict) while the Cajun went through his violent pantomime of violent evacuation, ejection, scooping something invisible into his arms and hurling it out and downward, and in the instant of completing the gesture changing from instigator to victim of that which he had set into pantomimic motion, clasping his head and, bowed over and not otherwise moving, seeming to be swept on and away before it, crying "Boom! Boom! Boom!", the convict watching him, his jaw not chewing now, though for just that moment, thinking, *What? What is it he is trying to tell me?* thinking (this a flash too, since he could not have expressed this, and hence did not even know that he had ever thought it) that though his life had been cast here, circumscribed by this environment, accepted by this environment and accepting it in turn (and he had done well here—this quietly, soberly indeed, if he had been able to phrase it, think it instead of merely knowing it—better than he had ever done, who had not even known until now how good work, making money, could be), yet it was not his life, he still and would ever be no more than the water bug upon the surface of the pond, the plumbless and lurking depths of which he would never know, his only actual contact with it being the instants when on lonely and glaring mudspits under the pitiless sun and amphitheatred by his motionless and riveted semicircle of watching pirogues, he accepted the gambit which he had not elected, entered the lashing radius of the armed tail and beat at the thrashing and hissing head with his lightwood club, or this failing, embraced without hesitation the armored body itself with the frail web of flesh and bone in which he walked and lived, and sought the raging life with an eight-inch knife-blade.

So he and the woman merely watched the Cajun as he acted out the whole charade of eviction—the little wiry man, gesticulant and wild, his hysterical shadow leaping and falling upon the rough wall as he went through the pantomime of abandoning the cabin, gathering in pantomime his meagre belongings from the walls and corners —objects which no other man would want and only some power or force like blind water or earthquake or fire would ever dispossess him of, the woman watching too, her mouth slightly open upon a mass of chewed food, on her face an expression of placid astonishment, saying, "What? What's he saying?"

"I don't know," the convict said. "But I reckon if it's something we ought to know we will find it out when it's ready for us to." Because he was not alarmed, though by now he had read the other's meaning plainly enough. *He's fixing to leave,* he thought. *He's telling me to leave too*—this later, after they had quitted the table and the Cajun and the woman had gone to bed and the Cajun had risen from the pallet and approached the convict and once more went through the pantomime of abandoning the cabin, this time as one repeats a speech which may have been misunderstood, tediously, carefully repetitional as to a child, seeming to hold the convict with one hand while he gestured, talked, with the other, gesturing as though in single syllables, the convict (squatting, the knife open and the almost-finished paddle across his lap) watching, nodding his head, even speaking in English: "Yah; sure. You bet. I got you,"—trimming again at the paddle but no faster, with no more haste than on any other night, serene in his belief that when the time came for him to know whatever it was, that would take care of itself, having already and without even knowing it, even before the possibility, the question, ever arose, declined, refused to accept even the thought of moving also, thinking about the hides, thinking, *If there was just some way he could tell me where to carry my share to get the money,* but thinking this only for an instant between two delicate strokes of the blade because almost at once he thought, *I reckon as long as I can catch them I won't have no big trouble finding whoever it is that will buy them.*

So the next morning he helped the Cajun load his few belongings—the pitted rifle, a small bundle of clothing (again they traded, who could not even converse with one another, this time the few cooking vessels, a few rusty traps by definite allocation, and something embracing and abstractional which included the stove, the crude bunk, the house or its occupancy—something—in exchange for one alligator hide)—into the pirogue, then, squatting and as two children divide sticks they divided the hides, separating them into two piles, one-for-me-and-one-for-you, two-for-me-and-two-for-you, and the Cajun loaded his share and shoved away from the platform and paused again, though this time he only put the paddle down, gathered something invisibly into his two hands and flung it violently upward, crying "Boom? Boom?"

on a rising inflection, nodding violently to the half-naked and savagely scoriated man on the platform who stared with a sort of grim equability back at him and said, "Sure. Boom. Boom." Then the Cajun went on. He did not look back. They watched him, already paddling rapidly, or the woman did; the convict had already turned.

"Maybe he was trying to tell us to leave too," she said.

"Yah," the convict said. "I thought of that last night. Hand me the paddle." She fetched it to him—the sapling, the one he had been trimming at nightly, not quite finished yet though one more evening would do it (he had been using a spare one of the Cajun's. The other had offered to let him keep it, to include it perhaps with the stove and the bunk and the cabin's freehold, but the convict had declined. Perhaps he had computed it by volume against so much alligator hide, this weighed against one more evening with the tedious and careful blade) and he departed too with his knotted rope and mace, in the opposite direction, as though not only not content with refusing to quit the place he had been warned against, he must establish and affirm the irrevocable finality of his refusal by penetrating even further and deeper into it. And then, and without warning, the high fierce drowsing of his solitude gathered itself and struck at him.

He could not have told this if he had tried—this not yet midmorning and he going on, alone for the first time, no pirogue emerging anywhere to fall in behind him, but he had not expected this anyway, he knew that the others would have departed too; it was not this, it was his very solitude, his desolation which was now his alone and in full, since he had elected to remain; the sudden cessation of the paddle, the skiff shooting on for a moment yet while he thought, *What? What?* Then, *No. No. No,* as the silence and solitude and emptiness roared down upon him in a jeering bellow: and now reversed, the skiff spun violently on its heel, he the betrayed driving furiously back toward the platform where he knew it was already too late, that citadel where the very crux and dear breath of his life—the being allowed to work and earn money, that right and privilege which he believed he had earned to himself unaided, asking no favor of anyone or anything save the right to be let alone to pit his will and strength against the sauric protagonist of a land, a region, which he had not asked to be projected into—was being threatened, driving the home-made paddle in grim fury, coming in sight of the platform at last and seeing the motor launch lying alongside it with no surprise at all but actually with a kind of pleasure as though at a visible justification of his outrage and fear, the privilege of saying *I told you so* to his own affronting, driving on toward it in a dreamlike state in which there seemed to be no progress at all, in which, unimpeded and suffocating, he strove dreamily with a weightless oar, with muscles without strength or resiliency, at a medium without resistance, seeming to watch the skiff creep infinitesimally across the sunny water and up to the platform while a man in the launch (there were five of them in all) gobbled at him in that same tongue he had been hearing constantly now for ten days and still knew no word of, just as a second man, followed by the woman carrying the baby and dressed again for departure in the faded tunic and the sunbonnet, emerged from the house, carrying (the man carried several other things but the convict saw nothing else) the paper-wrapped bundle which the convict had put behind the rafter ten days ago and no other hand had touched since, he (the convict) on the platform too now, holding the skiff's painter in one hand and the bludgeon-like paddle in the other, contriving to speak to the woman at last in a voice dreamy and suffocating and incredibly calm. "Take it away from him and carry it back into the house."

"So you can talk English, can you?" the man in the launch said. "Why didn't you come out like they told you to last night?"

"Out?" the convict said. Again he even looked, glared, at the man in the launch, contriving even again to control his voice: "I ain't got time to take trips. I'm busy," already turning to the woman again, his mouth already open to repeat, as the dreamy buzzing voice of the man came to him and he turning once more, in a terrific and absolutely unbearable exasperation, crying, "Flood? What flood? Hell a mile, it's done passed me twice months ago! It's gone! What flood?" and then (he did not think this in actual words either but he knew it, suffered that flashing insight into his own character or destiny: how there was a peculiar quality of repetitiveness about his present fate, how not only the almost seminal crises recurred with a certain monotony, but the very physical circumstances followed a stupidly unimaginative pattern) the man in the launch said, "Take him," and he was on his feet for a few minutes yet, lashing and striking in panting fury, then once more on his back on hard unyielding planks while the four men swarmed over him in a fierce wave of hard bones and panting curses and at last the thin dry vicious snapping of handcuffs.

"Damn it, are you mad?" the man in the launch said. "Can't you understand they are going to dynamite that levee at noon today?—Come on," he said to the others. "Get him aboard. Let's get out of here."

"I want my hides and boat," the convict said.

"Damn your hides," the man in the launch said. "If they don't get that levee blowed pretty soon you can hunt plenty more of them on the capitol steps at Baton Rouge. And this is all the boat you will need and you can say your prayers about it."

"I ain't going without my boat," the convict said. He said it calmly and with complete finality, so calm, so final that for almost a minute nobody answered him, they just stood looking quietly down at him as he lay, half-naked, blistered and scarred, helpless and manacled hand and foot, on his back, delivering his ultimatum in a voice peaceful and quiet as that in which you talk to your bed-fellow before going to sleep. Then the man in the launch moved; he spat quietly over the side and said in a voice as calm and quiet as the convict's:

"All right. Bring his boat." They helped the woman, carrying the baby and the paper-wrapped parcel, into the launch. Then they helped the convict to his feet and into the launch too, the shackles on his wrists and ankles clashing. "I'd unlock you if you'd promise to be-have yourself," the man said. The convict did not answer this at all.

"I want to hold the rope," he said.

"The rope?"

"Yes," the convict said. "The rope." So they lowered him into the stern and gave him the end of the painter after it had passed the towing cleat, and they went on. The convict did not look back. But then, he did not look forward either, he lay half sprawled, his shackled legs before him, the end of the skiff's painter in one shackled hand. The launch made two other stops; when the hazy wafer of the intolerable sun began to stand once more di-rectly overhead there were fifteen people in the launch; and then the convict, sprawled and motionless, saw the flat brazen land begin to rise and become a greenish-black mass of swamp, bearded and convoluted, this in turn stopping short off and there spread before him an expanse of water embraced by a blue dissolution of shore line and glittering thinly under the noon, larger than he had ever seen before, the sound of the launch's engine ceasing, the hull sliding on behind its fading bow-wave. "What are you doing?" the leader said.

"It's noon," the helmsman said. "I thought we might hear the dynamite." So they all listened, the launch lost of all forward motion, rocking slightly, the glitter-broken small waves slapping and whispering at the hull, but no sound, no tremble even, came anywhere under the fierce hazy sky; the long moment gathered itself and turned on and noon was past. "All right," the leader said. "Let's go." The engine started again, the hull began to gather speed. The leader came aft and stooped over the convict, key in hand. "I guess you'll have to behave now, whether you want to or not," he said, unlocking the manacles. "Won't you?"

"Yes," the convict said. They went on; after a time the shore vanished completely and a little sea got up. The convict was free now but he lay as before, the end of the skiff's painter in his hand, bent now with three or four turns about his wrist; he turned his head now and then to look back at the towing skiff as it slewed and bounced in the launch's wake; now and then he even looked out over the lake, the eyes alone moving, the face grave and expressionless, thinking, *This is a greater immensity of water, of waste and desolation, than I have ever seen before;* perhaps not; thinking three or four hours later, the shoreline raised again and broken into a clutter of sailing sloops and power cruisers, *These are more boats than I believed existed, a maritime race of which I also had no cognizance* or perhaps not thinking it but just watching as the launch opened the shored gut of the ship canal, the low smoke of the city beyond it, then a wharf, the launch slowing in; a quiet crowd of people watching with that same forlorn passivity he had seen before, and whose race he did recognize even though he had not seen Vicksburg when he passed it—the brand, the unmistakable hallmark of the violently homeless, he more so than any, who would have permitted no man to call him one of them.

"All right," the leader said to him. "Here you are."

"The boat," the convict said.

"You've got it. What do you want me to do—give you a receipt for it?"

"No," the convict said. "I just want the boat."

"Take it. Only you ought to have a bookstrap or something to carry it in."—"Carry it in?" the plump convict said. "Carry it where? Where would you have to carry it?"—

He (the tall one) told that: how he and the woman disembarked and how one of the men helped him haul the skiff up out of the water and how he stood there with the end of the painter wrapped around his wrist and the man bustled up, saying, "All right. Next load! Next load!" and how he told this man too about the boat and the man cried, "Boat? Boat?" and how he (the convict) went with them when they carried the skiff over and racked, berthed, it with the others and how he lined himself up by a cocacola sign and the arch of a drawbridge so he could find the skiff again quick when he returned, and how he and the woman (he carrying the paper-wrapped parcel) were herded into a truck and after a while the truck began to run in traffic, between close houses, then there was a big building, an armory—

"Armory?" the plump one said. "You mean a jail."

"No. It was a kind of warehouse, with people with bundles laying on the floor."—And how he thought maybe his partner might be there and how he even looked about for the Cajun while waiting for a chance to get back to the door again, where the soldier was and how he got back to the door at last, the woman behind him and his chest actually against the dropped rifle.

"Gwan, gwan," the soldier said. "Get back. They'll give you some clothes in a minute. You can't walk around the streets that way. And something to eat too. Maybe your kinfolks will come for you by that time." And he told that too: how the woman said,

"Maybe if you told him you had some kinfolks here he would let us out." And how he did not; he could not have expressed this either, it too deep, too ingrained; he had never yet had to think it into words through all the long generations of himself—his hill-man's sober and jealous respect not for truth but for the power, the strength, of lying—not to be niggard with lying but ra-

ther to use it with respect and even care, delicate quick
and strong, like a fine and fatal blade. And how they
fetched him clothes—a blue jumper and overalls, and then
food too (a brisk starched young woman saying, "But the
baby must be bathed, cleaned. It will die if you don't"
and the woman saying, "Yessum. He might holler some,
he ain't never been bathed before. But he's a good baby.")
and now it was night, the unshaded bulbs harsh and
savage and forlorn above the snorers and he rising, gripping the woman awake, and then the window. He told
that: how there were doors in plenty, leading he did not
know where, but he had a hard time finding a window
they could use but he found one at last, he carrying the
parcel and the baby too while he climbed through first—
"You ought to tore up a sheet and slid down it," the
plump convict said.—But he needed no sheet, there were
cobbles under his feet now, in the rich darkness. The city
was there too but he had not seen it yet and would not
—the low constant glare; Bienville had stood there too, it
had been the figment of an emasculate also calling himself Napoleon but no more, Andrew Jackson had found it
one step from Pennsylvania Avenue. But the convict
found it considerably further than one step back to the
ship canal and the skiff, the coca-cola sign dim now, the
drawbridge arching spidery against the jonquil sky at
dawn: nor did he tell, any more than about the sixty-foot
levee, how he got the skiff back into the water.

The lake was behind him now; there was but one direction he could go. When he saw the River again he
knew it at once. He should have; it was now ineradicably
a part of his past, his life; it would be a part of what he
would bequeath, if that were in store for him. But four
weeks later it would look different from what it did now,
and did: he (the Old Man) had recovered from his de-
bauch, back in banks again, the Old Man, rippling placidly
toward the sea, brown and rich as chocolate between
levees whose inner faces were wrinkled as though in a

frozen and aghast amazement, crowned with the rich
green of summer in the willows; beyond them, sixty feet
below, slick mules squatted against the broad pull of mid-
dle-busters in the richened soil which would not need to
be planted, which would need only to be shown a cotton
seed to sprout and make; there would be the symmetric
miles of strong stalks by July, purple bloom in August, in
September the black fields snowed over, spilled, the mid-
dles dragged smooth by the long sacks, the long black
limber hands plucking, the hot air filled with the whine
of gins, the September air then, but now June air heavy
with locust and (the towns) the smell of new paint and
the sour smell of the paste which holds wall paper—the
towns, the villages, the little lost wood landings on stilts
on the inner face of the levee, the lower storeys bright
and rank under the new paint and paper and even the
marks on spile and post and tree of May's raging water-
height fading beneath each bright silver gust of summer's
loud and inconstant rain; there was a store at the levee's
lip, a few saddled and rope-bridled mules in the sleepy
dust, a few dogs, a handful of Negroes sitting on the steps
beneath the chewing tobacco and malaria medicine signs,
and three white men, one of them a deputy sheriff can-
vassing for votes to beat his superior (who had given him
his job) in the August primary, all pausing to watch the
skiff emerge from the glitter-glare of the afternoon water
and approach and land, a woman carrying a child stepping out, then a man, a tall man who, approaching,
proved to be dressed in a faded but recently washed and
quite clean suit of penitentiary clothing, stopping in the
dust where the mules dozed and watching with pale cold
humorless eyes while the deputy sheriff was still making
toward his armpit that gesture which everyone present
realized was to have produced a pistol in one flashing motion for a considerable time while still nothing came of it.
It was apparently enough for the newcomer, however.

"You a officer?" he said.

"You damn right I am," the deputy said. "Just let me get this damn gun—"

"All right," the other said. "Yonder's your boat, and here's the woman. But I never did find that bastard on the cottonhouse."

V

One of the Governor's young men arrived at the Penitentiary the next morning. That is, he was fairly young (he would not see thirty again, though without doubt he did not want to, there being that about him which indicated a character which never had and never would want anything it did not, or was not about to, possess), a Phi Beta Kappa out of an Eastern university, a colonel on the Governor's staff who did not buy it with a campaign contribution, who had stood in his negligent Eastern-cut clothes and his arched nose and lazy contemptuous eyes on the galleries of any number of little lost backwoods stores and told his stories and received the guffaws of his overalled and spitting hearers, and with the same look in his eyes fondled infants named in memory of the last administration and in honor (or hope) of the next, and (it was said of him and doubtless not true) by lazy accident the behinds of some who were not infants any longer though still not old enough to vote. He was in the Warden's office with a briefcase, and presently the deputy warden of the levee was there too. He would have been sent for presently though not yet, but he came anyhow, without knocking, with his hat on, calling the Governor's young man loudly by a nickname and striking him with a flat hand on the back, and lifted one thigh to the Warden's desk, almost between the Warden and the caller, the emissary. Or the vizier with the command, the knotted cord, as began to appear immediately.

"Well," the Governor's young man said, "you've played the devil, haven't you?" The Warden had a cigar.

He had offered the caller one. It had been refused, though presently, while the Warden looked at the back of his neck with hard immobility even a little grim, the deputy leaned and reached back and opened the desk drawer and took one.

"Seems straight enough to me," the Warden said. "He got swept away against his will. He came back as soon as he could and surrendered."

"He even brought that damn boat back," the deputy said. "If he'd a throwed the boat away he could a walked back in three days. But no sir. He's got to bring the boat back. 'Here's your boat and here's the woman but I never found no bastard on no cottonhouse.'" He slapped his knee, guffawing. "Them convicts. A mule's got twice as much sense."

"A mule's got twice as much sense as anything except a rat," the emissary said in his pleasant voice. "But that's not the trouble."

"What is the trouble?" the Warden said.

"This man is dead."

"Hell fire, he ain't dead," the deputy said. "He's up yonder in that bunkhouse right now, lying his head off probly. I'll take you up there and you can see him." The Warden was looking at the deputy.

"Look," he said. "Bledsoe was trying to tell me something about that Kate mule's leg. You better go up to the stable and—"

"I done tended to it," the deputy said. He didn't even look at the Warden. He was watching, talking to, the emissary. "No sir. He ain't—"

"But he has received an official discharge as being dead. Not a pardon nor a parole either: a discharge. He's either dead, or free. In either case he doesn't belong here." Now both the Warden and the deputy looked at the emissary, the deputy's mouth open a little, the cigar poised in his hand to have its tip bitten off. The emissary spoke pleasantly, extremely distinctly: "On a report of death forwarded to the Governor by the Warden of the Penitentiary." The deputy closed his mouth, though otherwise he didn't move. "On the official evidence of the officer delegated at the time to the charge and returning of the body of the prisoner to the Penitentiary." Now the deputy put the cigar into his mouth and got slowly off the desk, the cigar rolling across his lip as he spoke:

"So that's it. I'm to be it, am I?" He laughed shortly, a stage laugh, two notes. "When I done been right three times running through three separate administrations? That's on a book somewhere too. Somebody in Jackson can find that too. And if they can't, I can show—"

"Three administrations?" the emissary said. "Well, well. That's pretty good."

"You damn right it's good," the deputy said. "The woods are full of folks that didn't." The Warden was again watching the back of the deputy's neck.

"Look," he said. "Why don't you step up to my house and get that bottle of whiskey out of the sideboard and bring it down here?"

"All right," the deputy said. "But I think we better settle this first. I'll tell you what we'll do—"

"We can settle it quicker with a drink or two," the Warden said. "You better step on up to your place and get a coat so the bottle—"

"That'll take too long," the deputy said. "I won't need no coat." He moved to the door, where he stopped and turned. "I'll tell you what to do. Just call twelve men in here and tell him it's a jury—he never seen but one before and he won't know no better—and try him over for robbing that train. Hamp can be the judge."

"You can't try a man twice for the same crime," the emissary said. "He might know that even if he doesn't know a jury when he sees one."

"Look," the Warden said.

"All right. Just call it a new train robbery. Tell him it happened yesterday, tell him he robbed another train while he was gone and just forgot it. He couldn't help himself. Besides, he won't care. He'd just as lief be here as out. He wouldn't have nowhere to go if he was out. None of them do. Turn one loose and be damned if he ain't right back here by Christmas like it was a reunion or something, for doing the very same thing they caught him at before." He guffawed again. "Them convicts."

"Look," the Warden said. "While you're there, why don't you open the bottle and see if the liquor's any good. Take a drink or two. Give yourself time to feel it. If it's not good, no use in bringing it."

"O. K.," the deputy said. He went out this time.

"Couldn't you lock the door?" the emissary said. The Warden squirmed faintly. That is, he shifted his position in his chair.

"After all, he's right," he said. "He's guessed right three times now. And he's kin to all the folks in Pittman County except the niggers."

"Maybe we can work fast then." The emissary opened the briefcase and took out a sheaf of papers. "So there you are," he said.

"There what are?"

"He escaped."

"But he came back voluntarily and surrendered."

"But he escaped."

"All right," the Warden said. "He escaped. Then what?" Now the emissary said look. That is, he said,

"Listen. I'm on per diem. That's tax-payers, votes. And if there's any possible chance for it to occur to anyone to hold an investigation about this, there'll be ten senators and twenty-five representatives here on a special train maybe. On per diem. And it will be mighty hard to keep some of them from going back to Jackson by way of Memphis or New Orleans—on per diem."

"All right," the Warden said. "What does he say to do?"

"This. The man left here in charge of one specific officer. But he was delivered back here by a different one."

"But he surren—" This time the Warden stopped of his own accord. He looked, stared almost, at the emissary. "All right. Go on."

"In specific charge of an appointed and delegated officer, who returned here and reported that the body of the prisoner was no longer in his possession; that, in fact, he did not know where the prisoner was. That's correct, isn't it?" The Warden said nothing. "Isn't that correct?" the emissary said, pleasantly, insistently.

"But you can't do that to him. I tell you he's kin to half the—"

"That's taken care of. The Chief has made a place for him on the highway patrol."

"Hell," the Warden said. "He can't ride a motorcycle. I don't even let him try to drive a truck."

"He won't have to. Surely an amazed and grateful State can supply the man who guessed right three times in succession in Mississippi general elections with a car to ride in and somebody to run it if necessary. He won't even have to stay in it all the time. Just so he's near enough so when an inspector sees the car and stops and blows the horn of it he can hear it and come out."

"I still don't like it," the Warden said.

"Neither do I. Your man could have saved all of this if he had just gone on and drowned himself, as he seems to have led everybody to believe he had. But he didn't. And the Chief says do. Can you think of anything better?" The Warden sighed.

"No," he said.

"All right." The emissary opened the papers and uncapped a pen and began to write. "Attempted escape from the Penitentiary, ten years' additional sentence," he said. "Deputy Warden Buckworth transferred to Highway Patrol. Call it for meritorious service even if you want to. It won't matter now. Done?"

"Done," the Warden said.

"Then suppose you send for him. Get it over with."
So the Warden sent for the tall convict and he arrived
presently, saturnine and grave, in his new bed-ticking,
his jowls blue and close under the sunburn, his hair recently cut and neatly parted and smelling faintly of the
prison barber's (the barber was in for life, for murdering
his wife, still a barber) pomade. The Warden called him
by name.

"You had bad luck, didn't you?" The convict said nothing. "They are going to have to add ten years to your
time."

"All right," the convict said.

"It's hard luck. I'm sorry."

"All right," the convict said. "If that's the rule." So
they gave him the ten years more and the Warden gave
him the cigar and now he sat, jackknifed backward into
the space between the upper and lower bunks, the unlighted cigar in his hand while the plump convict and
four others listened to him. Or questioned him, that is,
since it was all done, finished, now and he was safe again,
so maybe it wasn't even worth talking about any more.

"All right," the plump one said. "So you come back
into the River. Then what?"

"Nothing. I rowed."

"Wasn't it pretty hard rowing coming back?"

"The water was still high. It was running pretty hard
still. I never made much speed for the first week or two.
After that it got better." Then, suddenly and quietly,
something—the inarticulateness, the innate and inherited
reluctance for speech, dissolved and he found himself,
listened to himself, telling it quietly, the words coming
not fast but easily to the tongue as he required them:
How he paddled on (he found out by trying it that he
could make better speed, if you could call it speed, next
the bank—this after he had been carried suddenly and
violently out to midstream before he could prevent it

and found himself, the skiff, travelling back toward the region from which he had just escaped, and he spent the better part of the morning getting back inshore and up to the canal again from which he had emerged at dawn) until night came and they tied up to the bank and ate some of the food he had secreted in his jumper before leaving the armory in New Orleans, and the woman and the infant slept in the boat as usual and when daylight came they went on and tied up again that night too, and the next day the food gave out and he came to a landing, a town, he didn't notice the name of it, and he got a job. It was a cane farm—

"Cane?" one of the other convicts said. "What does anybody want to raise cane for? You cut cane. You have to fight it where I come from. You burn it just to get shut of it."

"It was sorghum," the tall convict said.

"Sorghum?" another said. "A whole farm just raising sorghum? *Sorghum?* What did they do with it?" The tall one didn't know. He didn't ask, he just came up the levee and there was a truck waiting full of niggers and a white man said, "You there. Can you run a shovel plow?" and the convict said, "Yes," and the man said, "Jump in then," and the convict said, "Only I've got a—"

"Yes," the plump one said. "That's what I been aiming to ask. What did—" The tall convict's face was grave, his voice was calm, just a little short:

"They had tents for the folks to live in. They were behind." The plump one blinked at him.

"Did they think she was your wife?"

"I don't know. I reckon so." The plump one blinked at him.

"Wasn't she your wife? Just from time to time kind of, you might say?" The tall one didn't answer this at all. After a moment he raised the cigar and appeared to examine a loosening of the wrapper because after another moment he licked the cigar carefully near the end. "All right," the plump one said. "Then what?" So he worked there four days. He didn't like it. Maybe that was why: that he too could not quite put credence in that much of what he believed to be sorghum. So when they told him it was Saturday and paid him and the white man told him about somebody who was going to Baton Rouge the next day in a motor boat, he went to see the man and took the six dollars he had earned and bought food with it and tied the skiff behind the motor boat and went to Baton Rouge. It didn't take long and even after they left the motor boat at Baton Rouge and he was paddling again it seemed to the convict that the River was lower and the current not so fast, so hard, so they made fair speed, tying up to the bank at night among the willows, the woman and baby sleeping in the skiff as of old. Then the food gave out again. This time it was a wood landing, the wood stacked and waiting, a wagon and team being unladen of another load. The men with the wagon told him about the sawmill and helped him drag the skiff up the levee; they wanted to leave it there but he would not so they loaded it onto the wagon too and he and the woman got on the wagon too and they went to the sawmill. They gave them one room in a house to live in here. They paid two dollars a day and furnish. The work was hard. He liked it. He stayed there eight days.

"If you liked it so well, why did you quit?" the plump one said. The tall convict examined the cigar again, holding it up where the light fell upon the rich chocolate-colored flank.

"I got in trouble," he said.

"What trouble?"

"Woman. It was a fellow's wife."

"You mean you had been toting one piece up and down the country day and night for over a month, and now the first time you have a chance to stop and catch your breath almost you got to get in trouble over another one?" The tall convict had thought of that. He remembered it: how there were times, seconds, at first when if it had not been for the baby he might have, might have tried. But they were just seconds because in the next instant his whole being would seem to flee the very idea in a kind of savage and horrified revulsion; he would find himself looking from a distance at this millstone which the force and power of blind and risible Motion had fastened upon him, thinking, saying aloud actually, with harsh and savage outrage even though it had been two years since he had had a woman and that a nameless and not young Negress, a casual, a straggler whom he had caught more or less by chance on one of the fifth-Sunday visiting days, the man—husband or sweetheart—whom she had come to see having been shot by a trusty a week or so previous and she had not heard about it: "She ain't even no good to me for that."

"But you got this one, didn't you?" the plump convict said.

"Yah," the tall one said. The plump one blinked at him. "Was it good?"

"It's all good," one of the others said. "Well? Go on. How many more did you have on the way back? Sometimes when a fellow starts getting it it looks like he just can't miss even if—" That was all, the convict told them. They left the sawmill fast, he had no time to buy food until they reached the next landing. There he spent the whole sixteen dollars he had earned and they went on. The River was lower now, there was no doubt of it, and sixteen dollars' worth looked like a lot of food and he thought maybe it would do, would be enough. But maybe there was more current in the River still than it looked like. But this time it was Mississippi, it was cotton; the plow handles felt right to his palms again, the strain and squat of the slick buttocks against the middle-buster's blade was what he knew, even though they paid but a dollar a day here. But that did it. He told it: they told him it was Saturday again and paid him and he told about it—night, a smoked lantern in a disc of worn and barren earth as smooth as silver, a circle of crouching figures, the importunate murmurs and ejaculations, the meagre piles of worn bills beneath the crouching knees, the dotted cubes clicking and scuttering in the dust; that did it. "How much did you win?" the second convict said.

"Enough," the tall one said.

"But how much?"

"Enough," the tall one said. It was enough exactly; he gave it all to the man who owned the second motor boat (he would not need food now), he and the woman in the launch now and the skiff towing behind, the woman with the baby, and the paper-wrapped parcel beneath his peaceful hand, on his lap; almost at once he recognized, not Vicksburg because he had never seen Vicksburg, but the trestle beneath which on his roaring wave of trees and houses and dead animals he had shot, accompanied by thunder and lightning, a month and three weeks ago; he looked at it once without heat, even without interest as the launch went on. But now he began to watch the bank, the levee. He didn't know how he would know but he knew he would, and then it was early afternoon and sure enough the moment came and he said to the launch owner: "I reckon this will do."

"Here?" the launch owner said. "This don't look like anywhere to me."

"I reckon this is it," the convict said. So the launch put inshore, the engine ceased, it drifted up and lay against the levee and the owner cast the skiff loose.

"You better let me take you on until we come to something," he said. "That was what I promised."

"I reckon this will do," the convict said. So they got out and he stood with the grapevine painter in his hand while the launch purred again and drew away, already curving; he did not watch it. He laid the bundle down and made the painter fast to a willow root and picked up the bundle and turned. He said no word, he mounted the levee, passing the mark, the tide-line of the old raging, dry now and lined, traversed by shallow and empty cracks like foolish and deprecatory senile grins, and entered a willow clump and removed the overalls and shirt they had given him in New Orleans and dropped them without even looking to see where they fell and opened the parcel and took out the other, the known, the desired, faded a little, stained and worn, but clean, recognizable, and put them on and returned to the skiff and took up the paddle. The woman was already in it.

The plump convict stood blinking at him. "So you come back," he said. "Well well." Now they all watched the tall convict as he bit the end from the cigar neatly and with complete deliberation and spat it out and licked the bite smooth and damp and took a match from his pocket and examined the match for a moment as though to be sure it was a good one, worthy of the cigar perhaps, and raked it up his thigh with the same deliberation—a motion almost too slow to set fire to it, it would seem—and held it until the flame burned clear and free of sulphur, then put it to the cigar. The plump one watched him, blinking rapidly and steadily. "And they give you ten years more for running. That's bad. A fellow can get used to what they give him at first, to start off with, I don't care how much it is, even a hundred and ninety-nine years. But ten more years. Ten years more, on top of that. When you never expected it. Ten more years to have to do without no society, no female companionship—" He blinked steadily at the tall convict. But he (the tall convict) had thought of that too. He had had a sweetheart. That is, he had gone to church singings and picnics with her—a girl a year or so younger than he, short-legged, with ripe breasts and a heavy mouth and dull eyes like ripe muscadines, who owned a baking-powder can almost full of ear-rings and brooches and rings bought (or presented at suggestion) from ten-cent stores. Presently he had divulged his plan to her, and there were times later when, musing, the thought occurred to him that possibly if it had not been for her he would not actually have attempted it—this a mere feeling, unworded, since he could not have phrased this either: that who to know what Capone's uncandled bridehood she might not have dreamed to be her destiny and fate, what fast car filled with authentic colored glass and machine guns, running traffic lights. But that was all past and done when the notion first occurred to him, and in the third month of his incarceration she came to see him. She wore ear-rings and a bracelet or so which he had never seen before and it never became quite clear how she had got that far from home, and she cried violently for the first three minutes, though presently (and without his ever knowing either exactly how they had got separated or how she had made the acquaintance) he saw her in animated conversation with one of the guards. But she kissed him before she left that evening and said she would return the first chance she got, clinging to him, sweating a little, smelling of scent and soft young female flesh, slightly pneumatic. But she didn't come back though he continued to write to her, and seven months later he got an answer. It was a postcard, a colored lithograph of a Birmingham hotel, a childish X inked heavily across one window, the heavy writing on the reverse slanted and primer-like too: *This is where were honny-monning at. Your friend (Mrs) Vernon Waldrip*

The plump convict stood blinking at the tall one, rapidly and steadily. "Yes, sir," he said. "It's them ten more years that hurt. Ten more years to do without a woman, no woman a tall a fellow wants—" He blinked steadily and rapidly, watching the tall one. The other did not move, jackknifed backward between the two bunks, grave and clean, the cigar burning smoothly and richly in his clean steady hand, the smoke wreathing upward across his face, saturnine, humorless, and calm. "Ten more years——"

"Women——!" the tall convict said.

7

MODERN TIMES

Editor's Note

By the end of the 1920s, the old slaveholding families had almost disappeared from Yoknapatawpha County. The name of Sartoris was borne only by a middle-aged woman and her half-grown son; the name of Compson only by an irascible bachelor; the name of McCaslin only by a childless hunter then in his late sixties; while other names like Sutpen, Grenier, and Beauchamp had survived, some of them in the Negro quarters, but most of them only in courthouse records. With the old families had vanished the code they tried to observe in their human relations; the only code followed by most of their successors was that of grab-and-git. Popeye (in *Sanctuary*, 1931), the impotent killer with his tight black clothes and his eyes like rubber pushbuttons, was the symbol of the time.

Of the four stories in this section, "Death Drag" appeared in *Doctor Martino* (1934) and later in the *Collected Stories*. It grew out of the same interest in the mechanized lives of barnstorming aviators that produced Faulkner's novel *Pylon* (1935). "Uncle Bud and the Three Madams" is the hilarious Chapter XXV of *Sanctuary*. "Percy Grimm" is from Chapter XIX of *Light in August*; it is not the best passage in that powerful novel, but it is almost the only one that tells a complete story in itself. Faulkner said in a letter, "I invented Grimm in 1931.

I didn't realize until after Hitler got into the newspapers that I had created a Nazi before he did." Incidentally the title of the novel refers primarily to Lena Grove and her baby. In the Mississippi backwoods it is sometimes said of a pregnant woman, but more often of a mare or a cow, that she will be *light* in August or September.

"Delta Autumn" is a sequel to "The Bear" and comes from the same book, *Go Down, Moses* (1942). Uncle Ike McCaslin, the hero of that novel (or cycle of stories), is the most saintlike of Faulkner's characters in his life as a whole and in his relation to the Negroes. Through Sam Fathers, his master in woodlore, he had also become a spiritual heir of the Chickasaws, and therefore it is right that he should give a final judgment on the Yoknapatawpha story from the beginning. "No wonder," he thinks on his last trip into the wilderness, "the ruined woods I used to know don't cry for retribution! The people who have destroyed it will accomplish its revenge."

1928

Death Drag

The airplane appeared over town with almost the abruptness of an apparition. It was travelling fast; almost before we knew it there it was already at the top of a loop; still over the square, in violation of both city and government ordinance. It was not a good loop either, performed viciously and slovenly and at top speed, as though the pilot were either a very nervous man or in a hurry, or (and this queerly: there is in our town an ex-army aviator. He was coming out of the post office when the airplane appeared going south; he watched the hurried and ungraceful loop and he made the comment) as though the pilot were trying to make the minimum of some specified maneuver in order to save gasoline. The airplane came over the loop with one wing down, as though about to make an Immelmann turn. Then it did a half roll, the loop three-quarters complete, and without any break in the whine of the full-throttled engine and still at top speed and with that apparition-like suddenness, it disappeared eastward toward our airport. When the first small boys reached the field, the airplane was on the ground, drawn up into a fence corner at the end of the field. It was motionless and empty. There was no one in sight at all. Resting there, empty and dead, patched and shabby and painted awkwardly with a single thin coat of dead black, it gave again that illusion of ghostliness, as though it might have flown there and made that loop and landed by itself.

585

Our field is still in an embryonic state. Our town is built upon hills, and the field, once a cotton field, is composed of forty acres of ridge and gully, upon which, by means of grading and filling, we managed to build an X-shaped runway into the prevailing winds. The runways are long enough in themselves, but the field, like our town, is controlled by men who were of middle age when younger men first began to fly, and so the clearance is not always good. On one side is a grove of trees which the owner will not permit to be felled; on another is the barnyard of a farm: sheds and houses, a long barn with a roof of rotting shingles, a big haycock. The airplane had come to rest in the fence corner near the barn. The small boys and a Negro or two and a white man, descended from a halted wagon in the road, were standing quietly about it when two men in helmets and lifted goggles emerged suddenly around the corner of the barn. One was tall, in a dirty coverall. The other was quite short, in breeches and puttees and a soiled, brightly patterned overcoat which looked as if he had got wet in it and it had shrunk on him. He walked with a decided limp.

They had stopped at the corner of the barn. Without appearing to actually turn their heads, they seemed to take in at one glance the entire scene, quickly. The tall man spoke. "What town is this?"

One of the small boys told him the name of the town.

"Who lives here?" the tall man said.

"Who lives here?" the boy repeated.

"Who runs this field? Is it a private field?"

"Oh. It belongs to the town. They run it."

"Do they all live here? The ones that run it?"

The white man, the Negroes, the small boys, all watched the tall man.

"What I mean, is there anybody in this town that flies, that owns a ship? Any strangers here that fly?"

"Yes," the boy said. "There's a man lives here that flew in the war, the English army."

"Captain Warren was in the Royal Flying Corps," a second boy said.

"That's what I said," the first boy said.

"You said the English army," the second boy said.

The second man, the short one with the limp, spoke. He spoke to the tall man, quietly, in a dead voice, in the diction of Weber and Fields in vaudeville, making his *wh*'s into *v*'s and his *th*'s into *d*'s. "What does that mean?" he said.

"It's all right," the tall man said. He moved forward. "I think I know him." The short man followed, limping, terrific, crablike. The tall man had a gaunt face beneath a two days' stubble. His eyeballs looked dirty, too, with a strained, glaring expression. He wore a dirty helmet of cheap, thin cloth, though it was January. His goggles were worn, but even we could tell that they were good ones. But then everybody quit looking at him to look at the short man; later, when we older people saw him, we said among ourselves that he had the most tragic face we had ever seen; an expression of outraged and convinced and indomitable despair, like that of a man carrying through choice a bomb which, at a certain hour each day, may or may not explode. He had a nose which would have been out of proportion to a man six feet tall. As shaped by his close helmet, the entire upper half of his head down to the end of his nose would have fitted a six-foot body. But below that, below a lateral line bisecting his head from the end of his nose to the back of his skull, his jaw, the rest of his face, was not two inches deep. His jaw was a long, flat line clapping-to beneath his nose like the jaw of a shark, so that the tip of his nose and the tip of his jaw almost touched. His goggles were merely flat pieces of window-glass held in felt frames. His helmet was leather. Down the back of it, from the top to the hem, was a long savage tear, held together top and bottom by strips of adhesive tape almost black with dirt and grease.

From around the corner of the barn there now appeared a third man, again with that abrupt immobility, as though he had materialized there out of thin air; though when they saw him he was already moving toward the group. He wore an overcoat above a neat civilian suit; he wore a cap. He was a little taller than the limping man, and broad, heavily built. He was handsome in a dull, quiet way; from his face, a man of infrequent speech. When he came up the spectators saw that he, like the limping man, was also a Jew. That is, they knew at once that two of the strangers were of a different race from themselves, without being able to say what the difference was. The boy who had first spoken probably revealed by his next speech what they thought the difference was. He, as well as the other boys, was watching the man who limped.

"Were you in the war?" the boy said. "In the air war?"

The limping man did not answer. Both he and the tall man were watching the gate. The spectators looked also and saw a car enter the gate and come down the edge of the field toward them. Three men got out of the car and approached. Again the limping man spoke quietly to the tall man: "Is that one?"

"No," the tall man said, without looking at the other. He watched the newcomers, looking from face to face. He spoke to the oldest of the three. "Morning," he said. "You run this field?"

"No," the newcomer said. "You want the secretary of the Fair Association. He's in town."

"Any charge to use it?"

"I don't know. I reckon they'll be glad to have you use it."

"Go on and pay them," the limping man said.

The three newcomers looked at the airplane with that blank, knowing, respectful air of groundlings. It reared on its muddy wheels, the propeller motionless, rigid, with a quality immobile and poised and dynamic. The nose was big with engine, the wings taut, the fuselage streaked with oil behind the rusting exhaust pipes. "Going to do some business here?" the oldest one said.

"Put you on a show," the tall man said.

"What kind of show?"

"Anything you want. Wing-walking; death-drag."

"What's that? Death-drag?"

"Drop a man onto the top of a car and drag him off again. Bigger the crowd, the more you'll get."

"You will get your money's worth," the limping man said.

The boys still watched him. "Were you in the war?" the first boy said.

The third stranger had not spoken up to this time. He now said: "Let's get on to town."

"Right," the tall man said. He said generally, in his flat, dead voice, the same voice which the three strangers all seemed to use, as though it were their common language: "Where can we get a taxi? Got one in town?"

"We'll take you to town," the men who had come up in the car said.

"We'll pay," the limping man said.

"Glad to do it," the driver of the car said. "I won't charge you anything. You want to go now?"

"Sure," the tall man said. The three strangers got into the back seat, the other three in front. Three of the boys followed them to the car.

"Lemme hang on to town, Mr. Black?" one of the boys said.

"Hang on," the driver said. The boys got onto the running boards. The car returned to town. The three in front could hear the three strangers talking in the back. They talked quietly, in low, dead voices, somehow quiet and urgent, discussing something among themselves, the tall man and the handsome one doing most of the talking. The three in front heard only one speech from the limping man: "I won't take less . . ."

"Sure," the tall man said. He leaned forward and raised

his voice a little: "Where'll I find this Jones, this secretary?"

The driver told him.

"Is the newspaper or the printing shop near there? I want some handbills."

"I'll show you," the driver said. "I'll help you get fixed up."

"Fine," the tall man said. "Come out this afternoon and I'll give you a ride, if I have time."

The car stopped at the newspaper office. "You can get your handbills here," the driver said.

"Good," the tall man said. "Is Jones's office on this street?"

"I'll take you there, too," the driver said.

"You see about the editor," the tall man said. "I can find Jones, I guess." They got out of the car. "I'll come back here," the tall man said. He went on down the street, swiftly, in his dirty coverall and helmet. Two other men had joined the group before the newspaper office. They all entered, the limping man leading, followed by the three boys.

"I want some handbills," the limping man said. "Like this one." He took from his pocket a folded sheet of pink paper. He opened it; the editor, the boys, the five men, leaned to see it. The lettering was black and bold:

DEMON DUNCAN
DAREDEVIL OF THE AIR
DEATH DEFYING SHOW WILL BE GIVEN
UNDER THE AUSPICES OF . . . .
THIS P.M. AT TWO P.M.

COME ONE COME ALL AND SEE DEMON DUNCAN
DEFY DEATH IN DEATH DROP & DRAG OF DEATH

"I want them in one hour," the limping man said.

"What you want in this blank space?" the editor said.

"What you got in this town?"

"What we got?"

"What auspices? American Legion? Rotary Club? Chamber of Commerce?"

"We got all of them."

"I'll tell you which one in a minute, then," the limping man said. "When my partner gets back."

"You have to have a guarantee before you put on the show, do you?" the editor said.

"Why, sure. Do you think I should put on a daredevil without auspices? Do you think I should for a nickel maybe jump off the airplane?"

"Who's going to jump?" one of the later comers said; he was a taxi-driver.

The limping man looked at him. "Don't you worry about that," he said. "Your business is just to pay the money. We will do all the jumping you want, if you pay enough."

"I just asked which one of you all was the jumper."

"Do I ask you whether you pay me in silver or in greenbacks?" the limping man said. "Do I ask you?"

"No," the taxi-driver said.

"About these bills," the editor said. "You said you wanted them in an hour."

"Can't you begin on them, and leave that part out until my partner comes back?"

"Suppose he don't come before they are finished?"

"Well, that won't be my fault, will it?"

"All right," the editor said. "Just so you pay for them."

"You mean, I should pay without a auspices on the handbill?"

"I ain't in this business for fun," the editor said.

"We'll wait," the limping man said.

They waited.

"Were you a flyer in the war, Mister?" the boy said.

The limping man turned upon the boy his long, misshapen, tragic face. "The war? Why should I fly in a war?"

"I thought maybe because of your leg. Captain Warren

limps, and he flew in the war. I reckon you just do it for fun?"

"For fun? What for fun? Fly? *Grüss Gott*. I hate it, I wish the man what invented them was here; I would put him into that machine yonder and I would print on his back, Do not do it, one thousand times."

"Why do you do it, then?" the man who had entered with the taxi-driver said.

"Because of that Republican Coolidge. I was in business, and that Coolidge ruined business; ruined it. That's why. For fun? *Grüss Gott*."

They looked at the limping man. "I suppose you have a license?" the second late-comer said.

The limping man looked at him. "A license?"

"Don't you have to have a license to fly?"

"Oh; a license. For the airplane to fly; sure, I understand. Sure. We got one. You want to see it?"

"You're supposed to show it to anybody that wants to see it, aren't you?"

"Why, sure. You want to see it?"

"Where is it?"

"Where should it be? It's nailed to the airplane, where the government put it. Did you thought maybe it was nailed to me? Did you thought maybe I had a engine on me and maybe wings? It's on the airplane. Call a taxi and go to the airplane and look at it."

"I run a taxi," the driver said.

"Well, run it. Take this gentleman out to the field where he can look at the license on the airplane."

"It'll be a quarter," the driver said. But the limping man was not looking at the driver. He was leaning against the counter. They watched him take a stick of gum from his pocket and peel it. They watched him put the gum into his mouth. "I said it'll be a quarter, Mister," the driver said.

"Was you talking to me?" the limping man said.

"I thought you wanted a taxi out to the airport."

"Me? What for? What do I want to go out to the airport for? I just come from there. I ain't the one that wants to see that license. I have already seen it. I was there when the government nailed it onto the airplane."

II

Captain Warren, the ex-army flyer, was coming out of the store, where he met the tall man in the dirty coverall. Captain Warren told about it in the barber shop that night, when the airplane was gone.

"I hadn't seen him in fourteen years, not since I left England for the front in '17. 'So it was you that rolled out of that loop with two passengers and a twenty model Hisso smokepot?' I said.

" 'Who else saw me?' he said. So he told me about it, standing there, looking over his shoulder every now and then. He was sick; a man stopped behind him to let a couple of ladies pass, and Jock whirled like he might have shot the man if he'd had a gun, and while we were in the café some one slammed a door at the back and I thought he would come out of his monkey suit. 'It's a little nervous trouble I've got,' he told me. 'I'm all right.' I had tried to get him to come out home with me for dinner, but he wouldn't. He said that he had to kind of jump himself and eat before he knew it, sort of. We had started down the street and we were passing the restaurant when he said: 'I'm going to eat,' and he turned and ducked in like a rabbit and sat down with his back to the wall and told Vernon to bring him the quickest thing he had. He drank three glasses of water and then Vernon brought him a milk bottle full and he drank most of that before the dinner came up from the kitchen. When he took off his helmet, I saw that his hair was pretty near white, and he is younger than I am. Or he was, up there when we were in Canada training. Then he told me what the name of his nervous trouble was. It was named Ginsfarb. The little one; the one that jumped off the ladder."

"What was the trouble?" we asked. "What were they afraid of?"

"They were afraid of inspectors," Warren said. "They had no licenses at all."

"There was one on the airplane."

"Yes. But it did not belong to that airplane. That one had been grounded by an inspector when Ginsfarb bought it. The license was for another airplane that had been wrecked, and some one had helped Ginsfarb compound another felony by selling the license to him. Jock had lost his license about two years ago when he crashed a big plane full of Fourth-of-July holidayers. Two of the engines quit, and he had to land. The airplane smashed up some and broke a gas line, but even then they would have been all right if a passenger hadn't got scared (it was about dusk) and struck a match. Jock was not so much to blame, but the passengers all burned to death, and the government is strict. So he couldn't get a license, and he couldn't make Ginsfarb even pay to take out a parachute rigger's license. So they had no license at all; if they were ever caught, they'd all go to the penitentiary."

"No wonder his hair was white," some one said.

"That wasn't what turned it white," Warren said. "I'll tell you about that. So they'd go to little towns like this one, fast, find out if there was anybody that might catch them, and if there wasn't, they'd put on the show and then clear out and go to another town, staying away from the cities. They'd come in and get handbills printed while Jock and the other one would try to get underwritten by some local organization. They wouldn't let Ginsfarb do this part, because he'd stick out for his price too long and they'd be afraid to risk it. So the other two would do this, get what they could, and if they could not get what Ginsfarb told them to, they'd take what they could and then try to keep Ginsfarb fooled until it was too late. Well, this time Ginsfarb kicked up. I guess they had done it too much on him.

"So I met Jock on the street. He looked bad; I offered him a drink, but he said he couldn't even smoke any more. All he could do was drink water; he said he usually drank about a gallon during the night, getting up for it.

" 'You look like you might have to jump yourself to sleep, too,' I said.

" 'No, I sleep fine. The trouble is, the nights aren't long enough. I'd like to live at the North Pole from September to April, and at the South Pole from April to September. That would just suit me.'

" 'You aren't going to last long enough to get there,' I said.

" 'I guess so. It's a good engine. I see to that.'

" 'I mean, you'll be in jail.'

"Then he said: 'Do you think so? Do you guess I could?'

"We went on to the café. He told me about the racket, and showed me one of those Demon Duncan handbills. 'Demon Duncan?' I said.

" 'Why not? Who would pay to see a man named Ginsfarb jump from a ship?'

" 'I'd pay to see that before I'd pay to see a man named Duncan do it,' I said.

"He hadn't thought of that. Then he began to drink water, and he told me that Ginsfarb had wanted a hundred dollars for the stunt, but that he and the other fellow only got sixty.

" 'What are you going to do about it?' I said.

" 'Try to keep him fooled and get this thing over and get to hell away from here,' he said.

" 'Which one is Ginsfarb?' I said. 'The little one that looks like a shark?'

"Then he began to drink water. He emptied my glass too at one shot and tapped it on the table. Vernon brought him another glass. 'You must be thirsty,' Vernon said.

" 'Have you got a pitcher of it?' Jock said.

" 'I could fill you a milk bottle.'

" 'Let's have it,' Jock said. 'And give me another glass while I'm waiting.' Then he told me about Ginsfarb, why his hair had turned gray.

" 'How long have you been doing this?' I said.

" 'Ever since the 26th of August.'

" 'This is just January,' I said.

" 'What about it?'

" 'The 26th of August is not six months past.'

"He looked at me. Vernon brought the bottle of water. Jock poured a glass and drank it. He began to shake, sitting there, shaking and sweating, trying to fill the glass again. Then he told me about it, talking fast, filling the glass and drinking.

"Jake (the other one's name is Jake something; the good-looking one) drives the car, the rented car. Ginsfarb swaps onto the car from the ladder. Jock said he would have to fly the ship into position over a Ford or a Chevrolet running on three cylinders, trying to keep Ginsfarb from jumping from twenty or thirty feet away in order to save gasoline in the ship and in the rented car. Ginsfarb goes out on the bottom wing with his ladder, fastens the ladder onto a strut, hooks himself into the other end of the ladder, and drops off; everybody on the ground thinks that he has done what they all came to see: fallen off and killed himself. That's what he calls his death-drop. Then he swaps from the ladder onto the top of the car, and the ship comes back and he catches the ladder and is dragged off again. That's his death-drag.

"Well, up till the day when Jock's hair began to turn white, Ginsfarb, as a matter of economy, would do it all at once; he would get into position above the car and drop off on his ladder and then make contact with the car, and sometimes Jock said the ship would not be in the air three minutes. Well, on this day the rented car was a bum or something; anyway, Jock had to circle the field four or

five times while the car was getting into position, and
Ginsfarb, seeing his money being blown out the exhaust
pipes, finally refused to wait for Jock's signal and dropped
off anyway. It was all right, only the distance between the
ship and the car was not as long as the rope ladder. So
Ginsfarb hit on the car and Jock had just enough soup to
zoom and drag Ginsfarb, still on the ladder, over a high-
power electric line, and he held the ship in that climb for
twenty minutes while Ginsfarb climbed back up the ladder with his leg broken. He held the ship in a climb with
his knees, with the throttle wide open and the engine
revving about eleven hundred, while he reached back
and opened that cupboard behind the cockpit and
dragged out a suitcase and propped the stick so he could
get out on the wing and drag Ginsfarb back into the ship.
He got Ginsfarb in the ship and on the ground again and
Ginsfarb says: 'How far did we go?' and Jock told him
they had flown with full throttle for thirty minutes and
Ginsfarb says: 'Will you ruin me yet?' "

III

The rest of this is composite. It is what we (groundlings, dwellers in and backbone of a small town interchangeable with and duplicate of ten thousand little dead
clottings of human life about the land) saw, refined and
clarified by the expert, the man who had himself seen
his own lonely and scudding shadow upon the face of the
puny and remote earth.

The three strangers arrived at the field, in the rented
car. When they got out of the car, they were arguing in
tense, dead voices, the pilot and the handsome man
against the man who limped. Captain Warren said they
were arguing about the money.

"I want to see it," Ginsfarb said. They stood close; the
handsome man took something from his pocket.

"There. There it is. See?" he said.

"Let me count it myself," Ginsfarb said.

"Come on, come on," the pilot hissed, in his dead, tense voice. "We tell you we got the money! Do you want an inspector to walk in and take the money and the ship too and put us in jail? Look at all these people waiting."

"You fooled me before," Ginsfarb said.

"All right," the pilot said. "Give it to him. Give him his ship too. And he can pay for the car when he gets back to town. We can get a ride in; there's a train out of here in fifteen minutes."

"You fooled me once before," Ginsfarb said.

"But we're not fooling you now. Come on. Look at all these people."

They moved toward the airplane, Ginsfarb limping terrifically, his back stubborn, his face tragic, outraged, cold. There was a good crowd: country people in overalls; the men a general dark clump against which the bright dresses of the women, the young girls, showed. The small boys and several men were already surrounding the airplane. We watched the limping man begin to take objects from the body of it: a parachute, a rope ladder. The handsome man went to the propeller. The pilot got into the back seat.

"Off!" he said, sudden and sharp. "Stand back, folks. We're going to wring the old bird's neck."

They tried three times to crank the engine.

"I got a mule, Mister," a countryman said. "How much'll you pay for a tow?"

The three strangers did not laugh. The limping man was busy attaching the rope ladder to one wing.

"You can't tell me," a countrywoman said. "Even he ain't that big a fool."

The engine started then. It seemed to lift bodily from the ground a small boy who stood behind it and blow him aside like a leaf. We watched it turn and trundle down the field.

"You can't tell me that thing's flying," the country-woman said. "I reckon the Lord give me eyes. I can see it ain't flying. You folks have been fooled."

"Wait," another voice said. "He's got to turn into the wind."

"Ain't there as much wind right there or right here as there is down yonder?" the woman said. But it did fly. It turned back toward us; the noise became deafening. When it came broadside on to us, it did not seem to be going fast, yet we could see daylight beneath the wheels and the earth. But it was not going fast; it appeared rather to hang gently just above the earth until we saw that, be-yond and beneath it, trees and earth in panorama were fleeing backward at dizzy speed, and then it tilted and shot skyward with a noise like a circular saw going into a white oak log. "There ain't nobody in it!" the country-woman said. "You can't tell me!"

The third man, the handsome one in the cap, had got into the rented car. We all knew it: a battered thing which the owner would rent to any one who would make a deposit of ten dollars. He drove to the end of the field, faced down the runway, and stopped. We looked back at the airplane. It was high, coming back toward us; some one cried suddenly, his voice puny and thin: "There! Out on the wing! see?"

"It ain't!" the countrywoman said. "I don't believe it!"

"You saw them get in it," some one said.

"I don't believe it!" the woman said.

Then we sighed; we said, "Aaahhhhhhh"; beneath the wing of the airplane there was a falling dot. We knew it was a man. Some way we knew that that lonely, puny, falling shape was that of a living man like ourselves. It fell. It seemed to fall for years, yet when it checked sud-denly up without visible rope or cord, it was less far from the airplane than was the end of the delicate pen-slash of the profiled wing.

"It ain't a man!" the woman shrieked.

"You know better," the man said. "You saw him get in it."

"I don't care!" the woman cried. "It ain't a man! You take me right home this minute!"

The rest is hard to tell. Not because we saw so little; we saw everything that happened, but because we had so little in experience to postulate it with. We saw that battered rented car moving down the field, going faster, jouncing in the broken January mud, then the sound of the airplane blotted it, reduced it to immobility; we saw the dangling ladder and the shark-faced man swinging on it beneath the death-colored airplane. The end of the ladder raked right across the top of the car, from end to end, with the limping man on the ladder and the capped head of the handsome man leaning out of the car. And the end of the field was coming nearer, and the airplane was travelling faster than the car, passing it. And nothing happened. "Listen!" some one cried. "They are talking to one another!"

Captain Warren told us what they were talking about, the two Jews yelling back and forth at one another: the shark-faced man on the dangling ladder that looked like a cobweb, the other one in the car; the fence, the end of the field, coming closer.

"Come on!" the man in the car shouted.

"What did they pay?"

"Jump!"

"If they didn't pay that hundred, I won't do it."

Then the airplane zoomed, roaring, the dangling figure on the gossamer ladder swinging beneath it. It circled the field twice while the man got the car into position again. Again the car started down the field; again the airplane came down with its wild, circular-saw drone which died into a splutter as the ladder and the clinging man swung up to the car from behind; again we heard the two puny voices shrieking at one another with a quality at once ludicrous and horrible: the one coming out of the very air itself, shrieking about something sweated out of the earth and without value anywhere else:

"How much did you say?"

"Jump!"

"What? How much did they pay?"

"Nothing! Jump!"

"Nothing?" the man on the ladder wailed in a fading, outraged shriek. "Nothing?" Again the airplane was dragging the ladder irrevocably past the car, approaching the end of the field, the fences, the long barn with its rotting roof. Suddenly we saw Captain Warren beside us; he was using words we had never heard him use.

"He's got the stick between his knees," Captain Warren said. "Exalted suzerain of mankind; saccharine and sacred symbol of eternal rest." We had forgot about the pilot, the man still in the airplane. We saw the airplane, tilted upward, the pilot standing upright in the back seat, leaning over the side and shaking both hands at the man on the ladder. We could hear him yelling now as again the man on the ladder was dragged over the car and past it, shrieking:

"I won't do it! I won't do it!" He was still shrieking when the airplane zoomed; we saw him, a diminishing and shrieking spot against the sky above the long roof of the barn: "I won't do it! I won't do it!" Before, when the speck left the airplane, falling, to be snubbed up by the ladder, we knew that it was a living man; again, when the speck left the ladder, falling, we knew that it was a living man, and we knew that there was no ladder to snub him up now. We saw him falling against the cold, empty January sky until the silhouette of the barn absorbed him; even from here, his attitude froglike, outraged, implacable. From somewhere in the crowd a woman screamed, though the sound was blotted out by the sound of the airplane. It reared skyward with its wild, tearing noise, the empty ladder swept backward beneath it. The sound of the engine was like a groan, a groan of relief and despair.

IV

Captain Warren told us in the barber shop on that Saturday night.

"Did he really jump off, onto that barn?" we asked him.

"Yes. He jumped. He wasn't thinking about being killed, or even hurt. That's why he wasn't hurt. He was too mad, too in a hurry to receive justice. He couldn't wait to fly back down. Providence knew that he was too busy and that he deserved justice, so Providence put that barn there with the rotting roof. He wasn't even thinking about hitting the barn; if he'd tried to, let go of his belief in a cosmic balance to bother about landing, he would have missed the barn and killed himself."

It didn't hurt him at all, save for a long scratch on his face that bled a lot, and his overcoat was torn completely down the back, as though the tear down the back of the helmet had run on down the overcoat. He came out of the barn running before we got to it. He hobbled right among us, with his bloody face, his arms waving, his coat dangling from either shoulder.

"Where is that secretary?" he said.

"What secretary?"

"That American Legion secretary." He went on, limping fast, toward where a crowd stood about three women who had fainted. "You said you would pay a hundred dollars to see me swap to that car. We pay rent on the car and all, and now you would—"

"You got sixty dollars," some one said.

The man looked at him. "Sixty? I said one hundred. When you would let me believe it was one hundred and it was just sixty; you would see me risk my life for sixty dollars. . . ." The airplane was down; none of us were aware of it until the pilot sprang suddenly upon the man who limped. He jerked the man around and knocked him down before we could grasp the pilot. We held the pilot, struggling, crying, the tears streaking his dirty, unshaven face. Captain Warren was suddenly there, holding the pilot.

"Stop it!" he said. "Stop it!"

The pilot ceased. He stared at Captain Warren, then he slumped and sat on the ground in his thin, dirty garment, with his unshaven face, dirty, gaunt, with his sick eyes, crying. "Go away," Captain Warren said. "Let him alone for a minute."

We went away, back to the other man, the one who limped. They had lifted him and he drew the two halves of his overcoat forward and looked at them. Then he said: "I want some chewing gum."

Some one gave him a stick. Another offered him a cigarette. "Thanks," he said. "I don't burn up no money. I ain't got enough of it yet." He put the gum into his mouth. "You would take advantage of me. If you thought I would risk my life for sixty dollars, you fool yourself."

"Give him the rest of it," some one said. "Here's my share."

The limping man did not look around. "Make it up to a hundred, and I will swap to the car like on the handbill," he said.

Somewhere a woman screamed behind him. She began to laugh and to cry at the same time. "Don't . . ." she said, laughing and crying at the same time. "Don't let . . . " until they led her away. Still the limping man had not moved. He wiped his face on his cuff and he was looking at his bloody sleeve when Captain Warren came up.

"How much is he short?" Warren said. They told Warren. He took out some money and gave it to the limping man.

"You want I should swap to the car?" he said.

"No," Warren said. "You get that crate out of here quick as you can."

"Well, that's your business," the limping man said. "I got witnesses I offered to swap." He moved; we made way and watched him, in his severed and dangling over-coat, approach the airplane. It was on the runway, the engine running. The third man was already in the front seat. We watched the limping man crawl terrifically in beside him. They sat there, looking forward.

The pilot began to get up. Warren was standing beside him. "Ground it," Warren said. "You are coming home with me."

"I guess we'd better get on," the pilot said. He did not look at Warren. Then he put out his hand. "Well . . ." he said.

Warren did not take his hand. "You come on home with me," he said.

"Who'd take care of that bastard?"

"Who wants to?"

"I'll get him right, some day. Where I can beat hell out of him."

"Jock," Warren said.

"No," the other said.

"Have you got an overcoat?"

"Sure I have."

"You're a liar." Warren began to pull off his overcoat.

"No," the other said; "I don't need it." He went on toward the machine. "See you some time," he said over his shoulder. We watched him get in, heard the airplane come to life, come alive. It passed us, already off the ground. The pilot jerked his hand once, stiffly; the two heads in the front seat did not turn nor move. Then it was gone, the sound was gone.

Warren turned. "What about that car they rented?" he said.

"He give me a quarter to take it back to town," a boy said.

"Can you drive it?"

"Yes, sir. I drove it out here. I showed him where to rent it."

"The one that jumped?"

"Yes, sir." The boy looked a little aside. "Only I'm a little scared to take it back. I don't reckon you could come with me."

"Why, scared?" Warren said.

"That fellow never paid nothing down on it, like Mr. Harris wanted. He told Mr. Harris he might not use it, but if he did use it in his show, he would pay Mr. Harris twenty dollars for it instead of ten like Mr. Harris wanted. He told me to take it back and tell Mr. Harris he never used the car. And I don't know if Mr. Harris will like it. He might get mad."

1929

Uncle Bud and the Three Madams

The tables had been moved to one end of the dance floor. On each one was a black table-cloth. The curtains were still drawn; a thick, salmon-colored light fell through them. Just beneath the orchestra platform the coffin sat. It was an expensive one: black, with silver fittings, the trestles hidden by a mass of flowers. In wreaths and crosses and other shapes of ceremonial mortality, the mass appeared to break in a symbolical wave over the bier and on upon the platform and the piano, the scent of them thickly oppressive.

The proprietor of the place moved about among the tables, speaking to the arrivals as they entered and found seats. The Negro waiters, in black shirts beneath their starched jackets, were already moving in and out with glasses and bottles of ginger ale. They moved with swaggering and decorous repression; already the scene was vivid, with a hushed, macabre air a little febrile.

The archway to the dice-room was draped in black. A black pall lay upon the crap-table, upon which the overflow of floral shapes was beginning to accumulate. People entered steadily, men in dark suits of decorous restraint, others in the light, bright shades of spring, increasing the atmosphere of macabre paradox. The women—the younger ones—wore bright colors also, in hats and scarves; the older ones in sober gray and black and navy blue, and glittering with diamonds: matronly figures resembling housewives on a Sunday afternoon excursion.

The room began to hum with shrill, hushed talk. The waiters moved here and there with high, precarious trays, their white jackets and black shirts resembling photograph negatives. The proprietor went from table to table with his bald head, a huge diamond in his black cravat, followed by the bouncer, a thick, muscle-bound, bullet-headed man who appeared to be on the point of bursting out of his dinner-jacket through the rear, like a cocoon.

In a private dining-room, on a table draped in black, sat a huge bowl of punch floating with ice and sliced fruit. Beside it leaned a fat man in a shapeless greenish suit, from the sleeves of which dirty cuffs fell upon hands rimmed with black nails. The soiled collar was wilted about his neck in limp folds, knotted by a greasy black tie with an imitation ruby stud. His face gleamed with moisture and he adjured the throng about the bowl in a harsh voice:

"Come on, folks. It's on Gene. It don't cost you nothing. Step up and drink. There wasn't never a better boy walked than Red." They drank and fell back, replaced by others with extended cups. From time to time a waiter entered with ice and fruit and dumped them into the bowl; from a suitcase under the table Gene drew fresh bottles and decanted them into the bowl; then, proprietorial, adjurant, sweating, he resumed his harsh monologue, mopping his face on his sleeve. "Come on, folks. It's all on Gene. I ain't nothing but a bootlegger, but he never had a better friend than me. Step up and drink, folks. There's more where that come from."

From the dance hall came a strain of music The people entered and found seats. On the platform was the orchestra from a downtown hotel, in dinner coats. The proprietor and a second man were conferring with the leader.

"Let them play jazz," the second man said. "Never nobody liked dancing no better than Red."

"No, no," the proprietor said. "Time Gene gets them all ginned up on free whiskey, they'll start dancing. It'll look bad."

"How about the 'Blue Danube'?" the leader said.

"No, no; don't play no blues, I tell you," the proprietor said. "There's a dead man in that bier."

"That's not blues," the leader said.

"What is it?" the second man said.

"A waltz. Strauss."

"A wop?" the second man said. "Like hell. Red was an American. You may not be, but he was. Don't you know anything American? Play 'I Can't Give You Anything but Love.' He always liked that."

"And get them all to dancing?" the proprietor said. He glanced back at the tables, where the women were beginning to talk a little shrilly. "You better start off with 'Nearer, My God, to Thee,'" he said, "and sober them up some. I told Gene it was risky about that punch, starting it so soon. My suggestion was to wait until we started back to town. But I might have knowed somebody'd have to turn it into a carnival. Better start off solemn and keep it up until I give you the sign."

"Red wouldn't like it solemn," the second man said. "And you know it."

"Let him go somewheres else, then," the proprietor said. "I just done this as an accommodation. I ain't running no funeral parlor."

The orchestra played "Nearer, My God, To Thee." The audience grew quiet. A woman in a red dress came in the door unsteadily. "Whoopee," she said, "so long, Red. He'll be in hell before I could even reach Little Rock."

"Shhhhhhhh!" voices said. She fell into a seat. Gene came to the door and stood there until the music stopped.

"Come on, folks," he shouted, jerking his arms in a fat,

sweeping gesture, "come and get it. It's on Gene. I don't want a dry throat or eye in this place in ten minutes." Those at the rear moved toward the door. The proprietor sprang to his feet and jerked his hand at the orchestra. The cornetist rose and played "In That Haven of Rest" in solo, but the crowd at the back of the room continued to dwindle through the door where Gene stood waving his arm. Two middle-aged women were weeping quietly beneath flowered hats.

They surged and clamored about the diminishing bowl. From the dance hall came the rich blare of the cornet. Two soiled young men worked their way toward the table, shouting, "Gangway. Gangway," monotonously, carrying suitcases. They opened them and set bottles on the table, while Gene, frankly weeping now, opened them and decanted them into the bowl. "Come up, folks. I couldn't a loved him no better if he'd a been my own son," he shouted hoarsely, dragging his sleeve across his face.

A waiter edged up to the table with a bowl of ice and fruit and went to put them into the punch bowl. "What the hell you doing?" Gene said, "putting that slop in there? Get to hell away from here."

"Ra-a-a-a-y-y-y-y!" they shouted, clashing their cups, drowning all save the pantomime as Gene knocked the bowl of fruit from the waiter's hand and fell again to dumping raw liquor into the bowl, sploshing it into and upon the extended hands and cups. The two youths opened bottles furiously.

As though swept there upon a brassy blare of music the proprietor appeared in the door, his face harried, waving his arms. "Come on, folks," he shouted, "let's finish the musical program. It's costing us money."

"Hell with it," they shouted.

"Costing who money?"

"Who cares?"

"Costing who money?"

"Who begrudges it? I'll pay it. By God, I'll buy him two funerals."

"Folks! Folks!" the proprietor shouted. "Don't you realize there's a bier in that room?"

"Costing who money?"

"Beer?" Gene said. "Beer?" he said in a broken voice. "Is anybody here trying to insult me by—"

"He begrudges Red the money."

"Who does?"

"Joe does, the cheap son of a bitch."

"Is anybody here trying to insult me by—"

"Let's move the funeral, then. This is not the only place in town."

"Let's move Joe."

"Put the son of a bitch in a coffin. Let's have two funerals."

"Beer? Beer? Is somebody—"

"Put the son of a bitch in a coffin. See how he likes it."

"Put the son of a bitch in a coffin," the woman in red shrieked. They rushed toward the door, where the proprietor stood waving his hands above his head, his voice shrieking out of the uproar before he turned and fled.

In the main room a male quartet engaged from a vaudeville house was singing. They were singing mother songs in close harmony; they sang "Sonny Boy." The weeping was general among the older women. Waiters were now carrying cups of punch in to them and they sat holding the cups in their fat, ringed hands, crying.

The orchestra played again. The woman in red staggered into the room. "Come on, Joe," she shouted, "open the game. Get that damn stiff out of here and open the game." A man tried to hold her; she turned upon him with a burst of filthy language and went on to the shrouded crap table and hurled a wreath to the floor. The proprietor rushed toward her, followed by the bouncer. The proprietor grasped the woman as she lifted another floral piece. The man who had tried to hold her intervened, the woman cursing shrilly and striking at both of them impartially with the wreath. The bouncer caught the man's arm; he whirled and struck at the bouncer, who knocked him halfway across the room. Three more men entered. The fourth rose from the floor and all four of them rushed at the bouncer.

He felled the first and whirled and sprang with unbelievable celerity, into the main room. The orchestra was playing. It was immediately drowned in a sudden pandemonium of chairs and screams. The bouncer whirled again and met the rush of the four men. They mingled; a second man flew out and skittered along the floor on his back; the bouncer sprang free. Then he whirled and rushed them and in a whirling plunge they bore down upon the bier and crashed into it. The orchestra had ceased and were now climbing onto their chairs, with their instruments. The floral offerings flew; the coffin teetered. "Catch it!" a voice shouted. They sprang forward, but the coffin crashed heavily to the floor, coming open. The corpse tumbled slowly and sedately out and came to rest with its face in the center of a wreath.

"Play something!" the proprietor bawled, waving his arms; "Play! Play!"

When they raised the corpse the wreath came too, attached to him by a hidden end of a wire driven into his cheek. He had worn a cap which, tumbling off, exposed a small blue hole in the center of his forehead. It had been neatly plugged with wax and was painted, but the wax had been jarred out and lost. They couldn't find it, but by unfastening the snap in the peak, they could draw the cap down to his eyes.

As the cortège neared the downtown section more cars joined it. The hearse was followed by six Packard touring cars with the tops back, driven by liveried chauffeurs and filled with flowers. They looked exactly alike and were of the type rented by the hour by the better class agencies. Next came a nondescript line of taxis, roadsters, sedans, which increased as the procession moved slowly through the restricted district, where faces peered from beneath lowered shades, toward the main artery that led back out of town, toward the cemetery.

On the avenue the hearse increased its speed, the procession stretching out at swift intervals. Presently the private cars and the cabs began to drop out. At each intersection they would turn this way or that, until at last only the hearse and the six Packards were left, each carrying no occupant save the liveried driver. The street was broad and now infrequent, with a white line down the center that diminished on ahead into the smooth asphalt emptiness. Soon the hearse was making forty miles an hour and then forty-five and then fifty.

One of the cabs drew up at Miss Reba's door. She got out, followed by a thin woman in sober, severe clothes and gold nose-glasses, and a short plump woman in a plumed hat, her face hidden by a handkerchief, and a small bullet-headed boy of five or six. The woman with the handkerchief continued to sob in snuffy gasps as they went up the walk and entered the lattice. Beyond the house door the dogs set up a falsetto uproar. When Minnie opened the door they surged about Miss Reba's feet. She kicked them aside. Again they assailed her with snapping eagerness; again she flung them back against the wall in muted thuds.

"Come in, come in," she said, her hand to her breast. Once inside the house the woman with the handkerchief began to weep aloud.

"Didn't he look sweet?" she wailed. "Didn't he look sweet!"

"Now, now," Miss Reba said, leading the way to her room, "come in and have some beer. You'll feel better. Minnie!" They entered her room with its decorated dresser, its wall safe, its screen, its draped portrait of a meek-looking man with an enormous moustache. "Sit down, sit down," she panted, shoving the chairs forward. She lowered herself into one and stooped terrifically toward her feet.

"Uncle Bud, honey," the weeping woman said, dabbing at her eyes, "come and unlace Miss Reba's shoes."

The boy knelt and removed Miss Reba's shoes. "And if you'll just reach me them house slippers under the bed there, honey," Miss Reba said. The boy fetched the slippers. Minnie entered, followed by the dogs. They rushed at Miss Reba and began to worry the shoes she had just removed.

"Scat!" the boy said, striking at one of them with his hand. The dog's head snapped around, its teeth clicking, its half-hidden eyes bright and malevolent. The boy recoiled. "You bite me, you thon bitch," he said.

"Uncle Bud!" the fat woman said, her round face, rigid in fatty folds and streaked with tears, turned upon the boy in shocked surprise, the plumes nodding precariously above it. Uncle Bud's head was quite round, his nose bridged with freckles like splotches of huge summer rain on a sidewalk. The other woman sat primly erect, in gold nose-glasses on a gold chain and neat iron-gray hair. She looked like a school-teacher. "The very idea!" the fat woman said. "How in the world he can learn such words on an Arkansaw farm, I don't know."

"They'll learn meanness anywhere," Miss Reba said. Minnie leaned down a tray bearing three frosted tankards. Uncle Bud watched with round cornflower eyes as they took one each. The fat woman began to cry again.

"He looked so sweet!" she wailed.

"We all got to suffer it," Miss Reba said. "Well, may it be a long day," lifting her tankard. They drank, bowing formally to one another. The fat woman dried her eyes; the two guests wiped their lips with prim decorum. The thin one coughed delicately aside, behind her hand.

"Such good beer," she said.

"Ain't it?" the fat one said. "I always say it's the greatest pleasure I have to call on Miss Reba."

They began to talk politely, in decorous half-completed sentences, with little gasps of agreement. The boy had moved aimlessly to the window, peering beneath the lifted shade.

"How long's he going to be with you, Miss Myrtle?" Miss Reba said.

"Just till Sat'dy," the fat woman said. "Then he'll go back home. It makes a right nice little change for him, with me for a week or two. And I enjoy having him."

"Children are such a comfort to a body," the thin one said.

"Yes," Miss Myrtle said. "Is them two nice young fellows still with you, Miss Reba?"

"Yes," Miss Reba said. "I think I got to get shut of them, though. I ain't specially tender-hearted, but after all it ain't no use in helping young folks to learn this world's meanness until they have to. I already had to stop the girls running around the house without no clothes on, and they don't like it."

They drank again, decorously, handling the tankards delicately, save Miss Reba who grasped hers as though it were a weapon, her other hand lost in her breast. She set her tankard down empty. "I get so dry, seems like," she said. "Won't you ladies have another?" They murmured, ceremoniously. "Minnie!" Miss Reba shouted.

Minnie came and filled the tankards again. "Reely, I'm right ashamed," Miss Myrtle said. "But Miss Reba has such good beer. And then we've all had a kind of upsetting afternoon."

"I'm just surprised it wasn't upset no more," Miss Reba said. "Giving away all that free liquor like Gene done."

"It must have cost a good piece of jack," the thin woman said.

"I believe you," Miss Reba said. "And who got anything out of it? Tell me that. Except the privilege of having his place hell-full of folks not spending a cent." She had set her tankard on the table beside her chair. Suddenly she turned her head sharply and looked at it. Uncle Bud was now behind her chair, leaning against the table. "You ain't been into my beer, have you, boy?" she said.

"You, Uncle Bud," Miss Myrtle said. "Ain't you ashamed? I declare, it's getting so I don't dare take him nowhere. I never see such a boy for snitching beer in my life. You come out here and play, now. Come on."

"Yessum," Uncle Bud said. He moved, in no particular direction. Miss Reba drank and set the tankard back on the table and rose.

"Since we all been kind of tore up," she said, "maybe can prevail on you ladies to have a little sup of gin?"

"No; reely," Miss Myrtle said.

"Miss Reba's the perfect hostess," the thin one said. "How many times you heard me say that, Miss Myrtle?"

"I wouldn't undertake to say, dearie," Miss Myrtle said.

Miss Reba vanished behind the screen.

"Did you ever see it so warm for June, Miss Lorraine?" Miss Myrtle said.

"I never did," the thin woman said. Miss Myrtle's face began to crinkle again. Setting her tankard down she began to fumble for her handkerchief.

"It just comes over me like this," she said, "and them singing that 'Sonny Boy' and all. He looked so sweet," she wailed.

"Now, now," Miss Lorraine said. "Drink a little beer. You'll feel better. Miss Myrtle's took again," she said, raising her voice.

"I got too tender a heart," Miss Myrtle said. She snuffled behind the handkerchief, groping for her tankard. She groped for a moment, then it touched her hand. She looked quickly up. "You, Uncle Bud!" she said. "Didn't I tell you to come out from behind there and play? Would you believe it? The other afternoon when we left here I was so mortified I didn't know what to do. I was ashamed to be seen on the street with a drunk boy like you."

Miss Reba emerged from behind the screen with three glasses of gin. "This'll put some heart into us," she said. "We're setting here like three old sick cats." They bowed formally and drank, patting their lips. Then they began to talk. They were all talking at once, again in half-completed sentences, but without pauses for agreement or affirmation.

"It's us girls," Miss Myrtle said. "Men just can't seem to take us and leave us for what we are. They make us what we are, then they expect us to be different. Expect us not to never look at another man, while they come and go as they please."

"A woman that wants to fool with more than one man at a time is a fool," Miss Reba said. "They're all trouble, and why do you want to double your trouble? And the woman that can't stay true to a good man when she gets him, a free-hearted spender that never give her a hour's uneasiness or a hard word . . ." looking at them, her eyes began to fill with a sad, unutterable expression, of baffled and patient despair.

"Now, now," Miss Myrtle said. She leaned forward and patted Miss Reba's huge hand. Miss Lorraine made a faint clucking sound with her tongue. "You'll get yourself started."

"He was such a good man," Miss Reba said. "We was like two doves. For eleven years we was like two doves."

"Now, dearie; now, dearie," Miss Myrtle said.

"It's when it comes over me like this," Miss Reba said. "Seeing that boy laying there under them flowers."

"He never had no more than Mr. Binford had," Miss Myrtle said. "Now, now. Drink a little beer "

Miss Reba brushed her sleeve across her eyes. She drank some beer.

"He ought to known better than to take a chance with Popeye's girl," Miss Lorraine said.

"Men don't never learn better than that, dearie," Miss Myrtle said. "Where you reckon they went, Miss Reba?"

"I don't know and I don't care," Miss Reba said. "And how soon they catch Popeye and burn him for killing that boy, I don't care neither. I don't care none."

"He goes all the way to Pensacola every summer to see his mother," Miss Myrtle said. "A man that'll do that can't be all bad."

"I don't know how bad you like them, then," Miss Reba said. "Me trying to run a respectable house, that's been running a shooting-gallery for twenty years, and him trying to turn it into a peep-show."

"It's us poor girls," Miss Myrtle said, "causes all the trouble and gets all the suffering."

"I heard two years ago Popeye wasn't no good that way," Miss Lorraine said.

"I knew it all the time," Miss Reba said. "A young man spending his money like water on girls and not never going to bed with one. It's against nature. All the girls thought it was because he had a little woman out in town somewhere, but I says, mark my words, there's something funny about him. There's a funny business somewhere."

"He was a free spender, all right," Miss Lorraine said.

"The clothes and jewelry that girl bought, it was a shame," Miss Reba said. "There was a Chinee robe she paid a hundred dollars for—imported, it was—and perfume at ten dollars an ounce; next morning when I went up there, they was all wadded in the corner and the perfume and rouge busted all over them like a cyclone. That's what she'd do when she got mad at him, when he'd beat her. After he shut her up and wouldn't let her leave the house. Having the front of my house watched like it was a . . ." She raised the tankard from the table to her lips. Then she halted it, blinking. "Where's my—"

"Uncle Bud!" Miss Myrtle said. She grasped the boy by the arm and snatched him out from behind Miss Reba's chair and shook him, his round head bobbing on his shoulders with an expression of equable idiocy. "Ain't you ashamed? ain't you *ashamed?* Why can't you stay out of these ladies' beer? I'm a good mind to take that dollar back and make you buy Miss Reba a can of beer, I am for a fact. Now, you go over there by that window and stay there, you hear?"

"Nonsense," Miss Reba said. "There wasn't much of it left. You ladies are about ready too, ain't you? Minnie!"

Miss Lorraine touched her mouth with her handkerchief. Behind her glasses her eyes rolled aside in a veiled, secret look. She laid the other hand to her flat spinster's breast.

"We forgot about your heart, honey," Miss Myrtle said. "Don't you reckon you better take gin this time?"

"Reely, I—" Miss Lorraine said.

"Yes; do," Miss Reba said. She rose heavily and fetched three more glasses of gin from behind the screen. Minnie entered and refilled the tankards. They drank, patting their lips.

"That's what was going on, was it?" Miss Lorraine said.

"First I knowed was when Minnie told me there was something funny going on," Miss Reba said. "How he wasn't here hardly at all, gone about every other night, and that when he was here, there wasn't no signs at all the next morning when she cleaned up. She'd hear them quarrelling, and she said it was her wanting to get out and he wouldn't let her. With all them clothes he was buying her, mind, he didn't want her to leave the house, and she'd get mad and lock the door and wouldn't even let him in."

"Maybe he went off and got fixed up with one of these glands, these monkey glands, and it quit on him," Miss Myrtle said.

"Then one morning he come in with Red and took him up there. They stayed about an hour and left, and Popeye didn't show up again until next morning. Then him and Red come back and stayed up there about an hour.

When they left, Minnie come and told me what was going on, so next day I waited for them. I called him in here and I says 'Look here, you sonofabuh—'" She ceased. For an instant the three of them sat motionless, a little forward. Then slowly their heads turned and they looked at the boy leaning against the table.

"Uncle Bud, honey," Miss Myrtle said, "don't you want to go and play in the yard with Reba and Mr. Binford?"

"Yessum," the boy said. He went toward the door. They watched him until the door closed upon him. Miss Lorraine drew her chair up; they leaned together.

"And that's what they was doing?" Miss Myrtle said.

"I says 'I been running a house for twenty years, but this is the first time I ever had anything like this going on in it. If you want to turn a stud in to your girl' I says 'go somewhere else to do it. I ain't going to have my house turned into no French joint.'"

"The son of a bitch," Miss Lorraine said.

"He'd ought to've had sense enough to got a old ugly man," Miss Myrtle said. "Tempting us poor girls like that."

"Men always expects us to resist temptation," Miss Lorraine said. She was sitting upright like a schoolteacher. "The lousy son of a bitch."

"Except what they offers themselves," Miss Reba said. "Then watch them. . . . Every morning for four days that was going on, then they didn't come back. For a week Popeye didn't show up at all, and that girl wild as a young mare. I thought he was out of town on business maybe, until Minnie told me he wasn't and that he give her five dollars a day not to let that girl out of the house nor use the telephone. And me trying to get word to him to come and take her out of my house because I didn't want nuttin like that going on in it. Yes, sir, Minnie said the two of them would be nekkid as two snakes, and Popeye hanging over the foot of the bed without even his hat took off, making a kind of whinnying sound."

"Maybe he was cheering for them," Miss Lorraine said. "The lousy son of a bitch."

Feet came up the hall; they could hear Minnie's voice lifted in adjuration. The door opened. She entered, holding Uncle Bud erect by one hand. Limp-kneed he dangled, his face fixed in an expression of glassy idiocy. "Miss Reba," Minnie said, "this boy done broke in the icebox and drunk a whole bottle of beer. You, boy!" she said, shaking him, "stan up!" Limply he dangled, his face rigid in a slobbering grin. Then upon it came an expression of concern, consternation; Minnie swung him sharply away from her as he began to vomit.

1930

Percy Grimm

In the town of Jefferson lived a young man named Percy Grimm. He was about twenty-five and a captain in the State National Guard. He had been born in the town and had lived there all his life save for the periods of the summer encampments. He was too young to have been in the European War, though it was not until 1921 or '22 that he realized that he would never forgive his parents for that fact. His father, a hardware merchant, did not understand this. He thought that the boy was just lazy and in a fair way to become perfectly worthless, when in reality the boy was suffering the terrible tragedy of having been born not alone too late but not late enough to have escaped first-hand knowledge of the lost time when he should have been a man instead of a child. And now, with the hysteria passed away and the ones who had been loudest in the hysteria and even the ones, the heroes who had suffered and served, beginning to look at one another a little askance, he had no one to tell it, to open his heart to. In fact, his first serious fight was with an ex-soldier who made some remark to the effect that if he had to do it again, he would fight this time on the German side and against France. At once Grimm took him up. "Against America too?" he said.

"If America's fool enough to help France out again," the soldier said. Grimm struck him at once; he was smaller

than the soldier, still in his teens. The result was fore-
gone; even Grimm doubtless knew that. But he took his
punishment until even the soldier begged the bystand-
ers to hold the boy back. And he wore the scars of that
battle as proudly as he was later to wear the uniform itself
for which he had blindly fought.

It was the new civilian-military act which saved him.
He was like a man who had been for a long time in a
swamp, in the dark. It was as though he not only could
see no path ahead of him, he knew that there was none.
Then suddenly his life opened definite and clear. The
wasted years in which he had shown no ability in school,
in which he had been known as lazy, recalcitrant, without
ambition, were behind him, forgotten. He could now see
his life opening before him, uncomplex and inescapable
as a barren corridor, completely freed now of ever again
having to think or decide, the burden which he now assumed and carried as bright and weightless and martial as
his insignatory brass: a sublime and implicit faith in physical courage and blind obedience, and a belief that the
white race is superior to any and all other races and that
the American is superior to all other white races and that
the American uniform is superior to all men, and that all
that would ever be required of him in payment for this
belief, this privilege, would be his own life. On each national holiday that had any martial flavor whatever he
dressed in his captain's uniform and came down town.
And those who saw him remembered him again on the
day of the fight with the ex-soldier as, glittering, with his
marksman's badge (he was a fine shot) and his bars, grave,
erect, he walked among the civilians with about him an
air half belligerent and half the selfconscious pride of a
boy.

He was not a member of the American Legion, but
that was his parents' fault and not his. But when Joe
Christmas, the mulatto, was fetched back from Mottstown

on that Saturday afternoon, accused of killing Miss Jo-
anna Burden, he had already been to the commander of
the local Post. His idea, his words, were quite simple and
direct. "We got to preserve order," he said. "We must
let the law take its course. The law, the nation. It is the
right of no civilian to sentence a man to death. And we,
the soldiers in Jefferson, are the ones to see to that."

"How do you know that anybody is planning anything
different?" the Legion commander said. "Have you heard
any talk?"

"I don't know. I haven't listened." He didn't lie. It
was as though he did not attach enough importance to
what might or might not have been said by the civilian
citizens to lie about it. "That's not the question. It's
whether or not we, as soldiers, that have worn the uniform, are going to be the first to state where we stand.
To show these people right off just where the government of the country stands on such things. That there
won't be any need for them even to talk." His plan was
quite simple. It was to form the Legion Post into a platoon,
with himself in command vide his active commission.
"But if they don't want me to command, that's all right
too. I'll be second, if they say. Or a sergeant or a corporal."
And he meant it. It was not vain glory that he wanted. He
was too sincere. So sincere, so humorless, that the Legion
commander withheld the flippant refusal he was about
to make.

"I still don't think that there is any need of it. And if
there was, we would all have to act as civilians. I couldn't
use the Post like that. After all, we are not soldiers now.
I don't think I would, if I could."

Grimm looked at him, without anger, but rather as if
he were some kind of bug. "Yet you wore the uniform
once," he said, with a kind of patience. He said: "I suppose you won't use your authority to keep me from talking to them, will you? As individuals?"

"No. I haven't any authority to do that, anyway. But just as individuals, mind. You mustn't use my name at all."

Then Grimm gave him a shot on his own account. "I am not likely to do that," he said. Then he was gone. That was Saturday, about four o'clock. For the rest of that afternoon he circulated about the stores and offices where the Legion members worked, so that by nightfall he had enough of them also worked up to his own pitch to compose a fair platoon. He was indefatigable, restrained yet forceful; there was something about him irresistible and prophetlike. Yet the recruits were with the commander in one thing: the official designation of the legion must be kept out of it—whereupon and without deliberate intent, he had gained his original end: he was now in command. He got them all together just before suppertime and divided them into squads and appointed officers and a staff; the younger ones, the ones who had not gone to France, taking proper fire by now. He addressed them, briefly, coldly: ". . . order . . . course of justice . . . let the people see that we have worn the uniform of the United States . . . And one thing more." For the moment now he had descended to familiarity: the regimental commander who knows his men by their first names. "I'll leave this to you fellows. I'll do what you say. I thought it might be a good thing if I wear my uniform until this business is settled. So they can see that Uncle Sam is present in more than spirit."

"But he's not," one said quickly, immediately; he was of the same cut as the commander, who by the way was not present. "This is not government trouble yet. Kennedy might not like it. This is Jefferson's trouble, not Washington's."

"Make him like it," Grimm said. "What does your Legion stand for, if not for the protection of America and Americans?"

"No," the other said. "I reckon we better not make a

parade out of this. We can do what we want without that. Better. Ain't that right, boys?"

"All right," Grimm said. "I'll do as you say. But every man will want a pistol. We'll have a small arms' inspection here in one hour. Every man will report here."

"What's Kennedy going to say about pistols?" one said.

"I'll see to that," Grimm said. "Report here in one hour exactly, with side arms." He dismissed them. He crossed the quiet square to the sheriff's office. The sheriff was at home, they told him. "At home?" he repeated. "Now? What's he doing at home now?"

"Eating, I reckon. A man as big as him has got to eat several times a day."

"At home," Grimm repeated. He did not glare; it was again that cold and detached expression with which he had looked at the Legion commander. "Eating," he said. He went out, already walking fast. He recrossed the empty square, the quiet square empty of people peacefully at suppertables about that peaceful town and that peaceful country. He went to the sheriff's home. The sheriff said No at once.

"Fifteen or twenty folks milling around the square with pistols in their pants? No, no. That won't do. I can't have that. That won't do. You let me run this."

For a moment longer Grimm looked at the sheriff. Then he turned, already walking fast again. "All right," he said. "If that's the way you want it. I don't interfere with you and you don't interfere with me, then." It didn't sound like a threat. It was too flat, too final, too without heat. He went on, rapidly. The sheriff watched him; then he called. Grimm turned.

"You leave yours at home, too," the sheriff said. "You hear me?" Grimm didn't answer. He went on. The sheriff watched him out of sight, frowning.

That evening after supper the sheriff went back downtown—something he had not done for years save when urgent and inescapable business called. He found a picket of Grimm's men at the jail, and another in the courthouse, and a third patrolling the square and the adjacent streets. The others, the relief, they told the sheriff, were in the cotton office where Grimm was employed, which they were using for an orderly room, a P.C. The sheriff met Grimm on the street, making a round of inspection. "Come here, boy," the sheriff said. Grimm halted. He did not approach; the sheriff went to him. He patted Grimm's hip with a fat hand. "I told you to leave that at home," he said. Grimm said nothing. He watched the sheriff levelly. The sheriff sighed. "Well, if you won't, I reckon I'll have to make you a special deputy. But you ain't to even show that gun unless I tell you to. You hear me?"

"Certainly not," Grimm said. "You certainly wouldn't want me to draw it if I didn't see any need to."

"I mean, not till I tell you to."

"Certainly," Grimm said, without heat, patiently, immediately. "That's what we both said. Don't you worry. I'll be there."

Later, as the town quieted for the night, as the picture show emptied and the drugstores closed one by one, Grimm's platoon began to drop off too. He did not protest, watching them coldly; they became a little sheepish, defensive. Again without knowing it he had played a trump card. Because of the fact that they felt sheepish, feeling that somehow they had fallen short of his own cold ardor, they would return tomorrow if just to show him. A few remained; it was Saturday night anyhow, and someone got more chairs from somewhere and they started a poker game. It ran all night, though from time to time Grimm (he was not in the game; neither would he permit his second in command, the only other there who held the equivalent of commissioned rank, to engage) sent a squad out to make a patrol of the square. By this time the night marshal was one of them, though he too did not take a hand in the game.

Sunday was quiet. The poker game ran quietly through the day, broken by the periodical patrols, while the quiet church bells rang and the congregations gathered in decorous clumps of summer colors. About the square it was already known that the special Grand Jury would meet tomorrow. Somehow the very sound of the two words with their evocation, secret and irrevocable and something of a hidden and unsleeping and omnipotent eye watching the doings of men, began to reassure Grimm's men in their own makebelieve. So quickly is man unwittingly and unpredictably moved that without knowing that they were thinking it, the town had suddenly accepted Grimm with respect and perhaps a little awe and a deal of actual faith and confidence, as though somehow his vision and patriotism and pride in the town, the occasion, had been quicker and truer than theirs. His men anyway assumed and accepted this; after the sleepless night, the tenseness, the holiday, the suttee of volition's surrender, they were almost at the pitch where they might die for him, if occasion rose. They now moved in a grave and slightly awe-inspiring reflected light which was almost as palpable as the khaki would have been which Grimm wished them to wear, wished that they wore, as though each time they returned to the orderly room they dressed themselves anew in suave and austerely splendid scraps of his dream.

This lasted through Sunday night. The poker game ran. The caution, the surreptitiousness, which had clothed it was now gone. There was something about it too assured and serenely confident to the braggadocio; tonight when they heard the marshal's feet on the stairs, one said, "Ware M.P.'s," and for an instant they glanced at one another with hard, bright, daredevil eyes; then one said, quite loud: "Throw the son of a bitch out," and another through pursed lips made the immemorial sound. And so the next morning, Monday, when the first country cars and wagons began to gather, the platoon was again intact. And they now wore uniforms. It was their faces. Most of them were of an age, a generation, an experience. But it was more than that. They now had a profound and bleak gravity as they stood where crowds milled, grave, austere, detached, looking with blank, bleak eyes at the slow throngs who, feeling, sensing without knowing, drifted before them, slowing, staring, so that they would be ringed with faces rapt and empty and immobile as the faces of cows, approaching and drifting on, to be replaced. And all morning the voices came and went, in quiet question and answer: "There he goes. That young fellow with the automatic pistol. He's the captain of them. Special officer sent by the governor. He's the head of the whole thing. Sheriff ain't got no say in it today."

Later, when it was too late, Grimm told the sheriff: "If you had just listened to me. Let me bring him out of that cell in a squad of men, instead of sending him across the square with one deputy and not even handcuffed to him, in all that crowd where that damned Buford didn't dare shoot, even if he could hit a barn door."

"How did I know he aimed to break, would think of trying it right then and there?" the sheriff said. "When Stevens had done told me he would plead guilty and take a life sentence."

But it was too late then. It was all over then. It happened in the middle of the square, halfway between the sidewalk and the courthouse, in the midst of a throng of people thick as on Fair Day, though the first that Grimm knew of it was when he heard the deputy's pistol twice, fired into the air. He knew at once what had happened, though he was at the time inside the courthouse. His reaction was definite and immediate. He was already running toward the shots when he shouted back over his shoulder at the man who had tagged him now for almost forty-eight hours as half aide and half orderly: "Turn in the fire alarm!"

"The fire alarm?" the aide said. "What—"

"Turn in the fire alarm!" Grimm shouted back. "It don't matter what folks think, just so they know that something . . ." He did not finish; he was gone.

He ran among running people, overtaking and passing them, since he had an objective and they did not; they were just running, the black, blunt, huge automatic opening a way for him like a plow. They looked at his tense, hard, young face with faces blanched and gaped, with round, toothed orifices; they made one long sound like a murmuring sigh: "There . . . went that way . . ." But already Grimm had seen the deputy, running, his pistol aloft in his hand. Grimm glanced once about and sprang forward again; in the throng which had evidently been pacing the deputy and the prisoner across the square was the inevitable hulking youth in the uniform of the Western Union, leading his bicycle by the horns like a docile cow. Grimm rammed the pistol back into the holster and flung the boy aside and sprang onto the bicycle, with never a break in motion.

The bicycle possessed neither horn nor bell. Yet they sensed him somehow and made way; in this too he seemed to be served by certitude, the blind and untroubled faith in the rightness and infallibility of his actions. When he overtook the running deputy he slowed the bicycle. The deputy turned upon him a face sweating, gaped with shouting and running. "He turned," the deputy screamed. "Into that alley by—"

"I know," Grimm said. "Was he handcuffed?"

"Yes!" the deputy said. The bicycle leaped on.

Then he can't run very fast, Grimm thought. *He'll have to hole up soon. Get out of the open, anyway.* He turned into the alley, fast. It ran back between two houses, with a board fence on one side. At that moment the fire siren sounded for the first time, beginning and mounting to a slow and sustained scream that seemed at last to pass beyond the realm of hearing, into that of sense, like soundless vibration. Grimm wheeled on, thinking swiftly, logically, with a kind of fierce and constrained joy. *The first thing he will want is to get out of sight,* he thought, looking about. On one hand the lane was open, on the other stood the board fence six feet high. At the end it was cut short off by a wooden gate, beyond which was a pasture and then a deep ditch which was a town landmark. The tops of tall trees which grew in it just showed above the rim; a regiment could hide and deploy in it. "Ah," he said, aloud. Without stopping or slowing he swept the bicycle around and pedalled back down the lane toward the street which he had just quitted. The wail of the siren was dying now, descending back into hearing again, and as he slewed the bicycle into the street he saw briefly the running people and a car bearing down upon him. For all his pedalling the car overtook him; its occupants leaned shouting toward his set, forwardlooking face. "Get in here!" they shouted. "In here!" He did not answer. He did not look at them. The car had overshot him, slowing; now he passed it at his swift, silent, steady pace; again the car speeded up and passed him, the men leaning out and looking ahead. He was going fast too, silent, with the delicate swiftness of an apparition, the implacable undeviation of Juggernaut or Fate. Behind him the siren began again its rising wail. When next the men in the car looked back for him, he had vanished completely.

He had turned full speed into another lane. His face was rocklike, calm, still bright with that expression of fulfillment, of grave and reckless joy. This lane was more rutted than the other, and deeper. It came out at last upon a barren knoll where, springing to earth while the bicycle shot on, falling, he could see the full span of the ravine along the edge of town, his view of it broken by two or three Negro cabins which lined the edge of it. He was quite motionless, still, alone, fateful, like a landmark almost. Again from the town behind him the scream of the siren began to fall.

Then he saw Christmas. He saw the man, small with

distance, appear up out of the ditch, his hands close together. As Grimm watched he saw the fugitive's hands
glint once like the flash of a heliograph as the sun struck
the handcuffs, and it seemed to him that even from here
he could hear the panting and desperate breath of the
man who even now was not free. Then the tiny figure
ran again and vanished beyond the nearest Negro cabin.

Grimm ran too now. He ran swiftly, yet there was no
haste about him, no effort. There was nothing vengeful
about him either, no fury, no outrage. Christmas saw that,
himself. Because for an instant they looked at one another
almost face to face. That was when Grimm, running, was
in the act of passing beyond the corner of the cabin. At
that instant Christmas leaped from the rear window of it,
with an effect as of magic, his manacled hands high and
now glinting as if they were on fire. For an instant they
glared at one another, the one stopped in the act of
crouching from the leap, the other in midstride of running, before Grimm's momentum carried him past the
corner. In that instant he saw that Christmas now carried
a heavy nickelplated pistol. Grimm whirled and turned
and sprang back past the corner, drawing the automatic.

He was thinking swiftly, calmly, with that quiet joy:
*He can do two things. He can try for the ditch again, or
he can dodge around the house until one of us gets a
shot. And the ditch is on his side of the house.* He reacted
immediately. He ran at full speed around the corner
which he had just turned. He did it as though under the
protection of a magic or a providence, or as if he knew
that Christmas would not be waiting there with the pistol. He ran on past the next corner without pausing.

He was beside the ditch now. He stopped, motionless
in midstride. Above the blunt, cold rake of the automatic
his face had that serene, unearthly luminousness of angels
in church windows. He was moving again almost before
he had stopped, with that lean, swift, blind obedience
to whatever Player moved him on the Board. He ran

to the ditch. But in the beginning of his plunge downward into the brush that choked the steep descent he turned, clawing. He saw now that the cabin sat some two feet above the earth. He had not noticed it before, in his haste. He knew now that he had lost a point. That Christmas had been watching his legs all the time beneath the house. He said, "Good man."

His plunge carried him some distance before he could stop himself and climb back out. He seemed indefatigable, not flesh and blood, as if the Player who moved him for pawn likewise found him breath. Without a pause, in the same surge that carried him up out of the ditch again, he was running again. He ran around the cabin in time to see Christmas fling himself over a fence three hundred yards away. He did not fire, because Christmas was now running through a small garden and straight toward a house. Running, he saw Christmas leap up the back steps and enter the house. "Hah," Grimm said. "The preacher's house. Hightower's house."

He did not slow, though he swerved and ran around the house and to the street. The car which had passed him and lost him and then returned was just where it should have been, just where the Player had desired it to be. It stopped without signal from him and three men got out. Without a word Grimm turned and ran across the yard and into the house where the old disgraced minister lived alone, and the three men followed, rushing into the hall, pausing, bringing with them into its stale and cloistral dimness something of the savage summer sunlight which they had just left.

It was upon them, of them: its shameless savageness. Out of it their faces seemed to glare with bodiless suspension as though from haloes as they stooped and raised Hightower, his face bleeding, from the floor where Christmas, running up the hall, his raised and armed and manacled hands full of glare and glitter like lightning bolts, so that he resembled a vengeful and furious god pronouncing a doom, had struck him down. They held the old man on his feet.

"Which room?" Grimm said, shaking him. "Which room, old man?"

"Gentlemen!" Hightower said. Then he said: "Men! Men!"

"Which room, old man?" Grimm shouted.

They held Hightower on his feet; in the gloomy hall, after the sunlight, he too with his bald head and his big pale face streaked with blood, was terrible. "Men!" he cried. "Listen to me. He was here that night. He was with me the night of the murder. I swear to God—"

"Jesus Christ!" Grimm cried, his young voice clear and outraged like that of a young priest. "Has every preacher and old maid in Jefferson taken their pants down to the yellowbellied son of a bitch?" He flung the old man aside and ran on.

It was as though he had been merely waiting for the Player to move him again, because with that unfailing certitude he ran straight to the kitchen and into the doorway, already firing, almost before he could have seen the table overturned and standing on its edge across the corner of the room, and the bright and glittering hands of the man who crouched behind it, resting upon the upper edge. Grimm emptied the automatic's magazine into the table; later someone covered all five shots with a folded handkerchief.

But the Player was not done yet. When the others reached the kitchen they saw the table flung aside now and Grimm stooping over the body. When they approached to see what he was about, they saw that the man was not dead yet, and when they saw what Grimm was doing one of the men gave a choked cry and stumbled back into the wall and began to vomit. Then Grimm too sprang back, flinging behind him the bloody butcher knife. "Now you'll let white women alone, even in hell," he said. But the man on the floor had not moved. He just lay there, with his eyes open and empty of everything save consciousness, and with something, a shadow, about his mouth. For a long moment he looked up at them with peaceful and unfathomable and unbearable eyes. Then his face, body, all, seemed to collapse, to fall in upon itself, and from out the slashed garments about his hips and loins the pent black blood seemed to rush like a released breath. It seemed to rush out of his pale body like the rush of sparks from a rising rocket; upon that black blast the man seemed to rise soaring into their memories forever and ever. They are not to lose it, in whatever peaceful valleys, beside whatever placid and reassuring streams of old age, in the mirroring faces of whatever children they will contemplate old disasters and newer hopes. It will be there, musing, quiet, steadfast, not fading and not particularly threatful, but of itself alone serene, of itself alone triumphant. Again from the town, deadened a little by the walls, the scream of the siren mounted toward its unbelievable crescendo, passing out of the realm of hearing.

1940

Delta Autumn

Soon now they would enter the Delta. The sensation was familiar to old Isaac McCaslin. It had been renewed like this each last week in November for more than fifty years —the last hill, at the foot of which the rich unbroken alluvial flatness began as the sea began at the base of its cliffs, dissolving away beneath the unhurried November rain as the sea itself would dissolve away.

At first they had come in wagons: the guns, the bedding, the dogs, the food, the whiskey, the keen heart-lifting anticipation of hunting; the young men who could drive all night and all the following day in the cold rain and pitch a camp in the rain and sleep in the wet blankets and rise at daylight the next morning and hunt. There had been bear then. A man shot a doe or a fawn as quickly as he did a buck, and in the afternoons they shot wild turkey with pistols to test their stalking skill and marksmanship, feeding all but the breast to the dogs. But that time was gone now. Now they went in cars, driving faster and faster each year because the roads were better and they had farther and farther to drive, the territory in which game still existed drawing yearly inward as his life was drawing inward, until now he was the last of those who had once made the journey in wagons without feeling it and now those who accompanied him were the sons and even grandsons of the men who had ridden for twenty-four hours in the rain or sleet behind the steaming mules. They called him "Uncle Ike" now, and he no longer told anyone how near eighty he actually was because he knew as well as they did that he no longer had any business making such expeditions, even by car.

In fact, each time now, on that first night in camp, lying aching and sleepless in the harsh blankets, his blood only faintly warmed by the single thin whiskey-and-water which he allowed himself, he would tell himself that this would be his last. But he would stand that trip—he still shot almost as well as he ever had, still killed almost as much of the game he saw as he ever killed; he no longer even knew how many deer had fallen before his gun— and the fierce long heat of the next summer would renew him. Then November would come again, and again in the car with two of the sons of his old companions, whom he had taught not only how to distinguish between the prints left by a buck or a doe but between the sound they made in moving, he would look ahead past the jerking arc of the windshield wiper and see the land flatten suddenly and swoop, dissolving away beneath the rain as the sea itself would dissolve, and he would say, "Well, boys, there it is again."

This time though, he didn't have time to speak. The driver of the car stopped it, slamming it to a skidding halt on the greasy pavement without warning, actually flinging the two passengers forward until they caught themselves with their braced hands against the dash. "What the hell, Roth!" the man in the middle said. "Can't you whistle first when you do that? Hurt you, Uncle Ike?"

"No," the old man said. "What's the matter?" The driver didn't answer. Still leaning forward, the old man looked sharply past the face of the man between them, at the face of his kinsman. It was the youngest face of them all, aquiline, saturnine, a little ruthless, the face of his ancestor too, tempered a little, altered a little, staring

sombrely through the streaming windshield across which
the twin wipers flicked and flicked.

"I didn't intend to come back in here this time," he
said suddenly and harshly.

"You said that back in Jefferson last week," the old
man said. "Then you changed your mind. Have you
changed it again? This ain't a very good time to——"

"Oh, Roth's coming," the man in the middle said. His
name was Legate. He seemed to be speaking to no one,
as he was looking at neither of them. "If it was just a buck
he was coming all this distance for, now. But he's got a
doe in here. Of course a old man like Uncle Ike can't be
interested in no doe, not one that walks on two legs—
when she's standing up, that is. Pretty light-colored, too.
The one he was after them nights last fall when he said
he was coon-hunting, Uncle Ike. The one I figured maybe
he was still running when he was gone all that month last
January. But of course a old man like Uncle Ike ain't
got no interest in nothing like that." He chortled, still
looking at no one, not completely jeering.

"What?" the old man said. "What's that?" But he had
not even so much as glanced at Legate. He was still
watching his kinsman's face. The eyes behind the spectacles were the blurred eyes of an old man, but they were
quite sharp too; eyes which could still see a gunbarrel
and what ran beyond it as well as any of them could. He
was remembering himself now: how last year, during the
final stage by motor boat in to where they camped, a box
of food had been lost overboard and how on the next
day his kinsman had gone back to the nearest town for
supplies and had been gone overnight. And when he
did return, something had happened to him. He would
go into the woods with his rifle each dawn when the
others went, but the old man, watching him, knew that
he was not hunting. "All right," he said. "Take me and
Will on to shelter where we can wait for the truck, and
you can go on back."

"I'm going in," the other said harshly. "Don't worry. Because this will be the last of it."

"The last of deer hunting, or of doe hunting?" Legate said. This time the old man paid no attention to him even by speech. He still watched the young man's savage and brooding face.

"Why?" he said.

"After Hitler gets through with it? Or Smith or Jones or Roosevelt or Willkie or whatever he will call himself in this country?"

"We'll stop him in this country," Legate said. "Even if he calls himself George Washington."

"How?" Edmonds said. "By singing 'God Bless America' in bars at midnight and wearing dime-store flags in our lapels?"

"So that's what's worrying you," the old man said. "I ain't noticed this country being short of defenders yet, when it needed them. You did some of it yourself twenty-odd years ago, before you were a grown man even. This country is a little mite stronger than any one man or group of men, outside of it or even inside of it either. I reckon, when the time comes and some of you have done got tired of hollering we are whipped if we don't go to war and some more are hollering we are whipped if we do, it will cope with one Austrian paper-hanger, no matter what he will be calling himself. My pappy and some other better men than any of them you named tried once to tear it in two with a war, and they failed."

"And what have you got left?" the other said. "Half the people without jobs and half the factories closed by strikes. Half the people on public dole that won't work and half that couldn't work even if they would. Too much cotton and corn and hogs, and not enough for people to eat and wear. The country full of people to tell a man how he can't raise his own cotton whether he will or won't, and Sally Rand with a sergeant's stripes and not

even the fan couldn't fill the army rolls. Too much not-
butter and not even the guns———"

"We got a deer camp—if we ever get to it," Legate
said. "Not to mention does."

"It's a good time to mention does," the old man said.
"Does and fawns both. The only fighting anywhere that
ever had anything of God's blessing on it has been when
men fought to protect does and fawns. If it's going to
come to fighting, that's a good thing to mention and remember too."

"Haven't you discovered in—how many years more
than seventy is it?—that women and children are one
thing there's never any scarcity of?" Edmonds said.

"Maybe that's why all I am worrying about right now
is that ten miles of river we still have got to run before
we can make camp," the old man said. "So let's get on."

They went on. Soon they were going fast again, as
Edmonds always drove, consulting neither of them about
the speed just as he had given neither of them any
warning when he slammed the car to a stop. The old man
relaxed again. He watched, as he did each recurrent November while more than sixty of them passed, the land
which he had seen change. At first there had been only
the old towns along the River and the old towns along
the hills, from each of which the planters with their
gangs of slaves and then of hired laborers had wrested
from the impenetrable jungle of water-standing cane and
cypress, gum and holly and oak and ash, cotton patches
which, as the years passed, became fields and then plantations. The paths made by deer and bear became roads
and then highways, with towns in turn springing up along
them and along the rivers Tallahatchie and Sunflower
which joined and became the Yazoo, the River of the
Dead of the Choctaws—the thick, slow, black, unsunned
streams almost without current, which once each year
ceased to flow at all and then reversed, spreading, drowning the rich land and subsiding again, leaving it still richer.

Most of that was gone now. Now a man drove two hundred miles from Jefferson before he found wilderness to hunt in. Now the land lay open from the cradling hills on the east to the rampart of levee on the west, standing horseman-tall with cotton for the world's looms—the rich black land, imponderable and vast, fecund up to the very doorsteps of the Negroes who worked it and of the white men who owned it; which exhausted the hunting life of a dog in one year, the working life of a mule in five and of a man in twenty—the land in which neon flashed past them from the little countless towns, and countless shining this-year's automobiles sped past them on the broad plumb-ruled highways, yet in which the only permanent mark of man's occupation seemed to be the tremendous gins, constructed in sections of sheet iron and in a week's time though they were, since no man, millionaire though he be, would build more than a roof and walls to shelter the camping equipment he lived from, when he knew that once each ten years or so his house would be flooded to the second storey and all within it ruined;— the land across which there came now no scream of panther but instead the long hooting of locomotives: trains of incredible length and drawn by a single engine, since there was no gradient anywhere and no elevation save those raised by forgotten aboriginal hands as refuges from the yearly water and used by their Indian successors to sepulchre their fathers' bones, and all that remained of that old time were the Indian names on the little towns and usually pertaining to water—Aluschaskuna, Tillatoba, Homochitto, Yazoo.

By early afternoon, they were on water. At the last little Indian-named town at the end of pavement they waited until the other car and the two trucks—the one carrying the bedding and tents and food, the other the horses—overtook them. They left the concrete and, after another mile or so, the gravel too. In caravan they ground on through the ceaselessly dissolving afternoon, with skid-chains on the wheels now, lurching and splashing and sliding among the ruts, until presently it seemed to him that the retrograde of his remembering had gained an inverse velocity from their own slow progress, that the land had retreated not in minutes from the last spread of gravel but in years, decades, back toward what it had been when he first knew it: the road they now followed once more the ancient pathway of bear and deer, the diminishing fields they now passed once more scooped punily and terrifically by axe and saw and mule-drawn plow from the wilderness' flank, out of the brooding and immemorial tangle, in place of ruthless mile-wide parallelograms wrought by ditching the dyking machinery.

They reached the river landing and unloaded, the horses to go overland down stream to a point opposite the camp and swim the river, themselves and the bedding and food and dogs and guns in the motor launch. It was himself, though no horseman, no farmer, not even a countryman save by his distant birth and boyhood, who coaxed and soothed the two horses, drawing them by his own single frail hand until, backing, filling, trembling a little, they surged, halted, then sprang scrambling down from the truck, possessing no affinity for them as creatures, beasts, but being merely insulated by his years and time from the corruption of steel and oiled moving parts which tainted the others.

Then, his old hammer double gun which was only twelve years younger than he standing between his knees, he watched even the last puny marks of man— cabin, clearing, the small and irregular fields which a year ago were jungle and in which the skeleton stalks of this year's cotton stood almost as tall and rank as the old cane had stood, as if man had had to marry his planting to the wilderness in order to conquer it—fall away and vanish. The twin banks marched with wilderness as he remembered it—the tangle of brier and cane impenetrable even to sight twenty feet away, the tall tremendous

soaring of oak and gum and ash and hickory which had
rung to no axe save the hunter's, had echoed to no machinery save the beat of old-time steam boats traversing
it or to the snarling of launches like their own people
going into it to dwell for a week or two weeks because it
was still wilderness. There was some of it left, although
now it was two hundred miles from Jefferson when once
it had been thirty. He had watched it, not being conquered, destroyed, so much as retreating since its purpose was served now and its time an outmoded time, retreating southward through this inverted-apex, this ▽-
shaped section of earth between hills and River until what
was left of it seemed now to be gathered and for the time
arrested in one tremendous density of brooding and inscrutable impenetrability at the ultimate funnelling tip.

They reached the site of their last-year's camp with
still two hours left of light. "You go on over under that
driest tree and set down," Legate told him. "—if you can
find it. Me and these other young boys will do this." He
did neither. He was not tired yet. That would come later.
Maybe it won't come at all this time, he thought, as he
had thought at this point each November for the last five
or six of them. *Maybe I will go out on stand in the morning too*; knowing that he would not, not even if he took
the advice and sat down under the driest shelter and did
nothing until camp was made and supper cooked. Because it would not be the fatigue. It would be because
he would not sleep tonight but would lie instead wakeful and peaceful on the cot amid the tent-filling snoring
and the rain's whisper as he always did on the first night
in camp; peaceful, without regret or fretting, telling himself that was all right too, who didn't have so many of
them left as to waste one sleeping.

In his slicker he directed the unloading of the boat—
the tents, the stove, the bedding, the food for themselves
and the dogs until there should be meat in camp. He sent
two of the Negroes to cut firewood; he had the cook-

tent raised and the stove up and a fire going and supper cooking while the big tent was still being staked down. Then in the beginning of dusk he crossed in the boat to where the horses waited, backing and snorting at the water. He took the lead-ropes and with no more weight than that and his voice, he drew them down into the water and held them beside the boat with only their heads above the surface, as though they actually were suspended from his frail and strengthless old man's hands, while the boat recrossed and each horse in turn lay prone in the shallows, panting and trembling, its eyes rolling in the dusk, until the same weightless hand and unraised voice gathered it surging upward, splashing and thrashing up the bank.

Then the meal was ready. The last of light was gone now save the thin stain of it snared somewhere between the river's surface and the rain. He had the single glass of thin whiskey-and-water, then, standing in the churned mud beneath the stretched tarpaulin, he said grace over the fried slabs of pork, the hot soft shapeless bread, the canned beans and molasses and coffee in iron plates and cups,—the town food, brought along with them—then covered himself again, the others following. "Eat," he said. "Eat it all up. I don't want a piece of town meat in camp after breakfast tomorrow. Then you boys will hunt. You'll have to. When I first started hunting in this bottom sixty years ago with old General Compson and Major de Spain and Roth's grandfather and Will Legate's too, Major de Spain wouldn't allow but two pieces of foreign grub in his camp. That was one side of pork and one ham of beef. And not to eat for the first supper and breakfast neither. It was to save until along toward the end of camp when everybody was so sick of bear meat and coon and venison that we couldn't even look at it."

"I thought Uncle Ike was going to say the pork and beef was for the dogs," Legate said, chewing. "But that's right; I remember. You just shot the dogs a mess of wild turkey every evening when they got tired of deer guts."

"Times are different now," another said. "There was game here then."

"Yes," the old man said quietly. "There was game here then."

"Besides, they shot does then too," Legate said. "As it is now, we ain't got but one doe-hunter in——"

"And better men hunted it," Edmonds said. He stood at the end of the rough plank table, eating rapidly and steadily as the others ate. But again the old man looked sharply across at the sullen, handsome, brooding face which appeared now darker and more sullen still in the light of the smoky lantern. "Go on. Say it."

"I didn't say that," the old man said. "There are good men everywhere, at all times. Most men are. Some are just unlucky, because most men are a little better than their circumstances give them a chance to be. And I've known some that even the circumstances couldn't stop."

"Well, I wouldn't say——" Legate said.

"So you've lived almost eighty years," Edmonds said, "and that's what you finally learned about the other animals you lived among. I suppose the question to ask you is, where have you been all the time you were dead?"

There was a silence; for the instant even Legate's jaw stopped chewing while he gaped at Edmonds. "Well, by God, Roth——" the third speaker said. But it was the old man who spoke, his voice still peaceful and untroubled and merely grave:

"Maybe so," he said. "But if being what you call alive would have learned me any different, I reckon I'm satisfied, wherever it was I've been."

"Well, I wouldn't say that Roth——" Legate said.

The third speaker was still leaning forward a little over the table, looking at Edmonds. "Meaning that it's only because folks happen to be watching him that a man behaves at all," he said. "Is that it?"

"Yes," Edmonds said. "A man in a blue coat, with a badge on it watching him. Maybe just the badge."

"I deny that," the old man said. "I don't——"

The other two paid no attention to him. Even Legate was listening to them for the moment, his mouth still full of food and still open a little, his knife with another lump of something balanced on the tip of the blade arrested halfway to his mouth. "I'm glad I don't have your opinion of folks," the third speaker said. "I take it you include yourself."

"I see," Edmonds said. "You prefer Uncle Ike's opinion of circumstances. All right. Who makes the circumstances?"

"Luck," the third said. "Chance. Happen-so. I see what you are getting at. But that's just what Uncle Ike said: that now and then, maybe most of the time, man is a little better than the net result of his and his neighbors' doings, when he gets the chance to be."

This time Legate swallowed first. He was not to be stopped this time. "Well, I wouldn't say that Roth Edmonds can hunt one doe every day and night for two weeks and was a poor hunter or a unlucky one neither. A man that still have the same doe left to hunt on again next year——"

"Have some meat," the man next to him said.

"——ain't so unlucky—What?" Legate said.

"Have some meat." The other offered the dish.

"I got some," Legate said.

"Have some more," the third speaker said. "You and Roth Edmonds both. Have a heap of it. Clapping your jaws together that way with nothing to break the shock." Someone chortled. Then they all laughed, with relief, the tension broken. But the old man was speaking, even into the laughter, in that peaceful and still untroubled voice:

"I still believe. I see proof everywhere. I grant that

man made a heap of his circumstances, him and his living neighbors between them. He even inherited some of them already made, already almost ruined even. A while ago Henry Wyatt there said how there used to be more game here. There was. So much that we even killed does. I seem to remember Will Legate mentioning that too—" Someone laughed, a single guffaw, still-born. It ceased and they all listened, gravely, looking down at their plates. Edmonds was drinking his coffee, sullen, brooding, inattentive.

"Some folks still kill does," Wyatt said. "There won't be just one buck hanging in this bottom tomorrow night without any head to fit it."

"I didn't say all men," the old man said. "I said most men. And not just because there is a man with a badge to watch us. We probably won't even see him unless maybe he will stop here about noon tomorrow and eat dinner with us and check our licenses——"

"We don't kill does because if we did kill does in a few years there wouldn't even be any bucks left to kill, Uncle Ike," Wyatt said.

"According to Roth yonder, that's one thing we won't never have to worry about," the old man said. "He said on the way here this morning that does and fawns—I believe he said women and children—are two things this world ain't ever lacked. But that ain't all of it," he said. "That's just the mind's reason a man has to give himself because the heart don't always have time to bother with thinking up words that fit together. God created man and He created the world for him to live in and I reckon He created the kind of world He would have wanted to live in if He had been a man—the ground to walk on, the big woods, the trees and the water, and the game to live in it. And maybe He didn't put the desire to hunt and kill game in man but I reckon He knew it was going to be there, that man was going to teach it to himself, since he wasn't quite God himself yet——"

"When will he be?" Wyatt said.

"I think that every man and woman, at the instant when it don't even matter whether they marry or not, I think that whether they marry then or afterward or don't never, at that instant the two of them together were God."

"Then there are some Gods in this world I wouldn't want to touch, and with a damn long stick," Edmonds said. He set his coffee cup down and looked at Wyatt. "And that includes myself, if that's what you want to know. I'm going to bed." He was gone. There was a general movement among the others. But it ceased and they stood again about the table, not looking at the old man, apparently held there yet by his quiet and peaceful voice as the heads of the swimming horses had been held above the water by his weightless hand. The three Negroes— the cook and his helper and old Isham—were sitting quietly in the entrance of the kitchen tent, listening too, the three faces dark and motionless and musing.

"He put them both here: man, and the game he would follow and kill, foreknowing it. I believe He said, 'So be it.' I reckon He even foreknew the end. But He said, 'I will give him his chance. I will give him warning and foreknowledge too, along with the desire to follow and the power to slay. The woods and fields he ravages and the game he devastates will be the consequence and signature of his crime and guilt, and his punishment.'—Bed time," he said. His voice and inflection did not change at all. "Breakfast at four o'clock, Isham. We want meat on the ground by sunup time."

There was a good fire in the sheet-iron heater; the tent was warm and was beginning to dry out, except for the mud underfoot. Edmonds was already rolled into his blankets, motionless, his face to the wall. Isham had made up his bed too—the strong, battered iron cot, the stained mattress which was not quite soft enough, the worn, often-washed blankets which as the years passed were less and less warm enough. But the tent was warm; presently,

when the kitchen was cleaned up and readied for breakfast, the young Negro would come in to lie down before
the heater, where he could be roused to put fresh wood
into it from time to time. And then, he knew now he
would not sleep tonight anyway; he no longer needed to
tell himself that perhaps he would. But it was all right
now. The day was ended now and night faced him, but
alarmless, empty of fret. *Maybe I came for this,* he
thought: *Not to hunt, but for this. I would come anyway,
even if only to go back home tomorrow.* Wearing only
his bagging woolen underwear, his spectacles folded
away in the worn case beneath the pillow where he could
reach them readily and his lean body fitted easily into
the worn groove of mattress and blankets, he lay on his
back, his hands crossed on his breast and his eyes closed
while the others undressed and went to bed and the last
of the sporadic talking died into snoring. Then he opened
his eyes and lay peaceful and quiet as a child, looking up
at the motionless belly of rain-murmured canvas upon
which the glow of the heater was dying slowly away and
would fade still further until the young Negro, lying on
two planks before it, would sit up and stoke it and lie
back down again.

They had a house once. That was sixty years ago, when
the Big Bottom was only thirty miles from Jefferson and
old Major de Spain, who had been his father's cavalry
commander in '61 and '2 and '3 and '4, and his cousin
(his older brother; his father too) had taken him into the
woods for the first time. Old Sam Fathers was alive then,
born in slavery, son of a Negro slave and a Chickasaw
chief, who had taught him how to shoot, not only when
to shoot but when not to; such a November dawn as
tomorrow would be and the old man led him straight to
the great cypress and he had known the buck would pass
exactly there because there was something running in
Sam Fathers' veins which ran in the veins of the buck too,
and they stood there against the tremendous trunk, the

old man of seventy and the boy of twelve, and there was nothing save the dawn until suddenly the buck was there, smoke-colored out of nothing, magnificent with speed: and Sam Fathers said, 'Now. Shoot quick and shoot slow:' and the gun levelled rapidly without haste and crashed and he walked to the buck lying still intact and still in the shape of that magnificent speed and bled it with Sam's knife and Sam dipped his hands into the hot blood and marked his face forever while he stood trying not to tremble, humbly and with pride too though the boy of twelve had been unable to phrase it then: *I slew you; my bearing must not shame your quitting life. My conduct forever onward must become your death*; marking him for that and for more than that: that day and himself and McCaslin juxtaposed, not against the wilderness but against the tamed land, the old wrong and shame itself, in repudiation and denial at least of the land and the wrong and shame, even if he couldn't cure the wrong and eradicate the shame, who at fourteen when he learned of it had believed he could do both when he became competent, and when at twenty-one he became competent he knew that he could do neither but at least he could repudiate the wrong and shame, at least in principle, and at least the land itself in fact, for his son at least: and did, thought he had: then (married then) in a rented cubicle in a back-street stock-traders' boarding-house, the first and last time he ever saw her naked body, himself and his wife juxtaposed in their turn against that same land, that same wrong and shame from whose regret and grief he would at least save and free his son and, saving and freeing his son, lost him.

They had the house then. That roof, the two weeks of each November which they spent under it, had become his home. Although since that time they had lived during the two fall weeks in tents and not always in the same place two years in succession and now his companions were the sons and even the grandsons of them with

whom he had lived in the house, and for almost fifty years
now the house itself had not even existed, the conviction,
the sense and feeling of home, had been merely transferred into the canvas. He owned a house in Jefferson, a
good house though small, where he had had a wife and
lived with her and lost her, ay, lost her even though he
had lost her in the rented cubicle before he and his old
clever dipsomaniac partner had finished the house for
them to move into it: but lost her, because she loved him.
But women hope for so much. They never live too long to
still believe that anything within the scope of their passionate wanting is likewise within the range of their passionate hope: and it was still kept for him by his dead
wife's widowed niece and her children, and he was com-
fortable in it, his wants and needs and even the small trying harmless crochets of an old man looked after by
blood at least related to the blood which he had elected
out of all the earth to cherish. But he spent the time
within those walls waiting for November, because even
this tent with its muddy floor and the bed which was not
wide enough nor soft enough nor even warm enough,
was his home and these men, some of whom he only saw
during these two November weeks and not one of whom
even bore any name he used to know—De Spain and
Compson and Ewell and Hogganbeck—were more his
kin than any. Because this was his land——

The shadow of the youngest Negro loomed. It soared,
blotting the heater's dying glow from the ceiling, the
wood billets thumping into the iron maw until the glow,
the flame, leaped high and bright across the canvas. But
the Negro's shadow still remained, by its length and
breadth, standing, since it covered most of the ceiling,
until after a moment he raised himself on one elbow to
look. It was not the Negro, it was his kinsman; when he
spoke the other turned sharp against the red firelight the
sullen and ruthless profile.

"Nothing," Edmonds said. "Go on back to sleep."

"Since Will Legate mentioned it," McCaslin said, "I remember you had some trouble sleeping in here last fall too. Only you called it coon-hunting then. Or was it Will Legate called it that?" The other didn't answer. Then he turned and went back to his bed. McCaslin, still propped on his elbow, watched until the other's shadow sank down the wall and vanished, became one with the mass of sleeping shadows. "That's right," he said. "Try to get some sleep. We must have meat in camp tomorrow. You can do all the setting up you want to after that." He lay down again, his hands crossed again on his breast, watching the glow of the heater on the canvas ceiling. It was steady again now, the fresh wood accepted, being assimilated; soon it would begin to fade again, taking with it the last echo of that sudden upflare of a young man's passion and unrest. Let him lie awake for a little while, he thought; He will lie still some day for a long time without even dissatisfaction to disturb him. And lying awake here, in these surroundings, would soothe him if anything could, if anything could soothe a man just forty years old. Yes, he thought; Forty years old or thirty, or even the trembling and sleepless ardor of a boy; already the tent, the rain-murmured canvas globe, was once more filled with it. He lay on his back, his eyes closed, his breathing quiet and peaceful as a child's, listening to it—that silence which was never silence but was myriad. He could almost see it, tremendous, primeval, looming, musing downward upon this puny, evanescent clutter of human sojourn which after a single brief week would vanish and in another week would be completely healed, traceless in the unmarked solitude. Because it was his land, although he had never owned a foot of it. He had never wanted to, not even after he saw plain its ultimate doom, watching it retreat year by year before the onslaught of axe and saw and log-lines and then dynamite and tractor plows, because it belonged to no man. It belonged to all; they had only to use it well, humbly and with pride. Then suddenly he knew why he had never wanted to own any of it, arrest at least that much of what people called progress, measure his longevity at least against that much of its ultimate fate. It was because there was just exactly enough of it. He seemed to see the two of them—himself and the wilderness—as coevals, his own span as a hunter, a woodsman, not contemporary with his first breath but transmitted to him, assumed by him gladly, humbly, with joy and pride, from that old Major de Spain and that old Sam Fathers who had taught him to hunt, the two spans running out together, not toward oblivion, nothingness, but into a dimension free of both time and space, where once more the untreed land warped and wrung to mathematical squares of rank cotton for the frantic old-world people to turn into shells to shoot at one another, would find ample room for both—the names, the faces of the old men he had known and loved and for a little while outlived, moving again among the shades of tall unaxed trees and sightless brakes where the wild strong immortal game ran forever before the tireless belling immortal hounds, falling and rising phoenixlike to the soundless guns.

He had been asleep. The lantern was lighted now. Outside in the darkness the oldest Negro, Isham, was beating a spoon against the bottom of a tin pan and crying, "Raise up and get yo foa clock coffy. Raise up and get yo foa clock coffy," and the tent was full of low talk and of men dressing, and Legate's voice, repeating: "Get out of here now and let Uncle Ike sleep. If you wake him up, he'll go out with us. And he ain't got any business in the woods this morning."

So he didn't move. He lay with his eyes closed, his breathing gentle and peaceful, and heard them one by one leave the tent. He listened to the breakfast sounds from the table beneath the tarpaulin and heard them depart—the horses, the dogs, the last voice until it died away and there was only the sounds of the Negroes clearing breakfast away. After a while he might possibly even hear the first faint clear cry of the first hound ring through the wet woods from where the buck had bedded, then he would go back to sleep again— The tent-flap swung in and fell. Something jarred sharply against the end of the cot and a hand grasped his knee through the blanket before he could open his eyes. It was Edmonds, carrying a shotgun in place of his rifle. He spoke in a harsh, rapid voice:

"Sorry to wake you. There will be a——"

"I was awake," McCaslin said. "Are you going to shoot that shotgun today?"

"You just told me last night you want meat," Edmonds said. "There will be a——"

"Since when did you start having trouble getting meat with your rifle?"

"All right," the other said, with that harsh, restrained, furious impatience. Then McCaslin saw in his hand a thick oblong: an envelope. "There will be a message here some time this morning, looking for me. Maybe it won't come. If it does, give the messenger this and tell h— say I said No."

"A what?" McCaslin said. "Tell who?" He half rose onto his elbow as Edmonds jerked the envelope onto the blanket, already turning toward the entrance, the envelope striking solid and heavy and without noise and already sliding from the bed until McCaslin caught it, divining by feel through the paper as instantaneously and conclusively as if he had opened the envelope and looked, the thick sheaf of banknotes. "Wait," he said. "Wait:"— more than the blood kinsman, more even than the senior in years, so that the other paused, the canvas lifted, looking back, and McCaslin saw that outside it was already day. "Tell her No," he said. "Tell her." They stared at one another—the old face, wan, sleep-raddled above the tumbled bed, the dark and sullen younger one at once furious and cold. "Will Legate was right. This is what you called coon-hunting. And now this." He didn't raise the envelope. He made no motion, no gesture to indicate it. "What did you promise her that you haven't the courage to face her and retract?"

"Nothing!" the other said. "Nothing! This is all of it. Tell her I said No." He was gone. The tent flap lifted on an in-waft of faint light and the constant murmur of rain, and fell again, leaving the old man still half-raised onto one elbow, the envelope clutched in the other shaking hand. Afterward it seemed to him that he had begun to hear the approaching boat almost immediately, before the other could have got out of sight even. It seemed to him that there had been no interval whatever: the tent flap falling on the same out-waft of faint and rain-filled light like the suspiration and expiration of the same breath and then in the next second lifted again—the mounting snarl of the outboard engine, increasing, nearer and nearer and louder and louder then cut short off, ceasing with the absolute instantaneity of a blown-out candle, into the lap and plop of water under the bows as the skiff slid in to the bank, the youngest Negro, the youth, raising the tent flap beyond which for that instant he saw the boat—a small skiff with a Negro man sitting in the stern beside the upslanted motor—then the woman entering, in a man's hat and a man's slicker and rubber boots, carrying the blanket-swaddled bundle on one arm and holding the edge of the unbuttoned raincoat over it with the other hand: and bringing something else, something intangible, an effluvium which he knew he would recognize in a moment because Isham had already told him, warned him, by sending the young Negro to the tent to announce the visitor instead of coming himself, the flap falling at last on the young Negro and they were alone—the face indistinct and as yet only young and with dark eyes, queerly colorless but not ill and not that of a country woman despite the garments she wore, looking down at him where he sat upright on the cot now, clutching the

envelope, the soiled undergarment bagging about him
and the twisted blankets huddled about his hips.

"Is that his?" he cried. "Don't lie to me!"

"Yes," she said. "He's gone."

"Yes. He's gone. You won't jump him here. Not this
time. I don't reckon even you expected that. He left you
this. Here." He fumbled at the envelope. It was not to
pick it up, because it was still in his hand; he had never
put it down. It was as if he had to fumble somehow to
co-ordinate physically his heretofore obedient hand with
what his brain was commanding of it, as if he had never
performed such an action before, extending the envelope
at last, saying again, "Here. Take it. Take it:" until he
became aware of her eyes, or not the eyes so much as the
look, the regard fixed now on his face with that immersed
contemplation, that bottomless and intent candor, of a
child. If she had ever seen either the envelope or his
movement to extend it, she did not show it.

"You're Uncle Isaac," she said.

"Yes," he said. "But never mind that. Here. Take it.
He said to tell you No." She looked at the envelope, then
she took it. It was sealed and bore no superscription. Nevertheless, even after she glanced at the front of it, he
watched her hold it in the one free hand and tear the
corner off with her teeth and manage to rip it open and
tilt the neat sheaf of bound notes onto the blanket without even glancing at them and look into the empty envelope and take the edge between her teeth and tear it
completely open before she crumpled and dropped it.

"That's just money," she said.

"What did you expect? What else did you expect?
You have known him long enough or at least often
enough to have got that child, and you don't know him
any better than that?"

"Not very often. Not very long. Just that week here
last fall, and in January he sent for me and we went west,
to New Mexico. We were there six weeks, where I could

at least sleep in the same apartment where I cooked for him and looked after his clothes——"

"But not marriage," he said. "Not marriage. He didn't promise you that. Don't lie to me. He didn't have to."

"No. He didn't have to. I didn't ask him to. I knew what I was doing. I knew that to begin with, long before honor, I imagine he called it, told him the time had come to tell me in so many words what his code, I suppose he would call it, would forbid him forever to do. And we agreed. Then we agreed again before he left New Mexico, to make sure. That that would be all of it. I believed him. No, I don't mean that; I mean I believed myself. I wasn't even listening to him any more by then because by that time it had been a long time since he had had anything else to tell me for me to have to hear. By then I wasn't even listening enough to ask him to please stop talking. I was listening to myself. And I believed it. I must have believed it. I don't see how I could have helped but believe it, because he was gone then as we had agreed and he didn't write as we had agreed, just the money came to the bank in Vicksburg in my name but coming from nobody as we had agreed. So I must have believed it. I even wrote him last month to make sure again and the letter came back unopened and I was sure. So I left the hospital and rented myself a room to live in until the deer season opened so I could make sure myself and I was waiting beside the road yesterday when your car passed and he saw me and so I was sure."

"Then what do you want?" he said. "What do you want? What do you expect?"

"Yes," she said. And while he glared at her, his white hair awry from the pillow and his eyes, lacking the spectacles to focus them, blurred and irisless and apparently pupilless, he saw again that grave, intent, speculative and detached fixity like a child watching him. "His great great— Wait a minute—great great *great* grandfather was your grandfather. McCaslin. Only it got to be Edmonds. Only it got to be more than that. Your cousin McCaslin was there that day when your father and Uncle Buddy won Tennie from Mr. Beauchamp for the one that had no name but Terrel so you called him Tomey's Terrel, to marry. But after that it got to be Edmonds." She regarded him, almost peacefully, with that unwinking and heatless fixity—the dark, wide, bottomless eyes in the face's dead and toneless pallor which to the old man looked anything but dead, but young and incredibly and even ineradicably alive—as though she were not only not looking at anything, she was not even speaking to anyone but herself. "I would have made a man of him. He's not a man yet. You spoiled him. You, and Uncle Lucas and Aunt Mollie. But mostly you."

"Me?" he said. "Me?"

"Yes. When you gave to his grandfather that land which didn't belong to him, not even half of it, by will or even law."

"And never mind that too," he said. "Never mind that too. You," he said. "You sound like you have been to college even. You sound almost like a Northerner even, not like the draggle-tailed women of these Delta peckerwoods. Yet you meet a man on the street one afternoon just because a box of groceries happened to fall out of a boat. And a month later you go off with him and live with him until he got a child on you: and then, by your own statement, you sat there while he took his hat and said goodbye and walked out. Even a Delta peckerwood would look after even a draggle-tail better than that. Haven't you got any folks at all?"

"Yes," she said. "I was living with one of them. My aunt, in Vicksburg. I came to live with her two years ago when my father died; we lived in Indianapolis then. But I got a job, teaching school here in Aluschaskuna, because my aunt was a widow, with a big family, taking in washing to sup——"

"Took in what?" he said. "Took in washing?" He

sprang, still seated even, flinging himself backward onto
one arm, awry-haired, glaring. Now he understood what
it was she had brought into the tent with her, what old
Isham had already told him by sending the youth to bring
her in to him—the pale lips, the skin pallid and dead-look-
ing yet not ill, the dark and tragic and foreknowing eyes.
Maybe in a thousand or two thousand years in America,
he thought. *But not now! Not now!* He cried, not loud,
in a voice of amazement, pity, and outrage: "You're a nigger!"

"Yes," she said. "James Beauchamp—you called him
Tennie's Jim though he had a name—was my grandfather. I said you were Uncle Isaac."

"And he knows?"

"No," she said. "What good would that have done?"

"But you did," he cried. "But you did. Then what do
you expect here?"

"Nothing."

"Then why did you come here? You said you were
waiting in Aluschaskuna yesterday and he saw you. Why
did you come this morning?"

"I'm going back North. Back home. My cousin brought
me up the day before yesterday in his boat. He's going
to take me on to Leland to get the train."

"Then go," he said. Then he cried again in that thin
not loud and grieving voice: "Get out of here! I can do
nothing for you! Can't nobody do nothing for you!" She
moved; she was not looking at him again, toward the
entrance. "Wait," he said. She paused again, obediently
still, turning. He took up the sheaf of banknotes and laid
it on the blanket at the foot of the cot and drew his hand
back beneath the blanket. "There," he said.

Now she looked at the money, for the first time, one
brief blank glance, then away again. "I don't need it. He
gave me money last winter. Besides the money he sent
to Vicksburg. Provided. Honor and code too. That was all
arranged."

"Take it," he said. His voice began to rise again, but he stopped it. "Take it out of my tent." She came back to the cot and took up the money; whereupon once more he said, "Wait:" although she had not turned, still stooping, and he put out his hand. But, sitting, he could not complete the reach until she moved her hand, the single hand which held the money, until he touched it. He didn't grasp it, he merely touched it—the gnarled, bloodless, bone-dry old man's fingers touching for a second the smooth young flesh where the strong old blood ran after its long lost journey back to home. "Tennie's Jim," he said. "Tennie's Jim." He drew the hand back beneath the blanket again: he said harshly now: "It's a boy, I reckon. They usually are, except that one was its own mother too."

"Yes," she said. "It's a boy." She stood for a moment longer, looking at him. Just for an instant her free hand moved as though she were about to lift the edge of the raincoat away from the child's face. But she did not. She turned again when once more he said Wait and moved beneath the blanket.

"Turn your back," he said. "I am going to get up. I ain't got my pants on." Then he could not get up. He sat in the huddled blanket, shaking, while again she turned and looked down at him in dark interrogation. "There," he said harshly, in the thin and shaking old man's voice. "On the nail there. The tent-pole."

"What?" she said.

"The horn!" he said harshly. "The horn." She went and got it, thrust the money into the slicker's side pocket as if it were a rag, a soiled handkerchief, and lifted down the horn, the one which General Compson had left him in his will, covered with the unbroken skin from a buck's shank and bound with silver.

"What?" she said.

"It's his. Take it."

"Oh," she said. "Yes. Thank you."

"Yes," he said, harshly, rapidly, but not so harsh now and soon not harsh at all but just rapid, urgent, until he knew that his voice was running away with him and he had neither intended it nor could stop it: "That's right. Go back North. Marry: a man in your own race. That's the only salvation for you—for a while yet, maybe a long while yet. We will have to wait. Marry a black man. You are young, handsome, almost white; you could find a black man who would see in you what it was you saw in him, who would ask nothing of you and expect less and get even still less than that, if it's revenge you want. Then you will forget all this, forget it ever happened, that he ever existed—" until he could stop it at last and did, sitting there in his huddle of blankets during the instant when, without moving at all, she blazed silently down at him. Then that was gone too. She stood in the gleaming and still dripping slicker, looking quietly down at him from under the sodden hat.

"Old man," she said, "have you lived so long and forgotten so much that you don't remember anything you ever knew or felt or even heard about love?"

Then she was gone too. The waft of light and the murmer of the constant rain flowed into the tent and then out again as the flap fell. Lying back once more, trembling, panting, the blanket huddled to his chin and his hands crossed on his breast, he listened to the pop and snarl, the mounting then fading whine of the motor until it died away and once again the tent held only silence and the sound of rain. And cold too: he lay shaking faintly and steadily in it, rigid save for the shaking. This Delta, he thought: This Delta. *This land which man has de-swamped and denuded and derivered in two generations so that white men can own plantations and commute every night to Memphis and black men own plantations and ride in Jim Crow cars to Chicago to live in millionaire's mansions on Lake Shore Drive; where white men rent farms and live like niggers and niggers crop on shares*

*and live like animals; where cotton is planted and grows
man-tall in the very cracks of the sidewalks, and usury
and mortgage and bankruptcy and measureless wealth,
Chinese and African and Aryan and Jew, all breed and
spawn together until no man has time to say which one
is which nor cares. . . .* No wonder the ruined woods I
used to know don't cry for retribution! he thought: The
people who have destroyed it will accomplish its revenge.

The tent flap jerked rapidly in and fell. He did not
move save to turn his head and open his eyes. It was Legate. He went quickly to Edmonds' bed and stooped,
rummaging hurriedly among the still-tumbled blankets.

"What is it?" he said.

"Looking for Roth's knife," Legate said. "I come back
to get a horse. We got a deer on the ground." He rose,
the knife in his hand, and hurried toward the entrance.

"Who killed it?" McCaslin said. "Was it Roth?"

"Yes," Legate said, raising the flap.

"Wait," McCaslin said. He moved, suddenly, onto his
elbow. "What was it?" Legate paused for an instant beneath the lifted flap. He did not look back.

"Just a deer, Uncle Ike," he said impatiently. "Nothing extra." He was gone; again the flap fell behind him,
wafting out of the tent again the faint light and the constant and grieving rain. McCaslin lay back down, the blanket once more drawn to his chin, his crossed hands once
more weightless on his breast in the empty tent.

"It was a doe," he said.

8

THE UNDYING PAST

Editor's Note

"The past is never dead," Gavin Stevens says in *Requiem for a Nun* (1951), and he adds, "It's not even past." In this judgment as in many others, Stevens appears to be speaking for the author. Faulkner himself was obsessed with a feeling that the past endures in every moment of our lives. He kept scrutinizing the past with a sort of anguish, in the hope that it would explain a present dilemma. That was one reason for his writing inordinately long sentences. "My ambition," he said, "is to put everything into one sentence—not only the present but the whole past on which it depends and which keeps overtaking the present, second by second."

The ambition comes nearest to fulfillment in "The Jail," a narrative written as prologue to the last act of *Requiem for a Nun*. There the first sentence is of only thirty-two words, but the second flows unbrokenly through the rest of the narrative—through the building of the jail, the expulsion of the Chickasaws, the mustering of volunteers for the Civil War, and the girl's name scratched on a window pane that preserved her memory into the age of nylon and neon—until those events of the past have illuminated the meaning of a final phrase that seems to be spoken by the dead girl, in 1951, but that might have been spoken by Faulkner himself in regard to his work as a whole: *"Listen, stranger; this was myself: this was I."*

"Appendix: The Compsons" was written for the present volume when I was putting it together in the autumn of 1945. I had remarked to Faulkner in a letter that the last or Dilsey section of *The Sound and the Fury* was the one I preferred to use, but that it didn't quite stand by itself. He thereupon offered to furnish "a page or two of synopsis to preface it, a condensation of the first 3 sections, which simply told why and when (and who she was) and how a 17 year old girl robbed a bureau drawer of hoarded money and climbed down a drain pipe and ran off with a carnival pitchman." What he wrote instead —yielding to his sense of the past enduring in the present—was a genealogy that traced the Compson family from the Battle of Culloden in 1745 to the end of World War II. Faulkner was pleased with the genealogy, or "Appendix," as he called it. "I should have done this when I wrote the book," he said. "Then the whole thing would have fallen into place like a jigsaw puzzle when the magician's wand touched it." The 1945 Appendix has been included in all subsequent editions of *The Sound and the Fury*, but in a version that—as a result of accidents and afterthoughts—is slightly different from the one in the Portable. Faulkner approved both versions.

The Jail (Nor Even Yet Quite Relinquish—)

So, although in a sense the jail was both older and less old than the courthouse, in actuality, in time, in observation and memory, it was older even than the town itself. Because there was no town until there was a courthouse, and no courthouse until (like some unsentient unweaned creature torn violently from the dug of its dam) the floorless lean-to rabbit-hutch housing the iron chest was reft from the log flank of the jail and transmogrified into a by-neo-Greek-out-of-Georgian-England edifice set in the center of what in time would be the town Square (as a result of which, the town itself had moved one block south—or rather, no town then and yet, the courthouse itself the catalyst: a mere dusty widening of the trace, trail, pathway in a forest of oak and ash and hickory and sycamore and flowering catalpa and dogwood and judas tree and persimmon and wild plum, with on one side old Alec Holston's tavern and coaching-yard, and a little farther along, Ratcliffe's trading-post-store and the blacksmith's, and diagonal to all of them, *en face* and solitary beyond the dust, the log jail; moved—the town—complete and intact, one block southward, so that now, a century and a quarter later, the coaching-yard and Ratcliffe's store were gone and old Alec's tavern and the blacksmith's were a hotel and a garage, on a main thoroughfare true enough but still a business side-street, and the

jail across from them, though transformed also now into
two storeys of Georgian brick by the hand ((or anyway
pocketbooks)) of Sartoris and Sutpen and Louis Grenier,
faced not even on a side-street but on an alley);

And so, being older than all, it had seen all: the mutation and the change: and, in that sense, had recorded them
(indeed, as Gavin Stevens, the town lawyer and the
county amateur Cincinnatus, was wont to say, if you
would peruse in unbroken—ay, overlapping—continuity
the history of a community, look not in the church regis-
ters and the courthouse records, but beneath the successive layers of calcimine and creosote and whitewash on
the walls of the jail, since only in that forcible carcera-
tion does man find the idleness in which to compose, in
the gross and simple terms of his gross and simple lusts
and yearnings, the gross and simple recapitulations of his
gross and simple heart); invisible and impacted, not only
beneath the annual inside creosote-and-whitewash of
bullpen and cell, but on the blind outside walls too, first
the simple mud-chinked log ones and then the symmetric brick, not only the scrawled illiterate repetitive unimaginative doggerel and the perspectiveless almost prehis-
toric sexual picture-writing, but the images, the panorama not only of the town but of its days and years until
a century and better had been accomplished, filled not
only with its mutation and change from a halting-place:
to a community: to a settlement: to a village: to a town,
but with the shapes and motions, the gestures of passion
and hope and travail and endurance, of the men and
women and children in their successive overlapping generations long after the subjects which had reflected the
images were vanished and replaced and again replaced,
as when you stand say alone in a dim and empty room
and believe, hypnotised beneath the vast weight of man's
incredible and enduring *Was*, that perhaps by turning
your head aside you will see from the corner of your eye

the turn of a moving limb—a gleam of crinoline, a laced wrist, perhaps even a Cavalier plume—who knows? provided there is will enough, perhaps even the face itself three hundred years after it was dust—the eyes, two jellied tears filled with arrogance and pride and satiety and knowledge of anguish and foreknowledge of death, saying no to death across twelve generations, asking still the old same unanswerable question three centuries after that which reflected them had learned that the answer didn't matter, or—better still—had forgotten the asking of it—in the shadowy fathomless dreamlike depths of an old mirror which has looked at too much too long;

But not in shadow, not this one, this mirror, these logs: squatting in the full glare of the stump-pocked clearing during those first summers, solitary on its side of the dusty widening marked with an occasional wheel but mostly by the prints of horses and men: Pettigrew's private pony express until he and it were replaced by a monthly stagecoach from Memphis, the race horse which Jason Compson traded to Ikkemotubbe, old Mohataha's son and the last ruling Chickasaw chief in that section, for a square of land so large that, as the first formal survey revealed, the new courthouse would have been only another of Compson's outbuildings had not the town Corporation bought enough of it (at Compson's price) to forefend themselves being trespassers, and the saddle-mare which bore Doctor Habersham's worn black bag (and which drew the buggy after Doctor Habersham got too old and stiff to mount the saddle), and the mules which drew the wagon in which, seated in a rocking chair beneath a French parasol held by a Negro slave girl, old Mohataha would come to town on Saturdays (and came that last time to set her capital X on the paper which ratified the dispossession of her people forever, coming in the wagon that time too, barefoot as always but in the purple silk dress which her son, Ikkemotubbe, had brought her back from France, and a hat crowned with the royal-colored plume of a queen, beneath the slave-held parasol still and with another female slave child squatting on her other side holding the crusted slippers which she had never been able to get her feet into, and in the back of the wagon the petty rest of the unmarked Empire flotsam her son had brought to her which was small enough to be moved; driving for the last time out of the woods into the dusty widening before Ratcliffe's store where the Federal land agent and his marshal waited for her with the paper, and stopped the mules and sat for a little time, the young men of her bodyguard squatting quietly about the halted wagon after the eight-mile walk, while from the gallery of the store and of Holston's tavern the settlement—the Ratcliffes and Compsons and Peabodys and Pettigrews ((not Grenier and Holston and Habersham, because Louis Grenier declined to come in to see it, and for the same reason old Alec Holston sat alone on that hot afternoon before the smoldering log in the fireplace of his taproom, and Doctor Habersham was dead and his son had already departed for the West with his bride, who was Mohataha's granddaughter, and his father-in-law, Mohataha's son, Ikkemotubbe))—looked on, watched: the inscrutable ageless wrinkled face, the fat shapeless body dressed in the cast-off garments of a French queen, which on her looked like the Sunday costume of the madam of a rich Natchez or New Orleans brothel, sitting in a battered wagon inside a squatting ring of her household troops, her young men dressed in their Sunday clothes for traveling too: then she said, "Where is this Indian territory?" And they told her: West. 'Turn the mules west,' she said, and someone did so, and she took the pen from the agent and made her X on the paper and handed the pen back and the wagon moved, the young men rising too, and she vanished so across that summer afternoon to that terrific and infinitesimal creak and creep of ungreased wheels, herself im-

mobile beneath the rigid parasol, grotesque and regal,
bizarre and moribund, like obsolescence's self riding off
the stage enthroned on its own obsolete catafalque, looking not once back, not once back toward home);

But most of all, the prints of men—the fitted shoes which
Doctor Habersham and Louis Grenier had brought from
the Atlantic seaboard, the cavalry boots in which Alec
Hoston had ridden behind Francis Marion, and—more
myriad almost than leaves, outnumbering all the others
lumped together—the moccasins, the deerhide sandals
of the forest, worn not by the Indians but by white men,
the pioneers, the long hunters, as though they had not
only vanquished the wilderness but had even stepped
into the very footgear of them they dispossessed (and
meet and fitting so, since it was by means of his feet and
legs that the white man conquered America; the closed
and split U's of his horses and cattle overlay his own
prints always, merely consolidating his victory);—(the
jail) watched them all, red men and white and black—
the pioneers, the hunters, the forest men with rifles, who
made the same light rapid soundless toed-in almost heelless prints as the red men they dispossessed and who in
fact dispossessed the red men for that reason: not because
of the grooved barrel but because they could enter the
red man's milieu and make the same footprints that he
made; the husbandman printing deep the hard heels of
his brogans because of the weight he bore on his shoulders: axe and saw and plow-stock, who dispossessed the
forest man for the obverse reason: because with his saw
and axe he simply removed, obliterated, the milieu in
which alone the forest man could exist; then the land
speculators and the traders in slaves and whiskey who
followed the husbandmen, and the politicians who followed the land speculators, printing deeper and deeper
the dust of that dusty widening, until at last there was
no mark of Chickasaw left in it any more; watching (the

jail) them all, from the first innocent days when Doctor Habersham and his son and Alex Holston and Louis Grenier were first guests and then friends of Ikkemotubbe's Chickasaw clan; then an Indian agent and a land-office and a trading-post, and suddenly Ikkemotubbe and his Chickasaws were themselves the guests without being friends of the Federal Government; then Ratcliffe, and the trading-post was no longer simply an Indian trading-post, though Indians were still welcome, of course (since, after all, they owned the land or anyway were on it first and claimed it), then Compson with his race horse and presently Compson began to own the Indian accounts for tobacco and calico and jeans pants and cooking-pots on Ratcliffe's books (in time he would own Ratcliffe's books too) and one day Ikkemotubbe owned the race horse and Compson owned the land itself, some of which the city fathers would have to buy from him at his price in order to establish a town; and Pettigrew with his tri-weekly mail, and then a monthly stage and the new faces coming in faster than old Alex Holston, arthritic and irascible, hunkered like an old surly bear over his moldering hearth even in the heat of summer (he alone now of that original three, since old Grenier no longer came in to the settlement, and old Doctor Habersham was dead, and the old doctor's son, in the opinion of the settlement, had already turned Indian and renegade even at the age of twelve or fourteen) any longer made any effort, wanted, to associate names with; and now indeed the last moccasin print vanished from that dusty widening, the last toed-in heelless light soft quick long-striding print pointing west for an instant, then trodden from the sight and memory of man by a heavy leather heel engaged not in the traffic of endurance and hardihood and survival, but in money —taking with it (the print) not only the moccasins but the deer-hide leggins and jerkin too, because Ikkemotubbe's Chickasaws now wore Eastern factory-made jeans and shoes sold them on credit out of Ratcliffe's and Compson's general store, walking in to the settlement on the white man's Saturday, carrying the alien shoes rolled neatly in the alien pants under their arms, to stop at the bridge over Compson's creek long enough to bathe their legs and feet before donning the pants and shoes, then coming on to squat all day on the store gallery eating cheese and crackers and peppermint candy (bought on credit too out of Compson's and Ratcliffe's showcase) and now not only they but Habersham and Holston and Grenier too were there on sufferance, anachronistic and alien, not really an annoyance yet but simply a discomfort;

Then they were gone; the jail watched that: the halted ungreased unpainted wagon, the span of underfed mules attached to it by fragments of Eastern harness supplemented by raw deer-hide thongs, the nine young men—the wild men, tameless and proud, who even in their own generation's memory had been free and, in that of their fathers, the heirs of kings—squatting about it, waiting, quiet and composed, not even dressed in the ancient forest-softened deerskins of their freedom but in the formal regalia of the white man's inexplicable ritualistic sabbaticals: broadcloth trousers and white shirts with boiled-starch bosoms (because they were traveling now; they would be visible to outworld, to strangers:—and carrying the New England-made shoes under their arms too since the distance would be long and walking was better barefoot), the shirts collarless and cravatless true enough and with the tails worn outside, but still board-rigid, gleaming, pristine, and in the rocking chair in the wagon, beneath the slave-borne parasol, the fat shapeless old matriarch in the regal sweat-stained purple silk and the plumed hat, barefoot too of course but, being a queen, with another slave to carry her slippers, putting her cross to the paper and then driving on, vanishing slowly and terrifically to the slow and the terrific creak and squeak of the ungreased wagon—apparently and apparently only, since in reality it was as though, instead of putting an inked cross at the foot of a sheet of paper, she had lighted the train of a mine set beneath a dam, a dyke, a barrier already straining, bulging, bellying, not only towering over the land but leaning, looming, imminent with collapse, so that it only required the single light touch of the pen in that brown illiterate hand, and the wagon did not vanish slowly and terrifically from the scene to the terrific sound of its ungreased wheels, but was swept, hurled, flung not only out of Yoknapatawpha County and Mississippi but the United States too, immobile and intact—the wagon, the mules, the rigid shapeless old Indian woman and the nine heads which surrounded her—like a float or a piece of stage property dragged rapidly into the wings across the very backdrop and amid the very bustle of the property-men setting up for the next scene and act before the curtain had even had time to fall;

There was no time; the next act and scene itself clearing its own stage without waiting for property-men; or rather, not even bothering to clear the stage but commencing the new act and scene right in the midst of the phantoms, the fading wraiths of that old time which had been exhausted, used up, to be no more and never return: as though the mere and simple orderly ordinary succession of days was not big enough, comprised not scope enough, and so weeks and months and years had to be condensed and compounded into one burst, one surge, one soundless roar filled with one word: town: city: with a name: Jefferson; men's mouths and their incredulous faces (faces to which old Alex Holston had long since ceased trying to give names or, for that matter, even to recognise) were filled with it; that was only yesterday, and by tomorrow the vast bright rush and roar had swept the very town one block south, leaving in the tideless backwater of an alley on a side-street the old jail which, like the old mirror, had already looked at too much too long, or like the patriarch who, whether or not he de-creed the conversion of the mud-chinked cabin into a mansion, had at least foreseen it, is now not only content but even prefers the old chair on the back gallery, free of the rustle of blueprints and the uproar of bickering architects in the already dismantled living-room;

It (the old jail) didn't care, tideless in that backwash, insulated by that city block of space from the turmoil of the town's birthing, the mud-chinked log walls even car-cerant of the flotsam of an older time already on its rapid way out too: an occasional runaway slave or drunken In-dian or shoddy would-be heir of the old tradition of Ma-son or Hare or Harpe (biding its time until, the court-house finished, the jail too would be translated into brick, but, unlike the courthouse, merely a veneer of brick, the old mud-chinked logs of the ground floor still intact be-hind the patterned and symmetric sheath); no longer even watching now, merely cognizant, remembering: only yesterday was a wilderness ordinary, a store, a smithy, and already today was not a town, a city, but the town and city: named; not a courthouse but *the* court-house, rising surging like the fixed blast of a rocket, not even finished yet but already looming, beacon focus and lodestar, already taller than anything else, out of the rapid and fading wilderness—not the wilderness reced-ing from the rich and arable fields as tide recedes, but rather the fields themselves, rich and inexhaustible to the plow, rising sunward and airward out of swamp and mo-rass, themselves thrusting back and down brake and thicket, bayou and bottom and forest, along with the copeless denizens—the wild men and animals—which once haunted them, wanting, dreaming, imagining, no other—lodestar and pole, drawing the people—the men and women and children, the maidens, the marriageable girls and the young men, flowing, pouring in with their tools and goods and cattle and slaves and gold money,

behind ox- or mule-teams, by steamboat up Ikkemotubbe's old river from the Mississippi; only yesterday Pettigrew's pony express had been displaced by a stagecoach, yet already there was talk of a railroad less than a
hundred miles to the north, to run all the way from Memphis to the Atlantic Ocean;

Going fast now: only seven years, and not only was the
courthouse finished, but the jail too: not a new jail of
course but the old one veneered over with brick, into two
storeys, with white trim and iron-barred windows: only
its face lifted, because behind the veneer were still the
old ineradicable bones, the old ineradicable remembering: the old logs immured intact and lightless between
the tiered symmetric bricks and the whitewashed plaster,
immune now even to having to look, see, watch that new
time which in a few years more would not even remember that the old logs were there behind the brick or had
ever been, an age from which the drunken Indian had
vanished, leaving only the highwayman, who had wagered his liberty on his luck, and the runaway nigger
who, having no freedom to stake, had wagered merely his
milieu; that rapid, that fast: Sutpen's untameable Paris
architect long since departed, vanished (one hoped) back
to wherever it was he had made that aborted midnight
try to regain and had been overtaken and caught in the
swamp, not (as the town knew now) by Sutpen and Sutpen's wild West Indian headman and Sutpen's bear
hounds, nor even by Sutpen's destiny nor even by his
(the architect's) own, but by that of the town: the long
invincible arm of Progress itself reaching into that midnight swamp to pluck him out of that bayed circle of dogs
and naked Negroes and pine torches, and stamped the
town with him like a rubber signature and then released
him, not flung him away like a squeezed-out tube of
paint, but rather (inattentive too) merely opening its
fingers, its hand; stamping his (the architect's) imprint

not on just the courthouse and the jail, but on the whole
town, the flow and trickle of his bricks never even falter-
ing, his molds and kilns building the two churches and
then that Female Academy a certificate from which, to a
young woman of North Mississippi or West Tennessee,
would presently have the same mystic significance as an
invitation dated from Windsor castle and signed by
Queen Victoria would for a young female from Long Island or Philadelphia;

That fast now: tomorrow, and the railroad did run unbroken from Memphis to Carolina, the light-wheeled
bulb-stacked wood-burning engines shrieking among the
swamps and cane-brakes where bear and panther still
lurked, and through the open woods where browsing
deer still drifted in pale bands like unwinded smoke: because they—the wild animals, the beasts—remained,
they coped, they would endure; a day, and they would
flee, lumber, scuttle across the clearings already overtaken and relinquished by the hawk-shaped shadows of
mail planes; they would endure, only the wild men were
gone indeed, tomorrow, and there would be grown men
in Jefferson who could not even remember a drunken Indian in the jail; another tomorrow—so quick, so rapid, so
fast—and not even a highwayman any more of the old
true sanguinary girth and tradition of Hare and Mason
and the mad Harpes; even Murrell, their thrice-com-
pounded heir and apotheosis, who had taken his heritage
of simple rapacity and bloodlust and converted it into a
bloody dream of outlaw-empire, was gone, finished, as
obsolete as Alexander, checkmated and stripped not even
by man but by Progress, by a pierceless front of middle-
class morality, which refused him even the dignity of ex-
ecution as a felon, but instead merely branded him on
the hand like an Elizabethan pickpocket—until all that
remained of the old days for the jail to incarcerate was
the runaway slave, for his little hour more, his little min-

ute yet while the time, the land, the nation, the American earth, whirled faster and faster toward the plunging precipice of its destiny;

That fast, that rapid: a commodity in the land now which until now had dealt first in Indians: then in acres and sections and boundaries:—an economy: Cotton: a king: omnipotent and omnipresent: a destiny of which (obvious now) the plow and the axe had been merely the tools; not plow and axe which had effaced the wilderness, but Cotton: petty globules of Motion weightless and myriad even in the hand of a child, incapable even of wadding a rifle, let alone of charging it, yet potent enough to sever the very taproots of oak and hickory and gum, leaving the acre-shading tops to wither and vanish in one single season beneath that fierce minted glare; not the rifle nor the plow which drove at last the bear and deer and panther into the last jungle fastnesses of the river bottoms, but Cotton; not the soaring cupola of the courthouse drawing people into the country, but that same white tide sweeping them in: that tender skim covering the winter's brown earth, burgeoning through spring and summer into September's white surf crashing against the flanks of gin and warehouse and ringing like bells on the marble counters of the banks: altering not just the face of the land, but the complexion of the town too, creating its own parasitic aristocracy not only behind the columned porticoes of the plantation houses, but in the counting-rooms of merchants and bankers and the sanctums of lawyers, and not only these last, but finally nadir complete: the county offices too: of sheriff and tax-collector and bailiff and turnkey and clerk; doing overnight to the old jail what Sutpen's architect with all his brick and iron smithwork, had not been able to accomplish—the old jail which had been unavoidable, a necessity, like a public comfort-station, and which, like the public comfort-station, was not ignored but simply by mutual concord, not seen, not looked at, not named by its purpose and aim, yet which to the older people of the town, in spite of Sutpen's architect's face-lifting, was still the old jail—now translated into an integer, a moveable pawn on the county's political board like the sheriff's star or the clerk's bond or the bailiff's wand of office; converted indeed now, elevated (an apotheosis) ten feet above the level of the town, so that the old buried log walls now contained the living-quarters for the turnkey's family and the kitchen from which his wife catered, at so much a meal, to the city's and the county's prisoners—perquisite not for work or capability for work, but for political fidelity and the numerality of votable kin by blood or marriage—a jailor or turnkey, himself someone's cousin and with enough other cousins and inlaws of his own to have assured the election of sheriff or chancery- or circuit-clerk—a failed farmer who was not at all the victim of his time but, on the contrary, was its master, since his inherited and inescapable incapacity to support his family by his own efforts had matched him with an era and a land where government was founded on the working premise of being primarily an asylum for ineptitude and indigence, for the private business failures among your or your wife's kin whom otherwise you yourself would have to support—so much his destiny's master that, in a land and time where a man's survival depended not only on his ability to drive a straight furrow and to fell a tree without maiming or destroying himself, that fate had supplied to him one child: a frail anemic girl with narrow workless hands lacking even the strength to milk a cow, and then capped its own vanquishment and eternal subjugation by the paradox of giving him for his patronymic the designation of the vocation at which he was to fail: Farmer; this was the incumbent, the turnkey, the jailor; the old tough logs which had known Ikkemotubbe's drunken Chickasaws and brawling teamsters and trappers and flatboatmen (and—for that one short summer night

—the four highwaymen, one of whom might have been the murderer, Wiley Harpe), were now the bower framing a window in which mused hour after hour and day and month and year, the frail blonde girl not only incapable of (or at least excused from) helping her mother cook, but even of drying the dishes after her mother (or father perhaps) washed them—musing, not even waiting for anyone or anything, as far as the town knew, not even pensive, as far as the town knew: just musing amid her blonde hair in the window facing the country town street, day after day and month after month and—as the town remembered it—year after year for what must have been three or four of them, inscribing at some moment the fragile and indelible signature of her meditation in one of the panes of it (the window): her frail and workless name, scratched by a diamond ring in her frail and workless hand, and the date: *Cecilia Farmer April 16th 1861;*

At which moment the destiny of the land, the nation, the South, the State, the County, was already whirling into the plunge of its precipice, not that the State and the South knew it, because the first seconds of fall always seem like soar: a weightless deliberation preliminary to a rush not downward but upward, the falling body reversed during that second by transubstantiation into the upward rush of earth; a soar, an apex, the South's own apotheosis of its destiny and its pride, Mississippi and Yoknapatawpha County not last in this, Mississippi among the first of the eleven to ratify secession, the regiment of infantry which John Sartoris raised and organised with Jefferson for its headquarters, going to Virginia numbered Two in the roster of Mississippi regiments, the jail watching that too but just by cognizance from a block away: that noon, the regiment not even a regiment yet but merely a voluntary association of untried men who knew they were ignorant and hoped they were brave, the four sides of the Square lined with their fathers or grandfathers and their mothers and wives and sisters and sweethearts, the only uniform present yet that one in which Sartoris stood with his virgin sabre and his pristine colonel's braid on the courthouse balcony, bareheaded too while the Baptist minister prayed and the Richmond mustering officer swore the regiment in; and then (the regiment) gone; and now not only the jail but the town too hung without motion in a tideless backwash: the plunging body advanced far enough now into space as to have lost all sense of motion, weightless and immobile upon the light pressure of invisible air, gone now all diminishment of the precipice's lip, all increment of the vast increaseless earth: a town of old men and women and children and an occasional wounded soldier (John Sartoris himself, deposed from his colonelcy by a regimental election after Second Manassas, came home and oversaw the making and harvesting of a crop on his plantation before he got bored and gathered up a small gang of irregular cavalry and carried it up into Tennessee to join Forrest), static in *quo*, rumored, murmured of war only as from a great and incredible dreamy distance, like far summer thunder: until the spring of '64, the once-vast fixed impalpable increaseless and threatless earth now one omnivorous roar of rock (a roar so vast and so spewing, flinging ahead of itself, like the spray above the maelstrom, the preliminary anesthetic of shock so that the agony of bone and flesh will not even be felt, as to contain and sweep along with it the beginning, the first ephemeral phase, of this story, permitting it to boil for an instant to the surface like a chip or a twig—a match-stick or a bubble, say, too weightless to give resistance for destruction to function against: in this case, a bubble, a minute globule which was its own impunity, since what it—the bubble—contained, having no part in rationality and being contemptuous of fact, was immune even to the rationality of rock) —a sudden battle centering around Colonel Sartoris's plantation house four miles to the north, the line of a creek held long enough for the main Confederate body to pass through Jefferson to a stronger line on the river heights south of the town, a rear-guard action of cavalry in the streets of the town itself (and this was the story, the beginning of it; all of it too, the town might have been justified in thinking, presuming they had had time to see, notice, remark and then remember, even that little)— the rattle and burst of pistols, the hooves, the dust, the rush and scurry of a handful of horsemen led by a lieutenant, up the street past the jail, and the two of them— the frail and useless girl musing in the blonde mist of her hair beside the window-pane where three or four (or whatever it was) years ago she had inscribed with her grandmother's diamond ring her paradoxical and significantless name (and where, so it seemed to the town, she had been standing ever since), and the soldier, gaunt and tattered, battle-grimed and fleeing and undefeated, looking at one another for that moment across the fury and pell mell of battle;

Then gone; that night the town was occupied by Federal troops; two nights later, it was on fire (the Square, the stores and shops and the professional offices), gutted (the courthouse too), the blackened jagged topless jumbles of brick wall enclosing like a ruined jaw the blackened shell of the courthouse between its two rows of topless columns, which (the columns) were only blackened and stained, being tougher than fire: but not the jail, it escaped, untouched, insulated by its windless back-water from fire; and now the town was as though insulated by fire or perhaps cauterised by fire from fury and turmoil, the long roar of the rushing omnivorous rock fading on to the east with the fading uproar of the battle: and so in effect it was a whole year in advance of Appomattox (only the undefeated undefeatable women, vulnerable only to death, resisted, endured, irreconcilable); already,

before there was a name for them (already their prototype before they even existed as a species), there were
carpetbaggers in Jefferson—a Missourian named Redmond, a cotton and quartermaster-supplies speculator,
who had followed the Northern army to Memphis in '61
and (nobody knew exactly how or why) had been with
(or at least on the fringe of) the military household of
the brigadier commanding the force which occupied
Jefferson, himself—Redmond—going no farther, stopping,
staying, none knew the why for that either, why he
elected Jefferson, chose that alien fire-gutted site (himself one, or at least the associate, of them who had set the
match) to be his future home; and a German private, a
blacksmith, a deserter from a Pennsylvania regiment, who
appeared in the summer of '64, riding a mule, with (so
the tale told later, when his family of daughters had become matriarchs and grandmothers of the town's new aristocracy) for saddle-blanket sheaf on sheaf of virgin and
uncut United States banknotes, so Jefferson and Yoknapatawpha County had mounted Golgotha and passed beyond Appomattox a full year in advance, with returned
soldiers in the town, not only the wounded from the battle
of Jefferson, but whole men: not only the furloughed
from Forrest in Alabama and Johnston in Georgia and
Lee in Virginia, but the stragglers, the unmaimed flotsam
and refuse of that single battle now drawing its final constricting loop from the Atlantic Ocean at Old Point Comfort, to Richmond: to Chattanooga: to Atlanta: to the Atlantic Ocean again at Charleston, who were not deserters
but who could not rejoin any still-intact Confederate unit
for the reason that there were enemy armies between, so
that in the almost faded twilight of that land, the knell
of Appomattox made no sound; when in the spring and
early summer of '65 the formally and officially paroled
and disbanded soldiers began to trickle back into the
county, there was anticlimax; they returned to a land
which not only had passed through Appomattox over a

year ago, it had had that year in which to assimilate it,
that whole year in which not only to ingest surrender
but (begging the metaphor, the figure) to convert, me-
tabolise it, and then defecate it as fertilizer for the four-
years' fallow land they were already in train to rehabilitate a year before the Virginia knell rang the formal
change, the men of '65 returning to find themselves alien
in the very land they had been bred and born in and had
fought for four years to defend, to find a working and already solvent economy based on the premise that it could
get along without them; (and now the rest of this story,
since it occurs, happens, here: not yet June in '65; this
one had indeed wasted no time getting back: a stranger,
alone; the town did not even know it had ever seen him
before, because the other time was a year ago and had
lasted only while he galloped through it firing a pistol
backward at a Yankee army, and he had been riding a
horse—a fine though a little too small and too delicate
blooded mare—where now he rode a big mule, which
for that reason—its size—was a better mule than the
horse was a horse, but it was still a mule, and of course
the town could not know that he had swapped the mare
for the mule on the same day that he traded his lieutenant's sabre—he still had the pistol—for the stocking full
of seed corn he had seen growing in a Pennsylvania field
and had not let even the mule have one mouthful of it
during the long journey across the ruined land between
the Atlantic seaboard and the Jefferson jail, riding up to
the jail at last, still gaunt and tattered and dirty and still
undefeated and not fleeing now but instead making or at
least planning a single-handed assault against what any
rational man would have considered insurmountable
odds ((but then, that bubble had ever been immune to
the ephemerae of facts)); perhaps, probably—without
doubt: apparently she had been standing leaning musing
in it for three or four years in 1864; nothing had happened since, not in a land which had even anticipated

Appomattox, capable of shaking a meditation that rooted,
that durable, that veteran—the girl watched him get
down and tie the mule to the fence, and perhaps while
he walked from the fence to the door he even looked for
a moment at her, though possibly, perhaps even probably,
not, since she was not his immediate object now, he was
not really concerned with her at the moment, because he
had so little time, he had none, really: still to reach Alabama and the small hill farm which had been his father's
and would now be his, if—no, when—he could get there,
and it had not been ruined by four years of war and neglect, and even if the land was still plantable, even if he
could start planting the stocking of corn tomorrow, he
would be weeks and even months late; during that walk
to the door and as he lifted his hand to knock on it, he
must have thought with a kind of weary and indomitable
outrage of how, already months late, he must still waste
a day or maybe even two or three of them before he could
load the girl onto the mule behind him and head at last
for Alabama—this, at a time when of all things he would
require patience and a clear head, trying for them
((courtesy too, which would be demanded now)), patient and urgent and polite, undefeated, trying to explain,
in terms which they could understand or at least accept,
his simple need and the urgency of it, to the mother and
father whom he had never seen before and whom he
never intended, or anyway anticipated, to see again, not
that he had anything for or against them either: he simply
intended to be too busy for the rest of his life, once they
could get on the mule and start for home; not seeing the
girl then, during the interview, not even asking to see her
for a moment when the interview was over, because he
had to get the license now and then find the preacher: so
that the first word he ever spoke to her was a promise
delivered through a stranger; it was probably not until
they were on the mule—the frail useless hands whose only
strength seemed to be that sufficient to fold the wedding

license into the bosom of her dress and then cling to the belt around his waist—that he looked at her again or ((both of them)) had time to learn one another's middle name);

That was the story, the incident, ephemeral of an afternoon in late May, unrecorded by the town and the county because they had little time too: which (the county and the town) had anticipated Appomattox and kept that lead, so that in effect Appomattox itself never overhauled them; it was the long pull of course, but they had —as they would realise later—that priceless, that unmatchable year; on New Year's Day, 1865, while the rest of the South sat staring at the northeast horizon beyond which Richmond lay, like a family staring at the closed door to a sick-room, Yoknapatawpha County was already nine months gone in reconstruction; by New Year's of '66, the gutted walls (the rain of two winters had washed them clean of the smoke and soot) of the Square had been temporarily roofed and were stores and shops and offices again, and they had begun to restore the courthouse: not temporary, this, but restored, exactly as it had been, between the two columned porticoes, one north and one south, which had been tougher than dynamite and fire, because it was the symbol: the County and the City: and they knew how, who had done it before; Colonel Sartoris was home now, and General Compson, the first Jason's son, and though a tragedy had happened to Sutpen and his pride—a failure not of his pride nor even of his own bones and flesh, but of the lesser bones and flesh which he had believed capable of supporting the edifice of his dream—they still had the old plans of his architect and even the architect's molds, and even more: money, (strangely, curiously) Redmond, the town's domesticated carpetbagger, symbol of a blind rapacity almost like a biological instinct, destined to cover the South like a migration of locusts; in the case of this man, arriv-

ing a full year before its time and now devoting no small
portion of the fruit of his rapacity to restoring the very
building the destruction of which had rung up the curtain
for his appearance on the stage, had been the formal visa
on his passport to pillage; and by New Year's of '76, this
same Redmond with his money and Colonel Sartoris and
General Compson had built a railroad from Jefferson
north into Tennessee to connect with the one from Memphis to the Atlantic Ocean; nor content there either,
north or south: another ten years (Sartoris and Redmond
and Compson quarreled, and Sartoris and Redmond
bought—probably with Redmond's money—Compson's
interest in the railroad, and the next year Sartoris and
Redmond had quarreled and the year after that, because
of simple physical fear, Redmond killed Sartoris from am-
bush on the Jefferson Square and fled, and at last even
Sartoris's supporters—he had no friends: only enemies
and frantic admirers—began to understand the result of
that regimental election in the fall of '62) and the railroad was a part of that system covering the whole South
and East like the veins in an oak leaf and itself mutually
adjunctive to the other intricate systems covering the rest
of the United States, so that you could get on a train in
Jefferson now and, by changing and waiting a few times,
go anywhere in North America;

No more into the United States, but into the *rest* of the
United States, because the long pull was over now; only
the aging unvanquished women were unreconciled, irreconcilable, reversed and irrevocably reverted against
the whole moving unanimity of panorama until, old un-
ordered vacant pilings above a tide's flood, they themselves had an illusion of motion, facing irreconcilably
backward toward the old lost battles, the old aborted
cause, the old four ruined years whose very physical scars
ten and twenty and twenty-five changes of season had

annealed back into the earth; twenty-five and then thirty-five years; not only a century and an age, but a way of thinking died; the town itself wrote the epilogue and epitaph: 1900, on Confederate Decoration Day, Mrs. Virginia Depre, Colonel Sartoris's sister, twitched a lanyard and the spring-restive bunting collapsed and flowed, leaving the marble effigy—the stone infantryman on his stone pedestal on the exact spot where forty years ago the Richmond officer and the local Baptist minister had mustered in the Colonel's regiment, and the old men in the gray and braided coats (all officers now, none less in rank than captain) tottered into the sunlight and fired shotguns at the bland sky and raised their cracked quavering voices in the shrill hackle-lifting yelling which Lee and Jackson and Longstreet and the two Johnstons (and Grant and Sherman and Hooker and Pope and McClellan and Burnside too for the matter of that) had listened to amid the smoke and the din; epilogue and epitaph, because apparently neither the U.D.C. ladies who instigated and bought the momument, nor the architect who designed it nor the masons who erected it, had noticed that the marble eyes under the shading marble palm stared not toward the north and the enemy, but toward the south, toward (if anything) his own rear—looking perhaps, the wits said (could say now, with the old war thirty-five years past and you could even joke about it—except the women, the ladies, the unsurrendered, the irreconcilable, who even after another thirty-five years would still get up and stalk out of picture houses showing *Gone With the Wind*), for reinforcements; or perhaps not a combat soldier at all, but a provost marshal's man looking for deserters, or perhaps himself for a safe place to run to: because that old war was dead; the sons of those tottering old men in gray had already died in blue coats in Cuba, the macabre mementos and testimonials and shrines of the new war already usurping the earth before the blasts of blank shotgun shells and the weightless collapsing of bunting had unveiled the final ones to the old;

Not only a new century and a new way of thinking, but of acting and behaving too: now you could go to bed in a train in Jefferson and wake up tomorrow morning in New Orleans or Chicago; there were electric lights and running water in almost every house in town except the cabins of Negroes; and now the town bought and brought from a great distance a kind of gray crushed ballast-stone called macadam, and paved the entire street between the depot and the hotel, so that no more would the train-meeting hacks filled with drummers and lawyers and court-witnesses need to lurch and heave and strain through the winter mud-holes; every morning a wagon came to your very door with artificial ice and put it in your icebox on the back gallery for you, the children in rotational neighborhood gangs following it (the wagon), eating the fragments of ice which the Negro driver chipped off for them; and that summer a specially-built sprinkling-cart began to make the round of the streets each day; a new time, a new age: there were screens in windows now; people (white people) could actually sleep in summer night air, finding it harmless, uninimical: as though there had waked suddenly in man (or anyway in his womenfolks) a belief in his inalienable civil right to be free of dust and bugs;

Moving faster and faster: from the speed of two horses on either side of a polished tongue, to that of thirty then fifty then a hundred under a tin bonnet no bigger than a wash-tub: which from almost the first explosion, would have to be controlled by police; already in a back yard on the edge of town, an ex-blacksmith's-apprentice, a grease-covered man with the eyes of a visionary monk, was building a gasoline buggy, casting and boring his own cylinders and rods and cams, inventing his own coils and plugs and valves as he found he needed them, which would run, and did: crept popping and stinking out of the alley at the exact moment when the banker Bayard Sartoris, the Colonel's son, passed in his carriage: as a result of which, there is on the books of Jefferson today a law prohibiting the operation of any mechanically-propelled vehicle on the streets of the corporate town: who (the same banker Sartoris) died in one (such was progress, that fast, that rapid) lost from control on an icy road by his (the banker's) grandson, who had just returned from (such was progress) two years of service as a combat airman on the Western Front and now the camouflage paint is weathering slowly from a French point-seventy-five field piece squatting on one flank of the base of the Confederate monument, but even before it faded there was neon in the town and A.A.A. and C.C.C. in the county, and W.P.A. ("and XYZ and etc.," as "Uncle Pete" Gombault, a lean clean tobacco-chewing old man, incumbent of a political sinecure under the designation of United States marshal—an office held back in reconstruction times, when the State of Mississippi was a United States military district, by a Negro man who was still living in 1925—fire-maker, sweeper, janitor and furnace-attendant to five or six lawyers and doctors and one of the banks— and still known as "Mulberry" from the avocation which he had followed before and during and after his incumbency as marshal: peddling illicit whiskey in pint and half-pint bottles from a cache beneath the roots of a big mulberry tree behind the drugstore of his pre-1865 owner— put it) in both; W.P.A. and XYZ marking the town and the county as war itself had not: gone now were the last of the forest trees which had followed the shape of the Square, shading the unbroken second-storey balcony onto which the lawyers' and doctors' offices had opened, which shaded in its turn the fronts of the stores and the walkway beneath; and now was gone even the balcony itself with its wrought-iron balustrade on which in the long summer afternoons the lawyers would prop their feet to talk; and the continuous iron chain looping from wooden post to post along the circumference of the court-house yard, for the farmers to hitch their teams to; and the public watering trough where they could water them, because gone was the last wagon to stand on the Square during the spring and summer and fall Saturdays and trading-days, and not only the Square but the streets leading into it were paved now, with fixed signs of interdiction and admonition applicable only to something capable of moving faster than thirty miles an hour; and now the last forest tree was gone from the courthouse yard too, replaced by formal synthetic shrubs contrived and schooled in Wisconsin greenhouses, and in the courthouse (the city hall too) a courthouse and city hall gang, in miniature of course (but that was not its fault but the fault of the city's and the county's size and population and wealth) but based on the pattern of Chicago and Kansas City and Boston and Philadelphia (and which, except for its minuscularity, neither Philadelphia nor Boston nor Kansas City nor Chicago need have blushed at) which every three or four years would try again to raze the old courthouse in order to build a new one, not that they did not like the old one nor wanted the new, but because the new one would bring into the town and county that much more increment of unearned federal money;

And now the paint is preparing to weather from an anti-tank howitzer squatting on rubber tires on the opposite flank of the Confederate monument; and gone now from the fronts of the stores are the old brick made of native clay in Sutpen's architect's old molds, replaced now by sheets of glass taller than a man and longer than a wagon and team, pressed intact in Pittsburgh factories and framing interiors bathed now in one shadowless corpse-glare of fluorescent light; and, now and at last, the last of silence too: the county's hollow inverted air one resonant boom and ululance of radio: and thus no more Yoknapatawpha's air nor even Mason and Dixon's air, but America's: the patter of comedians, the baritone screams of female vocalists, the babbling pressure to buy and buy and still buy arriving more instantaneous than light, two thousand miles from New York and Los Angeles; one air, one nation: the shadowless fluorescent corpse-glare bathing the sons and daughters of men and women, Negro and white both, who were born to and who passed all their lives in denim overalls and calico, haggling by cash or the installment-plan for garments copied last week out of *Harper's Bazaar* or *Esquire* in East Side sweat-shops: because an entire generation of farmers has vanished, not just from Yoknapatawpha's but from Mason and Dixon's earth: the self-consumer: the machine which displaced the man because the exodus of the man left no one to drive the mule, now that the machine was threatening to extinguish the mule; time was when the mule stood in droves at daylight in the plantation mule-lots across the plantation road from the serried identical ranks of two-room shotgun shacks in which lived in droves with his family the Negro tenant- or share- or furnish-hand who bridled him (the mule) in the lot at sunup and followed him through the plumb-straight monotony of identical furrows and back to the lot at sundown, with (the man) one eye on where the mule was going and the other eye on his (the mule's) heels; both gone now: the one, to the last of the forty- and fifty- and sixty-acre hill farms inaccessible from unmarked dirt roads, the other to New York and Detroit and Chicago and Los Angeles ghettos, or nine out of ten of him that is, the tenth one mounting from the handles of a plow to the springless bucket seat of a tractor, dispossessing and displacing the other nine just as the tractor had dispossessed and displaced the other eighteen mules to whom that nine would have been complement; then Warsaw and Dunkerque displaced that tenth in his turn,

and now the planter's not-yet-drafted son drove the tractor: and then Pearl Harbor and Tobruk and Utah Beach
displaced that son, leaving the planter himself on the seat
of the tractor, for a little while that is—or so he thought,
forgetting that victory or defeat both are bought at the
same exorbitant price of change and alteration; one nation, one world: young men who had never been farther
from Yoknapatawpha County than Memphis or New Orleans (and that not often), now talked glibly of street
intersections in Asiatic and European capitals, returning
no more to inherit the long monotonous endless unend-
able furrows of Mississippi cotton fields, living now (with
now a wife and next year a wife and child and the year
after that a wife and children) in automobile trailers or
G.I. barracks on the outskirts of liberal arts colleges, and
the father and now grandfather himself still driving the
tractor across the gradually diminishing fields between
the long looping skeins of electric lines bringing electric
power from the Appalachian mountains, and the sub-
terrene steel veins bringing the natural gas from the
Western plains, to the little lost lonely farmhouses glittering and gleaming with automatic stoves and washing
machines and television antennae;

One nation: no longer anywhere, not even in Yoknapatawpha County, one last irreconcilable fastness of strong-
hold from which to enter the United States, because at
last even the last old sapless indomitable unvanquished
widow or maiden aunt had died and the old deathless
Lost Cause had become a faded (though still select)
social club or caste, or form of behavior when you remembered to observe it on the occasions when young men
from Brooklyn, exchange students at Mississippi or Arkansas or Texas Universities, vended tiny Confederate battle
flags among the thronged Saturday afternoon ramps of
football stadia; one world: the tank gun: captured from
a regiment of Germans in an African desert by a regiment

of Japanese in American uniforms, whose mothers and fathers at the time were in a California detention camp for enemy aliens, and carried (the gun) seven thousand miles back to be set halfway between, as a sort of secondary flying buttress to a memento of Shiloh and The Wilderness; one universe, one cosmos: contained in one America: one towering frantic edifice poised like a card-house over the abyss of the mortgaged generations; one boom, one peace: one swirling rocket-roar filling the glittering zenith as with golden feathers, until the vast hollow sphere of his air, the vast and terrible burden beneath which he tries to stand erect and lift his battered and indomitable head—the very substance in which he lives and, lacking which, he would vanish in a matter of seconds—is murmurous with his fears and terrors and disclaimers and repudiations and his aspirations and dreams and his baseless hopes, bouncing back at him in radar waves from the constellations;

And still—the old jail—endured, sitting in its rumorless cul-de-sac, its almost seasonless backwater in the middle of that rush and roar of civic progress and social alteration and change like a collarless (and reasonably clean: merely dingy: with a day's stubble and no garters to his socks) old man sitting in his suspenders and stocking feet, on the back kitchen steps inside a walled courtyard; actually not isolated by location so much as insulated by obsolescence: on the way out of course (to disappear from the surface of the earth along with the rest of the town on the day when all America, after cutting down all the trees and leveling the hills and mountains with bulldozers, would have to move underground to make room for, get out of the way of, the motor cars) but like the trackwalker in the tunnel, the thunder of the express mounting behind him, who finds himself opposite a niche or crack exactly his size in the wall's living and impregnable rock, and steps into it, inviolable and secure while de-

struction roars past and on and away, grooved ineluctably
to the spidery rails of its destiny and destination; not
even—the jail—worth selling to the United States for
some matching allocation out of the federal treasury; not
even (so fast, so far, was Progress) any more a real
pawn, let alone knight or rook, on the County's political
board, not even plum in true worth of the word: simply
a modest sinecure for the husband of someone's cousin,
who had failed not as a father but merely as a fourth-rate
farmer or day-laborer;

It survived, endured; it had its inevictable place in the
town and the county; it was even still adding modestly
not just to its but to the town's and the county's history
too: somewhere behind that dingy brick façade, between
the old durable hand-molded brick and the cracked creo-
sote-impregnated plaster of the inside walls (though few
in the town or county any longer knew that they were
there) were the old notched and mortised logs which
(this, the town and county did remember; it was part of
its legend) had held someone who might have been
Wiley Harpe; during that summer of 1864, the federal
brigadier who had fired the Square and the courthouse
had used the jail as his provost-marshal's guard-house;
and even children in high school remembered how the
jail had been host to the Governor of the state while he
discharged a thirty-day sentence for contempt of court
for refusing to testify in a paternity suit brought against
one of his lieutenants: but isolate, even its legend and
record and history, indisputable in authenticity yet a little
oblique, elliptic or perhaps just ellipsoid, washed thinly
over with a faint quiet cast of apocryphy: because there
were new people in the town now, strangers, outland-
ers, living in new minute glass-walled houses set as neat
and orderly and antiseptic as cribs in a nursery ward, in
new subdivisions named Fairfield or Longwood or
Halcyon Acres which had once been the lawn or back

yard or kitchen garden of the old residences (the old obsolete columned houses still standing among them like
old horses surged suddenly out of slumber in the middle
of a flock of sheep), who had never seen the jail; that is,
they had looked at it in passing, they knew where it was,
when their kin or friends or acquaintances from the East
or North or California visited them or passed through Jefferson on the way to New Orleans or Florida, they could
even repeat some of its legend or history to them: but
they had had no contact with it; it was not a part of their
lives; they had the automatic stoves and furnaces and
milk deliveries and lawns the size of installment-plan
rugs; they had never had to go to the jail on the morning
after June tenth or July Fourth or Thanksgiving or Christmas or New Year's (or for that matter, on almost any
Monday morning) to pay the fine of houseman or gardener
or handyman so that he could hurry on home (still wearing his hangover or his barely-stanched razor-slashes)
and milk the cow or clean the furnace or mow the lawn;

So only the old citizens knew the jail any more, not old
people but old citizens: men and women old not in years
but in the constancy of the town, or against that constancy, concordant (not coeval of course, the town's
date was a century and a quarter ago now, but in accord
against that continuation) with that thin durable continuity born a hundred and twenty-five years ago out of
a handful of bandits captured by a drunken militia squad,
and a bitter ironical incorruptible wilderness mail-rider,
and a monster wrought-iron padlock—that steadfast and
durable and unhurryable continuity against or across
which the vain and glittering ephemerae of progress and
alteration washed in substanceless repetitive evanescent
scarless waves, like the wash and glare of the neon sign
on what was still known as the Holston House diagonally
opposite, which would fade with each dawn from the old
brick walls of the jail and leave no trace; only the old

citizens still knew it: the intractable and obsolescent of the town who still insisted on wood-burning ranges and cows and vegetable gardens and handymen who had to be taken out of hock on the mornings after Saturday nights and holidays; or the ones who actually spent the Saturday- and holiday-nights inside the barred doors and windows of the cells or bullpen for drunkenness or fighting or gambling—the servants, housemen and gardeners and handymen, who would be extracted the next morning by their white folks, and the others (what the town knew as the New Negro, independent of that commodity) who would sleep there every night beneath the thin ruby checker-barred wash and fade of the hotel sign, while they worked their fines out on the street; and the County, since its cattle-thieves and moonshiners went to trial from there, and its murderers—by electricity now (so fast, that fast, was Progress)—to eternity from there; in fact it was still, not a factor perhaps, but at least an integer, a cipher, in the county's political establishment; at least still used by the Board of Supervisors, if not as a lever, at least as something like Punch's stuffed club, not intended to break bones, not aimed to leave any permanent scars;

So only the old knew it, the irreconcilable Jeffersonians and Yoknapatawphians who had (and without doubt firmly intended to continue to have) actual personal dealings with it on the blue Monday mornings after holidays, or during the semi-yearly terms of Circuit or Federal Court:—until suddenly you, a stranger, an outlander say from the East or the North or the Far West, passing through the little town by simple accident, or perhaps relation or acquaintance or friend of one of the outland families which had moved into one of the pristine and recent subdivisions, yourself turning out of your way to fumble among road signs and filling stations out of frank curiosity, to try to learn, comprehend, understand what had brought your cousin or friend or acquaintance to elect to live here—not specifically here, of course, not specifically Jefferson, but such as here, such as Jefferson —suddenly you would realise that something curious was happening or had happened here: that instead of dying off as they should as time passed, it was as though these old irreconcilables were actually increasing in number; as though with each interment of one, two more shared that vacancy: where in 1900, only thirty-five years afterward, there could not have been more than two or three capable of it, either by knowledge or memory of leisure, or even simple willingness and inclination, now, in 1951, eighty-six years afterward, they could be counted in dozens (and in 1965, a hundred years afterward, in hundreds because—by now you had already begun to understand why your kin or friends or acquaintance had elected to come to such as this with his family and call it his life—by then the children of that second outland invasion following a war, would also have become not just Mississippians but Jeffersonians and Yoknapatawphians: by which time—who knows?—not merely the pane, but the whole window, perhaps the entire wall, may have been removed and embalmed intact into a museum by an historical, or anyway a cultural, club of ladies—why, by that time, they may not even know, or even need to know: only that the window-pane bearing the girl's name and the date is that old, which is enough; has lasted that long: one small rectangle of wavy, crudely-pressed, almost opaque glass, bearing a few faint scratches apparently no more durable than the thin dried slime left by the passage of a snail, yet which has endured a hundred years) who are capable and willing too to quit whatever they happen to be doing—sitting on the last of the wooden benches beneath the last of the locust and chinaberry trees among the potted conifers of the new age dotting the courthouse yard, or in the chairs along the shady sidewalk before the Holston House, where a breeze always blows—to lead you across the street and

into the jail and (with courteous neighborly apologies
to the jailor's wife stirring or turning on the stove the peas
and grits and side-meat—purchased in bargain-lot quanti-
ties by shrewd and indefatigable peditation from store to
store—which she will serve to the prisoners for dinner or
supper at so much a head—plate—payable by the
County, which is no mean factor in the sinecure of her
husband's incumbency) into the kitchen and so to the
cloudy pane bearing the faint scratches which, after a
moment, you will descry to be a name and a date;

Not at first, of course, but after a moment, a second,
because at first you would be a little puzzled, a little impatient because of your illness-at-ease from having been
dragged without warning or preparation into the private
kitchen of a strange woman cooking a meal; you would
think merely *What? So what?* annoyed and even a little
outraged, until suddenly, even while you were thinking
it, something has already happened: the faint frail illegible
meaningless even inference-less scratching on the ancient
poor-quality glass you stare at, has moved, under your
eyes, even while you stared at it, coalesced, seeming
actually to have entered into another sense than vision:
a scent, a whisper, filling that hot cramped strange room
already fierce with the sound and reek of frying pork-fat:
the two of them in conjunction—the old milky obsolete
glass, and the scratches on it: that tender ownerless obsolete girl's name and the old dead date in April almost a
century ago—speaking, murmuring, back from, out of,
across from, a time as old as lavender, older than album
or stereopticon, as old as daguerreotype itself;

And being a stranger and a guest would have been
enough, since, a stranger and a guest, you would have
shown the simple courtesy and politeness of asking the
questions naturally expected of you by the host or anyway volunteer guide, who had dropped whatever he was

doing (even if that had been no more than sitting with others of his like on a bench in a courthouse yard or on the sidewalk before a hotel) in order to bring you here; not to mention your own perfectly natural desire for, not revenge perhaps, but at least compensation, restitution, vindication, for the shock and annoyance of having been brought here without warning or preparation, into the private quarters of a strange woman engaged in something as intimate as cooking a meal; but by now you had not only already begun to understand why your kin or friend or acquaintance had elected, not Jefferson but such as Jefferson, for his life, but you had heard that voice, that whisper, murmur, frailer than the scent of lavender, yet (for that second anyway) louder than all the seethe and fury of frying fat; so you ask the questions, not only which are expected of you, but whose answers you yourself must have if you are to get back into your car and fumble with any attention and concentration among the road signs and filling stations, to get on to wherever it is you had started when you stopped by chance or accident in Jefferson for an hour or a day or a night, and the host—guide—answers them, to the best of his ability out of the town's composite heritage of remembering that long back, told, repeated, inherited to him by his father; or rather, his mother: from her mother: or better still, to him when he himself was a child, direct from his great-aunt: the spinsters, maiden and childless out of a time when there were too many women because too many of the young men were maimed or dead: the indomitable and undefeated, maiden progenitresses of spinster and childless descendants still capable of rising up and stalking out in the middle of *Gone With the Wind*;

And again one sense assumes the office of two or three: not only hearing, listening, and seeing too, but you are even standing on the same spot, the same boards she did that day she wrote her name into the window and on the

other one three years later watching and hearing through
and beyond that faint fragile defacement the sudden rush
and thunder: the dust: the crackle and splatter of pistols:
then the face, gaunt, battle-dirty, stubbled-over; urgent
of course, but merely harried, harassed; not defeated,
turned for a fleeing instant across the turmoil and the fury,
then gone: and still the girl in the window (the guide—
host—has never said one or the other; without doubt
in the town's remembering after a hundred years it has
changed that many times from blonde to dark and back
to blonde again: which doesn't matter, since in your own
remembering that tender mist and vail will be forever
blonde) not even waiting: musing; a year, and still not
even waiting: meditant, not even unimpatient: just pa-
tienceless, in the sense that blindness and zenith are colorless; until at last the mule, not out of the long northeast-
ern panorama of defeat and dust and fading smoke, but
drawn out of it by that impregnable, that invincible, that
incredible, that terrifying passivity, coming at that one
fatigueless unflagging jog all the way from Virginia—the
mule which was a better mule in 1865 than the blood
mare had been a horse in '-2 and '-3 and '-4, for the reason
that this was now 1865, and the man, still gaunt and undefeated: merely harried and urgent and short of time
to get on to Alabama and see the condition of his farm—
or (for that matter) if he still had a farm, and now the
girl, the fragile and workless girl not only incapable of
milking a cow but of whom it was never even demanded,
required, suggested, that she substitute for her father in
drying the dishes, mounting pillion on a mule behind a
paroled cavalry subaltern out of a surrendered army who
had swapped his charger for a mule and the sabre of his
rank and his defeatless pride for a stocking full of seed
corn, whom she had not known or even spoken to long
enough to have learned his middle name or his preference
in food, or told him hers, and no time for that even now:
riding, hurrying toward a country she had never seen, to

begin a life which was not even simple frontier, engaged only with wilderness and shoeless savages and the tender hand of God, but one which had been rendered into a desert (assuming that it was still there at all to be returned to) by the iron and fire of civilization;

Which was all your host (guide) could tell you, since that was all he knew, inherited, inheritable from the town: which was enough, more than enough in fact, since all you needed was the face framed in its blonde and delicate vail behind the scratched glass; yourself, the stranger, the outlander from New England or the prairies or the Pacific Coast, no longer come by the chance or accident of kin or friend or acquaintance or roadmap, but drawn too from ninety years away by that incredible and terrifying passivity, watching in your turn through and beyond that old milk-dim disfigured glass that shape, that delicate frail and useless bone and flesh departing pillion on a mule without one backward look, to the reclaiming of an abandoned and doubtless even ravaged (perhaps even usurped) Alabama hill farm—being lifted onto the mule (the first time he touched her probably, except to put the ring on: not to prove nor even to feel, touch, if there actually was a girl under the calico and the shawls; there was no time for that yet; but simply to get her up so they could start), to ride a hundred miles to become the farmless mother of farmers (she would bear a dozen, all boys, herself no older, still fragile, still workless among the churns and stoves and brooms and stacks of wood which even a woman could split into kindlings; unchanged), bequeathing to them in their matronymic the heritage of that invincible inviolable ineptitude;

Then suddenly, you realise that that was nowhere near enough, not for that face—bridehood, motherhood, grandmotherhood, then widowhood and at last the grave —the long peaceful connubial progress toward matriarchy in a rocking chair nobody else was allowed to sit in, then a headstone in a country churchyard—not for that passivity, that stasis, that invincible captaincy of soul which didn't even need to wait but simply to be, breathe tranquilly, and take food—infinite not only in capacity but in scope too: that face, one maiden muse which had drawn a man out of the running pell mell of a cavalry battle, a whole year around the long iron perimeter of duty and oath, from Yoknapatawpha County, Mississippi, across Tennessee into Virginia and up to the fringe of Pennsylvania before it curved back into its closing fade along the headwaters of the Appomattox river and at last removed from him its iron hand: where, a safe distance at last into the rainy woods from the picket lines and the furled flags and the stacked muskets, a handful of men leading spent horses, the still-warm pistols still loose and quick for the hand in the unstrapped scabbards, gathered in the failing twilight—privates and captains, sergeants and corporals and subalterns—talking a little of one last desperate cast southward where (by last report) Johnston was still intact, knowing that they would not, that they were done not only with vain resistance but with indomitability too; already departed this morning in fact for Texas, the West, New Mexico: a new land even if not yet (spent too—like the horses—from the long harassment and anguish of remaining indomitable and undefeated) a new hope, putting behind them for good and all the loss of both: the young dead bride— drawing him (that face) even back from this too, from no longer having to remain undefeated too: who swapped the charger for the mule and the sabre for the stocking of seed corn: back across the whole ruined land and the whole disastrous year by that virgin inevictable passivity more inescapable than lodestar;

Not that face; that was nowhere near enough: no symbol there of connubial matriarchy, but fatal instead with all insatiate and deathless sterility; spouseless, barren, and undescended; not even demanding more than that: simply requiring it, requiring all—Lilith's lost and insatiable face drawing the substance—the will and hope and dream and imagination—of all men (you too: yourself and the host too) into that one bright fragile net and snare; not even to be caught, over-flung, by one single unerring cast of it, but drawn to watch in patient and thronging turn the very weaving of the strangling golden strands—drawing the two of you from almost a hundred years away in your turn—yourself the stranger, the outlander with a B.A. or (perhaps even) M.A. from Harvard or Northwestern or Stanford, passing through Jefferson by chance or accident on the way to somewhere else, and the host who in three generations has never been out of Yoknapatawpha further than a few prolonged Saturday nights in Memphis or New Orleans, who has heard of Jenny Lind, not because he has heard of Mark Twain and Mark Twain spoke well of her, but for the same reason that Mark Twain spoke well of her: not that she sang songs, but that she sang them in the old West in the old days, and the man sanctioned by public affirmation to wear a pistol openly in his belt is an inevictable part of the Missouri and the Yoknapatawpha dream too, but never of Duse or Bernhardt or Maximilian of Mexico, let alone whether the Emperor of Mexico even ever had a wife or not (saying—the host—: 'You mean, she was one of them? maybe even that emperor's wife?' and you: 'Why not? Wasn't she a Jefferson girl?')—to stand, in this hot strange little room furious with frying fat, among the roster and chronicle, the deathless murmur of the sublime and deathless names and the deathless faces, the faces omnivorous and insatiable and forever incontent: demon-nun and angel-witch; empress, siren, Erinys: Mistinguette, too, invincible possessed of a half-century more of years than the mere three score or so she bragged and boasted, for you to choose among, which one she was—not *might* have been, nor even *could* have been, but *was:* so vast, so limitless in capacity is man's imagination to disperse and burn away the rubble-dross of fact and probability, leaving only truth and dream— then gone, you are outside again, in the hot noon sun: late; you have already wasted too much time: to unfumble among the road signs and filling stations to get back onto a highway you know, back into the United States; not that it matters, since you know again now that there is no time: no space: no distance: a fragile and workless scratching almost depthless in a sheet of old barely transparent glass, and (all you had to do was look at it a while; all you have to do now is remember it) there is the clear undistanced voice as though out of the delicate antennaskeins of radio, further than empress's throne, than splendid insatiation, even than matriarch's peaceful rocking chair, across the vast instantaneous intervention, from the long long time ago: *'Listen, stranger; this was myself: this was I.'*

Appendix: The Compsons

IKKEMOTUBBE. A dispossessed American king. Called *l'Homme* (and sometimes *de l'Homme*) by his foster-brother, a Chevalier of France, who, had he not been born too late, could have been among the brightest in that glittering galaxy of knightly blackguards who were Napoleon's marshals, who thus translated the Chickasaw title meaning "The Man"; which translation Ikkemotubbe, himself a man of wit and imagination as well as a shrewd judge of character, including his own, carried one step further and anglicized it to "Doom." Who granted out of his vast lost domain a solid square mile of virgin north Mississippi dirt as truly angled as the four corners of a cardtable top (forested then because these were the old days before 1833 when the stars fell and Jefferson, Mississippi, was one long rambling one-storey mudchinked log building housing the Chickasaw Agent and his trading-post store) to the grandson of a Scottish refugee who had lost his own birthright by casting his lot with a king who himself had been dispossessed. This in partial return for the right to proceed in peace, by whatever means he and his people saw fit, afoot or ahorse provided they were Chickasaw horses, to the wild western land presently to be called Oklahoma: not knowing then about the oil.

JACKSON. A Great White Father with a sword. (An old duellist, a brawling lean fierce mangy durable im-

704

perishable old lion who set the well-being of the nation above the White House, and the health of his new political party above either, and above them all set, not his wife's honor, but the principle that honor must be defended whether it was or not because defended it was whether or not.) Who patented, sealed, and countersigned the grant with his own hand in his gold tepee in Wassi Town, not knowing about the oil either: so that one day the homeless descendants of the dispossessed would ride supine with drink and splendidly comatose above the dusty allotted harborage of their bones in specially built scarlet-painted hearses and fire-engines.

These were Compsons:

QUENTIN MacLACHAN. Son of a Glasgow printer, orphaned and raised by his mother's people in the Perth highlands. Fled to Carolina from Culloden Moor with a claymore and the tartan he wore by day and slept under by night, and little else. At eighty, having fought once against an English king and lost, he would not make that mistake twice and so fled again one night in 1779, with his infant grandson and the tartan (the claymore had vanished, along with his son, the grandson's father, from one of Tarleton's regiments on a Georgia battlefield about a year ago) into Kentucky, where a neighbor named Boon or Boone had already established a settlement.

CHARLES STUART. Attainted and proscribed by name and grade in his British regiment. Left for dead in a Georgia swamp by his own retreating army and then by the advancing American one, both of which were wrong. He still had the claymore even when on his homemade wooden leg he finally overtook his father and son four years later at Harrodsburg, Kentucky, just in time to bury the father and enter upon a long period of being a split personality while still trying to be the schoolteacher which he believed he wanted to be, until he gave up at last and became the gambler he actually was and which no Compson seemed to realize they all were, provided the gambit was desperate and the odds long enough. Succeeded at last in risking not only his neck but the security of his family and the very integrity of the name he would leave behind him, by joining the confederation headed by an acquaintance named Wilkinson (a man of considerable talent and influence and intellect and power) in a plot to secede the whole Mississippi Valley from the United States and join it to Spain. Fled in his turn when the bubble burst (as anyone except a Compson schoolteacher should have known it would), himself unique in being the only one of the plotters who had to flee the country: this not from the vengeance and retribution of the government which he had attempted to dismember, but from the furious revulsion of his late confederates now frantic for their own safety. He was not expelled from the United States; he talked himself countryless, his expulsion due not to the treason but to his having been so vocal and vociferant in the conduct of it, burning each bridge vocally behind him before he had even reached the place to build the next one: so that it was no provost marshal nor even a civic agency but his late co-plotters themselves who put afoot the movement to evict him from Kentucky and the United States and, if they had caught him, probably from the world too. Fled by night, running true to family tradition, with his son and the old claymore and the tartan.

JASON LYCURGUS. Who, driven perhaps by the compulsion of the flamboyant name given him by the sardonic embittered woodenlegged indomitable father who perhaps still believed with his heart that what he wanted to be was a classicist schoolteacher, rode up the Natchez Trace one day in 1820 with a pair of fine pistols and one meagre saddlebag on a small light-waisted but strong-hocked mare which could do the first two furlongs in definitely under the halfminute and the next two in not appreciably more, though that was all. But it was enough: who reached the Chickasaw Agency at Okatoba (which in 1860 was still called Old Jefferson) and went no further. Who within six months was the Agent's clerk and within twelve his partner, officially still the clerk though actually halfowner of what was now a considerable store stocked with the mare's winnings in races against the horses of Ikkemotubbe's young men which he, Compson, was always careful to limit to a quarter or at most three furlongs; and in the next year it was Ikkemotubbe who owned the little mare and Compson owned the solid square mile of land which some day would be almost in the center of the town of Jefferson, forested then and still forested twenty years later, though rather a park than a forest by that time, with its slave quarters and stables and kitchen gardens and the formal lawns and promenades and pavilions laid out by the same architect who built the columned porticoed house furnished by steamboat from France and New Orleans, and still the square intact mile in 1840 (with not only the little white village called Jefferson beginning to enclose it but an entire white county about to surround it, because in a few years now Ikkemotubbe's descendants and people would be gone, those remaining living not as warriors and hunters but as white men—as shiftless farmers or, here and there, the masters of what they too called plantations and the owners of shiftless slaves, a little dirtier than the white man, a little lazier, a little crueller—until at last even the wild blood itself would have vanished, to be seen only occasionally in the nose-shape of a Negro on a cottonwagon or a white sawmill hand or trapper or locomotive fireman); known as the Compson Domain then, since now it was fit to breed princes, statesmen and generals and bishops, to avenge the dispossessed Compsons from Culloden and Carolina and Kentucky; then known as the Governor's house because sure enough in time it did produce or at least spawn a governor—Quentin MacLachan again, after the Culloden grandfather—and still known as the Old Governor's even after it had spawned (1861) a general— (called so by predetermined accord and agreement by the whole town and county, as though they knew even then and beforehand that the old governor was the last Compson who would not fail at everything he touched save longevity or suicide)—the Brigadier Jason Lycurgus II who failed at Shiloh in '62 and failed again, though not so badly, at Resaca in '64, who put the first mortgage on the still intact square mile to a New England carpetbagger in '66, after the old town had been burned by the Federal General Smith and the new little town, in time to be populated mainly by the descendants not of Compsons but of Snopeses, had begun to encroach and then nibble at and into it as the failed brigadier spent the next forty years selling fragments of it off to keep up the mortgage on the remainder: until one day in 1900 he died quietly on an army cot in the hunting and fishing camp in the Tallahatchie River bottom where he passed most of the end of his days.

And even the old governor was forgotten now; what was left of the old square mile was now known merely as the Compson place—the weedchoked traces of the old ruined lawns and promenades, the house which had needed painting too long already, the scaling columns of the portico where Jason III (bred for a lawyer, and indeed he kept an office upstairs above the Square, where entombed in dusty filingcases some of the oldest names in the county—Holston and Sutpen, Grenier and Beauchamp and Coldfield—faded year by year among the bottomless labyrinths of chancery: and who knows what dream in the perennial heart of his father, now completing the third of his three avatars—the one as son of a brilliant and gallant statesman, the second as battleleader of brave and gallant men, the third as a sort of privileged pseudo Daniel Boone-Robinson Crusoe, who had not returned to juvenility because actually he had never left it—that that lawyer's office might again be the anteroom to the governor's mansion and the old splendor) sat all day long with a decanter of whiskey and a litter of dog-eared Horaces and Livys and Catulluses, composing (it was said) caustic and satiric eulogies on both his dead and his living fellowtownsmen, who sold the last of the property, except that fragment containing the house and the kitchengarden and the collapsing stables and one servant's cabin in which Dilsey's family lived, to a golf-club for the ready money with which his daughter Candace could have her fine wedding in April and his son Quentin could finish one year at Harvard and commit suicide in the following June of 1910; already known as the Old Compson place even while Compsons were still living in it on that spring dusk in 1928 when the old governor's doomed lost nameless seventeen-year-old great-greatgranddaughter robbed her last remaining sane male relative (her uncle Jason IV) of his secret hoard of money and climbed down a rainpipe and ran off with a pitchman in a travelling streetshow, and still known as the Old Compson place long after all traces of Compsons were gone from it: after the widowed mother died and Jason IV, no longer needing to fear Dilsey now, committed his idiot brother, Benjamin, to the State Asylum in Jackson and sold the house to a countryman who operated it as a boarding house for juries and horse- and muletraders; and still known as the Old Compson place even after the boardinghouse (and presently the golfcourse too) had vanished and the old square mile was even intact again in row after row of small crowded jerrybuilt individuallyowned demiurban bungalows.

And these:

QUENTIN III. Who loved not his sister's body but some concept of Compson honor precariously and (he knew well) only temporarily supported by the minute fragile membrane of her maidenhead as a miniature replica of all the whole vast globy earth may be poised on the nose of a trained seal. Who loved not the idea of the incest which he would not commit, but some presbyterian concept of its eternal punishment: he, not God, could by that means cast himself and his sister both into hell, where he could guard her forever and keep her forevermore intact amid the eternal fires. But who loved death above all, who loved only death, loved and lived in a deliberate and almost perverted anticipation of death, as a lover loves and deliberately refrains from the waiting willing friendly tender incredible body of his beloved, until he can no longer bear not the refraining but the restraint, and so flings, hurls himself, relinquishing, drowning. Committed suicide in Cambridge Massachusetts, June 1910, two months after his sister's wedding, waiting first to complete the current academic year and so get the full value of his paid-in-advance tuition, not because he had his old Culloden and Carolina and Kentucky grandfathers in him but because the remaining piece of the old Compson mile which had been sold to pay for his sister's wedding and his year at Harvard had been the one thing, excepting that same sister and the sight of an open fire, which his youngest brother, born an idiot, had loved.

CANDACE (CADDY). Doomed and knew it; accepted the doom without either seeking or fleeing it. Loved her brother despite him, loved not only him but loved in him that bitter prophet and inflexible corruptless judge of what he considered the family's honor and its doom, as he thought he loved, but really hated, in her what he considered the frail doomed vessel of its pride and the foul instrument of its disgrace; not only this, she loved him not only in spite of but because of the fact that he himself was incapable of love, accepting the fact that he must value above all not her but the virginity of which she was custodian and on which she placed no value whatever: the frail physical stricture which to her was no more than a hangnail would have been. Knew the brother loved death best of all and was not jealous, would have handed him (and perhaps in the calculation and deliberation of her marriage did hand him) the hypothetical hemlock. Was two months pregnant with another man's child, which regardless of what its sex would be she had already named Quentin after the brother whom they both (she and the brother) knew was already the same as dead, when she married (1910) an extremely eligible young Indianian she and her mother had met while vacationing at French Lick the summer before. Divorced by him 1911. Married 1920 to a minor movingpicture magnate, Hollywood, California. Divorced by mutual agreement, Mexico 1925. Vanished in Paris with the German occupation, 1940, still beautiful, and probably still wealthy too, since she did not look within fifteen years of her actual forty-eight, and was not heard of again. Except there was a woman in Jefferson, the county librarian, a mouse-sized and -colored woman who had never married, who had passed through the city schools in the same class with Candace Compson and then spent the rest of her life trying to keep *Forever Amber*, in its orderly overlapping avatars, and *Jurgen* and *Tom Jones* out of the hands of the highschool juniors and seniors who could reach them down, without even having to tiptoe, from the back shelves where she herself would have to stand on a box to hide them. One day in 1943, after a week of a distraction bordering on disintegration almost, during which those entering the library would find her always in the act of hurriedly closing her desk drawer and turning the key in it (so that the matrons, wives of the bankers and doctors and lawyers, some of whom had also been in that old highschool class, who came and went in the afternoons with the copies of the *Forever Ambers* and the volumes of Thorne Smith carefully wrapped from view in sheets of Memphis and Jackson newspapers, believed she was on the verge of illness or perhaps even loss of mind), she closed and locked the library in the middle of the afternoon and with her handbag clasped tightly under her arm and two feverish spots of determination in her ordinarily colorless cheeks, she entered the farmers' supply store where Jason IV had started as a clerk and where he now owned his own business as a buyer of and dealer in cotton, striding on through that gloomy cavern which only men ever entered—a cavern cluttered and walled and stalagmite-hung with plows and discs and loops of tracechain and singletrees and mulecollars and sidemeat and cheap shoes and horse liniment and flour and molasses, gloomy because the goods it contained were not shown but hidden rather since those who supplied Mississippi farmers, or at least Negro Mississippi farmers, for a share of the crop did not wish, until that crop was made and its value approximately computable, to show them what they could learn to want, but only to supply them on specific demand with what they could not help but need—and strode on back to Jason's particular domain in the rear: a railed enclosure cluttered with shelves and pigeonholes bearing spiked dust-and-lint-gathering gin receipts and ledgers and cotton samples and rank with the blended smell of cheese and kerosene and harness oil and the tremendous iron stove against which chewed tobacco had been spat for almost a hundred years, and up to the long high sloping counter behind which Jason stood, and, not looking again at the overalled men who had quietly stopped talking and even chewing when she entered, with a kind of fainting desperation she opened the handbag and fumbled something out of it and laid it open on the counter and stood trembling and breathing rapidly while Jason looked down at it—a picture, a photograph in color clipped obviously from a slick magazine—a picture filled with luxury and money and sunlight—a Riviera backdrop of mountains and palms and cypresses and the sea, an open powerful expensive chromium-trimmed sports car, the woman's face hatless between a rich scarf and a seal coat, ageless and beautiful, cold serene and damned; beside her a handsome lean man of middleage in the ribbons and tabs of a German staffgeneral—and the mouse-sized mouse-colored spinster trembling and aghast at her own temerity, staring across it at the childless bachelor in whom ended that long line of men who had had something in them of decency and pride, even after they had begun to fail at the integrity and the pride had become mostly vanity and selfpity: from the expatriate who had to flee his native land with little else except his life, yet who still refused to accept defeat, through the man who gambled his life and his good name twice and lost twice and declined to accept that either, and the one who with only a clever small quarterhorse for tool avenged his dispossessed father and grandfather and gained a principality, and the brilliant and gallant governor, and the general who, though he failed at leading in battle brave and gallant men, at least risked his own life too in the failing, to the cultured dipsomaniac who sold the last of his patrimony, not to buy drink but to give one of his descendants at least the best chance in life he could think of.

"It's Caddy!" the librarian whispered. "We must save her!"

"It's Cad, all right," Jason said. Then he began to laugh. He stood there laughing above the picture, above the cold beautiful face now creased and dogeared from its week's sojourn in the desk drawer and the handbag. And the librarian knew why he was laughing, who had not called him anything but Mr. Compson for thirty-two years now, ever since the day in 1911 when Candace, cast off by her husband, had brought her infant daughter home and left the child and departed by the next train, to return no more, and not only the Negro cook, Dilsey, but the librarian too, divined by simple instinct that Jason was somehow using the child's life and its illegitimacy to blackmail the mother not only into staying away from Jefferson for the rest of her life, but into appointing him sole unchallengeable trustee of the money she would send for the child's maintenance, and had refused to speak to him at all since that day in 1928 when the daughter climbed down the rainpipe and ran away with the pitchman.

"Jason!" she cried. "We must save her! Jason! Jason!" —and still crying it even when he took up the picture between thumb and finger and threw it back across the counter toward her.

"That Candace?" he said. "Don't make me laugh. This bitch ain't thirty yet. The other one's fifty now."

And the library was still locked all the next day too when at three o'clock in the afternoon, footsore and spent yet still unflagging and still clasping the handbag tightly under her arm, she turned into a neat small yard in the Negro residence section of Memphis and mounted the steps of the neat small house and rang the bell and the door opened and a black woman of about her own age looked quietly out at her. "It's Frony, isn't it?" the librarian said. "Don't you remember me—Melissa Meek, from Jefferson—"

"Yes," the Negress said. "Come in. You want to see Mama." And she entered the room, the neat yet cluttered bedroom of an old Negro, rank with the smell of old people, old women, old Negroes, where the old woman herself sat in a rocker beside the hearth where even though it was June a fire smoldered—a big woman once, in faded clean calico and an immaculate turban wound round her head above the bleared and now apparently almost sightless eyes—and put the dogeared clipping into the black hands which, like those of the women of her race, were still as supple and delicately shaped as they had been when she was thirty or twenty or even seventeen.

"It's Caddy!" the librarian said. "It is! Dilsey! Dilsey!"

"What did he say?" the old Negress said. And the librarian knew whom she meant by "he"; nor did the librarian marvel, not only that the old Negress would know that she (the librarian) would know whom she meant by the "he," but that the old Negress would know at once that she had already shown the picture to Jason.

"Don't you know what he said?" she cried. "When he realized she was in danger, he said it was her, even if I hadn't even had a picture to show him. But as soon as he realized that somebody, anybody, even just me, wanted to save her, would try to save her, he said it wasn't. But it is! Look at it!"

"Look at my eyes," the old Negress said. "How can I see that picture?"

"Call Frony!" the librarian cried. "She will know her!" But already the old Negress was folding the clipping carefully back into its old creases, handing it back.

"My eyes ain't any good any more," she said. "I can't see it."

And that was all. At six o'clock she fought her way through the crowded bus terminal, the bag clutched under one arm and the return half of her roundtrip ticket in the other hand, and was swept out onto the roaring platform on the diurnal tide of a few middleaged civilians, but mostly soldiers and sailors enroute either to leave or to death, and the homeless young women, their companions, who for two years now had lived from day to day in pullmans and hotels when they were lucky, and in daycoaches and busses and stations and lobbies and public restrooms when not, pausing only long enough to drop their foals in charity wards or policestations and then move on again, and fought her way into the bus, smaller than any other there so that her feet touched the floor only occasionally, until a shape (a man in khaki; she couldn't see him at all because she was already crying) rose and picked her up bodily and set her into a seat next the window, where still crying quietly she could look out

upon the fleeing city as it streaked past and then was behind, and presently now she would be home again, safe in
Jefferson, where life lived too with all its incomprehensible passion and turmoil and grief and fury and despair,
but there at six o'clock you could close the covers on it
and even the weightless hand of a child could put it back
among its unfeatured kindred on the quiet eternal shelves
and turn the key upon it for the whole and dreamless
night. *Yes* she thought, crying quietly, *that was it; she
didn't want to see it know whether it was Caddy or not
because she knows Caddy doesn't want to be saved hasn't
anything any more worth being saved for nothing worth
being lost that she can lose.*

JASON IV. The first sane Compson since before Culloden and (a childless bachelor) hence the last. Logical,
rational, contained and even a philosopher in the old
stoic tradition: thinking nothing whatever of God one
way or the other, and simply considering the police and
so fearing and respecting only the Negro woman who
cooked the food he ate, his sworn enemy since his birth
and his mortal one since that day in 1911 when she too
divined by simple clairvoyance that he was somehow using his infant niece's illegitimacy to blackmail her mother.
Who not only fended off and held his own with Compsons, but competed and held his own with the Snopeses,
who took over the little town following the turn of the
century as the Compsons and Sartorises and their ilk
faded from it (no Snopes, but Jason Compson himself,
who as soon as his mother died—the niece had already
climbed down the rainpipe and vanished, so Dilsey no
longer had either of these clubs to hold over him—committed his idiot younger brother to the state and vacated
the old house, first chopping up the vast once splendid
rooms into what he called apartments and selling the
whole thing to a countryman who opened a boarding-
house in it), though this was not difficult since to him all

the rest of the town and the world and the human race too except himself were Compsons, inexplicable yet quite predictable in that they were in no sense whatever to be trusted. Who, all the money from the sale of the pasture having gone for his sister's wedding and his brother's course at Harvard, used his own niggard savings out of his meagre wages as a storeclerk to send himself to a Memphis school where he learned to class and grade cotton, and so established his own business, with which, following his dipsomaniac father's death, he assumed the entire burden of the rotting family in the rotting house, supporting his idiot brother because of their mother, sacrificing what pleasures might have been the right and just due and even the necessity of a thirty-year-old bachelor, so that his mother's life might continue as nearly as possible to what it had been; this not because he loved her but (a sane man always) simply because he was afraid of the Negro cook whom he could not even force to leave, even when he tried to stop paying her weekly wages; and who despite all this, still managed to save $2840.50 (three thousand, as he reported it on the night his niece stole it) in niggard and agonized dimes and quarters and halfdollars, which hoard he kept in no bank because to him a banker too was just one more Compson, but hid in a locked steel box beneath a sawn plank in the floor of his locked clothes closet in the bedroom whose bed he made each morning himself, since he kept the room's door locked all the time save for a half hour each Sunday morning when, himself present and watching, he permitted his mother and Dilsey to come in long enough to change the bedlinen and sweep the floor. Who, following a fumbling abortive attempt by his idiot brother on a passing female child, had himself appointed the idiot's guardian without letting their mother know and so was able to have the creature castrated before the mother even knew it was out of the house, and who following the mother's death in 1933 was able to free himself forever not only from the idiot brother and the house but from the Negro woman too, moving into a pair of offices up a flight of stairs above the supplystore containing his cotton ledgers and samples, which he had converted into a bedroom-kitchen-bath, in and out of which on weekends there would be seen a big, plain, friendly, brazenhaired pleasantfaced woman no longer very young, in round picture hats and in its season an imitation fur coat, the two of them, the middleaged cottonbuyer and the woman whom the town called, simply, his friend from Memphis, seen at the local picture show on Saturday night and on Sunday morning mounting the apartment stairs with paper bags from the grocer's containing loaves and eggs and oranges and cans of soup, domestic, uxorious, connubial, until the late afternoon bus carried her back to Memphis. He was emancipated now. He was free. "In 1865," he would say, "Abe Lincoln freed the niggers from the Compsons. In 1933, Jason Compson freed the Compsons from the niggers."

BENJAMIN. Born Maury, after his mother's only brother: a handsome flashing swaggering workless bachelor who borrowed money from almost anyone, even Dilsey although she was a Negro, explaining to her as he withdrew his hand from his pocket that she was not only in his eyes the same as a member of his sister's family, she would be considered a born lady anywhere in any eyes. Who, when at last even his mother realized what he was and insisted weeping that his name must be changed, was rechristened Benjamin by his brother Quentin (Benjamin, our lastborn, sold into Egypt). Who loved three things: the pasture which was sold to pay for Candace's wedding and to send Quentin to Harvard, his sister Candace, firelight. Who lost none of them, because he could not remember his sister but only the loss of her, and firelight was the same bright shape as going to sleep, and the pasture was even better sold than before, because now he and Luster could not only follow timeless along the fence the motions which it did not even matter to him were human beings swinging golfsticks, Luster could lead them to clumps of grass or weeds where there would appear suddenly in Luster's hand, small white spherules which competed with and even conquered what he did not even know was gravity and all the immutable laws, when released from the hand toward plank floor or smokehouse wall or concrete sidewalk. Gelded 1913. Committed to the State Asylum, Jackson, 1933. Lost nothing then either because, as with his sister, he remembered not the pasture but only its loss, and firelight was still the same bright shape of sleep.

QUENTIN. The last. Candace's daughter. Fatherless nine months before her birth, nameless at birth and already doomed to be unwed from the instant the dividing egg determined its sex. Who at seventeen, on the one thousand eight hundred ninetyfifth anniversary of the day before the resurrection of Our Lord, swung herself by a rainpipe from her window to the locked window of her uncle's locked and empty bedroom and broke a pane and entered the window, and with the uncle's firepoker ripped off the locked hasp and staple of the closet door and prized up the sawn plank and got the steel box (and they never did know how she had broken the lock on it, how a seventeen-year-old girl could have broken that lock with anything, let alone a poker) and rifled it (and it was not $2840.50 or three thousand dollars either, it was almost seven thousand. And this was Jason's rage, the red unbearable fury which on that night and at intervals recurring with little or no diminishment for the next five years, made him seriously believe it would at some unwarned instant destroy him, kill him as instantaneously dead as a bullet or a lightning bolt: that although he had been robbed not of a mere petty three thousand dollars but of almost seven thousand he couldn't even tell anybody; he could not only never receive justification—he did not want sympathy—from other men unlucky enough to have one bitch for a sister and another for a niece, he couldn't even demand help in recovering it. Because he had lost four thousand dollars which did not belong to him he couldn't even recover the three thousand which did, since those first four thousand dollars were not only the legal property of his niece as a part of the money supplied for her support and maintenance by her mother over the last sixteen years, they did not exist at all, having been officially recorded as expended and consumed in the annual reports he submitted to the district Chancellor, as required of him as guardian and trustee by his bondsmen: so that he had been robbed not only of his thievings but his savings too, and by his own victim; he had been robbed not only of the four thousand dollars which he had risked jail to acquire, but of the three thousand which he had hoarded at the price of sacrifice and denial, almost a nickel and a dime at a time, over a period of almost twenty years: and this not only by his own victim but by a child who did it at one blow, without premeditation or plan, not even knowing or even caring how much she would find when she broke the box open; and now he couldn't even go to the police for help: he who had considered the police always, never given them any trouble, had paid the taxes for years which supported them in parasitic and sadistic idleness; not only that, he didn't dare pursue the girl himself because he might catch her and she would talk, so that his only recourse was a vain dream which kept him tossing and sweating on nights two and three and even four years after the event, when he should have forgotten about it: of catching her without warning, springing on her out of the dark, before she had spent all the money, and murdering her before she had time to open her mouth) and climbed down the same rainpipe in the dusk and ran away with the pitchman who was already under sentence for bigamy.

And so vanished; whatever occupation overtook her would have arrived in no chromium Mercedes; whatever snapshot would have contained no general of staff.

And that was all. These others were not Compsons. They were black:

TP. Who wore on Memphis' Beale Street the fine bright cheap intransigent clothes manufactured specifically for him by the owners of Chicago and New York sweatshops.

FRONY. Who married a pullman porter and went to Saint Louis to live and later moved back to Memphis to make a home for her mother since Dilsey refused to go further than that.

LUSTER. A man, aged 14. Who was not only capable of the complete care and security of an idiot twice his age and three times his size, but could keep him entertained.

DILSEY.
> They endured.

Address upon Receiving the Nobel Prize for Literature

STOCKHOLM, DECEMBER 10, 1950

I feel that this award was not made to me as a man, but to my work—a life's work in the agony and sweat of the human spirit, not for glory and least of all for profit, but to create out of the materials of the human spirit something which did not exist before. So this award is only mine in trust. It will not be difficult to find a dedication for the money part of it commensurate with the purpose and significance of its origin. But I would like to do the same with the acclaim too, by using this moment as a pinnacle from which I might be listened to by the young men and women already dedicated to the same anguish and travail, among whom is already that one who will some day stand here where I am standing.

Our tragedy today is a general and universal physical fear so long sustained by now that we can even bear it. There are no longer problems of the spirit. There is only the question: When will I be blown up? Because of this, the young man or woman writing today has forgotten the problems of the human heart in conflict with itself which alone can make good writing because only that is worth writing about, worth the agony and the sweat.

He must learn them again. He must teach himself that the basest of all things is to be afraid; and, teaching himself that, forget it forever, leaving no room in his workshop for anything but the old verities and truths of the heart, the old universal truths lacking which any story is ephemeral and doomed—love and honor and pity and pride and compassion and sacrifice. Until he does so, he labors under a curse. He writes not of love but of lust, of defeats in which nobody loses anything of value, of victories without hope and, worst of all, without pity or compassion. His griefs grieve on no universal bones, leaving no scars. He writes not of the heart but of the glands.

Until he relearns these things, he will write as though he stood among and watched the end of man. I decline to accept the end of man. It is easy enough to say that man is immortal simply because he will endure: that when the last ding-dong of doom has clanged and faded from the last worthless rock hanging tideless in the last red and dying evening, that even then there will still be one more sound: that of his puny inexhaustible voice, still talking. I refuse to accept this. I believe that man will not merely endure: he will prevail. He is immortal, not because he alone among creatures has an inexhaustible voice, but because he has a soul, a spirit capable of compassion and sacrifice and endurance. The poet's, the writer's, duty is to write about these things. It is his privilege to help man endure by lifting his heart, by reminding him of the courage and honor and hope and pride and compassion and pity and sacrifice which have been the glory of his past. The poet's voice need not merely be the record of man, it can be one of the props, the pillars to help him endure and prevail.